THE BOREAN SEA

AVALIS

JERAWUN

ILLENDALE

SOLARIS PLAIN

PILBAN

KYLENSHAR

KALIMITH

PERTHANA

RIPARIAN
WOOD

MIRRORMERE

SOWEL PASS

MYRRH RIVER

SERPENTSPINE MOUNTAINS

DRAXX

NARIL

MYRRH RIVER

GRIMKNOLL

TERSAL

HIGHLANDS

DURGEN
RANGE

AZE

HATHOR
PASS

AGROTHAR

SALIA RIVER

ZINDAN

DEMAL

MIST
WOOD

KALSHIRU VELDT

For Ibrahim —
Thank you so much
for your support and friendship.
It means more to me than you
will ever know.

MYTHICA

GENESIS

Brett B. Culley

247 of 333

MYTHICA

GENESIS

SCOTT S.
COLLEY

All rights reserved. Published in the United States of America by Krullstone Publishing, LLC, Springville, Alabama.

www.krullstonepublishing.com
www.worldofmythica.com
www.scottscolley.com

Cataloging-in-Publication Data is on file with the Library of Congress.

ISBN: 978-0-9833237-0-9

PRINTED IN THE UNITED STATES OF AMERICA

10   9   8   7   6   5   4   3   2   1

First Edition

For Neslihan:

My life, my love, my inspiration,

and the one who makes every day worth living

And for Daddy Woe Ivey,
whose seemingly inconsequential decision over 50 years ago
has been instrumental in making a dream come true

PROLOGUE

IN LEGENDS AND myths handed down through hundreds of generations, it is said that long ago, thousands of years before the world took its current shape, Man ruled the earth. Dozens of kingdoms and countries spanned the entire globe, each with its own culture and customs. Dominated by sciences far advanced beyond anything this world knows, the Old World was characterized by massive structures of iron and stone that reached into the sky, carriages made of steel driven by strange energies, even flying machines that men used to sail the heavens. The magic that permeates our societies today was non-existent in the world of old.

Sadly, despite all their wondrous creations and immense knowledge, mankind could not cure the eons-old ailments of greed and desire. Poverty, famine, war, and oppression were always present in the world of Men. Consumed by the need to elevate themselves above those around them, the stronger repressed the weaker, using any means necessary to appear superior to their neighbors. Kingdoms employed spying, disruption, and other disreputable tactics to give them power over others, while individuals resorted to deception, corruption, even violence to put themselves on top. Mankind engaged its vast knowledge to create horrifying diseases and weapons of unimaginable power for use against his enemies.

Eventually mankind's unchecked growth exhausted the earth's natural resources, resulting in mass poverty and the collapse of entire empires. Revolts began in the cities as the oppressed rose up against their oppressors, giving strength to the weak and cause to the disillu-sioned. Larger kingdoms mobilized their technologically superior armies to invade smaller territories under the false pretense of restoring order. The concept of peace through mutually assured destruction crumbled under the irrepressible lust for power and wealth. The fear of global war became reality when those in power ruled out dialogue for peace in favor of striking first against potential antagonists. Terrifying weapons of mass destruction were unleashed upon the earth, ravaging the environment and its inhabitants. Fire rained from the sky, obliterat-ing whole civilizations in the blink of an eye, while unstoppable diseases decimated populations, heralding the end of mankind's reign over the earth.

With the destruction of mankind's vast empires and the subse-quent collapse of the environment, Nature's fury was unleashed. Countless species were driven to extinction during the ensuing period of chaos as vicious storms raged across the world, and massive earth-quakes tore apart the land, forever changing its face. Unnatural winter plunged the planet into a new Ice Age, and a lasting darkness fell upon the land, which the sun could not penetrate for a thousand years. Yet Life always finds a way to survive. When the storms ceased and the sun's warmth returned to melt the ice, small pockets of life began to re-emerge from hiding.

In the five thousand years that followed the great holocaust known as the Lost Age, life slowly recovered from near extinction. Mankind, reduced to a primitive existence, found itself competing with many new races and creatures for survival. Beings such as Elves, Dwarves, Trolls, Faeries, Giants, and a plethora of others, many of whom were long thought to be confined to dreams and nightmares, began to appear and carve their own niches in the new world. With their old knowledge nearly completely forgotten, Men found that they were no longer the dominant power in the world. Lost in a dark time where everything but the basic means of survival had disappeared, most of the races wandered the land in primitive clans or tribes. Fighting amongst each other for land and food introduced an era of slaughter and blood-shed, which gave birth to extreme hostility between many of the races.

This age-old hatred led to countless wars and senseless conflicts.

When the Ice Age ended and the earth began to recover from the damage inflicted upon it, Valin Icarus, the leader of the largest tribe of humans, founded the city of Caer Dorn in an attempt to unite the human race and ensure its continued existence. Separated from the other races, mankind's new stronghold grew quickly and expanded. Men from all across the land flocked to this new kingdom — called Valinar after its founder — seeking a safe haven from the perils of the harsh environment of the new world.

Near the end of the Lost Age magic was rediscovered, and its use became commonplace within just a few generations. This mystical power, based on the inherent energy contained within all life and indeed the very earth, became a useful tool for the races that helped them climb from the quagmire of barbarism and enter a new era of discovery and advancement. At the peak of its power, Valinar was the most prosperous and learned empire in the world. Their schools of thought and sorcery rivaled even those of the Elves and brought many new advances in science and the arts.

However, a gifted young sorcerer known as Asaru grew greedy for knowledge beyond what the universities could offer. He delved into the dark arts, seeking the secrets of ultimate power, performing forbidden experiments and rituals in secrecy. When the Council of Mages discovered this, Asaru was banned from their halls and exiled into the wilderness. Within the barren wastelands he found an ancient place of great mystical power, a nexus of the magical currents that crisscross the world. There Asaru continued his quest for power in solitude. In his hidden study in the wilderness, he mastered the black art of necromancy and discovered how to reanimate and control the corpses of the dead.

Driven insane by his years of isolation and consumed with hatred of the Valinarians, Asaru began a campaign to obliterate their empire, now known as the War of the Dead. Though discouraged and demoralized by the massive, grotesque armies commanded by Asaru, the Valinarians fought courageously, thwarting annihilation for over sixty years. Yet despite their bravery and valor, one by one their citadels fell, while their fallen comrades rose again to fight against them. In the end the mighty armies of Valinar were defeated; Asaru's unholy minions slaughtered her horror-stricken citizens while the cities burned to the ground.

Today very little of Valinar remains, except for the few scattered ruins of crumbling castles and decaying buildings, most of them haunted by evil spirits or prowled by undead. Without military support and other aid from the homeland, most of Valinar's colonies also fell into ruination, abandoned by their peoples. All hope was not lost, however, for as the country collapsed, survivors flocked to the safety of Illendale. Settled almost a hundred years before the war began and far from the troubles of the Old World, it was a veritable paradise.

More recently, due to the influence of Queen Cailyn of House Emory, relations with other amicable nations have begun in an effort to stimulate the healing of the land and maintain a peaceful environment for all who reside within it. Despite centuries of raids and incursions from the violent Orcs to the south and other invaders, the people of Illendale have prospered and thus far have been able to live in relative peace.

Until now.

I NEW ARRIVALS

A LIGHT WIND swept across the forested hills of the Durgen Range as the distant sun burned brightly in the noonday sky. It was a cool day in late fall, and as the breeze whistled through the trees and the bare branches rattled against each other, it seemed the land itself was lamenting the loss of summer. Although the thin wisps of white clouds drifting through the atmosphere did not block the sun's light, its rays offered no warmth on this day.

Kairayn tightened his cloak about him, trying to ward off the chill. He was lost in thought, riding at the head of his caravan, weary of the long march that lay behind them and of the road that yet lay ahead. With his dark brown topknot flying in the wind, clad in black studded leather armor, weapons strapped all over his body, he was a truly fearsome sight, like the Horseman War come to claim men's souls. From his saddle on small chains hung various skulls and bones, trophies of his conquest and glory on the battlefield. Kairayn was the Grand Slavemaster, responsible for the capture, re-education, and keeping of all the slaves in the service of the Orc mages. He was a remorseless Orc, feeling neither pity for those he enslaved nor for those negatively affected by his dark trade. To his mind those he pressed into the Orcs' service were lesser beings and were rightfully bound to offer up their lives to their superiors. In his opinion they served a greater purpose than whatever meaningless endeavors they might pursue if given the choice.

He was in a foul mood today, in some small part due to the irritation suffered by the long road he must travel, but mostly his mind was filled with a sense of foreboding. A dark cloud had hung about him since his troop had set out from Grimknoll nearly a month earlier under orders from the High Summoner. Raids for fresh slave stock were not uncommon but highly unusual this late in the season. For this reason he was deeply disturbed. He did not care to learn what dark secrets the Druhedar kept or what plot they were involved in now, but a nagging premonition told him black days were in store for his people.

Now the journey was nearly over.

Kairayn glanced over his shoulder to glare at the iron-barred cages atop the wagons creaking along slowly. He felt his anger rise a notch as he pondered the significance of the Simoril slaves held within. The stupid, brutish ape-men had made excellent slave stock for the Orcs for nearly three hundred years, but he had to disbelieve that this group of women and children were even remotely as valuable as the two dozen good warriors who had been sacrificed to capture them. His journey had gone from irritable to dreadful when snows had blocked the mountain passes, and they were forced to travel south through the Kalshiru Veldt and the Centaurs that claimed them as home.

No hatred was spared between Orc and Centaur, and when the horsemen had ambushed them on the open plains, the battle had been vicious and bloody. Kairayn's anger slipped another notch as the memory replayed in his mind. There would be no revenge for the warriors he had lost. All he had to show for the loss was a handful of useless beings who were hardly worth the trouble. He ground his teeth to drown out the wrath that threatened to break free. There had better be a good reason for all this.

Slowly but surely, Kairayn could see the dark battlements of Grimknoll looming on the horizon grow larger. He could finally be free of this wasteful expedition. He could see a trail of dust extending from the main gate toward his caravan, no doubt an escort of riders to guide them home. It was unnecessary, of course, but it was traditional courtesy to meet and accompany returning warriors on the final leg of their journey.

There were five riders, dressed in the ringmail and midnight blue of the Nightwatch, the protectors of the Druhedar and their keep.

They approached at a quick trot, two abreast with their captain at the head of their small column. At about fifty paces they reined in their stallions and stood waiting at attention for the caravan to meet them.

"Hail and well met, Slavemaster," spoke the captain when Kairayn had closed the distance between them. His cloak billowed lightly in the breeze as his hard, yellow eyes fixed on the Slavemaster. His face and hands were crisscrossed with numerous scars, a testament to the captain's many years in the service of the Druhedar. "I trust you have returned with honor."

Kairayn returned the sizable Orc's stare with an icy gaze of his own. The captain did not care about Kairayn's honor; he was really asking if his expedition had been successful without insulting him. "Well met, Captain. I have kept my honor, and many of my warriors gave their lives to ensure it."

"They shall be honored as heroes as our custom dictates they must be." He raised one fist to his chest and thumped it loudly, paying tribute to the fallen warriors. "For now let us escort you to the keep, where fresh food and drink await you. The High Summoner is anxious for your report. He awaits your arrival at the main gate."

"Very well," replied Kairayn. "You stay here and escort the caravan. I will ride ahead and meet the High Summoner."

Not waiting for a response, he spurred his horse onward. He was weary, hungry, and aching from the long pressed march and eagerly looked forward to some warm food and a good bottle of ale. The sun had passed its zenith, gradually descending upon the horizon and casting long shadows across his path.

"Grubbash can deal with the slaves when they arrive at the gate," Kairayn thought out loud. "I have nothing more to do with this; they are his problem now."

Grimknoll loomed dark and mysterious, towering over him. The fortress of the Druhedar was constructed entirely of gray granite, giving it a dull and gloomy look. Kairayn thought it an apt image considering what went on within those walls. Its hexagonal shape rose nearly one hundred and fifty feet into the sky, topped by several small spires. Except for a few carved into the solid stone of the higher towers, there were no windows. The huge gate served as the only entrance and was made of iron-studded oak timbers three feet thick. The door was recessed into the building far enough to fit a single wagon inside the entryway without opening the door. An iron portcullis could be lowered from the ceiling along the outer wall, either to trap attackers or to prevent those inside from fleeing.

Thirty years ago they had constructed this hold on the orders of Grubbash Grimvisage, the High Summoner and master of the Druhedar. His desire had been to separate his sect from the chaos and constant infighting that plagued the loosely associated jumble of city-states and villages that comprised the Orc lands. Safe in their stronghold, far from prying eyes, they could continue their quest for arcane knowledge in peace and be left to their own devices. Until recently, the Druhedar had been content to work in the shadows, quietly prompting and guiding, always deep in some plot to increase their power that only they were aware of. With Grubbash's power building and a strong following behind him, he had begun to openly incite war and preach Orc superiority.

Preoccupied with the constant warfare between city-states, the Orcs remained ever divided, and Grubbash's rhetoric faded into the shadows. They were up to something, Kairayn knew, but what he could not tell. He was only sure that he did not wish to be on the receiving end when Grubbash's latest plot was revealed.

As Kairayn approached the gate he could see the High Summoner waiting, surveying the land about him as though he had not a care in the world. As he strode up, Grubbash turned and waited patiently for Kairayn to join him.

Grubbash was short for an Orc, standing less than six feet tall, but his harsh countenance made up for this lack. He was bald, as most Orcs were, his right canine tooth sheared off neatly, and he had a large pinkish scar running down the right side of his face from the top of his rounded forehead to his chin, which made an unpleasant contrast to the greenish tone of his skin. His stormy gray eyes had a way of locking on to people, transfixing them with his piercing stare. He was well muscled, as far as mages went, but that was pretty hard to tell beneath the black robes the Druhedar always wore. His smile was as mirthless as his laugh, and both caused those around him to squirm uneasily, probably because he only smiled or laughed when a truly diabolical thought crossed his mind. Grubbash was a prodigy, gifted in the ways of sorcery and equally adept at swaying the minds of those around him. He had apprenticed to the most talented of mages, and when his master died conducting a dangerous ritual, he had declared himself High Summoner and founded the Druhedar order. Some believed that his mentor's death was not accidental at all, which wasn't far from the truth, but none dared to directly challenge a sorcerer of Grubbash's power. He had been swift in uniting the various mage guilds under his banner, eliminating those who opposed him and having Grimknoll constructed as the Druhedar's headquarters.

"*Greb dokreg nar,* Slavemaster," Grubbash greeted in their traditional tongue.

"*Egrob du,* Summoner," Kairayn replied as he reigned in his steed and dismounted. "*Naggash akmal grek.*"

"How was your journey? Were you able to procure what I requested?" There was a glimmer of expectation in his eyes.

"I don't understand why you ordered this expedition, Grubbash, especially so late in the season. Heavy snows blocked the pass behind us, and we were forced to take the long route." A hint of frustration and anger was in Kairayn's voice now; he could not hide his disdain for the Summoner's apparent lack of foresight. "It hardly seems worth the lives of two dozen good warriors for a handful of slaves; women and children aren't of much use as manual labor either."

"I sense your anger, Kairayn," Grubbash soothed, "and believe me, they are worth the sacrifice. Tell me what happened."

"Ambushed, by Centaurs on the open plains. They rode in from the east at dawn. We did not even hear them coming until it was too late. We were able to save your precious cargo, however. We captured about thirty of them in the highlands." Kairayn spat the words as though they were poison.

"You have served your people well, Kairayn. I should like to inspect your catch as soon as possible."

"Do you care nothing for the lives of our warriors?" Kairayn was livid with anger, his jaw set and his fists clenched. "You wasted the lives of my Orcs! You sent us on a fool's errand to capture worthless prey at the worst time. My Orcs died for nothing!"

"Calm yourself, Slavemaster." There was warning in his tone, hinting that a dangerous line was about to be crossed.

"I do not fear your magic any more than you fear my blade," Kairayn replied simply, resting his hand on the pommel of the scimitar at his waist, "and your lack of respect for the lives of my Orcs disturbs me."

"Peace, Kairayn! There is no need for violence between us. Your warriors' deaths were not in vain, and what you have brought back with you is not worthless. Come with me, and I will explain to you the significance of my request." With that he turned and walked toward the open gate, strolling deliberately away without looking back to see if Kairayn was following.

Kairayn felt suddenly wary. Seldom indeed was anyone allowed to enter the Druhedar keep. He had no desire to enter into this place, especially after just losing his temper with the High Summoner. He had very nearly provoked Grubbash into combat, and perhaps the sorcerer had not quite brushed off the encounter as casually as it seemed.

Grubbash was within a few strides of the entrance when he stopped to wait patiently for Kairayn to catch up. Kairayn sighed heavily, forcing down his trepidation to trudge wearily toward the yawning opening. He doubted the sorcerer meant to harm him despite his insubordination, but he could not help but dread what lay waiting inside this place for him. Dark secrets were kept within, secrets Kairayn felt were better left to those who cherished them.

When he arrived at the outer gate, Grubbash turned and walked inside without saying a word. Kairayn followed a step behind, matching his pace. They passed beneath the portcullis and approached the giant wooden doors of the inner gates. The doors were banded horizontally with steel, and each had a large ring attached about chest level. They were obviously too heavy for the rings to serve any purpose other than decoration; it would take twenty Orcs just to pull one of them open. They waited for a few seconds before the low rumble of machinery rose from within the keep. Slowly the doors opened outward, just enough to allow them access.

The two quickly stepped inside to a large round chamber. With a loud groan the doors closed behind them, and the sound of locks clicking into place echoed across the room. Kairayn's gaze swept the room, seeing for the first time the inner sanctum of the Druhedar. The ceiling was high above them, perhaps the height of three or four Orcs, and was braced by huge wooden beams the size of trees. The beams were evenly spaced about the outer wall of the chamber and rose all the way to the domed ceiling where they jutted toward the middle of the room, joining in the center like the legs of a spider. Intricately crafted and gilded sconces that basked the room in flickering yellow light were spread about. Banners adorned with the seal of the Druhedar hung from the walls in places, as well as fine woven tapestries and murals. A few piles of wooden crates were stacked in the center of the room atop a giant flaming crescent carved into the rough stone floor, the standard of the Druhedar. Dead silence filled the hall; even the handful of Initiates skittering around, hurrying off to some important task or hauling the crates to storage rooms, made little noise other than a faint rustling of robes.

A half a dozen doors around the perimeter led to the other areas within the keep, but all stood closed. Grubbash silently walked toward the door directly across the room with Kairayn in tow. The Summoner stopped briefly and whispered something inaudible into an Initiate's ear, who quickly scurried away and disappeared behind one of the doors. Kairayn thought that the great hall felt more like a tomb than anything else.

"Very few outside the order enter these walls," Grubbash said softly to Kairayn. "Stay close to me and do not stray; intruders are not well received here."

Kairayn wanted to demand why he had been allowed entrance, but Grubbash was already moving away, a wraith at home in his haunt. Kairayn followed quickly, feeling largely out of place and overwhelmed. He should not be here.

When they reached the door at the back of the hall, Grubbash halted. He reached out with his hands and felt along the stone wall adjacent to the door until he found the hidden trigger that would unlock it. With a loud snap the locks released, and the door swung open, revealing a flight of stairs spiraling down into blackness. A rush of stale air greeted them, strong with the odor of earth and stone. The two companions slipped inside, and Grubbash shut the door behind them. The small landing was plunged into utter darkness, and once again Kairayn heard the familiar sound of locks sliding into place.

Kairayn waited calmly in the dark for Grubbash to light a torch, suppressing the sudden surge of vulnerability he felt as the weight of the keep settled upon him. Abruptly, a flash of green light filled the chamber. A small globe of luminescent energy hovered above the sorcerer's outstretched palm, surrounding the two in a halo of light just large enough to see the beginning of the flight of stairs ahead of them, three strides at most.

Obviously the Druhedar had planned against unwelcome guests; depriving them of torches would require a mage to escort them through the pitch black.

Grubbash gave him a mirthless smile and moved to the first stair. The orb of green light floated ahead of them as they began to descend the seemingly endless flight of steps. Soon Kairayn lost his sense of direction entirely, the constant downward helix confusing his internal compass. He noticed the walls and steps changed suddenly from mortar and stone to a crude tunnel carved straight out of the bedrock. With every stride Kairayn felt despair welling within him, an unsettling aura of gloom gathering around and stifling his breath.

"You're sweating. Relax, Kairayn; there is nothing to fear here." Grubbash's sudden words startled Kairayn, causing him to jump and almost lose his footing on the steps. "Just take a deep breath," he spoke again, "and count to ten."

Kairayn did so, placing his hands against the walls. Instantly he felt better, calmer. He took a moment to steady himself and then continued on down the steps. Grubbash walked alongside him, hands folded neatly in front of him. The sphere of green light drifted through the air a few paces ahead, still lighting their way. Kairayn wondered how far down in the earth they had gone now and how far the complex stretched beneath the surface.

"I am surprised that you feel so uncomfortable underground; your ancestors were not so inclined," Grubbash said suddenly.

"My ancestors?" Kairayn asked, confused. "Orcs have always lived here in the Durgen Range, always above ground."

"More than four thousand years ago, when mankind still ruled the earth, Orcs did not exist. In fact, none of the races existed, excepting of course Men and Elves," Grubbash lectured.

"The Elves?" Kairayn gave him an incredulous look.

"Listen and learn, my friend." Grubbash gave him a knowing smile. "The Elves have always been there, although not quite in their current form, even before Men. It is believed the Elves are the eldest of all the races, created first by the Gods under an accord to care for the earth. They were charged with preserving the planet and its beauty. They survived mankind's domination of the globe, hidden in the shadows, though they could not prevent the destruction Men wrought upon the land. They have survived the Great Holocaust and re-established themselves in the New World.

"Little more than three thousand years ago, when the Ice Age ended and the earth began to recover from the foolishness of Men, the new races began to emerge. Among them were our cousins, the Goblins. They dwelled primarily within caverns carved into the mountains, as they still do. It is unknown exactly how they got there or where their ancestry traces back to; no records exist of where they came from.

"Two thousand five hundred years ago one clan of Goblins, ostracized by the others due to their unusual strength and large stature, elected to abandon their subterranean lairs and claim lands of their own. Led by Krulag the Mad, they migrated here to the Durgen Range."

"I know the rest of the story. Is there a point behind this history lesson, Grubbash? I never cared much for book learning." Kairayn was growing impatient. The Summoner had brought him into the annals of the stronghold for a reason; now he just wanted Grubbash to get to the point and release him.

As Kairayn spoke, they reached the bottom of the flight of stairs. Still there were no torches or sconces to light their way, only a dark tunnel ahead of them, yawning open like the hungry maw of some giant beast eager to swallow them up. Grubbash ignored his question and led him several hundred paces to a junction. Two passages led to either side, both equally dark and uninviting.

"This way." Grubbash motioned him to the left.

They resumed their march once again, passing several wooden doors until they came to another junction. This time the tunnels went off in three directions; one lay straight ahead, while the others jutted off at right angles. Grubbash took him left again, and they walked for about a hundred paces before they came to yet another junction of halls. They turned down the path to the right. As they walked on, Kairayn noticed the steady trickle of water echoing off the walls, issuing forth from somewhere in the black.

"While excavating these passages we came across a vast underground lake," Grubbash said as though reading Kairayn's thoughts. "It is fed by an underground river that flows right out of the Serpentspine. We use it as a source of water; it helps us remain independent of the outside world."

"The Druhedar have already separated themselves from the rest of society. Any more independence and you will have to create your own kingdom," Kairayn muttered sarcastically.

"Our separation is necessary to maintain an objective stance as the advisors and scholars of our society. The Overlords have a way of pulling everyone into their politics," Grubbash replied coolly. He stopped in front of an inconspicuous door constructed of vertical black oak planks bound together with iron. The portal was overgrown with moss in some places, its hinges rusted. The apparent disuse caused the door to blend in with the rock around it, making it almost unnoticeable; one could walk right past it and never know it was there.

"We are here," he said, as he touched a hidden latch on the wall next to the door.

The door swung open noiselessly, and the two entered a small chamber. The ceiling was a bit higher than the tunnels outside, and the walls were lined with shelves stacked with tomes and rolls of parchment. In the center of the room was a wooden table that had several open books and scrolls spread across it. Two uncomfortable looking chairs sat next to the table, and candelabras stood unlit upon stands in the corners. A small side table held a large bottle with a pair of clay mugs, as well as a plate with half a loaf of bread and some cheese on it.

"Please sit." Grubbash motioned to the pair of chairs. "We have much to discuss."

As Kairayn lowered himself into a chair, Grubbash uttered a few arcane words and motioned toward the candelabras. Abruptly they burst into flame, and light sprang into the room. Grubbash waved a hand, and the green sphere disappeared in a burst of smoke.

"Drink?" Grubbash asked, as he walked over to the small side table. "You must be exhausted from your long journey."

Kairayn nodded his head while glancing about the room. Grubbash returned and placed a mug full of ale in front of Kairayn, as well as one for himself before taking the seat across the table. He eyed Kairayn for a few moments before he spoke again, as if trying to divine his thoughts.

"Krulag the Mad," he continued his lecture in a hushed tone, "kept a record of his experiences when his tribe arrived here. According to his notes, while exploring the wilderness he came upon an ancient site, two cylindrical towers made of fused stone. When he entered the towers, he was incapacitated by an unknown force, made blind and unable to walk. His skin began to blister, and he fell to the ground, awaiting death. It was then that the prophecy was made. Visions of our ultimate victory over the other races and our continued dominance throughout the ages coursed like fire through his veins, burning forever the truth of our existence into his brain. Terrified by what he was experiencing, he crawled away. Hours later, a search party from his tribe's encampment found him unconscious upon a hillock overlooking the area. As they carried his body back to their camp, the party claims an unimaginably powerful explosion destroyed the whole site.

"According to his journal, Krulag was bedridden for weeks, trying to recover from the episode. He drifted in and out of consciousness, suffering from intense hallucinations. During this time his body began to change. He grew larger, his muscle mass increased, and eventually he became the original model of Orc anatomy. When Krulag fully recovered, he packed up his tribe and led them back to the site. There he ordered the construction of their new home, the same place where Agrothar now stands." Grubbash had walked over to the side table and taken the bread. He bit into the loaf and tore off a large piece, chewing loudly.

"The rest of the tribe began to transform soon after they settled," he progressed while striding back to his seat, "and within several generations Orcs as we are today came into being."

"You believe the ramblings of a madman dead for two thousand years? That is the basis for your belief in our supremacy?"

"Perhaps, perhaps not." Grubbash pushed an open book towards Kairayn that appeared as ancient as the earth itself. "This is Krulag's journal; there is much more than what I have told you contained within it." Grubbash reached for his mug and raised it to his lips. Kairayn flipped through the old manuscript's pages, scanning through the lines of text. To him it looked like meaningless gibberish.

"Why are you telling me all of this, Grubbash?" Kairayn asked softly.

"I know you believe in our race's superiority as I do, but I want you to understand it as well," Grubbash replied. "I require your services; our people need you."

"I do not wish to become involved in your plots, sorcerer," Kairayn shot back defiantly.

"Think about it, Kairayn!" Grubbash declared. "We are the inheritors of the Earth. This new world is a testing ground; the strongest will outlast the others and reign supreme. Who is stronger than the Orcs? Who can stand against us? Mankind had his chance. They ruled the globe for thousands of years before our people even existed, and they threw it away, nearly destroying it while trying to destroy each other. The Elves before them were not strong enough to prevent Man from consuming the planet.

"Yet through all of their folly, they still survive." Grubbash grew excited now, gesturing wildly with his hands. He stood quickly, knocking his chair over, and began pacing around the room. "Men and Elves have grown weak. The Elves lost their immortality eons ago, punishment for their failure I presume, and most of their arcane lore has been lost over the ages. They cannot withstand the might of the Orcs. And Men? They have always been weak. It was only due to a lack of competition that they were able to control the earth in ages past. If you looked at recent history alone, you would find them undeserving. Their original homeland was destroyed by their own greed. No, Men do not deserve this earth, and I will not allow them to have it.

"Who else, then, can stand against us if not Men and Elves? The Dwarves can hardly defend themselves against our Goblin cousins. They have been at war for centuries, never gaining ground. The Trolls haven't the stomach for conquest, or they would have pounded the Elves to dust by now. I ask you, who will prevent us from claiming our birthright?"

Kairayn thought for a moment and let all that Grubbash had said sink in. The sorcerer had not revealed his complete plan, but his words suggested that wheels were being put in motion. War was on the horizon, the Orcs' destiny at hand. Kairayn felt himself grow excited at the prospect of charging into battle against the armies of the weaker races and utterly crushing them.

"If the other races were to unite," Kairayn realized suddenly, "their combined might would prove overwhelming."

"Yes, I have considered that," Grubbash smirked. "The Dwarves will not leave their country undefended, not while the Goblins lurk on their doorstep. Our brethren will keep them occupied. To the east the Trolls will keep the Elven army engaged while we are left to deal with the humans."

"So the Goblins and Trolls have already pledged their support?" The disdain in Kairayn's voice was almost palpable. "We don't need their kind."

"Hardly. The Goblins will continue to fight the Dwarves

because they are too stupid to do any different." Grubbash recovered his chair and sat across from Kairayn, leaning in close. "The Trolls hate the Elves more than anything; a little pressure in the right places will throw the two into war. You just have to know where to push."

"And how do you intend to unite us? Blood feuds have divided our nation for hundreds of years, bleeding our country of good warriors." Kairayn scowled at the thought.

"To answer that I must counter with another question. What makes us fight each other? Why do the states war against one another?" Grubbash paused for a moment, waiting for an answer he knew would not come. "I'll tell you. We fight each other because we have been tricked into believing that there is nothing else. Those in power have squashed our faith in our own supremacy and replaced it with a frustration and apathy that we have only ourselves to take it out on. If we are to unite, we must be given a common goal, a common enemy to fight. All they need is a sign that our time has come, that the moment of our ascension is at hand. All they need is a spark.

"I will provide that spark by summoning four Daemon Lords from the Abyss, whose armies will give our own strength and courage beyond imagining. The Overlords wouldn't dare oppose the will of our entire nation. With the strength of the demons behind us and our people united, we will crush the pathetic humans of Illendale. Once they have been annihilated, the rest of the world is ours for the taking."

"You're mad! Demons cannot be trusted! They will destroy us and wreak havoc on this world!" Kairayn was shocked at this new revelation. How could Grubbash possibly believe that the Lords of Hell would aid them? "We have known each other for a lifetime, Grubbash, but I cannot allow you to go through with this. Surely you are aware of the maelstrom you intend to unleash."

"I am aware; that is why I need you." Grubbash fixed him with his hard gray eyes, the seriousness of them enthralling Kairayn. Grubbash stood anew and strode to one of the shelves on the wall. He removed a single tome bound in leather and came back to the table. He opened the book to a marked page and placed it before Kairayn for him to review.

"This volume was recovered centuries ago from the ruins of Valinar by an expedition sent to determine the fate of the human empire. It describes in detail many of the magical artifacts created by the humans during that era. The page you are looking at describes one such piece."

"The Krullstone?" Kairayn read the description. There was a sketch on the opposite page of a gauntlet gilded with mystical runes and bedecked with small gemstones. In the palm of the glove was set a large, finely cut stone, oval in shape yet very thin. "What purpose does this stone serve?" asked Kairayn.

"Read on and discover its purpose for yourself," Grubbash responded.

Kairayn perused the eccentric handwriting on the paper. It explained that the Krullstone was intended to counteract the necromancer Asaru's growing power by siphoning it away from him. The gem embedded in the palm of the construct was found at an ancient site that predated the Old World. During experiments to test its magical qualities, it was discovered that the stone could absorb the power of other objects into itself and grant them to the bearer. It was later crafted into the gauntlet, which was inscribed with powerful runes that would allow the wearer to command the Krullstone's power. Kairayn finished reading and looked up at his friend, mollified.

"Surely you do not intend to use this on the Daemon Lords?"

"Not at all, Kairayn," Grubbash assuaged him. "That trinket will merely serve as an insurance policy against any shifts in their devotion to our cause." Grubbash smiled wide, stretching the pink scar on his face. Kairayn did not care to know what was going through his mind at that moment.

"What is it I am required to do?" Kairayn inquired quietly.

"You must go in search of the Krullstone. It must be returned here as soon as possible." Grubbash leaned across the table, very close to Kairayn's face, and whispered, "It is absolutely imperative that no one is aware of your quest. The Daemon Lords must not be alerted, as they certainly will not appreciate our doubt of their conviction."

"Where will I seek this Krullstone? Surely it has been lost over so many years." Kairayn wondered how he could find such a small device in such a large world. Who knew how far the winds of time had taken it from its original resting place?

"It was crafted in Valinar. I suspect it is still there, hidden in some vault. Asaru was never aware of its construction, and I have reason to believe it has never left its sepulcher." Grubbash sounded convinced, but Kairayn was still skeptical.

"Send someone else. Surely an Initiate or Master will serve you better than I in this arena."

"It must be you," Grubbash pressed. "I cannot trust the Druhedar in this matter; they are too easily corrupted by the lures of power. We have been friends for more than half a century, and I trust you implicitly."

Kairayn stared at the mage, his gaze boring into him, weighing the truth of his words. "Then I will go. When shall I leave?" Kairayn asked.

"As soon as you can assemble your party. I will send two Masters with you to help you succeed and anything else you require. None in your party will be aware of the true purpose of this undertaking; that I must insist upon." Grubbash stood then and tucked his chair under the table. He re-summoned the green sphere of light and extinguished the candles with a wave of his hand, casting the room in an eerie emerald glow.

"I have already given orders that you are to be assisted in any way possible. Whatever you require to begin your journey will be provided. The luminorb will guide you back to the main hall," Grubbash stated, pointing to the hovering ball of luminescence. "Now if you'll excuse me, I have much to do. *Dokal neb uknirog*, old friend."

"Luck to you as well," Kairayn said. He reached for his mug of ale, which he had not touched since arriving, and drained its contents. He was pleased to be leaving the underbelly of Grimknoll, but he was not ecstatic at being left alone with a floating orb to find his way out.

He stood and clasped hands with the sorcerer, then excused himself. The orb floated a few paces in front of him, somehow programmed to discern the path back to the surface. Kairayn stepped out the door and followed the light down the hallway, leaving Grubbash in darkness. As he followed the trail chosen for him, Kairayn reflected on the events that had just transpired. Grubbash had not needed to convince him of the Orcs' supremacy; he had believed it all his life. All Orcs did. It had been bred into the very fiber of their being.

Now Grubbash had revealed a way for his people to realize their destiny. He had not wanted to be involved in the politics of the Druhedar, and the prospect of summoning demons to their aid made his blood curdle. In the end, however, Grubbash had proven his genius. His fervor and dedication to the cause inspired Kairayn, and he accepted his task with pride. He now served a greater purpose, irrevocably placed in the center of what would prove to be the Orcs' finest hour.

As he ascended the final steps that led out of the catacombs below, Kairayn steeled himself for the duty now fallen to him. When he reached the upper landing and passed through the door to the main hall, he found several Initiates waiting for him. He began dispatching them, and they bounded off to gather what he requested without question. Kairayn sent the last Initiate to rouse the Masters he was promised and then strode out the front gate with newfound pride to assemble his warriors.

Grubbash watched him go from the back of the hall, a faint smirk on his face and a gleam in his eyes.

II THE SUMMONING

GRUBBASH GRIMVISAGE WATCHED from the highest parapet of his keep as night slowly descended, reveling in the earth's inevitable surrender to the night. There would be no moon, and the thought brought a smile to his greenish lips.

"Fitting, considering the events to come," he said to himself. All the pieces had fallen into place as he had designed, and now the game was all but set. Tonight would herald the culmination of years worth of scheming and plotting. From the day he had been chosen as a youth to be initiated into the arcane arts, he had dreamed of the day he would wield ultimate power. He had been a child prodigy, his intelligence and talent for sorcery unparalleled. He was dedicated to the ideal that the petty squabbling between Orcs could be stifled and their race exalted to their rightful place as rulers of the world.

In a nearby village, little more than a smudge on the fields below his perch, Kairayn was preparing his excursion to recover the Krullstone and supervising his hand-picked warriors as they organized their supplies. The Slavemaster had required surprisingly little prodding. Of course, Grubbash had not told him everything. It was not essential or prudent to divulge all his secrets, even to an old friend. Kairayn did not need to be distracted by the details Grubbash had neglected to share.

In the halls below the tower where he stood, Grubbash could already hear the night's work begun. The ominous sound of drums beating in steady rhythm, coupled with the deep chanting of his followers, was truly haunting. The sanctuary had been prepared earlier. The newly arrived slaves had been the only missing piece from the arrangements needed for tonight's ritual. Kairayn had returned with them just in time. The stunning alignment of required circumstances only occurred once in a lifetime. Lunar phases, planetary alignments, the ebb and flow of the earth energies, the solstice — everything was in its proper place — and now Grubbash simply waited for the correct hour to begin the summoning.

Grubbash's spine tingled at the thought of what was about to occur. A lifetime of preparation and desire would finally be realized. It had taken half a century to come to this point. After his twenty-year apprenticeship, Grubbash had begun to seek ways to empower himself and his brethren. He had spent years pouring over ancient manuscripts and tomes of power, searching for the keys that would unlock the doors of omnipotence. Piecing together scraps of lost spells and rituals and analyzing what the natural laws would allow and what had been done in past experiments, he had finally discovered how to contact beings from other dimensions.

Over time he had mastered spirit walking, a method of meditation by which the soul leaves the body and is free to wander the ethereal planes. It was during one of these meditations, while his spirit wandered between realms, that the Daemon Lord Serathes had made his presence known. Grubbash had seen many things that night: all that was, is, and has yet to be.

Grubbash remembered how terrifying and yet liberating it had felt to be in such close proximity to a being of nearly infinite power. He realized this was his opportunity to seize control of Fate and shape the future. Grubbash had questioned what was needed to fulfill the Orcs' destiny, and Serathes had explained everything to him.

To create the dimensional rift that would allow Serathes and his lieutenants — Athiel, the Lord of Uncertainty; Adimiron, The Bloody One; and Satariel, The Deceiver — to enter this world would take massive amounts of energy, more than any one mortal could muster. Serathes had instructed Grubbash on the rituals, the required arrangements, and the essential timing necessary to free the four Daemon Lords from their imprisonment in outer darkness. It would take the combined energy of an army of mages and then some.

Grubbash's reverie was interrupted suddenly by the sound of heavy footsteps climbing the winding staircase behind him. His temper flared briefly; he had given specific instructions that he was not to be disturbed. He did not bother to turn and see who had intruded upon his privacy. He could tell by the weighty footfalls that it was Bogran, Lord and Master of the city-state of Naril.

"I did not call for you; you have no business here," Grubbash scolded him. He turned abruptly and fixed his fiery gaze upon him.

Bogran was colossal; his enormous muscles rippled as he walked toward Grubbash and stretched the finely woven gray wool tunic and breeches he wore almost to the point of bursting. His long dark cloak fluttered behind him as he moved, revealing a wicked looking axe secured through his belt loop. About his neck on a golden chain hung a large dragon's talon, his personal sigil. He was probably the greatest warrior in the Empire; his expertise in military strategy and undeniable mastery of combat were unmatched. His breath rattled in his chest as he struggled to recover from his long climb, and Bogran's yellow eyes gleamed as they returned Grubbash's harsh stare.

"Be calm, Summoner. Our agreement warrants my presence here." His surly voice sounded like a barely-contained thunderstorm.

Grubbash had recruited Bogran into his plot years ago, bribing him with promises of power and wealth in exchange for his support. "I am very intimate with the details of our agreement," Grubbash growled. "You are gravely mistaken if you believe it gives you free reign over my keep."

"I did not come here to intrude, Summoner." His apologetic tone did not fool Grubbash. Bogran yielded to no living thing. "Everything is proceeding according to plan; the divided armies will meld seamlessly to create the most powerful fighting force in the world. Once a few loose ends are tied up, I can begin mobilizing our forces."

"Excellent! In just a few hours' time I will complete the final phase of our plan. The Overlords will be dealt with; they will either submit or be swept away like the useless relics they have become." A malicious grin spread across Grubbash's face, bestowing upon him a demonic look in the failing light.

"You are certain this can be done?" Bogran asked, a hint of skepticism creeping into his voice.

"Bogran, do not doubt that I can and will succeed in my endeavors tonight. I have waited too long for this day to falter now." The determination on his face declared that nothing would stand in his way.

"Very well. It is reassuring to see that you are up to the task. I also have waited long for this day, and I would hate for this opportunity to be wasted due to any miscalculation on your part."

They locked gazes for a moment, each probing the strength of the will of the other. Bogran was eager; he belonged on a battlefield, and his eyes belied his desire. Yet, despite his intimidating demeanor, it was he who turned away first. Grubbash's dedication to their success was fanatical, bordering on insanity.

"We understand each other then," Bogran muttered as he lowered his glance. "I will await further instructions from you in Naril."

Grubbash nodded his consent. Bogran spun deftly and marched toward the steps leading down from the tower. Silently Grubbash watched him leave, and as his momentous steps faded into nothing, he turned to survey the landscape once more.

The sun had slipped below the mountains to the west, and darkness was blanketing the land. Bogran did not know of the expedition Kairayn was leading to recover the missing Krullstone, and neither knew of its true purpose. The intricate web of plots he had woven was rapidly falling into place, and very soon no one would have the power to oppose him. Grubbash allowed himself to drift into a daydream, envisioning his new empire. Everything he beheld would be within his sole grasp. He would be the pinnacle of the world, and all things would be put in their rightful order according to his enlightened understanding.

Once more he was pulled from his musing by the reverberation of huge gongs from within the keep. Slowly the pounding noise sounded out the hour; it was eleven, and still there was so much to do before the night was done. Time was rapidly overtaking him.

Abandoning his perch and his imagination, Grubbash glided briskly to the steps that would carry him into the depths of the keep.

As he descended into the catacombs, the ominous chanting of his gathered sect rose up to meet him. He trekked past locked doors and dark passageways until he came to the end of the locus he was traveling. His path forward was blocked by a heavy iron-bound door, from behind which came the portentous mantra that had filled the stronghold since dusk. He opened the door with ease and drifted down the flight of stairs before him like a shadow, traveling even further into the gullet of the earth. At long last he came to his final destination.

Be calm. Focus.

His inner voice was urging him to contain a sudden rush of adrenaline. His anticipation was building; the excitement of completing a lifelong journey was about to boil over. Concentration was paramount now. Summoning rites of this nature had never been attempted, to his knowledge, and any slip on his part could quite possibly destroy him. He took a moment to ground himself and prepare mentally for the task he must now perform. Without further hesitation he swung open the door and strode regally into the shrine of the Druhedar.

Within was a huge cavern roughly carved out of the solid bedrock of the Durgen Range that was so large that Grubbash could hardly see the far wall. The sanctuary was lit by the soft glow of thousands of candles spread about the room, situated on altars, stone tables, even the cold stone floors. Dozens of mages dressed in dark robes encircled the walls and knelt with their heads to the floor, repeating the same litany unceasingly. Nestled against the far wall was a cadre of large kettledrums attended to by Initiates who pounded out the rhythm of the chant.

A huge pentacle within a circle had been carved into the rocky floor, an altar of obsidian adorned with strange runic markings placed within the center. Archaic runes were also patterned into the stone around the circle and pentacle, completing the system. Upon the altar rested the *Arcanomicon*, the great book of the Druhedar, which housed the compilation of all their mystical knowledge.

Grubbash surveyed the room before he proceeded, insuring that all had been prepared as he had ordered. In three of the empty spaces between the five points of the pentacle were painted geometric triangles as he had instructed. On the plane of each triangle, strapped by strong cords to poles of wood, two of the Simoril slaves that Kairayn had brought back with him were bound. Around the perimeter of the circle, three at each of the five points of the pentacle, more of the slaves were bound with leather straps to wooden tables specially crafted for the ritual.

Grubbash proceeded to his place at the altar in the center of the chamber. The book before him was already opened to the correct place, prepared by him earlier. Grubbash closed his eyes and focused his attention, letting his followers' dirge wash over him and pull him into a trance-like state. While raising his hands to the sky, fists clenched, and bowing his head, he began to recite the rite in a booming voice that echoed off the cavernous walls around him.

The chanting reached a feverish pitch, the drums beating in an ever-increasing cadence. As Grubbash continued, his disciples rose singly from the outer circle until one was standing behind each of the bound slaves at the points of the pentacle.

As the chanting reached a crescendo, they drew curved blades from beneath their robes and approached the captives bound to the tables. The drums hammered a final note as Grubbash bellowed the last word of the incantation. At the same moment the standing Initiates smoothly reached out and cut the throats of the shackled slaves.

Dead silence fell across the grotto; the resounding drums went ominously quiet, and the only sound was that of the final dying gasps of the slaves as the life-blood drained from their rent jugular veins.

The blood was collected in special gutters constructed into the tables that ran down into the carved pentacle on the chamber floor. As the carving filled with the blood of innocent sacrifices, the Druhedar began to chant anew, softly yet hauntingly. An eerie red glow emanated from within the pentacle as the low voices slowly began to rise.

Grubbash was filled with a sense of power. The gift of sacrifice granted potent mystical energies. He began to form intricate designs in the air with his outstretched fingers, beginning the final recitation as tracers of red and orange and yellow mist gave life to the arcane symbols he was creating.

Once more the chanting reached its climax, the booming of the drums and the clamor of the Druhedar rising to a deafening roar. The triangles set within the circle began to gleam with yellow light, shining upwards toward the ceiling. The Simorils still living, tied to their posts about the triangles, began to scream frantically with the realization of their fate, adding fuel to the cacophony filling the air.

As Grubbash finished the last line of the rite, the air above the triangles began to crackle and shimmer with energy, arcs forking into the center of the room. Without warning the air before the altar seemed to tear itself apart, and a rift began to appear, engulfing the room in a faint scarlet glow. As the rift grew larger, the slaves nearby gave a final tortured sigh, and then their very souls were torn from their bodies, disappearing in a flash of gray smoke into the widening portal. A low rumble rose out of the earth, and the whole room began to shake, causing streamers of dust to fall from the ceiling. Only an impenetrable black void lay beyond, disturbingly silent and serene. The earth groaned in protest as the portal touched the floor, a new shower of dust and small rocks falling from the canopy.

Black shapes began to manifest in the emptiness on the other side of the opening before the Druhedar, somehow darker even than the world in which they dwelled. Then suddenly it was as if a great veil was lifted, and a nightmare scene of a magnitude never before imagined possible unfolded before them. A harsh, hot wind blew out, sweeping about the room, extinguishing the candles and stealing the breath of the occupants with its foulness. Many of the mages shrank back in terror.

Grubbash stared in morbid fear, his mouth agape as he watched the specters issue forth from a dimension so horrible as to be unspeakable. Words could not describe the utter torment and anguish one saw in that fleeting glimpse into Hell. Grubbash wondered if he had gone wrong somewhere, if somehow he had overlooked some tiny detail and condemned them all to a fate worse than death.

Creatures began to emerge from the scarlet doorway, gigantic and forbidding. A pervasive sense of imminent doom filled the air, and some of the Initiates collapsed in a heap, scratching at their eyes. Shades and wraiths spilled forth from the breach.

As the screams of the tortured souls rose, etching themselves forever in the memories of those present, huge forms began to materialize in the portal. Grubbash cowered in fear, edging backward until he was pressed against the wall. The breath caught in Grubbash's throat as the benefactors of his work took shape in the crimson glow and stepped firmly from one world into another. The spirits writhing through the shadows darted back into their own dimension, their wails fading as they exited.

The portal flared with unexpected fervor and winked out. Unnerving silence gripped the hall as it plunged into blackness, and Grubbash dared not move lest his sanity be challenged again by the horrors he had just beheld. He was overcome with fatigue, his psyche frayed almost beyond recovery.

Then something began to move through the utter blackness. Grubbash could hear great breaths being drawn as four sets of lumbering footsteps, so heavy they shook the stone beneath them, closed in on him.

Serathes released a deafening roar that shook the foundations of the cavern, threatening to bring the tons of rock above them crashing down. The candles that had lit the room previously sprang to life again, filling the sanctuary with their warm glow. Grubbash raised his eyes, and his mind went numb as the being before him fixed him with its piercing gaze. Grubbash felt a bottomless pit open inside of him, and darkness welled within his soul. Unconsciousness took him then, and Grubbash collapsed to the floor in a heap.

Kairayn awoke refreshed and ready at sunrise, a familiar feeling of excitement rushing through his veins as he oversaw the final preparations. He had turned in shortly after nightfall, resolving to get as much rest as possible before setting out on yet another journey that might drag on even longer than the last. Before the sun had crested the horizon, he and the members of his party had already risen and were readying themselves for the long road ahead.

After leaving Grubbash in the catacombs yesterday, he had moved quickly to gather his party and the necessary resources for their trek. He had felt positively inspired by Grubbash's conviction, and the pride he felt from being chosen to serve on such an important endeavor was immeasurable. He had roused the Masters who had been assigned to him — vicious sorcerers trained by the Druhedar order to inflict maximum pain and destruction with their magic — and hand-picked the warriors who would join them on their quest. Altogether there would be twelve of them traveling to the old kingdom of Valinar. Very little should be able to stand in their way.

Now, the Initiates helping to procure their supplies were loading the last of the packhorses, and their personal steeds had arrived from the stables earlier that morning. Kairayn strolled regally around the muster area, which was situated in a small village that served as an auxiliary outpost just to the south of Grimknoll. He checked the horses and stores that were contained within saddlebags and crates that were tied atop the pack animals.

"Master," one of the servants greeted him as he fell into step, "all of the supplies have been secured on the beasts. Everything is in order as you requested."

"Very good," Kairayn replied. "We will depart immediately. I want to cover good ground today."

"As you wish, master. I will inform the High Summoner of your departure. Glory and honor to you." The Orc banged his fist sharply against his chest in salute before walking away.

"Mount up!" Kairayn ordered sharply as he pulled himself into his saddle. "We're moving out now, double file. Grok and Dorg, you're in charge of the packhorses."

Saying nothing further, the Orcs fell into place within the column and trotted down the road. Kairayn rode at the head of the party and kept a sharp eye out for any who might try to shadow them. Later he would send a couple of his Orcs to circle back and make sure they were not being tracked, but for now it would only rouse suspicion.

Kairayn looked to his right at the looming monolith of Grimknoll. He was curious why Grubbash had not turned out to see them off this morning, but if everything had gone as planned the night before, he would not risk compromising this mission by overseeing its departure. It was best if the demons did not know the two were connected. He wondered for a moment if Grubbash had been successful.

He wondered darkly what, if anything, within those walls was watching them leave.

III A DRINK AMONG FRIENDS

LAZARUS ARKENSTONE PUT the quill back in the ink jar and pushed his chair away from the polished oak desk. He had been cooped up inside this office all day filling out the paperwork that had been piling up while he was away. Requisitions for supplies, transfer orders, work orders for blacksmiths, and dispatches created a mound of paper that he had spent all morning trying to work through. Since sunrise he had been signing away, frantically trying to catch up with the bureaucratic red tape.

His company had returned to Kylenshar late in the evening last night from a long patrol of the eastern border. They had been dispatched on orders to investigate reports of a tribe of Ratmen who had crossed the Myrrh River and raided trade routes and villages north of Kalimith. As the commanding officer of the Phoenix Legion, he could have relegated the mission to one of the other officers, but he felt that it was his duty to lead his soldiers into battle personally.

The Phoenix Legion was usually dispatched to deal with these types of threats, serving as their country's shock troops and first response to hostility. The Phoenix Legion was the elite fighting force in Illendale, its warriors trained to the very limit of human capability.

Small wisps of Lazarus' long blond hair managed to escape his ponytail and drift in front of his brown eyes. He reached out across the stack of completed papers for his mug of black herb tea, long since gone cold, and grimaced as he finished drinking the contents. He thought briefly about calling to the clerk on the other side of the closed door to bring fresh tea but instead decided to get up and move around a bit.

He rose from his chair, his lean form moving with cat-like grace. Lazarus was slightly taller than average, making him look thin under the loose-fitting forest green tunic he wore. He was well muscled, though not overly strong, and was gifted with lightning quick reflexes. His deep brown eyes reflected his calm and cool-headed demeanor. His high-set cheekbones and fair complexion added to his charming look, giving an impression of youth not befitting his station.

Lazarus had apprenticed to a Blademaster when he was fourteen years old, devoting his life at that moment to learning the art of combat and modern warfare. He had learned quickly enough, and when he had reached his eighteenth year, he joined the army. He had been promoted to sergeant after he had completed the standard military training and given command of his own squad. Over the next six years he worked his way through the ranks, enduring skirmishes and battles with the enemies of Illendale. His experience fending off Orcs, Kobolds, Ratmen, and others had honed his already masterful skills. At twenty-four he was granted the title of Blademaster; two years later Commander Durham retired from service, and Lazarus was given command of the Legion. That was six years ago. Having spent half of his life in the Phoenix Legion, it was an easy transition; most of the men already knew him on sight and trusted him as a competent leader. He was an honorable man and above all loyal to his men and kingdom.

He stretched briefly, his aching muscles reminding him of how uncomfortable the unpadded wooden seat really was, and looked about the sparsely decorated office. Aside from the desk there was little else in the small room; a small table on the wall opposite his desk sat unadorned next to the only entrance. A single curtained window let in a dash of sunlight from the outside world, and a couple of small potted plants were placed in the corners for some decoration. It wasn't the most inviting room, but then again Lazarus hardly spent any time in his office. He preferred to be outside, not stuck behind a desk writing and signing orders.

Lazarus walked around the desk, collected the stack of paper-work he had been working on, and strode toward the door. Holding his effects in one hand, he opened the wooden door with a creak of hinges and stepped into the reception area outside. There was a bit more dec-oration out here: potted and hanging plants, serene paintings of nature, and chairs for those who were waiting to be seen. Several other doors identical to the one Lazarus had just exited led to the other offices. A set of double wooden doors on the far wall led outside to the square inside the military complex, and the clerk's large desk sat against the plaster wall on his left.

"Had enough for today, sir?" the bald aide asked sarcastically over the rims of his thick glasses.

"Good morning to you, too, Tully," Lazarus replied with a smile as he dropped the stack of finished paperwork on the desk. "I see you've gotten up on the wrong side of the bed again."

"Sitting behind a desk all day and missing such wonderful weather will do that to you, Commander Arkenstone. Oh, it's not morn-ing anymore either. You've worked most of the day through. It's well past midday," Tully admonished, gesturing unenthusiastically at the window.

Lazarus looked and was startled to realize that he had indeed worked all through the morning into the afternoon. He had intended to finish his report on the mission and then spend the rest of the day relax-ing, but duty had swept the day away from him.

"Would you please forward my report to General Markoll, as well as deliver these requisitions, Sergeant?" Lazarus asked politely. It usually was not a good idea to give orders to Sergeant Tully, despite Lazarus' superior rank. Tully was getting old, and he had a tendency to get grumpy when younger folk did not show proper respect for their elders, regardless of his zealous adherence to military discipline.

Tully nodded his acquiescence and returned to the stack of orders and requests he had been working on. Lazarus walked toward the closed doors, the hinges creaking slightly as he pulled one open and stepped out into the waning afternoon sunlight.

Outside a high wall of stone surrounded a dirt courtyard.

Several barracks lined the wall to the left of the command post he had just exited. The main gate was immediately to the right; beyond that were the stables and the various workshops of the artisans who supplied equipment and services to the army. In the center of the yard, a circle of rough gray stones surrounded several flagpoles upon which were raised the standards of each legion. Units of men were moving all about, some performing training exercises while others marched off to other duties.

Lazarus walked down the few steps that led from the command post's wooden porch and began to lazily meander across the yard. He was immediately enveloped by the sounds of activity that permeated the grounds. Blacksmiths' hammers rang in the near distance as they struck heavy steel anvils; soldiers recited military rhymes as they marched around the yard, and the *clack clack clack* of practice weapons filled the air where soldiers were training for combat.

A slight breeze picked up as Lazarus crossed the courtyard, gently tossing his golden hair. Some of the men he passed recognized him and saluted even though he wasn't in uniform. He saluted back and smiled, glad to be out of the office, and continued on his way. As he strolled across the grounds, he soaked up the sunlight, reveling in the cool day that had not yet yielded to winter's icy grip.

Lazarus stopped at the ring of flagpoles in the center of the yard and gazed up at the emblems for each legion, his own included. He looked around, admiring the sights and sounds of the bustling center of military might for his nation. In a small grassy area nestled between two of the barracks, he noticed something that caught his attention. Two men were facing off, wooden swords in hand, while two other men sat on a nearby bench watching the event. Instantly he recognized the men and began walking in their direction.

The two men sparring were his younger brothers, Vinson and Aldric. Relaxing on the bench were his best friends, Major Layek Ogras and Azrael. As he approached, his brothers began their duel, feigning and thrusting, trying to gain an edge against each other.

Vinson was short and stocky, a powerfully built man with short, spiky brown hair. He was a captain in the Phoenix Legion, as was

Aldric, and an accomplished soldier. He was somewhat of an anomaly, having learned to wield minor magics to complement his fighting skills. As the two brothers battled back and forth across the area, Vinson was shouting taunts at his younger brother, trying to goad him into making a mistake.

Aldric, the youngest of the three, had also apprenticed to a master warrior when he was old enough. Like Lazarus, he was tall and wiry, his motions fluid and rapid like quicksilver. He wore his hair short like Vinson, using a wax derivative to spike it up like a porcupine's quills. Aldric had a wicked temper that had a tendency to get the best of him when he became frustrated or confused. His apprenticeship had taught him to harness that inherent weakness and use it as a deadly weapon against his opponents. He had been training for years, and when he became enraged, he was all but unstoppable, impervious to pain and the wounds inflicted upon him.

"Beautiful day, isn't it, boys?" Lazarus said, as he finally reached the small lawn and stood next to the bench that Layek and Azrael were sitting on.

"Welcome back, Laz! You're just in time for the show." Layek looked up at him with a whimsical grin and stretched out his hand in greeting to his old friend. Layek was a giant of a man, a huge mass of bulging muscles. He wore his short, sandy brown hair flat on his head, and his serene hazel eyes were a sharp contrast to the combative look of his large stature. His voice was deep and rough, yet surprisingly gentle. His sense of humor was as liberal as the size of his muscles; Layek was famous for his wit and lack of seriousness.

Lazarus had met Layek during his apprenticeship, and the two had quickly become friends. They had both been assigned to the Phoenix Legion when they had completed their training, and although Layek was a few years his senior, they had advanced together through the ranks. When Lazarus had been promoted to commander of the Legion, he had immediately named Layek his second in command and would be hard pressed to find a better man for the job. Layek was a dedicated and disciplined soldier despite his comic attitude. His courage and bravery were unsurpassed as was his loyalty to his friends, and his experience with the Legion made him a lethal opponent.

Vinson and Aldric were still circling their makeshift arena, skillfully testing each other, each switching fluidly from offense to defense and back again. The sound of their wooden weapons echoed off the walls of the nearby buildings, creating the illusion of more combatants battling than there actually were. Vinson was still taunting his younger brother, but by now Aldric was shooting back his own playful comments.

"Don't let him distract you, Aldric. Concentrate," Lazarus instructed his sibling.

"How long before he gets frustrated and loses it, do you think, Laz?" Layek quipped.

"How about the two of you leave them alone and let them take care of themselves?" Azrael interjected, annoyed at Layek's attempt to distract his friend for his own amusement. His dark penetrating eyes flared momentarily, and a slight breeze briefly caused his black robes to billow. He was tall and skinny, and his dark hair added to his intimidating visage. Azrael, unlike his friends, was a sorcerer. He was gifted with a natural talent to channel the Earth's energies. None of them were sure of Azrael's true origins; as an orphan with no place else to go, he had apprenticed to the University of Sorcery. He had never said where his family was or what happened to them, and when anyone asked him about the subject, he became solitary and aloof. He was taciturn by nature, preferring to watch and listen rather than dive headlong into conversation.

He had grown into a powerful sorcerer, his years of training honing his raw potential into an efficient skill. He was not a ranking officer in the Legion like his companions were; he was a member of the platoon of sorcerers assigned to the Phoenix Legion. Of course, the sorcerers were not forced to join the army, but Azrael preferred traveling with his friends to being trapped within the confines of the University's halls.

"Sounds like you've been spending too much time with Sergeant Tully, Azrael." Lazarus' jest evoked a staunch chuckle from Layek.

The duel between the two brothers was picking up pace now, the two clashing swords with a loud crack. They stood there for a moment, swords crossed, trying to force the other to give way. Vinson tried to sweep Aldric's leg with a swift low kick, but he was too quick to fall prey to the maneuver. Aldric jumped backwards lightly and then lunged right back into the fray, bringing his sword down in a vertical slash. Vinson sidestepped the blow and spun around, bringing his sword level and trying to catch Aldric across the back as his momentum carried him forward. Once again the younger Arkenstone was too quick, reversing his vertical slash to parry the blow and then tucking into a roll that carried him a few feet away. Instantly he jumped up again, just in time to meet Vinson's new onslaught.

"Wow! They're really going at it," Lazarus expressed. "Anyone care to tell me why this started in the first place?"

"It's just a friendly duel between two brothers," Layek replied.

"They wanted to test each other to see who was better with the sword, without magic, of course," Azrael put in with a sour glance at Layek.

"All I said was that paltry spells were no match for a good weapon in the hands of a skilled warrior," Layek defended. "Or as honorable," he added quietly.

"Well, so long as they both understand that it's a friendly contest. You know how their tempers can be," Lazarus said.

"Don't worry, Lazarus," Azrael soothed. "Neither of them will be hurt. I can heal any damage they might inflict on each other."

"That's very comforting, Azrael," Lazarus replied skeptically.

Vinson and Aldric were still locked in combat, pushing each other back and forth across the makeshift arena. Vinson made a quick jab at Aldric's torso, and when Aldric brought his blade down to avert the blow, Vinson's wooden blade was shattered. Splinters flew off in all directions as his weapon disintegrated, momentarily throwing them both off guard.

Vinson recovered first and, realizing his weapon was lost, lunged at Aldric with his bare hands. Aldric tried to bring his weapon around and fend off the assault, but for once he was too slow. Vinson slammed into him, sending both their bodies tumbling onto the ground. They wrestled, rolling back and forth, each trying to pin the other and end the duel. Vinson managed to get on top of Aldric and pin his arms.

"Yield?" Vinson asked, breathing heavily.

"Never!" Aldric shot back.

With that Aldric thrust his legs upward, throwing Vinson's unbalanced weight forward and off of his chest. Vinson was not expecting this sudden shift and rolled away, falling face first in the grass. Aldric pulled himself off the earth and recovered his weapon, wheeling sharply to find where his brother had landed. He saw Vinson resting on his knees with his back turned several paces away, trying to brush the grass and dirt off his face. He began advancing on his brother quietly, intent on subduing him and forcing his surrender with the wooden weapon.

As he was closing in, Vinson regained his senses and turned. Seeing that Aldric was nearly on top of him, he quickly jumped to his feet. Aldric raised the tip of his sword, prepared to continue the duel if his brother would not admit defeat.

"Do you surrender, Vinny?"

"Would you really attack an unarmed man if I didn't?" Vinson inquired of his younger brother, gesturing at the wooden sword in his hands.

"You're hardly defenseless, Vinny," Aldric said with a wide grin, "although you do move like a sloth."

"Oh," Vinson laughed. "In that case I don't surrender. Any sloth should be able to handle somebody with the ferocity of a bunny."

Aldric chuckled at the comeback. Neither of them would give up, but now he had an advantage. Vinson had to know that his chances of disarming him were slim, and yet he still would not surrender. Lazarus seemed to notice the direction this fight was heading and smoothly intervened to prevent things from getting out of hand.

"How about we all head over to the Blue Moon for a round or two?"

"I second that motion," Layek said, his eyes lighting up. He loved good drink more than anything.

"Sounds like a plan to me. What do you think?" Aldric asked without lowering his guard.

"I think it sounds like you're trying to save yourself from a beating," Vinson said playfully.

"Did that fall jar the sense right out of you?" Aldric retorted. "You should accept this generous offer of peace before you get your head cracked."

"Very well," Vinson said laughing. "Well fought, brother," he added as he walked towards Aldric, extending his hand to shake and cement the truce.

Lazarus began to walk over to where the remains of Vinson's practice blade had fallen so that it could be disposed of, while Azrael and Layek stood up and started strolling toward the main gate.

Aldric was still grinning when he reached out to grasp his brother's hand, thinking that their combat had come to a satisfactory conclusion. Vinson, on the other hand, had other plans. When he was finally within reach of Aldric, instead of taking his hand in friendship, he took a quick step forward. Aldric gasped in surprise as his older brother firmly planted his right leg behind his own at the knee, placed his outstretched palm on his chest, and pushed.

Aldric was totally unprepared for this ambush and completely lost his balance. As he fell backward, he dropped his weapon and reached up to grab Vinson's tunic with both hands. Both brothers plummeted to the ground; Vinson's face plunged once again into the soft, finger length blades of grass.

"You dim-witted buffoon! You weren't supposed to drag me down with you!" Vinson exclaimed as he tried to spit out the grass he had inadvertently consumed.

"How's the grass taste?" Aldric responded.

The others came running up, believing the battle between the two younger Arkenstones had taken a turn for the worse. Upon closer inspection, however, they found Aldric and Vinson laughing hysterically and throwing clumps of grass at each other. Azrael began laughing, too, joined shortly by Layek and Lazarus.

"If the two of you are done grazing, maybe we can get underway here," Lazarus said playfully between laughs. He looked to the sky to see the sun lazily sinking toward the horizon. "If we leave now, we can still get a table before the inn gets too crowded."

Layek reached down with his huge arms and bodily lifted both brothers off the ground. After a brief moment to brush themselves off, the five of them strolled off together. Their ultimate destination was a popular tavern named the Blue Moon Inn. The soldiers of the army held it in very high esteem, and by dusk the establishment would be packed full.

The five friends meandered across the courtyard, past the ring of flagpoles with their standards waving lazily in the delicate breeze. They passed through the heavy wooden gate and into the streets of Kylenshar. The sun was nearly below the horizon, casting long shadows in the lanes and byways of the capital. Traffic was relatively light as some folk made their way home from a long day's work, while others were still perusing the shops and vendors that lined the wide street.

The area surrounding the barracks on the eastern side of the city was dominated primarily by industry. Warehouses full of finished goods and raw materials stood like silent sentinels in the background waiting to be called to life. Vendors stood in doorways and next to wooden carts announcing their wares in loud voices that wafted over the passersby like a fog.

They continued unimpeded for several blocks, catching up on events for the last couple of weeks before turning north up a side street, which looked much like the one they had just left.

Just a few buildings down was their destination. The Blue Moon Inn was a two-story wooden building painted a lighter shade of blue with several shuttered windows on each floor facing out into the street. A carved sign hung out from the doorway, identifying the establishment. The paint on the building was old and faded, giving it a rundown and unkempt look. The narrow street blocked out most of the remaining daylight, adding to the dark and dreary atmosphere. Light filtered through the shuttered windows, and the sounds of entertainment and laughter echoed off the other nearby buildings.

"I hope there's still a seat for us," Layek grumbled as they approached the double doors.

As Layek reached for the handle, a handful of drunken soldiers threw open the door and stumbled out into the dim light of the street. On their sleeves was the insignia of the Chimaera Legion, also stationed in Kylenshar. The group stood aside as the men awkwardly made their way down the short steps.

"Looks like the party started without you, Layek," Vinson said with a grin.

"So long as they haven't emptied the barrels yet and there's still some chaps at the dice table willing to lose their money, I'm happy," Layek replied in an optimistic tone. He loved gambling almost as much as drinking, even though he rarely won anything.

The five friends continued in through the door and found that the place wasn't quite filled to capacity. In stark contrast to the exterior, the interior was neat and well maintained; a dozen lanterns hung from the rafters high overhead to provide ample lighting. Oak chairs and tables filled the room from one end to the other, and directly to the rear the bar was situated. Kegs and barrels filled with all types of liquor lined the wall behind the smooth polished serving bar, which stretched nearly the whole length of the back wall except for a single door that led to the kitchens and access to the upper level. Two large stone fireplaces with mantels dominated the walls to either side, still unlit because the weather had not yet gotten cold enough to warrant their use.

On their right, near the entrance, were situated several tables designed for playing dice and cards, with a dozen or so gamblers already huddled around them. The tall stools that sat at the bar were all filled, but a few of the tables spread around the square room were not yet occupied. The friends chose a table near the gambling den and sat down.

"So, Laz. How was your little vacation?" Azrael asked as he pulled out his chair and sat down.

"Yeah, and tell us why we weren't invited while you're at it," Aldric added.

Before Lazarus had a chance to respond, a tall woman wearing a plain brown tunic and pants approached their table. Her short curly hair was black as soot, and her dark, watchful eyes scanned the room as she walked. She wore a white apron stained with food and grease from working in the kitchen and moved with purpose, carrying a large round tray stacked with five tall mugs of ale.

"Good evening, boys," she said as she sat the tray on the table and began placing one cup in front of each of them.

"Hello, Sermin," Lazarus greeted. "Busy tonight?"

"Oh, busy enough I guess. With all these well-muscled soldiers about, the serving girls I hire would rather flirt than do any work so I get stuck doing it all myself. Anyway, I saw you come in and brought you a round of my best ale." Sermin shot harsh stares at her hired help as she talked.

"You're too good to us, Sermin." Layek was positively bubbling with joy at the sight of the brew.

"What corner of the world is this from?" asked Aldric, ever interested in the lands beyond Illendale's borders.

"This particular brew came straight from the Dwarven lands," she enlightened them. "Ibrahim brought it back with him from one of his trading journeys. The Dwarves call it Golden Rock. Mighty fine stuff, too," she added.

"How is old Ibrahim?" asked Vinson. "We haven't seen him for awhile."

"He spends most of his time traveling," she said woefully. "His merchant venture has him running all over to find the best products. He just returned from a trip to the Dwarven capital. He's at the warehouse now supervising while his cargo gets unloaded."

Her husband, Ibrahim, was a trader who dealt in all manner of goods. He traveled all across the lands seeking exotic wares to bring back to Illendale and sell. He did quite well financially, although he had to spend most of his time away from home.

"Well, gentlemen," she sighed as she collected her tray, "I had best get back to work. Somebody's got to keep the hired help in line."

"Thanks for the drinks," Aldric responded.

"Send Ibrahim our best wishes and good luck with the servers," Vinson said with a wink.

Sermin smiled back and marched toward the kitchen, chastising a blonde-haired serving girl as she went. Several more small groups of customers had come in while they were talking. Only a couple of tables still remained empty, and the hall was filled with the mingled voices and laughter of men enjoying good drink and company. The five friends turned to their drinks while yet more people came in through the front door.

"Looks like we got here just in time to beat the crowd," Lazarus said.

"Yeah, but you still haven't answered why you didn't bring us with you on your mission." Aldric glared at his eldest brother. He did not appreciate being left behind while there was action in the wilderness.

"There wasn't much to see or do," Lazarus said defensively. "We tracked this tribe of Ratmen around the village of Brookhollow for a week or so. A few skirmishes broke out, and eventually they led us right to their stronghold."

"I still don't understand why you wouldn't bring us along, Laz," Layek grumbled as he drained his glass.

"There just wasn't any need for it," Lazarus said in a low voice. "There were less than five hundred of them and almost a thousand of us. I took the whole first company. Ratmen may be crafty and volatile, but they are also cowards. When we assaulted their fortress and they found themselves outnumbered by at least two to one, they turned and ran without much of a fight. More to the point, I would hate to bring along the only family I have and then see them get hurt or killed unnecessarily."

Lazarus and his two younger brothers were all that remained of the Arkenstone family. Their parents had died of yellow fever when they were still very young after an epidemic had nearly wiped out their whole village. The three brothers survived and were sent to their only relative, an uncle who lived in the mining city of Pilban on the northern spur of the Serpentspine Mountains. He had subsequently been killed in an accident. After that the brothers were placed in an orphanage. As soon as they had been old enough, each of them apprenticed to the military to escape the dreadful orphanage life.

"Killed?" Vinson blurted. "By Ratmen? It would never happen."

"Still playing protector, Laz," Layek admonished. "Sooner or later you're going to have to accept that your brothers are soldiers, too; accomplished soldiers at that. You can't keep them out of danger forever."

"He's right, Laz," Azrael added. "Vinny and Aldric are grown men. They may not have the experience you do, but they are well-trained and capable of taking care of themselves."

"Besides that, who are you going to rely on when the Orcs come charging over the river?" Vinson inquired. "Some day our barbaric neighbors to the south are not going to settle for petty raids."

"When they do, they'll find the invincible Phoenix Legion waiting for them!" Layek expressed emphatically. "We'll send them packing with their tails tucked between their legs!"

"You'd better knock on wood, Layek, before you curse us all," Lazarus said seriously.

They finished their drinks, and Layek raised his arm to signal a passing barmaid for more. She bent low to Layek so he could give her their order over the din that had risen with the continual arrival of new guests. Layek whispered something into her ear, and she giggled as she trotted off.

When the barmaid returned with her tray, there were two glasses for each of the five friends seated at the table. Layek put a few silver coins on her tray to pay for their drinks, along with a little extra for her efforts.

"Did you get enough for us to drink?" Azrael jested as he stared at the two large glasses situated in front of him.

"Drink up, guys!" Layek lifted the first glass to his lips. Before any of them could even say anything, he had gulped down the entire contents of his mug. He slammed it down on the table when he was finished.

"Getting a head start on a good night, Layek?" Lazarus asked sarcastically. The rest of them raised their glasses as well and began to chug down the golden hued brew, slamming down their glasses when they were finished.

"Like I always say," Layek said as he lifted his second glass, "if you can't fight, drink!"

"I'll drink to that," Vinson put in as he followed Layek's lead.

"What are a few good drinks among friends anyway?" Lazarus raised his glass, too.

When their glasses were finished, they ordered another round and continued to drink to all manner of things: health, honor, battle, good ale, and anything else that Layek could think of.

When Layek was sufficiently intoxicated, he stood up from his chair and excused himself to head over to the gambling tables where a multitude of drunken soldiers were tossing dice. Aldric opted to join the action and stumbled after him.

The bar had filled up completely by now. Darkness had settled on the city for the night, and off-duty soldiers and citizens came in to relieve the stress from a hard day's work. All the seats in the house were filled, leaving many to hover around tables already occupied by their friends or just to wander around the room in search of quality companionship. Occasional shouts of dismay and happiness came from the dice tables off to the side whenever somebody won or lost.

Lazarus was enjoying an in-depth conversation with Azrael and Vinson when a young boy dressed in the red garb of the Crimson Guard, the branch of the army responsible for policing the cities, came bursting in through the door, gasping for breath. Few noticed his dramatic entrance aside from Lazarus. The hair on the back of his neck bristled.

The boy's eyes scanned the room briefly, seeking the target of his visit. He spied Sermin coming through the door in the back and walked briskly over to her. Their discussion was inaudible, but when Sermin turned and pointed in his direction, he knew the messenger was there for him. The boy nodded as he fixed his eyes on Lazarus and began easing his way through the crowd toward their table.

"I wonder who wants to see me now," Lazarus sighed in resignation. "A soldier's duties are never finished it seems."

"Maybe General Markoll wants you to report in person," Vinson suggested.

"I doubt it," was Lazarus' reply. "Markoll wouldn't send for me this late, and even if he did, he would send someone from headquarters. Somebody wants to see me, though I cannot think who."

"Perhaps someone from the High Council needs you for something," Azrael offered.

"It's possible," Lazarus mused, "but I still doubt it. In any case, we'll find out soon enough."

"Good evening, Commander Arkenstone," the boy said nervously as he saluted. Obviously he wasn't sure how Lazarus would take the intrusion. "I'm sorry for disturbing you, but I have an urgent message."

"You don't have to salute, lad; I'm not in uniform. Have a seat if you like," Lazarus said kindly as he gestured towards the open chair next to him.

"Thank you, sir." The boy's stance softened visibly as he spoke. "The Queen requires your presence at the palace immediately. She requests that you come quickly and without delay."

A warning flag shot up in Lazarus' mind. "What is this about?"

"I don't know, sir; the Queen and her advisor will speak to no one but you. I fear something terrible has happened, sir."

"Very well. Send word to the palace that I will be there as soon as possible."

"Yes, sir." The messenger saluted once again before turning on his heel and working his way back to the door.

"What's going on, Lazarus?" Azrael asked quietly. "This is highly unusual."

"I don't know, Azrael. I've got a bad feeling about this." Lazarus rose and tucked his chair back under the table. "I guess I had better get going."

"Well, good luck to you, brother, whatever happens," Vinson said.

"I'll fill you in tomorrow," Lazarus replied. "Until then, drink up and have a good night. Tell Layek and Aldric not to lose all their money."

Lazarus eased his way through the crowd. As he stepped outside, the cool night air wrapped around him like a cloak, raising goose bumps on his skin and making him wish he had brought some warmer clothes. The street was dark and quiet, the night sky empty and cavernous against the thin sliver of the moon. Lazarus was alone in the silence with nothing but the sound of his own footfalls to keep him company.

He looked around momentarily before he began his short trek. The palace grounds were little more than a mile away, and even at a leisurely pace it would not take him long to get there. He whistled as he walked to keep the growing stillness at bay.

Suddenly the hair on Lazarus' neck rose up stiffly, and he had the unmistakable sensation of eyes watching him. He stopped dead in his tracks, straining to catch any noise that might give the hidden watcher away. For several minutes he waited, but nothing happened. He thought perhaps it might be footpads or a pickpocket who probably realized his chosen prey was not so defenseless and went on in search of easier targets.

Lazarus walked a little more briskly now, pushing his sense of dread deep down inside to pay more attention to where he was going. He knew that worrying about what dire circumstances could require his presence this late would only hamper his ability to reason. Fear was a soldier's worst enemy. He focused on the road ahead and thought nothing more of what awaited him.

As Lazarus walked away, the cold emotionless eyes of the doppelganger watched him go.

IV DARK VISIONS

MELYNDA WOKE FROM her sleep in a cold sweat. With a gasp and a sudden jerk she sat up straight in her bed, throwing off the silk sheets. She glanced at the gilded clock on the nightstand next to her, squinting to make out the time. Eleven o'clock. She sighed and lay back against her down pillows. Dark dreams had troubled her rest.

Closing her eyes momentarily, she let herself come fully awake and allowed the cascade of images that had been her dream settle into her mind. Her shoulder length light brown hair was damp and matted to her head. She shivered lightly, not because it was cold in her chamber within the Royal Palace but because she knew better than to brush such a dream casually aside as a meaningless nightmare. She had the unique gift of foresight; her psychic and empathic abilities were famous across the kingdom.

She had experienced dream visions before, though not usually so terrifying. All of them paled in comparison to the severity and darkness of this one.

As the full weight of her knowledge settled onto her shoulders, Melynda stood up shakily. She thought about calling for the guards who were without doubt keeping watch but thought better of it. The magnitude of the situation called for discretion lest she create an unnecessary panic. Donning a thick white cotton robe over her nightgown and stepping into her slippers, she staggered to the door. She took a moment to steady herself. So shaken was she by the horrible realization that her nightmarish vision was dangerously close to becoming reality that she had to fight back the urge to collapse to the floor and cry.

Once she had solidified her composure, Melynda opened the mahogany paneled door and stepped cautiously into the dark hallway. At this hour most of the tenants of the Palace were asleep. Only a few members of the housekeeping staff would be awake and, of course, the guards on duty that evening. Most of the arched hall was shrouded in darkness, but a few lit oil lamps mounted to the stone walls cast pools of dim light.

She made her way down the marble tiled floor, her pattering footsteps echoing lightly off the walls, walking briskly from one circle of yellow light to the next, heading for the great foyer. There would be guards posted there whose service she could acquire. What she needed now was to wake the Queen. She must be alerted of these dark visions immediately. And she needed someone to find Commander Lazarus Arkenstone.

∽   ∽   ∽

Lazarus approached one of the four gates that led into the palace grounds. It had taken him a little less than twenty minutes to walk from the Blue Moon Inn and through the Tranquil Gardens that ringed the high walls that separated the castle from the rest of the city. Two men of the Crimson Guard stood on either side of the reinforced wooden gates, blanketed in a halo of light created by large braziers that hung from the archway on either side of the entrance.

Lazarus approached the men calmly, materializing out of the darkness as though from thin air. The guards immediately noticed and snapped to attention, peering warily at the man before them. They were obviously uneasy; something had heightened their suspicions this night.

"Halt!" one of the men said in a commanding tone. "Who goes there?"

"Commander Arkenstone of the Phoenix Legion," Lazarus stated as he came to a stop ten paces before the guards. "I believe I am expected."

"Aye, sir. You are indeed." The two men relaxed visibly at

discovering Lazarus' identity. One of the men knocked twice on a barely noticeable side door. A small peephole opened, and the guard muttered something inaudible into the black opening. The sound of an iron bar being lifted pierced the silence, and then the door abruptly opened inward. Three men cautiously stepped out into the light. Lazarus presumed by the golden stripes on his sleeve that the foremost among them was the ranking officer.

"Commander Arkenstone," the sergeant addressed him in a deep gravelly voice. "Your presence has been requested by the Queen. I am to show you to her study; they're waiting for you."

"Very well." Lazarus tried to hide his dismay over the strange circumstances. "What's this all about, Sergeant?"

"I don't know, sir." The lean man's eyes darted around nervously, and he spoke in a hushed tone. "It's the seer. I think she's had a vision."

The fear in his words was as noticeable as the agitated manner of his body language. Certainly the sergeant recognized the unusual disregard for protocol and feared the worst. Very rarely were guests admitted into the Royal Palace at such an hour.

"Show me in then." Lazarus motioned for the soldier to lead the way.

With Lazarus in tow the sergeant marched back toward the side door. Inside they passed through a small, undecorated antechamber and into a short hallway just wide enough to fit one man. At the end of the short hall was another iron-bound door, which the soldier unlocked and opened. The two stepped out into the courtyard on the other side of the main gate.

Stretching out before him was a gravel path that wound through the gardens that surrounded the Royal Palace. The darkness shrouded the garden in mystery, but Lazarus could make out the shapes of large trees, pruned shrubs and bushes, and flower beds lined with stone. Lazarus had seen the palace grounds in daylight when they were at their most beautiful, yet there was some magnetism to them at night. Still and quiet, the gardens called to those who entered, inviting one to stay and lose oneself in their serenity.

Without a word the sergeant led Lazarus down the path of shiny white pebbles. It took only a few minutes for the two to reach the high parapets and glistening white walls of the palace. They entered through a side door that led into a short passageway near the guest quarters. After Lazarus' guide had locked the door behind them, they continued down the passageway to a door at the far end. This door was unlocked, and the two passed through into the grand halls of the Royal Palace.

Like the gardens Lazarus had just left, the palace was cloaked in darkness save for a few lit oil lamps fastened to the walls. Nothing stirred in the abandoned halls as Lazarus and his guide marched through; only the sound of their boots echoing off the cavernous walls broke the stillness.

As they walked, Lazarus surveyed his surroundings, admiring the great paintings and luxurious tapestries that hung on the walls of the hall. Above him he could barely make out the outline of the grand arches that held up the vaulted ceilings; marble statues, gilded ornaments, and various plants filled the empty spaces between the giant pillars that supported the levels overhead. Doors and arches jutted off the hall in many places, leading into other sections of the castle.

The sergeant abruptly wheeled to the left under an arch that fronted yet another, though smaller, hall. Here the decorations were more widely spaced, and doors lined the walls. Lazarus kept pace with the silent watchman, standing to his right and a step behind. He had been inside the palace before, though not recently — and never at night — and it seemed lonely and desolate without the usual bustle of servants, nobles, and court-goers roaming around.

Lazarus was deep in thought about what grim circumstance could warrant his invitation to the palace at such an hour when the man leading him stopped so abruptly that he didn't even notice they had reached their destination and nearly ran into the guard.

"The Queen's advisor is waiting for you inside." Almost as an afterthought the guard added, "Good luck, Commander."

Lazarus nodded and took a moment to steady his mind, taking a deep breath. Once he had calmed the uneasy feeling that had been rising in his stomach from the moment he had left the tavern, he stepped up to the door. Reaching down to grasp the smooth brass knob, he steeled himself for whatever might be waiting for him within.

He turned the knob and pushed gently on the polished mahogany door. It swung inward soundlessly, and Lazarus stepped into a plush reading room occupied solely by the Queen's Advisor. Mahogany inlaid with burl and white marble lined the four walls filled with books and tomes. A single reading table, also constructed of hand-carved mahogany and polished to a high luster, rested in the center of the large study. Around the table were four high-backed chairs, each upholstered with luscious purple velvet cushions. Exquisite Gnome-crafted carpets covered the floor in vivid patterns, and beeswax candles set into elegant brass lamps with crystal chandeliers adorned several spots along the walls. A single door on the opposite end offered the only other exit from the study. A solitary candle in a brass stand lit the room from the table, casting shadows about in all directions.

Melynda was sitting in one of the comfortable looking chairs, resting her head on her hand. She was still in her nightgown Lazarus noticed; apparently whatever was going on could not wait long enough for her to change clothes. Her disheveled hair hung down into her face, partially obscuring her hazel eyes as they fixed on him.

"Welcome, Commander Arkenstone," she said soothingly. "I'm sorry to disrupt your evening, but this matter cannot wait."

Lazarus had met Melynda on several previous occasions and was well aware of her abilities. "I can't imagine what dire circumstance would warrant my presence or why you would seek me out instead of approaching General Markoll."

"Please sit, Lazarus," Melynda said, motioning toward the chair next to hers.

Lazarus walked over to the open seat and lowered himself into the cushion. He pulled the chair up to the table and folded his hands in front of him.

"Dire circumstance would be an understatement, Lazarus. As you have probably already guessed, I have had a vision." She wrapped her robe tighter around her body as if to ward off a sudden chill.

"I assumed it was so. I assume also that I have been summoned here because somehow, in a way I do not yet understand, this involves me."

"You are correct in your assumptions. However, words can only go so far in describing the extent of the crisis facing our land; you must experience the vision for yourself." She paused for a moment to allow her words to sink in fully.

"But that's impossible..." Lazarus began, but Melynda cut him off.

"You have been called here tonight because the vision I have experienced involves you directly. You and your brothers as well. I can share what I have seen with you; I have that power. If you are willing, you must open your mind to me."

Lazarus squirmed uneasily. "I do not understand what's going on here. If this vision spells disaster for our country, why are you not sharing these visions with the Queen instead of me?"

"I have already informed the Queen; she is in the library as we speak, seeking information which may help us. You and your brothers are an integral part of my vision, and it is imperative that you understand what is required of you."

"Please, Melynda. Your words are cryptic; they make little sense to me. I'm just a simple soldier. Why have I been brought here tonight?"

"In order to gain the answers you seek, you must trust me. Open your mind to me, and everything that can will be revealed to you." She leaned in close and placed her hand over his, trying to allay his distress.

"Very well, do what you will."

"Are you certain that you are ready for this?" Melynda questioned him. "It can be quite unsettling."

"I am as ready as I ever will be. What am I to do?" Lazarus was very uneasy; he had never heard of visionaries transferring their experiences to others. On the other hand, if these visions involved his family in some way, he was more than willing to endure whatever he must to gain the knowledge needed to aid them.

"Relax your body," Melynda was saying to him. "Clear your mind of all thought and breathe deeply." Her soft voice was peaceful and calming, like listening to a small stream as it flowed over a rocky bed.

Lazarus closed his eyes and leaned back. The velvet cushions cradled his body as he slipped deeper and deeper into complete relaxation. Melynda spoke to him as he was drifting, calming him even further and driving the uncertainty from his mind. His breathing slowed, and Melynda reached out with her hands, placing her fingertips on Lazarus' temples. Lazarus immediately felt a warm glow flow through him, engulfing him. He felt weightless, as though he might float away at any moment if he were not anchored down.

Then he felt Melynda's presence, not as a physical feeling but as a mental force, invading his consciousness. It was not painful, only uncomfortable. Slowly her essence worked its way inside his mind. Lazarus tried to resist this strange sensation briefly, but the more he tried to fight it the harder she pushed. White searing light filled his mind's eye abruptly, startling him. He thrust his face skyward in an attempt to escape, but Melynda persisted, maintaining her grip on his skull. Instantly the feeling subsided and was replaced by a myriad tapestry of interwoven events. One by one they came to him, giving him little glimpses of what the future might hold. Each one seemed not like an ethereal picture but an actual physical reality complete with sounds, emotions, and sensory perception. Lazarus felt himself drift away from his body and out of substance. He became a formless wraith unable to touch the realm he had entered, allowed only to witness the events happening around his ghostly form.

Abruptly Lazarus found himself drifting on the winds, up and out of the Royal Palace into the night sky. He was drawn southward, and with frightening speed he was whisked away to the Durgen Range. There he descended on a lone tower reaching up into the darkness. He found he knew its name: Grimknoll, refuge of Orc sorcerers. He passed through its walls, unhindered by the stone, and descended deep into the bowels of the earth. Through dirt and rock he flew until he emerged inside the innermost sanctum. The drums pounded in his ears, the haunting voices of the Druhedar echoing in the cavern. He saw the portals open and the four Daemon Lords step into this world for the first time. His mind screamed for this torture to cease when the grotesque form of Serathes came into sight.

Without warning the scene changed. Again he was drifting, north this time. He was swept over the Solaris Plain and then wheeled sharply west. Lazarus knew the geography well. He saw a party of humans traveling across the grasslands, his brothers among them. As they endured hardship after hardship their numbers dwindled, devoured by a nameless evil that pursued them. Through the forbidding and dangerous Morah Weald they traveled into the lands of Valinar.

His spectral form descended on the ruins of Caer Dorn, once again passing through the earth to an underground chamber. There he found an ancient artifact, the Krullstone. He knew intuitively what this stone was capable of. He knew that it was the only worldly means of destroying Serathes and the Daemon Lords. It would be Vinson's duty to carry the stone and when the time came, wield it against Serathes and his minions. Yet he sensed something dark waiting for them there — an ancient evil so powerful it could transcend death itself. It rested there in the ruins of Caer Dorn, biding its time, and it would not give up the Krullstone easily.

Then he was spirited away again, back to his homeland. A massive army of Orcs was assaulting Illendale, trying to force their way across the Myrrh River and through Sowel Pass. He saw the Phoenix Legion defending the pass, trying in vain to hold off an army that hopelessly outnumbered them. He could hear the ringing of blades and the cries of the wounded on the battlefield. He saw himself, surrounded by his enemies, trying desperately to reach his brothers who were cut off from the rest of the Legion. He knew that if he did not reach them, they would die. He cried out in agony as first one brother and then the other were cut down by the horde pressing through the keep.

Crushed by the image of his brothers' deaths, he watched on in horror as the armies of Illendale were forced back, unable to stand alone against such a vast opponent. One by one the cities of Illendale were overrun and razed. Illendale was forever erased from the land. The destruction did not end there, however; the Orcs turned their hostility against other realms, and eventually all of the known lands were conquered. In time the demons turned against their masters, and the whole of the Orc nation was annihilated. Serathes and his minions pillaged and burned the earth, poisoning the environment and hunting the races like animals to their extinction.

There were more — many, many more. Some he understood all too well; others were as mysterious as they were fleeting. The visions unfolded before him like a series of plays, his mind transfixed and forced to watch the horror reveal itself. Images of friends and acquaintances slaughtered by the encroaching Orcs plagued his mind. Grubbash Grimvisage would seek out the Krullstone, and if he were permitted, he would use it against the demons to claim ultimate power for himself. He saw the earth as it would be not too far into the future. Charred and blackened, his world would become a playground for monstrous beings born of nightmares.

Melynda dropped her hands from his head, and the visions ceased. Lazarus shuddered once and sagged into his chair, haunted by the memory of the terror he had witnessed. He tried to make sense of everything, but his mind was numb, his thoughts tied in a knot that would not be undone.

Several things were immediately clear to him. First, he and his brothers must seek out the Krullstone. For whatever reason they had been chosen to be its bearers, and it was the only way Serathes would be vanquished. Second, Illendale must prepare for war. If the visions were to be believed, then there wasn't much time left before the Orc hordes came charging across their border. Lastly, he must find a way to keep his brothers alive and penetrate the keep where the Daemon Lords and their master were residing so that they could be destroyed.

Lazarus' mouth felt like he had not had anything to drink for days. He had no idea how he was to accomplish what was needed of him. His heart grew heavy with doubt. When he finally opened his mouth to speak, his voice sounded harsh and cracked. "You are certain these visions are true?"

"Lazarus," Melynda whispered, reaching out to take his hands into hers, "they are always true to some extent. The future is always in motion. What you have been shown is only one future out of an infinite number of possibilities. Now that you have seen for yourself, you understand what comes and what must be done to prevent the unthinkable."

"No!" Lazarus retracted his hands. "I do not understand. I do not understand why it must be me or why my brothers must be involved. There must be others more capable than we."

"For whatever reason, Lazarus," she replied, unshaken by his denial, "you and your brothers have been chosen by Fate. I too do not know why it must be you. I only know that unless you can fulfill the needs that this kingdom and indeed the whole world require of you, then the visions you have seen will come to pass.

"The end is near. The Daemon Lords have been summoned forth from their infernal pit. The combined armies of darkness will wash over this world like a black tide and drown the earth in destruction and oppression. An unspeakable evil is about to be unleashed. The earth will burn in unholy fire, and her peoples will perish or be enslaved."

"And you are certain that these events have already been set in motion?" Lazarus asked, still trying to cling to the possibility that he could somehow escape this terrible responsibility.

"Yes. Subtle symbols embedded within the visions, whose meanings escape you, tell me that the demons are already here. This Grubbash Grimvisage summoned them four days ago. Even now they are preparing for war. If you refuse to accept this and do nothing, it will be up to Fate to decide who will rule this earth, the Orcs or the demons. If the demons survive, this world will become a permanent outpost of Hell, blasted and barren. The Daemon Lords' mere presence will have a very negative effect on the earth. The weather patterns will change, warming the earth. If enough time passes, the seasonal rains will cease, and no new growth will sprout. The sun will beat down on our land as if it were inside an oven, killing all vegetation. Our land will become a wasteland, inhabitable only by the Daemon Lords and their brethren."

"And what of Valinar? No one has ever returned from that wretched place."

Melynda leaned in very close now, her voice dropping to a

whisper. "Grimvisage will seek out the Krullstone for himself, and eventually he will find it. If he succeeds and uses it against Serathes and his minions, he will absorb their power. Assuming the stone does not destroy him, he will use that power to subjugate all the races. Those who stand against him will be annihilated, and the survivors will become slaves, hunted like animals. The Orcs will spread across the whole of the world. Their lack of respect for nature will upset the natural balance, and just like the Great Holocaust of old, the earth will be destroyed again. Only this time, nobody may live through it."

"Then I must go in search of the Krullstone," Lazarus breathed. "It must be recovered before the Orcs can find it. If the visions are to be believed, it is our only hope." Lazarus resigned himself to the inevitable. It appeared that he had no choice in the matter; Fate had made the decision for him. He could not sit idle while his country was in peril, but perhaps he could keep his brothers safe by leaving them in Illendale.

"No, Lazarus," Melynda whispered back. "You will be needed here. Vinson and Aldric must go. Only your brothers can locate the stone and safely return it."

"I cannot and will not send my brothers off alone," Lazarus stated determinedly. "You forget that Valinar is a cursed land. No one has ever returned from there since the destruction of the Old Kingdom. They have not seen the visions. Someone who knows where it can be found and knows of the dangers they will face must go. They should stay."

"Vinson must go," she said irritably. "He is the only one among the three of you who can successfully wield the stone and not be corrupted by its power. Others who attempt to use it against a being such as Serathes would likely be destroyed outright, but your family has been chosen. If you will not send them alone, then the three of you must go together."

Lazarus took a deep breath. "So be it."

As Lazarus finally accepted the reality that his brothers would have to come with him into the wilds and be placed in grave peril, the Queen entered the study through the door opposite where he was sitting.

Her husband and protector, Ukiah, came after her, looking more than just a little perturbed. He carried with him several large tomes from the library. Lazarus rose to bow before the Queen.

Queen Cailyn Emory, though nearly fifty years old, was a stunningly beautiful woman. Hazel eyes that were both hard and compassionate twinkled like emeralds from beneath fine eyebrows that accentuated her fair complexion. Auburn hair hung nearly down to her waist and trailed after her like a silk shawl. She wore a green dress, vibrant yet simple, and gold jewelry dangled from her neck and ears. The Queen was tall for a woman, just short of six feet, her slender physique complementing her natural charm.

Women were more empathetic and caring rulers and not usually prone to the fits of rage and violence and greed that so often beset men. Women had a greater affinity towards the people they ruled and their environment than men typically exhibited. Thus, long ago, the people of Illendale had determined that women would function better as rulers of the kingdom. House Emory had been ruling Illendale for more than two hundred years, Queen Cailyn for nearly Lazarus' whole life.

For as long as Illendale had been an independent nation the men of royalty had served as the protectors of its queens. Ukiah was a big man, well muscled and powerfully built. He was not wearing the leather armor he usually did, but he had not forgotten his weapons. A sword was strapped across his waist, and a long knife had been hastily thrust into his belt. His hair was graying slightly at the temples, and his stormy gray eyes measured everything they surveyed. Although his demeanor seemed hard, beneath the steely surface he was quite warm and kind. He was somewhat tousled, his usual composure disrupted by the night's strange goings-on.

The Queen glided to the nearest chair and sat down. Ukiah set his burden down and seated himself next to Cailyn with a cursory nod. "Commander Arkenstone, welcome," Queen Cailyn greeted him, her voice calm and consoling like a light breeze on a warm summer night. "I'm sorry to have spoiled your evening, but as you can see, we have great need of you. I trust Melynda has enlightened you as to the situation?"

"Yes, Your Highness," Lazarus responded. "The situation has been made painfully clear to me." His body language expressed his level of discomfort.

"I apologize again. I do not want to separate your brothers from you, but it must be so. Illendale will need all the good men it can get in the coming fight. Do not worry for them," she added. "They are good men, as good as any. I am certain they will succeed."

"As am I, Your Highness." Lazarus looked her hard in her eyes. "Because I am going with them." The conviction in his voice would brook no argument; he was going with or without her approval.

The Queen fixed him with her stare. "Make no mistake, Commander. This is the greatest challenge our kingdom has ever faced. I do not agree that you should accompany your brothers, but I will not order you to stay. I'm sure Melynda has already tried to make you choose otherwise." She paused for a moment before continuing. "As Melynda has surely told you, Fate has chosen you and your brothers as our champions. I am confident that you are more than capable of succeeding in this quest."

Lazarus was going to say nothing, but his doubts got the best of him. "I hope that a grave mistake is not being made by putting the fate of so much in the hands of so few. The visions have already revealed what the probable outcome of this quest will be. As Melynda has seen it, my brothers will lose their lives, and Illendale will fall anyway. Perhaps we are not strong enough to fulfill the charge given to us."

"Do not be so modest," Ukiah chided. "We have the utmost faith in you. You will succeed because you must; the whole world depends on it."

"Remember, Lazarus, that what I have seen is only a possible future. The visions are a guide, a glimpse of what may be. We must choose to continue on the path the visions show us or do something different to alter the future as we have seen it," Melynda said with conviction.

"Though it may not be what I would have chosen, I will do everything in my power to defend my country. Hopefully we can make a difference," Lazarus stated, resigned to his fate, yet happy still that the Queen did not insist that he remain behind.

"It is decided then," Cailyn spoke. "Vinson, Aldric, and you will go in search of the Krullstone. I will leave it to you as the leader of this expedition to arrange all the details."

"We are agreed then. When shall we leave?" Lazarus asked.

"As soon as possible," Cailyn told him. "In the morning the four of us will meet with the High Council to inform them of the situation. You should take the rest of the day to organize your team and the supplies you will require."

"That shouldn't take long. I will choose ten others from the Phoenix Legion; including my brothers and I, that will make us thirteen strong." A slight grin crossed Lazarus' face. "It's my lucky number, and we're going to need all the luck we can get."

"Were I you, I would put my faith in good solid steel, not super- stitious numbers," Ukiah retorted affably.

"Point taken," Lazarus replied soberly. "But it can't hurt to have luck on our side. Anyway, my party will be prepared to leave by week's end."

"It is settled then." Cailyn sat back in relief. She was visibly distraught by the events of the evening, her face drawn and weariness reflected in her eyes. "I will send someone for you in the morning; until then, get some rest, Lazarus. You're going to need it. Thank you, Commander."

"It is my duty to serve, Highness," Lazarus said with pride. "I will do what I must."

"Goodnight then, Lazarus. We'll see you in the morning."

"Goodnight, Milady." He bowed to his queen and slipped off.

As Lazarus walked he considered the events of the evening — how he had volunteered his brothers and himself to join this crazy crusade to save the world from a threat that as yet had not shown any visible signs of existence. He wondered if he had made the right choice or if he had even had a choice to begin with. It had seemed like all the cards were stacked against him.

No matter what his arguments were, the truth was that if Melynda was right, he could not afford to dismiss the whole story out of hand. Not only was it his job to defend his people but also his sense of honor and loyalty would not allow him to abandon them, even if the things that he was asked to do seemed foolish and reckless. For most of his life his duty had been to protect his country, and he would not fail them now.

Lazarus ambled down the cobblestone streets, heading back to his small lodge within the barracks grounds, wondering if he could somehow spare his friends and family from the pain and sorrow that was sure to follow. If it were not necessary for his brothers to accompany him, he would have left them here safe within the walls of the capital city.

However, if the visions turned out to be true, his brothers' service would be needed desperately, and besides that, they would not be safe no matter where Lazarus left them. So far as he knew Melynda had never been wrong. He saw no reason why she should be wrong this time, though he wished that were the case.

He arrived back at his simple room and lay down to sleep, the rest of the city either asleep or in the taverns drinking and gambling their night away. His mind reeled from the burden that had been placed on his shoulders, and he wished that it could have been given to another. He worried that he would not be able to live up to his obligations, but most of all he worried that he might fail his family and friends.

When sleep finally overcame him, his fears and doubts were there waiting for him. He tossed and turned restlessly, haunted by nightmares spawned by the visions shown to him. He saw the Orcs, their army massive and undefeatable, and watched as demons rampaged across the countryside, destroying everything and everyone. Across the landscape of his mind he fought to stay one step ahead of the enemy he could not seem to overcome. Relentlessly he sought the Krullstone, the ethereal hope that would not be found. He watched in agony as the homeland he loved became a terrible battlefield where he competed with faceless foes for supremacy and inevitably was forced to give way to their overwhelming might. Always he came back to that vision of his brothers, unable to reach them in time to save their lives and having to watch them be cut down by their ruthless foes.

Once or twice he awoke with a scream only to fall asleep and be forced to face them again.

V THE HIGH COUNCIL

WHEN THE GUARDSMAN woke him in the morning with his summons to the High Council, Lazarus was exhausted. He was weary from lack of sleep, yet something more bothered him still. He felt hollow and cold, his spirit tortured by the nagging belief that he could not save the people he cared for most. He would be the one to lead them into the abyss, and he could not guarantee he could lead them out again.

He washed himself and dressed in his uniform mechanically, eating his breakfast of fruit and bread without tasting it. Like an automaton he marched off towards the Council chambers, staring blankly ahead as he walked. His eyes played fiendish tricks on him, making him believe he saw demons and evil things around every turn, in every corner, and in the faces of the people he passed in the street. Phantoms appeared briefly at the edge of his vision and then vanished insidiously when he turned to challenge them. The morning shadows stretched out to snare him, their tendrils icy on his skin, seeking to pull him in and swallow him whole.

He plodded wearily onward, the streets beginning to bustle with the day's activities. Vendors were preparing their storefronts for business, while others were hurrying off to work or some other endeavor. Lazarus saw none of this; he was lost to the world around him, consumed entirely by his own torturous imagination.

He finally arrived at the large circular building where the High Council of Illendale convened. Sculpted columns of marble supported a golden domed roof with a single spire atop it that shot into the sky like a needle. Pane glass windows ran around the outer wall to allow light into the structure. Gardens filled with azaleas, irises, and marigolds ringed the building except where a dozen stone block steps led up to the recessed main entrance.

Lazarus ascended the steps and passed between the giant columns toward a pair of massive oak doors inlaid with ivory and gold leaf scrollwork. A squad of guards dressed in fine chain mail armor and bearing hefty halberds stood watch at the entrance.

The guards did not move to bar his entrance as he approached. Seeing his rank displayed upon his uniform, two of the men moved forward to grasp the giant brass handles and push the doors open. Without a word Lazarus entered and proceeded through a short hallway. Doors and inconspicuous passages extended into the offices and small meeting rooms that occupied this section of the building, but Lazarus walked past them without a glance.

He stopped short when he came to the entrance to the main chamber, which was constructed in the same daunting manner as the exterior doors. To the right sat a veteran guard behind a modest desk. Lazarus faced the man.

"Good morning, Corporal."

"Morning, sir," replied the guard, who stood and saluted sharply. "How may I help you?"

"I have been summoned by the Queen to appear before the Council," Lazarus informed him. "I am Commander Arkenstone."

"Yes, of course, sir. Her Majesty and the High Council have been expecting you. They await your arrival within." The guard skirted his desk and moved toward the door with measured steps. Reaching out to grasp the large handle of one door, the corporal pulled it open with a heave. "After you, Commander." He ushered him in with a wave of his hand.

Lazarus entered through the partially opened door into an elaborately crafted hall, circular in shape like the rest of the building, with high vaulted ceilings. The chamber was divided into two distinct sections by sculpted columns similar to those outside and a low oak railing. The first was two arcs of seats fronted by polished tables, the smaller set in front of the larger, facing the Queen's throne that sat raised on a small dais set against the far wall. The first row of lavish chairs was reserved for the senior ministers of the High Council, while the second row housed the General Assembly. On either side of the throne were two smaller, yet equally luxurious, high-backed chairs for the Queen's Protector and Advisor. The second section was comprised of rows of plain wooden benches for the public audience that ran all the way back to the walls, circling most of the room.

Today, only the seven seats of the ministers of the High Council were occupied. The Queen, dressed in a radiant green silk gown, sat stoutly on her throne, flanked by Ukiah and Melynda. The most powerful and respected members of their nation were all present. The ministers ceased their quiet conversation when the guard who had led Lazarus in announced his name and title for those in attendance. As one all the eyes in the room turned to him, their stares a mix of curiosity, suspicion, and disinterest.

Abruptly Queen Cailyn spoke, but the eyes never left the newcomer. "Come forward, Commander. Corporal Kemer, no one is to be admitted. We are not to be disturbed under any circumstance."

"Yes, Your Highness," replied the corporal. He about-faced and closed the door behind him. Lazarus heard the security bar slide into place.

"We've been waiting for you, Commander," Queen Cailyn addressed him. "Please sit." She lifted one ringed finger and pointed to the empty row behind the Council members.

Lazarus began his trek across the room, the eyes of the High Council following his every step, the sound of his footfalls echoing ominously off the chamber walls. He lowered himself into his chair, sitting with his back straight as a board, trying to maintain the composure expected of an officer. He returned the stares of the ministers levelly, determined not to show the extent of his discomfort.

Lee Hanlan, the presiding Chief Minister, watched him coolly from his plush chair at the center of the row. The Chief Minister was a tall and wiry man with short gray hair that was slightly receding at his brow line. His piercing green eyes weighed and measured everything he saw.

To the right sat General Dean Markoll, the Minister of Defense and leader of Illendale's army. Lazarus knew him well from his years in the service. Markoll was perhaps the finest military mind the kingdom had ever known. Next to the General sat the Foreign Minister, David Bolge, and at the end of the row sat Ozlem Ruel, the Minister of Finance.

On the other side of the Chief Minister sat Rebecca Markoll, the Interior Minister and Dean Markoll's wife. Next to her sat the Minister of Commerce, Elvan Faris, a middle-aged woman with dark skin and golden brown hair. Douglas Armand, the Minister of Industry, sat at the end.

Cailyn cleared her throat, drawing everyone's attention. "Let us begin now that everyone is present." Several of the ministers nodded in agreement. "You have been called here because our nation is in grave peril."

The men and women of the council glanced at each other nervously. Some murmured quietly to those next to them, and Lazarus could see skepticism evident in more than one face. Many a questioning glance was cast in his direction.

"What manner of crisis threatens our nation, Highness?" questioned Lee Hanlan. "We have heard no news here in the capital."

"Patience, Minister," the Queen replied. "All will be revealed to you in due course. You have been called here today to address a growing threat against our lands. If nothing is done to challenge this threat, if we take no action, then our entire world shall perish. Everything we know and love will be destroyed."

She paused, looking into the eyes of each person. After a long silence she continued, "You all know of Melynda, my advisor. You are all familiar with her talents. Last night she had a vision, a revelation that contains horror beyond our wildest imaginations. I believe Melynda's vision to be true. I have known her long enough not to doubt her abilities. Many of you have known her almost as long as I. We have been given an opportunity to avert this disaster before it catches our people unprepared. I will allow her to explain the details to you, for she knows them better than I. Melynda, if you would please."

All eyes shifted to Melynda, expectant and worried. Several of the ministers had served in their office long enough to know all too well how accurate Melynda's visions were.

Lazarus studied the faces of the ministers as Melynda narrated the specifics of her vision. She spared them no details in painting a graphic picture within their minds of the destruction that loomed on the horizon. Lazarus watched as the doubt and worry in their eyes gave way to outright fear.

She told them about the sorcerer, Grubbash Grimvisage, and his plot to overthrow the current Orc leadership with the aid of Serathes, how the demons had already been summoned, and how Grimvisage would rally the armies of the Orcs and their allies to make war against the other races. She elucidated that the Orcs and their evil allies would conquer the whole land, starting with Illendale, if nothing were done to stop them. She told them how the demons would eventually depose the Orcs and rule the earth through their unwitting lackeys. She explained how the Daemon Lords could not be overcome by any mortal means and how they would ultimately destroy the earth and her peoples, turning the land into a barren wasteland where nightmare creatures would stalk the helpless races. The land they called home would, in the long run, become a permanent outpost of hell, twisted beyond recovery.

The Ministers of the High Council shifted uneasily as the seer went into stark detail about what might come to pass. Some were shocked to find their homeland in such great danger. Some were observably skeptical, hesitant to believe such a wild and uncorroborated tale. They stared at each other in deepening silence, glancing from face to face.

It was General Markoll who broke the silence, his intense brown eyes darting about the room. "You are certain that these events will come to pass?"

"It has already begun," Melynda answered him. "I spoke with the Mages' Guild this morning. Many among them felt a massive disruption in the energy currents five nights ago. The presence of the demons is already affecting our world, Ministers," she continued. "The Mages' Guild has also reported small disturbances in the balance of nature. They have concluded that these disturbances are connected to the disruption they felt earlier, and that if the disturbances continue, they could have disastrous side effects on the environment. It is important that you know they have not been informed of my vision."

Once again the chamber fell into silence as those present pondered this new information. Lazarus looked from face to face, trying to judge their reaction to the startling news. Queen Cailyn sat calmly upon her throne, allowing them time to digest the outrageous testimony they had been given.

This time it was David Bolge who broke the silence. "I cannot believe that our nation could be under such great threat without any visible proof. I have little faith in the reports of sorcerers; their power is whimsical and circumstantial at best. If indeed a massive invasion from the south is at hand, then why are there no reports from our garrisons at the borders of this supposedly unstoppable army of Orcs?" The Foreign Minister's skepticism was obvious. Either he could not or did not want to believe that such an attack was possible or feasible.

"The Orcs are not limited to assaulting us from the south," General Markoll pointed out. "Do not forget that they could come from Sowel Pass. Or they could march around the Serpentspine and attack us from the Solaris Plain where our defenses are weakest. They could even assault us from the east where we would least expect an attack because they must cross the Myrrh twice to get there. If this army is as large as has been said, it is possible and even likely that the Orcs will attack from more than one direction."

"A wise observation, General," Queen Cailyn said. "It is true that as yet we have had no warnings from the borders. It is also possible, although I do not believe it to be so, that the Mages' Guild is incorrect in their assumptions." The Queen rose from her chair then and stepped down off the dais to stand before the Council. "The invasion Melynda has foreseen could be days, weeks, even months away. Some of you may doubt her abilities, but I have known her long enough to realize when action must be taken. Her visions have helped us avert disasters before. Certainly she is human and therefore capable of error. The real question is, Ministers, can we afford not to prepare for what might be looming on the horizon?" She let her question hang on the air for several moments.

"If we cannot defeat this army, assuming there is one, what hope have we?" asked Douglas Armand. "What are we to do if we cannot hope to defeat our enemies?"

"Surely we will fight," Markoll said strongly. "We have a well-trained army, and we can defend our own country even against such seemingly insurmountable odds."

"Your faith in the army is encouraging, General," Elvan Faris interjected. "However, even if we can defeat the Orc army, what are we to do about the demons? Certainly you don't believe the army can destroy them as well."

General Markoll had nothing to say about this, but Melynda did have an answer for him.

"You are correct," she said. "Our army cannot defeat the demons. No offense intended, General, but it cannot withstand the might of the Orcs either." General Markoll started to reply, but she silenced him with a raised hand. "Without doubt our army can and must hold the Orcs for as long as possible. There is another way to save our land. Commander Arkenstone, please rise."

Lazarus did as he was asked and rose from his chair to stand before the High Council. Their eyes sought his, wondering what purpose he would serve in the defense of their country.

"Many of you know Commander Arkenstone," continued Melynda. "He has served in the army for fourteen years, six of them as the commanding officer of the Phoenix Legion. His legion is the most highly trained fighting force in Illendale, perhaps the entire world. They have fought to defend our borders for as long as anyone can remember.

"There is something which I have not told you until now. In one part of my vision, I watched as a group of men traveled across the Solaris Plain to the ancient land of Valinar. They sought an ancient artifact, created long before the armies of the undead destroyed our ancestral homeland. It was made known to me that this artifact was the salvation of our people, the only hope for our survival. It is called the Krullstone. Mages from the old empire discovered the stone at a site of primeval power and harnessed it, incorporating it into a gauntlet that would allow it to be wielded by one of sufficient power and wisdom.

"In my vision the Krullstone was shown to me as the only means to eliminate Serathes and his minions. It was also made known to me that only his brothers," she pointed one long finger at Lazarus, "are capable of retrieving it safely and wielding it against the demons."

Melynda looked to the Queen, who continued the narration. "Commander Arkenstone will lead an expedition to Valinar to recover the Krullstone. It is the only hope for our people and must be found and brought back safely. We must hold the Orc hordes at bay until they can return."

"How can we be certain that the Krullstone can be found?" asked Lee Hanlan.

Lazarus found it strange that he should be skeptical; given his past experiences, Lee should know better than any among the Ministers the extent and accuracy of Melynda's visions.

"As I have said, it must be found if we are to be saved," Melynda stated, "and Valinar is where it shall be discovered."

"It seems to me that we have no choice but to prepare," Rebecca interposed. "The consequences are too great if we fail to heed this warning, and it proves to be true." Her steely gaze fell on the other Ministers like a ton of bricks. "If Melynda says this is the way, then so be it."

"I agree," added General Markoll. "We cannot wait until physical proof of an invasion exists. By then, it would be too late to mobilize and provision the army as it must be to defend our country against a superior force."

Most of the other Ministers nodded in concurrence. Even if the invasion never came and the vision turned out to be false, it was better to be prepared. Lee Hanlan and David Bolge still maintained their disbelieving stance, but they could not argue with this logic.

"I will also seek support from the other races," Queen Cailyn declared. "We must at least warn them of what may be approaching, and perhaps we can even convince them to stand with us. United we may be powerful enough to challenge the enemy in the event that Commander Arkenstone's mission fails."

"Excellent judgment, Highness," General Markoll praised her. "We must assume that the journey to recover the Krullstone will fail and be prepared for that contingency."

Indeed, Lazarus mused, it was probably likely that his party would never return. Since the fall of Valinar to the armies of Asaru, no expedition had ever returned from there. The last group who attempted was led by the famed archaeologist Aslihan Cavetti nearly one hundred years ago. They had simply vanished. Every journey ever sent had disappeared without a trace, and now nobody was foolish or brave enough to venture into that forbidden land. It seemed Lazarus' task to find the Krullstone there was a suicide mission.

Lazarus knew very well the danger. Aside from the rumors of monstrous creatures and nightmares stalking the woods in that region, the visions had shown him that something darker still waited for them there. Yet the visions had shown him that the dangers could be overcome, and that gave him a spark of hope. He would take every precaution necessary to ensure that his companions would succeed where others had always failed.

"I will mobilize and outfit the army," General Markoll was saying. "That will take some time, especially if I am to call up the reserves."

"I do not think the reserves should be called up as yet," Ozlem said, joining the discussion. "News of the reserves being reinstated would spread like wildfire."

"She is right," Rebecca put in. "We do not want to create a panic. If we start recalling soldiers, they will fear the worst. Once the truth of the situation gets out, people will abandon the southern cities. We'll have anarchy."

"Point taken," Queen Cailyn said. "We must keep the truth hidden for now. We don't want to alert the Orcs that we know of their intentions. If they think us unprepared, they will be overconfident and therefore more foolish."

"That may be true, but I think it would be prudent to at least secretly order the garrisons in those cities to prepare for a full scale evacuation," General Markoll said, rubbing at the stubble on his chin.

"If it can be done in secrecy, then let it be so. Commander Arkenstone will prepare his team to leave as soon as possible."

"I will see to it," replied the General. "I will also send my best scouts into the Durgen Range to try to ascertain when the invasion might begin and the strength of the enemy."

When nobody offered anything further, the Queen dismissed the Council with a request that the Ministers keep the details of their meeting confidential. They rose as one and moved towards the exit, not speaking as they were leaving. Lazarus rose from his seat as well, noting that the Ministers of the High Council looked more like dazed and confused children than the leaders of a nation. General Markoll approached him as he stood and motioned him off to the side.

"Have you given any thought to whom you will take with you?" he inquired. "I could recommend a few good men if you require them."

"For the most part I have them all selected," Lazarus answered. "Obviously, my brothers and I must go. Major Ogras will go, as will Azrael. I will choose seven others from my legion."

"Thirteen then?"

Lazarus shrugged. "It is my lucky number. My soldiers know and trust me. That will make it easier for them to follow me where they might otherwise not go. Besides," Lazarus added, "there are none better suited than the men of the Phoenix Legion."

"Who will command while you're away?" Markoll asked him.

"Captain Sterl Reich will command in my stead. He's a good man, been with us for ten years. Reich has a good head on his shoulders and the experience to know how to use it."

"A good choice," Markoll mused. "Lazarus, I'm ordering the Phoenix Legion to the Myrrh."

"It would have been my advice. It is the best fighting force we can field."

"Aye, it is. When the invasion comes, it will most likely come at us from more than one direction, as I've said, but I'm certain that they will try to cross the Myrrh. It is the most direct route into our land. I want to make them pay dearly to cross it."

"Agreed," Lazarus nodded. "It would be best if we had some defensive positions already in place. Have you considered where they will cross?"

"Indeed. I believe they will try to force a crossing south of Perthana at The Narrows. If their army is as large as Melynda says it is, they will not think to outmaneuver us, but rather just overpower us as quickly as possible."

"I'm sure you are right. In any case, at least we'll have forces in the region," Lazarus said.

"Exactly." Markoll clasped his hands behind his back. "I would send more, but it will take time to outfit the rest of the army. The Phoenix Legion will have to stand alone until I can bring up the bulk of our forces."

"The Phoenix Legion will hold them, if for no other reason than that they must," Lazarus assured him. "They will fight to the last man if necessary."

"Let us hope that is not the case. Very well." The man put his hand on Lazarus' shoulder. "If you should need anything, don't hesitate to ask. It sounds like you're going to need all the help you can get. Good luck, Commander."

The General extended his hand. Lazarus gripped it strongly and said his own farewell. Markoll walked to the doors, his stride marked by a sense of purpose and duty. Lazarus turned to find the Queen and saw that she was standing next to her throne, talking quietly with Melynda and Ukiah.

Cailyn smiled warmly as he approached them. "Go and gather your team. Tell them what you must, but remember that as yet nobody outside the High Council knows of your mission."

"Those I have chosen to accompany me will not violate our secrecy. They are good men, all."

"Without doubt," the Queen assured him. "Do what you must to prepare for your journey. I have already sent emissaries to the other races. I do not know how many will answer the call in these dark times, but hopefully those who will can gather quickly. I will send for you if your presence is required. Until then, rest and prepare."

"As you wish, Your Highness." Lazarus bowed. He nodded to Melynda and Ukiah before he turned toward the doors that led outside. Melynda grabbed his hand as he was leaving.

"Be wary, Lazarus," she said softly to him. "The Daemon Lords certainly are aware of the Krullstone and may attempt to recover it. They will send spies into our kingdom to discover what we are about as well. They may already have agents within the city. We are all depending on you, Lazarus. Be careful and good luck."

"I will do what I can," was all Lazarus replied. Melynda forced a smile and hugged him emphatically.

"Take care of yourself, Lazarus," Ukiah called after him.

Lazarus left the Council chambers and walked down the avenue outside. He strolled east through the heavily congested street. It was nearing noon as Lazarus made his way among the throngs of people toward the Grand Bazaar, only a few blocks east of the Council building.

He thought about how he would tell his brothers what the future held and what must be done to prevent it. People he passed on the street noticed the rank displayed on his uniform and stepped aside for him, making his passage easier as he walked through the marketplace.

The Grand Bazaar occupied a large fragment of the city just south of the Tranquil Gardens that surrounded the palace grounds. Small tents lined the wide boulevard, and vendors sold their wares from wagons and carts everywhere. Taverns, inns, and shops hunkered down behind the rows of tents like sleeping behemoths. Vendors cried out prices and slogans, straining to be heard over the din created by the masses of people. One could purchase almost anything in the Grand Bazaar: from gold jewelry to gemstones, fine cloth and silks, dyes and weapons, fruits and vegetables, livestock and anything in between.

It was a rich tapestry of sights, smells, and sounds that Lazarus had seen a thousand times. Today he ignored the shouts and cries as he wove his way between the stalls and carts. He reached the center of the marketplace where several roads intersected at a large fountain and turned north toward the Tranquil Gardens.

As he continued on his way he decided that first he would seek out Layek and then break the news to his brothers. Layek was a good friend and would understand the sensitive nature of the situation. He was the one Lazarus could share his fears and doubts with, the one who would offer him sound advice and support him in his judgments.

The Tranquil Gardens were separated from the rest of the city by an iron-grated fence that stood chest high. Where the road led into the gardens from the Grand Bazaar there was a small wooden shack, and as Lazarus approached, the soldiers standing watch snapped to attention.

"Good afternoon, sir," the sergeant greeted him, a short, balding man with a bulging stomach.

"Good day, Sergeant," Lazarus returned. "I need a runner. Can you spare a man?"

"Of course, sir. McKenna here is the fastest I've got; he can deliver your message in no time." He motioned to a tall red-haired soldier who stepped over to them quickly. Freckles dotted his face, and he looked too young to be a soldier by at least two years.

"Yes, sir?" the boy asked.

"Seek out Major Ogras and tell him to meet me here within the gardens," Lazarus ordered. "He should be at the barracks. Tell him he is to come alone, no one else. I will be waiting for him on the bench near the big willow tree not far from here. You know which one I mean?"

"Yes, sir. I know it well."

"Very well. Carry on." Lazarus dismissed the young guard and turned to the sergeant. "Thank you, that will be all."

"Yes, sir, glad to be of assistance. It gets a little dull at this post. Not much for us to do these days," he added with a shrug.

"Be grateful. There are worse fates than boredom," Lazarus replied somberly.

"Are you all right, sir?" the sergeant asked. "You seem a little out of sorts. Can I get you some refreshment, or perhaps there is something else?"

"No, thank you. Let's just say that boredom isn't my curse in life. Good day, Sergeant."

"Good day, Commander." The guard saluted sharply and then turned back to his little guard post.

Lazarus returned the guard's salute and continued through the gate and into the Tranquil Gardens. He walked along a dirt trail marked by white stones that wound its way around the perimeter of the gardens for about a quarter of a mile before he reached the great willow tree he had spoken of to the guard at the watch post. The tree's drooping limbs formed a secluded hollow where one could sit in mild privacy and enjoy the sweet fragrances and sounds of the gardens.

Lazarus left the trail and stooped beneath the hanging branches. Next to the aged trunk of the old willow, which was twice as wide as his body, stood a simple stone bench. Lazarus seated himself and tried to get comfortable on the worn granite. It would be at least a half an hour before the young guard he had dispatched could locate Layek and bring him here, time Lazarus could use to ease his troubled mind.

He leaned back against the rough bark and rubbed his eyes. A slight autumn breeze blew through the willow and surrounding oaks, ash, and elms, creating a relaxing sound like the sighing of Nature herself, Lazarus thought. An entire symphony of birdcalls drifted through the air, and the sweet fragrances of hyacinth, jasmine, and iris wafted through the walls of his makeshift shelter to fill his nostrils.

Lazarus breathed in deeply and closed his eyes. Slowly he felt his muscles begin to slacken, and the stress that he had been under since the night before gradually melted away. For just a few precious moments at least he could let go and enjoy the peacefulness of the gardens.

VI RUDE AWAKENING

"HEY!" SOMEBODY BARKED as he shook him wildly. "Wake up, slacker!"

Lazarus snapped open his eyes, realizing he had dozed off. He did not know for how long he had been asleep, but it was still light outside so it couldn't have been too long. He rubbed the sleep out of his eyes and looked around groggily. Layek was standing over him, vigorously trying to pull him out of the peaceful slumber that had overcome him. He sat up straight and stretched his muscles for a moment. He felt rested, and a sense of calmness had settled over him. *These gardens really are magical,* he thought to himself.

"How long have I been asleep?" he asked his old friend.

"A couple of hours I imagine," Layek answered him. "That boy you sent said it took him two hours just to find me."

"Where were you? I would've thought you would still be asleep or nursing a hangover," Lazarus said playfully. The hazy weariness that had possessed him earlier in the day had vanished completely.

"I was looking for you, cotton-brain," Layek shot back. "When I got up today, Azrael told me you had been summoned to the palace last night. I went to find out what was going on, but you had already left. I found out you were summoned to the High Council so I went there only to find that you were gone. I looked everywhere for you. Finally the guard caught up with me, and here I am."

Lazarus yawned lazily. "Sounds like quite an adventure."

"Everybody else is looking for you, too," Layek said. "We

thought you'd run off again without us. Vinson and Aldric are mad as hornets."

"You didn't tell them you were meeting me here?" Lazarus asked him, looking around suspiciously.

"No. The guard told me I was to come alone. Besides, there aren't enough hours in the day for me to track down your entire family." He smiled wryly.

"Good," was all Lazarus replied, remembering why he had brought his friend here.

"What's all this cloak and dagger stuff about, Laz? What's going on?" A worried look creased his face. "Is something wrong?"

"I'm afraid so, Layek."

"You're going to tell me, right? I am assuming that's why you've brought me here." Layek seated himself on the bench next to Lazarus.

"It is. And this time I can't keep you guys out of it."

"Come on then, out with it," Layek grumbled. "No more riddles. Or I could just shake it out of you," he said mischievously, reaching out to grasp Lazarus' shoulders.

"That won't be necessary." Lazarus pushed his hands away. "I will tell you because I must, but promise me: this stays between us until I say otherwise. Swear it."

"Done. It stays between us." Layek's eyes grew serious again. "Now what's going on?"

"Melynda has had a vision."

"That's it?" Layek stated contemptuously. "You really believe in that nonsense?"

"I do. I have seen it for myself. She shared her vision with me through some sort of mental link," Lazarus explained to his skeptical friend. "What she has shown me terrifies me."

"Tell me."

So Lazarus did. He explained everything that had happened since he left the Blue Moon the night before. In gruesome detail he described for his old friend the visions that Melynda had shared with him.

Layek listened intently as Lazarus chronicled the events that would lead to the end of their world. When he had finished his tale, Layek leaned back against the tree and sighed heavily.

"That's pretty intense." For a long moment those were the only words he could muster. "Charging off to Valinar in search of some long lost talisman is practically suicide, and the Orcs have never been organized enough to launch a full-scale assault. This cannot be true."

"Nevertheless, Layek, it is true. We must go."

"Is there any proof other than the seer's word? Any news from the border?"

"Nothing from the border, quiet as ever. Has Azrael said anything to you about a strange disturbance several nights ago?" Lazarus asked him.

Layek thought for an instant before answering, stroking his flat hair. "Come to think of it, he did say something yesterday about bizarre fluctuations and energy ripples. I wasn't really listening, though. Why?"

"During the meeting with the High Council, Melynda said the Mages' Guild had reported to her that there was a massive disruption in the mana flows in the environment; the same night she says the Daemon Lords were summoned by this Grubbash Grimvisage," Lazarus explained. "She also said that the Mages' Guild is not aware of her vision as yet. They're keeping it very low profile."

"Interesting coincidence." Layek dismissed the connection.

"If you believe in coincidence."

"She could be wrong."

"But she's not, Layek. Anyway, can we afford not to be prepared in the event that what she says does happen?" One eyebrow raised questioningly at his friend.

"This is madness," Layek exclaimed. "Even if you somehow manage to escape Valinar with your life and the Krullstone, how are you ever going to get close enough to Serathes to use it?"

"I don't know." Lazarus shook his head, letting out a long sigh. "There was nothing in the vision to suggest how that would be accomplished. I guess we'll have to track them down after we find the stone."

"That's not a very sound plan," Layek retorted.

"I must go, Layek. Even if I fail, I have to at least try. I don't know why Fate has chosen us for this task, and it doesn't really matter. I cannot rest until I have done everything in my power to save our people and country; my conscience won't allow for anything less."

"You're convinced — I can see it in your eyes. You can't keep Vinson and Aldric out of it this time. That's what bothers you about this whole business, isn't it?" It was more a statement of fact than a question.

"In the vision I saw," Lazarus began solemnly, "my brothers will both lose their lives in a battle against the Orc army. If that happens, I will not be able to wield the Krullstone against the demons. The enemy will win, Layek. Where is my hope? They must come with me, or the world will fall. If they come with me, they will die." There was despair in his voice, the kind of despair that possesses men when they have lost the will to go on. Layek reached up and placed a hand on his shoulder to comfort him.

"Fate does not always have the last word, Lazarus," he told him softly. "If you follow the vision exactly as it was shown to you, then perhaps that is what will happen. Making a different choice, no matter how slightly it deviates from the path shown to you, can have great effect on what may yet be."

Lazarus' smile was hollow and sad. Once in a while Layek could actually offer great wisdom, but this time it did little to comfort him. "You must come with me as well, Layek. I need more than one pair of eyes to watch after them."

"I wouldn't have it any other way, brother," Layek replied. "We have a unique advantage in this situation. We already know what's coming our way. When do we leave?"

"As soon as possible. How do you think Vinny and Aldric will react?" Lazarus searched his friend's eyes.

"Are you kidding?" Layek looked surprised that he would even ask. "Vinson will believe the story in an instant. We'll have to chain Aldric to a post to keep him from scampering off to Valinar right now. They'll jump at the opportunity."

"That's what I'm afraid of," Lazarus groaned. "Layek, do not tell them about their deaths. I don't want them getting fatalistic."

"If you say so. I think you should tell them, though. They have a right to know their own future."

"Perhaps I will," he replied. "When the time is right. First we have to find them."

Lazarus stood and stretched, straightening out his uniform. Layek rose with him, and together they stepped out into the late afternoon light. They decided that they had the best chance of finding Vinson and Aldric back at the barracks, thinking they would have given up their search of the city by now and returned to the Legion head-quarters. They followed the trail to the eastern side of the gardens, walking in silence. They encountered only a handful of people, others enjoying the stillness of the gardens in the waning afternoon, but none paid any attention to the two soldiers.

They passed through the east gate and into the city streets still crowded with traffic. Occasionally Layek broke their silence with witty remarks and comical memories, but for the most part they walked wrapped in their own thoughts. They passed easily through the host of people on the street; most stepped aside when they noticed the ranks of the two men.

The sun was just beginning to sink into the horizon as they entered the barracks complex, and their shadows grew long as they made their way toward the command post. The training yard was all but empty; only a handful of soldiers lingered this late in the day. The forges and other workshops were silent and dark, slumbering beasts awaiting a new dawn to restore them to life. A peaceful stillness settled over the grounds like a warm blanket.

They ascended the few steps that led up to the headquarters building and entered. Sergeant Tully had already gone home for the evening, and another soldier had taken up his post for the remainder of the day. Layek and Lazarus approached the desk and addressed the middle-aged sergeant seated behind it, but the clerk told them that Vinson and Aldric had not checked in today, nor had he seen them since he came on duty. Lazarus exited, disappointed, yet strangely relieved that he would not have to face his brothers right away, and sat down on the front steps.

Layek dropped down next to him and leaned back on his hands. They sat there for several minutes in silence, enjoying the sunset.

"They must be really upset if they still haven't come back," Layek mused.

Lazarus didn't answer right away; he knew how much Vinson and Aldric hated it when they got left behind. Like him, they were fascinated with war. Soldiery was their life; it was in their blood.

"Any idea where we might find them?" Lazarus asked finally. "I don't want to rush this, but there are preparations to be made."

"Be patient, Laz," Layek replied. "You'll have plenty of time to arrange things tomorrow."

"Maybe we should go look for them," Lazarus suggested.

"Let's head over to the Blue Moon. I could use a drink; I think you could use one, too." When Lazarus started to protest, Layek added, "We can leave a message with the clerk. If they come back before we do, at least they'll know where to find us."

"All right then. I'll be right back."

Lazarus heaved himself off the porch and walked back inside the building. He emerged again a moment later to find Layek waiting for him, tapping his foot impatiently. He rose quickly, and together they ambled over to the main gate.

Before they exited the complex Lazarus insisted on leaving a message with the guards on duty at the entrance as well. He told them to inform his brothers that there was a message waiting for them within the command post if they should return without him. Once he was satisfied, the two friends continued on their way, traversing the familiar path between the barracks and the Blue Moon Inn.

When they arrived at their destination, the tavern was mostly empty. Half a dozen patrons huddled over mugs of cold ale and talked in calm voices. It was still early; the rowdier customers would not turn up until after full dark settled in. They took a table near the back, distanced enough from the rest of the clientele so that their conversation could not be overheard.

Sermin greeted them as usual and stopped to chat for a moment before hurrying off to get their order. They sat for a while, sipping their drinks without speaking. Neither wanted to further discuss Melynda's vision; both had accepted the fact that soon enough they would be leaving their home and very possibly might never return. They finished their ale in silence and promptly ordered a second round. The second round became the third, and when the cold drinks started to ease the weight off their shoulders, they began to speak.

At first they reminisced about other, happier times and completely avoided any conversation about the task they were about to undertake. Hours went by as they chuckled gaily at old memories and shared experiences. Customers began to trickle in, one or two at a time, and their conversation shifted to their current obligations. They discussed the best route to Valinar, how they might navigate the impenetrable Morah Weald, what manner of supplies to bring, and who would accompany them.

Suddenly Aldric, Vinson, and Azrael came bursting through the door. Collectively, their eyes settled on Lazarus and Layek, who stopped their exchange to return the hot stares of the three newcomers. Without delay the trio tramped over to the table they were occupying.

"Where in the blazes have you been?" Aldric demanded hotly.

"We've been combing the entire city all day," Azrael added in the same tone.

"We thought you had run off without us again," Vinson finished.

"Now calm down," Lazarus beseeched them, raising his hands innocently. "There's no need to get upset. After all, as you can see, I'm still here."

"What the devil's going on here?" Aldric pressed. "First you get summoned to the palace in the middle of the night; then you disappear for an entire day. Now we find you here, conspiring no doubt, to conveniently leave us here twiddling our thumbs."

"Relax, brother." Lazarus stood and clapped his younger sibling on the shoulder. "We were doing no such thing. Would I have left a message of where to find me if I was planning to leave without you?"

Aldric considered this new concept for a moment. He looked to Vinson and Azrael for encouragement, but they simply shrugged in defeat. Lazarus had a point, and they could not argue against it.

"Something's going on anyway," Vinson stated matter-of-factly. "I know it."

"Indeed something is," Layek said.

"We should go somewhere a little more private," Lazarus affirmed. "What I have to say is not for just any ear."

Vinson looked at his two companions quizzically; a hint of understanding flashed in Azrael's eyes but was gone an instant later. Aldric nodded in acceptance. Lazarus waved Sermin over to their table and politely asked her if she could lend them a private room to continue their dialogue. She nodded and trotted off to the back. Moments later she re-emerged with a set of keys and motioned for them to follow.

She led them up the stairs to the second floor. A narrow hallway led in a single direction toward the other side of the building. Without hesitating she took them down the hall and stopped in front of the first door to their left. Sermin placed the key in the lock and turned it. There was a sharp click as the latch released, and the door swung inward; she ushered them into the room.

Inside was a small study of sorts. There was a long wooden table with half a dozen plain chairs in the center. Half-filled bookshelves lined one wall while the other had a small fireplace. Dressers decorated with flowers and little knick-knacks sat on either side of the unlit hearth. A single window, closed and shuttered, adorned the wall opposite the door. Sermin urged them to take up seats as she lit the single oil lamp in the middle of the table.

"This is my private study," she said. "Never cared much for reading but it's a nice spot to relax a bit. Can I get you boys anything to eat or drink?"

Lazarus requested a round of drinks for them. "Thank you, Sermin, for your hospitality," he said. "I hope we're not imposing ourselves on you too much."

"Nonsense, dear," she replied cheerily. "It's always a pleasure having you boys around. I'll be right back with your drinks. Please, make yourselves at home."

With that she scurried off, closing the door gently behind her. They waited patiently for about ten minutes before she returned with their refreshments, rapping softly on the door before entering with a tray laden with ceramic mugs.

"Here you are," she stated as she plopped a full tankard of ale in front of each of them. "I'd stay to chat, but somebody has to keep an eye on things downstairs. You know how things can get out of hand in a jiffy. You probably want some privacy anyway."

She gave them a knowing wink before announcing that she would return a little later to check on them. The five companions thanked her again for her generosity as she turned for the door. Lazarus rose from his chair and followed after her, closing it softly behind her. He turned the latch and heard the lock snap into place but waited until Sermin's footsteps had receded down the hall before returning to his seat.

"So, Laz, what's all the secrecy about?" Aldric asked as Lazarus pulled his chair up to the table and sipped from his mug.

"Does it have anything to do with the discord I've been feeling in the mana flows?" Azrael inquired, his eyes intense.

"Yes, Azrael," Lazarus answered. "In a way it does. Our lands are in severe peril."

"From what?" Vinson questioned his older brother. "Illendale has no real enemies, except for the Orcs, but they have never posed a serious threat to us."

"It is true that in the past the Orcs have not been able to challenge our military," Lazarus said. "Until now, they have been a disorganized mob barely able to maintain their coherence as a nation. That has changed."

"What changed? Have the Orcs finally organized an offensive?" Aldric's eyes flared with excitement at the possibility.

"There has been a coup, and under their new leadership they are preparing an invasion of our lands." Lazarus looked them each solidly in the eyes.

"How do you know all this, Laz?" Azrael continued his interrogation. "And what does this have to do with the disturbances I've felt?"

"Melynda has had a vision," Lazarus stated simply.

Collectively, his brothers and Azrael inhaled sharply in surprise. They knew of Melynda and her abilities, though before her visions had never involved any of them directly.

"This vision predicts a massive Orc invasion, so massive that our army in all probability cannot withstand it," Lazarus told them. "A sorcerer known as Grubbash Grimvisage is in the process of seizing power in the Orc lands. He may already have accomplished this. Once rule of the Orcs is his, he will rally their armies for war. Illendale, being his closest and most powerful neighbor, will be among his first targets."

"There is something else; otherwise you would not have been summoned to the palace so late last night," Vinson pointed out.

"There is more, Vinny. Much more," Lazarus replied ominously.

Lazarus explained Melynda's vision in full once again, leaving out only the portion that had shown Lazarus of his brothers' deaths.

Vinson, Aldric, and Azrael listened intently, dumbfounded by the overwhelming suddenness of the prospect Lazarus had presented to them. When he had finished, none of them spoke; they simply stared in stunned silence.

It was Vinson who first recovered. "Why have I been chosen to wield the Krullstone if any of us three can use it?"

"The Krullstone is immensely powerful. Using it for any amount of time becomes addicting to the user. It is possible to become obsessed with that power and lose touch with reality completely," Lazarus lectured. "As a hybrid warrior, you are the only one of us three able to wield magic, Vinny. Perhaps this will serve you well in resisting the temptation the Krullstone will set against you. I think that's why you have been chosen."

"If we can recover the Krullstone, how are we going to get through the entire Orc army to use it against the Daemon Lords?" Azrael asked.

"I asked the same thing," Layek said. "Unless the Daemon

Lords plan on riding at the head of the army, how are we supposed to find them?"

"I'm sorry," Lazarus said sincerely. "I don't have the answers to your questions. Let me tell you this: I believe in Melynda's vision. I believe that if we do nothing, the apocalypse she has foreseen will come to pass. I must do whatever I can to help our people, and though I may not have all the information I need, I must continue on faith alone. What other choice is there?"

"I don't like it one bit," Azrael opined. "We must know more before any semblance of sound judgment can be made."

"If the Orc army is as awesome as Laz says it is, the only way to save our land appears to lie with this Krullstone," Layek noted. "I don't see any other alternative."

"If it is as Laz says," Aldric said, "then we must make haste. We should leave immediately."

"Do not be rash, Aldric," Lazarus admonished his youngest brother. "Do not forget that nobody has ever returned from Valinar. Undertaking this quest could very well lead to your death."

There was a hint of surprise on Layek's face; he had not expected Lazarus to allude to his brothers' foreseen demise so soon. He said nothing, however, remembering his promise to his friend.

Aldric was unfazed by Lazarus' words. "If our army cannot withstand the forthcoming invasion, then we cannot wait until the Orcs are at our doorstep to go looking for this talisman," he stated ardently.

"I agree with Aldric," Vinson said simply. "We cannot afford to delay. Procrastination now could cost us more than we can imagine."

"Well, I'm coming, too," Azrael blurted. "No way I'm going to get left behind this time."

"I'm happy to have you with us, Azrael. The Queen is contacting the other races to seek aid from them in case we fail," Lazarus explained. "Hopefully she can convince them to aid us. Either way, we must succeed. Our combined armies can't defeat the Daemon Lords; they are beyond mortal weapons. The army must buy us the time to find the Krullstone so we can use it to destroy them."

"It is wise to ask the other races for help, but I doubt they will volunteer without physical proof." Vinson toyed with his mug of ale as his thoughts coalesced. "The Dwarves have been at war for centuries. They will be very hesitant to send us military support unless they can see some gain for themselves in it. The Elves might be persuaded to assist us, but they have problems of their own, and Illendale is a long way to march an army to fight an enemy that doesn't directly threaten them. Like Laz said, we must succeed in finding the stone, and we must successfully wield it against the Daemon Lords, or our world is doomed. Failure is not an option."

"We have the vision to guide us at least," Lazarus added. "That will help us prepare for the pitfalls that await us and avoid them." Lazarus stole a quick glance at Layek, and they exchanged a knowing look.

"You have told us everything?" Azrael asked, noticing the fleeting look Lazarus and Layek had given each other. "You would not keep anything from us, not in this situation."

"Laz?" Layek looked to his friend to answer the question. It was plain in his eyes that he wanted Lazarus to divulge the secret he had been keeping throughout their conversation.

"Yes," Lazarus lied flatly. "I have told you everything."

"Good," Vinson cut in. "Then let's get on with this business. There is much to be done."

"Indeed there is. We need to leave the day after tomorrow."

"So you're not going to try to talk us into staying behind this time, Laz?" asked Aldric. "I would have thought that for a task as dangerous as this you would do everything in your power to keep us here."

"This time," Lazarus said, lowering his head, "I have no choice. Believe me, if it could be any other way, I would have it so. However, it has been made clear to me that only together can we hope to recover the Krullstone and return safely."

"Don't worry, brother," Vinson soothed him. "We can watch out for each other. Who better to undertake such a mission than the people you trust most?"

"He's right, Laz," Aldric said softly. "Together we can and will fulfill the trust that has been given us. Lay your fears aside for now; together there is nothing we cannot accomplish."

"I hope you are right," Lazarus replied.

"Laz and I have discussed this a little as we were waiting for you guys to arrive," Layek said, switching the focus of the conversation. "We both agree that our best route of travel is across the Solaris Plain to the Morah Weald. From there we will make our way through the forest to the ruins of Caer Dorn where we will locate the Krullstone. Once we find the stone, we will return along the same route. It is the quickest way."

So they began to plan for their upcoming journey, the supplies they would need to carry with them, and candidates who were best suited to join their expedition. Everyone had input, and they argued the merits of their individual suggestions well into the night. Sermin checked on them a few times while they talked, bringing them fresh drinks and some snacks whenever she had a moment to spare from the common room below them.

Several rounds of drinks later they had the whole plan worked out. Everything had been carefully thought out and well discussed. They had all agreed on the route they would follow to their destination; crossing the plains was the simplest and straightest road to travel and would facilitate their need for haste.

They had determined the eight other soldiers who would accompany them. Among the chosen were Aurora Skall, the senior sorceress of the Phoenix Legion; Emeris Dallen, arguably one of the best horsemen in the kingdom, master strategist, and captain of the cavalry in the Phoenix Legion; and Joseph Corsin, probably the best scout in the Legion, as well as five other hand-picked soldiers, stout men of the infantry who could make such a long, forced march easily.

Once their business had been concluded, they collected their glasses, and Lazarus led them out of the room, unlocking the door and stepping out into the hallway. When they arrived in the common room, civilians and soldiers alike crowded around, enjoying drinks and good company. Lazarus stood at the bottom of the stairs for a few moments, seeking out Sermin. He spotted her after awhile, weaving her way through the host of patrons with a tray in her hands laden with empty mugs. He moved to intercept her, his company in tow.

"Finished already?" she asked politely as she plopped her tray onto the serving bar.

"Yes, we are," Lazarus replied as he removed his purse from his belt to pay their tab. "Thank you for your hospitality."

"Don't mention it, sweetie."

Lazarus could see that she was swamped with work so he promptly counted out the coins to cover their bill. He placed them gently in her hand, including a few extra silver pieces for her kindness. She thanked him before graciously excusing herself to attend to her other customers. Collectively the five companions progressed their way through the throng that crowded the popular bar.

Outside the night air was crisp and cool, causing their breath to cloud thickly. Lazarus wrapped his arms about himself to protect his body from the chill while the others gathered around him.

"Well," he said, "let's go home and get some sleep. We have a lot of work to do tomorrow."

"Yeah," Vinson commiserated. "I think I've had enough for one night."

Layek put his hand on Vinson's shoulder. "Agreed. There have been enough surprises for one day."

They walked in silence, brooding over the journey that awaited them. None of them wanted to speak about the dangers that confronted them or the possibility of injury or death. None wanted to consider what it might mean for them if the war came as had been prophesied. They had always been together, as friends and as brothers, and though it went unspoken, none of them could imagine life without the others.

When they neared the entrance to the barracks, Azrael said his goodbyes. Not being in the Legion, his home was outside the grounds within the surrounding city. Each officer within the army was granted his own living quarters, and although they were quite small, the homes afforded the officers some measure of personal space.

The group arrived first at Lazarus' residence and paused at the front steps to bid each other good night before parting ways. Vinson and Aldric walked away, vanishing into the night like ghosts. When Lazarus and Layek were alone, Layek turned to his friend.

"I still think you should have told them," Layek scowled.

"When the time is right," came Lazarus' casual reply. "They are already aware of the dangers that face us; they don't need that cloud hanging over their heads. It will only complicate matters further."

"I seriously disagree. But if that's the way you want to play your cards, then so be it." The big man shifted uncomfortably before beginning again. "Are you sure about this, Laz? I know you believe wholeheartedly in this prophecy nonsense, but I worry about you sometimes. Sometimes I think you take too much responsibility upon yourself."

"I hope so," Lazarus sighed heavily. "There are too many variables in this business, and I can't be certain that the decisions I make are the right ones, but what choice do I have? I have always tried to keep my brothers safe; they are the last of my family, and I do not think I could go on if I lost them. Now I am forced to subject them to a challenge they may not be able to conquer. I must go on faith alone, and I only hope that faith will be enough to bring us all safely through."

"Worry not, my friend. Together we will come out of this okay. Try to get some sleep tonight. Long days are ahead of us, and you will need as much strength as you can muster." Layek slapped him lightly on the back as he spoke, ushering him toward the door of his quarters.

The two friends said goodnight, taking each other's hand before Layek trudged wearily off into the darkness. Heavy hearted, Lazarus walked straight to his bed, pausing only to shake the boots off of his feet. Although he had resigned himself to destiny, explaining it all to his brothers and admitting to himself that he must trust them to take care of themselves had taken every ounce of his energy. He didn't even bother to undress; he simply threw himself onto the mattress and immediately fell asleep.

VII PERSISTENT SHADOWS

GRUBBASH AIMLESSLY WANDERED the halls of his keep, carefully mulling over events and how they fit into his schemes. Everything was proceeding just as he had charted. His risky venture was well underway, and although it had not yet paid off, someday soon it would. The Orc nation would kneel before him, and once he had them in his thrall, the rest of the world would follow suit in due time.

He was in the upper passages of Grimknoll; he turned left through an archway that led to a stone veranda overlooking the northern territory of the Durgen Range. Grubbash enjoyed the long views granted from the higher reaches of his sanctuary, and today he chose this vantage point because it faced the same direction as his ambitions. Here he could be isolated from the mundane daily grind and be left alone with his thoughts. Here his guests would not disturb him.

Their presence was so intolerable to him that he almost wished he had never summoned them. He thought that perhaps he did not need their power to fulfill his desires. In the end he decided that though he may not need their power, it should be his anyway. He would be the pinnacle of life on earth, the all-powerful being through which life on this world would be defined.

He had successfully summoned Serathes and the three Daemon Lords, a feat that had nearly killed him. The ritual had sapped his energy almost to the point of death. He had been left badly weakened and unconscious for three days, a dangerous position for him to be in. He considered himself quite lucky to be alive. Grubbash knew he had many enemies, even among the members of his order, who coveted his title and power more than enough to kill for it.

How fortuitous that none of his adversaries had capitalized on the opportunity when it had presented itself. Now he was awake. So far his plans had succeeded, and once Kairayn returned bearing the Krullstone he would be invincible. Nobody would be able to stand against him once he had commandeered Serathes' and the Daemon Lords' power.

The Daemon Lords spent the majority of their time in the catacombs beneath the keep, and he preferred not to spend too much time around them. He despised them. He hated the charade of servitude he was forced to uphold until the Krullstone was brought to him. He hated the commanding and demeaning tone the demons used when speaking to him. Most of all, he hated the fact that their power was greater than his.

Only for a short while, he whispered within the secrecy of his mind. He must endure until the time came when he could reveal the trap he had devised; then it would be too late for them to escape.

He looked to the ground below his perch and noticed a train of wagons with the familiar iron-barred cages atop them. Another shipment of fodder for the Daemon Lords to dismember and consume. They demanded fresh meat and souls to feed on so Grubbash brought them Simoril slaves. He cared nothing for the stupid creatures, but he cared even less for the manner in which the Daemon Lords tortured their meals. Some they would drain the life force from, feeding off the souls of the slaves and leaving little but empty husks behind before throwing the remains as scraps to the demon minions they continually brought from their world. Others would be dismembered one limb at a time so that the slaves could watch in horror as their companions were devoured piece by piece. Some would be eaten in a manner that would keep them alive as long as possible so that the demons could delight in their agony as they took pleasure from the flesh of their victims. It seemed to Grubbash that the Daemon Lords fed as much on misery and suffering as they did on souls, flesh, and blood.

Not much longer, he reminded himself.

He wondered about Kairayn and how his expedition was faring. It had been nearly a week since his departure, and by now he would be entering the Tersal Highlands on his trek north. They should be making excellent speed, and with any luck Kairayn would return just as the armies of Orcs began to march.

Very soon.

 formatting಄   ಄   ಄

Kairayn crouched low to the ground next to his horse. It was shortly after dawn on the fifth day since he had left Grimknoll on his covert mission to recover the Krullstone for the High Summoner. The eleven other Orcs in his party were huddled around him in a tight circle, listening to the report of the scout who had returned from his patrol less than half an hour before.

His team had moved quickly after leaving Grimknoll, setting out at dawn each day and riding until they could no longer see the terrain in front of them. They had made excellent time, already reaching the southern bend of the Serpentspine Mountains and approaching the border of the Tersal Highlands. He had been here little more than two weeks ago, though he had been heading in the opposite direction, and he knew the area well.

They had encountered no one in their march south, and Kairayn had felt confident that they had escaped the keen eyes of the Daemon Lords. Now he was not so certain. He had dispatched his best scout, Lagor, last night as they made camp to backtrack and be certain that they were not being followed. Now that scout had returned, and the news he bore was not pleasing in the least.

"There are eight of these creatures at the most," Lagor relayed. "They move quickly without stopping for rest or food. They will catch us by nightfall."

Kairayn looked at the burly Orc. Large and imposing, he was a masterful scout and tracker nevertheless. Kairayn had utilized his talents before and listened intently as he conveyed the information he had gathered.

The morning air misted as Kairayn exhaled, and he pulled his cloak close to his body to ward off the chill. They had broken camp before the sun had risen and prepared to leave upon Lagor's return, not wanting to waste anymore daylight than was necessary.

"You are certain that these creatures track us?" Kairayn posed the question, though he already knew the answer. Someone had seen them leave and roused the suspicion of the Daemon Lords. Now they were sending their minions to find out what his purpose was. He doubted that these things intended to attack, especially when they had them outnumbered, but he did not like being followed or spied upon.

"Without doubt, Master," Lagor said with certainty. "They make a line straight for our position. If they intended to attack us, I think they would have ambushed us last night as we slept. It seems they are just shadowing our movements, biding their time. I believe they have been following us since we departed. Their movements suggest that they know how we operate; otherwise they might have stumbled upon us in the night, or we may have spotted them in the daylight hours. They stay well back, yet close enough to keep an eye on us."

Kairayn spat. He could not allow these hell-spawned fiends to compromise his mission's secrecy. He could attempt to lose them in the vast wilderness around them, but his intuition told him they would be able to track his party wherever they went and no matter how skillfully they disguised their trail.

That meant he would have to kill them. He didn't mind; they were nothing to him. It was the time it would take that was upsetting. Setting up an ambush would cost precious hours, maybe even the lives of his soldiers, and he would have need of all of them if they were to find the missing Krullstone. There was also the possibility that one or more of these demons might escape. If that happened, they were all doomed.

"Do you recognize these creatures, Lagor?" If the scout could provide any information about what tracked them, maybe he could use it to their advantage.

"Nothing that I've ever seen before," the scout replied flatly. "They are small, not even half the height of an Orc. They are highly agile, and they possess the tracking skills of a master. I used every trick I know to hide our trail, but they knew right where to find us. It may seem strange, but I don't think they even look for tracks. I observed them earlier, and I didn't notice them even searching the earth for our signs; they just keep coming like they already know where to find us."

"Do they know we are aware of their presence?"

"As yet, no." Lagor shifted his weight to ease his cramping muscles. "I was not seen, and they would have no other reason to believe that we know of them. We have been camouflaging our tracks since the beginning so the efforts I made today should not have alerted them."

Kairayn thought for a few moments, working out the details of his new plan before responding. "Excellent. If they do not know we are aware of their presence, then they should not be able to see what we have in store for them. Lagor, you will continue to counter-track our shadows and keep an eye on their movements. Take a mage with you and try to identify these things. The rest of us," Kairayn finished his layout of their plan, "will continue on our route northward as if nothing has changed; we do not want our guests to become suspicious. If we can lure these creatures in close enough, we can rid ourselves of them for good."

Kairayn raised himself off the ground. "Well done, Lagor. Get yourself something to eat, and then I want you back out there. Roktar will go with you to see if he can identify these beasts."

The Orcs dispersed to their assigned tasks. Roktar waited patiently for Lagor to finish a hasty breakfast of dried beef and bread before the two of them slipped away to locate their pursuers. Kairayn sent two of his warriors, Kilreg and Dreeg, ahead to scout the territory. Their orders were simple: find a suitable place for them to stage an ambush.

Kairayn led his group northward, guiding his horse through the increasingly rocky terrain as he considered this turn of events. His Orcs did not know their true purpose for this long march. So far as they knew, the High Summoner had ordered them to recover ancient manuscripts from Valinar. Except for the Druhedar, his warriors knew nothing of the Daemon Lords; only an abundance of rumors of war had reached their ears. News of war spread fast in the Orc lands.

Now they were being tracked by demons. *What questions would that bring up in their minds,* he wondered darkly, *especially the Druhedar.* His warriors might pass it off as meaningless, but how long before the mages began wondering why demons would be tailing them through the wilderness? Sooner or later they were bound to put two and two together. Already they must be suspicious. And sooner or later the two Masters would figure out that this expedition was after more than mere manuscripts.

Kairayn let the thought pass through him. There was nothing to be done about it now. If the sorcerers fell out of line, he would adjust their attitude as necessary. His warriors, at least, would remain loyal to him to the end. *No,* he told himself, *the mages would not be a problem.* He had absolutely no qualms about burying them here in this forsaken land if they jeopardized his mission.

The band of warriors continued their trek, passing without much difficulty through the rough hills of the Tersal Highlands. Far to the north Kairayn could see storm clouds gathering, a dark mass of natural fury borne southeast on the prevailing winds. It looked to be a particularly vicious storm, but with any luck the winds would shift, and it would blow over the mountains before it could reach them.

At least the demons will not be able to track us in such a storm, Kairayn thought dismally.

Midday came and went, and still they had no word from their scouts. Kilreg and Dreeg had not returned, nor had Lagor and his escort. They stopped for a quick lunch of dried meat, bread, and cheese and to rest their horses, taking shelter under a stand of leafless elms. They spoke little as they ate, preferring instead to keep company with their thoughts.

Less than an hour after resuming their march Lagor joined up with them. As Kairayn rounded a set of large boulders, he found Lagor there waiting; the mage Roktar was there as well, sitting a few paces off with his head lowered. The big Orc rose immediately upon seeing his master and saluted as he stepped out to meet him.

"What have you found, Lagor?" Kairayn asked simply, keeping his eye on the mage still seated ahead of him.

"Our shadows continue the pursuit, keeping a safe distance from us. They still do not know we are aware of them. Roktar has identified the beasts, Master." The Orc gestured to the mage who had lifted his head to look into Kairayn's eyes.

Kairayn saw the suspicion in that glare, lurking just below the surface, held carefully in check. He would have to watch this one for certain, which meant he would have to watch the other one as well. Druhedar were thick as thieves.

"What say you, mage?"

Roktar stared at him for a moment, not speaking. Kairayn could see the wheels working behind his eyes as he debated whether to tell him his findings straight out or to confront him about his suspicions. In the end he decided against challenging Kairayn's authority, for the moment at least.

"I have discovered the identity of our pursuers," he began plainly. His tone remained even as he spoke, carefully keeping his true thoughts masked. "They are called imps. Mischievous beings. They could be stalking us for sport, or it is possible they believe we hold something of value and mean to waylay us and claim it for themselves. It is even conceivable the imps were sent here by another to sabotage our mission; it is not uncommon to find imps in the service of more powerful demons."

The subtle suggestion did not go unnoticed by Kairayn. He was playing Kairayn against himself, gently probing him to see if his expressions would give away some hidden knowledge to validate his mistrust. Kairayn ignored it. He was not about to start playing mind games with a Druhedar. He had better things to do with his time. Besides, he did not want to inadvertently give anything away; sorcerers were very perceptive, and they gleaned meaning from even the most ordinary responses.

"How dangerous are these imps?" Kairayn asked evenly.

"Imps are small and weak generally speaking. They wield some magic, but they should not pose a threat to us."

"Good. How are they tracking us? What weaknesses can we exploit?"

"The imps are using their magic to track us. They are following the ethereal scent of our life essences. A simple trick really but more effective than trying to follow any physical evidence we may leave in our passing," Roktar finished, still holding Kairayn's gaze.

"Can you use your magic to manipulate this 'trail'?" Kairayn inquired, seeing an opportunity to set the trap he had been planning.

"Yes, Master. I can alter the scent to seem older, making it appear as though we are farther ahead of them."

"Good. I will call for you when I require your services again. You have done well." Kairayn dismissed the mage and turned his horse to rejoin the rest of the party.

Kilreg and Dreeg returned unsuccessful from their search, and Kairayn bade them all gather round and laid out his plan. He sent Lagor ahead of them now to find an appropriate location for their snare. They would ride on as normal until a site was found. Once Lagor returned they would prepare the trap while the mages used their power to trick the imps into believing they were still riding hard ahead of them. The Orcs would spread out to form a rough half circle about the imps, and when Kairayn gave the signal, they would collapse in on their enemies from all sides. He made it abundantly clear that none were to escape.

They wasted no time in moving on, traveling forward at an average pace to allow Lagor the time he needed to procure the right spot. It only took him a couple of hours to return, but by then it was well into the afternoon. He rode in swiftly and immediately approached Kairayn, explaining what he had found. The site he had chosen was well suited to the task. Kairayn called out to Roktar, and when the sorcerer appeared before him, he set him to his designated task.

Roktar trotted off to one side and began working his magic. He uttered the words of power in the strange tongue of the mystics while weaving his hands smoothly through the air to form the symbols that would give his spell life. It took only a few minutes to complete the minor ritual, and when he was finished, he looked over to Kairayn and said simply, "It is done, Master."

Kairayn gave the signal and sharply kicked his horse in the flanks. The others followed suit, spurring their steeds into a gallop behind their leader. No more than two miles ahead of them was the place Lagor had chosen for them to stage their ambush. It was a small clearing with low hills to either side forming a shallow ravine. Rocks and large boulders dotted the hills while a thicket of tangled bushes covered the far banks of a stream that ran through the center of the valley. It wasn't much, but it would certainly serve their purpose.

Kairayn directed his warriors to occupy the hills to either side, dividing them up evenly. He gave them instructions to close in behind the imps and cut off their escape when he gave the signal to engage them. He positioned the two Masters and Lagor with himself within the hedge at the north end of their little vale.

With everything in place, the Orcs settled in to await their prey. It would not be long before they came charging up the stream toward them, Kairayn thought. When Roktar cast his spell, they must have realized that their targets were far ahead of them and would make great speed to ensure that they did not lose their quarry in the vast highlands. Kairayn counted the minutes, thinking that at any moment the enemy would materialize in front of them. He waited, growing more and more edgy with each passing moment. "Something is wrong. It should not have taken them this long to catch up to us," Kairayn growled to himself. After what seemed like an hour, Kairayn could wait no longer. He shuffled silently over to where Lagor was crouched and whispered into the scout's ear. Lagor disappeared soundlessly into the hills behind them.

Something was definitely not right; it should not have taken the imps this long to fall into their trap. The sun was beginning to set on his right, deepening the gloom of the valley. If it got much darker before the imps arrived, it would be hard to see them in the expanding darkness. With every passing minute the chances grew that one of them might slip through their net and escape to tell the Daemon Lords what had happened.

Lagor returned less than half an hour later, winded by the haste with which he had carried out his charge. The light was faltering swiftly, too swiftly for them to execute their plans on this night. Kairayn would have to wait for another day to rid himself of the pestering demons. If his patience lasted long enough.

"Well?" Kairayn asked impetuously.

"Master," Lagor paused briefly to catch his breath, "the imps are not coming."

"What? Where are they, Lagor?" Kairayn's voice was a barely contained maelstrom of rage waiting to be unleashed.

"My Lord, the imps are just east of our position. They do not move. It appears that they know where we are. Our plan has failed, Master. I believe they know what we are up to."

"Roktar, you fool!" Kairayn yelled as his temper snapped. "I should have known better than to trust a sorcerer!"

Kairayn called the rest of his warriors to him and ordered them to make camp. As they prepared to settle in for the evening, Kairayn strode about the makeshift camp, yelling and swearing, cursing the Druhedar and anything that crossed his path. At one point he drew his sword and began relentlessly attacking a nearby birch tree, hacking away at its skeletal limbs until he had whittled it down to a stump. Roktar stayed well away from Kairayn until his rage had calmed.

If the imps knew that the Orcs had tried to ambush and kill them, then the Daemon Lords would soon know as well. Once they heard the news he would be finished. They would certainly be more curious as to what he was doing out here in the wilderness; they would send more of their lackeys to track him, perhaps capture or kill him. If the Daemon Lords discovered what he was about, he was certainly dead, and Grubbash would quickly follow him to the grave.

Eventually his vehemence passed, and after posting a watch, the Orcs turned in for the night. Kairayn remained awake for some time, devising new ways to eliminate this threat to his mission. Before he fell asleep he wished that he had skinned Roktar alive for complicating matters worse than they already had been. Someday soon, he promised himself, Roktar would pay the price for his failure.

The Orcs rose with the sun in the morning. None said a word as they collected their gear and prepared for another day of marching. Kairayn immediately dispatched Lagor to locate their shadows. He had several new ideas on how to deal with these pests.

Lagor returned less than an hour later and informed Kairayn that the imps were once again on their trail. Kairayn immediately split the party into two groups, ordering one to continue en route while he and the rest rode around behind their enemies. Kairayn charged off into the wilderness, leading them in a wide arc to avoid detection until they were following the trail of their comrades. They galloped at full speed toward the rest of the party, trying to catch the imps in between the two.

The imps would not be caught that easily, however. Just when Kairayn thought he should be catching them, he found himself face to face with his own Orcs again. Once again he sent Lagor to find the imps, who maddeningly were not far off. This time he divided them into four units and ordered them each to close in on their foes from a different direction. The warriors rode off to their designated points and then wheeled sharply towards their enemy's position.

His plan failed again, the imps somehow managing to slip between them into the wild. Kairayn became frustrated and belligerent, obsessed now with ending the lives of these creatures that agitated him so.

The storm he had seen to the north yesterday was closing in, thunder rolling on the cold wind, driving into them and chilling them to the core. Lightning forked to the ground where the storm had broken, and Kairayn figured in less than three hours it would be on top of them. They would be hard pressed to trap their prey in such a furious storm.

The Orcs separated into their respective groups and once again charged off into the highlands. They closed in on their enemies, forming a loose circle that Kairayn thought they could not possibly escape this time. Once again he was disappointed when his Orcs rejoined in the empty space that should have been occupied by the hapless imps.

Kairayn was so enraged at this point that he didn't bother to instruct his Orcs on how to proceed next. Instead he flew off into the wind, intent on riding down these nuisances and putting them out of his misery. His Orcs rode after him, struggling to keep up in the growing darkness as the storm drew nearer.

Kairayn spurred his horse on, forcing it dangerously near exhaustion. However fast and hard they rode, the Orcs could not over-take their quarry. *If they had not known what was going on last night, they certainly know now*, Kairayn thought blackly. Now there was no turning back. He must kill these loathsome beasts.

He reined in his horse and dismounted. He halted so suddenly that those who had managed to keep up nearly ran him down. The storm was right on top of them now; large raindrops were beginning to fall all around him. The wind had picked up, driving the rain into his face and eyes. Thunder boomed out of the sky, and lightning flashed almost as plentiful as the raindrops. It was only midday, but the black clouds overhead blocked out most of the day's sunlight so that the landscape became so gray and hazy he could barely see thirty paces in front of him. When the rest of the Orcs caught up to him, he immediately consigned Lagor to again locate the imps. Kairayn settled himself on a nearby rock, unperturbed by the storm breaking all around him. The others dismounted and did the same silently, trying not to invoke the wrath of their leader. The lightning storm increased, some bolts striking the hilltops near where they rested, and the rain began to fall in steady sheets. The horses became restless, frightened by the fierce storm, but Kairayn was as motionless as the rock he sat on.

Lagor returned shortly, materializing out of the haze like a wraith, and hastily went to Kairayn. Kairayn did not even look up at his scout's approach so focused was he in his rage.

"Master," Lagor said excitedly, "the imps have changed course. They are rapidly closing in on our position, only a few minutes behind me."

Kairayn looked up, startled by the news. He had expected them to continue running away, all the way back to Grimknoll. "Very persistent. Why would they turn around when they know we are hunting them?"

"It's the storm!" Roktar shouted above the crashing thunder. "The lightning is disrupting their sense of our location. They must stay within sight or risk losing us completely!"

Kairayn jumped up at these last words. This was his opportunity. If they had to stay within visual range of him, he could lure them into a trap like he had originally planned. Kairayn remounted his horse and bid his warriors do the same. He explained that he would ride ahead with Kilreg and Dreeg to find a suitable location for an ambush. He instructed the rest to follow slowly and to make sure they were seen so as not to lose the imps in the tempest.

When Kairayn and his two subordinates were far enough ahead, he ordered Kilreg and Dreeg to fan out across the highlands to search for an adequate location for the ambush they had planned, meeting up again every fifteen minutes to report their findings. For several hours they continued their search without much luck; Kairayn was very picky in choosing the site. He wanted the perfect place; he needed this to go flawlessly.

As they moved through the highlands they left small signs for the rest of their party to follow so that they would know in which direction to proceed. Kairayn was becoming severely annoyed by the unaccommodating landscape; his desire to be rid of their shadows grew with each passing minute. The storm continued to worsen, the wind howling through the rocks and trees as it blew across the highlands.

For nearly four hours they explored the region before Kairayn's irritation was finally appeased. When he arrived at their next meeting point, he found Dreeg waiting for him, resting comfortably in his saddle and indifferently staring off into the rain-soaked distance.

Kairayn rode up to him and immediately demanded his report. "What have you got, Dreeg?"

"Master," Dreeg addressed him, "I have found what we seek."

"Take me there. Have you seen Kilreg?"

"No, Master. He has not yet returned."

"Very well. When he returns, we'll all set out together."

Kairayn did not want to raise a false alarm by leaving a man behind. He did not know how long they would spend scouting the location Dreeg had found, but if they left without Kilreg and did not come back soon enough, he might return to the rest of the party and cause an unnecessary stir.

They sat there on their mounts like stone statues, atop a small rise watching the lightning in silence, apparently immune to the rain and chilly blasts of wind. They did not have to wait long for Kilreg, however. He led his horse up the rise at a walk barely ten minutes after

Kairayn had arrived. He joined them at the top of the mound, navigating its rocky, rain-slicked surface to round out the rough circle the three of them formed.

"Master, still I have not found a suitable position."

"It is of no consequence," Kairayn dismissed his negative report impatiently. "Dreeg says he has found what we have been searching for. Lead on, Dreeg. We must finish our business here before it becomes too dark to see."

Dreeg led them to the northwest for about a mile before they came to their destination. Dreeg pointed it out to his companions as they approached, and Kairayn was instantly pleased. This was what he needed.

Dreeg had discovered a dry wash that led out of a series of particularly rocky mounts. The steep slopes would not allow the passage of horses, and the wash wound through a deep, narrow file for several hundred feet before emerging into a small bowl formed by surrounding hills strewn with large rocks and trees. It was the perfect spot for an ambush. If the things that tracked them followed their trail through the wash, the Orcs could assault them on the other side and close off their escape route by circling around on foot.

"Well done, Dreeg," Kairayn congratulated the Orc. "This will do nicely."

Kairayn surveyed the location for a few moments longer before turning his horse about. Dreeg and Kilreg fell into step behind him, and together the three trotted off to the south.

They joined up with the rest of the party nearly an hour later. By then it was late in the afternoon, and the light had diminished considerably. The trail was becoming difficult to discern, and the storm continued to rage all around them. Lagor confirmed that the imps were close behind and increasingly nearer, determined not to lose them in the worsening weather.

Kairayn familiarized the rest of the party with his plan. It was quite simple and easily understood. They would ride swiftly to the location discovered earlier by Dreeg. Once they reached their destination they would assume positions behind the rocks and trees on the hills surrounding the small glen. The imps behind them would think the Orcs were trying to lose them in the storm and charge headlong into the trap. Kairayn made it clear that the attack was not to begin until he signaled and that the imps should be given sufficient time to move away from the narrow file so that they could be surrounded and exterminated.

Satisfied that everyone understood their part, Kairayn led them forward at a gallop. Kilreg had done an excellent job of marking the trail back, and despite the gloom closing in about them, the Orcs had no trouble reaching the chosen spot. There was only enough space for them to pass through the constricted crevasse in single file, but they made it through to the other side quickly.

Once there, Kairayn divided them up, sending Kilreg and three others up the western slope, Dreeg and three Orcs up the eastern slope, and the rest with him at the north end of the valley. The Orcs settled into their positions to wait for the imps to emerge. Constant flashes of lightning lit the small dale for spare moments and then plunged them into darkness once again.

Kairayn waited ten minutes, and still the imps did not show. He began to wonder if they had outmaneuvered him again. He waited longer still. The rain continued to fall steadily, and runoff began to fill the once dry riverbed they had traveled through to get here.

Just when he was about to give up, Roktar grabbed his arm. Without saying a word he pointed in the direction of the chasm that loomed less than fifty paces in front of them. At first Kairayn saw nothing; the rain and the dark obscured his vision so that he could barely make out the rock wall.

His patience was gone, and he briefly considered removing the Master's head to satisfy his dark mood. A sudden shimmer from the clouds above changed his mind instantly. In the valley below him he had seen the glint of yellow eyes as they reflected the flash of the storm.

He held his breath, his eyes riveted on the valley before him. Finally, after two days, he would have retribution against these beasts for the aggravation they had caused him. Slowly and silently he freed his giant scimitar from its scabbard at his waist. Next to him Lagor fitted an arrow into his bow, waiting for Kairayn's signal to unleash silent death upon his enemies.

A second thunderclap illuminated the area for a few precious seconds, and Kairayn got his first look at his opponents. Crouched next to a rock just outside the opening of the chasm was a short, ugly thing barely half his own height. Dark green skin fit snugly against an emaciated, bony frame, and malicious yellow eyes peered out across the gloom from within thin slits, gleaming in the brief flashes of light. Sharp fangs protruded from its mouth; claws extended from its hands and feet. Oversized pointed ears pricked up, trying to catch any sound of their prey above the storm.

When the light faded, Kairayn could still see the creature's silhouette. It remained crouched there by the rocks for several minutes, unsure whether it should continue forward. Its companions were probably just out of sight, waiting for their leader's assurance before making a move. Apparently they had not forgotten earlier events.

Fortunately, the other Orcs obeyed Kairayn's orders and remained hidden. When the lead imp was certain that they were not walking into a trap, he moved further out into the open. Slowly at first, then without warning, it sprang out into the open glen, swift as an arrow. It stood there for a few moments and then turned about and motioned with one clawed hand. Seconds later, seven other imps came bounding into the valley.

Thunder boomed overhead, deafening in its ferocity. The imps conversed in a strange, guttural language and then slowly moved forward, looking about cautiously. Now that Kairayn had them within his trap, he didn't care if they suspected what he was up to. The imps could be as vigilant as they wanted, but the moment they drew near enough to his hiding place he would send them back to whatever hell had spawned them.

"When I tell you, Roktar," Kairayn whispered in the mage's ear, "I want light all over this valley."

The mage nodded in accordance. Kairayn turned to Lagor who had now notched his arrow and drawn back his bow, taking careful aim at the closest imp. Kairayn held up his hand, signaling him to hold his shot. He waited on edge as the seconds crept by. He counted the steps between him and his targets.

Thirty. Twenty. Ten.

In one fluid motion Kairayn dropped his hand and leapt from behind his cover. He heard the twang of Lagor's bow and felt the arrow sail past him, burying itself in the skull of the foremost imp. An instant later greenish light flooded the area, revealing the imps in an eerie emerald glow. Kairayn yelled out his battle cry and was promptly answered by the cries of his companions.

Then all hell broke loose.

Kairayn charged forward, and through his peripheral vision he could see the rest of his Orcs closing from all directions. The imps, suspecting they might come under attack, were not caught completely off guard. Blasts of energy flew from their outstretched palms; bolts of lightning fell from the sky all around.

Abruptly a wall of fire went up before Kairayn just as he was almost on top of his foes. A bolt of lightning struck to his left, knocking him off his feet. He regained his footing a second later and, enraged now beyond thought, charged through the fire blocking his path forward. On the other side of the flames he came face to face with the demons who had annoyed him so. Three already lay dead in the rain-soaked dirt, arrows jutting out of their lifeless bodies. He immediately faced three of the imps, shrieking in rage and fear.

One of them shot a fireball at him from a single clawed hand. The shot flew wide, and the thing screeched in dismay. Kairayn responded with his own cry of wrath and charged forward. One powerful stroke cleaved the foul beast's head at the neck. Black blood sprayed as its headless body fell backward.

The other two sprang at Kairayn, one from each side, clinging to him, biting and clawing. Kairayn roared in anger and pain. He dropped his sword and grappled with the imps for a few seconds before clamping his mighty hands about one's neck. He bellowed in triumph as he effortlessly twisted the imp's head, snapping its spine like a twig.

The demon who still clung to his arm loosened its grip upon seeing its comrade torn asunder by this Orc and turned and ran shrieking into the night. Kairayn did not hesitate. He reached down to the earth, finding his great scimitar lying in the mud where he had dropped it. With a grunt he flung the sword. The blade caught the imp mid-stride square in the back and buried itself deep in the little monster's flesh. The imp collapsed in a heap and did not move again.

The sounds of battle had died around him, and his fury faded. Kairayn sought out the rest of his warriors. He called out to them in the black of the storm, drawing them to him, but only eight answered his call.

Aside from the three who were missing, they had only suffered minor injuries, mostly burns and small scratches from the claws of the imps. They searched the battlefield for their fallen companions and found Dreeg first, lying on his back next to a gutted imp with his throat torn out. Ugdor, another warrior, was found less than ten paces away face down in the dirt. They had some trouble recognizing him, so badly was his body charred and scorched. On the northern slopes they found Roktar, a hole burned clear through his chest.

Kairayn was relieved to find that none of the imps had escaped when they counted the bodies. The loss of Dreeg and Ugdor upset him, especially because they could not be given proper burial rites due to the rain. No dry wood for a funeral pyre would be found in this weather, and they did not have time to wait for dryer days. Roktar he did not mourn at all. He did not care for the Druhedar to begin with, and this one would surely have caused him problems down the road.

Those who weren't significantly injured were ordered to bury their dead and prepare their equipment. Lagor tended to the wounded while the others worked, bandaging their lacerations and burns. The sooner they got away from this place the harder it would be for others to follow their trail and take up where the imps had left off.

The Orcs took a few minutes to rest themselves after the day's long chase and the battle, eating a sparse meal from the rations they carried. Kairayn took the time to collect his sword and a trophy from the fallen imps, seeking out the one he had beheaded. He lifted the head from the mud where it had fallen and lashed it to his saddle with a strip of leather cord. Fifteen minutes later the Orcs mounted their horses and vanished into the rain.

VIII HUNTERS OF THE NIGHT

DEEP IN THE catacombs of Grimknoll all was silent. Night had fallen on the Durgen Range like a death shroud but nowhere as heavy as on the sanctuary of the Druhedar. Nothing stirred in the caverns and hallways of the fortress, and stillness hung on the air like a hungry beast, daring any to disturb its slumber.

The resident Druhedar had all turned in at sundown, more out of fear than discipline. None wanted to be caught wandering the halls when the dark brought out the hunters of the night. Demons were a hard lot to control, and more than one mage had disappeared mysteriously while traversing the hallways of their keep alone after dusk.

In the temple beneath the keep, Serathes waited patiently. Bones and carcasses littered the once sacred shrine, the remains of morbid feasting. A few large braziers were lit around the perimeter of the circular chamber, their muted yellow glow battling fitfully against the encroaching darkness. Shadows danced gleefully throughout the dreadful room, and the smell of death and decay permeated the stale air. He rather liked the new décor. His brothers would be coming soon, bearing news of the progression of their plans. He could sense their presence drawing close. Surely they must suspect, as he did, what the Orcs were up to.

The door creaked open slowly. A solitary crow flapped through the gaping entryway, followed by a black wolf and an unusually large serpent. His brothers. These were not their true forms; the confined spaces of the keep prevented them from moving freely in their natural state, for the Daemon Lords were far too large. Their magic was powerful enough to allow them to alter their appearance to facilitate their needs, albeit for a short while.

The three beasts settled in a row in front of him. Before Serathes' eyes the charade began to fade. Heavy mist began to form around the three, engulfing them completely in seconds. The mist grew into thick clouds, obscuring all vision of the Daemon Lords as they reverted to their original forms.

"Welcome, brothers," Serathes greeted them as the haze cleared, his voice deep and rough. "What news have you?"

Adimiron spoke first. "Hail, Serathes. I bring word of our plans in Illendale."

"And how are our pale-skinned little friends?"

"My spies have infiltrated their government," Adimiron relayed in his tortuous voice. "The Queen of Illendale has a visionary in her service; she has foreseen our coming. She knows of the Krullstone. The humans will send an expedition to recover it from Valinar."

Serathes thought for a moment. "We can no longer trust that the Necromancer will stop them from reaching their goal. Eliminate this threat."

"As you wish, Lord." Adimiron bowed his head ever so slightly in acquiescence. "Shall I remove anyone else to disrupt their preparations for war?" the demon asked hopefully.

"Do as you see fit," Serathes granted him. "Strike at their leaders. Without their leadership the humans will be lost. It will cripple their ability to oppose us."

"It shall be done, Lord. Tonight."

Serathes' gaze fell upon Satariel. "How are things with the Elves and the Trolls, Deceiver?"

"My plans are moving forward, Lord," Satariel stated, his voice thin as smoke. "Soon enough they will not be able to answer any calls for aid from Illendale."

"Very well. See that it is done. Let the races tear each other apart. They will find it difficult to oppose us once they have finished slaughtering one another."

Athiel came forward to speak now. "Lord, the spirit-link with our spies in the highlands has been severed. I no longer see what the Orcs are doing."

"Our imps have been slain," Serathes said, a hint of dissatisfaction surfacing. "I suspected that the Orcs would also seek the Krullstone. Now it seems we have proof."

"Damn Grimvisage for his deception! We should feast on that traitorous mage's soul!" Adimiron growled a curse in the hateful tongue of demons.

"Patience, brother," Serathes said calmingly. "The time is not ripe for the mage's suffering to begin. He is our link to the Orcs, and we require his services — alive. His time will come."

"And what of this Slavemaster, Kairayn?" questioned Athiel. "We should not allow him to continue, knowing what he seeks."

"Agreed. It shall be your task to see that they are repaid in full for their careless destruction of our servants. Send the hellhounds."

"Consider it done, Lord." Athiel smiled wickedly in delight.

�
ঞ   ঞ   ঞ

The sun had not yet risen when Aldric awoke, which was not unusual for him. He had always been an early riser, taking the early morning hours for himself, walking about and enjoying the peaceful city before it rose from its nightly repose.

Something was different this morning; he could feel it. As he emerged from his quarters, he noticed the dark storm clouds gathering on the western horizon. It looked to be a pretty nasty storm; already the mountains it glided over carried telltale white tips, signaling that snow was on its way. Frost coated the ground, and his breath misted before him as he exhaled. The gusting southeasterly wind carried Winter's touch and brought winter weather ever closer to his home. By tomorrow the storm would have reached Kylenshar.

The coming storm did not bother him, though. Something was

wrong. It wasn't the silence that hung in the air or the cold weather. Perhaps it was that sense of Death's touch in the chill morning. The knot in his stomach told him it was something more than just the weather.

He thought to check in on his brothers and decided against waking them this early. It would only make them cross. They were all on edge these days with their upcoming journey and all the talk of demons and Orcs. No, it was better to leave them at rest.

The barracks compound seemed to be in order in any event so he decided to wander the city for a couple of hours. A good long walk might help him clear this foreboding feeling. So he set out, passing through the gates and into the streets of the industrial sector. All was quiet; very few people were up and about.

He turned left down the empty avenue, walking towards the castle and the Tranquil Gardens. He took his time, in no particular hurry to be anywhere. He ambled past the entrance to the gardens and on towards the Grand Bazaar. As he walked through the vacant market-place he felt the unmistakable sensation that he was being watched. The hair on the back of his neck bristled, and the cold seemed to seep deeper into his bones.

He slowed his pace considerably, inconspicuously eyeing the area, trying to spot the source of this agitation. Nothing moved. Nothing seemed out of the ordinary. He didn't see anyone: no concealed face peering at him from the gray shadows of buildings or through foggy windows, no movement in the streets or alleyways.

The impression faded as he continued on his path, but the perception that something was seriously awry intensified. He trudged onward through the cold. The sun's first rays were beginning to creep over the tops of the surrounding buildings, slowly chasing away the gray limbo world between dusk and dawn.

The residents of Kylenshar were still sleeping, and the streets belonged only to him for the time being. He strolled down the thorough-fare, enjoying the peace that would soon be shattered by the throngs of citizens within the city.

Despite the solitude of the empty streets, the apprehension he felt persisted and would not be driven away. As he rounded a small bend in the road, the Council Chambers came into view, the familiar domed roof glinting dully in the half-light. The morning frost still clung to the flowers within their beds surrounding the building, a vision of crystalline perfection.

He continued his slow pace, pondering the frailty of flowers and the coming winter, when he was caught off guard by torchlight emanating from within the open doorway to the Council Chambers. Nobody should be there at this hour; it was too early for any meetings to be taking place.

He changed course, heading for the entrance of the building. As he neared the front steps he was taken aback when he beheld soldiers standing at the entrance. He quickly bounded up the steps and nearly ran headlong into the four guards who were warding the doorway. His curiosity was piqued by the strange circumstances and severity of his notion that something was terribly wrong. The four brawny men barred his path with their long halberds, crossing them in front of him at chest level.

"You may not enter," one bearded guard said. Aldric saw fear in those eyes, the kind of fear that came from realizing one's own mortality.

"I am Captain Arkenstone, Phoenix Legion." Aldric threw back his heavy cloak to reveal the rank displayed on his uniform.

"I'm sorry, sir," the guard stammered. "Inspector Kolmon has given specific instructions; none are to be admitted without his express consent."

"What's going on here?" Aldric questioned the man.

"I'm not at liberty to say, sir. I'm sorry."

"It's all right; Kolmon sent for me," Aldric lied flatly. He had to know what was going on in there.

The guard eyed him suspiciously for a minute, trying to discern if the man standing before him was telling the truth. "My apologies, Captain." The middle-aged guard decided it was best not to question the word of a senior officer. "You may enter."

The guards removed their weapons from his path, and Aldric cautiously stepped forward into the dimly lit corridor, hearing the guards mumble something about evil deeds and having a strong stomach. Only a couple of torches stood lit in their wall brackets, blanketing the hallway in deep shadows.

Aldric continued in the direction of the main chamber where he heard low voices conversing. He stood within the shadows of the entryway for several moments, catching bits and pieces of their conversation.

"... No signs of forced entry. Must've known the killer ..."

"... Sure to check outside for tracks. Poor souls."

"... No witnesses ... no chance to flee ..."

The great doors stood open; there were no guards watching this entrance to the main chamber. Aldric could see a handful of men standing near the High Council seats, basking in the flickering glow of the torches they held aloft. The room felt hollow and dismal like a permanent shadow had taken up residence within. A macabre silence layered the room as if Death had come to visit and had not yet left. It made the hair on Aldric's neck stand.

He walked quietly up to the men with the torches who were furiously studying the floor around them. As he drew nearer Aldric noticed that the desks and chairs were broken and scattered. The cold feeling in his stomach magnified as he approached.

When he entered the circle of light cast by the brands, the guards all jumped in surprise. They drew weapons quickly and prepared to defend themselves against this perceived enemy who had materialized out of thin air. Aldric held up his hands complacently, and when the men recognized his uniform beneath his cloak, they lowered their weapons, if only slightly.

"Who are you, and why are you here?" the apparent leader demanded of him.

Aldric was too horrified to answer. What he saw within the wavering gleam of torchlight froze him in his tracks and numbed him to the core. He stood there, his jaw hanging slackly, and his eyes widened in shock for several long minutes as he took in the grisly scene.

Most of the desks and chairs of the High Council lay shattered and broken about the hall, carelessly thrown aside during the gruesome

events that had taken place. Blood was splattered everywhere: on the
scattered and smashed furniture, on the wooden rails that fenced off the
area, on the columns that supported the roof. The blood congealed in
large pools on the floor before him. Bodies were strewn about the room,
perhaps half a dozen of them. It was hard to tell. The bodies had been
torn apart in diabolical fashion. Heads and limbs were separated from
grotesquely mutilated corpses and scattered around the room like some
sick puzzle waiting to be reassembled.

Aldric's heart raced. His mind screamed at him to flee this
house of death. What on this earth was capable of such mindless
destruction, such atrocity? His mind could only return a single answer.

Demons!

Questions clouded his mind, questions he could not seem to
answer. How had they gotten inside? What purpose did this serve?
Who else had fallen prey to this malicious unseen foe? He was light-
headed and dizzy. The whole room seemed to be spinning. His legs
turned to jelly beneath him and gave out. He tried to correct himself but
found he was unable to. Like a tree someone had taken an axe to, he
slowly toppled forward, his eyes rolling back into his head.

The man who had spoken to him only moments ago rushed
forward to catch him, followed quickly by the others around him. Aldric
was out cold for only a few minutes, and when he came to, he was lying
on his back on the cold stone floor with three men kneeling over him.
He was lost and disoriented for a moment until the vileness of what he
had witnessed came rushing back to him. He tried to speak but found
he could not make the words come out.

"Hold it together, man," said one man. "I'm gonna wring
Garvey's neck for lettin' any old body just waltz right in."

"It's not his fault," Aldric said finally, regaining his power of
speech. His voice was still a little shaky, but he quickly regained his
composure. "I lied to him. I told him I was sent for."

"And who are you?" questioned the man contemptuously.

"I am Captain Aldric Arkenstone, Phoenix Legion," he replied
indignantly. Aldric forced himself up to a sitting position. "I was
walking by, and I noticed things seemed out of sorts so I came to

investigate."

The man who had been speaking to him stood and extended his hand downward, offering to help Aldric off the cold stone. "I'm Inspector Kolmon; I'm in charge here."

"What the hell happened, Inspector?" Aldric took the man's hand and rose up off the floor. "Who are these people?"

"We're still tryin' to figure that out." Kolmon turned back to the gruesome display. "It appears three of 'em are members of the High Council, though which members we can't tell. The other three appear to be bodyguards or personal assistants." Kolmon pointed them out as he spoke, turning Aldric's attention to the fine clothes that hung ragged off the remains. "We won't be able to identify which Council members they are until we can track down the rest of them. I've got men seeking them out as we speak."

"What under the stars is capable of such monstrosity?"

"You'd be surprised what some creatures are capable of," Kolmon said, almost sadly. "I've seen some pretty horrifying things in my time, but this one steals the bread. Whatever it was, it managed to kill six people in a matter of minutes without letting any of them escape the room. It wasn't human either."

Kolmon walked around the area, leading Aldric back towards the entrance. He knelt down to the floor and indicated a peculiar pattern of blood smears on the polished tile. It was a series of partial footprints Aldric realized, something with three clawed toes and a spiked heel. He had never seen a track like this before. It was definitely not human or any other creature he had ever encountered in his life.

The sudden impact of the realization of what was going on hit him like a ton of bricks. He wavered for a moment, shaking like a tree in the wind, dangerously close to falling over. Kolmon put a strong hand on his shoulder to steady him. He couldn't believe he hadn't seen it from the beginning it was so obvious. The demons had begun their assault on Illendale by assassinating its leaders. These few were not the only casualties from last night, he would bet. He had to get back to the barracks as quickly as possible.

"You'd better send more men to find the other members of

the High Council, Inspector," Aldric said glumly. "This is just the beginning."

"Is there somethin' I should know, sir?" Kolmon asked him suspiciously. "Do you know somethin' about this?"

"Just a hunch, Kolmon."

Aldric exited the building as quickly as he could. He was still a little light headed, but he made it out to the street without too much strain. Business was beginning to get underway in the city, and a few people were already out on the roads. Nobody seemed to notice the unusual goings-on at the Council building, and the people passed by without a second glance.

Aldric walked briskly past the guards at the front doors and down the steps. He hit the street at a dead run, hoping that he was not too late. If the demons could strike wherever they chose in Illendale and were wise enough to hit their leaders, then perhaps they also knew of their mission to recover the Krullstone. If that were true, then the demons would certainly try to eliminate them before they could set out. That meant his brothers and his friends would be targets, as well as himself, and perhaps some of those targets had been executed during the night like those in the building he had just left.

He ran through the gathering crowds at the Grand Bazaar and into the barracks grounds without slowing. He charged up the steps to Lazarus' quarters and pounded on the door. His heart raced as he waited to hear the sound of booted feet coming to open the door.

None came.

He waited for several minutes, knocking again and again, but there was no answer. The blood pounded in his ears like kettledrums. It took him ten minutes to build up the courage to try the latch. He found that it was unlocked, and the door swung inward noiselessly. Aldric stepped slowly into the front room, scanning for any sign of struggle or foul play. Everything seemed to be in order here. He continued on to the back where the door to the bedroom stood closed.

Please, Light! Not my family!

Slowly he opened the door and peered inside, expecting to see a mirror image of the bloodbath he had witnessed earlier. To his complete surprise and utter relief, the room was empty. The bed was made neatly, and everything was well organized, as was Lazarus' habit. There were no signs of the disaster he had feared.

That meant his brother was safe. He was exalted at the discovery and sprinted off to Vinson's house to see if he was all right as well. His spirits had lifted considerably, and he was not so worried when Vinson did not appear to answer his knock. He checked inside just to be sure, but everything was fine.

So where were they? He had been left behind again. He hated that feeling so much. Still excited about his discovery, he trotted off toward the headquarters building to see if he could locate them.

In the command post Aldric discovered that his brothers had left for the palace more than an hour ago on urgent business. In a whirlwind of motion he shot out the door. He blazed past the guards at the gate and into the avenue, rushing for the palace. When he arrived at the main entrance to the castle, he was winded and had to take a moment to catch his breath before he could explain to the soldiers on guard what his business there was.

Between gasps he told the guards his rank and purpose for being there. They let him pass without incident, but Aldric noticed security was tighter than usual. Indeed the number of Crimson Guard on duty had at least doubled.

He did not let this slow him, however, and he hurried into the palace. Once inside the grand entryway and its majestic halls Aldric asked the nearest man where he could find Commander Arkenstone. The guard pointed him in the direction of the guest quarters, mumbling something about all the commotion.

In the man's eyes Aldric had seen the same evidence of worry and fear as he had seen at the Council Chambers. Something had happened here as well during the night; he could sense it. He hoped with all his heart that the Queen was safe. Illendale might not survive such an unexpected blow.

Aldric walked down the decorated halls toward the guest wing, passing dozens of doors and side corridors. He heard several voices conversing around the corner at the next intersection of hallways and turned left, hoping to finally locate his siblings. Sure enough, in the hallway with a handful of Crimson Guard and a few others he did not recognize, there was Lazarus and Vinson. Layek and Azrael were with them as well, and the look on Layek's face was more worrisome than when the tavern ran out of his favorite ale. The situation must be very dire indeed to bring Layek down.

"Aldric!" Lazarus exclaimed. "Where in the blazes have you been?"

"I went for an early morning walk. I've been looking for you. We need to talk."

"You can say that again; we've been worried sick about you," Lazarus said. "These are no times for us to be wandering alone." There was something in his voice that alluded to hidden danger, something Aldric was no longer oblivious to.

"I am perfectly capable of taking care of myself, thank you very much," Aldric quipped. He understood the severity of the situation, but being the youngest of the three, he had grown up under the shadow of his brothers. They had always felt the need to protect him from harm, and that need had been carried forward into adulthood.

"Let's talk," Lazarus told him, ushering him towards one of the doors nearby.

Layek, Vinson, and Azrael followed close on their heels, as did two others whom Aldric did not recognize. They filed into the room, a lushly decorated antechamber complete with a writing desk, four low-backed cushioned seats, and a table. Paintings hung from the walls next to silver oil lamps, and flowers decorated the finely crafted table. Two doors led into the sleeping chambers of the guest suite, one on either wall. Lazarus offered his friends chairs while he and the other two who had followed them in remained standing near the entryway.

"Have you heard, Aldric?" Azrael asked anxiously as he took the seat next to him.

"Yes. I walked by the Council Chambers this morning. The Crimson Guard were already on the scene, but I convinced them to let me through." He spoke nervously as he remembered what he had witnessed in that dark place. "Have they discovered which Council members were murdered?" Aldric inquired.

"Who got murdered?" Vinson blurted in surprise. "What happened?"

"Tell us everything," Lazarus said fervently.

"I thought you already knew. Isn't that why you're all here?"

Layek stole an unmistakable glance at the two strangers. "This is news to us. We've been, uh, preoccupied."

Aldric finally realized the strangers were Elves. But why were the Elves allowed to listen in on their conversation? Wasn't their whole mission supposed to be a secret?

"What's going on here?" Aldric looked over at the Elves in total bewilderment.

"The demons have come," Azrael whispered.

"Tell me something I don't know. What do these two have to do with it?"

They returned his gaze evenly when Aldric looked at them. The closest to him was a man, tall and slender as was the manner of Elves. He had dark brown hair and green eyes that scanned every inch of the room without leaving his for a second. His stance was easy, yet Aldric detected tenseness there, like a cat about to pounce. A well-groomed goatee adorned his chin, and his skin was tanned and weathered; he obviously spent a lot of time outdoors. By Aldric's guess he was probably a tracker.

His companion had a decidedly different look to her. Beautiful auburn hair cascaded down past her shoulders, partially obscuring her immeasurably deep emerald eyes. Her skin had a deep bronze tone that complemented the shapely figure marvelously, which was hardly disguised by the flowing, gold-threaded velvet dress she wore. Gem studded jewelry hung upon her wrist and neck, and large ruby earrings graced her ears, mirroring the fire in her eyes. She was stunningly beautiful, even for an Elf. There was an aura of intensity about her, a fire that lurked beneath the serenity of her beauty that seemed to draw one in. There was an unidentifiable attractiveness to her, something that included her fire and beauty, yet something more still just out of view. Aldric noticed that Lazarus was quite intrigued by her mystery from the way he continually shifted his gaze back to her.

"Aldric, this is Neslyn of House Alluris and her comrade Zafer." Lazarus introduced them. "They are with an Elven delegation to Illendale. Zafer is an Elven Ranger. Neslyn is a sorceress and second daughter to the King of the Elves.

"Last night, demons snuck into the castle, presumably with the intent to assassinate Queen Cailyn. They came in through the entrance in the guest wing apparently from the gardens outside. Nobody knows how they got that far, and were it not for the Elves, they might have succeeded in their plans. It was sheer coincidence that the Elves were still up and about at that hour. Five of them turned a corner to find themselves face to face with the demons, two Lurkers from what the Elves have described to me. Neslyn and Zafer alone survived the encounter." Lazarus finished his short narration.

"The demons tried to kill the Queen as well? I should have seen it coming," Aldric said. "At least three members of the High Council are also dead, murdered last night in the Council building. The investigator in charge still wasn't sure what their identities were, but it was obvious that the killer wasn't human. I know it was the demons."

"It is safe to assume then that we are in grave peril. Perhaps they already know of our plans," Vinson warned.

"It appears things have taken a turn for the worse," Layek stated.

"Indeed," Lazarus confirmed. "Time slips away from us."

"May we be of assistance in some way?" Neslyn asked in a voice that was smooth as silk.

"Thank you, but no. You have helped us as much as you can. Look to your friends now."

"Do not think that we are blind, Commander." Zafer fixed Lazarus with his stare. "A great evil has descended upon this kingdom. Three of our countrymen and friends have already fallen to this malicious force. Obviously there is some plot that you are involved in to fight this evil. There is much that you have not told us."

Lazarus mulled over in his head how much they had already gleaned from their conversation. Three of their friends had died fighting the demons already, which gave them some right to know what was going on. Illendale certainly needed all the allies she could muster; perhaps they had found some in these two Elves. He looked surreptitiously to Layek for his feelings on the matter. Layek simply shrugged. What difference could it make, except for the greater good.

"Tell them, Laz," Azrael urged him. "I believe they have earned it."

So Lazarus told them everything. He explained in great detail Melynda's visions, the coming Orc invasion, the demons, and their quest to find the Krullstone to save their country. He left out nothing, save the prophesied demise of his brothers.

The two Elves listened intently to what Lazarus had to say without interrupting. When he had finished, they looked at each other for several moments before Neslyn turned to Lazarus and said simply, "We're coming with you."

Her tone left no room for argument, but Lazarus contested anyway. "My Lady," he said, "where we go is far too dangerous for royalty. We cannot guarantee your safety. There is a great chance that we may not return at all."

"If what you say is true, you will need all the help you can get," Zafer reminded him.

"We do not have time to play babysitter for the little princess' adventure," Layek said gruffly.

Neslyn's eyes flared at Layek's words. "You are a fool, Major," she breathed, "to believe that you are more suited to this task than I." As she spoke she raised her arms, palms uplifted. Fire sprang forth, igniting the table in the center of the room. Aldric and the others seated in the chairs sprang back in surprise, Azrael falling backwards to the floor. Lazarus looked on in stunned silence.

The table was reduced to ashes in a matter of seconds, and as the fire began to spread to the rug and around the room, Neslyn brought her arms up above her head. A breeze whipped up, growing more forceful by the moment. Paintings began to fly off the walls, and the oil lamps flickered wildly in protest. The temperature plunged until frost began to cover the whole room. The flames were slowly dying, unable to survive in the iciness overtaking the room.

Neslyn lowered her arms, the wind and cold fading as she did so. She extended one hand toward the destroyed table. Before their eyes a new table of crystalline ice materialized, perfect in its construction. For many long minutes nobody knew what to say; they just stood there like statues.

"Amazing," Azrael finally whispered. "Where did you learn how to do that?"

"Secrets of the Elves," Neslyn winked mischievously at him. "Still think I can't go, Major?" The Elf's eyes dared him to say yes.

"Uh," Layek stammered, "no." He started to say something more but decided better of it and shut his mouth with a loud clap.

"Good. When do we leave?"

"In light of recent events, I think it is important that we leave immediately. As Vinny stated, we must assume the demons know of our plans and therefore most likely will attempt to eliminate us as well."

"We shouldn't leave in broad daylight though," Vinson said. "Stealth will be our greatest ally if the demons are hunting us."

"I need to consult with the Queen," Lazarus said. "Perhaps Melynda will have more insight for us. Layek, Vinny, and Aldric, prepare the supplies and gather the others. Try to be inconspicuous. I'll come for all of you when it's time."

"Very well," Layek agreed. "We'll be waiting for you at the Blue Moon."

"Sounds good," Lazarus replied. "Watch yourselves out there. Bring Aurora Skall, Emeris Dallen, and Joseph Corsin. Find Marcell, Mihan, and Devoll as well. They already know what is required of them."

"See you soon," Azrael said.

"Neslyn and Zafer," Lazarus turned to the two Elves, "go with them." Neslyn's eyes flared again, thinking that perhaps this was some trick to lose them before they left the city. "That way I don't have to track you down when the time comes."

"Very well, Commander."

Lazarus followed the rest of them back to the main foyer. There they parted company, promising to meet up again by dusk. Lazarus made his way deeper into the palace, seeking out the Queen and Melynda.

It took him a little less than ten minutes to reach the familiar study where Cailyn and Melynda were congregating. The guards outside made him wait in the hall while they got permission to admit him, but once it was granted they let him pass without comment. Inside he was ushered to a seat and offered tea.

The three discussed the gruesome events of the day and how it affected their plans. Lazarus told them of the Elves and their insistence to be brought along, while Melynda relayed to him the latest news on the murdered officials at the Council Chamber. Ozlem Rhul, David Bolge, Elvan Faris, and Douglas Armand were all dead. The latter three had been killed at the Council building while the former had been slain in her home as she slept. All had died in the same brutal manner, indicating that the same creature had committed all four crimes. Chief Minister Lee Hanlan had been reported as missing when all the members of the Council were notified of the danger and moved to safer locations.

All agreed that Lazarus and his party should leave immediately without drawing attention to themselves, of course. Queen Cailyn did not agree that the Elven princess Neslyn Alluris should accompany them, but Lazarus explained her display in the guest wing and the two Elves' refusal to be left behind after discovering their secret.

They finished their tea, having said everything that needed to be said. With a few final words of encouragement from Melynda and a reminder to keep her visions fresh in his mind, Lazarus exited the room. His meeting with the Queen had taken him nearly two hours, and he wasted no time getting out of the palace. By now, Layek and the others would have everything in order and would be waiting for him.

The storm clouds that had been hovering over the Serpentspine Mountains had finally drifted in, obscuring the sun's rays and plunging the valley into gray haziness. The wind had picked up, and a light rain had begun to fall. Lightning sporadically flashed in the sky, accompanied by rolling thunder that seemed to split it apart. By nightfall it would be pouring.

Instead of heading straight to the tavern where his friends would be waiting, Lazarus decided to take a little time to himself to be alone and think. It wasn't quite time for them to be leaving yet anyway; he had decided it would be best if they departed after dark, especially if the storm let loose. The wet weather would make it very difficult to track them, and he had to assume that they were being watched.

He made his way into the Tranquil Gardens where his favorite spot beneath the familiar willow tree awaited him. He sat on the bench and listened to the rain falling, protected by the tree's thick tangle of branches. The noise had a certain soothing effect, and right now he needed it. In just a few short hours he would be embarking on a journey he had been dreading since the beginning.

He didn't really want to go; he wanted even less for his brothers to follow him. He had no choice, however; Fate had taken that away from him. Now he was only left with duty. The moment of truth was upon him, and there was no avoiding it.

He went over the plan in his head. It was quite simple: they would cross the Solaris Plain through the Morah Weald and into the ancient city of Caer Dorn. Once they had located the Krullstone somewhere within the city, they would turn around and come back as quickly as possible. They would have to avoid being tracked and found by the demons, outwit whatever dangers lurked within the Morah Weald and Caer Dorn, and return in time to save their people from total annihilation.

He drifted off into a daydream, trying to imagine what horrors he would have to face on his journey. He pieced together the visions Melynda had shown him, trying to keep them at the forefront of his memory. Always the vision of his brothers' deaths haunted him. He tried to force that thought out of his head, tried to ignore it. Slowly time slipped away. The rain worsened, and the light failed as the clouds grew thicker overhead. It became cold and damp outside, and Lazarus wrapped his cloak tighter around his body to keep warm.

Finally he decided it was time to go. It was well past sunset when he emerged from his place of solitude. The rain was coming down in a steady drizzle, and a light mist had sprung up from the ground, giving the gardens a decidedly gloomy feel. His visual range grew short as fog clouded the air.

Lazarus hugged his heavy cloak tighter around himself to ward off the chill and walked briskly toward the egress from the gardens. The guards at the gates stopped him briefly on his way to ask him a few questions about his purpose for being out so late, but they let him pass without too much delay. The streets had emptied of all traffic due to the weather, and he hurried on to the Blue Moon where his friends would be waiting for him.

When he finally arrived, he found the place was well occupied as usual. Bodies filled the room from end to end. Every available seat was taken, and the gambling tables were overflowing with men ready to risk it all on the next toss of the dice.

He made his way through the crowd to one of the two fireplaces, which were now lit to counteract the dropping temperature. He stood by the hearth, shaking off his cloak and trying to dry out. As he stood with his back to the crackling flames, he searched the room for the friends he was supposed to meet.

He spotted them, the whole group, occupying a set of tables in the far corner. They did not look particularly jovial, sitting hunched over their mugs without drinking, without talking. Apparently they were as caught up in events as he was. Neslyn and Zafer were with them, conversing with each other in whispers. The soldiers chosen to accompany them were also there, sharply keeping an eye out for any signs of trouble. He walked over to his waiting companions and seated himself in the space they had reserved for him.

"Welcome, brother," Vinson greeted. "What took you so long? We've been here for hours."

"I'm sorry. Is everything ready?"

"Of course," Aldric said. "All the equipment is prepared and waiting for us at the stable. You've got good timing. Layek's been getting pretty edgy. It's taken every ounce of energy I have to keep him away from the gambling tables."

"Thank you for that, Aldric," Lazarus replied. "The weather has turned in our favor; we leave now."

"How is the weather anyway?" Layek asked. "It was looking pretty nasty when we came in."

"Cold and wet, old friend. Perfect for a little vacation," Lazarus answered sarcastically.

"Great," Layek muttered back.

"Zafer and Neslyn, are you ready?"

"Indeed we are, Commander." Zafer stood from his chair. "We have left word with the rest of our delegation that we will be absent for a few weeks. We will not be missed."

"Let's get going then," Lazarus said as he stood up.

The rest of the newly-formed group joined him, and together the thirteen members of the party left the Blue Moon. The rain had gotten worse while they had been inside, and now it was coming down in buckets. Large puddles were beginning to form in the barren streets, and the thunder boomed all around them. It was the perfect time to leave the city if you didn't want to be seen or followed; nobody in their right mind went outside in this kind of storm.

The group wrapped their cloaks tightly about their bodies in a futile attempt to keep themselves dry and ran for the stable within the barracks grounds. As promised, all their gear was packed and ready to go, set in neatly organized piles for easy distribution.

Lazarus directed Devoll, Mihan, and Marcell to stow their equipment on the packhorses. Corsin and Zafer watched the entrance to make sure nobody noticed them, while Emeris Dallen began bringing out their mounts.

It took them half an hour to complete the whole process, and when they were done, Lazarus went through everything again with Layek to be sure nothing was being left behind. Once he was satisfied they took their steeds by the reins and prepared to head out into the miserable weather. Joseph Corsin took an extra moment to reveal a special surprise for everyone; he had requisitioned specially treated cloaks to help keep them dry in the rain. They accepted their gifts graciously and donned them immediately, throwing them on over the heavy cloaks they already wore.

The thirteen companions mounted their horses and rode silently out of the stable. They stuck close together in the blackness to avoid losing each other as they passed through the wind and the rain like shadows. They made for the western wall of the city, setting an easy pace for the long ride ahead. Lazarus led them through a rarely used and unguarded entrance.

Like wraiths they navigated through the neighborhoods beyond the city walls and out onto the surrounding plains. All eyes looked forward as they plodded steadily onward, watching the terrain in front of them. None of them saw the dark shape skulking through the shadows behind.

IX A NEW DYNASTY

GRUBBASH GRIMVISAGE SAT atop his black horse overlooking the sprawling city of Naril from a wooded bluff. He had called the Overlords — the rulers of the five largest cities and most powerful Orcs in the lands — to a meeting, and surprisingly they had granted his request. His patience had all but run out, and he was in no mood to ride back and forth across the kingdom to individually see those who currently stood between him and his destiny.

Predictably, it had taken them forever to agree to this meeting. They would rather stay in their grand halls, feasting and drinking. *Those days are over*, Grubbash thought with a smile. Today would mark the end of the pathetic excuse for leadership the Overlords represented, and a new era would begin, an age in which Orcs no longer used their strength against their brothers but rather their enemies. Their influence would spread across the lands, and all the races would be made to serve their rightful masters.

He looked around for his escorts, a cadre of the Nightwatch, and found them waiting patiently for him to continue on. They would reach the city well before midday when the meeting was set to occur. He had already arranged for a special appearance by the Daemon Lords, and they would remove the irritating presence of the Overlords from his life once and for all.

He signaled to his underlings that they were moving on, and together they made their way down off the bluff toward the gates of the city. Naril was probably the second largest of the Orc cities, a haphazard collection of rounded mud huts stacked on top of one another. The red-brown color of the buildings was a sharp contrast to the black and gray construction of the large citadel in the center of the city. The castle of Naril was situated on a small hill, and the massive fortress rose high into the sky, a thick tangle of towers and spires, battlements and parapets.

The promise of power had delivered Bogran into his hands, and his loyalty to the cause was why he had chosen this place to conduct the meeting. Bogran's word was final within this forbidding keep, which limited the surprises the Overlords might otherwise attempt to spring upon him.

They kept a moderate pace, slowly but surely closing the distance between them and the slums that ringed the outer edge of the city. A few of the Orcs they passed in the streets recognized the High Summoner and quickly turned away. Most feared his power rather than respected it.

They traversed the dirty and polluted streets of the city unimpeded and made their way to the front gate. Bogran was there to greet them, and he offered to have his servants take their horses and escort them into the hold where refreshments awaited until the summit convened. Grubbash accepted his offer and gave his horse over to the stable hand. Without waiting for the rest of his group he marched into the keep. They walked through it to a small waiting room near the main audience chamber. Inside the sparsely decorated room the two conspirators sat in high-backed wooden chairs and drank cold ale with a helping of fresh meat while they discussed their plans.

"Are they here?" Bogran asked of Grubbash at one point, referring to the Daemon Lords. There was a hint of fear in his eyes as he spoke, a bit of reluctance at having to accommodate demons in his keep.

"Do not fret, Bogran. They are nearby, awaiting my call. When the moment arrives, they will be on hand to do what is required of them."

For several hours they conversed, talking over strategy and the order of events once the Overlords were removed. Bogran was well prepared to take up his position as commanding officer and had already made preparations to mobilize and organize the army, but it would be Grubbash's duty to win the support of the leaders who would replace those currently in power. Once their armies were assembled and ready Bogran would lead them into battle.

At long last came the summons. They were ready to receive him. Bogran took his leave to take up his seat at the council while Grubbash finished his ale. When he swallowed the last of the soothing liquid, he rose from his chair and, gathering his loose robes around him, followed the aide who had remained behind to guide him. His excitement was almost palpable as he was led to the meeting hall.

Grubbash waited outside the giant double doors to be admitted for what seemed like forever, but at last a pair of guards appeared and motioned for him to enter. Grubbash followed them into the large chamber.

The meeting hall was a huge domed room, the roof far above them, supported by thick rough timbers taken from the surrounding woodlands. The chamber had a decidedly cold feel to it, constructed of the same black and gray stone as the exterior of the castle. Rich and extravagant tapestries and murals decorated the walls except where large round windows broke through to the open air outside. Torches hung in iron brackets along the walls, and sconces were scattered about the room, providing ample light for the grand hall.

The Overlords sat in the center of the circular room on lavish seats behind a series of wooden plank tables set end to end in a wide arc, the standards of their house and dominion set into the stone floor directly behind them. Each was allowed one aide and one personal guard; visitors were allowed none.

Bogran was situated in the center of the arc, flanked on both sides by the Overlords of the cities of the Orc Empire. On his left sat Gurdir of Agrothar and Drogan of Demal. Nerghal of Zindan and Keogh of Draxx took up the right side. All stared unwaveringly as Grubbash crossed the expanse between them to stand in the center of the arc formed by their tables.

Excepting Bogran, all four of the Orcs shared similar features.

They were all of average height and build, although most of them were beginning to bulge noticeably in their middle sections. Gurdir was the only one among them who had any hair worth mentioning; it was braided into a tight knot that hung down his back like a thick length of rope.

They have grown lazy and decadent, Grubbash thought, *unfit to rule their people.*

The only thing they cared about now was how much food and ale would be at the next feast.

"Welcome, High Summoner," Gurdir greeted him in a booming voice. His salutation was hollow, and Grubbash could see from the look in his eyes that he was not happy to see the sorcerer again. "What would you seek of us?"

Grubbash decided to throw propriety to the wolves and get right to the point. "You know all too well why I come before you, Lord."

"You will show proper respect while in our presence!" Drogan shouted at him. "We do not have time for your insolence!"

Grubbash stared at the Orc without moving. If his gaze had been a dagger, Drogan would have been dead. "You will listen to what I have to say because this is your last opportunity. I will not waste my efforts trying to persuade you of the error of your ways again." His tone was acidic and volatile as he spoke. "This is your last warning."

"I see no reason why we should bow to your will, Summoner," Drogan shot at him. "You would have Orcs spread to the far edges of the lands, killing anything they come across without a care for the integrity of our people."

"We have held this discussion before," Gurdir interjected. "Our decisions are not open for debate. We will not start war with our neighbors simply because you believe we should, especially when our people are so divided."

"Hypocrites!" Grubbash barked, pointing an accusing finger at them. "You can stand here together and pass judgment on me, yet you cannot prevent our brothers from slaughtering each other in the streets. The truth is, our people are divided because you do nothing to prevent it!"

"Silence, maggot!" Gurdir bellowed, knocking his chair over as he jumped up. "We will not tolerate your insubordination any longer. You have strayed far, Grubbash. Your mind has become twisted beyond recovery. You are a danger to the stability of our lands and would seek to undermine our authority through your meddling. Guards! Seize him!"

Grubbash was now livid with rage. The doors to the great halls burst open, and four Orcs came rushing into the room to take him prisoner. Grubbash realized that they had planned this all along. He had suspected that the Overlords would try to eliminate him once they heard what he had to say, but now he knew that they had agreed to this meeting in the first place, knowing what he would bring before them. They had used it as an opportunity to eliminate the greatest threat to their continued sovereignty.

Of course, this expected turn of events made it easier for him. They underestimated his power greatly, a mistake they would not live to repeat. As the guards came rushing at him, he raised his hands toward them. Muttering the arcane words he had memorized, he bound them in invisible cords. The guards froze in their tracks, bewildered and frightened to discover that they could no longer move.

Grubbash turned to the Overlords, who were staring at him in amazement. He walked toward them menacingly, hands raised and pointed at them like weapons. Their bodyguards sprang forward to defend their masters. Grubbash threw out bolts of lightning from his hands, which forked in midair to strike the five warriors confronting him. Their lifeless bodies were thrown backward with the force of Grubbash's spell, crashing them into the rear wall before coming to rest on the cold stone floor. The Overlords jumped up from their chairs and turned to flee, except for Bogran, of course, but it was too late for them. Grubbash paralyzed them in their tracks.

"Fools! To think that you were greater than me! You should have listened when you had the chance. You'd rather sit in your halls, fattening yourselves up like cattle while our people kill themselves in meaningless feuds and power struggles, than embrace your true nature. We are a warrior people, the strongest of the races on this earth. This world is ours by right, ripe for the taking."

As Grubbash spoke a great crow came flying in through one of the open windows to settle on the tables. Through the open door behind Grubbash, a lone black wolf and a huge serpent inched their way forward to join the crow. The Overlords could tell there was something unusual about these beasts, and fear sprang into their eyes. They struggled against the invisible bonds that held them but could not break free.

"I would like you to meet Satariel, The Deceiver; Adimiron, The Bloody One; and Athiel, the Lord of Uncertainty." Grubbash's tone was ice. "Your hands have held the Orcs back long enough, and they are here to see to it that you will never do so again."

As he spoke the animals began to dissolve into a thick mist that rose up into the rafters. When the mist cleared, the Orcs found to their horror that they were faced with three terrifying giants. They began to plead with Grubbash for mercy.

The three were nearly identical in appearance, standing well past the height of two Orcs in a vaguely humanoid form with blood-red skin. All three were characterized by their sharp fangs, wicked looking claws that extended from their hands and feet, and eyes that burned with unnatural flame. Adimiron had long spikes that protruded from his joints and spine. Athiel seemed to be shrouded in a darkness that clung only to him, making his features blurry and difficult to discern. Satariel had vicious horns that grew out from his forehead and cheeks, twisted and deformed.

"Enjoy the feast," Grubbash said morbidly and turned to leave the room. "Come, Bogran. We have work to do."

Bogran followed close on his heels as Grubbash exited the room, not wishing to be caught in the unspeakable horrors that were about to take place in that meeting hall. He was glad that he had plenty of servants to clean up the mess. Grubbash picked up the pace, and Bogran requisitioned two of his warriors to shut the doors behind them. Screams echoed throughout the halls of Bogran's castle, the haunting and soul-wrenching noise of some demonic symphony.

"Bogran," Grubbash said, "go to the quarters of their kin and summon them to the alternate meeting hall. I will be waiting for you there. And Bogran, make certain that word gets out of what happened here. Make sure every ear in the Empire hears of the power I command."

"Very well. It will be done." Grubbash's impressive display of power had made Bogran wary, and he realized that there was no turning back now. He must serve the High Summoner and serve him well or face a similar fate. The Orc leaders' frightening screams still resounded in his mind. It would be a long time before he could force them from his memory.

Grubbash stood in the hallway and watched Bogran hurry off to gather the successors of the deposed Overlords. They would not be pleased at all when they discovered what had become of their kin at the hands of the High Summoner. Things were so far proceeding according to his plan; all he needed now was to convince the new leaders to serve him. He suspected that it wouldn't be that difficult; the Orcs who would take over were a young and restless lot. He could appeal to their youthful zeal, greed, and love of violence to win them over.

He did not head straight to the secondary meeting place; instead he turned around and went back to the main hall where the meeting had taken place. He did not really care to return to that room, but the trip was absolutely necessary. When he reached the closed and guarded door that led into the chamber, all was quiet.

Grubbash decided that rather than enter himself and deal with the Daemon Lords and the mess they had undoubtedly created inside, he would order the two guards on duty to go in and retrieve what he required. The two Orcs were not very enthusiastic about their new duty, but they went in anyway, not wishing to cross the Orc who had just ended the centuries-long rule of the Overlords.

Moments later they reappeared through the massive iron-bound door looking pale and fearful. Grubbash knew well the manner in which the Daemon Lords treated their prey and paid it no mind. The Overlords had sealed their fate when they had denied the inevitable change their society was about to undergo.

The two heavily built Orcs produced a wool bag containing the items he had requested they recover. Grubbash took it from them and looked inside, making sure everything he had requested was present. When he was satisfied with its contents, he dismissed the guards and turned away.

He walked briskly through the domed hallways of Bogran's keep, paying no attention to the plethora of gilded decorations that were displayed everywhere. He proceeded unhindered to a secondary and somewhat smaller chamber on the same floor. Grubbash took a moment to steady himself before reaching out and taking the iron handle and pulling the door open.

It was a secluded place, entered through a single door of inconspicuous construction. Inside was a plain, undecorated room of stone walls and floors with a dozen wooden chairs scattered about. A small table sat in the middle of the room, adorned only by a large clay pitcher and a handful of mugs.

Grubbash closed the door behind him and looked around the room at the Orcs who had ceased their hushed conversations to suspiciously eye their new visitor. Bogran sat in one corner alone, keeping separate from the rest of them. Scattered around the room were the next of kin to the now dead Overlords, eighteen in total. Several members of each ruling house from each city were present — brothers, sons, and cousins of the Orcs he had given over to the Daemon Lords less than an hour ago. There was anger in those faces, and Grubbash knew vengeance lurked just behind it. It would take some effort to convince those gathered to join his cause, but then, of course, he could always just kill them if they didn't conform.

"Good afternoon," Grubbash greeted them. "I trust you know why you have been brought here."

Gurgor, son of Gurdir, stood from his chair and looked around the room. Fury smoldered in his eyes as he addressed those present. "You are a fool, sorcerer. You cannot sweep away a thousand years of tradition to further your own causes and get away with it."

"You refer to the Overlords," Grubbash stated simply.

"This mage has killed our leaders and kin. I say we repay him in kind."

Gurgor reached to his side where a long dagger rested in his sash.

Grubbash raised a hand in warning, and the Orc halted. "You are the fool, Gurgor, son of Gurdir, if you believe that the rulers of old served any great purpose to our people. You are the next in line to take their place, which is why you have been brought before me." Grubbash paused for a moment, looking at each of the Orcs in turn, measuring their character with his stony gaze. Most in that room found it impossible to meet his stare for more than a moment.

"I have eliminated a system of government that has ruled our people for a millennia, yes. Ask yourselves this: What good have they ever done for the Orcs? And where have they led us?" Grubbash raised one eyebrow inquisitively. "Where, other than into decadence and degradation? I think you will find the answer quite easily."

None in the room knew how to answer. It had never crossed their minds, never occurred to them, that there could be another way. The Orcs hadn't been a single, cohesive people for a thousand years or more. Grubbash gave them several moments to think about it before continuing.

"In a thousand years, how many wars have we fought? None. In a thousand years how many cities have we sacked? None. How many of our foes lie dead or dying on the battlefield after opposing an Orc army? None.

"The point is, they have never done anything to further Orc supremacy in this world. They have never led us outside our lands to war. Ours is the strongest of all civilizations. The Overlords and their ilk have done nothing to lead the Orcs to their rightful destiny as rulers of this world. Never have they brought glory and honor to our warriors on the battlefield.

"For centuries we have remained in our lands, neglecting what is rightfully ours. I pleaded for years to unite our brothers and stop the senseless infighting. They did nothing. I say no more. No more will our warriors settle for the blood of their brothers on the battlefield. No more will I stand by and watch our people destroy themselves. If the rulers of our people cannot uphold the rudimentary beliefs of Orc society, then I will!"

"This is outrageous!" Gurgor cried. "You would plunge us into war while we are still divided. You would destroy our people."

"That is why I need your help," Grubbash replied. "I cannot unite our people alone. You are the heirs of your respective forebears. Only you can stop the bloodshed and mindless feuds amongst our people."

Krud, the first cousin to Drogan, rose to speak. He was well respected among those present for his cooler reasoning and slow temper. "Why should we believe you, Summoner?" he asked. "What is to stop you from murdering us as you did the Overlords?"

"Serve your people as they should have, and you are safe from my wrath," Grubbash told him quietly. "If you would rather lazily sit in your halls collecting the tribute from your lands, waiting for the next great feast and plotting how to usurp your brother's power, then you should fear me. If you would rather lead your people to glory and increase your wealth with the spoils of war, then I consider you my ally."

Grubbash stepped toward the center of the room, lifting up the wool bag he still held in his hands for all to see. "Within this sack is contained the symbols of your predecessors' authority. I will return them to you in return for your oath of fealty to me. A new dynasty has risen in our empire. I will lead our people to the destiny they were promised in ages past. With me as your chosen leader we cannot and will not fail."

"We still have no reason to believe you can fulfill these promises you give us, Summoner," Gurgor stated icily.

"Aside from the considerable power that I already command," Grubbash said, raising his empty hand into the air, his eyes narrowing into thin slits as blue fire sprang forth, soundless and cold, "I have brought forth four Daemon Lords from the abyss to aid us in our cause."

"Demons!" Nergal uttered in dismay. "You *are* mad!"

"Then I encourage you to embrace my madness," Grubbash snapped. "Already we have begun to set in motion events beyond your vision. The demons are under my control and will serve us well.

Already I have made use of them to weaken our enemies. The time has come for you to accept what you have known all your life."

Grubbash could see the looks displayed on their faces changing from doubt and anger to wonderment. Mirrored in each set of eyes was the realization of an opportunity like none had believed possible. He could practically smell the greed. Most in this room were prepared to accept him as their new sovereign. Some, he speculated, were quite eager to take up this new cause.

"What would you ask of us if we accept your proposal?" Krud asked calmly.

"With you or without you," Grubbash said, making it clear that their options were very limited, "all hostilities between Orcs will cease immediately. I will no longer allow my brethren to slaughter each other. Each city will raise an army; every Orc fit for battle will march to my citadel at Grimknoll. There we will assemble the greatest army ever seen in this world. Through strength of arms we will claim what is ours by birthright.

"For your service, I will allow each to take his fill of the spoils of war." Grubbash emptied the contents of the bag he was holding, spilling the pendants each of the Overlords had worn as his symbol of leadership onto the small table before him. "The choice is yours. Choose wisely."

For many long minutes no one moved or spoke. Grubbash stood and waited patiently for them to deliberate. A few of the Orcs began to whisper in low tones amongst their comrades, debating whether or not to oppose the one who had usurped the power of the Overlords and forced them into a position they could not escape. They knew their only options were acceptance or death. Bogran, who had kept silent through-out the whole discussion, now rose and walked over to where Grubbash stood.

"I am the last surviving Overlord," Bogran announced loud enough for everyone present to hear him. Heads turned to regard him critically, and voices hushed. "I still breathe only because I accept the High Summoner's vision of the future. I saw firsthand the lack of vision and dedication to our people. When he came before us and laid down the gauntlet, I accepted his leadership. I believe he is the one to lead us to our destiny, and I will take my oath on it."

Bogran kneeled before Grubbash, placing both hands on one knee. "I, Bogran, son of Durgran, hereby recognize the High Summoner as my lord and master. By my blood," he said as he removed a small dagger from its sheath at his waist, "I swear to serve him until my dying breath. Long live the emperor!" He closed his fist around the blade of the dagger and quickly withdrew it. He clenched his fist, as he remained knelt before Grubbash, letting the blood drip from his wounded hand onto the floor.

"Rise," Grubbash commanded him in a regal manner. Bogran lifted himself off the floor, walking around Grubbash to stand behind him. "Your loyalty shall be rewarded greatly."

One by one the rest came forward to swear allegiance to the new emperor. As they did so, Grubbash bestowed upon them the sigil of their predecessor, signifying his acceptance of their oath of loyalty. Gurgor was the last to come forward, and he did so reluctantly, but there was no other choice. He did not share his father's views and did not wish to join him in death. So he swore his fealty to the High Summoner.

"You have all chosen wisely," Grubbash commended them. "Together we will elevate our people to their rightful status as rulers of these lands. Our enemies will be crushed by our might. That which has stood in our way will no longer bar us from our destiny." The new Overlords bowed before him.

The faintest smirk tugged at the corners of Bogran's mouth. "What is your command, My Lord?"

"As I have said," Grubbash stated empirically, "hostilities between all factions will cease immediately. You will exercise control over your warriors. Return to your cities and rally your soldiers to your banner. Before the new moon, advance your armies to Grimknoll where we will begin the long march to glory."

The Orcs bowed in compliance before departing the room. Within the hour each had left the castle with their entourage, bound for their keeps to uphold the word they had given to their new master. Many among them had been unsure of their standing during their meeting, but now they understood the magnitude of the situation. They understood that the future was upon them and that they could embrace it and make it their own or be swept away as remnants of the old ways. Many found that finally, after so many years, they would be doing what they had felt should have been done all along.

Rumors spread like wildfire throughout the city, and by sunset the whole area was in an uproar. Excitement was in the air as Orc society came alive for what seemed like the first time in a thousand years. Hammers rang as they struck anvils, echoing throughout the metropolis, and everywhere there was commotion.

Grubbash watched the action from a tower high on the walls of Bogran's keep, a grin of satisfaction stretched across his face. Everything had gone exceedingly well. The Overlords were no more, and their replacements had fallen in line nicely. Gurgor he would have to keep an eye on, but that was easily handled. Later on the Orc would attempt to seek revenge for his father; Grubbash could see it in his eyes, but for now he would serve as he had sworn to. The Orcs had been given purpose and meaning in their lives beyond their expectations. They belonged at war; battle was the rudimentary building block of their lives. Now that primordial instinct had been given direction.

For several hours Grubbash stood atop the castle, reveling in the sounds of his people making ready for war. Within days this scene would be mirrored in the other great cities in the kingdom. By the new moon the Orc armies would be assembled and ready for battle. Then the invasions would begin, and Grubbash would start down the path that would make this world his.

Grubbash watched for some time before turning away from the view. He went back into the castle to the sleeping chambers provided for him to get some rest. He would leave in the morning for his own keep to oversee matters there; some details required his direct attention. He lay in bed for a time before falling asleep, recapping in his mind the steps that had been taken and those that were yet to come. His plan was moving forward exactly as he had designed. Very soon his vision would be realized.

The world would tremble at the mention of his name.

X FEAR AND DOUBT

CAILYN EMORY ROSE sluggishly from her down-filled bed. Her sleep had been light and tumultuous, haunted by the dark phantoms of her subconscious mind. In her dreams she was relentlessly hunted by horrors too terrible to mention. They hunted her upon waking as well, the shadows and wraiths of her fears springing forth from her dreams to find purchase in her peripheral vision and the dark spots within her bedchamber, causing her to cast about suspiciously. Ever since the demons had penetrated the city and murdered half of the High Council she had been on edge. She could not shake the feeling that her days were numbered.

They had tried to kill her as well on that same fateful night, and if not for the bravery of the visiting Elves, she might be dead right now. Lazarus and his brothers had left the city sometime after the attack; she didn't know when. It was probably best; those who did not know could not be made to tell. Surely by now the demons were aware of their plot to recover the Krullstone and would do everything in their power to stop the three brothers.

She lowered her feet onto the cold tile of her bedchamber and slid them into her fur slippers. It was already past sunrise, but very little light filtered through the frosted panes of the windows. The rain continued to fall outside in a gray haze, adding to the Queen's reluctance to get out of bed.

Today she would meet with the dignitaries of the races who had answered her call and try to convince them that the threat the Orcs and their dark allies posed was real.

The Dwarves had finally arrived yesterday, as had the Gnomes. As soon as they had settled in, Cailyn had arranged for them to convene at noon. She hoped that they would maintain an open mind. They could only collectively survive this crisis if they banded together.

She dressed mechanically as she rehearsed the arguments she would put forward. She did not want to mislead or leave out anything. She must eloquently and respectfully address the ambassadors of the races if she expected to gain their support.

Cailyn made her way down to the dining room for a little breakfast, and as she ate her meal she continued to drill herself about the upcoming meeting. Ukiah came in through a side door and proceeded to sit next to her. He remained at her side in silence until she had finished. When she finally pushed her chair away from the table, he asked softly, "Are you ready for this?"

"As ready as I ever will be," she replied with a half-hearted smile. "There's only so much I can say. Hopefully it will make some difference."

"Everything happens for a reason. Either they will choose to help us, or they won't. In any event, things will work out as they are meant to."

"I only hope that they aren't meant to work out the way Melynda sees them."

"Lazarus will not fail," Ukiah assured her.

They stood, and Ukiah hugged his wife close, kissing her forehead lightly. For many long minutes they embraced, standing in the deserted dining hall. He whispered reassurances to Cailyn as he held her, promising her that those they had chosen as their champions would not fall short and that some help at least could be gained from the other races.

After awhile they let each other go, refreshed and ready to take on the tasks set before them. The meeting was still several hours away, but there were other things to attend to until then. Since the murders she now had to take up the slack, filling in for the unwittingly absent Council members.

Cailyn sent Ukiah to track down General Markoll to check on his progress in secretly mobilizing the army and developing a defense strategy while she saw to the affairs of the kingdom. It gave her something to do. It kept her mind off the reality of the situation, which threatened to pull her down into a bottomless well of hopelessness.

Her footfalls echoed off the arched halls as she walked to the throne room where the officials from the High Council would be waiting for her to attend to the needs of their country. Servants and maids bowed to her as she passed, but she did not acknowledge them or slow her pace. Crimson Guard were scattered about in twos and threes, eyes darting warily from one place to the next, never lingering for more than a moment. A pair of them opened the carved double doors that led into the audience chamber as she approached.

The throne room was a rectangular hall with high vaulted ceilings and imperial marble columns. Marble tiles stretched across the whole of the floor, divided down the center of the room by a strip of lush red carpeting that led to an elevated dais. Upon the dais rested the throne of Illendale. Hand carved of ash wood, its intricate patterns were accentuated by gilding of silver and gold and bedecked with a dazzling array of colorful gems.

A handful of representatives from the High Council were already gathered nearby. They stood in a small circle, whispering to each other in hushed voices. When they saw her approach, they turned as one to greet her, smiling disarmingly. She did not care much for dealing with the aides and clerks of the High Council; it seemed to her that their predilection for courtly gossip far outweighed their usefulness. Cailyn greeted them kindly as she seated herself on the throne. The entourage gathered around her, each taking their turn at presenting reports, documents to be signed, and affairs that needed authorization. She listened disinterestedly, her mind wandering once again to the particulars of what was to come. Her eyes wandered as well, shifting from one face to the next across the darker spaces of the hall, wondering from where the next attack would come.

And it would come, Cailyn knew. The question was when and where? Would today be the day? Was she already drawing the last breath she would take in this life? Who among them was not what they seemed? Which was the wolf amidst the sheep? With growing suspicion she tried to match the faces she saw with memories from a time when she had been safe and secure within her own home.

"... reports that the grain houses are well stocked and secured. Contamination is at a minimum, although warehouses in the south district ..."

"Ladies and gentlemen, we will finish this later. No arguments." She raised her hand to halt the protests forming on their lips.

The clerks gathered up their papers and strode purposefully away. Cailyn watched them go, satisfied to be free of their nagging presence. When the giant doors closed behind them, she turned her attention to the servants industriously going about setting the hall for the meeting.

She drifted, quite accidentally, into a peaceful trance. Sitting there on the throne, watching the workers buzz about like determined bees, she floated to memories of less troubling times when she was not haunted by the threat of destruction or the helplessness she felt now. Times when her strength of character and will had been enough to sustain her people.

Slowly the settings began to take shape. Tables set with colorful flowers and flanked by cushioned, high-backed chairs formed a rough circle in the center of the hall. A row of tables sat off to one side, overflowing with cakes, muffins, and other assorted refreshments. All appeared to be in readiness; only the attendees of this makeshift conference were missing.

Seeing the arrangements nearly completed reminded her of her duty, and she snapped suddenly back to reality, bringing her head upright with a quick jerk. The delegations from the other nations would be arriving soon. She stood up, feeling slightly calmer. She crossed the room, stopping one of the passing servants to inquire about the hour.

"It's nearly midday, Your Highness," the plump woman replied with a cheerful smile, nodding her head slightly before hurrying on.

Cailyn let the woman pass and walked toward the entrance, and a pair of guards opened the doors for her. Splashes of red-garbed guards were everywhere in the main hallway beyond, wicked looking halberds and pikes glinting reassuringly amidst the bustle of traffic. Ukiah appeared out of an adjoining hallway and walked briskly over to where the Queen stood.

"Everything is prepared." His eyes never met hers; they were constantly scanning the area for threats. He had not been at ease since the attacks.

"Did you find Markoll?" she asked, reaching down to clasp his hand.

"I did." He turned to face her. "The Phoenix Legion is ready to march; they will depart in the morning for the Myrrh. The rest of the legions will take some time to gather and equip; it may be weeks before they are ready. More if the reserves are to be called up."

"We may not have weeks. I find it hard to believe that we could be so unprepared."

Ukiah had nothing to say to this. He knew as well as she did the suddenness with which the threat to their lands had surfaced. Until now, there had been little need for the army. The seven legions worked on rotating tours of duty, four on leave while the other three were scattered about the country. It took time to gather them all again.

Preferring not to dwell on matters she could not help, Cailyn switched to more immediate business. "Have our guests been summoned?"

"Of course. They should be arriving any moment now," he said as he scanned the room to see if any of the expected emissaries had appeared. "General Markoll should be on his way as well."

"Good. He's better at explaining military matters anyway."

They stood in silence for several long minutes. Cailyn suddenly began to feel dangerously exposed. Her heartbeat quickened, and she clenched her fingers around Ukiah's arm as a knot of fear settled into her stomach.

Then the sound came.

It started gently, a barely noticeable rush of wind that built upon itself until it filled the ears of everyone in the hall, causing them to pause in fear and search frantically for the source. It grew and climaxed, a leathery chorus of wings that beat down upon those constrained to the ground. Cailyn's grip on Ukiah's arm grew tighter, her teeth clenched in anticipation of the horror she was expecting. Ukiah rested his hand on the pommel of the sword at his waist, his muscles coiling like a spring, waiting.

The bloodcurdling howl that followed sent ice rushing through her veins as it echoed off the walls of the great hall. Screams and shouts of warning rose up to challenge it as eyes turned skyward. Cailyn's breath caught in her throat as the attackers revealed themselves from high in the buttresses. How these creatures had slipped past the guards was a thought almost as frightening as their actual presence.

"Howlers!" Ukiah shouted as he yanked free his sword, standing protectively in front of his wife. "Guards, to arms! Fight for your lives!"

Dozens of the demons appeared and, as their wails reached a crescendo, began swooping down upon the hapless crowds. Instantly Ukiah was moving, backing away as he pushed Cailyn toward the exit, never taking his eyes from the battle. The Crimson Guard sprang into action, rushing from their posts to meet the demons as they descended on the helpless citizens.

Cailyn got her first good glimpse of the monsters as one dropped not more than a dozen paces in front of her, shrieking in glee as it tore into one of the guardsmen rushing out to join the fight. Its quill-covered body bristled as it swooped in for the kill, its talons raking the man's armor as its wolf's head split wide to reveal row upon row of jagged fangs. The guard screamed as the great bat-like wings enfolded him as he tried in vain to bring his halberd to bear on the cat-quick demon.

More and more of the demons plummeted from the rafters, appearing faster than the guards could react and rapidly overwhelming them. Alarms rose dully throughout the castle as the demons moved to seal the exits.

Too slow, Cailyn thought as the screams of the dying echoed off the cavernous walls and filled her ears.

Ukiah sprang into action. Two of the demons dropped in front of him as he moved to aid the guards, and no sooner had they touched the tile floor than he had sliced through them like a hot knife through butter.

"Guards, to me!" he shouted, holding his sword up high. "Form up on me!"

The doors began to slam shut. The demons were closing them in, and the Queen's men became outnumbered. So many dead littered the floor, Cailyn had to turn her eyes away or risk purging her roiling stomach. Muffled shouts reached out to them as reinforcements tried to break their way in.

Only a dozen men answered Ukiah's call, far fewer than should have been present. The screams of the civilians were dying out, as those who had not been able to flee to safety fell to their ferocious attackers.

"Protect the Queen," Ukiah ordered those who had gathered around him. "Whatever happens, she is not to be taken."

The men formed a protective wedge around Cailyn as their enemies, who were dozens strong, began to advance on them. They backed into an alcove where they would have a superior defensive position. There was no doubt about the ultimate outcome if help did not arrive soon.

The demons came slowly at first, whining and howling in anticipation, circling the beleaguered humans. Had it not been for the scrape of claws on the walls above, the Queen's protectors would have realized the ruse too late. The guards at the rear called out to their comrades as more of the monsters fell from the ceiling, and at their moment of distraction the Howlers advancing on the ground rushed them head on.

Ukiah stepped forward to meet the rush as the men behind him fell back to defend the Queen. He could hear that things were not going well for them. He risked a quick glance back. Cailyn was huddled in a corner; three of the guards were down, as were several demons, but the others seemed to be holding their ground well enough.

The howl of his attackers was the only thing that saved his life. His head snapped back and his sword came up just in time to sever the outstretched arms of the lead Howler. They had closed the distance too quickly. As his stroke felled the first, those that followed rapidly over-whelmed him. Ukiah roared as claws and quills tore into his flesh, and a red haze of pain washed over him. He heard the men behind him cry out, and he dropped to one knee under the weight of the demons pressing down on him.

From behind him he heard Cailyn scream. He tried to turn his head but could not see through the swarm surrounding him. His anger flared, fueled by the fear that he would not be able to protect his wife as he had sworn to do. He reached for that calm place within, where pain and fatigue held no sway and where only steely determination remained.

Bellowing in rage Ukiah thrust upward, scattering the beasts that clung to him. He slashed again and again, and the demons fell away, abandoning their dead and dying in the face of his fury. He turned his attention to those behind him.

The guards were all dead, save one who fought desperately to fend off the dozen or so demons that besieged him. His skin was pale with fear and blood loss, but he knew he was the only thing that stood between the demons and his Queen.

Methodically, eyes afire with rage, Ukiah charged into the Howlers. A great sweep of his sword sent three of the monsters to the floor, their internal organs spilling out from their shredded midsections. He hacked and slashed like a madman as the others turned to meet this new rush. Limbs and gore splattered across the battlefield as Ukiah slaughtered his enemies.

He reached his pale-faced and shivering wife. Her eyes met his, and the terror he saw there only fueled his wrath. He placed a steady-ing hand on her shoulder. It never occurred to him that the fear he saw in her eyes was for his life, not her own.

Turning to face the demons he instinctively knew were encircling him, he gently pushed Cailyn deeper into the corner. There was a ringing in his ears that drowned out his ragged breath, the heavy pounding on the main entrance as the Crimson Guard sought desper-ately to rescue them, the menacing hisses of his foes. His mind was crystal clear, the inevitability of his victory already determined. The trifling details of how that would be established were as meaningless as the lives he meant to extinguish.

The Howlers surrounded them as they formed a wide crescent and slowly began to inch their way forward, wary now of the one they faced. Ukiah stepped out to meet them, taking the form of The Crane and motioning his enemies forward.

The Howlers charged, screeching ferociously.

Without missing a beat, Ukiah steadied himself to meet them. Seeing him as the last threat to the accomplishment of their mission, the demons quickly encircled him, intent on silencing his defiant war cry.

As if in slow motion, Ukiah watched them come. When the first was within range, he issued a quick sideward slash, and it fell to the floor, skidding across the blood-slicked tile. As the circle grew tighter Ukiah moved like quicksilver. A series of sweeping cross slashes dropped three more of his attackers. The last stroke carried him into a right spin, and as he turned he brought his sword in a downward arc, splitting the skull of the Howler directly behind him.

The blade lodged itself there, and as the lifeless body toppled forward, Ukiah tucked into a forward roll. The two Howlers rushing in from the sides collided, claws ripping into each other. He carried the roll for a few more yards, scooping up the halberd of a fallen guard as he did so. Then he spun on his knees, propping up the polearm just in time to impale the demon following on his heels. Fluidly, he scooped up a sword from the floor and thrust it into the gut of a slathering Howler on his right. Reaching down to his belt, he slid his long knife from its sheath and jammed it into the eye of the demon attacking on his left. He withdrew the sword from the gurgling monster as it died and swept it upward, splitting the next Howler from stem to sternum.

The force of the stroke lifted him to his feet, and he spun as he leapt backward. The momentum carried him into the waiting arms of two more Howlers, and the ferocious whip of his sword cut them clean in half. The scrape of claws on stone betrayed the position of the demon closing behind him, and Ukiah fell flat onto his back, thrusting his sword up through the chin of the beast as it fell atop him. With both legs he heaved the lifeless body and sent it crashing into an approaching trio.

Ukiah rolled to the side, narrowly avoiding the talons of

another demon as it dropped to where he had been lying. He thrust his sword into its side and left it there. Flipping back onto his feet, he scooped up an ownerless pike. Swinging it in a wide arc, he forced back the Howlers gathering around him. The slowest caught the blade across the neck, showering Ukiah in blood.

Using the pole as a support, he vaulted, drop kicking one in the chest with such force he heard its bones crack. Thrusting behind him, he impaled another, withdrawing his weapon just in time to hook the leg of another Howler as it charged. Ukiah brought the blade up in a sweeping arc and jammed it into the fallen demon's chest so hard he felt it strike stone and entrench itself there. A swift roundhouse kick knocked the next challenger to its back. He grabbed the wrist of an outstretched arm and pulled the owner close, striking its head against the shaft of the jammed pike hard enough to crack its skull. The Howler grappled with him, and striking with lightning force, Ukiah ripped its throat clean out with his bare hand.

Ukiah retracted his arm riddled with quills as the demon fell away. He ignored the pain. His eyes scanned the battlefield for his wife and found her just as she skewered an attacking Howler with a wicked-looking poleax. The momentary distraction cost him, and as he turned back to the battle at hand, a body slammed into him from behind.

The force of the blow knocked the wind out of him and sent him sprawling to the floor. Pain wracked his body as his attacker's quills dug in. Desperately he struck at the creature's head with his elbows, trying to dislodge it while he fought to regain his breath. The effort proved futile, and Ukiah heard the howls of glee as the others closed in to finish him off. Spots danced before his eyes. He could feel the black well of unconsciousness tugging at the corners of his vision.

Then suddenly the weight was ripped off of him. The howls of victory became cries of fear and anger. Ukiah could hear the ringing of swords and the clank of metal armor as booted feet rushed into the hall. He found the strength to look up to see that the men of the Crimson Guard had finally arrived to rescue them.

General Markoll's voice was unmistakable in his ear, strong and confident. "Rest easy, My Lord. We'll take care of the last of them. It's a good thing we arrived when we did; otherwise there might not have been any left for us."

℘   ℘   ℘

Hours later, wounds cleaned and dressed and new clothes donned, Cailyn sat between her husband and General Markoll, waiting for the arrival of those races who would heed her invitation to meet. The servers provided them with refreshments, though they sat largely untouched on the table before them. Cailyn glanced at her husband, bandaged and wrapped in almost every conceivable place. His wounds had been extensive, and she shuddered to think what would have been the outcome if Markoll had not arrived when he did. Ukiah was truly an impressive man, radiating an aura of confidence and strength. Despite the grievous wounds he had sustained, her husband had refused to leave her side. Cailyn silently prayed that the weight of his conviction alone would sway their guests.

The Elves were the first to enter the hall. Cailyn rose to greet them as the three strode regally across the room. Seyhan Alluris, eldest daughter of the king, led them, her chestnut hair flowing behind her as she walked. Two others followed a step behind. Cailyn greeted them formally, smiling warmly as she bid them take their seats.

The Dwarven delegation came plodding in on the heels of the Elves; the sound of their heavy boots made it seem like a whole platoon was marching in. There were five, Kagan Ochak and Vani Carchim at their head. Cailyn had never met them, and they seemed like a rough pair; the group as a whole looked unkempt and haggard. They marched directly to her and, defying her perceptions, introduced themselves cordially. Cailyn showed them to their places, turning just in time to see the last of the meeting's attendees enter.

Through the great double doors came a handful of tiny Gnomes, the tops of their heads barely reaching Cailyn's waist. They were garlanded with generous amounts of gold, silver, and gemmed jewelry. Wealth was a Gnome's first concern; everything else was secondary. They greeted the Queen respectfully, bowing deeply, and Cailyn returned the gesture.

Once all were seated, Cailyn instructed her personnel to leave them in privacy. She ordered the guards to wait outside until the meeting was finished and gave them strict orders they were not to be disturbed.

When everyone was out and the great double doors were secured, Cailyn stood to address those assembled. She quickly scanned the rafters to calm her frayed nerves, taking a deep, steadying breath as she did so. Nothing there.

"Thank you all for coming," she said as she tapped a fork against a crystal glass. "I apologize for the arrangements. Unfortunately, our customary meeting hall has been compromised by recent events."

Most of those gathered nodded in understanding. The news of earlier events had spread like wildfire through the palace and the city beyond. The Elves might as well have been carved in stone they were so stationary.

Cailyn took several minutes to introduce everyone present, making sure to include all the proper titles and observe formal protocol. The last thing she needed right now was to insult these people. *Better to butter them up before putting them over the fire,* she thought sardonically.

"Ladies and gentlemen," Cailyn said, taking them all in with her steady gaze. "You have been called here because a rising menace threatens us all. Evil gathers and endangers our right to be free people. Shadows spread across the land and threaten to shroud us forever in darkness."

She paused for a moment, measuring the effect of her words. "The Orcs in the Durgen Range are mobilizing. They have summoned powerful demons from the abyss and allied themselves with an unspeakable evil. Unless we unite under one banner we cannot hope to survive."

Jamin T'rul, head of the Gnome delegation, spoke. A long crooked nose pierced through the center with a gold ring dominated his sharply-pointed features. The orange cast of his skin gave him a decidedly mischievous look. "We have heard no such news, Your Highness. If what you say were true, word would fly like seeds in a strong gust of wind."

"Nevertheless, it is true." Cailyn locked her gaze on the Gnome. "Little more than a week ago my advisor Melynda had a vision."

Whispers erupted from those seated before her as she spoke. "This vision prophecies a massive invasion of our lands by the Orc hordes, aided by demon allies and led by the evil sorcerer Grubbash Grimvisage. Our kingdom will be among the first to fall as the armies of evil sweep across the lands. If we do not stand together, one by one our people will be enslaved."

"Tell us exactly what the vision entails," Seyhan of the Elves requested. The murmurs ceased when the Elf spoke. "We must know what we are dealing with before making any judgments."

Cailyn began her narration, relating the details of the vision in stark detail. As she explained the plot that threatened them, fear and doubt registered on the faces of those present. She held them transfixed with her words as she told them of the coming of the demons and their masters. She painted within their minds a vivid picture of the destruction and horror that would be visited upon them, one by one, if they failed to heed her warnings.

When she finished, no one spoke for a long time. Silence hung thickly in the air like a monstrous thing, daring any to speak and break its hold on the room.

Finally, the disbelief as evident upon his face as a painted sign, Jamin addressed them. "This is ludicrous. How can you be so certain? Not only do the Orcs lack the unity it would take to launch such a campaign, but if their armies are as vast as you say they are, what makes you believe they will focus solely on Illendale?"

"I have enough experience with visions to respect their validity." Her gaze burned into the Gnome. "However, I believe General Markoll can answer your question better than I. General, if you would please."

"The visions show that Illendale will be among the first to fall," Markoll said as he rose from his chair. "We believe we will be the first for two reasons. For sure, we are the closest and most tangible threat, and if they march against anyone else first, they risk leaving their own lands undefended and being flanked by our army. Only the Myrrh River separates us from them."

Markoll's solemn voice echoed off the cavernous walls of the hall as he continued. "Second, despite the massiveness of their armies, if they divide their forces on multiple fronts, it is much easier for them to be defeated. Better to remain one entity and take us on singly so they can make the most of their advantage in numbers."

The logic behind his theory was undeniable. All but the Gnomes nodded in agreement.

"Is there any proof to support these allegations?" Vani Carchim asked softly.

"Have you ever heard of Lurkers? Perhaps Howlers?" Cailyn searched their faces. "Nor had I until recently. Just three nights past a pair of these loathsome and frightening beasts stole into this palace with the intention of assassinating me. If it had not been for the bravery of the Elves, surely they would have succeeded. The second attempt occurred just before you arrived. The demons failed, but as you can see, they strike at their leisure. Before long they will have the strength and numbers to assault us head on. It is only a matter of time before your own homelands experience this horror firsthand."

Her guests squirmed and looked about uneasily. They were not comfortable knowing that the demons could strike anywhere they chose.

"Princess Seyhan," Kagan said, turning to the Elf, "is this claim true?"

"Indeed," Seyhan replied sadly. "Five of my kinsmen encountered these fiends, including my sister. Only my sister and one other survived."

"That same evening four members of our High Council were murdered. The identity of their killer remains unknown. A fifth Councilman is missing." Cailyn searched the faces of her peers. "Our nation has already fallen under attack. If you do not stand with us against this evil, it will undoubtedly spread to your lands."

"With all due respect, Your Majesty," Jamin cut in, "you say that according to the prophecy of your advisor, we cannot defeat the Orcs so what good will it do for us to band together?"

"Yes," Kagan said, taking over for the Gnome, speculating further. "Even if the Orcs are defeated, how will you defeat their demon allies? Surely the more powerful among them are beyond mortal weapons."

"Excellent observation, master Dwarf," Cailyn replied. "Lurkers and such ilk are little more than nuisances compared to their masters. The power of the Daemon Lords is beyond imagining. We here do not possess the means to destroy them."

"Then you admit it!" cried Jamin. "It is folly to oppose them. Why, then, have you summoned us?"

"Patience, Lord." Seyhan's venomous gaze silenced the Gnome's outburst. "Certainly there is a way to defeat the demons, or we would not be here."

Vani backed her. "The lady is right. Let's hear what the Queen has to say."

"Thank you," Cailyn said. "We cannot defeat the Orcs or the demons with strength of arms alone. The vision has foretold as much. Yet the vision shows the existence of a talisman that can destroy the Daemon Lords. It is called the Krullstone. Our armies can only hope to delay the Orc advance until it can be recovered."

Jamin scoffed in disgust. "And where are we supposed to find this trinket?"

"In the ancient land of Valinar." Cailyn fixed her gaze on him once more. It was obvious he would be the most difficult to persuade. "Already our finest soldiers seek the stone. With any luck they will return before it is too late."

"My sister travels with them." Seyhan rose abruptly from her chair. "She left several days ago, leaving only a short note. She under-stands the magnitude of the threat we face. I am certain she has gone to ensure that the Krullstone is returned safely, and she will not fail."

"This is absurd!" Jamin T'rul blurted, slamming his fist on the table for emphasis. "We are supposed to stand and fight a hopeless battle against an enemy we cannot defeat while some ragtag band of soldiers and a princess charge into a wilderness no one has returned from in a hundred years or more to find a talisman no one has ever heard of? Lunacy!"

"Lord T'rul," Seyhan replied, eyes smoldering as she sought to contain her anger. "You are a fool. Rather than ridiculing the solution presented, why don't you try making yourself useful and offer some suggestions of your own?"

Jamin shook his head, rattling the numerous gold and silver chains that hung about his neck. "Even if the Orcs are mounting an assault, which I seriously doubt, I see no reason to believe it is anything other than a continuation of a feud that has existed between your races for decades."

"Enough!" Ukiah snapped. "This bickering is pointless. We need to work together, or we will all pay the ultimate price."

Jamin T'rul, though still obviously displeased, slouched back into his chair and reached for the mug of ale on the table in front of him. Cailyn paused for a few minutes, allowing everyone time to calm down. She took a sip from her untouched glass of water.

"In the end, each of you must decide for yourself the truth behind what I have told you," Cailyn said finally. "Know this: we must stand together or risk being swept away completely. The assault has already begun; the demons strike wherever they choose, and no one is safe as Lady Seyhan and the Elves can attest. Our only hope lies in the Krullstone. We must delay any offensive until it can be found, or we are all doomed. What say you? Will you help us?"

For a long time the room was bathed in silence. Heavy rain fell outside, accompanied by brief flashes of lightning. Thunder rumbled out of the sky, rattling the glass panes of the windows in their casings. The room felt suddenly cold and gloomy to those gathered as they brooded over the choice presented to them.

They whispered among themselves, though to Cailyn it did not seem like there should have been much to discuss. Ukiah reached over to clasp her hand gently in his, offering her whatever reassurance he could. She waited patiently for them to reach their conclusions; she did not want to rush them. She was confident that she had done what she could to convince them that the threat they faced was real. Surely the Elves understood. Seyhan was a smart woman, and given the fact that the Elves had already experienced the danger firsthand, certainly they would support them.

Perhaps the Dwarves would, too. Elves and Dwarves had been good friends for hundreds of years, and the trust shared between the two might push both of them in her favor. She hoped so. Illendale needed all the help it could get.

As for the Gnomes, she would find no satisfaction there. Jamin T'rul had already made up his mind; they would not support her or Illendale. She watched them as they whispered secretively amongst themselves and tried to discern something of what they were thinking. Not that it really mattered. The Gnomes were not much in the way of warriors. Although they were crafty and highly intelligent, the Gnome kingdoms had not had a standing army since their inception.

Eventually the whispering ceased. Decisions had been reached. Cailyn rose from her seat, releasing Ukiah's hand as she stood. "Have you reached a conclusion?" she asked, trying to conceal the hope in her voice.

Seyhan of the Elves spoke first. "Having met this threat first-hand, we understand what we are facing and how it affects all free people, not just Illendale."

Cailyn held her breath.

"Certainly, Your Highness, you can appreciate the need to defend our own country," Seyhan continued. "However, knowing the danger the Orcs and their demon allies pose, the Elves will not abandon our friends. It is necessary for all of us to stand together in these perilous times. We will answer your call for aid."

Cailyn exhaled slowly. "Thank you, Lady Alluris. We are indebted to you."

"We are in agreement with our wise friends, the Elves," Kagan said with a nod to Seyhan. "As you know we have been at war with the Goblin clans for centuries. While we cannot leave our own country undefended, we will send whatever aid we can spare to help defend against this new threat."

"Thank you, Lords." Cailyn bowed deeply. She turned then to the Gnomes, her voice thick with contempt. "Lord T'rul. Dare I ask where you stand?"

Jamin leaned forward in his chair. He did not stand like the others had, but perhaps it was more because of his stature than his displeasure over the situation. "War is not the province of our people," he began calmly. "In our entire history we have never fought a war or needed to. I do not see a need to change that."

His eyes grew cold as he continued. "You say that Orcs, supported by demon hordes summoned from some netherworld, are marching against you, yet you have no proof. You say that this supposed enemy threatens all our freedom, and yet we have had no encounters with the evil you speak of. What little evidence you have to support your claims is based on nothing more than one person's whimsical gift."

Cailyn thought momentarily to interrupt his speech, to argue against him. It had been obvious from the beginning that the Gnomes would not support them, but she could not help feeling that there must be something she could say to change their minds.

"The Gnome peoples have nothing to gain by charging off to join a war that may or may not happen," Jamin continued. "Furthermore, we are perfectly safe within our own lands. In over a thousand years no outsider has ever successfully navigated the Nithal Maze. The Orcs and their demon allies will find that we are beyond their reach if ever they decide to move against us. We will remain within our own lands; we will not join this farcical crusade against an enemy that has yet to appear."

"By the time you receive the proof you require to act, Lord T'rul, it will be too late for you and your people," Cailyn said frostily.

Jamin T'rul stood abruptly, his cohorts following him up. Without a word he turned and marched pompously out of the hall. The others watched in silent resentment as the Gnomes left. Cailyn stared after them for a few minutes, frustrated by their ignorance and her failure to rally them to the cause. Though she was angry, inwardly she despaired and hoped that the Gnomes did not pay the ultimate price for their lack of trust.

She hoped they all did not have to pay that price.

Cailyn indulged in a late lunch with the Elves and Dwarves, not wanting her guests to leave hungry. She found that she was ravenous.

There was little discussion while they ate; mostly the talk involved General Markoll's defense strategy for the kingdom. Seyhan was eager to learn more of the expedition to recover the Krullstone. Her sister had traveled with Lazarus and his brothers, and she wanted to know everything she could about what they might face in the wilderness. Cailyn did her best to satisfy Seyhan's inquisitiveness, divulging what little she knew of their plans.

After lunch had finished and the topics of discussion exhausted, the Elves and Dwarves took their leave. Cailyn offered her gratitude for their promise of aid and bid them a safe journey. The Dwarves were the first to go, offering their thanks for her hospitality before riding out, followed closely by Seyhan and the Elves. Cailyn stood watching until long after they had disappeared into the horizon.

Later that evening Cailyn found herself staring out the foggy windows of a high balcony into the gray expanse of the valley. The rain had continued unabated all day, mixed now with sleet and ice, and the land was enfolded in the hazy darkness of twilight.

She found herself reflecting on the events of the day, wishing she had done something more. The Elves and the Dwarves had both agreed to send soldiers to aid them in defending Illendale, despite the threats each already faced. It was the Gnomes' stance that troubled her most. Understandably, they did not want to fight. None of them wanted a war. It was deeply distressing to her that they refused to stand with them. She had not expected them to raise an army overnight and charge off to battle; she had hoped that the Gnomes would accept the danger posed to them and at least be prepared to face it in the event that it reared its ugly head in their corner of the world. As it was, they had dismissed her pleadings out of hand without even attempting to understand, without paying any heed to her warnings. She worried for them, despite her anger over the manner in which Jamin T'rul had represented his people; she worried that when the shadow fell on the

Gnomes, they would be caught completely unprepared.

Ukiah approached her, gently assuring her that everything would work out for the best and not to worry. She smiled and hugged him affectionately, feeling slightly better just having him near. It felt good to know there were still some things she could rely on. Her fears and doubts persisted, however, lurking just beneath the surface like iron chains wrapped about her. Thinking of all the things that could go wrong and the sheer precariousness by which they held on brought a new wave of despair washing over her. Illendale's armies could not hold off the Orc hordes for long, even if they could survive the initial assault. The demons could strike at will throughout her kingdom, stripping away her sense of security, leaving her feeling naked and vulnerable. All her hopes rested on the shoulders of Lazarus and his brothers, and yet the chances of them succeeding seemed nonexistent.

So she stood, staring out into hazy nothingness, battling with her emotions and trying desperately not to lose hope.

XI A PERILOUS PATH

FOR THREE DAYS Lazarus and his company rode across the sodden and muddy plains toward the north rim of the Serpentspine Mountains. The rain, now mixed with sleet, continued to fall in buckets, soaking them through despite their foul-weather gear. Their spirits were as saturated as their clothes, and they hadn't had a warm meal since departing. Tempers were short and nerves frayed as they all continually cast suspicious glances over their shoulders, fearful of the demons they were certain must be hunting them.

There was little talking. The monotony of their trek was masked in silence broken only by the steady rainfall. What little conversation that did take place was short and to the point, uttered in low voices. Corsin was leading, guiding them along the trail. Devoll, Marcel, and Mihan were fanned out along the front and flanks, with the rest of the group huddled in the center of the vanguard formed by the soldiers.

Lazarus plodded wearily onward atop his dappled roan, trailing the rest of the group and trying in vain not to look behind him. It was nearing midday. By nightfall they would reach the mining town of Pilban, where they could dry themselves out a bit before continuing on their journey. Between furtive glances to the land behind, he occupied his time thinking about how they would proceed once beyond Illendale's borders.

At least he tried to.

He tried to stay focused and sharp, to keep his attention on the task at hand, but his mind kept wandering back to the Elven princess,

Neslyn. He could not help it, and the more he tried to fight it the more she haunted him. More often than not, when his thoughts drifted to her memory, his eyes followed.

He watched her as she rode ahead of him. She was beautiful, a lithe vision of femininity so finely wrought she seemed more like a mirage than a flesh and blood creature. The robes and heavy cloak she wore did little to hide the sensuality of the woman beneath. He frequently found himself watching her surreptitiously, enthralled by her every action — by the mesmerizing sway of her walk, the sweet song of her voice, the infinite well of her emerald eyes. He studied her whenever she was near, etching in his memory the lines and angles of her face, the smooth, ageless quality of her skin, and he always felt like a part of him was dying when she moved away.

Lazarus tried not to think of her, tried instead to concentrate on more pressing matters. As the leader of the group there was some amount of pressure on him to have all the answers to their dilemmas. There were considerable challenges lurking just around the corner, lying in wait for them just beyond the jagged line of mountains that loomed before him. Even obscured in the hazy grayness surrounding him, Lazarus could feel their capacious presence, feel the weight of them pressing down on him.

Once they left Illendale they would have to cross the Solaris Plain. Under normal circumstances it wouldn't have been hard at all, but with its broad expanses there would be little cover for them. That would make it much easier for the demons to track them and harder for them to defend themselves if their enemies caught them. Then, of course, they had to successfully navigate the Morah Weald, an endless mass of tangled trees and brush that was home to any number of untold dangers. If they managed to get through the woodlands, they then had to locate the ancient city of Caer Dorn, the once-great capital of Valinar. Within the city they would have to find the Krullstone and take it from the unknown evil that brooded there, likely by force. Then they would have to escape to Illendale and hope that they were not too late to save their people. He had studied maps of the lands drawn before the War of the Dead had destroyed Valinar, but who knew exactly how accurate they were? He knew the general direction, and somehow he would have to make do with what limited knowledge he possessed.

Yes, there was much to consider, much to worry about. Doubts and fears plagued him, teased him in his waking hours and his sleep. They rode next to him and slept with him at night. They glided on the wind, whispering in his ears, reminding him of all the dark things the future held. Snippets of Melynda's vision crept insidiously into his thoughts and imbedded themselves there, waiting to spring on him like a stalking cat. He struggled within his mind, and he fought each and every hour not to fall into the black well of misery and despair that threatened to consume him.

Lazarus wiped irritably at the raindrops clouding his vision. He was strangely weary despite the easy pace they had set. Since leaving Kylenshar his fears had magnified in his mind, and he had grown taciturn and introverted, avoiding any conversation about events to come. He tried to dislodge his discomfort by vigorously shaking his head, an action that did little but draw odd glances from his companions.

They stopped in a stand of sprawling hickory and ate a cold meal of dried meat and nuts with some bread, washing it all down disinterestedly with draughts from their water skins. They rested their horses for a time, wandering off in groups of two or three, not straying too far and yet putting at least a little distance between themselves and the rest of the company. Aldric and Vinson clustered around Zafer, sharing old hunting stories and tales of adventure. They had quickly grown to be friends during their journey, often talking and joking with each other. Emeris Dallen and Aurora Skall drifted off into the trees to be alone, intent on finding at least some measure of companionship in this dark and forbidding trek. Corsin and the other soldiers sat together, keeping a watchful eye on things as they ate.

Lazarus stayed near the horses, chewing absently on a piece of dried beef. He picked a spot underneath one of the nearby trees where it was still dry and sat with his back against the rough bark. He saw Neslyn briefly, walking among the old trees, lost in thought. She flashed that dazzling smile when she saw him watching and changed course to come over and sit with him.

Sitting cross-legged in front of him, she studied him intently, obviously waiting for him to say something. He watched silently as she brushed at a stray wisp of her auburn hair. Precipitation clung to her face in a fine sheen, casting her sculpted features in a muted glow and making her appear almost angelic.

Say something, you fool. Anything!

But he could not. She was so beautiful. He felt like he could tell her anything, any of the million thoughts that were racing through his mind at the moment, but every time he tried to latch onto one, they scattered like dry leaves in a strong wind. His voice was frozen, as if he had never spoken before in his life. The words simply would not come. His heart raced. He could not focus his mind enough to form a coherent sentence. Her eyes glittered when he looked into them, and Lazarus felt like he could sink into them and disappear into their emerald bliss forever.

"Confounded rain," he said finally, lamely. "I wish the sun would come out again. The rain always makes me feel depressed."

Neslyn did not reply right away, apparently seeking a deeper meaning in the words he had spoken. "I like the rain. It has a sort of cleansing quality to it. After a storm the earth always feels cleaner, looks more vibrant, as if all the dirt and stress and sorrow have been washed away."

Long minutes slipped past as they stared at each other, sheltered from the rain and gloom by the trees.

"Why did you decide to come, knowing the danger we would face?" Lazarus asked her suddenly.

"I'm not sure," she said after a moment. "It seemed like the right thing to do."

"I'm sure Layek telling you that you couldn't come had nothing to do with it."

"Only partly," she confessed, suppressing a mischievous grin.

"Life is so sheltered when you're the king's daughter. So much is forbidden. Everything is masked and hidden away, as if being a princess makes me too fragile to handle the truth. Rarely am I allowed to venture out into the wilderness and even then only when well guarded. I guess I came partly to get away, partly to prove that I am capable enough to be out on my own, and also because I believe in your cause. Why are you here?"

"I am here because it must be so," Lazarus stated resignedly. "Melynda's vision says that only my brothers can find the Krullstone and return with it."

"Yes, but why are you here?" Neslyn probed, not satisfied with his rhetorical answer. "Certainly you do not go along just because somebody says you must."

"It is the only way; otherwise we are all lost. I go because there is no one else, because for whatever reason, Fate has chosen me to champion my people."

"You are afraid." It was a statement of fact, not demeaning or impertinent, but rather intended to draw out something more. Neslyn waited patiently for a response.

"Yes."

She sensed his hesitation mirrored in his succinct answer. Impulsively she reached out and took his hand in her own. "Your fear runs deep, Lazarus Arkenstone. I sense it, see it cloaked in your eyes. If it would make you feel better talking about it, I am here to listen."

"Thank you." The warmth of her touch spread through him, lifting his darkened spirits. He wondered if she could sense the affection he held for her like she sensed his fears. He searched her eyes for any sign that she knew what he hid within.

"Tell me," she said after he did not speak.

"Where do I begin?" Lazarus lowered his eyes. "Yes, I am afraid. Afraid of too many things to count. The hopes and dreams of an entire people rest on my shoulders. I fear that the trust bestowed upon me has been misplaced. What if I am not strong enough to do what is necessary? What if I fail? So many things can go wrong, so many variables. How am I to maintain control of the situation?"

"We do what we can with what we have," Neslyn reassured him. "No one can ask any more than that. The weight of the world is too great a burden for one man to carry alone. Events and circumstances often take us far from where we would rather be, but we must carry on nonetheless. To do otherwise is unthinkable."

Lazarus sagged back into the tree, feeling the rough bark chafe at his skin through his tunic and cloak. "I know, but I can't help thinking that somehow it will not be enough. Those I lead are my friends and family; they depend on me to see them safely through this mess. How will I live with myself if I fail them? Not everyone will survive this journey I fear, and the blood of the fallen will be on my hands."

"Leadership is not without its burdens," she said. "Your friends trust your judgment enough to follow you even knowing what they face. They are prepared to sacrifice whatever is demanded of them, including their lives if the situation calls for it. The only way to fail your friends here would be to abandon them. I do not think you are that sort of man."

"And what if the situation demands sacrifices I am not prepared to make?"

Neslyn immediately sensed the change in him; there was something in the way his eyes narrowed and his body stiffened. He was talking about something specific she intuited, something he had hidden from all of them from the beginning.

"What sacrifices, Lazarus?" She leaned forward until her face was only inches from his.

"It was a hypothetical question," Lazarus evaded, turning quickly away.

"No," she reached out, placing her hand gently on his cheek and turning him back to meet her intense emerald eyes. "You are hiding something. What sacrifices, Lazarus?"

Lazarus held her gaze, captivated by the fervor he saw in them. Her hand on his face sent a wave of electricity down his spine, and once again he found himself studying the angles of her delicate face. The sharp Elven features, smoothed by the softness of her voice and dazzling green eyes, caused his heart to ache so sharply he felt that it would break in two. He had the sudden, irresistible urge to run his fingers through her silken hair and throw back the cowl of her cloak so that he might kiss her. The longing he felt for her was almost overwhelming. Never before had he seen a creature so beautiful.

He flushed with the thought and tried to pull away from her, but she held him fast.

"What sacrifices?" she pressed again.

"Some of us may die during this venture," he began slowly. He had not wanted to reveal his secrets, but it seemed he could not deny Neslyn anything so powerful was her hold on him. "For most of us it is little more than a risk, a finality that will be decided by chance and skill. For others the path has already been defined. Vinson and Aldric, my brothers, the only family I have, are doomed to die."

Neslyn breathed in sharply. She knew Lazarus had been hiding something, but she had not expected something so dark as this. She sat motionless, stunned into silence. Tears welled in his eyes as the memory surged from the dark corner of his mind he had confined it to. "Melynda has foreseen their deaths," Lazarus continued shakily. "They will die in the coming war with the Orcs, and I will not be able to defeat the demons on my own."

"Do they know this?" she asked him gently.

"No. I could not tell them. I'm afraid that if I do, it will cripple their ability to act, and everything depends on them. They are the ones who will wield the stone in battle." He took a deep breath to steady himself, determined that all his secrets should be laid bare now. "The truth is, I shouldn't be here. I was to remain in Illendale to defend our country. I came to insure that my brothers live through this; they must if we are to win, but more than that, I cannot live with myself if the only thing I have in this world is lost. I must be there for them when the time comes. Somehow I must thwart Fate."

"You are afraid that you cannot save them. Lazarus, you lack faith in yourself. Visions are not solid, unchangeable truths. By nature they are little more than glimpses into what the future might hold. The future is not set in stone; it is an ever-changing collage of events, a tapestry of circumstance whose pattern can be altered and redefined with the simplest of gestures."

She cradled his face in both her hands, whispering now. "Do not fear, Lazarus. Already you change the future by doing what you feel is necessary and not what you are told must be done. You carry a burden of guilt for things that have not yet come to pass. Lay that aside along with your fears. When push comes to shove, you will do what you must, and that will be enough. In the end, everything will work out as it was meant to."

"That's what scares me," Lazarus whispered back. "What if this was meant to be, and there is nothing I can do to prevent it?"

"I do not think that is what the Gods have planned for us," she smiled faintly, a slight tugging motion at the corners of her mouth that somehow made her even more beautiful in the gloomy half-light. "Be at peace. Your heart is true, and you are well intentioned. Have faith that what you do is right and that good will prevail over the evil that threatens."

"You are indeed a noble woman, Neslyn. Thank you." Lazarus took her hands in his and squeezed them lightly. "Promise me that you will keep this conversation between us."

Neslyn opened her mouth to protest, but he placed a single finger over her lips. "Shhh. When the time is right, the truth will be revealed. Until then you must promise to say nothing to the others."

She nodded grudgingly.

The conversation refreshed Lazarus; his strength of will returned, and for at least a little while his fears and doubts were cast aside. He rose slowly, helping Neslyn up as he did. They stood there for a moment while they eased their cramped muscles. Lazarus hugged Neslyn impulsively in gratitude. To his surprise she hugged him back. The other members of the group began to return, ready to begin their trek west once again. With hardly a word they mounted their horses and trotted off.

The rain had slightly abated while they had rested, coming down now in a light drizzle. The hazy mist continued to gather, obscuring their view as they rode steadily on. Trees materialized out of the gloom like sentinels set at watch and were gone just as quickly. The miasma hung thickly on the air and drained away the color of the land, turning everything into lifeless specters that watched them as they passed, taunting them with the promise that Lazarus and his friends would soon join them in their tortured emptiness. Their vision was limited to little more than twenty paces in front of them, and they clustered together to keep from losing each other. The gray clouds hid the sun, a thick layer of gauze that descended from the sky and wrapped about them.

They had been riding for about an hour when Lazarus had the unmistakable feeling of being watched. His scalp crawled, and he turned to find the source of discomfort, only to see gray emptiness staring back at him. He continued to search the murk that enclosed them, taunted by the shifting haze and the ghostly shapes that appeared momentarily and then faded back into limbo.

He was about to dismiss his intuition altogether and credit it to the dreariness that surrounded him when Aldric abruptly declared that they were being followed. The others turned in surprise. Neslyn said that she also felt it, and they halted for a moment to see what might appear from the mists, forming themselves in a rough circle so they could see in every direction.

Shadows skulked through the swirling haze as they watched, but nothing came forward. They stood watching expectantly for several minutes, each not entirely sure what to expect and at the same time expecting the worst. Disembodied sounds drifted through the heavy air, ominous and threatening and yet lacking any discernable source. A flock of birds suddenly burst forth from their roost in some nearby trees. Everyone jumped in surprise; Mihan and Marcell instantly had their weapons out. Still nothing showed itself, and the company of thirteen stood watch uneasily.

"It's nothing," Layek muttered irritably. "Just your imagination playing tricks on you."

There were uncertain whispers of agreement as the company turned their horses west to continue on. Corsin took the lead once again, disappearing into the fog. The others followed him, except Aldric, who hung back to be alone with Lazarus.

Lazarus watched as the gray swallowed up his companions like a hungry beast one by one and spurred his horse on to catch up. Aldric maneuvered his mount next to Lazarus as they moved forward into the gloom.

"Something's back there," he said with a quick glance over his shoulder. "I can feel its eyes watching us."

"Whatever it is, it's keeping well out of sight, waiting until we let our guard down, and then it will have us."

"Do you think the demons have found us?"

"I don't know." Lazarus looked at his brother levelly. "We tread a perilous path. Whatever is back there, you can bet it's not friendly. Best keep a sharp eye out."

Aldric nodded. He rode at Lazarus' side for a time and then broke away. Lazarus was left alone again, trailing the rest of the company. He kept himself occupied, trying to puzzle through the questions that were still unanswered. There were just too many unknowns in this business and no way for him to divine the details that were hidden from him. His mind tired quickly of fretting over the things he could not control or change.

The shadows grew, gathering in dark pools that swallowed up what little light was present, as the day slowly gave way to dusk. The path became less distinguished, and their pace slowed. The thirteen companions cast cautious glances into the gathering darkness. None wanted to spend another night out in the open, not with their unseen pursuer still fresh on their minds.

Minutes stretched into hours, and still they plodded onward. The landscape began to change, becoming more rocky and rough as they entered the foothills of the Serpentspine. Deciduous trees gave way to fir and cedar and pine; the grasses of the plains thinned and were replaced by scrub and rock that crunched beneath the hooves of their horses. The rain stopped altogether, but the mist remained, an impenetrable wall of grayness that closed in around them like a thick blanket. Lights began to appear in the fog, hazy and distorted, a beacon that beckoned to them and whispered of warmth and comfort. Corsin led them onto a road that headed toward their destination, pitted and rutted from heavy use. Large puddles frequently blocked their path, and they slogged through them, drawn to the haven of the city like moths to a flame.

Then without warning buildings began to appear out of the shadows. Only a few at first, darkened shacks and huts that sagged under the weight of their age, holding together out of sheer stubbornness. Soon newer, better-kept cottages of stone, plaster, and wood planking replaced the rundown hovels. Light seeped through the windows and cracks in the boards. Warehouses loomed up beside them, dark and silent like sleeping giants, and the smell of ash and coal invaded their nostrils. They passed several forges and metal works brightened by the glow of the fires within that were never allowed to cool.

They continued along the road, encountering only the occasional person hurrying home. Raucous laughter and the clink of glasses echoed out of the pleasure dens and taverns they passed, the night still young for those who were looking for companionship and entertainment. Corsin led them down the thoroughfare without deviating; the rest of the group bunched protectively behind him. Pilban was a mining town, the heart of the industry in Illendale, and it could be a rough place if one wasn't careful. Brawls and bar fights were a common occurrence in the taverns, and there was the usual gathering of thieves and criminals stalking the alleyways waiting for an easy target to present itself.

Corsin turned right at an adjoining street and led them on a short distance before stopping in front of a stable. Directly across the street was a large inn with a stone base and slat-board walls; a painted sign named it the Twinkling Star. The sounds of activity were less apparent on this street, and it appeared to be a well-kept establishment. Lazarus nodded his approval when Corsin looked at him, and the man knocked loudly on the door of the stable.

There was the sound of locks being slid free, the door swung open, and a fat, balding man holding a lantern appeared before them. Corsin spoke with the man, arranging for their horses to be cared for and housed for the night. The man yelled inside, and several young men appeared to take them. Lazarus and his companions dismounted, handed over the reins to the boys, and after collecting their gear proceeded across the street.

They gathered under the portico of the porch, and Lazarus reached out to open the arched double doors. Inside they saw a slight departure from the usual atmosphere of inns in a mining town. There were the familiar rows of benches and tables, the booths partitioned from the rest of the room for privacy and the expected oversized hearth with logs ablaze to ward off the night's chill. The room was well lit by oil lamps placed on the tables and hanging from the rafters overhead. A polished oak serving bar occupied the far corner, and delicious smells of food wafted into the room from a set of swinging doors that led back into the kitchens. A wide set of stairs rested on the other side of the large room, leading up to the sleeping quarters. The typical crowds of boisterous miners and workers were missing; a gentle and relaxing silence filled the void. The inn was warm and inviting, a welcome respite from their dismal journey.

The place was very clean and tidy, everything ordered neatly in its place. There weren't any gambling tables to Layek's dismay, and only a dozen or so patrons occupied the common room, talking idly amongst themselves and smoking long-stemmed pipes. A middle-aged woman casually swept the floor while a tall man washed glasses behind the bar with a cloth. Both looked up when they entered.

Lazarus and his company removed their heavy cloaks and stood numbly in the doorway for a few moments, feeling the warmth of the room wash over them and chase away the cold that had permeated them during their journey. The patrons who were scattered about the room didn't even look up; they had come to the right place if they wanted to go unnoticed.

Lazarus stepped forward, and the woman leaned her broom against a nearby table. She walked briskly towards them, wiping her hands absently on her white apron as she moved.

"Good evening," the woman said as she approached them, her voice soft and smooth. Light brown hair tumbled down to her shoulders, and a smile warm enough to melt a mountain of snow creased her youthful face. "I'm Stefini. How can I help you?"

"Hello," Lazarus greeted her. "We need rooms for the evening. And a warm meal would be most welcome."

"Certainly. Rabbit stew is on the menu tonight, but perhaps you would like to get settled first."

Lazarus nodded in agreement, and she motioned for them to

follow her. The woman led them up the stairs and down a hall to a set of four adjoining rooms. Each room was lightly furnished and spacious: four simple beds with a table and chairs and a set of cabinets for storing belongings. After their sodden journey the rooms looked cozy. They divided up and settled themselves into their quarters, storing their gear before trudging back downstairs where the thick smell of warm food teased their nostrils.

They sat together in a corner of the common room, talking softly among themselves as they consumed their meal. Their spirits had risen markedly since they had arrived. It seemed everyone was content with a good hot meal and a warm bed to sleep in, if only for the night. Layek was ecstatic just to be near a keg of ale again. All thoughts of demons were forgotten, suffocated by their renewed vivacity. Their previous misgivings and fears were banished, gratefully set aside while they enjoyed the comfort of the inn. Jokes and stories were exchanged, past histories revealed, the bonds of friendship strengthened and nurtured.

Time passed quickly, and the hour grew late. All of the other guests had already strayed to their beds for the evening, leaving the room shrouded in a silence that was strangely relaxing. Yawning and sleepy-eyed, the company began to shuffle off to their rooms. Lazarus arranged for a watch to be set, explaining that it was better to be prepared than to be caught off guard. He did, however, give them some measure of comfort by delaying their departure until midmorning.

Lazarus remained seated, not yet ready for sleep, and watched them go. Layek remained behind as well, intent on taking his fill of the ale stores before they moved on tomorrow. Mihan and Marcell took up places near the front door, worrying over mugs of ale as they made sure their companions were safe in their slumber. Layek stood and walked over to the bar where the bartender was sitting on a tall stool, twirling a strangely crafted club. Lazarus followed him after a moment, deciding on one more glass before heading off to sleep.

The bartender, who identified himself as Jake, refilled their ceramic mugs and set them down in front of them. "There ya go, lads," he said in a peculiar accent. "Cannae sleep tonight, eh?"

"Not yet." Layek took a long sip from his cup. "Can't let all this fine drink go to waste. What's that you got there? I've never seen a weapon like that before," he said, pointing to the club.

"This? This be no weapon; tis an apparatus for an ancient game, handed down through me family fer generations, since the old days," he beamed, handing the thing over to Layek for him to inspect.

Lazarus leaned in to have a look. On closer inspection he saw that it was little more than a three-foot shaft of oak with a triangular head attached at one end and leather strips wrapped on the other.

"What game is this?" Lazarus asked. He had never heard of such a thing.

"Ya take the club an' use it to strike a stone wrapped in leather. The object is to try to get the stone in a hole in the ground in as few strokes as possible."

Layek looked at him askance. "Is it any fun? It doesn't sound nearly as amusing as drinking or dice."

"O'course tis!" he explained. "Lemme explain it to ya. . . ."

Lazarus slipped away quietly as Layek and Jake continued their discussion, which mostly included Jake detailing the rules of his sport and Layek guzzling down ale by the pint. He was quite tired by now and decided to get some fresh air before going to his room.

He went through the kitchens, the smells of food faded and the stoves now cold, and out through the back door where Zafer kept watch. He nodded perfunctorily to the Elf as he passed by to the yard behind the inn. It seemed deadly quiet outside, and he checked himself quickly to be sure he still had his long knife tucked into his belt. The mists had cleared somewhat, and patches of the bejeweled night sky peeked through the clouds. Lazarus wrapped his arms around his chest to fight the cold and followed a rough path to a gazebo surrounded by spruce trees at the far end of the courtyard. He sat there for long minutes, marveling at the pervasive silence around him and trying to ignore the ringing in his ears. He drifted in a mix of serenity and fatigue, lost in his own meandering thoughts of times past, and slowly his eyes grew heavy. He rested his chin in the palm of his hand, his eyes closing altogether, and fell asleep.

        ა   ა   ა

Outside the Twinkling Star, crouched back in the shadows and well hidden from the eyes that kept watch, the doppelganger waited. It had waited for days as it had carefully studied its prey, patiently following when they left Kylenshar in secret. Not even the rain and mist had been enough to lose it in the wilderness. Now, it seemed, its patience was about to pay off.

The humans who had gone in search of the Krullstone had thought to avoid pursuit by leaving during the night after discovering the murders in Kylenshar, murders it had committed. It had killed those members of the High Council, posing as the Chief Minister. Mostly though, it had done it because it pleased it. It loved games of subterfuge and deception. That's all anything was in the end: a game. A game it played well, and it had never lost.

Now it served a new master. The High Summoner had offered it the opportunity to test itself against a bloodline despised by the demons above all others. It was an invitation it could not resist. All that was required of it in return was to ensure that the Krullstone was returned to its new lord.

So it had tracked the humans across the plains, teasing them on occasion with its presence without ever revealing itself. It had carefully chosen the one among them who would serve its purpose best. The three brothers were off limits to it; they were needed to recover the stone, according to the seer. But there were others within their group who it might become, and under their guise it could veil its true intentions until the time came when it would reveal the truth. Until then it would enjoy toying with them, much like a cat with a mouse that it has captured. Give the prey false hope by allowing it to escape — then pounce.

The doppelganger circled the building to where the rear entrance opened into the yard. It hung back in the shadows for a long while. It watched as Lazarus exited the inn, catching a brief glimpse inside at the Elf keeping watch over the door. They would be changing the watch soon. Its eyes gleamed wickedly in the darkness. It was almost time. It was about to make its move when half a dozen shadows detached from the black to its right.

Lurkers. Pure killing machines.

It thought back to a week before when demons like them had been sent to assassinate the Queen of Illendale. Had it not been for its aid they would never have gained entrance into the palace. Too bad those meddling Elves happened to be there at just the right moment. Perhaps if the Lurkers had been slightly more inconspicuous, they would have succeeded in their goal. The doppelganger surely would have. Lurkers had no sense of stealth or trickery, no understanding of the sport.

They had better not ruin my plan, it thought darkly. It watched as they circled the building, scouting. Would they prove to be too great a match for the humans? The doppelganger doubted it. The humans were prepared for this, perhaps even expecting it. They were smart enough to assume that the demons would be hunting them.

The Lurkers continued to circle the building, disappearing from sight. Two remained behind to guard the rear entrance and to make sure none escaped. Not too bright at all. Apparently they had decided on a frontal assault of the inn.

It waited until the other demons were out of sight. It would have to kill these two, of course, but they meant nothing to it. Just two more pieces on the board for it to outsmart. With the element of surprise they would be no match for it. It could kill them quickly and steal inside during the confusion of the attack and do its work.

Swiftly the doppelganger charged out of its concealment, silent as death and equally as quick. By the time the Lurkers realized its presence the doppelganger already had hold of them, its dreadful claws ripping. In seconds they lay dead, their throats torn out.

It inched toward the door, reaching out to take the handle in its bloodied grip. Then the door opened slowly. Caught completely off guard, the doppelganger started. It smiled when it saw what had come to see it. The individual must have heard the scuffle and come to investigate. Fortunately for the doppelganger, this was the one it was seeking.

The being froze in terror when it saw the doppelganger. Quick as thought, the doppelganger pounced. *Like a cat,* it thought, as its claws tore into the flesh of its target, rending and shredding with supernatural malevolence.

Euphoria rushed through the doppelganger as it reveled in the thrill of its kill. It relished its victory for only a moment. It had a mission to accomplish, and there would be plenty of time to celebrate later. The doppelganger felt its magic spark in response to its desire, and it began to take on new form. There was sudden, intense pain as its skeletal structure began to alter, bones cracking and breaking before re-knitting to fit its new manifestation. Skin and cartilage wove to fill in the spaces. In a matter of moments the transformation was complete — a change as drastic as night from day, utterly flawless in its design. Not only did the doppelganger look and feel exactly as its target, the process also siphoned away everything that the prey had ever been; all the memories, experiences, and emotions now belonged to it. No one would ever know the difference between the original and the copy.

It was about to conceal the evidence of its deception when a great crash broke the stillness of the night, shattering the silence like glass. Shouts of alarm rose from the room as the sentries rushed to repel the invaders.

The assault on the Twinkling Star had begun.

XII DARK ALLIANCE

LAZARUS AWOKE WITH a start.

How did I fall asleep out here? How late is it?

He stood up, relieving his aching muscles, shivering against the freezing cold. He must have been more tired than he had thought; otherwise it would have been far too uncomfortable in the gazebo to fall asleep. The moon and stars had retreated behind the thick layer of clouds overhead, leaving the yard behind the inn black as pitch. He had barely taken two steps towards the darkened inn that loomed before him when he heard the sound.

There was a great crash and the noise of wooden boards splintering and snapping apart. Then the shouts began. Frantic cries of alarm and fear rose into the night like wraiths born of darkness come to haunt him. A vast black pit opened in his stomach and threatened to swallow him whole. He knew what was happening.

The demons had found them.

Lazarus slid his long knife from his belt and sprinted for the inn. He stumbled and went down, his foot catching on something heavy and limp. He kicked his leg free and jumped back up. Looking down chilled him to the bone as he recognized the lifeless eyes of a Lurker staring back at him. He looked around warily. How many more were out there with him, stalking the shadows? He quickly dismissed the idea. The demons would already be inside, and if there were any others out here with him, he would probably already be dead.

He turned and ran for the rear entrance to the inn, and grasping at the handle, threw the door open wide. He darted inside, momentarily blinded by the light, and nearly ran headlong into a stunned Azrael.

Lazarus straightened himself, seeing now the blood that was sprayed all over the hallway. On the floor lay what used to be a person. Lazarus fought the urge to wretch. The corpse was totally unrecognizable. It looked like it had been turned inside out.

"What happened?"

"I don't know! I was in the back getting a drink when all hell broke loose. This is what I found when I came out of the kitchen," Azrael gasped, wildly shaking his head.

Shouts and the sounds of battle burst through the doors at the end of the hall like a stampeding herd of elephants. Lazarus quickly sped to the common room, long knife in hand. His breath caught in his throat.

The arched double doors that served as the main entrance were torn completely off their hinges and lay broken on opposite sides of the room, leaving a gaping hole in the wall. Chairs and tables lay smashed all about. Several small fires burned where oil lamps had been knocked over, and they were spreading quickly.

A trio of Lurkers had forced their way in and were wreaking havoc as they fought with the humans they had been sent to kill. Mihan, Marcell, and Vinson were clashing with two of the creatures on one side of the room while Layek tried to keep the third one from tearing him to pieces on the other. A fourth was hunched down near the demolished doorway, gnawing wildly at Devoll's lifeless body.

Lazarus had never seen a living Lurker, had not even heard of them until several of them had been dispatched to assassinate the Queen. They were truly fearsome monsters, something akin to a giant dog. Even on all fours they were at least as tall as he was. Fur that was blacker than the darkest night and that seemed to swallow up the light covered them from head to tail, bristling like spikes. The Lurkers appeared to blend and mix with the darkness wherever they met it, giving the impression that the shadows themselves had come to life. Yellowed rows of razor sharp fangs protruded from their muzzles, and claws equally as deadly jutted from their paws. Golden eyes glowed maliciously from within their recessed sockets, eyes that exposed the madness that consumed the things from within.

The Lurker that was despoiling what had been Devoll turned to Lazarus and Azrael when they exploded into the room. Baring its fangs and growling, a sound like bone scraping on stone, the demon stalked toward them. It licked its bloodied chops greedily as it neared them, emitting a sickening whine that carried the essence of need and the promise of agony through the air.

With only his long knife, Lazarus knew he was seriously disadvantaged. "Azrael..."

He never finished. As soon as he spoke, the beast flung itself with a speed that was frightening, hurtling through the air like a missile. Lazarus stood his ground, taking the full brunt of the assault. Falling backwards, he jammed his legs into its gut, allowing its momentum to work against it. In that same instant he drove his knife up through the monster's jaw and into its brain. The Lurker yelped, harsh and piercing, and was carried over Lazarus to crash into the wall behind him. It fell to the floor, convulsed once, and did not move again.

"Azrael! We've got to get out before the whole place goes up!" Lazarus cried as he regained his feet.

Flames were spreading uncontrollably, consuming everything. Already the stairs were blocked by the conflagration. Those trapped upstairs would have to find another way out.

"Go help Vinson and the others; I'll see to Layek."

Azrael nodded. Lazarus looked to Layek and found his old friend, lying on his back, trying desperately to keep the Lurker atop him at bay. Mihan, a fraction too slow, was swatted and sent flying by one great paw. Vinson and Marcell rushed to his aid, thrusting and feigning to force the Lurkers back from their fallen comrade.

Lazarus darted across the room to where Devoll lay, his sword still sheathed on his lifeless body. He needed a weapon if he were to be of any use to his friend.

Layek abruptly roared in pain as the demon he grappled with sank its teeth into his forearm. Having only made it halfway to the weapon he needed, Lazarus immediately changed course and beelined it for the Lurker and his flagging friend.   He sensed the urgency of Layek's condition in his cry; his friend could not hold out any longer.

Shoulder lowered and without slowing, Lazarus slammed into the Lurker. The beast tumbled away into the flames and disappeared. Lazarus helped his wounded friend to his feet, scooping up Layek's broadsword with his free hand. Layek sagged heavily into him. Blood stained his shredded tunic, so much so that Lazarus couldn't tell how many wounds he had sustained, and his left arm hung limp at his side. Lazarus scanned the room, looking for some trace of the Lurker.

The Lurker launched itself from behind the bar, fur ablaze and shrieking.

Lazarus pushed Layek aside and turned to meet the rush, raising the broadsword to defend himself. Too slow, the fiery monster crashed into him, knocking him flat on his back and emptying his lungs of air. Spots danced before his eyes as he gasped for breath. Fire seared his flesh where the Lurker held him pinned.

Lazarus thrust up with his legs, trying to dislodge the beast, but it sunk its claws into him at the shoulders and would not be moved. He batted futilely at its head with his fists, desperate to save himself from the nightmarish inferno on top of him. A red haze of pain clouded his vision as the claws sunk deeper into his skin. The stench of burning fur filled his nostrils, and the agonizing cry of the Lurker pierced his ears, drowning out everything else.

Then Layek was next to him.

Roaring furiously he attacked, stabbing relentlessly with his dagger, heedless of the flames that burned him. The Lurker turned to face this new assault, its strength waning from the killing fire and yet oblivious to the pain.

It yanked its claws out of Lazarus' shoulders and snapped wildly at Layek. Lazarus felt for the sword that had fallen from his hands as the Lurker turned to attack his friend. His hand found the pommel, and his grip tightened. Swift and silent as death, Lazarus brought the blade around and thrust it into the monster's side.

The Lurker shrieked in agony and trembled riotously, trying to shake loose its would-be killers. Lazarus and Layek continued to gore it, ichor spraying everywhere as their blades found home and withdrew again for another strike. For what seemed like forever this macabre dance played itself out, the Lurker lashing out violently in an attempt to fend off Lazarus and Layek, who dodged and weaved until they found an opening. Lazarus and his friend kept at it, the demon simply refusing to give in.

Vinson and those who battled on the other side of the room were in a similar position. One of the Lurkers already lay dead, its head hacked off and oozing blood from numerous other gashes. Vinson, Mihan, and Marcell had backed the other into a corner and were trying to break through its defenses without getting any limbs clawed off. Azrael was nowhere to be seen.

Lazarus had no time to think on it, though. The Lurker before him suddenly lunged, caught him across the face, and sent him reeling backwards.

The beast launched itself at Layek then, catching him off guard and landing square on his chest. Layek fell back under its weight, his own strength failing from loss of blood. As he fell, he plunged his sword deep into the monster's chest. Layek thumped heavily to the floor, carrying the lifeless body of the Lurker with him.

"Layek!" Lazarus rushed to his friend's side. "Layek."

His friend's eyes found his own. Layek was soaked in blood from head to toe. His eyes were distant and glassy when Lazarus looked into them.

"I can't feel anything, Lazarus."

"You're … you're going to be okay," Lazarus stammered. "Layek! Layek, look at me! You're going to be fine."

Lazarus rolled the corpse of the Lurker off his friend. He tore strips from his already shredded tunic and attempted to bind the worst of his wounds. The fire had spread quickly during their battle, and they were in danger of becoming trapped within the building as it burned. Timbers crashed to the floor, and the structure groaned in protest, an ominous voice that threatened to crush them all.

Vinson came running up to Lazarus as he knelt next to Layek, cradling his head in his hands.

"Laz, we have to get out of here! The whole building is going to collapse!" he shouted as he tugged at Lazarus' arm.

"Help me carry him, Vinny," Lazarus urged his brother, signaling him to take Layek's legs.

"It's no good, Laz," Layek whispered. "Leave me. Save yourself."

Lazarus ignored him. Together he and Vinson half carried, half dragged Layek to the door and out into the cool night air. They set him down in front of the stables across the street, cushioning his head with Vinson's tunic. Mihan and Marcell were scouting around, looking for the others of their group and making sure that nothing else lurked in the pervasive shadows of the deep night. Shouts of alarm rose from the city around him like winged beasts as the Crimson Guard slowly roused itself. Bells clanged somewhere in the distance as the fire brigade was rallied.

"Use your magic, Vinny. Heal him," Lazarus pleaded with his brother.

Vinson stooped over Layek's body; his breathing was shallow, an almost imperceptible rise and fall of his chest. He looked in disgust at the lacerations that covered him. He placed one hand on Layek's head, gripping his skull at the temples. A soft white glow emanated from his hand and flowed into Layek.

It lasted only a few brief moments before the light faded.

"He is wounded too badly, Lazarus. I have done what I can to help him, but I'm afraid I have done little but buy him some time."

"Where are the others?" Lazarus looked around, almost frantically. "Did they escape?"

"I sent Azrael upstairs to rouse them and get them out. I'm sure they are all fine."

Just then Neslyn rounded the corner of the inn, somewhat disheveled and wild-eyed, with Zafer close behind. Aldric and Azrael trailed after, rushing forward when they saw Lazarus hunched over Layek's motionless body. From the opposite side of the house Corsin, Dallen, and Skall came running from the darkness.

In a jumbled mass of bodies they approached Lazarus, crowding around him. For a few precious seconds a fragile silence hung over the air as each tried to figure out what had gone wrong. Then they all began talking at once.

"Quiet!" Lazarus yelled when he could stand no more. "Neslyn, Aurora, Azrael. Layek is in critical condition. Can you help him?"

"I will take care of him, Lazarus," Neslyn said reassuringly, placing a comforting hand on his shoulder. "Allow the others to tend to your wounds, and I will see to your friend."

"Do not worry, Laz. It will be all right. Come; let's get you all cleaned up. There's nothing more for you to do here." Azrael quickly grabbed him by the arms, lifting him to his feet.

"Where's Devoll?" Corsin asked.

"He didn't make it," Vinson replied somberly, lowering his head. "The Lurkers killed him."

Lazarus allowed himself to be led off to the side where Azrael sat him down against the wall of the stable. Suddenly, Lazarus realized that Zafer was there. Hadn't he been on watch when the Lurkers had attacked? Wasn't it his body he had seen? Obviously it couldn't have been because he was here. But if not Zafer, who had been killed at the back entrance? And who had killed the Lurkers in the yard? Azrael had not said anything about it to him. He made a mental note to get some answers once they were safely away from the city.

Aurora Skall came over and using her magic, healed his wounds. It was a mostly painless experience, the familiar white light flooding through his body as she worked, filling him with warmth. He closed his eyes and rested briefly until she was finished. When he opened them again many minutes later, he felt weak and light-headed. Blood was caked and dried where his wounds had been, but they were now almost entirely gone. For the most part only some scarring remained. His shoulders were still tender from where the Lurker's claws had dug into his skin, and a thin line of scarlet marked where the magic had not been able to fully wipe away the damage that had been done.

He pulled himself off the ground and huddled everyone except

Neslyn — who still sat with Layek — close to him in a small circle. A fresh wave of fatigue washed over him, and he swayed feebly. Corsin placed a steadying hand on his shoulder.

"As you all know," Lazarus said, "the demons have found us. Somehow Lurkers have tracked us from Kylenshar. They now know where we are, and if we are not quick, more will follow. We have to leave the city tonight. Right now in fact."

"What about Layek?" Azrael gestured to where the big man lay. "He's in no condition to ride. He's lucky even to be alive after the thrashing he took."

Lazarus frowned grimly. "It can't be helped. We'll carry him if we have to, but we cannot stay here. If we do, we are all dead."

Lazarus dispatched them to ready their equipment and horses. After having their wounds mended by Azrael, he set Mihan and Marcell at watch in case more demons appeared before they could escape the city. They gently moved Layek inside the stable where Neslyn could continue her healing undistracted.

Outside, a crowd had begun to gather as the flames consumed the inn. Crimson Guard were everywhere, keeping the people back and trying in vain to discover what had happened. Lazarus thought it best if they did not get involved with the guards; it was preferable for them to remain anonymous.

At one point, after the fire crews had shown up with their horse-drawn carts to try to salvage the inn, Lazarus saw Jake standing at the edge of the glow cast by the burning building. Stefini was wrapped in his arms, cradling a baby and crying uncontrollably into his shoulder.

A sharp tinge of guilt struck Lazarus, a knife blade that slipped smoothly between the ribs and into his heart. He had brought this upon them. It was his fault. He had chosen this inn as their place to rest for the night and thus brought the wrath of the demons down upon the innocent couple. He hurried inside the stable where he collected what little money the group had carried with them. He returned to where Jake and Stefini were standing, stone statues amid all the commotion, and handed them the small bag. They thanked him, of course, though it didn't make him feel any better.

Afterward he returned to the stable and helped the rest of the group prepare their gear. Neslyn remained with Layek, deep in concentration, touching him occasionally to administer healing for his wounds. They had been surprisingly lucky. When Neslyn and her companions had faced three Lurkers in Kylenshar, only two of them had survived. Despite the loss of Devoll, they were truly fortunate.

Little more than an hour after the attack, Lazarus led his dejected companions out from the stables and away from the city. The Twinkling Star collapsed as they rode past, a final farewell and Death's grim promise of a future appointment.

Layek had to be strapped into the saddle with leather cords; he was unconscious from exhaustion and the wounds he had sustained, but Neslyn had been true to her word. He would live. Given time to rest he would be good as new again.

And so they rode, gloomy and disconsolate, casting apprehensive glances into every nook and cranny. Their fragile sense of security had been brutally shattered and their own mortality thrust mockingly in their faces. Each of them knew that at any moment some new terror could come bursting from the darkness and send them to join their fallen comrade. They brooded in silence, raising invisible walls as impenetrable as the darkness that surrounded them, each thinking the worst, bleakly wondering when their time would come.

℘   ℘   ℘

The doppelganger rode amongst the members of the company from Kylenshar, pretending to be brooding over the events of the evening. In truth, it was studying those it was trying to emulate. From beneath the anonymity of its hooded cloak it watched, trying to discern the strengths and weaknesses of those who surrounded it. Eventually it would have to kill them all, those who survived anyway, once they had found the Krullstone.

It would take skill and masterful deception to succeed. These were not fools it was dealing with, not by any stretch. Four Lurkers had only managed to kill one of them, which meant they possessed some measure of skill. Even the Elves had not fared as well in the palace at Kylenshar.

Their leader, Lazarus, would especially have to be watched. He was clever enough. Already he could see the wheels turning behind the mask of his eyes. Clearly something about the events of this night had not settled right with him, and now he was trying to sort out the pieces of the puzzle to make them fit. Sooner or later he would realize the truth.

But by then it would be too late.

ဢ   ဢ   ဢ

Death.

It had always been and would always be for as long as life existed. Nothing was permanent. Eventually all things answered Death's undeniable call. It stalked the lands, an inanimate force that was somehow palpable just the same. It could be merciful or cruel, peaceful or violent, tragic or liberating. It was everywhere and yet nowhere all at once, striking when and where it chose according to its unfathomable design. It was an indiscriminate judge, caring nothing for race or age or social standing, only that those whose time had come were claimed. *Death was the only certainty in life,* Tellyr Laen thought, *as guaranteed as the Western sunset.*

He looked out across the clearing from his concealment in the heavy brush. Death had seen fit to manifest its darker side here, leaving an indelible footprint that only time would wash away.

Bodies littered the ground, perhaps a dozen or more, the remains of a Troll border patrol. The stench of decay was heavy on the air, a shameless beast that refused to hide its ugliness. Broken weapons and gear were strewn about, bearing mute testimony to the futility of their owners' resistance.

The others were there as well, though he could not see them from this vantage point. Six other Elves made up his little scouting party, charged with keeping a constant vigil over the border that separated the Elven kingdom from the Troll nations. It was their duty to patrol the region and investigate any disturbances or violations of their borders.

Tellyr crouched motionless, scanning the area for signs of danger. There were no sounds of nature here, deathly still in the absence of vibrant birdcalls and the buzzing of insects. Even the wind seemed to have abandoned this place in favor of more agreeable climates.

He whistled shrilly, shattering the pervasive silence. The answering call came quickly — once, then twice. All clear.

Swiftly, silently, Tellyr charged into the clearing. Two others, Vayan and Ferros, dashed in from opposite sides, and the three of them met in the center, back to back facing outward. The rest would stay hidden, of course, until they were positive there was no danger lurking under the cover of the thicket that surrounded the open space.

The three stood expectantly for several long minutes. When Tellyr was convinced that there was no lingering threat, he whistled once more, a low warble, and the rest of the Elves emerged from the trees.

While Tellyr, Vayan, and Ferros began to decipher the tracks and signs about the camp, the other four kept a steady watch at the perimeter. They strode back and forth across the area, taking note of footprints, signs of struggle, the disarray of the gear and supplies. After about half an hour they regrouped to share their findings.

"What do you think, Vayan?" Tellyr asked.

"Do you remember Elderwood?"

"All too well," Tellyr muttered.

The Elf was referring to the village they had left two days ago, a tiny border town at the edge of the great Siryth Forest. They had spotted the column of smoke rising from the remains of the village sometime around midday. When they had arrived, they had found a scene more gruesome than anything they had ever witnessed before. Men, women, and children had been slaughtered like animals — some dismembered, some burnt alive within the buildings of the town.

What was most troubling about the whole thing was the evidence that suggested a Troll war party had been the culprit. Lesser trackers perhaps would have fallen for the ruse, but not Tellyr Laen and his companions. Vayan and Ferros were the best trackers in the Elven nation, maybe the best anywhere.

Almost immediately they had discovered the truth. A scrape of claws here, a partial imprint there. The real perpetrators had gone to great lengths to make it look as though the Trolls were responsible; everywhere there were Troll arrows, weapons, footprints, and other signs. But the Elves had seen through the veneer. The most disturbing questions remained unanswered, however; who were the conspirators and why try to incriminate the Trolls?

So in search of answers they had traveled south, following a barely discernable trail left by their unknown quarry. Skilled as they were, the Elves had lost the trail numerous times and had been forced to backtrack to find it again. Their search had brought them here, though it had not ended as they had hoped.

"I've never seen anything like this." Ferros shook his head. "Somehow they have left tracks and signs that identify them as Elves. Weapons, boot tracks, arrow shafts — it all points to us. But there aren't any of our other patrols operating in this region. It's impossible."

"Somebody or something is trying to set us up. They're deliberately trying to provoke war. You know how the Trolls will react," Vayan said.

"Perhaps the Trolls will see through the lie as we have," Tellyr suggested.

Vayan spat. "I doubt it. Whoever struck Elderwood got sloppy. We were lucky to have noticed, and I see none of that carelessness here. The Trolls won't know the difference. Our own tracks are going to be all over this place now, too."

Tellyr sighed in resignation. What were they to do then? Trolls were a notoriously vindictive people, and once they discovered what they would consider unpardonable treachery by the Elves, they would gather their armies and march straight to war. Nothing the Elves said or did would stop them. The tentative peace between them had been shattered as surely as a crystal glass stepped on by a giant.

"Call the others, Ferros. We're leaving."

Tellyr walked briskly back into the trees. He had to get back to

Elysium immediately and warn the king. Vayan, Ferros, and the others melted back into the trees with him in a loose group.

War was coming.

He had only gone a hundred yards into the trees when he heard the sound. It rose up out of the surrounding vegetation in a disembodied crashing of limbs and leaves. It seemed to come from everywhere and nowhere all at once.

Tellyr pivoted, searching for the source of the noise. "Ferros!"

Ferros materialized next to him, Vayan a step behind. The three Elves stood back to back, weapons drawn, waiting for the source of the clamor to reveal itself.

"Where are the others, Vayan?" Tellyr asked.

There was a sudden shout and cries of alarm as the others of the group came face to face with the thing hidden in the trees. A piercing scream shot out, and the thrashing intensified. The three turned about, trying to determine in which direction they were needed.

Then the clamor ended almost as suddenly as it had started. Silence gripped the forest. Tellyr and his remaining companions waited with bated breath for something to appear.

What's out there?

Tellyr's heart pounded. Obviously whatever had slain the Trolls in the clearing had not left the area. Now it was eliminating his party to cover up the truth. Perhaps it had known all along that the Elves were tracking it and had been waiting for them to appear.

"Ferros," Tellyr whispered. "On my signal ..."

He never finished. Something came hurtling out of the underbrush and struck Vayan in the chest. The sturdy Elf went down like a sack of stones. Tellyr and Ferros ducked on reflex, turning as they did so in the direction the missile had come from.

Vayan cried out, and Tellyr turned to check on his fallen companion. He was covered in blood, but to Tellyr's horror none of it belonged to the Elf. A weapon had not struck him as they had thought; rather he had been brought down by what appeared to be half a torso. Bones protruded from the grotesque chunk of flesh, and entrails clung to Vayan's tunic. The Elf brushed disgustedly at it, his face stricken

SCOTT S. COLLEY

with horror.

From their left the assailant emerged, its massive form partially obscured by the trees and brush as it advanced purposefully on them. When it broke free of the undergrowth, Tellyr's breath caught in his throat. He had never seen a creature such as this. He doubted anyone ever had and lived to tell about it. The beast was all muscle and sinew, a juggernaut that exuded power with every measured step. It walked on all fours and looked vaguely like a skinned bear, tendons and ligaments rippling beneath its reddish hide. Yellow eyes gleamed wickedly, and its muzzle drew back to reveal rows of razor sharp teeth dripping with spittle and blood.

It stopped less than twenty yards from the Elves, stood on its hind legs, and sniffed experimentally at the air. It moved ponderously and slowly, almost lackadaisical in its approach. Tellyr was not fooled for one second by the façade. The beast fixed the three crouched figures with its eyes, huffing audibly. Then it emitted an ear splitting mewl, a nerve-racking sound that caused Tellyr to shrink back in revulsion.

The thing dropped back to all fours and started forward slowly, wagging its head lazily from side to side in time with its whimsical advance. Tellyr and his companions raised their weapons and backed away slowly, trying to keep distance between them and the thing.

"Whatever happens," Tellyr whispered to his companions without taking his eyes off of the beast, "one of us must escape to tell the truth of what happened here. The king must be warned. Ferros, you're quickest. Vayan and I will distract it. When I make my move, run for it."

The other two nodded in understanding. Already four of their friends had been struck down by this thing, experienced warriors who would have been more than a match for most anything. There was little doubt that they could not outrun it if they fled. There was also little doubt as to the outcome of any battle between them and this thing. Their only hope was to distract it long enough for one of them to escape.

As they slowly backed away, Vayan and Ferros fanned out to either side, giving enough space between them so that it could not attack one without exposing its flank to the others. The beast growled menacingly but continued its advance, focused on Tellyr.

In one fluid motion, lightning quick, Tellyr whipped out a long knife and hurled it at the beast. The strike was so quick and unexpected that the beast did not even have time to react. The blade buried itself to the hilt in the flesh of its thick neck. It reared up and roared in fury. Clawed paws wrapped clumsily about the offending metal shard and wrenched it free. Blood gushed from the wound, and the thing dropped back and licked lightly at it. It whimpered softly, not in pain but sick delight. Slowly its head swiveled to face Tellyr, anticipation and excitement as clear as day in its eyes.

With frightening speed the beast charged at them, clawed limbs tearing up the earth beneath it as it thundered toward Tellyr. He threw himself aside, barely quick enough to avoid being trampled, and felt a rush of air as claws swept passed. He landed on his side and struck out with his sword, catching the beast a glancing blow.

Tellyr rolled away and jumped back to his feet. The monster had already turned itself around and was coming for him again, jaws split wide. From the corner of his eye he caught a glimpse of Ferros as he darted away from the melee.

Vayan cried out as he counterattacked, rushing to the aid of his leader. The Elf slashed at the beast's flanks, trying to cripple it. Enraged, the thing stood on its hind legs and swatted Vayan with one great paw, sending him tumbling away.

Tellyr charged in at its exposed belly, slashing once, twice, three times, almost quicker than the eye could follow. The beast roared and lashed out as Tellyr darted back. He was too slow this time. Knife-edged claws ripped through his tunic and deep into the flesh of his arm and chest. He fell to his knees, pain rushing through his body. It loomed over him, moving in for the finish.

Still dazed and trying to recover, Tellyr would have been dead if not for Vayan. The brave Elf reappeared from the trees and flung himself at the beast. He hacked and stabbed relentlessly at it, his bloodied face set in grim determination. The creature turned to face him, unfazed by this new assault. Vayan dodged and weaved, attacking when he found an opening. Tellyr fought his way to his feet, leaning on his sword for support. Vayan tripped and went down, and the monster instantly set upon him. He cried out in pain as its claws dug into him, and he struggled wildly to break free.

Tellyr ignored the dizziness that clouded his vision and bounded to rescue his friend. With every ounce of strength he possessed, he brought his sword down, slicing through the tough hide and striking bone with jarring force. Instantly he jumped up onto the beast's back, reaching down for the knife in his boot.

The monster ignored the attack and continued to tear at the Elf it had pinned beneath it, crushing Vayan with its weight even as its claws ripped into him. Tellyr screamed in fury, stabbing at the creature's neck with his knife, desperate to kill it and save his friend. Vayan ceased to struggle, and the life faded from his eyes, his body broken and shredded.

Turning its attention to the attacker on its back, the beast roared and shook itself violently, throwing Tellyr to the ground. Spots danced before his eyes as he struggled to stand, his fingers still clutching the knife. He brandished it before him, knowing that the battle was already over. He was no match for this thing.

Be swift, Ferros, he thought as he lost his footing and dropped to his knees. *It falls to you now.* The beast lumbered toward him, having removed Tellyr's sword from its back, knowing that the Elf could not fight it anymore.

Tellyr looked up, trying to focus his eyes. *Come, thing. Finish it. Come see what I have for you.* He couldn't win this fight, he knew, but maybe he could get even.

The creature came up to him, leaned in close. Tellyr could smell the foulness of its breath. But the deathblow did not come as he expected. Instead, the beast wrapped him up in its massive arms, cradling him as a mother might a child. It lifted him off the ground, slowly standing up to its full height. Tellyr looked into its eyes. They shined gleefully with malice.

Then it began to squeeze. He felt the air slip from his lungs, bones beginning to crack. Tellyr felt the blackness rising within him.

Soon it would be over. He struggled. Somehow he slipped his arm that still held the knife free. With a final surge of anger he thrust the knife into the beast's eye.

It shrieked in pain and shook its head violently, trying to dislodge the killing blade. Furiously it flung him away and reached up to grasp at the knife. Tellyr crashed into a nearby tree and fell to the ground, limp and broken. Before sight failed him, he saw with great satisfaction as the monstrous thing fell lifelessly to the ground. His breathing slowed.

Far in the distance he heard Ferros' terrified scream.

Then everything faded into blackness.

Once again Grubbash found himself staring into space from the parapets of Grimknoll. He almost never went into the halls below anymore. Serathes and his minions had all but taken over his home and made it their own. The sanctuary had lost its entire past splendor and sacredness since the demons had moved in.

Now it was a rancid cesspool of death and putrefaction. Half-rotten corpses, bones, and random body parts littered the hall. The hallowed ornaments and decorations had been defiled and all but erased, replaced by effigies of death and torture more grisly than most mortals could bear to look at for more than a split second.

Every second that passed magnified his hatred of them. He despised them so deeply that it nearly drove him mad. He hated them for the lack of respect and dignity with which they treated his people and, most of all, himself. He knew now that they had no intention of abandoning this world once the Orcs had fulfilled their goals. He knew now that they had intended to use the Orcs for their own dark purposes from the beginning, to ride on the backs of a great and powerful people to victory and glory.

He would have his day he reminded himself whenever his hate threatened to consume him. Their power would be his, as it rightfully should be. It should have been his to begin with. These fools hadn't the first clue what to do with such power. They wasted their time toying with lives and worlds without ever realizing they could just reach out and take it. They were unfit to command such power.

There was a faint rumbling from far below, an ever so slight vibration of the stone and mortar that made up his keep. That would be the Daemon Lords once again forcing a rift in the very fabric of space and time to allow more of their brothers into this world. At least he had a use for them. The demons would march side by side with the Orcs, shock troops and fodder for his glorious crusade to claim what was rightfully his.

The Goblins were already unknowingly working for him, launching a new offensive at the Dwarves. They had even succeeded in breaching the fortress at Adar Nin. One day he would have to hear how they managed that. Adar Nin was said to be impenetrable by even the greatest army. The Elves and the Trolls were being tricked into war with each other, though they didn't yet know it. The Daemon Lords had proven true to their word — a rare occurrence — and managed to incite the Trolls' wrath against the Elves.

There would be no one to come to the aid of the pathetic humans in Illendale. His spy would have successfully infiltrated the party sent by their queen to recover the Krullstone by now, and like it or not, the humans would help him achieve his goal.

Ironic, he thought.

The very thing that they sought to save them and the very people they had sent to champion them would only serve him in the end.

XIII THE THORN WITHIN

THE SUN ROSE out of the eastern sky, a gradual changing of the firmament from black to deep purple to brilliant shades of orange and red when the fiery disk finally crested the horizon. Morning dew glittered on the long grasses of the Solaris Plain, thousands of tiny diamonds reflecting the early light and scattering it across the flats in a dazzling array. The clouds that had obscured the sky for days had finally broken apart and drifted away. The songs of birds filled the air in a peaceful symphony, and the sodden earth began to slowly dry. The day grew warm as the sun dragged across the blue sky.

The group of travelers from Kylenshar worked their way steadily across the plains, hunched over their mounts in exhaustion. They had ridden all night in an effort to put some distance between themselves and the demons they knew now without a doubt were hunting them, perhaps to put some distance between them and the apparition of their fears as well.

Lazarus called a halt late in the morning so that they could rest. The battle with the Lurkers had left them battered and worn. Layek had slept the night through passed out on his horse, still weak from his ordeal. Neslyn had worked a miracle in healing his wounds, but it was amazing that he had clung to life until she could save him; a lesser man would not have lasted half as long.

Lazarus volunteered to take the first watch while the others slept, and no one argued. The others rolled themselves into their cloaks and were asleep within minutes. He picked a spot among a patch of wildflowers a short distance from the others and slumped wearily to the ground.

He was dead tired, harrowed by the events of the previous evening, and it was all he could do to stay awake, yet he was grateful for the time alone. He let his mind wander for a time, content for the moment to take in the sounds and sweet fragrances of nature.

All too soon, though, reality came barging back to the forefront of his thoughts.

He was disturbed by the relative ease with which the demons had seemed to catch up to them. How had they known where to find them? The obvious answer was that his attempts at secrecy had failed. The demons had somehow followed them across the valley from Kylenshar and taken advantage of their vulnerability at the inn, or they had known their plan all along and had simply been lying in wait. The latter suggested that there could be a spy among those with whom he traveled or someone privy to the knowledge of their expedition in Kylenshar. He found it hard to believe that they had been followed across the plains to Pilban, but then again several of them had felt the presence of an unseen pursuer. On the other hand, if the demons knew of the Krullstone and their mission to recover it, they could simply wait for Lazarus and his company anywhere along the way.

If indeed there was a spy among them, he would have to be extremely vigilant. It also made sense that instead of trying to prevent them from recovering the stone, the demons would try to take it for themselves. Perhaps they had infiltrated his group and were simply biding their time until the Krullstone had been found, at which point the spy could attempt to steal it. But then why send the Lurkers? It occurred to him suddenly that the attack might have been nothing more than a diversion. If not to divert their attention, why not send enough demons to finish them all off?

He pondered further the strange events surrounding the attack in Pilban. Who had killed the Lurkers behind the inn and why? Azrael had not known of them. And who had been killed by the kitchen? The body had been unrecognizable, but it could not have been anyone within their group as they had all been accounted for. Something about the whole situation bothered him. Something didn't fit right. Some inner voice tugged at him, warned him that he had overlooked something, but what it was he couldn't quite put his finger on.

Not that it mattered anyway, he reminded himself, his mind weary of sifting through the quandary he was in. Spy or not, hunted or not, they must continue their search for the Krullstone. It was the only hope they had, and somehow they must overcome the dark forces set against them, or everything was lost. They would have to face whatever surprises came as they went. It would have been nice if everything could be as clear-cut as night and day, though.

Then his mind began to wander again, away from the things that puzzled and vexed him. He reflected briefly on the loss of Devoll. He hated losing men. Those under his command were his responsibility. It was his duty to keep them from harm, as much as was possible in their line of work, and not spend their lives lightly. Though outwardly he mourned the loss of a good soldier, deep down inside Lazarus was secretly thankful that it had been Devoll and not one of his brothers. It frustrated him that it should be so, that he should wish some die over others, and yet the feeling seemed somehow fitting.

He had nearly lost his best friend, an event that had never happened before and had never troubled his mind. Somehow he had felt that Layek would always be there, that he was in some way immune to Death's inevitable call. He had never worried for his friend before; Layek had never needed him to. He thought it strange and ironic that the one he had thought safe from harm had suffered the worst. Vinson and Aldric, whom he had watched over and protected his whole life, had escaped the attack with barely a scratch on them. Layek, who had never needed anyone to look after him, had very nearly lost his life. He realized how much his friend meant to him now, and the thought of losing him caused a sharp pain in his chest.

He was deeply grateful to Neslyn for saving his life. Lazarus turned his head to look at where the Elf lay sleeping. He watched the rise and fall of her chest as she breathed. She was an extraordinary woman; her physical beauty, while exceptional in every way, was but a pale reflection of the beauty within. She was kind and gentle, caring and compassionate, a warm presence that soothed and calmed. Yet there was an edge to her sharper than any blade; Neslyn was not someone to be crossed.

He marveled at her for only a few moments, forcing his affections for her aside as he tried to impose some order on his thoughts. He cast aside his fears for his friends as well, as there was little he could do at the moment to insure their safety. Instead he let himself drift on the sweet fragrances of wildflowers and the sounds of birdsong. He let the warmth of the day wrap around him like a blanket and take him in, setting him adrift on a sea of peace. Lazarus took in the sights and sounds of the golden fields surrounding him and felt the tension within slowly melt away. Muscles relaxed, his mind wandered freely, and for at least a little while all his worries were forgotten.

His eyes grew heavy with sleep, and he was having difficulty keeping them open when he heard footsteps approaching. He looked up, suddenly wary, and breathed a deep sigh of relief when he saw it was only Vinson.

"Maybe you should get some sleep," his brother said, seating himself on the ground next to him. "You look like hell."

"Why aren't you asleep?" Lazarus glanced at the sky. Puffs of white cloud drifted past lazily. "Your night was as rough as mine."

"I couldn't. I've been thinking about this whole business, been thinking about it since we left Kylenshar actually."

"What's on your mind, Vinny?" Lazarus asked.

Vinson shifted to get comfortable. "I was thinking about how you said it would be my responsibility to use the Krullstone against the demons, if we even manage to recover it. The whole reason we are going after it is to keep that Orc sorcerer from laying his hands on it. We have to stop him because if he uses it against the demons, it will make him powerful beyond reckoning."

"That's right. He will absorb the power of the Daemon Lords and make it his own. If that happens, he will be invincible."

"Right." Vinson didn't say anything more; instead he reached down and tugged free a cluster of blue flowers from the earth. He began pulling the petals off one by one.

"What is it that's bothering you, brother?"

"Won't the same thing happen to me if I use the Krullstone? Won't the power of the Daemon Lords be absorbed into me?" he finally asked, a cheerless tone creeping into his voice.

Lazarus had not considered this; indeed it had never even crossed his mind. What if? Vinson was right, of course. Logically, the same thing would happen to him if he employed the Krullstone against the Daemon Lords. But that couldn't be right; otherwise why would Melynda charge Vinson with the Krullstone's use? Unless she hadn't seen it in her visions. *Was it possible,* Lazarus asked himself silently, *that in all her numinous wisdom she had not realized that Vinson would be subject to the same laws and effects of the Krullstone as Grimvisage?*

"I hadn't thought of that," Lazarus said weakly. He felt the woe rise within, the now familiar chains wrapping about him, threatening to drag him down into nothingness. He also felt the dark apparitions of his fears rise against the barriers he had momentarily put in place to block them out.

"I can't stop thinking about it," Vinson replied. "I'm not sure I'm able to pay the price that is demanded of me."

"Melynda said, when she first revealed the vision to me, that you must be the one to wield the stone." Lazarus turned to face his brother, placing his hand on the other's shoulder to comfort him. "Knowing the ways of magic gives you a link to the stone that Aldric and I do not have. Perhaps that makes you better prepared to resist the stone's effects. Aldric or myself would likely succumb to the power of the stone and become that which we sought to destroy. If I thought for one moment that you would be harmed by the stone's use, I would not have agreed to let you go in search of it."

"I hope Melynda is right," he said, sounding unconvinced but noticeably relieved.

"I'll be right there by your side. To the end. Aldric as well. We began this journey together, and we'll finish it together."

They sat in silence for a while just enjoying the peaceful

environment that enveloped them.

Vinson spoke suddenly. "Do you ever wish that you had chosen a different life? If you had it all to do over again, would you?"

Lazarus thought for a moment. "No. I think I would choose the same. People make the choice that's right for them when the time comes. I think I chose a life that fits me better than any other. Here, I make a difference. I guess here is where I feel I do the most good."

"I'm not sure. Sometimes I think I would have been happier if I had done something else with my life," Vinson said sadly.

"You only say that because of the mess we're in now. I remember you were happy with your life before all this began."

"You're right. I guess I'm just feeling pressured by all these expectations being placed on us. It happened so fast I didn't really have time to think about it, but now I'm having second thoughts."

"Don't worry, brother. Everything is going to be just fine. You wait and see. In the meantime don't let the weight of the world crush you underneath. We do the best we can when the time comes; leave it at that."

"Thank you, Laz."

"That's what brothers are for." Lazarus brushed at his hair with a hand. "We look out for each other. You going to get some sleep now?"

"No," Vinson said. "I'd rather stay up for awhile, take in the sights. You go. You look like you need it more than I do anyway."

"Suit yourself." Lazarus pushed himself up, a wave of fatigue washing through him. He yawned and stretched, and with a final nod to Vinson he trudged off wearily to where the others lay sleeping still. He chose his spot on a bed of tall grasses and rolled into his cloak. Within seconds he was sound asleep.

For the first time since Melynda had revealed her vision to him, Lazarus slept soundly, undisturbed by the haunted dreams that had plagued him. It was with great reluctance and heavy regret that he opened his eyes when a hand shook him awake in what seemed like only moments after he had closed them. He blinked several times, fighting to keep his eyes open in the stark brightness of the afternoon. When at last he could see clearly, he looked up to find Emeris Dallen standing over him.

"You're going to want to see this," he said, his voice sonorous and rough. Without waiting for a reply he straightened and walked away.

Lazarus came fully awake and threw off his cloak, curious now as to what was happening. For a moment he was fearful that perhaps they had come under attack, but there were no signs of alarm or disorder. He rose hurriedly and walked briskly over to where the others were standing huddled in a tight circle. There he found, to his complete surprise and relief, that Layek was awake.

Aurora Skall was checking him over, making sure that his wounds were healing properly and that there were no residual effects. Layek was insisting vehemently that he was perfectly fine and that he did not need any looking after. The big man stood, a little shaky, but otherwise he seemed okay.

Lazarus ran up to him and embraced him so forcefully that he nearly knocked his friend over. "Layek, you blockheaded mule! It's a good thing you're alive, or I'd have to kill you!" Lazarus' grin spread from ear to ear as he released his friend and stepped back.

"Easy there, tiger," Layek chuckled. "It takes more than a few scratches to bring me down." He tested his limbs gingerly and took a few steps around to make sure everything was in order before sitting back down.

"He's still a little weak," Aurora said, "from loss of blood and the healing. It should pass in a day or so as long as he gets his rest and doesn't overexert himself."

"Nonsense," Layek cried. "I'm as good as new."

"Nevertheless, you're going to take it easy for the next couple of days. Don't argue. It's done." Lazarus waved away the protest that was forming on Layek's lips.

Understandably his friend didn't want to be left out or given special treatment, but Lazarus needed him fully healed and rested. If they were forced to stand and fight again, he needed everyone in good condition and capable of defending themselves. As much as he wished he could, he could not watch after everyone. He had to set priorities, and right now his brothers had to be at the top of the list.

"It's good to have you back, Layek," Lazarus said.

"It's good to be back," Layek grumbled. "Anyway, somebody has to be here to make sure you lace up your boots right, or you might trip and hurt yourself."

Lazarus couldn't help but chuckle.

They packed up their gear, most of which had been saved from the fire simply because it had been left in the stables, and headed out. Small streams crossed their path frequently, and the sun burned down on them from high up in the blue sky. By the time they stopped for a late lunch, the tufts of white cloud had disappeared completely. Tensions eased and spirits rose even though their pace was quick, as Lazarus thought it was best to put as much distance between them and Pilban as was possible. Jokes and stories were shared between the travelers, and all enjoyed the casual atmosphere.

They moved across the endless expanse of grassland easily and made good time. They stopped for the evening in a copse of old walnut trees, the limbs forming a canopy over them that offered only small glimpses of the clear night sky overhead. A small creek ran nearby, lapping and bubbling noisily over rocks on its way through the plains. Lazarus allowed a fire, and they ate a delicious meal of hot stew and bread.

After they had eaten and cleaned up, a watch was set, and those remaining lounged around the small fire, sharing thoughts and feelings, some smoking pipes of tobacco leaf. Eyes grew heavy, and yawns dominated the conversation after a time, and the members of the company from Kylenshar began to turn themselves into their bedrolls to sleep.

Lazarus, however, was averse to sleep just yet. It had been such a nice day that he was reluctant to let it go. He stood and walked out of the grove, breathing the cool night air, fresh and clean. A delicate breeze ruffled his hair, and he lifted his head to take it in. He looked up into the dark sky where a whole host of stars winked down at him. He walked for a distance, looking up into the heavens and enjoying the calm in general.

That's when he bumped into Vinson. He hadn't even seen his brother leave, and he was so preoccupied that he stumbled over him and nearly fell face first into the grass.

"Out for a stroll, brother?" Vinson rubbed at the shoulder Lazarus had inadvertently thumped with his knee.

"I didn't see you there," Lazarus said apologetically. "Sorry."

"It's okay. I just came out here to look at the stars. It seems like ages since the last time I saw them."

"Ironic how you don't appreciate the little pleasures in life until they're taken away from you, isn't it?"

Footsteps approached from the direction of their camp, and both turned to see who had come to join them or perhaps just to make sure they didn't get run over.

"What's going on out here?" Aldric's voice wafted out of the shadows as he materialized before them. "Midnight rendezvous?"

"Just taking a few moments to enjoy Nature's mysterious beauty," Lazarus replied.

"And trying not to get trampled in the process," Vinson added lightheartedly.

"Mind if I join you?" Aldric asked. "Couldn't sleep myself so I thought I'd come get some fresh air."

"Go right ahead; it's a big sky. There's plenty for all of us," Lazarus said as he lowered himself next to Vinson. Aldric followed him down.

They sat in silence for a while, savoring the ambience. Insects buzzed and clicked, the only noise to disturb the profound silence that blanketed the plains. The moon hung high in the sky, full and bright, its silvery glow bathing the land and casting everything in a surrealistic light.

"It's amazing how incredibly huge the universe is," Aldric said suddenly. "It makes you feel so small and unimportant."

"That's a depressing thought, Aldric," Vinson replied. "I think that every person on this world was put here for a specific purpose. Each of us has a goal in life we were destined to achieve; each has his own place in the tapestry that Fate weaves. Without everyone to do their part in life, the balance of the universe would be thrown off, and our world would fall apart."

"So you're saying that none of us really has a choice what happens to us in life; it's all predetermined by some greater force beyond our understanding?" Lazarus asked.

"In the larger sense, yes. All living things possess free will, and yet by exercising their freedom of choice they always choose what Fate has already decided."

"That's quite the logical quandary," Aldric mused.

Once again silence fell between the three brothers. They sat in peace, pondering whatever crossed their minds and enjoying their surroundings and each other's company.

Finally, Lazarus broke the silence. "There's something I have to tell you guys. Something I have kept hidden from you since we left Kylenshar."

Aldric and Vinson cocked their heads toward him, arching their eyebrows questioningly.

"You remember how I explained Melynda's vision to you? I wasn't completely honest. I left something out. Something important."

"Go on, let us have it," Vinson urged him anxiously. "Whatever it is, it can't be that bad."

Lazarus took a deep breath and let it out slowly. "According to the vision, both of you will die in a battle against the Orcs. If this happens, the Orcs will win."

Lazarus' brothers faced him, unspeaking for several minutes, hard-faced and taut. Then Vinson spoke. "Why didn't you tell us before? Why hide it this whole time?"

"I'm surprised you let us come at all," Aldric huffed. "We should be back in Kylenshar under lock and key."

Lazarus smiled in spite of himself. "I had no choice. Only the two of you together can find the Krullstone. As for not telling you, I didn't want you guys to become fatalistic. I was afraid you would be convinced that your fate had already been sealed."

"It's only a vision, Laz. It's not set in stone."

"I know, Vinny," Lazarus said, sounding unconvinced. "I should have trusted you. It's just that you are the only family I've got. Without the two of you I have nothing."

"We'll just have to be extra careful," Aldric added. "Besides, I'd be more worried about the demons than the Orcs. They seem to be the ones who always manage to find us."

"Speaking of which," Vinson said brusquely, "how do they manage to keep finding us?"

"Well, I've been thinking about that a lot. I can think of only three reasons why. The demons either followed us from Kylenshar, they could have a spy within the High Council, or there is a spy among us. The first possibility is highly unlikely given our caution and the weather conditions. The second and third scenarios are equally as likely as they are possible."

"But how would they know we would stop in Pilban?" Aldric asked.

"And why not send enough demons to be absolutely sure we did not survive the attack?" Vinson pointed out.

"Exactly. I think that there is a spy among us. That would explain how the demons knew where to find us and why they didn't make sure we all died in Pilban. Think about it," Lazarus said emphatically. "Why keep us from claiming the Krullstone when they could have it for themselves? The demons thrive on destruction and chaos and covet only power. If they think we can find it, why not wait until we have it and then take it from us?"

"Right," Vinson replied. "They would need someone on the inside to keep an eye on us."

"Why try to kill us then?" Aldric asked.

"Maybe they weren't trying to kill all of us. It could have been a diversion to keep our attention, give us something to focus on rather than what's right in front of us. Something we can see and fight so we don't consider what we can't." Lazarus leaned back, propping himself up on his elbows.

Vinson rubbed wearily at his eyes. "So who is it? Who's the spy?"

"I wish I knew," Lazarus replied. "I can't seem to reason that out. It could be anyone."

"Not one of us," Aldric said. "We can be sure of that."

"Of course, not," Vinson assured him. "But there are still ten others in this group who could have betrayed us."

"Not anymore," Lazarus said darkly. "Devoll's dead. That makes nine."

"So who?" Vinson posed the question again. "How do we find out which one of us is not who he claims to be?"

"I'm afraid we'll have to wait and see," Lazarus sighed. "We need to be extremely vigilant and attentive. Sooner or later our traitor will make a mistake, and then we'll have him."

"If there is one at all," Aldric said. He raised his hands to ward off the argument forming on Vinson's lips. "I'm not saying there isn't a spy, only that there might not be. All we have at this point is speculation. Until there is definitive proof of betrayal, we should keep this between ourselves."

"Agreed," Lazarus said. "We need to wait and see what happens. All things come to those who wait."

"Hopefully it's not too late for us when that time comes." There was no doubt in Vinson's mind.

"Well, we'd best get some sleep. We have a long journey ahead of us, and we'll need our strength if we are to survive," Lazarus said as he stood and turned toward the camp and their sleeping comrades.

"Laz," Vinson called after him. Lazarus halted. "You were right to tell us."

"Goodnight, Vinny. Aldric. Watch yourselves in the coming days. Until this is all over, none of us is safe."

ৎ   ৎ   ৎ

In the morning the little company from Kylenshar awoke sleepy-eyed to a magnificent golden sunrise and a steadily warming day. Drops of dew glistened on leaves and blades of grass. Branches swayed gently in the breeze, and the sweet fragrances of wildflowers filled the air.

Lazarus and his companions rose at dawn and after gathering up their gear, set out across the endless plains. They stopped frequently to water and rest the horses, keeping them fresh in case they were forced to press the mounts. In reality, the breaks were as much for the travelers as they were for their beasts of burden. It grew warmer as the sun climbed into the sky, warm enough that they began to shed their heavy cloaks. They had been prepared for cooler weather, expecting that Winter's icy touch would be their biggest concern.

Progress was slow but steady, and when night finally fell, they gratefully accepted the respite. The air cooled as the dark deepened around them, and they reveled in the evening calm. Mihan and Marcell found them a campsite near a grove of ash with a small stream that emptied into a still pond, providing them with fresh water. They cooked and ate a delicious stew of beef and vegetables prepared by Neslyn and Aurora Skall. The horses and pack animals were tethered near the stream where they could graze on the soft grasses that covered the ground that surrounded it. Lots were drawn, and a watch was set for the remainder of the night. They picked out their spots among the soft grasses and rolled themselves into their blankets. Within moments, all were sound asleep.

Lazarus was roused in the morning by a strong hand gripping his shoulder and shaking him vigorously. "What is it?" he asked irritably. He rolled onto his back and looked up through sleepy eyes to see Layek staring down at him. "Layek! You can't find a better way to wake up people?"

"Sorry, Laz," he said with a sly grin. "It's important. Something's happened."

Lazarus rose sluggishly, trying to rub the sleep from his eyes. He wasn't sure how it was possible, but he felt more tired now than before he had gone to sleep. The sun had not risen yet, and the camp was bathed in a deep purplish shadow. He stumbled about for a minute before he gained his bearings and, reaching down to grab his sword, followed after Layek.

Layek led him toward the stream where the horses had been tethered the night before. At first everything seemed ordinary. He brushed at his eyes again, attempting futilely to wake himself up.

"Layek, what's the meaning of all this? Is this some kind of ..." Lazarus trailed off as he realized something was missing. "Layek, where are the horses?"

"Your guess is as good as mine. Zafer noticed it earlier this morning and came straight to me. No one else knows yet."

Lazarus kneeled to the ground, studying. He made his way over to the severed tethering lines and grasped them in his hand. "These lines weren't cut. It looks like they snapped under stress. The horses ran off in that direction." He pointed south. "Something scared them enough to break the lines. Whatever caused them to bolt like that should have wakened us all. It makes no sense."

"You're telling me!" Layek waved his hands in exasperation. "Weird stuff has been going on since Kylenshar. It seems to have become a way of life for us."

"Who was on watch last night?"

"Emeris Dallen, Mihan, Marcell, and Zafer. In that order. You think one of them had something to do with it?"

"I'm not sure. Under normal circumstances I would say yes, but how is it that none of us heard?" Lazarus shook his head in confusion.

Layek shrugged. "I don't know. Like I said, weird stuff."

"Wake the others. Have Corsin take Mihan and Marcell with him and go find our horses."

Layek marched off to fill his request, leaving Lazarus in thought. It made no sense, of course; there was no way the horses could have been frightened enough to break their tethering lines without waking at least one of them. Yet it had happened. Maybe one of those on watch was the culprit, but what could they have done to scare the horses that badly?

In any case, the horses must be found. Without the horses to carry them they would have to cross the plains by foot. That would slow them down by a week at least. They would have to carry their gear and supplies as well, much of which would have to be left behind. The return trip would be very difficult in that case.

Layek returned shortly with Corsin, followed by everybody else. They stared wide-eyed for several moments, and then everyone began talking at once. Lazarus raised his hands in an effort to silence them. When at last he succeeded, he set Corsin to the task of tracking down their horses.

Joseph Corsin studied the tracks around the stream for several minutes and then took Mihan and Marcell with him southward to find their mounts. The rest stayed behind, discussing the possible explanations for what was happening. Lazarus questioned Zafer and Emeris Dallen about their shifts on watch, attempting to discover the truth of what happened during the night. Both explained to him that everything was normal, that there had been no signs of an intruder, and that neither had witnessed anything out of the ordinary. Corsin returned an hour later, most of the horses in tow, and went directly to Lazarus.

"Where are the packhorses?" Lazarus asked, immediately recognizing which horses were missing.

"I found these grazing in a field about two miles south of here. I followed the tracks of the others even further south until I found their bodies in a wash. They have been destroyed; there was no sign of what killed them or why they bolted in the first place."

Lazarus proceeded to question Mihan and Marcell but learned nothing from them. According to the two soldiers, everything had been as it should. It was growing late in the morning, and anxious to be underway again, he set his companions to preparing the morning meal and gathering up their gear. He took his brothers and Layek aside so that they could discuss the events in private.

"This is not a good sign," he said when they were out of earshot of the rest of the party. "Without those pack horses we won't be able to carry all of our supplies. There won't be enough food for the return trip."

"I think that's the idea," Aldric scoffed. "The saboteur doesn't want us equipped to make it back."

"Maybe we can ration our stores to last," Layek suggested hopefully.

"I'm afraid that won't be enough. But we'll have to anyway. Even more disturbing is how no one realized what was happening."

"Maybe our food was drugged," Layek offered. "That could have put us all out long enough for the traitor to scare off the horses."

"What about the watch, though?" Vinson asked. "They say that they were wide awake and alert."

"Then one of them is lying," Layek growled. "One of them must know something."

"There's something else. It could have been magic, Laz. A sleep spell would explain how nobody was wakened. It's the only explanation for why we didn't hear anything," Vinson said seriously.

"There are only four in this camp capable of wielding magic," Aldric pointed out. "Azrael, Aurora Skall, Neslyn, and you, Vinny."

"None of them were on watch last night," Lazarus replied.

"Of course, not," Layek spat. "If they weren't on watch, they wouldn't be suspected. It makes perfect sense."

Lazarus considered this for a moment. "Which one was it, though? There's no evidence that anyone left the camp last night. No tracks, nothing."

"That's easy enough to hide," Layek said. "Especially if you're a sorcerer."

"That leaves us three possibilities then since we know Vinny didn't do it." Aldric looked at them each in turn. "How do we know which it was?"

"That's easy, too," Layek continued. "Take what we know. We know it wasn't Vinny but another of our mages. So who could be a spy out of the three remaining? Certainly not an old friend, someone we've known for years and have trusted with our lives before."

"You mean Azrael. Of course, not him either," Vinson affirmed.

"And Aurora Skall, too," Layek reminded them. "She has been with us for a long time. That only leaves one other person. Neslyn Alluris."

"Don't forget that she saved your life, Layek," Lazarus said angrily. "You wouldn't be here were it not for her."

"Perhaps. Think about it. We don't know anything about those two Elves. They showed up under peculiar circumstances, and strange things have been happening since they joined us. The attacks in Kylenshar, the Lurkers in Pilban, and now the missing horses. It seems clear as day to me," Layek said.

"It makes perfect sense," Vinson agreed, placing a hand on Lazarus' shoulder to comfort him. "I know you have feelings for this Elf woman but don't let them stand between you and the truth."

"This is absurd!" Lazarus lost his temper, violently shaking off Vinson's hand. "It's nothing more than a coincidence. She saved your life, Layek. It could as easily have been Vinny or Azrael as her."

"You are defending her because you're infatuated with her!" Layek shouted. "You would place suspicion on your own brother rather than see that this woman has intentionally deceived you. She's playing you for a fool and turning you against us! Maybe she's not even really an Elf!"

"Shut up! Don't you dare say another word!" Lazarus shouted back, balling his fists and taking a menacing step forward.

"Easy, Laz." Aldric jumped between the two. "There's no need to get violent. Without some proof we can't be sure of anything, but you cannot doubt the validity of Layek's argument, Laz. It does make some sense."

"You're a bunch of fools," Lazarus breathed spitefully. He turned his back to them and stalked off, leaving them to stare after him uncertainly.

XIV TIES THAT BIND

LAZARUS KEPT HIS distance from his brothers and Layek after their conversation. The others did not know what had happened between them but could sense that something was wrong. They carefully avoided each other, Lazarus especially, who had grown short-tempered and volatile.

The group ate breakfast in silence. It was obvious from the start that without their pack animals they would have to leave much of the supplies behind. Everything that was not absolutely essential to their survival had to be dumped. Foodstuffs were sorted and packed, carefully rationed to last as long as possible. The rest was bundled together and stashed in a hollow log near the pond so that they could recover it on the return journey.

Nearing midday they finally set out across the plains, the sun out in full force warming the plains just enough for them to forego the use of their heavy travel cloaks. Browning leaves rattled and blew in the light breeze.

No one spoke. There was a sense that the bonds between them had grown strained and that even the slightest agitation would snap them completely. They spread out along their chosen path, keeping as much distance between each other as they could without separating entirely.

Each was left to his own thoughts, and for most their minds were occupied with pondering the circumstances of their journey or when the next surprise would jump out at them unexpectedly from the shadows. For Lazarus Arkenstone, thoughts were of little except the Elven princess he had defended against his best friend and only family.

He still couldn't understand why he had felt so enraged at the possibility that she was not who she claimed to be. He barely knew this girl, and at least a few of the suggestions made by Layek and Vinson had some logic behind them. When he thought about it, it made perfect sense. And yet he could not bring himself to believe that she was not being honest with him. There was a real connection there, a bond that defied explanation or reason. He could see it in her eyes when he looked at her, feel it in the conviction of her words. She was as forthcoming and candid as anyone he had ever known, as straight as an arrow in her faith and solid as a rock in her confidence.

He had spent some time with her along their journey but barely enough to know as much as he should to warrant the feelings he felt blossoming within him. In fact, with all that had happened to them since they left Kylenshar, he should be highly suspicious of her. He just couldn't help himself. The more he looked at her, the more the feeling grew. Somewhere deep inside Lazarus could sense that somehow this woman was tied to him, that Fate had placed her in his life and that she was meant for him.

So as they rode across the seemingly endless fields of golden grass, Lazarus battled back and forth across the landscape of his mind, fighting in turns his growing attraction for Neslyn and the logical sense that demanded caution.

Midday came and went, melting into twilight as the group continued its trek westward. They made camp for the night, and still Lazarus was no closer to resolving his conflict of interest. There was little talk as they mechanically executed their evening ritual. Lazarus took the second watch, and even though he had plenty of time to sleep, he lay awake into the early morning hours.

The following day was much the same, riding through the ever-growing heat, trying to hold on to his rationality. The hours dragged on, and time seemed to grind to a halt for Lazarus. There was no distinction between morning and afternoon, the phases of the day blending into an infinite parade of grasslands, streams, and the occasional grove of barren trees or thicket of scrub brush.

For days he continued on like that with nothing to break through the monotony of his journey. He felt immensely alone despite the company of those with whom he rode, and nothing could seem to break through the shell that had formed around him. On the horizon he could see the growing mass of ridgelines and peaks that made up the eastern end of the Cloudspire Mountains, and he took comfort in knowing that they were nearing their destination. A change of scenery would do him good.

Then things began to take a turn for the better. Lazarus and his companions began to break through the barriers that had sprung up between them in the previous days. Tensions eased, and moods improved. At one point Lazarus maneuvered his horse over to Layek.

"I'm sorry for the way I acted the other day," Lazarus apologized. "I overreacted."

"It's okay," his friend replied. "We're all under a lot of stress, and it's easy to lose your temper. I said some things that I probably shouldn't have said as well."

"It's amazing how you can manage to say the wrong thing even when you haven't been drinking," Lazarus jested, smiling openly.

"Yeah, my brain doesn't function right when I don't get my standard ration of ale. It's you I'm worried about, though." Layek looked at him sideways. "Just you make sure that new girlfriend of yours doesn't get you into trouble."

"She's not my girlfriend, and you know it."

"You defend her like you're already married." Layek couldn't help but smile.

"I guess we better keep an eye on each other then," Lazarus suggested seriously. "You make sure my choice in women is up to par, and I'll make sure you don't die from lack of drink."

"Deal!" Layek laughed and clapped him on the back cheerily. "You should go talk to Vinny, too. You weren't very nice to him either."

"I will … I told him and Aldric about the rest of the vision, you know."

"Really? I didn't think you would ever get around to it. Good for you, Laz. They had a right to know the truth."

Lazarus made his way over to where Vinson was riding, far off to the right of the rest of the group, lost in some private daydream. Lazarus rode casually up to his brother as though nothing were amiss between them. His brother greeted him with a nod.

"Hello, Vinny," he said simply. "Nice day, isn't it?"

"What's on your mind, Laz?" he asked tersely. "Don't beat around the bush."

"I wanted to apologize for my rudeness a couple of days ago; I was out of line. I didn't mean to suggest that you would betray us."

"But you did, Laz. You all but accused me of being the traitor."

"I know. I am sorry. It wasn't my intention."

"Now is the time when we have to be strong, unified. You would throw that unity away for a woman you barely know and as far as we know could easily be the enemy among us." Vinson looked at him crossly. "I thought blood was thicker than that."

"You're absolutely right, Vinny. And under normal circumstances I would agree with you and Layek that she is likely the one enemy among us. But there is something about her, some magnetism that I cannot explain. She is not the traitor, Vinny. I can feel it in my heart. I hope that you can understand that. I hope you will accept my apology." Lazarus lowered his head. "I really am sorry."

"Of course, I forgive you. I just wanted you to understand that my agreement with Layek the other day was based purely on solid logic. There isn't any proof so there can be no permanent judgment, but I can promise you I will be keeping a very close eye on her. I hope you are right about her, but right now I just don't see it."

"That makes two of us." Lazarus sighed heavily.

"I'm glad you came to talk to me, Laz. It means a lot."

"Thanks for listening," he said and turned away.

After his conversations with Layek and Vinson, Lazarus' mood improved markedly. He was grateful for the clear blue skies and magnificent sun that beat down upon him. *Better than snow and freezing weather,* he thought.

Gradually his tensions eased, his worries and fears dissolving into a deep sense of peace, amplified by the quiet inner voice within him that rose up to soothe his frayed nerves. *Everything is going to be fine,* it told him.

He no longer felt caged by the vast open spaces that surrounded him. He began to notice the serene beauty of the plains. A patch of wildflowers here, a bubbling stream there, the long grasses and the stands of oak, elm, and ash swaying gently, rhythmically in the slight afternoon breeze. Jackrabbits darted from the brush as they approached; birds glided past in bright flashes of color; a fox watched them cautiously from beneath a tangle of foliage. Each had its own place in Nature's order and added to the remarkable character of the land in its own little way.

Then he caught sight of Neslyn out of the corner of his eye as she angled her horse toward him. She looked amazing as usual, but with the sun shining down upon her, enveloped by the magnificence of the plains, the Elven princess appeared positively divine. Lazarus smiled broadly as she neared, and to his delight she smiled back.

"Good afternoon, Neslyn," Lazarus beamed as she closed in on him. "You look especially radiant today; I think even the sun is jealous. Indeed, fair as the weather you are, a revelation of perfection."

She blushed slightly as she drew her horse up next to his. "Somebody's in a good mood today."

"It's such a gorgeous day it's hard not to be. Life is so much more vibrant when nature is in full bloom. It makes me feel more alive. Helps me to appreciate life."

"You really enjoy the wild, don't you?" she asked.

"I do. I find nature's beauty intoxicating."

"You should visit my homeland sometime," she said. "The Elven lands would take your breath away, they are so stunning. Endless forests of tall green trees, the scent of flowers heavy on the air, the sky so big you think that at any moment it must collapse under its own weight. It is truly blessed by the gods."

"You speak highly of your home. I admire that. I would like to see your home someday. I rarely get the chance to travel outside the borders of my own kingdom. After this is all over, though, I think I'm going to need a vacation. If any of us survive this anyway," Lazarus added, a hint of pessimism creeping into his voice.

"Of course, we will." She looked at him incredulously. "Don't be so fatalistic."

"I'm sorry. I get a little down when I think about the odds we're up against."

"Then don't think about them," she replied matter-of-factly. "Your focus determines your reality so if you always focus on the negative, then negative things will always be foremost in your life."

"You are indeed a wise woman, Neslyn. We're lucky to have you among us."

"Lazarus," she said, her tone becoming serious. "The real reason I came to talk to you is that I wanted to thank you."

"I ... I don't understand. What do you have to thank me for?"

"For defending me against your brother and Layek."

"You were eavesdropping on our conversation?"

"No, absolutely not. I decided to go for a walk," she explained. "By accident I stumbled upon you arguing. I just wanted to say thank you for sticking up for me. Layek and Vinson seemed convinced that I was a spy and that I had betrayed everyone to our enemies."

"And have you?" Lazarus immediately regretted the question. "No, don't answer that. I'm sorry; that was a stupid thing to say."

"It's okay, Lazarus. The truth is, you have no way of knowing if I am a traitor or not. All you have is my word."

"If you heard our argument, then you know that I don't believe you have betrayed anyone," Lazarus reminded her. "There is no proof to incriminate you, nothing to suggest you are anything other than what you claim to be. It could just as easily have been any one of the others."

Neslyn thought for a moment before responding. "That is true, Lazarus, but why would you suspect your own brother as readily as me?"

"I was only trying to point out that there was no reason to suspect you over the others."

"Yes, but you grew so heated."

"The truth is, Neslyn," he said softly, "I like you a lot. I really feel in my heart that you are as true as you appear to be. To me, you are as immune to suspicion as my brothers are."

"Then who do you think it is?" she asked simply.

"I don't know." Lazarus threw up his hands in exasperation. "I really don't know. I trust everyone we travel with; that's why they were chosen. I guess that means I will have to suspect everyone equally."

"Don't worry too much, Lazarus," she told him. "Everything will turn out for the best."

"You keep telling me that. I hope you are right."

"Of course, I am," she said with a wink. "Don't you know that women are always right?"

Lazarus laughed. "You do have a sense of humor. I was beginning to think you were serious all the time."

They rode in silence for a time, just enjoying the closeness of each other. She smiled at him and pulled her horse close to his. She leaned over and grasped his hand, squeezing it once.

Abruptly, she spoke. "How do you do it? How can you handle leading your brothers into a situation where they could easily be killed? How do you deal with any man's death under your command?"

"It's never easy," Lazarus began slowly. "The role of the army is to serve and protect the people of Illendale, to uphold its laws and defend it with our lives if necessary. It is a dangerous line of work, even during times of peace. An officer's job is the most difficult because frequently we are placed in situations where we must give orders that endanger the lives of those we command. It is the burden of leadership, and it never gets any easier.

"I adhere to a simple principle and take what comfort I can from it. Preserve the lives of those under your command and do everything in your power to protect them by making informed decisions based on quality intelligence and sound judgment to minimize conflict and loss of life. That's my code."

"Do you get that from officer school? It sounds like it came from a textbook."

"No," Lazarus replied. "I invented it after I lost my first man to an Orc raiding party. I took it pretty hard, and ultimately I forgave myself by understanding I had done everything I could to prevent it."

"It's good," Neslyn told him. "Soundly logical and true to you and your men. I like it."

"Thanks. Sometimes, it's the only thing that gets me through. The men I command — they're my responsibility. Each time one of them falls, I have failed," he said sadly.

"You are a good man, Lazarus." She gripped his arm to comfort him. "Don't be so hard on yourself."

"Normally I'm not. Ever since this whole thing started I feel like I have betrayed my own convictions. The decisions I make are not based on any reliable information source. I know next to nothing in this business, and I am forced to make choices that will likely lead to the death of my friends. Already we have lost one; how many more deaths will be on my hands before the end?"

"Everyone here understands the danger we face, and yet they follow you willingly. That must count for something," she said. "As I've said before, don't be so hard on yourself. Everything will turn out fine if we just stick together."

Lazarus just smiled and nodded his head. "On a day like this, I could almost believe it."

They rode together for most of the day, joking and laughing, holding hands when it suited them. Neither had a care in the world, and for a time all else was forgotten. They ate lunch together when the group stopped, sharing their meal under the relaxing shade of an old shagbark hickory, and stayed close when they set out again, talking and laughing, discussing the history of their lives, completely oblivious to the curious stares of their companions.

Afternoon came and went, the daylight melting into the horizon, chased westward by the coming of night. Stars winked out at them from the darkening sky as they settled in. They ate a meal of dried beef, bread, and some fruit, and for a time they lay on their backs, gazing up at the stars, engaging in idle conversation. One by one they drifted off to sleep.

The following day began much the same as the others had, the company rising early and setting out across the plains before the sun crested the eastern horizon. The day grew steadily warmer, and the air shimmered with the heat, teasing the travelers with far off mirages.

All in all, their mood was high, enhanced by the tranquility of the lands surrounding them. Fears and doubts slipped away, lost in the heat of the day and the delight of simply being alive. They talked freely among each other as though they were on holiday and not a quest for salvation. Things might have gone that way indefinitely had they been traveling in other times.

Early in the afternoon, as they halted to consume their lunch, Corsin thought he caught sight of something slinking through the long grass. "It was there for a moment and then gone just as quickly," he explained. "Maybe it was nothing at all."

"Maybe it was something," Lazarus said seriously, recalling all too well how the demons had displayed a disturbing knack for finding them when they least expected it. "Better to be sure. We have been too relaxed in our vigilance these past few days."

"Come on, Laz," Layek pleaded with him. "It was probably just a wild boar or something. No need to get your feathers all ruffled."

"No, Layek. Now is the time for caution. Let's not forget what happened in Pilban."

The others nodded in agreement. None of them wanted a repeat of those events or to be caught with their guard down again.

Lazarus immediately sent out two separate groups of scouts to search the surrounding area while the rest of them prepared to move out. Joseph Corsin, Mihan, and Emeris Dallen made up the first group while Marcell, Layek, and Aldric comprised the second. Corsin led his team to where he thought he saw their pursuer, and Layek led his in a wide arc to encircle their position.

They returned little more than an hour later covered in dust. Neither team had anything of consequence to report. Corsin had found some tracks in the area where he had thought he had seen something, but they appeared to be nothing more than animal prints.

"I told you there was nothing out there," Layek grumbled.

"Better safe than sorry, old friend," Lazarus replied. "I'm glad that you didn't find anything."

"That doesn't mean that there's nothing out there. Maybe you just didn't see it," Vinson interjected. "We should keep our eyes open."

"Agreed," Lazarus said. "Tonight we'll set a double watch. Everyone stay vigilant. We don't want to take any chances."

They set out immediately, anxious to be off. They traveled at an easy pace, trying to gain as much ground as possible without wearing down their horses.

The group camped that night on top of a small hill in the plains where those on watch could see a long distance in all directions despite the dark of night. They took guard duty in pairs, uneasily peering out into the gloom, half expecting the shadows to jump to life. Nothing showed, however, and the night passed without event.

The next morning the twelve plodded cautiously onward across the plains. They watched furtively as they rode, eyeing suspiciously everything that might hide an enemy. Even Mother Nature seemed subdued on this day; songbirds rarely graced them with their serenades, and the life that had been so abundant the day before seemed to have all but disappeared.

Lazarus frequently sent Corsin to scout ahead and behind them just to be sure that there were no surprises along the way. He never went alone — that was far too risky. He was always accompanied by two of the others. Of course, they never found anything during their small scouting forays, but it made them feel that much safer.

Twice during the morning they heard a great, bone-grating growl from somewhere far in the distance. Each time they would halt and look around cautiously, searching for the source of the noise. Nothing would ever show, however, and they eventually concluded that it was nothing more than another of the numerous denizens of the grasslands.

So they continued, praying in the silence of their minds to make it across the plains without meeting any resistance. Their luck had held thus far, minus the sabotage of their horses and supplies. Yet somewhere deep within they could sense that all was not right. The character of the environment had changed dramatically; the land had grown hushed and expectant. It was beyond question that the demons would be hunting them and that eventually they would be found. They were simply hoping against hope that the time was not now.

The wind picked up, cold and brisk, and gray clouds began to drift in from the north with an ominous promise of storms to follow.

Late in the afternoon the growls returned, closer now than they had been before — so close that Lazarus was certain the creature was right on top of them. Weapons flashed out in an instant as they came to a sudden stop. They positioned themselves back to back, looking forward in all directions. Layek spotted something running through the tall grasses, but his glimpse was only momentary and not enough to identify it.

"Whatever it is," he said, "it's big and fast."

"It's a predator all right," Joseph Corsin added. "It's using the environment to its advantage, hiding in the tall grasses as it stalks us. We probably won't see much more than a blur until it strikes. Right now it's just waiting for the right moment."

"Is it a demon?" asked Aldric.

"I don't think so. Whatever it is, it knows we've spotted it. I think it's just toying with us. It wants to discourage us, hoping we'll let our guard down."

Lazarus grimaced. This was not good news. "We had best keep moving. Stay alert."

They accelerated their pace, pushing on as fast as they could without tiring the horses too quickly. Lazarus advised them to search for a defensible camping ground as afternoon drifted into early evening. They needed a place that was difficult to approach unseen and where they could not be caught off guard. The remainder of the day passed rapidly, and before they knew it the sun was setting, driving into them with its blinding rays.

Layek spotted a grove of oak trees to the south, its perimeter clear of the long grasses and foliage that dominated the Solaris Plain, and they decided it would be their best choice for a campsite. They could use the trees for cover while still maintaining sight of the land around them for twenty yards or more. It was as good a place as they were going to get. It would have to do.

Nervously, they hastily prepared their dinner of jerky and old bread, washing it down with fresh water without interest. A few engaged in idle conversation designed to drive away the fear and expectation they were all feeling. Lazarus forbade any sort of fire, and though they tried, it was a long time before anyone slept.

They stood watch three at a time, providing as much security as possible throughout the night. Lazarus took the last watch, in the deepest part of the night when sleep was heaviest and it was most likely they would come under attack. At least according to his logic he hoped that was how it worked. He wanted to be where he could have the greatest hand in the outcome of any encounter.

He lay on his back looking up through the branches of the trees, trying to catch a glimpse of the night sky. He shunned the small talk some of the others were making, preferring instead to be left to the solitude of his own thoughts. He was only slightly tired so he tried to occupy his mind with memories of peaceful days from his youth. He was not too successful in this endeavor, and notions of what might be kept creeping into his brain. He wrestled with them for a time, trying to force them away and focus on calmer, soothing things. Eventually he grew weary of the struggle and gave up, content to let his mind wander where it would while he simply listened to the wind pass through the trees.

Before he knew it, he was asleep.

And that's when the dream came to him. He found himself standing within their camp, cold and shivering from the sharp wind that had suddenly sprung up. The night sky was totally obscured, and there was almost no light, only a thick impenetrable blackness that surrounded him and wrapped about him like a living thing. He could make out the outline of the trees and the bedrolls where his companions had been when he had fallen asleep. They had abandoned him, disappeared into the night as surely as the sun.

He thought briefly that perhaps it was not a dream at all but reality. It seemed real enough, aside from the overwhelming sense of aloneness he felt and the instinctive realization that this was not waking life. It seemed to him that he might be the only living thing on this landscape his subconscious had painted for him, and he looked around hesitantly, not sure what purpose this dream had.

He began to despair, the feeling welling up inside him from no discernable source, only encouraged by the black void surrounding him. He tried to call out, to seek some companionship, and found that he had no voice. He panicked; his breathing became ragged and quick.

Then he felt a presence rise up, inexplicably everywhere and nowhere all at once, evil and malicious in its intentions. He could feel it stalking him, at home in the sinister gloom. He could not see it or even hear it, only sense that it was out there. If it ever found him, he knew he would die.

He ran, not knowing what else to do, having no other method to defend himself. All he could think of was escape. *Faster, faster! Run!* His mind screamed at him. *Get away!*

He flew through the empty and lifeless plains, running as fast as thought, as fast as his mind would let him. The plains seemed to stretch away into forever, an unending field that he could never escape alive. He could feel the thing's breath on his neck as it ran after him, tireless in its pursuit, but he dared not look back to see it.

The plains wore on and on, far beyond where Lazarus knew they should have ended. His legs grew tired, becoming heavy and wooden as his strength began to fail. He stumbled and went down. He tried to rise and found that he couldn't. His legs no longer worked. He could sense the thing standing over him, laughing at Lazarus' pointless attempt to escape, gleeful over his misery.

Lazarus knew he was about to die, but he refused to give up. He clawed his way forward, dragging himself bodily across the ground, continuing on will power alone. His limbs felt wooden and useless, his body like a lump of iron, a deadweight dragging him down. His arms gave out, and he could go no further. He rolled onto his back, closing his eyes in anticipation of the coming deathblow. His lungs burned like he had inhaled hot coals. The seconds crept by, and still the thing did not kill him.

He cracked his eyes open, determined now to see the source of his undoing. Slowly his eyes opened, and his attacker began to take shape. Then everything disappeared in the white haze of his endless scream.

XV THE RISING TIDE

KAIRAYN STARED STRAIGHT ahead as he led his dwindling column of warriors north across the Tersal Highlands. The skies were as clear and blue as he could ever remember them being, and he took what comfort he could in the pleasant weather. The sun shone brightly in the sky, and the temperature had risen steadily since dawn, giving the day a relaxing, summer-like feel. He didn't think on it too much though.

Grubbash had made it sound like recovering the Krullstone from the lost lands of Valinar would be little more than a stroll in the park. He had not expected things to be quite so simple, but things seemed to be spiraling out of control. His first priority had been secrecy, and he thought he had achieved that when they left Grimknoll. His only concern had been getting in and out of Valinar alive. Getting to and from their destination should have been little more than a long and dull march.

How naïve he had been.

Silently he cursed himself for his stupidity. He should have anticipated that the demons would be too clever to be kept in the dark. He should have known that they would try to stop him. Accustomed to being the hunter, now he was the hunted. He didn't like being the prey at all.

Several days ago they had been taken by surprise by a bunch of misshapen dog-things. The hellhounds, as they were called according to Urgor, had wreaked havoc upon them while they were camping for the night, and by the time the dust had settled the beasts had slain four of his warriors and destroyed most of their pack animals and supplies. Now, not even halfway across the highlands yet, he had already lost more than half of his group. Their foodstuffs would be gone in a week, but at least they still had horses. Walking the rest of the way would take forever. Then again, he thought to himself, if he got too hungry, he could just eat one of the horses.

He tried unsuccessfully to put it all behind him and just focus on the land ahead. Outwardly he looked calm and composed, but inwardly he was in complete turmoil. Rage and frustration roiled underneath his skin. He fought desperately to contain it and keep it from consuming him completely. Every moment he risked losing his sanity, and it was all he could do to keep from screaming uncontrollably. Lagor was out scouting ahead, picking out the easiest trail for them to follow and leaving small signs so those who came after would know which way to go. The rest of them plodded onward in total silence. They all knew Kairayn's temper, and none of them wanted to set him off. They jumped when he spoke and did exactly as they were told without complaint.

The days came and went, dragging on forever as if time had frozen. It seemed to Kairayn that they had been traveling for ages, that he had been going to or coming from somewhere for as long as he could remember. And yet he was here, in the middle of nowhere, searching for something that he might never find, trying to stay one step ahead of the monsters he knew were out there hunting him.

A new rush of anger surged through him, and he shook his head to drive it away. Flies buzzed around his head, and he slapped at them irritably. The heat of the day continued to grow, and he sweated freely. He never looked anywhere but straight ahead, ignoring the scenery surrounding him, heedless of anything but the trail before him.

Which is why he never saw the beast.

No one did until it was too late. It must have been tracking them for some time, waiting for the right moment to strike. It found its opportunity as they entered a small ravine less than ten yards wide where steep, brush covered-slopes rose up on either side of them.

It leapt soundlessly from the brush above, hurtling through the air with amazing speed. Kairayn caught a glimpse of it out of the corner of his eye as it descended on him. He shouted in warning and threw up his arms to deflect the attack, his reaction just quick enough to save his life.

The thing tore into him, claws and teeth ripping. His arms took the brunt of the attack as the weight of the beast knocked him from his horse and bore him to the ground, landing with an audible thud. Instinctively he rolled to the side as razor sharp claws raked the dirt where he had been. His companions started in surprise as other beasts charged out of the surrounding brush. Kairayn caught a glimpse of the thing that had unhorsed him as it tore into his shrieking mount and gritted his teeth.

More hellhounds. The Daemon Lords had sent more of their grotesque minions to make his life miserable.

The hellhounds looked much like an overgrown mutt, except that they were completely furless, and their skin was tinged flaming red. Muscles rippled with strength as they moved, quick and certain. They were ferocious in battle, ripping and tearing with their razor sharp claws and mouthful of fangs. Their eyes gleamed a maddened yellow, and the strong stench of sulfur followed wherever they went.

Kairayn looked on in disgust and aggravation. He counted at least eight; perhaps there were more that had not revealed themselves yet. His Orcs were trying desperately to hold them off, but they were on the defensive and quickly being overwhelmed. One was already down, and the others were fighting for their lives.

His horse had stopped kicking and screaming, and the hellhound atop it roared in triumph. Kairayn pushed himself to his feet and pulled free the scimitar from his waist. The hellhound turned toward him and growled menacingly. He heard one of his Orcs being torn to shreds behind him, but he couldn't be sure which one it was. Urgor shouted defiantly somewhere to his left. He would have to be quick before he was outflanked. He took a step closer to the hellhound and raised his sword, jaw set and grim-faced. The beast snarled in response to his challenge and bared its fangs, crouching low to the ground like a coiled spring. He glanced quickly to his right, trying to take some measure of how his companions were faring.

That's when the hellhound sprang. With a roar it launched itself at Kairayn, closing the distance between them much quicker than he would have thought possible. With jaws gaping wide it came for him. Kairayn brought his sword up. Too late, he realized. The flat of the blade slapped against the creature's head, but the blow didn't even phase it. One great paw swept up and knocked the weapon from his grasp. Kairayn brought his hands up to grapple the beast as the two fell backward, his sword clattering uselessly to the ground a few yards away.

He fell flat on his back, knocking the wind from his lungs. Spots danced before his eyes, and the smell of sulfur was heavy in his nostrils. The hellhound lunged in, striking for the jugular to finish him off, but Kairayn brought his arm up in defense. Pain rushed through him as the beast closed its jaws around his arm, a sharp burning sensation rushing up the appendage.

Kairayn roared and thrashed wildly, striking with his free hand at the hellhound's head, trying to dislodge it. But the beast had its front paws planted on his chest, and its superior weight kept him firmly pinned to the ground. The left paw drew back, sweeping down to smack him across the face. His vision faded momentarily at the force of the blow as the hellhound prepared for another strike. Kairayn reached up with his free hand through the haze of pain that wracked his body, catching the massive paw and holding it off. He brought up his knee and jammed it sharply into its ribcage again and again.

Releasing his arm from its jaws, the hellhound lunged again for his throat. With his wounded arm Kairayn gripped the beast around the throat, holding its head and bloody snout away from him. He could not hold out like this for long, he knew. He needed to do something to turn the tables, or he was dead.

The hellhound struggled vehemently to break free of Kairayn's grip. From out of nowhere a bolt of fire collided with the beast's midsection, momentarily knocking it off balance. Kairayn seized the opportunity and thrust upward with both legs, rolling it off of his chest. He heard Urgor's triumphant cry from somewhere nearby, taunting and spiteful, but kept his attention focused on his opponent.

The hellhound thrashed and flailed wildly, trying to right itself, but Kairayn buried his boot heels in its shoulders, pinning it to the ground. He released his grip on the thing's throat and drew a long knife from its sheath, adjusting his balance to keep the beast from breaking free. He slashed at one floundering limb, cutting so deeply he struck bone. Blood spurted out, splashing across Kairayn's upper torso. The hellhound howled in pain. Kairayn turned his attention to the beast's chest, slipping the blade between the third and fourth ribs, aiming for its vital organs.

He left the knife there and reached down to pull another from his belt. The hellhound continued to struggle and strain against Kairayn's weight, howling in agony. Kairayn sliced through the soft tissue of the hellhound's neck, and the beast's cries of pain faded into a sickening gurgle. It shuddered violently and went still.

Kairayn leapt to his feet. His sword lay on the ground a few paces away, and he took a step towards it. He noticed abruptly that the sounds of fighting had disappeared altogether around him, and he glanced around. What he saw enraged him. Urgor was nowhere to be seen, not even a body. The others of his party were strewn about, some in one piece, some not, but all dead. Most of the hellhounds lay dead next to them. He marveled at the carnage, and anger welled up within him. His whole team had been slaughtered.

Then he heard a familiar growl from behind him. He didn't need to look to know what was there. The only question was how many. He hadn't seen any except the dead about the battlefield. If he was lucky, there was only one. If he was very lucky, he could reach his sword before the beast tore him apart. He stood completely still, assessing the distance to his weapon and the speed of his enemy, hoping silently that there was only one. The growl came again, low and menacing.

Kairayn leapt for his sword without warning, hoping to gain an edge. He heard the scraping of claws on gravel as the hellhound launched itself at him. In a flash he reached his sword, his hand closing about the pommel. Without slowing he rolled, bound to his feet again and turned, sweeping his sword down in a wide arc.

The plan worked, and the blade of Kairayn's sword caught the beast in midair, square in the skull, slicing clean through the flesh and bone. He stepped aside, and the hellhound's lifeless body sailed past him, crashing to the ground beyond. He heard, rather than saw, the second beast charging at him from the left and turned to face the new threat. Blade lowered, he twisted just in time to catch the second hellhound as it leapt upon him. His free arm came up to grasp it about the neck to keep it from sinking its teeth into him. The creature's momentum carried it right into Kairayn and his ready sword, burying its blade to the hilt. The hellhound cried out in pain and fury, lashing out violently at Kairayn with its claws, slashing him across the ribs and torso. The creature struggled only briefly before its strength gave out, and the life drained from its eyes.

Kairayn staggered back a step as the demon dropped to the ground. Blood soaked his tunic, and his wounds burned with unnatural fire. His strength was fading quickly. He heard footsteps behind him and glanced over his shoulder. His shoulders sagged. Another hellhound. How many were there? He knew that he did not have the strength to wrestle another one. This one would have to die quickly, or it would be him lying lifeless on the ground.

He turned his head again, scanning the ground around him for any manner of weapon, anything he could use to defend himself. The closest was a spear, point thrust into the earth, a beacon of hope ten paces away. He wondered if he could reach it in time. His calculations were interrupted by the sound of claws scraping in the dirt behind him. He glanced back. The hellhound was on the move, circling, waiting for the moment to strike. The dance of Death had begun.

He didn't see any others. Apparently they were the only two survivors of the battle, left now to determine which side would be victorious. Kairayn turned slowly to face the beast, backing toward the spear he had seen, his only chance at survival. *Just a little further,* he prayed silently. Gradually the beast closed on him, circling still, drawing a little closer with each step.

At five paces the beast sprang. Lightning quick, it covered the distance between them before Kairayn had time to react. He knew in that instant it was over. He didn't have the strength to go toe to toe with this demon, and no one was left to come to his rescue. He was dead.

Then the impossible happened. Right when the beast was descending on him, jaws about to snap shut and end his life, a lightning bolt streaked across the ravine and struck the hellhound full on. It spun away, crashing into the corpse of a horse. The hellhound jumped off the ground, shrieking in rage and smoking where it had been hit. It charged at Kairayn again, a maddened nightmare that refused to quit. Another bolt struck it and sent it sprawling. Immediately it jumped up, roaring in pain and fury. This time Kairayn heard Urgor's defiant cry in response. The hellhound changed direction and ran straight for the mage, trailing smoke like a cape. Urgor sent fire lancing in torrents at the monster as it came at him, dodging and weaving, trying to avoid the wretched mage's spells. It caught several glancing blows, each turning it aside, and the smell of burning flesh filled the air.

Still it came on. Kairayn took the opportunity to retrieve the spear while the hellhound was focused on Urgor. He was pleased to see that at least one of his subordinates had survived the ambush, even if it was a Druhedar mage. Kairayn yanked the spear from the ground and hefted it, testing its weight. He took a moment to judge the distance and speed of his target and hurled the spear. It sailed through the air, whistling as it glided toward its target. It caught the hellhound mid-stride, piercing its hide and protruding out the other side. The hellhound fell over, crying out in agony and struggling to claw its way forward, refusing to give in even when mortally wounded. Urgor pointed an open palm at the beast and launched a stream of incinerating flames. A few moments later the hellhound was gone, and only a smoking pile of ash remained.

"I thought you were dead, Urgor," Kairayn yelled over to the sorcerer.

"Hardly. It took every ounce of energy I had to survive the initial assault; I had to retreat and regain my power."

"Glad you didn't wait too long." Kairayn sagged to his knees. "That hellhound would have had me for lunch."

Urgor sat down next to him. Kairayn noticed there wasn't a scratch on him. "You're wounded," the mage said. "We should clean those up and bind them."

"I'll live. First we need to get away from here. If we're lucky, the demons won't know we're still alive."

"I'll see what supplies I can salvage," Urgor told him. "I think I saw some of our horses run off to the north; maybe we can catch them."

Urgor walked off, rummaging through the remains of their troop to salvage whatever he could for them. Kairayn recovered his weapons, as well as a wicked looking poleax. Then he set to cleaning and bandaging his wounds. He found a couple of water skins that were still full and some clean cloth in a pack. He used the water to clean the lacerations he had received and then tore the cloth into strips and bound them tightly. The wounds still burned with fire, but at least the bleeding had stopped. He felt lightheaded and disoriented. He didn't think it was from loss of blood, but he didn't really know. Maybe it was another adverse effect of whatever poisons the hellhounds carried in their claws. He pushed the discomfort out of his mind. Nothing he could do about it now. He would just have to make do.

Urgor had scavenged what they could carry from the dead and organized them into several packs. Kairayn shouldered two of them and trudged off into the sweltering afternoon. His thoughts lingered on the images of his slaughtered companions. His hate burned hotter than the wounds he carried, driving him onward as surely as a master's whip. If nothing else, his hatred of the traitorous demons would see him through. He swore to himself that he would not rest until the Krullstone was found.

Then he would have his revenge.

꙳   ꙳   ꙳

Grubbash sat in his cushioned armchair, staring at maps and documents in his war room in the towers of Grimknoll. It was only mid-morning, and already his eyes were tired. He had been poring over these maps for days now, devising strategy with his generals. He had studied them so much that he knew them entirely from memory — every rock, tree, and river. They would all be his, subject to his will.

For now he was just waiting. Soon his armies would be gathered, and the world would tremble and bow before him. He wondered briefly how close Kairayn was to recovering the Krullstone. He hoped his old friend would return soon. The demons played along with his plans for now, but all too soon he feared they would outgrow their need for him. At least he still had the doppelganger. It never hurt to have a back-up plan, especially when in his situation. Failure was not an option because it meant death or worse. That was unacceptable. He would rule this earth. It was his destiny.

Soon he would have to go before the Daemon Lords to reveal to them his master plan for the invasion and subjugation of the free kingdoms of the world. The Daemon Lords had been opening gateways into their own dimension for some time now, bringing their minions over, building their own army. These demons would be added to his already considerable forces, and together they would crush everything that stood in their path. Nothing would be able to stand against their combined might. He just had to string Serathes along for a little while longer.

He rose from his chair and walked over to a small table set with pitchers and plates of food in the corner of the undecorated room and poured himself a drink. He gulped it down and poured another. This he carried back to his seat and once again resumed his empty stare at the maps that were spread before him. He hated waiting.

The door behind him creaked open slowly, and a servant poked his bald head in.

"My Lord?" the servant asked hesitantly. "Sorry to disturb you, My Liege, but Lord Bogran has sent for you. He says they are ready for you now."

A smile creased Grubbash's face. Finally. "You may go. Tell them I will be there shortly."

He had waited for days and days for this moment. His time was at hand at last. The waiting was over. *Let them wait on me for once,* he thought. He took his time finishing his drink and briefly considered pouring another. He decided against it. It had been long enough, and there would be plenty of time to savor the moment later. For now there was work to be done.

He quietly slipped out into the hallway beyond. It curved away in either direction; he turned left and followed the camber of the passageway around the tower. Doors came and went, but he ignored them. He continued until he came to a set of arched double doors that led out onto a veranda overlooking the open lands below the keep.

Grasping the handles, he threw the doors open wide. Half a dozen or so Orcs, headed by Bogran, turned to regard him coolly. They each nodded in deference and respect when they recognized him. These were the top class in his empire, and they had come as he had bidden them to fulfill his enlightened vision of their future.

"Welcome, Lords," Grubbash greeted them. "You have done well. Your people will revere you as gods, and the earth shall be laid at your feet."

The others nodded in agreement and bowed deeply before him. A smile creased his face, wrinkling the scar. He stepped forward, motioning for them to step aside. They did so, bowing as they went, parting down the center. Grubbash continued until he stood at the edge of the balcony, staring down at the fields below.

It was truly an impressive sight. Hundreds of thousands of Orcs, armed to the teeth and raring for battle, were settled on the field. Tents dotted the landscape by the thousands, and smoke from the hundreds of cooking fires filled the air. Hammers rang on anvils as smiths mended armor and sharpened weapons. The Orcs below milled about, eating, drinking, waiting for as far as the eye could see.

Grubbash signaled to Bogran to call them to attention so that he might address the army as a whole. Moments later horns sounded, deep and sonorous, and the Orcs scattered below began to fall in. It was by no means a quick exercise, but Grubbash kept his patience in check. He liked watching his army in motion. It reminded him of how close to fulfillment his dream was. Slowly the army took shape as the soldiers organized themselves into rows and companies and divisions, filling the air with dust. When the air cleared and the sounds died away, three hundred thousand pairs of eyes stared expectantly upward.

"Orcs of all lands! My brothers!" Grubbash's voice boomed out over the field, commanding the undivided attention of the army gathered below. "From all corners of the Empire you have gathered here, regardless of bloodline and class, in defiance of the stagnation and indolence that has gripped our people for centuries. No more! The hands that have held us back for so many years have been removed so that we might claim our birthright. From the ashes of the old a new dynasty has risen, a power dedicated to the dreams and aspirations of the Orcs, a leadership committed to the ideals and principals of our race."

Grubbash paused for a moment before continuing, letting his words sink in to the multitudes gathered below him. "You have answered the clarion call to battle. You have taken it upon your shoulders to ensure that our destiny is fulfilled. Look around you, and you will see the greatest army ever amassed. We are the strongest of the earth's peoples, the chosen of the gods. It is our right and our duty to rule this world. Through sacrifice and perseverance we shall prevail over those who would deprive us of what is rightfully ours. Many will die, but the glory for those with the courage to face our enemies upon the battlefield shall be immeasurable. And for those who are robbed of the glory and honor of death on the battlefield, the rewards shall be beyond imagining. Together we can create the perfect world, with Orcs at the helm as they should be.

"The future is now! A new era awaits us, a golden age that will stand the test of time and be remembered forever! Let the rivers run red with the blood of our foes! Let nothing stand in your way, and atop the bones of our adversaries we will recast this world as it was meant to be!"

Grubbash raised his arms, and a thunderous cry erupted from the horde. Banners waved, and swords rattled against shields, adding to the fervor. Grubbash remained standing there for many long minutes, reveling in the gratification he felt.

Finally he lowered his hands, satisfied that he had sufficiently inspired his new army, and turned back to his Overlords. They bowed respectfully to him, stirred themselves by his speech. He motioned for them to follow and walked back into the war room.

Grubbash faced the would-be leaders of his armies. "Well done, Lords. You have taken care of the business of melding the army together."

"It had better be worth it." Gurgor fixed him with his eyes.

"Speak carefully, Overlord," Grubbash said frostily. "Your position of authority is still on probation."

The threat was obvious, and the Orc shut his mouth. The other Overlords cast their eyes to the ground, not wishing to cross the High Summoner. Gurgor walked on thin ice, and none of them wanted to be near him when he fell through.

Grubbash rummaged through the papers on the desk and came up with several scrolls. "Here are your orders, in case you forget when you leave here. For now, I will explain it to you so there is no misunderstanding of what I expect."

He stood and walked to the far wall where a great map was posted. Several flags were pinned on a spot marked as Grimknoll, signifying the location and division of each army.

"Each flag on this map represents one division of the army, six in total," Grubbash instructed them. "Each of you will command a division, excepting Supreme Commander Bogran, who will oversee the whole army. Our first target is Illendale. The humans there are the closest threat to our dominance and must be dealt with immediately. The bulk of the army will be reserved to invade their lands. The Elves and the Trolls will not require our attention until Illendale has been subdued. The Goblins and Dwarves are preoccupied so we need not worry about them.

"Two divisions will cross the Myrrh into Illendale and engage the humans from the south. Three more divisions will attack from the west through the Tersal Highlands. Use the mountain passes if possible. If timed well, these combined assaults will overload their defenses. A small occupying force will be left to maintain our control of the highlands. The remaining division will march south to secure Mistwood and the surrounding lands. Pacify the Centaurs by any means necessary. Wipe them out if need be.

"The Daemon Lords have summoned legions of demons to

reinforce us. They will follow your command so do not hesitate to use them."

"What makes you so certain that the demons will bend to our will?" Krud asked. "I do not trust them."

"Nor should you," Grubbash replied. "I have assurances that they will follow orders. Remember that we still outnumber them. They are too weak to challenge us directly. Do not turn your back to them for one second, though."

"How do you intend to keep the demons under your thrall?" Gurgor asked disdainfully. "It is not in their nature to serve anyone."

Grubbash's harsh glare burned into the hardy Orc. "I do not give them the choice. Either they choose to serve me or I will send them back to the abysmal pit I summoned them from."

"You play a dangerous game, Summoner," Nergal declared. "Careful that you don't bite off more than you can chew."

"I'm touched by your concern," Grubbash mocked, "but you should worry more about yourself I think, since you will be the ones side by side with the demons on the battlefield. You would do well to remember that I am the only thing between you and their teeth. Now, are all divisions ready to march?"

"All but two, Master," Bogran informed him. "We are still striving to fully arm and provision them, but it will take some time. These two divisions will be stationed on the Myrrh until the rest of the army is in position. By then they should be fully prepared. Conscription and outfitting of twelve additional divisions is underway."

"Excellent. See to it that they are ready. The rest of the army should march immediately."

"It shall be so," the burly Orc assured him.

"Now, leave me." Grubbash waved them off. "There is much to be done, and I have matters that require my personal attention. Bogran, you stay."

The Overlords filed out of the room, some grumbling pessimistically, feeling a little uneasy about their alliance with the demons. For them, working in close quarters with the dark minions of the Daemon Lords was like playing with fire; it might keep an Orc warm through a cold night, but in an instant it could turn on him and consume him. It was a necessary evil, but that didn't mean they had to like it.

"Rough crew," Bogran commented when the door had closed behind the last of them.

Grubbash sighed deeply and leaned back into his chair. "Keep them in line, Bogran. It would be very hard to run three different armies by yourself."

"Vultures, the lot of them," Bogran spat. "Like a pack of hungry wolves, they wait and watch until they see weakness, and then they tear you to shreds. They already have their eyes on you, particularly Gurgor. He hates you more than anything. Best keep a close watch on them."

"Already taken care of," Grubbash smiled wickedly. "It is absolutely imperative that the demons continue to serve their purpose, and that depends entirely on maintaining our position of strength. We must be united. If the demons sense that we are coming apart at the seams, they will have the opportunity they need to take power from us. That cannot happen."

"I will do what I can," Bogran assured him.

"If any of the Overlords oversteps his bounds, then he will have to be removed and replaced very quietly."

Bogran nodded. "If it comes to that. So far all they do is grumble. You'd better have a good way of controlling the demons you haven't said anything about. Sooner or later they will turn on us."

"Relax, Bogran. I have everything well in hand. When we are finished with the demons, I can dispose of them as easily as I brought them here. You just worry about your end. Now go."

Bogran did as he was told, closing the door behind him as he left. Grubbash was left alone again to ponder the events that had transpired. He knew all too well how treacherous his chosen leaders and demon allies could be and how narrow a ledge he walked. It was a careful balance he maintained, and so far his gamble had paid off. He just needed the Krullstone returned to him, and then he would be unstoppable. The Orcs he could handle on his own, but the Daemon

Lords could easily overpower him. He needed the Krullstone to give him the upper hand and complete his plan.

From the halls below a great gong sounded out the hour. Dusk was nearing. Grubbash rose from his chair and padded toward the door. His armies were ready to march, and everything was going according to his design. Now he would go before the Daemon Lords to apprise them of his progress.

He held no illusions that when the demons felt the time was right, they would turn on the Orcs. If he did not have the Krullstone in his possession by then, they were all doomed. Now he must go into the depths of his keep, which was all but taken over by the multiplying demons, and mold them into his army and send them off to war. If he were lucky, Serathes would not seek to take a direct hand in matters. So far his luck had held; it just needed to hold out a little while longer.

He thought of Kairayn as he floated ghost-like through the halls of Grimknoll. He hoped that his old friend was succeeding, not because he really cared what happened to Kairayn but because his whole plan revolved around the Krullstone being found and brought into his custody. He stole through the keep, barely noticed by the Druhedar he passed in the halls who were engrossed in the tasks assigned to them. Grubbash descended from one level to the next until he reached the door that would take him into the catacombs beneath the stronghold.

Grubbash marveled at how much things had changed in his home. It seemed now a foreign place. Fewer Druhedar roamed the halls these days; many of them had been sent to join the army encamped without in preparation of the coming war. Yet there was something more. The once familiar silence that he had become so fond of now seemed like a living thing, an invisible beast waiting to pounce. Screams wafted up through the towers from far below more often than he cared for, ominous reminders of the things caged in the catacombs beneath the fortress. Tremors sometimes shook the whole of the keep, sending cascades of dust and silt showering down from the ceilings. Odious scents drifted on the air, filled with the stench of death and hate. The demons were commandeering his keep in more ways than one.

He took a moment to steady himself against the coming

encounter, breathing deeply. He reached out and grasped the carved handle of the door and thrust it open. A rush of stale air burst from the portal, embracing him like an old lover. It smelled faintly of decay and mold, the scent of death.

Grubbash stepped through the doorway and onto the familiar landing that led to the steps that would take him below. He gestured and whispered the words of power, and the luminorb materialized before him to light his way through the impenetrable darkness. The High Summoner started down. The stench of rot and putrescence filled the air, becoming more oppressive with each step. He tried to shield his nose with one sleeve of his robe to no avail. Small multi-legged insects scurried away at his approach, skirting the edges of the halo of light that surrounded him. Disembodied growls emerged from the black as he navigated the narrow tunnels toward the sanctuary. He reached the battered door to the once great shrine and stopped.

He thought momentarily that perhaps he should knock to announce his arrival. His anger flared. Why should he announce himself in his own house? He would never bow before these vile beings. They were only here because he allowed it to be so. It angered him much more that he had considered for even the slightest moment showing deference to these things. He grabbed the handle and violently pulled back the wooden slab, nearly tearing it from its hinges.

The High Summoner stormed into the room, oblivious to the danger he might be placing himself in. The stench was nearly unbearable, and Grubbash had to fight back the urge to wretch. His sanctuary had fallen greatly since the demons had taken over; it no longer commanded the respect and reverence it once had. The floors were littered with carcasses, half eaten and rotting. Effigies of evil were everywhere, hanging from the ceilings, etched into the walls and floors, scrawled in blood anywhere between. Grubbash was disgusted.

The first of the demons launched out of the darkness when he had taken less than four steps into the room — small, wiry things shrieking with madness. Grubbash raised his hands and gestured, sending forth an inferno of fire from his palms, burning them to ash. He charged forward into the room, caught up in his own rage. A dozen more demons materialized, bulky, spiked soldier demons, hissing with rage. Grubbash cried out, and a wall of flame engulfed them. A second later he was through the breach, stepping over the charred and smoking remains of his attackers.

A smoky haze filled the room, and more demons began to emerge, howling in fury. Grubbash braced himself for the rush as it was forming, fire sparking at his fingertips. Hatred burned in his eyes, and the need to destroy these hateful creatures consumed him.

"Enough!" a dark voice boomed from the shadows. "What is the meaning of this intrusion?"

Grubbash recognized the voice instantly. "It is I, Lord."

"Summoner," the voice growled. "There had better be an exceptional reason for your grievous violation of our domain. And an even better reason for the attack on my minions."

Grubbash winced at the obvious displeasure of Serathes. He immediately hated himself for it. "This is my domain, Lord," he snarled. "You are a guest in my house."

"I take what I will, Orc, and I have claimed this as mine," Serathes' icy tone echoed off the cavernous walls.

"As for your cronies," Grubbash ignored the comment, "they attacked me. I was merely defending myself. Unfortunately the price for their mistake was death."

Growls rose from the crowd of demons who had now encircled him as they slowly inched closer. Grubbash threw out his hands, casting light in a wide circle around him, bright as day. The demons shrieked in pain and shied away.

"I have come to inform you that my armies are prepared to march. The legions you have pledged are required to launch the invasion. My commanders and I have already devised a strategy. The humans to the north will be our primary target; the bulk of the army will be sent there." Grubbash finished his report and stood waiting.

"Very well," Serathes replied. "By morning our legions will be ready to join your army. I'm sure the tactics you have chosen to employ will suffice. However, my lieutenants will accompany your armies to ensure that everything runs smoothly. Athiel, Satariel, and Adimiron will each lead the demons that travel with your three armies."

Grubbash gritted his teeth. Not only did he not want the Daemon Lords traipsing around the countryside with his armies where they might be tempted to overthrow Orc leadership, but also he needed them here when the Krullstone finally arrived. It would be much harder to reach his ultimate goal if he had to track them down later. He wracked his brain for an argument, any logical reason that he might keep them here.

"No arguments, Summoner." Serathes seemed to read his thoughts. "This is not negotiable."

"As you wish, My Lord."

"And next time," the Daemon Lord stared him down, making him feel small and inconsequential, "knock before you enter. It may save your life."

"Yes, My Lord," Grubbash muttered and turned on his heel.

He marched straight for the door, ignoring the demons who followed in his wake. He slammed it as he left, a small outlet for the frustration he felt. He thought about wandering the catacombs for a while, slaughtering any demons he came across to satisfy his urge for bloodshed, scouring clean at least some small part of his home of the foulness that had consumed it. He thought better of it, though, and continued without stopping until he reached the surface.

When he reached the main level and had closed the thick door behind him, he sagged back into the alcove. He had been foolish to charge so brazenly into the demons' midst and attack them. He would have to do better at controlling his anger in the future. It would do him no good if they decided to kill him before he had the Krullstone in his possession.

Grubbash took a calming breath and walked out into the entry-way. He motioned over several mages he found there, dispatching them to see to the final preparations of the army. Then he went in search of Bogran to inform him of the changes in their plan. Maybe together they could find a way to turn this to their advantage. Maybe the Daemon Lords would prove easier to handle separated.

Maybe.

XVI INTO THE UNKNOWN

LAZARUS' EYES SNAPPED open.

His breathing was heavy and ragged, and he was bathed in sweat. Had the scream been real or simply a part of his dream, imagined like everything else? He thought he heard the sound echo through the trees. Was that what had awakened him? Or was it just the horror of the dream carried over into real life? He could not seem to focus. The grogginess padded his mind like thick wads of cotton, and he could not seem to reconcile the difference between reality and fantasy.

A horrible dream, nothing more.

It was still dark outside, cool and silent. The first tinges of light were becoming visible in the east, fading the blackness of night into lighter shades of blue and purple. The slight breeze from the previous day was still present, causing the branches above him to chafe against each other, creating a soothing, rushing noise like that of a lazy river.

His companions lay sleeping around him, undisturbed by his waking. He reached over to find the reassuring presence of his sword, grasping it with his fingers, the scabbard cool to the touch. He took several deep breaths and closed his eyes to let the fog clear from his brain. He looked around cautiously, trying to make out the shapes of the sentries he knew were there somewhere.

That's when he noticed how quiet it was.

There was no noise whatsoever. None of the telltale signs of life. The rustling of night creatures as they foraged for food, the buzzing of insects, all were absent. It reminded him of his dream, and he felt suddenly exposed and alone. He looked around again to assure himself that his companions were still there.

Somewhere close a twig snapped. Lazarus froze. He waited for several seconds, but nothing else happened. Something was wrong. He could feel it.

Slowly and silently he slid out of his blankets. He crouched next to his bedroll and quietly slid his blade free of its scabbard. On cat's paws he moved to where Vinson lay sleeping a few feet away. Sword held firm in one hand, both eyes scanning the darkness, he put a hand on his brother's shoulder.

Vinson's eyes opened immediately, and Lazarus put a finger to his lips, signaling for silence. A flicker of recognition crossed Vinson's face, and he swiftly rolled out of his blanket, scooping up his spiked mace as he did so.

Vinson looked at him questioningly. *What is it?*

Lazarus shook his head and motioned for him to wake the others quietly. Lazarus inched forward in the direction he had heard the noise, pushing forward painstakingly slow, trying not to make any sound that would give away his position.

Then a piercing scream shattered the stillness. Lazarus went rigid. The scream had come from behind him, outside the camp. It sounded like Mihan.

He turned and started to run. The others of the company were leaping from their slumber now, awakened by the noise, diving for their weapons and searching for the source of the disturbance. Fear was mirrored in their eyes. Lazarus ignored them and charged forward. A large, bulky shape appeared from the gloom ahead of him, stopping him dead in his tracks.

The beast lumbered closer, emitting a rattling growl as it did so. Lazarus recognized it immediately as the one they had heard yesterday. Whatever had been tracking them had finally revealed itself. It stepped guardedly forward, stopping just close enough for them to make out its repulsive features.

The creature was hideous. It had the body of a lion, with scaled legs, a long tail covered in spikes at its end, and a horribly disfigured human face. The face ended in a stubby snout with powerful jaws and rows of wicked looking teeth. It was a massive creature, its shoulders at least a foot above Lazarus' head.

Clenched in its jaws were the shredded remains of Mihan.

Lazarus gasped in dismay. *Not again.*

The beast took another step forward, pawing restlessly at the ground. It shook its head vigorously, its thick mane flaring out, spraying gore all over the place. It released Mihan's corpse from its jaws, launching the ravaged body across the grove. It cracked its bloody jaws. Lazarus could swear it was smiling in its own sick way as it released that bone-grating snarl again.

Where are Azrael and Marcell? The question rang in his mind. He heard Layek's battle cry from somewhere behind him and saw his friend surge past him toward the beast. He followed after, yelling at his companion to use caution. Layek ignored him and charged on. Vinson and Aldric were on their feet now, circling around the creature to attack its exposed flanks.

Ten paces from the beast he felt the heat of a fire bolt as it flew past him, striking it in the chest. Several more followed the first, hitting dead on, singeing its thick hide. The creature was not even phased by the sudden attack. Layek caught up to the monster, swinging his great battleaxe around, but it side-stepped his attack with frightening speed and swatted him with one massive paw. Layek grunted and tumbled away, crashing into a tree fifteen feet away. He did not get up again.

Lazarus darted in, slashing with his sword and quickly bounding away, avoiding the claws and fangs of the beast. Vinson and Aldric continued their attack from the rear and sides, striking at every opportunity while trying to steer clear of its spiked tail. Aldric dodged a half second too slow and caught a kick from one powerful leg which threw him off his feet. Lazarus immediately counterattacked to distract the creature, and out of the corner of his eye he saw Vinson pull Aldric, bloodied and dazed, to his feet, then lead him away from the battle.

It was just he and the beast now. He wondered briefly where the others had gotten off to, but then the creature came for him. He flowed smoothly from sword-form to sword-form as he had trained for the better part of his life, fighting to stay one step ahead of the thing. He slashed and stabbed relentlessly, but it seemed that the blows he landed were completely meaningless to his foe.

He took a moment to look around and see where the others of the company were. He couldn't figure out why none of them had come to his aid by now. He rolled to the side, barely quick enough to avoid being cleaved by the claws of the beast. Then he saw it. Neslyn and the others were fighting off another one of the monsters.

Two of them! It figures.

Layek had gotten to his feet again, and Vinson was looking to Aldric who was still reeling from the blow he had received. Lazarus turned his attention back to the immediate threat just in time to avoid a sweep of the monster's claws. He lashed out with his sword, striking again and again at its legs, trying to disable it.

Back and forth across the thicket they battled, Lazarus managing to stay just a step ahead of his foe. The beast cried out in frustration and rage, striking out in vain. Lazarus dodged and weaved, striking at its flanks and weak spots when openings were presented.

Then he stumbled on a tree root and went down. Instantly the beast was on him. He tried to fight it off, slashing and stabbing like a madman. He rolled away, claws tearing up the earth where his head had been. Another clawed paw came down at him, but this time he was too slow. He was struck a glancing blow to the head as he tried to wheel past the assault, knocking him off balance. The creature's tail swung around, striking him in the shoulder, burying its spikes into his flesh. He cried out in pain and fell over.

The beast stood over him, roaring in triumph, and reared up to finish him off. Lazarus was stunned but still had the presence of mind to defend himself. He thrust his sword out before him, stabbing deep into the monster's underbelly. The wound seemed to do little more than enrage it, seeing now how close it was to killing off this nuisance, and it closed in on him. Then Layek was there, battleaxe swinging, yelling in defiance. He hacked at the creature's tail as it swung around to strike him, lopping it completely off where it met the beast's body.

It screamed in pain, turning to face this new threat. Layek struck again, this time aiming for its forelegs, crushing one completely at the knee. The beast lurched forward and rose up on its hind legs, holding its wounded limb close to its body. Layek seized the opportunity and buried his axe in its midsection. It fell forward, landing on its stomach, growling and snarling. Layek didn't hesitate; he slammed his axe down into the creature's skull, splitting it wide and spraying blood everywhere.

Lazarus lay back, breathing deeply and clutching his arm to his side. Layek rushed up and knelt beside him. "You all right?" he asked, concern bright in his eyes.

"I'll be fine. How are the others? What about the other one?"

Layek looked up quickly to scan the area. "Vinny is taking care of Aldric; he took a pretty nasty blow, probably broke a couple of ribs, but he'll be fine. Neslyn and the others are finishing off the other thing right now."

"Help me up." Lazarus winced as he forced himself to a sitting position. "I want to talk to Azrael. Any sign of Marcell?"

"I'll send someone to look for him." He didn't seem optimistic about the soldier's chance of survival. "You just rest here for a minute. I'll bring over Azrael; he can see to your wounds while he's at it."

Layek stood and marched off, shouting orders to find Marcell, seeing to Mihan's body, and demanding that Azrael come over to where Lazarus was sitting. Neslyn rushed over to him and dropped to her knees. Sweat glistened on her forehead, and her hair was matted and tousled, yet to Lazarus she seemed as beautiful as ever.

"Can't seem to keep out of trouble I see." She smiled warmly. "Let me see what we have here."

"What were those things?" Lazarus asked, flinching as she pulled several quills from his shoulder.

"It's called a manticore. Evil creatures, they stalk whatever catches their eye and kill for pleasure more often than for food. Never heard of one this far north, though. They usually stay in the southern jungles. According to lore, they always hunt alone, never in groups." She stopped talking and focused her energy on healing Lazarus' wounds. A soft white glow spread from her fingertips into his shoulder, and warmth came with it. A moment later it was gone again. "It looks like you've fractured most of the bones in your shoulder."

"I'm not surprised," Lazarus scoffed. "We seem to attract all kinds of trouble and things that should not be. One way or another, it always leads to somebody getting hurt."

"You'll need to wear a brace for a couple days, and it will be a little sore," she told him. "But you'll be fine. A little worse for the wear but otherwise okay. I'll find some cloth so we can bind your arm."

"Thank you, Neslyn," Lazarus said as she turned away.

Layek returned with Azrael in tow. "How's your arm, Laz?" Azrael asked his friend.

"Nothing that won't heal with a little time," Lazarus replied. "What news have you brought for me?"

"Well, I'm afraid that Marcell has seen the end of this journey. We found his body not too far back; he had his throat torn out. Mihan, as you already know, didn't make it either," Layek informed him solemnly.

"Azrael," Lazarus said sternly, "what the hell happened? Where were you while all this was going on?"

"I don't know how they got so close without alerting us. One minute all was quiet, and the next thing I knew we were under attack. I took a hit to the head and blacked out. That's all I remember. I never even saw what hit me," he explained. "I came to with Layek yelling at me."

"Yeah, sorry about that," Layek said.

Lazarus sighed. "Well, you better have Vinny look at your head. What about everyone else?"

"Just fine," Layek answered. "A few scrapes and bruises but nothing serious."

"All right," Lazarus grunted as he lifted himself off the ground. "I want Mihan and Marcell buried properly. Then we strike camp and move on. The sooner we get off these plains and into the Morah Weald the harder it will be for these little surprises to follow us. Make it happen."

"Yes, sir! I'll get right on it."

An hour later, the march resumed across the grasslands that seemed to stretch on forever. It was still early in the morning, and yet the heat was already rising. Sweat beaded on their foreheads and stained their clothes. The sky above them was devoid of clouds, the sun beating down on them unobstructed and, coupled with the events of the morning, had left the ten remaining members of the company from Kylenshar irritable and introspective.

Lazarus barked out orders, and his subordinates engrossed themselves in the tasks he gave them to keep their minds off of the troubles that seemed to follow them wherever they went. They spread out in a protective formation, just enough to allow them space and to keep from jumping at each other's throats. Tempers had grown short and had a tendency to flare up without warning.

They trudged ever onward, avoiding each other as much as possible and trying desperately not to let the dark things that haunted their minds out into the world. The days wore on, seeming to last forever as the temperature continued to rise. The nights passed uneventfully, and they woke each day rested, if not any lighter in mood. After what seemed like an eternity, Corsin informed them that they would reach the outskirts of the Morah Weald by nightfall the next day if they could keep up the pace.

That night Lazarus tossed and turned for a long time, trying desperately to fall asleep. Around him, the others of the company had already succumbed to slumber. He rolled onto his back and looked up into the sky, studying the stars above him. Lazarus struggled within his mind, not sure if he was more averse to remaining within the open plains or the mysterious and forbidding forestlands no man had ever returned from. He knew that he had to go, that the decision had already been made. He only hoped that the demons would not be able to track them so easily once they were off the grasslands. Hope was about the only thing left to him at this point. His friends were dying around him, seemingly at every turn, and there was nothing he could do to prevent it. A meteor flashed across the darkened sky. Lazarus offered a silent wish in the privacy of his mind, hoping against hope for the salvation of his friends and kingdom. The wish became a litany of prayers that he repeated over and over until he finally fell asleep.

When he awoke in the morning, clouds had filled the sky, gray and heavy. They threatened rain, but much to Lazarus' gratitude rain had not yet begun. The journey was hard enough as it was. And it would only get worse he feared. There was a reason why no one had returned from the Morah Weald since the destruction of Valinar, and he fully expected to come face to face with that reason. He could only hope that he and his companions would prove to be a greater force than whatever evil awaited them.

He joined the others in a lackluster breakfast of old bread and dried fruit. Layek grumbled about the weather, and Neslyn bade everyone a good morning most cheerfully, but the atmosphere was anything but cheery. Dialogue was restrained and often gruff. Many of them tried to maintain a merry attitude by joking and teasing each other, but the somber tone would not be banished.

The cloudy grayness that filled the sky blocked out the sun's rays completely, and yet the day still grew steadily warmer. Not more than a couple hours after departing the rain began, a slow, steady drizzle barely enough to wet the parched ground that was both refreshing and depressing at the same time. It brought them some measure of relief from the growing heat, and yet the damp and gloom saturated their spirits more than their clothes.

They rode on, keeping careful vigilance over the shifting haze that surrounded them. Now, more than ever, they feared that at any moment hordes of nightmarish monsters would come charging from the mists. Thankfully, nothing appeared, and they continued on their way undisturbed.

They ate lunch around midday, stopping for a long time to rest themselves for the challenges ahead. Lazarus took the opportunity to go over strategy with Layek, discussing what they might come up against in the woodlands and how best to avoid its dangers. Lazarus insisted that they move through the forestland to the lost city of Caer Dorn and back out again as quickly as possible. He was ardently opposed to spending a second longer than was absolutely necessary in the forbidden lands. He argued that the place might still be home to the undead that destroyed the country so long ago and any number of untold dangers that had never been revealed. Layek heartily agreed with him. With Corsin scouting the trail before them, they headed out in single file. Far on the horizon they could see the dark line of the Morah Weald, growing slightly with each step forward. The rain stopped, and clouds broke up a little, allowing the last rays of daylight to sift through, setting the clouds afire in a splendid array of gold and orange. The forbidding wall of the woodlands rose up before them as the sun sank below the horizon. Lazarus called a halt.

"We'll rest here for the night and continue at first light," he explained. "We don't want to go in there in the dark of night."

Heads nodded in agreement, and the group broke up to do their separate tasks. The evening meal was prepared and eaten, the horses tethered and fed, and sleeping gear was unpacked. They sat restlessly in the growing dark, casting worried glances at the thick tangle of the woods to the west, deliberating what might be waiting for them there. It was too early to sleep, and none felt like talking so they huddled in a loose circle, gazing up into the sky and listening to the symphony of night sounds. Full dark settled upon them like a shroud, and they posted the night watch before rolling themselves into their sleeping gear. They slumbered fitfully, waking constantly from haunting dreams to fearfully search their surroundings.

Morning came and rain with it. The clouds had gathered overnight and gained strength. The group awoke sodden and dispirited, moving about their morning chores disinterestedly. They weren't particularly excited to get underway, and yet at the same time they weren't really eager to stay either. They decided to leave their horses behind, figuring that they would be more hindrance than help in the close quarters of the forest, and set them loose in the small stand of shagbark hickory. They were trained not to wander and should be safe enough in the copse until they returned.

If we return, Lazarus mused darkly.

Corsin led the way, and less than an hour later they stood staring at the massive wall of trees that rose up before them, marveling at the sharply defined border between grassland and forest. Aldric pointed out that the familiar birdsongs and wildlife had vanished. Silence gripped the threshold of the unknown, increasing the amazement and anxiety of those gathered there.

They stood staring for a long time before Layek spoke up. "The gods only know what's waiting for us in there."

"Not like we have a choice," Aldric quipped.

"The longer we stand here talking about it the longer it's going to take us to come back out again," Neslyn reminded them.

"Corsin," Lazarus said, "take us in. Everyone stay close and keep your eyes open. We've had enough surprises for one vacation."

Progress was slow at first as they wound their way uncertainly through the thick tangle of growth. About a mile in the massive trunks — most wider than several men standing abreast — became more widely spaced, and the underbrush thinned, allowing them much easier passage. The limbs intertwined above their heads, forming a thick blanket of leaves and branches that no sunlight could penetrate. It was hot and humid in the confines of the forest, and it smelled faintly of rot. Corsin set a stiff pace, and they made good time despite the uncomfortable stickiness.

They couldn't tell what time it was so thick was the canopy overhead so they broke their march for lunch when they thought it closest to midday. At first they saw no signs of wildlife, and the forest was ominously quiet. Then animals began to appear. Small ones at first, chipmunks and squirrels, small birds that burst from the high branches at their approach; then larger animals could be heard moving among the trees. They caught brief glimpses of some as they darted away, little more than hulking shadows. Nothing approached them as they moved on, and they did their best not to disturb the fragile calm that gripped the woodland.

At one point something that resembled a giant beetle crossed their path, catching them completely off guard. Apparently they looked a lot like lunch. The beetle-thing flared its massive mandibles and charged at them amazingly quick for its bulky size. Aurora Skall sent a bolt of energy at the thing, striking it right between the eyes. The beetle shrieked in pain and turned and ran in the opposite direction. Silence engulfed the woods once again.

They stood staring for several minutes to be sure that the thing had truly gone. When nothing appeared, they continued on, marching for what seemed like forever until the light began to fail. Lazarus started to wonder how safe it would be for them to sleep in a place such as this with no knowledge of the denizens and no choice of an even slightly defensible camp.

The shadows grew quickly, and before they knew it they were walking around in nearly complete darkness. Lazarus called a halt and gathered everyone to him. Layek half-seriously suggested they continue marching through the night just to avoid the vulnerability of sleep.

"Not much to work with," Lazarus mumbled to himself. He paced about for a minute until he found a spot where several trees grew right next to each other in a rough horseshoe. It was large enough to fit them all comfortably and enclosed enough that they would not have to watch their backs and flanks.

The group settled in, anxiously staring off into the dark as they consumed their evening meal. They drew lots for the watch and turned into their blankets, though none of them was about to fall asleep. The forest came alive with the night, rustling and crashing filling the black void that surrounded them as the nocturnal creatures began their nightly struggle for life and death. Disembodied growls and howls echoed off of the massive tree trunks, making it impossible to tell which direction they came from or even if it was one or many creatures making the noise.

Several times they heard the scratching of large creatures approaching their camp. Hands went instantly to weapons, and their breath caught in their throats as they waited for the assault to begin. Each time, though, whatever it was decided to go in search of easier meals and moved off into the darkness. It was a long time before any of them slept.

They rose in the morning, sore and tired, eager to move on and escape the confines of the forest. Lazarus noticed that everything seemed smaller and closer somehow, as if the trees were slowly hemming them in. He knew it was absurd, and yet he began to feel claustrophobic whenever he thought about it. The others agreed with him, uncomfortably eying the trees just to be sure that they were indeed still rooted to the earth.

They hurried on, quickening their pace as much as possible without tiring themselves out. Around what seemed to be midday Lazarus called a halt for lunch. He had grown worried that they might be traveling in circles, having no landmarks to guide them or being sure of their direction of travel. The forest looked the same in every direction, the layout uniform disorder throughout their limited line of vision. He consulted with Corsin to get his estimation. He seemed pretty certain that they were still traveling west, though how he could know was beyond Lazarus.

After they had finished their meal, he commissioned Aldric to climb a tree to see if he could get a view through the canopy and determine the direction of their route. Aldric wasn't very excited about climbing trees, but he was even less enthusiastic about being lost in the woods. So with a boost from Layek so he could reach the lower branches of a gigantic alder, the youngest Arkenstone scaled to the heights of the canopy.

The minutes crept by as they waited for Aldric to come back down. They grew nervous as a few minutes turned into what seemed like half an hour.

"Aldric!" Lazarus cupped his hands together to project his voice into the upper reaches. "What's taking so long? Are you okay?"

No answer. Lazarus waited for a couple more minutes for him to respond.

"That's it. I'm going up after him. Layek, give me a hand."

The two friends moved to the base of the tree, and Lazarus was about to begin his ascent when suddenly Aldric appeared, swinging down through the branches with the versatility of a monkey.

"What took so long?" Vinson demanded.

"What?" Aldric looked bewildered. "It's not exactly a short climb. These trees are massive."

"So what did you learn?" Lazarus asked anxiously.

"West is that way," he pointed off to the left. "We were heading in the right direction."

"Excellent. Let's get going then. This forest creeps me out," Emeris Dallen broke in.

"There's something else," Aldric said. "High up in the trees I came across several snares and webs. Big ones."

"Webs and snares?" Lazarus was confused. "Why would anyone put them way up in the trees?"

"They were spider webs. From some very large spiders."

Lazarus felt a chill run down his spine. He hated spiders. Giant spiders sounded absurd, but then again everything in this place seemed to be larger than normal. "As long as they stay up in the trees and we stick to the ground, we should be fine. Just keep one eye on the roof."

They marched on in silence, continually eyeing the branches overhead for any sign of danger. Nothing appeared, and they made good time, pressing hard to cover as much ground as possible before dark.

Then the light began to fade. Corsin still led the way, his internal compass beyond reproach now in Lazarus' opinion. It was growing dark very quickly, visibility dropping to within a few feet in the gray haze of dusk.

That was why Corsin didn't see the tripwire until it was too late. "Look out!" the scout cried as he flung himself aside.

The others ducked into a protective crouch as they waited to see what was happening. They sat motionless for several minutes. Lazarus heard Corsin thrashing around in the brush in front of him, and he slowly crept forward to where the scout lay on the ground.

To Lazarus it looked like he was rolling around in the dirt for no reason. "You all right?" he whispered.

"I hit a tripwire!" Corsin shot back. "Never even saw it!"

Lazarus inched forward until he was next to the scout. Sure enough, he was wrapped up in some sort of clear wire, thick as a finger.

He reached out to untangle Corsin, but when he touched the rope, his hand stuck to it. He tore his hand back immediately.

"Spider webs!" he hissed. "These things must be huge!"

"Well, get me out of here before they come to check. They're nocturnal hunters you know!"

The others had gathered around now and were staring in mute shock. Lazarus pulled his knife from his belt and began to saw at the thick cords that bound Corsin, careful to only touch them with the sharp edge so that they wouldn't stick to the blade. A couple of minutes later Corsin was free, and they were all scrambling back the way they had come.

"So much for staying up in the trees," Layek growled.

"Bigger prey on the ground," Zafer reminded him.

"I can't believe I didn't see it," Corsin breathed in astonishment. "Those cords are as clear as air."

"This is not good. When whatever laid that trap comes looking, it's going to wonder where its dinner went," Neslyn said. "We need to get away from here."

Lazarus nodded. "We'll backtrack until we find a good spot to camp. We'll continue on at first light."

Without another word they retraced their steps for several hundred yards, stumbling around almost completely blind. They found a spot where several mulberry bushes grew closely together with a hollow space between them, creating a sort of cave. It was cramped and uncomfortable when they all squeezed in, but they preferred that to staying out in the open. They nibbled idly at strips of dried beef as they sat in the dark, listening intently for any sound of intruders. They tried unsuccessfully to sleep and instead spent the night huddled fearfully in the dark, waiting for Death to show its ugly face.

It never did, and when morning began to brighten the shadows, they crawled out of their hiding spot, eagerly stretching their aching and cramped muscles. They looked around to make sure they were not being watched. Anxiously, the group set off to the west once again.

Almost immediately they came across the spot where Corsin had triggered the booby trap. The remains of the webbing lay on the ground, bits and pieces of dirt and leaves stuck to it. They carefully sidestepped it and with a sharp eye continued forward. Going was slow due to the difficulty they had spotting the tripwires. The traps became much more plentiful and complex as they progressed.

Several times they were forced to change directions because the webs became so numerous they could not slip past without tripping them. The day passed slowly, but progress was good. They ate as they marched, deciding it was better to keep going than waste time resting. They were tired, but they were highly averse to spending another night in this part of the forest. They had yet to see any of the monsters responsible for the webs, and none of them wanted to. The day wore on, and the light began to fade again. It was obvious they would not clear the woods this night. They found a spot that offered at least some semblance of protection and bedded down, sleeping in fits, more out of exhaustion than anything else.

The next day was exactly the same as the last, an endless parade past never-ending ranks of wooden sentries. They spent their time watching their steps closely, avoiding the tripwires and hidden nets of the unseen web-makers. Often they came across sprung traps with the lifeless husk of some creature suspended above the forest floor in a tangle of silvery gossamer threads. They hurried on quickly.

By nightfall they still had not reached the end of the maze of trees. They huddled close in what little protection they could find as the night passed, and at the first sign of light they were up and moving, itching to be free of the forest and its dark mysteries. They set a grueling pace, charging ahead as quickly as possible without risking entangling themselves in the snares laid out all around.

Morning melded into afternoon; afternoon faded into twilight. They began to despair that they would have to spend yet another night in the dark confines they so abhorred. They pushed on, Corsin in the lead, milking as much time as they could from the day.

Suddenly, the trees began to give way. Gradually at first and then there was a noticeable thinning as the terrain adjusted from forest to plains. The sun poked through the spaces in the branches, and they quickened their stride. They burst through the last of the giant sentinels into the open air of a ridge overlooking a large valley. Within the valley, to their amazement and relief, was the place they had been looking for.

"Caer Dorn," Lazarus whispered as he stared out across the ruins, squinting into the setting sun. "We'll camp here tonight and begin our search first thing in the morning."

With that, a surge of hope raced through every one of them.

XVII CLOSE ENCOUNTERS

THE MORNING AFTER the small band from Kylenshar had discovered the lost city of Caer Dorn brought an unwelcome change in the weather. Gray storm clouds covered the sky, threatening rain, and thunder rumbled ominously in the distance. Strong winds buffeted the foliage and howled mournfully through the crumbling walls of the once-great city. Strangely, the heat remained, though not as oppressive with wind and clouds present to abate it.

They stood atop a small rise on the edge of the Morah Weald, staring out across the bleak landscape, wondering with grim determination what surprises the ruins held for them. The complex was massive, stretching out across the land for several miles. Some of the buildings still stood, dilapidated and overgrown with vines and brush, patiently waiting to be swallowed by the earth.

Two things were immediately apparent to Lazarus: it would take a considerable amount of time to search the ruins in their entirety, and finding the Krullstone was going to be like looking for a needle in a haystack. A big haystack.

The wind whipped about them, and the first raindrops began to fall from the stony sky as Lazarus turned to address his small company. "We'll search in groups; we can cover more ground that way." He looked them over as he spoke. "Zafer and Neslyn, you're with me. Vinny, Azrael, Aldric, and Layek will make up the second team. Corsin,

Dallen, and Skall the third. Stay together; nobody goes anywhere alone. Ever. We all meet up here one hour before sunset."

"Come on, you superstitious old goat," Layek joked. "Have you suddenly grown afraid of the dark?"

Lazarus ignored his big friend's attempt at humor. "Let's not forget about what happened to this place or about the things that are hunting us."

"The walking dead," Vinson muttered in disgust.

"Has anyone ever even seen one?" Emeris Dallen questioned in disbelief.

"Just because you don't see them doesn't mean they don't exist," Neslyn replied.

Lazarus gathered them close and traced a rough sketch of the ruins in the dirt with a stick, dividing it into quadrants. "Each day we'll explore a different sector. Keep in mind that the Krullstone was probably kept in a well-guarded place, likely a vault. The main palace, universities, and major barracks will be our top priorities. In all probability that's where the stone would have been held so locating these sites is paramount. Just be careful and keep your eyes open; we can't afford any accidents."

They made a quick check of their weapons and gear, stashing any unnecessary equipment in a nearby thicket of overgrown ferns. They remained together until they crossed over the threshold of the city, which was marked by the rubble that had once been the protective wall surrounding Caer Dorn. Wishing each other luck, they split up into their separate teams and headed off to their assigned sections.

The rain worsened steadily as the day progressed, turning the wide avenues to mud and obscuring their vision. A heavy mist began to rise as the cool rain met the warm earth, swirling and shifting in the wind like a living thing. By midday the rain was coming down in a heavy deluge, soaking them through and forming small lakes in the low spots in the terrain that they constantly had to skirt. They scoured the ruins, venturing into every demolished building and dark space, hoping to find some clue to lead them on, but all they found was emptiness.

Late in the afternoon Lazarus came across a squat brick building that was still mostly intact. The large stone blocks were cracked and worn from decades of erosion, and it was partially covered over with vines. Lazarus thought it remarkably resembled a guardhouse, and he realized after a moment that it was. Excitedly he motioned his companions to follow, and together they made their way inside.

Most of the ceiling had collapsed, and the interior was filled with rubble. They carefully made their way through each of the many chambers inside, one by one. In several of them they found rusted and useless weapons and armor buried beneath the debris. Near the back of the building Zafer discovered a staircase leading down into blackness, eroded and half buried in wreckage. Cautiously they descended, Neslyn leading and lighting the way through the dark with her magic.

After a dozen steps the floor leveled and became a broad hallway carved from the rock. The passage smelled of mildew, and thick moss grew in many places. They made their way cautiously forward, unsure of what to expect yet hopeful that their search would get cut short. Dozens of wooden doors, rotted away by time, opened into small compartments on both sides of the passageway. They inspected each only to find empty crates and boxes as rotted as the doors that guarded them. All were empty.

They reached the end of the hallway and found yet another set of stairs leading down. They followed it, sinking ever deeper into the earth, swallowed by the surrounding darkness. They scanned the inkiness that engulfed them, and their ears strained to catch any sound that might suggest they were not alone. The second level was laid out in the same manner as the first, leading back in the opposite direction. Nothing of importance caught their eyes, and at the end of that channel another set of stairs led them down to a third level. They began to sweat despite the coolness of the underground complex as they carefully made their way down the slick stone steps.

The third level marked a change in the atmosphere. Their footfalls echoed ominously off the walls as they walked. The tunnel came to a junction and split into three, and they halted warily.

"Which way do we go?" Neslyn whispered, her breathing heavy and labored.

"You're guess is as good as mine," Lazarus said in frustration.

"We had better be careful not to lose our way down here," Zafer added. "Starving to death isn't on the top of my list of ways to die. If these tunnels intersect other tunnels, then we could easily lose our direction."

Lazarus frowned. "Then we better be careful. Let's try the left first."

Neslyn started forward once again. They had not gone far when iron-barred cells began to appear. They peered into the darkened chambers. Some had chains hammered into the walls while others had nothing at all in them. In more than one cell were the remains of what had once been the prisoners of the dungeon. They came across one large chamber with a solid iron door that stood ajar, and when they looked inside, they felt chills run down their spines. Torture devices were scattered all about the room, and rusted implements that could have come only from the grimmest of imaginations lined the walls. They hurried on quickly.

They turned a corner, and abruptly the passage ended. They turned and went back the way they had come, searching the other two tunnels and finding them much the same as the first they had explored. When the small group came to the end of the last, they found yet another set of stairs leading down; a heavy stone slab on hinges that was obviously used to seal the lower levels lay next to the opening. Lazarus wondered bleakly how far underneath the surface the warren ran.

They started slowly down the steps and immediately felt a change. It was hard to identify at first as they pressed forward. The tunnels had grown noticeably smaller, and the pervasive darkness devoured every sound they made. They became uneasy and restless. This passage seemed permeated somehow with sorrow and agony, as though the emotions were etched into the walls themselves, a part of the very shadows that engulfed them. They retreated into themselves, hiding away within the solid core of their being in an attempt to shut out the feeling that seemed to press down upon them with the weight of the earth itself.

Lazarus brought his friends to a halt and sank to the floor. "I don't think this is what we're looking for."

Neither of the two Elves responded; instead they sat next to him. Silence dominated the narrow cavern. They remained there for several minutes, trying to ignore the claustrophobia that threatened to overcome them in the confines of the passage.

"What is that?" Zafer said suddenly, fearfully.

Lazarus' breath caught in his throat, and his ears strained to catch whatever the Elf had detected. He fought past the ringing that filled his ears in the face of the overwhelming silence.

"I hear it, too," Neslyn whispered, her voice barely audible.

Then Lazarus heard it. A hissing sound, like a sigh from the earth, building on itself, borne through the shadows with an unmistakable malice that chilled Lazarus' blood. It came from the tunnel before them, growing steadily louder.

Neslyn extinguished the light created by her magic, and they inched silently backward. The hissing grew louder, a wild rushing in their ears, and the certainty that they were not alone gripped them like iron bands.

Neslyn launched light into the darkness before them, filling the tunnel with brightness reminiscent of the sun. What appeared out of the dark sent ice coursing through their veins and froze the breath in their lungs.

As far as the light stretched bodies filled the tunnel, returned beings born of suffering and hate and driven mad by the need for revenge, decaying flesh pulled close against a frame of bones. Fire burned in their eyes, fueled by their loathing of living things, and the hiss came from their voiceless throats. They seemed to Lazarus more like apparitions than flesh and blood creatures, floating rather than walking, approaching them with disturbing calmness. There was no sense of urgency in their assault, only a swift and certain advance that guaranteed death to those who stood in their path.

"Revenants!" Zafer cried.

"Run!" Lazarus yelled, yanking free his sword.

They turned and fled back down the tunnel, racing for the stairs that led to safety. They could feel the nightmarish monsters closing in on them, though they could not hear anything over the deafening shriek filling their ears. Lazarus never looked back. None of them wanted to find out how effective their weapons would be against these things.

Abruptly Neslyn stumbled and went down hard. Zafer hadn't noticed and kept going. Lazarus turned and darted back to where she lay and picked her up, jamming his sword into its scabbard and running on through the tunnel, cradling her in his arms. Neslyn came to a few moments later, and Lazarus set her on her feet without slowing, pushing her in front of him.

They hit the stairs at a dead run, barely slowing as they bounded up to the next level. Lazarus was the last through the portal, and he immediately turned and knelt to the floor where the stone slab lay.

"What are you doing?" Neslyn yelled when she realized he had stopped; a trickle of blood ran down her face from a cut on her forehead. Zafer slowed and turned; his weapon shone brightly in the false light cast by Neslyn's magic.

"We can't outrun them! Help me seal the tunnel! It's our only hope!"

Zafer rushed forward, and together they heaved against the stone block. It didn't budge. Neslyn sent fire racing down the steps into the tunnel beyond, and shrieks filled the air. Acrid smoke rose up out of the hole. Lazarus and Zafer redoubled their efforts, and the stone slab slowly began to rise. The shrieks rose once again, and Lazarus' nostrils filled with the foul stench of rotting and burning flesh.

Lazarus gave a final heave, and the slab lifted off the floor, slamming down over the stairwell and sealing away the revenants.

"Not sure how long that will hold them," Lazarus gasped. "We'd better get out of here."

"You don't have to tell me twice." Zafer shivered as he forced the rusted iron deadbolts into place.

They traced their way through the labyrinth of tunnels back to the surface. They stumbled frantically through the narrow halls in the muted glow of Neslyn's light and emerged finally into the ruined remains of the ground level. Heavy rain and howling winds greeted them enthusiastically, and blackness filled the sky above them. Thunder boomed loudly, seemingly right on top of them, and lightning flared in the sky, forking wickedly toward the ground before disappearing into the dark of night again.

Lazarus blinked in confusion. Had they really been gone that long?

"What do we do now?" Neslyn shouted above the wind.

Lazarus crouched low in the shadow of the wall next to him, pulling the two Elves down as he went. They couldn't possibly have been exploring the tunnels for that long. Lightning flared, and Lazarus' breath caught in his throat. Dark forms skulked in the open spaces outside their partial shelter. He blinked in surprise, thinking it had been a trick of the light. He waited until the lightning flared again, looking out at the ruins. They were everywhere, crawling over the ruins in droves. There was no mistaking their identity.

Lazarus inched backward slowly, motioning for Neslyn and Zafer to follow. Judging by the look in their eyes, they had witnessed the horror as well. They were surrounded. Obviously the undead did not know they were there, or they would be swarming all over them. Lazarus led his charges deeper into the shadows, back to the opening that led into the tunnels below. He ushered them down into the hole far enough inside to escape the rain and wind.

"They're everywhere!" Zafer gasped. "We can't go out there."

Neslyn shook her head. "I can't believe we were gone for that long. How could it be dark already?"

"It doesn't matter now. We'll have to wait here until daylight." Lazarus sighed heavily. "I don't think we can slip past those things. At least we have a defensible position here if they do discover us."

"Let's hope those other things can't get through the barricade and sneak up behind us," Zafer added.

He sounded calm, but the fear shone clearly in his eyes. He knew as well as Lazarus if the dark things found them, they were as good as dead. There was little hope that they could stand against the multitudes outside.

"I'll keep watch if you would like to get some sleep," Lazarus offered.

"Like that's going to happen," Neslyn snapped. "I'm sorry. I shouldn't have said that. You saved my life back there. I should be thanking you."

Lazarus shrugged. "You would have done the same for me. No offense taken. We're all a little edgy right now."

They sat in silence for a long time, listening to the dull thud of the thunder muffled by the thick stone above their heads, praying not to be found by the creatures that lurked overhead. There was no food to eat; they had not brought anything beyond the meager lunch they had consumed earlier in the day. They had expected to be back at their camp well before sunset. Their stomachs grumbled angrily, but there was no quieting them now.

After a time Neslyn nuzzled up to Lazarus, resting her head on his shoulder. In minutes she was asleep.

ço   ço   ço

Less than two miles away from where Lazarus and the two Elves were hidden from the undead denizens of the ruins, Vinson, Aldric, Azrael, Layek, Corsin, Emeris Dallen, and Aurora Skall sat under the sheltering branches of an ancient oak tree atop the small rise from which they had surveyed the city earlier that day, trying in vain to ignore the inclement weather and focus on the situation at hand. As agreed they had regrouped just before dusk, and as they waited patiently for the arrival of the missing three, they consumed their evening meal.

The wind whipped about them in a frenzy.

The seven stood in a rough semi-circle staring out into the maelstrom, torn between their loyalty to their leader and their better judgment. They had watched the undead crawl from their dens as the sun set. When Lazarus and the two Elves did not return before dark, the argument had begun.

"You can't possibly consider leaving him out there alone! You saw what is down there!" Vinson screamed at Layek, clenching his fists.

"We can't just abandon him!"

"You saw as well as I did." Layek was furious, but he held his anger in check. "There's no way we can slip past all those things, and we can't possibly fight through all of them. And damn you for suggesting that I would abandon Lazarus. There just isn't any way for us to get to him right now."

"You're a coward!" Vinson shouted.

Layek started forward, losing his grip on calmness. Vinson faced him in challenge, daring him to get within striking distance.

"Enough!" Aldric jumped between the two, holding them apart. "I hate to admit it, Vinny, but he's right. If we go down there, we're all dead. He's my brother, too. He's smart, and he's got the Elves with him. They'll be okay."

"Major Ogras," Emeris Dallen addressed him. "In the absence of the Commander, you lead. We follow your command. I'm sorry, Captain Arkenstone."

"Thank you, Captain Dallen." Layek gathered himself and stepped back, taking a deep breath. "We must wait until dawn. I swear to you, Vinny, at first light we will go searching, and I will not rest until I have found him."

"You had better be right," Vinson seethed and stalked off.

They settled in for the night, unsuccessfully trying to get some measure of sleep. Thoughts returned constantly to their missing friends. Hopes and prayers raced through their minds as they tried not to think of what would become of them if their rescue attempts were too late.

ꝙ   ꝙ   ꝙ

In the morning a hand clawing at his shoulder awakened Lazarus. He started, thinking he had fallen under attack as he dozed, and cried out, reaching for the sword that rested against the wall next to him. A hand grasped his and held it fast. His eyes opened, and he relaxed greatly when he saw it was only Zafer.

"Sun's up," he whispered. "We'd best get going. The others will be looking for us by now."

Lazarus nodded and looked to his shoulder where Neslyn was still snuggled up to him fast asleep. He shook her gently. She lifted her head, and her glittering hazel eyes found his, flashing that dazzling smile that melted away the cold that had seeped into his bones. Something unspoken passed between them in that moment, and a bond was forged that neither could fully define and yet instinctively felt the value of its worth.

They stood carefully and stretched their cramped muscles, walking gingerly up the stairs into the bright light of day. They blinked away the sleep as their eyes adjusted to the sudden change in brightness. Then they took a few moments to look around before Lazarus decided it would be best if they returned first to their camp. It was imperative for them to meet up with the rest of their group, as well as get some food.

The rain had stopped sometime during the night, and the clouds had broken up, though they had not disappeared entirely. The sun shone brightly in the sky as it drifted between the clouds, and the day quickly grew hot. They had not gone far when they found the rest of their friends. Apparently they had spotted the trio from atop the ruined wall as they walked down a wide, muddied avenue and rushed to catch them. Greetings were exchanged, the excitement at having been reunited palpable, and they shouted and laughed ecstatically. Lazarus had to go through their harrowing story of the previous night three times before anyone was satisfied. Vinson was furious that they had not been more careful and made sure that they had gotten out of the city before dark. Lazarus promised that it would not happen again.

"At least we know what we're up against," Layek mused. "I always thought it was just a myth meant to scare small children."

Lazarus couldn't help but smile at his friend's cynicism. "The most unbelievable things often prove to be true. At least we know now to take extra care."

"Or become history ourselves," Emeris Dallen scoffed. "Judging by what we saw from the camp last night, it's no wonder nobody has ever come back from this place."

Aurora Skall procured some water from a skin and some food from the pack she carried, which they devoured greedily. A few minutes later, after the three had been satiated, they gathered themselves to plan out the rest of their day.

"I know we had planned to search the city in quadrants," Lazarus announced, "but I think in light of our newfound knowledge, it's best to form a new strategy. Time is of the essence. The more time we spend roaming these ruins the more likely it is we will be discovered. A confrontation with the armies of the undead is not in our best interest. I say we skip everything else and focus on locating the palace and old university. That's our best chance for getting out of here quickly and safely."

They walked for a ways before finding a partially intact stone tower, which Lazarus scaled with Corsin and Zafer to determine a destination. They spotted what appeared to be the central part of the city and to their best guess, where the palace would have been located. The three climbed down, and they set off.

The clouds began to clear, and the sunshine and blue skies took the edge off the tension that gripped the group as they made their way through the ruins, and soon the furtive glances over their shoulders stopped. Lazarus began to whistle as he walked. Moods eased, and smiles crossed their faces as they took in the warm morning. There was no wildlife to speak of, and they sorely missed the sound of birdsong, but all in all the day was enjoyable despite the intimidating surroundings.

Shortly after noon they arrived at what they realized was the outer wall of the old palace. It was crumbled and destroyed but still a recognizable barrier. They stumbled over it excitedly. It seemed the old palace had been entirely leveled, and yet most of the surrounding buildings were still standing in remarkably good condition.

They poked around for the remainder of the day, digging through the rubble of the old palace to see if they could find anything and searching some of the auxiliary buildings. But their brief forays garnered nothing, and when the sun began to threaten the horizon, they quickly marched out of the city.

They gained the rise their camp had occupied the previous evening, and at Lazarus' behest they relocated to the south. He reasoned that if they kept changing locations, it would be harder for them to be discovered. Their tracks in the city were so confused from their search that it would take even the most skilled tracker a substantial amount of time to locate them, but Lazarus felt it was better to be safe than sorry, and everyone else heartily agreed.

As the stars emerged from the darkened sky, they watched in amazement as the undead emerged from their lairs to slink across the ruins. Hundreds of the abominable creatures spilled forth, covering the ground in a dark stain as they scoured the ancient city.

They slept uneasily and awoke in the morning unsettled by the frightful visions from the evening before. They set out hastily to explore the city once more, ever cautious of the monsters they knew were hiding somewhere. It seemed that they only came forward at night, perhaps to cleanse the ruins of unwanted visitors like Lazarus and his friends. In any case it made their search somewhat easier knowing that they would not likely meet any resistance so long as they were out of the city by nightfall.

They took up where they had left off the previous day, spreading out across the central core of the ruins as they searched building by building. Early on Aldric discovered what appeared to be a sealed entrance to some kind of underground complex. It came in the form of a solid alabaster stone cube, inscribed in strange runes that none of them could seem to decipher. It was oddly intact and clean of any decay or overgrowth. Neslyn, Azrael, and Aurora Skall sensed that the barrier was protected by a powerful magic and spent several hours trying to discover the way in, all to no avail.

Finally, frustrated and out of ideas, they moved on to other parts of the city. Afternoon came and went, and before they knew it the sun was setting once again. They rushed out of the city, anxious to be away from the ruins before the denizens of the place appeared for their nightly hunt. They moved their camp once again, circling the city farther to the west.

For days this fruitless search became their routine. Each night they watched the disturbing cabaret performed by the gruesome undead, and it slowly began to erode their confidence. Thoughts turned grim and constantly revisited the memory of the inexplicable wall. It was an anomaly that did not fit into the puzzle of Caer Dorn, an enigma that both baffled and frustrated them. Instinctively they felt that it was an important landmark, and yet it did not seem that they could solve its mystery.

The gray storm clouds returned, and the rains poured down on them unceasingly. Spirits dropped, and tempers flared as they grew more and more desperate. Their food supplies were beginning to run short despite their careful rationing, and many of them began to wonder if perhaps they had been sent on a fool's errand. They investigated the ruins tirelessly but could not seem to make any meaningful progress. They found the remains of the old university, identified by a faded inscription on the ancient stone blocks. They inspected it thoroughly but found nothing.

They began to lose hope. Morale fell dangerously low. On the sixth day Aldric insisted that they return to the odd edifice near the center and decode its purpose. He was confident that its mystery could be unveiled with a sufficient amount of thought, though the rest of the group were skeptical.

Aldric puzzled over the strange construct for many hours. The others had all lost interest long ago and sat listlessly on the surrounding rocks, engaging each other in idle conversation to pass the time. Lazarus had become convinced that this was their last hope and paced the grounds restlessly, wracking his brain for a solution. Occasionally one of the others would come stand next to Aldric and offer some suggestion as to how the barrier might be breached, but all efforts proved to be in vain.

It was well into the afternoon, and the sun had begun to droop in the sky as it traced its path westward when Aldric finally made a breakthrough. He had begun a couple of hours earlier to run his hands over the walls of the squat building in hopes of finding a crease or lever that might suggest there was an opening. As he came to the center of the wall on the east side, he traced the runes etched into the stone with his fingers.

Inadvertently he ran his hand across a small, razor sharp

outcropping and nicked his hand. Blood streamed from the wound onto the wall, running over some of the faded markings. There was a sudden flare of power as the dormant magic contained within sparked to life. Aldric jumped back in surprise. The rest of the group stared on in wonderment as a line of blue fire delineated the shape of a broad door. They flinched as the light brightened, and suddenly, as quickly as it had appeared, it was gone.

They were so stunned by Aldric's discovery that for several long minutes none of them moved. Lazarus was dumbfounded, and yet he was elated. He could feel in his bones that this was what they were seeking. Abruptly he remembered the chilling visions Melynda had shared with him in Kylenshar, the memory of the unseen evil bubbling to the surface that awaited them in Valinar. He hoped that whatever he had sensed in that vision would not be waiting for them within this secret chamber.

Aldric immediately insisted that they enter and explore the mysterious building.

"Aldric, Vinny, and myself will enter and have a look around," Lazarus said. "The rest of you will wait outside and guard our escape route."

Layek huffed irritably. "No way. You're not going in there without me."

"We're not going in there at all today," Neslyn interrupted quickly. "It's nearing dusk. We need to get out of here before those things come out to make their nightly rounds."

Lazarus knew she was right, but he just couldn't contain his excitement. He weighed the matter briefly, but in the end his curiosity got the best of him. "The three of us will just have a quick look around. We'll be gone less than an hour." Neslyn and the others started to protest, but Lazarus silenced them with a wave of his hand. "Just give us an hour. You have my word we'll be back before nightfall."

The others reluctantly agreed. Lazarus, Aldric, and Vinson double checked their weapons. Lazarus gathered up some deadwood and created several makeshift torches that they could use to light their way. With a deep breath and a moment to reassure themselves, the three brothers turned and disappeared into the dark passage.

Holding the brands before them protectively against the dark, they proceeded. The darkness was thick enough to cut with a knife, their torches only lighting a small circle around them. The passageway started out narrow but quickly broadened as it sloped downward into the earth. The path was smooth and free of projections, and they quickened their pace. It became steeper and began to snake left and right. Their footsteps echoed hollowly off the walls, and they heard the sound of water dripping into some underground pool.

Suddenly the walls gave way, and they felt themselves entering a vast subterranean chamber. They came to a stop and tried to allow their eyes to adjust to the darkness. After a few moments Vinson became frustrated by the lack of light.

"I can fix this," he muttered.

He reached down into a pouch at his belt and pulled forth a handful of silvery dust. He thrust the sparkling powder into the blackness and muttered something unintelligible. Light flared from the cloud of dust and quickly spread out into the black. In seconds the whole chamber was illuminated in a soft, pale glow.

Lazarus and his brothers marveled at the sight before them. The chamber was massive, extending far into the distance beyond their vision. Thick fluted columns laid out in geometric lines braced the ceiling. A shallow pool of water clear as crystal covered the floor.

"It must be a cistern," Lazarus breathed. "Probably used to supply the city with water. The perfect place to have a hidden vault because nobody would ever come down here. Amazing."

They stared on in amazement for a few minutes more before they pushed their way forward. They were a little reluctant at first to tread into the water, but after seeing that it was only about a foot deep they hurried on, realizing that time was running short for them. They marveled at the intricate designs carved into the columns; some were decorated with the reliefs of gorgon heads, which Lazarus found slightly disturbing. He figured it was one way to frighten off unwanted visitors, and at the same time he hoped it wasn't a preview of what was to come.

The water got deeper as they continued, slowly climbing until it was up to their waists. After what seemed like miles they came to a dry landing that led into yet another darkened tunnel. The trio held their torches before them and plunged into the blackness, their courage growing with the hope that this was the final resting place of the Krullstone.

The passage narrowed as it wound further into the earth. Lazarus wondered just how far it would take them before coming to an end. Shortly after the tunnel became even narrower, and small niches appeared, carved into the wall from top to bottom, most filled with skeletal remains. Dozens of side tunnels jutted off from the main passage, but Lazarus motioned for his brothers to continue straight ahead.

The tunnel became rougher, the smooth, carved walls giving way to sharp stalactites and jagged rock. They proceeded more carefully, having to crawl in several places to keep from bumping their heads against the spikes protruding from the ceiling. Then the tunnel began to broaden again until it was wide enough for the three of them to walk abreast, though they were still mindful of the protuberances hanging from the ceiling.

Then without warning the tunnel abruptly ended in a smooth, flat wall. The three brothers held their torches forth and studied the wall intently, elation welling inside them. An inscription was carved onto the wall, which they soon realized was a door that led into yet another chamber. They gathered closely around the portal as Lazarus read the markings on the door, amazingly engraved in the common tongue of the lands.

> *Herein lies the hope of the heroes of the ages.*
> *Herein is contained the power to fight the evil that would*
> *threaten and consume, that which will lead the righteous*
> *to victory over the forces of darkness.*
> *Whosoever holds virtue in his heart and follows the path of the*
> *true shall enter.*

Lazarus' heart soared. Finally they had reached what was promised them. There was still hope for their people and the rest of the world if they could figure out how to open the door, of course.

Vinson proved to be their savior in that arena. While Lazarus and Aldric were still staring at the door, Vinson was leaning against it, pressing his hands against its smooth surfaces. Within moments blue flame streaked across the seams. The engraving flared with magical energy, and the entrance swung open soundlessly. Light flooded into the small antechamber, and they stumbled forward into the glow.

Inside they found a nearly empty chamber, faultlessly carved into the solid rock. Murals depicting ancient battles and heroes were engraved onto every inch of the walls. In the center of the room was a waist high pedestal of solid white marble, flanked on four sides by smaller square platforms. Lining the walls were other platforms, chests, and stands, overflowing with treasures and trinkets that twinkled brightly in the torchlight. Runes carved into the pedestals pulsed with the life of magical energy. On three of the surrounding blocks, resting on golden stands, were swords, sheathed in intricately scrolled and gilded scabbards.

There on the center pedestal sat a gilded gauntlet with a flat, multi-faceted gemstone that seemed to glow in a rainbow of colors from within. Instantly the three brothers knew it was the object of their quest. For many long minutes they stared in astonishment. Then they rushed forward, crowding around the plinth to gaze at the artifact resting peacefully there. They stared in amazement, unable to speak or move, afraid that if they reached out to touch the Krullstone, it would prove to be nothing more than a mirage and would dissipate into thin air.

Slack-jawed, Vinson finally reached out to collect the Krullstone.

"Halt," a raspy voice called from beyond the chamber door.

XVIII THE KRULLSTONE AND THE NECROMANCER

NESLYN AND THE rest of the group sat huddled protectively around the entrance to the dark cavern. It had been nearly an hour since the three had ventured inside, and the Elven princess began to grow worried.

Something was wrong. She could feel it.

The shadows were growing larger and, emboldened by the sun's decline, slowly crept across the ground, swallowing whole patches of earth. It would not be long before full dark settled in for the night. If the Arkenstones did not return soon, they would not have enough time to escape the city before the undead emerged from their hiding places for their nightly hunt.

She shuddered at the thought, remembering their harrowing experience only a few nights ago. She did not care to repeat it.

Neslyn sat a little to the side from the others, preferring to be left to the solitude of her own thoughts than be part of the idle conversation that they were engaging in. Surely they were thinking the same thing she was and were merely trying to ignore the sense of impending doom by sharing in meaningless banter. At least it passed the time.

"If they're not back in fifteen minutes, we should go after them," Layek grumbled in discontent.

None answered him. They were all on edge, uneasy with their surroundings and disturbed by the wait that seemed to drag on forever.

The sun dipped below the horizon.

Then Neslyn heard a noise that sent chills up her spine, the sound of bone scraping on stone. The others fell silent; apparently they had heard it, too.

They formed a protective semi-circle around the entrance to the tunnel Lazarus and his brothers had gone into, facing out into the growing gloom. The noise increased and multiplied, and they drew weapons, dread filling them to the core.

Moments later they began to appear. Only a few at first, skeletal forms lurching into view almost mindlessly, yet with unmistakable purpose.

Then others began to appear, dozens upon dozens of them, until a wall of grotesque figures completely encircled them. Neslyn's heart fell as she prepared herself for the inevitable.

They were surrounded and hopelessly outnumbered. There would be no escape this time.

જ   જ   જ

Cailyn Emory ambled slowly through the gardens in the courtyard of the Royal Palace in Kylenshar. Melynda walked by her side, keeping her company. These walks were a ritual of Cailyn's that she adhered to religiously; it helped her to relax and cleared her mind of all the clutter that built up with the responsibilities and stress of her office, stress that seemed to multiply exponentially these days.

Since the murders in the High Council and the attempt on her life, rumors had been circling the city like vultures, whispers that war was on the horizon and that demons had come from the very depths of hell to claim the souls of each and every one of them. The bloodshed had not ended there either. Death was almost a nightly occurrence in the city now. Every morning it seemed a new grisly murder was discovered. A strict curfew had been enacted; no one was allowed out past dark. The city was just short of complete lockdown.

Fear was in the air, and the people were becoming panicked. She had considered making a public statement, but she was apprehensive that the truth of the situation might lead to greater unrest. Soon she would have to tell the people. With the army being assembled right inside the city, it would eventually become impossible to hide it.

She looked around until she located the trio of bodyguards who were now attached to her around the clock. Ukiah had insisted that she never be without protection. She had bowed to his wishes. The demons had tried twice now, and they would try again; the only question was when.

"It seems that their grip on this world strengthens with every passing hour," Melynda muttered at her side, reading her thoughts. "Time slips away from us."

Cailyn didn't respond. There was nothing to say that hadn't already been said. Everything that could be done was already in progress. General Markoll was marshalling their forces to meet the invading army when it presented itself; even now the Phoenix Legion was entrenched upon the southern banks of the Myrrh River. Scouts had returned bearing news that the Orcs were raising a massive army south of Perthana. According to the figures presented by the General, they were outnumbered at least twenty to one, not the most promising of odds. The Phoenix Legion would make the Orcs pay dearly to cross the river into Illendale, but they could not hope to hold them for long without reinforcements. General Markoll was still at least two weeks from marching with the full strength of their army. Reserves were being called up from every corner of the kingdom, but it took time to outfit and supply an entire army. The Elves and Dwarves had both pledged support, but as yet none had arrived, and there had been no word from either.

She thought briefly of Lazarus and his brothers, gone now several weeks, and wondered how they were faring. It had become quite clear that they were indeed the only hope for them. If the Orc army was half as large as the reports claimed, they were still outmatched. With the demons tearing them apart from within, they might not even live to see an invasion, she thought bleakly.

She continued her walk through the noonday sun and the stifling heat it brought with it. Rows of withering flowers decorated the extraordinary gardens, struggling to cope with the unseasonable temperatures that slowly drained them of life despite the best efforts of the masterful horticulturists employed to preserve them. She frowned. It appeared nothing was immune to the dark touch of the evil that threatened.

So engrossed was she in her own thoughts that she didn't see the black form until it was almost on top of her. Melynda cried out in fear and stumbled back at its approach. Cailyn looked up, whipping out the small dagger she had begun to carry so many days ago.

Hurtling at her with frightening speed was a tall, gangly creature with disproportionately large jaws, rows of razor sharp teeth, and an elongated, rounded skull. Its skin seemed to change colors to blend in with its surroundings, making it a barely traceable blur.

She cried out and stepped backwards, looking for the bodyguards who should have been there to protect her. Two were lying facedown in the dirt not far from her; the dark stain spreading out beneath them told her she would receive no help from that quarter.

The third, a quick and deadly young man named Gordon, launched himself from behind a tree to her right, colliding with the demon mid-stride. The two tumbled to the ground, clawing and hacking at each other. Cailyn watched in stunned surprise.

Seconds later Gordon was off the ground, his foe motionless as its lifeblood seeped into the parched earth, but the young guard had not escaped unscathed. Blood stained his tunic at his side, and one arm clutched tight against the wound.

Gordon backed toward her, holding his sword protectively in front of him, scanning the grounds for more attackers. Melynda had disappeared. Cailyn prayed silently that she had gone for help.

Suddenly several more forms detached themselves from the shrubs and trees of the gardens. Their camouflage was so complete that they may as well have been a part of the gardens, completely invisible until they moved. They looked ponderous and slow, moving in a disjointed saunter that was dangerously deceptive.

Slowly the queen and her bodyguard backed away, Gordon

trailing blood behind him. Cailyn wondered darkly how many more were hidden out there.

Out of the corner of her eye she caught a flash of movement. Two more of the blurry shapes appeared on their right, moving with dark intent toward them.

Cailyn cried out in warning, and Gordon shifted his attention briefly to this new threat. In that instant the demons attacked, rushing forward with uncanny speed. Her bodyguard cut down the first as soon as it came within striking distance. The second he slashed about mid-section just as it collided with him, and the two fell to the ground.

Before Gordon had even touched the ground, the rest of the demons were pouncing, ripping, and tearing at the brave soldier. He screamed in pain as they tore him apart, and his scream fell into silence. Cailyn held the dagger protectively in front of her as the three remaining demons began to inch toward her, jaws split wide and covered in blood. She knew she was dead. There was no chance she could defend herself against such lethal foes. Her shoulders sagged as the weight of her fate settled upon her.

Then they sprung. Purely on reflex Cailyn slashed with her short dagger, catching the foremost attacker across the throat. The demon gurgled and dropped to the ground, clutching at its throat as the black blood spilled from it.

Then she noticed the stinging in her side. Without taking her eyes off the two remaining demons, she reached down to her abdomen. Her hand came away wet with her own blood. She had been too slow and paid the price for it.

Rage and frustration boiled their way up through the despair she felt. Determination, hard as cooled iron, gripped her, and she fixed the demons with her eyes. If she must die, so be it, but she was not going down alone.

The demons began to circle her, one to each side. She circled with them, backing away as she tried to keep them both within her field of vision. She knew if they got behind her, she was finished.

She started as her back came up against the solid form of a tree trunk. They were toying with her, she realized. Just one of them was more than a match for her; now they were just relishing in her fear and despair. The thought incensed her, and she felt her judgment slip with her temper.

She took a step forward, brandishing her dagger.

Instantly the two demons charged, one from each side. She had seen them in action only moments earlier, but still the speed with which they moved startled her. A split second later they were on top of her, claws ripping into her flesh. She screamed in pain.

It's over, she thought. *How could it end like this?*

A frightening roar filled her ears, and a blurry shape crashed into the demons, knocking them aside. Cailyn, weak from loss of blood and pain, slumped to the ground beside the tree. She glimpsed the figure of Ukiah, his features an epitaph of rage, hacking mercilessly at the demons as her sight began to dim.

As though from within a black hole, she heard the hollow sound of Melynda's voice calling to her, assuring her that everything would be fine.

"There's a healer here," she heard her friend say, though the words didn't seem to make sense anymore.

She was slipping into blackness, and she could not seem to stop the sliding.

"You're going to be okay," Melynda whispered again.

She was aware of dozens of guards racing through the gardens, searching for any other demons. Ukiah was at her side, tears welling up in his eyes. She wanted to hold him, to talk to him, but her voice and limbs no longer obeyed her.

Lazarus Arkenstone, where in the name of the gods are you?

Then she closed her eyes and gave herself to endless silence.

As one, the three brothers turned, reaching for their weapons. A lone figure stepped into the light and raised a stick thin arm. Instantly Lazarus and his brothers were frozen in place as though invisible bands of iron had wrapped about them and held them fast.

Vinson gasped in surprise. "The Nameless One," he whispered in fear and loathing.

"Such a dismal label," the man replied. "That's no way to talk to the lord of the house." There was a hint of spite mixed with the contempt in his voice. He stepped closer into the light, and the three brothers got their first real look at their captor.

He was definitely human or at least had once been. He was tall and emaciated, his skin pulled tight against his frame. His tattered clothes hung loosely on his bones, a frayed vest over a simple shirt with breeches that barely extended to his ankles. His skin was pasty and gray and looked as though all the life had been drained from it ages ago. Black eyes, burning with unnatural fire and sunken back into their sockets, stared out at them from beneath stringy, white shoulder-length hair. He looked and smelled like he hadn't had a bath in a hundred years.

"So the heirs of Icarus have returned to claim their birthright," he rasped. "I knew you would come eventually. I have waited a long time."

Lazarus' mind reeled. *Heirs of Icarus? Birthrights?* It made no sense. He knew instinctively that this being was the evil that the vision had warned him of. It had just admitted lying in wait for them. Still, he sensed something was missing. Something obvious that he had over-looked and could not quite put his finger on.

"What are you talking about?" Aldric blurted out, frustrated by the man's cryptic words.

"Ah, yes," the man breathed. "We have not been properly intro-duced. I am Asaru. These lands and those that dwell within them are mine. I was responsible for the destruction of ancient Valinar and the creation of the undead hordes."

"That's impossible," Lazarus replied in disbelief. "That would make you more than three hundred years old!" Lazarus risked a glance at his brothers. Vinson simply stared dumbfounded at the figure before them.

"Death holds no power over those who embrace it," he shot back ominously. "I have mastered its secrets and therefore am not subject to its rules."

"What do you want from us?" Lazarus asked levelly. "And what do you mean *heirs of Icarus*?"

"Do you not know?" Asaru cackled in malevolent glee. "Yours is the bloodline of kings. You are the direct descendants of Valin Icarus, and therefore the relics of his kingdom are your birthright."

The air left Lazarus' lungs with the revelation. No wonder they had been sent to recover the Krullstone. It had been in the care of their ancestors before and was rightfully theirs to command. That was why they were able to open the doorways where others had failed. But how were they going to escape this ancient evil that had destroyed everything his forefathers had tried to build?

"Are you wondering how you will escape this with your lives?" Asaru asked, reading his mind. "The truth is, you are free to go."

"You expect us to believe that you will just let us go?" Aldric asked skeptically.

"Yes. Take the Krullstone and fulfill your charge to destroy the Daemon Lords. I will not stop you."

"You lie!" Vinson hissed. "How do you know we will not turn the Krullstone's power on you?"

"If you do not do as I say," he fixed Vinson with his cold eyes, "your friends will die. Then I will kill you and take the Krullstone for myself." The invisible bands around them tightened, slowly pressing the air from their lungs. "In life or in death, you will serve me."

Vinson was silenced, and a sudden pang of fear passed through the three brothers. Could they trust this man? He was solely responsible for the destruction of an entire kingdom, and he was certainly not their friend.

"What's the catch?" Lazarus eyed him suspiciously. "Why would you want us to destroy the Daemon Lords? You both seek the same end — total dominion over the lands."

Asaru's eyes smoldered. "Yours is a bloodline hated above all others. For millennia your ancestors have stood in the way of the Daemon Lords and their plans for this world. Three hundred years ago your ancestors stood in my path, and I destroyed them. I would do the same to you in a heartbeat but for we share a common enemy. You will survive this only because I allow it to be so. Your coming was foreseen ages ago, and patiently I have waited.

"Artemis Icarus, a great and powerful seer, prophesied the destruction of Valinar. She also prophesied that three brothers of the chosen line would return to claim the Krullstone and that their coming would herald the destruction of the Daemon Lords.

"Long ago I was contacted by the Daemon Lords. They had little to offer that I could not take for myself, and thus I refused to aid them in their quest to return to this world. As punishment for my defiance the Daemon Lords bound me to these lands with a powerful sorcery. This imprisonment has given me the time needed to foster and cultivate my power. My hatred of them has festered like an open wound until it has surpassed even my hatred of you and your kind.

"Do not mistake my intentions. I am not your ally. I am not your friend. Your pathetic existence is inconsequential to me. Yours and the other races of the world will ultimately bend to my will. You will take the Krullstone, and you will destroy the Daemon Lords. Not because I tell you to or because of your hatred of them, but because your conscience leads you to defend the inherent weakness of your way of life. That will be your undoing. And if we ever cross paths again, I will see to it that you meet your destiny!"

Lazarus was taken aback by the sudden tirade. There was such hatred, such volatility in his voice, he wondered briefly if the Nameless One might change his mind and kill them after all. He doubted they could do anything to stop him if he did. The necromancer was taking an awful risk in allowing them to take the Krullstone from him, but he supposed that there really wasn't a choice. If Asaru was telling the truth, and Lazarus believed he was, then he was literally trapped. He was using them to do his dirty work, and whether they liked it or not they had to comply.

He was speechless. He looked over at Vinson and Aldric and read the same dumbfounded expression that he was certain framed his own face. The thought of serving such a vile being was repulsive, even if only by proxy. He hated being a pawn, but there was no help for it.

They absolutely must destroy the Daemon Lords. It was the only way to save their people and way of life. Later, Asaru could be dealt with. The Krullstone would work just as well on him as the demons.

"Now go," Asaru hissed. "Be swift or pay the price."

Then the necromancer was gone. As suddenly as he had appeared, he returned again to the blackness of the cave, melding into the shadows as though they were little more than an extension of himself. The invisible forces holding them tight were released, and the three brothers heaved a sigh of relief. Still, it was several minutes before any of them moved.

Then Vinson turned toward the pedestal upon which rested the Krullstone. Gingerly he lifted it from the stand, holding it close to his face and studying the strange inscriptions upon it. He gazed deep into the stone, which sparkled unnaturally in the gloomy light of their torches. Lazarus and Aldric came up next to him.

"We had better hurry," Aldric cautioned them. "The others will be worried for us."

"They had better not be harmed," Vinson growled as he tucked the gauntlet into a belt pouch. "I will personally hunt that hellish fiend down and destroy him."

Lazarus prayed that would not be necessary.

He looked at the three filled stands next to the Krullstone. Carefully he read the inscriptions at the base of each. The Quietus Edge, Shadowsbane, and Soulreaver. Instantly he knew what they were. Excitedly he reached down and scooped up the one labeled as the Quietus Edge. The scabbard was an intricate masterpiece with amazing scrollwork and gilding. Slowly he drew the blade free and marveled at its masterful construction. The sword gleamed in the light, almost as if it had life of its own. Down the entire length of the blade runes were engraved, flawlessly set and arranged.

"Runeblades," Aldric whispered in disbelief. "Aren't they just a myth?"

"Apparently not," Lazarus managed to answer. "Absolutely amazing! The power crafted into these blades was supposed to be incredible! We cannot leave them behind."

Vinson nodded and grasped the one marked Shadowsbane, while Aldric took Soulreaver. They marveled at them for several more minutes, completely captivated by their miraculous fortune. This was more than they could ask for; here were the weapons that would protect them and lead them to ultimate victory over the demons.

A scuffling outside the vault brought their attention back to the real world. As one they turned to see what new horror would present itself to them, the malicious words of Asaru echoing ominously through their minds.

Be swift or pay the price.

Slowly they crept to the entrance of the small vault. Lazarus' gasp caught in his throat when he saw what was waiting for them. Ghostly figures floating on air, hissing in anticipation, awaiting them with an all too familiar icy calmness in the cavern beyond.

Revenants.

Slowly Lazarus drew forth the Quietus Edge, hoping dearly that whatever magic it had once held was still contained within it.

"So much for the easy way out," Aldric muttered.

"We go together," Lazarus said. "When I go, stay behind me. Stay right behind me."

Lazarus charged into the eagerly waiting crowd of monsters, jaws opened wide to greet him. The magic of his sword flared to life as he brought it down in a sweeping arc, blue fire racing up the length of blade and filling Lazarus with exhilarating power. Lazarus felt the magic reach down deep inside him, awakening a part of him that thirsted for blood and drawing it out.

The first line of Revenants exploded into ash when met with the blade of the Quietus Edge, feeding Lazarus' frenzy. Those who came behind were momentarily caught off guard, confused by the sudden emergence of this new power. Lazarus plowed into them without slowing, little by little losing himself in the bloodlust instilled by the sword's magic as he struck down the enemies before him.

Vinson and Aldric followed close on his heels, both amazed by the weapon's power and fearful of Lazarus' sudden transformation into an unstoppable instrument of death. Moments later Lazarus finished off the remaining Revenants, sending the survivors scurrying for safety down a side tunnel. Lazarus started to give chase, but Vinson grabbed him by the arm. Lazarus turned to face his brother, murder in his eyes.

"Get a grip, Lazarus!" Vinson shouted at him. "We have to get out of here, now! Let it go, Laz!"

It took a moment for Lazarus to come back to himself, but slowly the fire faded from his eyes, and he came back to his senses. He lowered the runesword, its magic drawing back into the blade, and he slumped slightly. Without the magic of the sword to sustain him, he felt weak and drained, as though he had not slept in days. Small shocks of energy traveled up and down his spine, the after-effects of the magic's use slowly beginning to become apparent to him.

"We had better hurry," Lazarus said, sagging against the chains that wrapped about him and threatened to pull him down.

They ran on down the tunnel through the cistern and back to the entrance that had brought them down. The Revenants did not reappear, and they ran unhindered through the crypt.

Minutes later they burst through the entrance that had admitted them and nearly ran headlong into the rest of their friends. Hemming them in was a sight none of the three brothers was prepared for. A sea of undead, stretching for as far as the eye could see, swaying like a forest of grisly trees in a breeze, surrounded them. There must have been thousands of the abominations, and there was no way they would be able to fight their way through all of them.

From atop the ruined walls of Caer Dorn, Asaru watched patiently as the Arkenstones emerged from the catacombs beneath the city and joined their besieged friends. Only a small portion of his minions were actually gathered there, but the effect was the same.

The Necromancer smiled.

They were resilient creatures. They had traveled across the plains despite the demons that were surely hunting them, navigated the forbidding Morah Weald, and found the vault containing the Krullstone.

They had fought their way through his Revenants and regained the surface.

Would they prove to be the bane of the Daemon Lords? He certainly hoped so.

He watched as they floundered outside the entrance to the catacombs, trying to find a way out of the bind they were in. He thought briefly of killing them. It would be so easy. They were the last of their bloodline, too, which meant their meddlesome kind would finally be exterminated. Then he could take the Krullstone and simply await the Daemon Lords in his own lands. Once they finished with the rest of the world they would surely come looking for their nemesis.

He thought better of it. It was best not to go against prophecy. By the time the demons came for him their power would have grown beyond a match for him, even with the Krullstone.

Asaru hated watching them go, but they served him best alive. With just a little luck the three would not survive their encounter with the Daemon Lords, and he could kill two birds with one stone. He sighed in resignation. He raised his hand, and the sea of undead parted to allow the small group to exit. Their time would come and so would his.

So many centuries wasted. What were a few more weeks?

He watched as Lazarus and his companions fled the ruins, his eyes burning with anticipation.

ൟ   ൟ   ൟ

"Where in the blazes have you been?" Neslyn asked heatedly. "You promised it would take less than an hour. Now look what we've got to deal with."

"We had some unexpected company," Aldric shot back.

"Looks like we have a common dilemma," Layek exclaimed. "Anyone care to tell me how we're going to get out of this?"

Lazarus brought up the Quietus Edge and prepared himself. "Stay close to me."

"Vinny, use the stone! Wipe them out," Aldric commanded

his brother.

"I don't know how! I haven't even had a chance to study it yet!" Vinson cried.

"Hold on," Layek interrupted. "You found it?"

"Yes," Vinson answered. "It was in a secret vault far below us."

Their friends were dumbstruck. Weapons slowly fell, and jaws went slack. For a moment the army of undead surrounding them was completely forgotten. Then they all started shouting at once, calling to see the stone, for him to use it against their enemies, demanding to know how it was they had come to possess it.

"Silence," Lazarus shouted at them. "There will be time later to hear the whole story! For now we need to get out of here!"

"He's right," Neslyn supported him. "What will we do, Lazarus?"

"We're going to walk right through them."

"Are you nuts?" Aurora Skall shouted. "They won't just step aside so we can pass!"

"Stay close." Lazarus ignored her protests and those of the others. He took a step toward the front ranks of undead. "Stand aside!" he commanded them. He brought up the runesword and called forth its magic, blue flame engulfing the blade once again.

Then there was a loud shuffling, the nerve-wracking sound of bone scraping against other bones, grating on rock. Slowly the crowd before him parted and gave way, creating a narrow channel for them to pass through. Lazarus took another step forward and stood within the hall created by the swaying bodies around him.

"Quickly now," he called to his companions. "Stay close to me and do not lag."

Vinson and Aldric pushed the rest forward, urging them to heed to Lazarus' instructions. Quickly they chased after their leader, the two brothers bringing up the rear and prodding their friends on ever faster. It was a nightmarish experience. Every direction they looked were the fearsome rotting faces of the dead, silently watching them as they passed. It seemed that the path carried on forever and that they might spend eternity running through this dreadful landscape.

At last it did end, and led by Lazarus, the group burst from the sea of corpses. They did not slow or look back, and together they charged forward into the night.

They ran for nearly a mile before Lazarus brought them to an uneasy halt. Eyes fixed on the darkness behind them as ears strained to pick up any sounds of pursuit.

"We need to pick up our supplies from the camp," Joseph Corsin reminded them.

"There isn't enough time!" Emeris Dallen blurted. "We have to get out of here before those things come looking for us. You saw how many of them there are; if we don't leave now, we're doomed."

"There isn't a choice," Layek said, breathing heavily. "We can't make it through the forest again without something to sustain us."

"Layek's right," Aldric added. "Besides, I don't think any of us want to go into that place in the dark."

Lazarus took a deep breath, fighting off the weariness that gripped him. "We can forage in the forest to feed ourselves along the way. We cannot stay here tonight. You remember what Asaru said."

Vinson and Aldric nodded. Lazarus was right. The Nameless One had given them fair warning and an impressive display of his power. Thus far he had been true to his word so they had no doubt that he would continue to keep it. They could not stay within his lands a moment longer than was absolutely necessary.

"Did you say Asaru?" Neslyn interrupted. "You mean *the* Asaru? The Nameless One?"

Recognition dawned on the faces of the three brothers' companions.

"You saw him?" Layek asked excitedly. "You actually talked to him?"

Aurora Skall broke in as well. "How did you escape him? And how did you get those undead to let us pass like that?"

So Lazarus told them — with a considerable amount of help from his brothers — all about their adventure in the crypt below the city. When the three had finished their tale, the rest of the group stared at them as though they were complete strangers.

"The most evil man known to this world let you go? Just like that." Layek, like the rest of them, was having a hard time swallowing the story. "And he just gave you the Krullstone and three runeswords to boot. Oh, by the way, you just happen to be related to a king. A very famous king."

"I find it as hard to believe as you do, Layek." Lazarus looked squarely at his friend. "I'm telling you that's exactly what happened."

"I'll be damned," Emeris Dallen whispered.

"The truth shall set you free," Zafer commented. "Sounds like the Necromancer has decided to test that theory."

"Plenty of time to discuss this on the way," Lazarus said, getting anxious. "We need to get out of here."

Having heard the story and seen for themselves the miracles that evening, the rest of the group were inclined to agree. Corsin took the lead with Zafer just a step behind, his sharp Elven eyes helping the tracker spot the trail for them, and they headed east. It was not long before the black wall of the Morah Weald greeted them like an unwelcome guest.

They halted for a moment to rest as they drew up to the threshold of the forest. They were tired and hungry, but those were secondary concerns. Lazarus would not permit them to stay, and despite their misgivings to entering the forest at night, none of them wanted to spend the night in the lands of Valinar after having met its occupants.

Zafer took the lead, his eyes better suited to picking out the trail in the dark of night. Together they plunged into the blackness, and in seconds the forest swallowed them up.

XIX THE LURE OF POWER

LAZARUS AND HIS companions walked slowly through the tangle of foliage that made up the outskirts of the Morah Weald. The branches overhead blocked out the moonlight and shuttered them in, blanketing them in blackness so thick it became difficult to discern anything around them.

They had not gotten far within the wood when he called a halt for the night. Progress was so slow as to be immeasurable in the near total darkness, and they were worn out from the day's events already. They found a spot that made for a decent camping site and immediately collapsed and fell asleep. A watch was posted, and regardless of the uncomfortable surroundings, the small group slept soundly through the night.

They awoke in the morning famished and only slightly refreshed but anxious to continue on their journey. They had achieved the impossible and survived the horrors of Caer Dorn, and food or no food they were chomping at the bit to get moving again. Instinctively they felt that if they could just clear this dismal forest, they were guaranteed to make it home.

Buoyed by their success, hopes soared, and moods were light. There were no complaints as they traveled, and even the reservations buried deep down inside them were momentarily squelched when Zafer foraged some roots and tubers for breakfast. It wasn't much, and they weren't particularly tasty, but it was enough to quell their grumbling stomachs.

They made good speed even though they stopped often to rest themselves. Lazarus insisted that they keep their strength up for whatever might lay ahead, and none were about to second-guess him in this place. The day passed uneventfully, and when night began to steal the color from the forest about them, they began to look for a place to hold out until dawn.

It took them only a short while to find what they were looking for, and they settled in quickly to await the coming darkness. Zafer and Neslyn made a short foray into the surrounding area to rummage up something to eat and came back with plenty more of the strange roots for everyone. They ate disinterestedly, and when darkness conquered, they quickly set up the watch and turned in for the night.

Dawn came without incident, and once again they resumed their march. It wasn't long before they began to see signs of the webbing that they remembered so well. Carcasses suspended in midair watched them in deathly silence as the group carefully made their way through the tangle of webs, avoiding with equal caution the traps that had already been sprung and the ones that had yet to trap a meal for their makers.

They were making their way carefully through a thicket that was particularly dense with the web snares when a lone bear-thing came barreling out of the brush. It made no sound as it approached, which is why they weren't aware of its presence until it was amidst them. It roared with fury as it cleared the surrounding foliage and went straight for Vinson.

Azrael cried out in warning but was too late. The beast, vaguely resembling a bear with massive limbs and feral eyes, windmilled into them, knocking Emeris Dallen flying before any of them had a chance to react.

It set upon Vinson as he turned to face it, claws sweeping in. Vinson was bowled over by its charge, and instantly the thing leapt upon him. Lazarus, cat-quick, drew his katana sword and jumped atop the beast's great back. With a grunt of force he thrust the sword deep into its back. The bear-thing roared in fury and reared up, trying to dislodge the killing blade. Lazarus was thrown from his perch and crashed into a nearby tree but was instantly on his feet again. The others rushed in to pull Vinson clear, who was dazed by the unexpected assault.

Weapons drawn, they rushed the thing, hacking and slashing at it. Though wounded, the beast was still a formidable foe, and it took them several minutes to bring it down. Finally it succumbed to the wounds they had inflicted upon it and fell to the ground. Emeris Dallen swooped in and severed its head with one deft blow.

They stood around momentarily, trying to recover from the shock of the sudden attack and to catch their breath.

Then several more beasts launched from their concealment, setting upon the group so quickly most of them didn't have time to set themselves. They knocked aside those who stood in their way and rushed at Vinson.

Aldric went down in a flurry of limbs and claws. More strange beasts emerged from the forest, a seemingly endless stream of hideous beings of every shape and size. Lazarus fought to reach Vinson, Zafer and Neslyn at his back. Azrael was flinging fire in every direction, sending monsters fleeing back into the woods. Smoke filled the air, choking them and stinging their eyes.

Layek's battle cry rose from the din as he pulled Aldric from underneath a tangle of screeching nightmares. In a crush they reached Vinson and stood back to back, fighting for their lives. Magic flared across the battlefield from the mages, and the rest cut down anything that came within reach.

Minutes later silence fell across the thicket as the last of the monsters fled from their fury. Smoke wafted through the trees, and bodies littered the ground.

"We have to get out of here before more of those things show up!" Lazarus breathed heavily, anxiously.

Zafer took the lead as they charged through the forest, trying to put as much distance between them and the killing ground as possible. Far off in the distance they heard the growls and cries of more creatures as they joined in the hunt.

They had not gone far when they were ambushed again.

More prepared this time, they met the rush head on, cutting a path through the dozen or so monsters that emerged to confront them. Without stopping they ran on.

Cries rose all around them. It seemed the whole forest was coming to life to hunt them down.

They continued like that the rest of the day, running when they could, standing to fight when they were forced to. By nightfall they were exhausted. Still the sounds of pursuit echoed throughout the cavernous forest.

Corsin found a hollow log and ushered them inside. It was cramped and smelled like rot, but it was defensible. It was closed on one end, which left only one way to get in but also only one way to get out.

They huddled close together and listened apprehensively to the sounds of their hunters outside. There was nothing to eat and very little to drink so with grumbling stomachs and parched throats they did their best to get comfortable and catch some sleep. None of them succeeded for much more than a few minutes because they were constantly being awakened by the sound of some beast or another as it passed close to their hiding spot.

Lazarus sat nearest the entrance, his sword drawn and resting on his lap, eyes watching the entrance to their makeshift stronghold with fearful vigilance. There had been no discussion of setting up a watch, but Lazarus was certain he would not sleep this night and did not mind guarding over his friends.

His mind raced with the events of the day and his own theories and musings. Constantly his thoughts returned to the words of Asaru and what they meant. If the Necromancer was telling the truth, and Lazarus' instincts told him he was, the Daemon Lords had known of them from the start. They must have known that they would go in search of the Krullstone and also that it was the only thing that could defeat them.

"Are you tired?" Vinson whispered, materializing next to him.

Lazarus jumped in spite of himself, his grip tightening on his sword. "Exhausted," he answered, "but there's no way I'm going to sleep with all this racket."

"What are you thinking?"

"I can't stop wondering about what the Necromancer said." Lazarus shifted in a vain attempt to relieve his cramped muscles. "If we really are the descendants of Valin Icarus and what that means if we are."

"That thing is not to be trusted," Vinson spat. "He would say anything to manipulate us."

"But why would he lie about that? What purpose does it serve him?"

"I don't know yet, but you can bet we haven't heard everything."

Lazarus sat silently for a moment. "I think Asaru was telling the truth."

"What difference does it make?" Vinson was exasperated. Not by his brother but by the unpleasant turns their adventure was taking. "We have to go on no matter what."

"True, but it helps to know all the details. History has a way of repeating itself. If what Asaru said is true, then this isn't the first time the Daemon Lords have tried to conquer our world. It also explains why we were sent to recover the Krullstone."

"Yes, but it still doesn't change anything." Vinson yawned.

Lazarus looked at his brother. "Perhaps you're right. Maybe I'm reading too much into this."

They were silent then for a time, each lost in his own thoughts, sorting through all the possibilities and outcomes of their quest.

Finally Vinson spoke. "Did you notice that all the things we fought today were coming after me?"

"Yes." Lazarus had hoped that the conversation wouldn't come to this point. "It's because of the Krullstone."

"You think so? You don't think Asaru had anything to do with it?"

Lazarus thought for a moment, considering the possibility. "No, he has no control over these creatures. And they're not demons. The lure of power is a dangerous thing."

"It scares me," Vinson whispered. "This whole time I've never really thought about where this was all leading. Now I can't stop."

"Don't worry," Lazarus consoled him. "We'll get through this."

"I never considered the prospect that we might not, but so many have died already, and we haven't even faced the real enemy yet."

"We have the Krullstone now," Lazarus pointed out. "Now we have a chance."

"What if I can't use it?" Vinson whispered, the doubt thick in his voice. "What if we don't make it out of this forest? Everywhere we go we are hunted; how long before we cannot surmount the challenge?"

"I won't lie to you and say that there isn't a chance we will fail. There is a good chance that we won't survive this. I have feared this day my whole life. That's why I always kept you and Aldric out of harm's way. I just wish that I could this time, too."

"I never understood that before this whole thing started," Vinson admitted, squirming against the confines of the log. "I'm glad you're here with me."

Lazarus grew solemn and serious, turning to face his brother and look him in the eye. "Vinny, listen to me. There may come a time when I won't be there to stand by you." He held up a hand to silence his younger brother's protest. "Just listen. There will come a time when you will have to use the Krullstone. Power is addictive and has a way of corrupting people against their will. I know you are trained to uphold order and stand for good and right in the face of great evil, but be wary. Do not use the stone in anger or hate. Do not succumb to the temptations that are surely in store for you."

"I will try."

"You must succeed no matter what happens to the rest of us." Lazarus gripped Vinson's arm. "Great trials are in store for us all, and I cannot promise that I will always be there to aid you."

"You forget that Melynda's vision predicts my death, not yours," Vinson reminded him softly.

"I swear to you that as long as I am alive I will not allow that to happen."

"You're a good brother, Laz." Vinson yawned, fighting to keep his eyes open. "I couldn't ask for a better man to share this quest with me."

Lazarus didn't answer him. He didn't have to. The ties between them were stronger than steel, and he swore to himself that this bond would protect his two brothers from whatever they faced. He swore that somehow they would all make it through this.

Whatever it took.

They spent the remainder of the night in silence, dozing on occasion, each taking turns trying to get whatever sleep he could in the uncomfortable confines of their safehold. The night passed slowly, and they constantly awoke to the sounds of the creatures stirring without, reaching uneasily for their weapons until the disturbance passed. Several times they heard thrashing and cries as predators found their victims, which only served to unsettle them more.

Morning came, and they slowly crawled out from their hiding place. Eyes darted around restlessly to make sure they were alone as they emerged from their log. They were greeted only by silence, and they took a moment to stretch their cramped and aching muscles.

Lazarus didn't let them rest long, however, feeling uncomfortable being out in the open. Zafer took the lead again, followed closely by the rest of them. They tried foraging as they walked, but their efforts did not yield much.

Snares made of the strange webbing lay at every turn, and they slowed their pace, trying desperately not to draw attention to themselves. They traveled for much of the day without any contact and without even hearing any sounds of the denizens of the forest. Lazarus guessed that most of the creatures were nocturnal hunters and would spend the daylight hours sleeping, giving him hope that they might escape a repeat of yesterday's harrowing march.

Then they reached a small clearing, where the silence was especially pervasive. Snares and webs were everywhere; some appeared as though the makers had not even attempted to conceal them.

"Based on what I've seen before," Zafer whispered as they huddled at the edge of the clearing, "these are new, made sometime last night."

"All of them?" Lazarus was surprised. "That would mean that they knew we would come this way."

"It's possible that there are other areas like this one all around us — that this is not a single instance but a wide attempt to snare anything that passes through," Corsin said but didn't sound convinced.

"Maybe it's just a fertile hunting ground for these creatures," Azrael offered. "Just a coincidence."

Lazarus' gut told him otherwise. He gazed out over the clearing and the tangle of webs within it. He lifted his gaze to the canopy above, and instantly his blood ran cold.

There, suspended high above them in the trees, were monsters straight out of his worst nightmare. Gigantic spiders, at least half a dozen of them, sat resting in their perches. Spindly legs curled tight around their black bulbous bodies; they appeared to be asleep.

"We'll go around," Lazarus whispered, pointing above the heads of his companions.

Gasps of surprise escaped the lips of several of them, and slowly they began to back away. They were almost clear, relieved that they had avoided disaster and still troubled by the seeming precognition of their hunters, when a twig snapped.

Instinctively they froze. They stood still for several minutes, waiting to see if the creatures sleeping above them had heard the sound. Minutes crept by, and nothing moved. Finally, satisfied that they had not been discovered, they began to tiptoe away.

Suddenly there was a shifting above them. There wasn't any noise to suggest it, but they all felt it.

Evil was stirring.

They looked skyward, and to their horror the spiders above them were shifting, slowly at first, stretching out their limbs and testing their supports. They were so engrossed with the ones they could see that they never considered the possibility that it was just a ruse.

Abruptly there was a rustling like leaves scraping against bark. And then Corsin screamed.

They turned about to see what had befallen their friend just in time to catch a glimpse of darkened limbs as Corsin was pulled up into the trees and out of sight. Zafer's bow sang in response to the attack, and half a dozen arrows sailed up into the canopy.

Neslyn was shouting in warning, and all of their eyes turned up. Dozens of the giant spiders were descending upon them, silent and deadly. Weapons were drawn hastily to meet the rush, and cries of warning rose up all around.

Azrael launched lightning bolts into the air, burning several of the monsters to a crisp before they hit the ground. Aurora Skall went down screaming, beset by several of the enormous creatures, and Emeris Dallen rushed to her aid. Neslyn and Zafer stood back to back, fighting to keep themselves from being whisked away.

Lazarus pulled free the Quietus Edge and instantly felt the magic surge through him. Yelling ferociously, he slashed at the things, hacking off limbs. Three of them fell lifelessly to the ground. Vinson and Aldric had their runeblades drawn as well, glowing with magic as they slashed through the enemies that beset them.

Confusion ruled on the battlefield. Shouts and cries filled the air, and more of the massive arachnids fell from the canopy. Growls began to rise from the forest around them as other beasts drew near, bloodthirsty and anxious to see what all the commotion was about.

Lazarus fought his way to his brothers, cutting through anything that stood in his path. Together they drove a wedge into the mass of bodies, hacking a path to rescue their friends. The sounds of ground-borne animals grew ever nearer, and monsters began to appear all around them.

"Run for it!" Lazarus shouted to his comrades as he opened a path for them.

In a knot they took off, Emeris Dallen in the center carrying an unconscious Aurora Skall. The others covered his flanks as Lazarus sliced his way through.

They broke into a dead run as they cleared the fray, opting to try to outpace their foes rather than stand and fight. Things rose up in front of Lazarus as they ran, and he cut them down without a second's thought, leaping over the bodies with quick glances back to be sure he had not lost his friends.

The sounds of pursuit grew distant, and they slowed to a brisk walk, winded and terrified. Finally they stopped altogether to regain their breath.

Emeris Dallen set Aurora down, and they huddled around her, worry lining their faces. Neslyn knelt next to the unconscious sorceress, feeling her neck for a pulse. Her breathing was shallow and her skin pale and drawn. Neslyn continued her examination, focusing her mind and probing her body for evidence of what ailed her.

"You have to save her," Emeris whispered, tears welling in his eyes. "She has to be all right. She has to be."

Emeris and Aurora had been lovers for many years; they had planned to be married during the summer. The two had been inseparable for as long as Lazarus had known them, which was nearly all of his time with the Legion. He hated to see them this way and silently cursed himself for not thinking his decision to bring them along a little more thoroughly before they had left. It was true that they were experts and he needed their experience, but if one or the other were to lose a life in this mess, he wasn't sure if he could forgive himself.

Far in the distance they could hear the sounds of the denizens of the Morah Weald as they hunted for them. Zafer and Layek glanced around anxiously.

"We should not linger here much longer," Zafer said uneasily.

"Lazarus." Emeris pulled him down next to him, his voice cracking with emotion. "You have to do something, Lazarus. You have to help Aurora."

"We will do everything that can possibly be done. Neslyn, what have you found?"

The sorceress lifted her face to meet Lazarus', resignation mirrored in the emerald pools of her eyes. "She was bitten by one of the spiders. I can't stop the poison. I can slow it, but she will have to fight for her own life."

Emeris Dallen began to cry, muttering unintelligibly as he knelt close to his partner. Lazarus placed a soothing hand on his shoulder. He thought to say something to encourage him, but the words simply escaped him.

Suddenly Layek cried out in warning.

Lazarus turned to see Zafer launching arrows up into the trees as fast as he could manage. There were several loud thumps as the targets fell from the foliage above, the Elf's arrows finding their mark. Lazarus didn't need to see a body to know what was up there.

"Move!" he yelled, pulling Neslyn to her feet. "Layek, take Aurora!"

Layek rushed over and threw the sorceress over his shoulder as though she weighed nothing at all and took off in a dead run, followed closely by Emeris Dallen, who refused to be more than a step away from her. Aldric and Vinson charged after them, keeping one eye on the limbs above. Lazarus came only a few steps behind, holding on protectively to Neslyn, leading her forward and fighting to keep up the grueling pace set by those ahead of him. She gripped his hand tightly as they ran, and his strength surged with her touch. Zafer covered their retreat with his bow, firing with deadly accuracy whenever sight or movement betrayed their attackers' locations.

Layek stumbled and went down, throwing Aurora to the ground. Emeris picked her up without losing a step and sailed past without even looking back. The two younger Arkenstones chased after, trying not to lose Emeris in the tangle of trees. Zafer surged forward and helped Layek to his feet, and together they ran on.

They went on like that for the rest of the day, running until they could run no more and resting until their enemies caught up with them. Twice they ran into groups of monsters and were forced to stand and fight. They battled their way through, miraculously unharmed.

Nightfall came, but their pursuers kept at them, and they gave up any hope of respite on this night. They were exhausted and starving, yet they hastened on, driven by fear and adrenaline. Dawn came, and they were still running, tired beyond comprehension or caring, persisting on willpower alone.

"Where does this cursed forest end?" Layek blurted out in frustration.

They came to a halt, breathing heavily and on the verge of collapse. They listened intently for several minutes, and when they didn't hear any sounds of pursuit, they sat down, heaving a sigh of relief. Emeris gently laid Aurora's limp body on the ground and sat down next to her, holding her hand and whispering soothingly in her ear. Zafer scrounged up some more roots and some nuts for them to eat, and they devoured the meager offering in seconds. Lazarus looked his friends over, judging their status by how ragged they looked. He offered to stand watch while they dozed or until they had to run again. Gratefully they accepted; most of them were asleep before their eyes had even closed.

Little more than half an hour into his vigil Lazarus' eyes grew heavy, and he was having a hard time keeping them open. He was afraid to fall asleep; his friends were counting on him to watch over them, and he had given his word that he would. He stood and paced around their makeshift camp, keeping himself awake through constant motion. Hours passed, and still he did not hear the sounds of pursuit like he expected to.

When it was about noon, according to Lazarus' calculations, he began to awaken his comrades. Groggy and foggy-eyed they woke from their slumber. They were a little surprised to find out how long they had been able to sleep but grateful still for the reprieve.

They scrounged up a little more to eat, watching the trees suspiciously, disbelieving that the calm would last. Lazarus and Zafer gathered some wood and constructed a makeshift stretcher to carry Aurora and gently laid her on it. They rested for a half an hour more before Lazarus became too antsy to sit around any longer. The more daylight they wasted meant more stumbling around at night, not a very appealing prospect after their latest nerve-racking evening.

Vinson and Aldric took the first shift carrying the stretcher, and slowly they set out. Lazarus led, with Neslyn close by his side. Since Aurora had fallen she had never strayed more than a few feet from him, and Lazarus felt comforted by her constant presence.

He set an easy pace, and they took short turns carrying Aurora to reserve their strength as much as possible for when they had to run again. There were no more surprises as they marched; in fact, the forest seemed quite serene and peaceful. If they didn't know better, they could almost believe that the Morah Weald was a sylvan paradise with its gigantic trees and calming quietude.

It was drawing near to dusk, the sunlight beginning to fade, deepening the shadows and the silence, when they crossed paths with their enemies once again. Lazarus was still leading with Neslyn at his side; Emeris and Azrael were carrying the stretcher with Zafer bringing up the rear. Vinson and Aldric were bunched up in the center near the stretcher when, without any warning, a net weaved of the thick webbing they had encountered before dropped from the trees above them.

Zafer saw the trap as it was sprung and cried out in warning to his companions, but it was too late. Their ambushers had weighted the ends of the net with large logs, and it tumbled down onto them swiftly. Without any time to react or even to draw their weapons, Vinson, Aldric, Azrael, Emeris, and the unconscious Aurora were snared. They thrashed out in confusion, which served only to entangle them more in the webbing.

Lazarus was instantly moving, yanking free his sword and rushing back to help, Neslyn only a step behind him. With deadly intent the spiders swiftly descended upon their prey. Zafer exhausted his remaining arrows, and several of their attackers fell lifeless to the ground, greenish blood oozing out of their pierced hides.

The arachnids ignored everyone but those caught within their snare. The more those within struggled, the tighter the net drew in around them, and the spiders moved in quickly to seal their fate and haul away their catch.

Several of the monsters moved to block Lazarus and the two Elves. Neslyn cried out in defiance and unleashed the fury of her magic, incinerating anything that stood in her way.

Lazarus leapt past the first line, and those spiders atop the netting turned to face him. Two of the dreadful beasts fell to his sword almost immediately. He deftly dodged and weaved, fighting off those spiders that challenged while at the same time slashing at the threads that held his brothers and friends captive.

More joined the fray and, realizing Lazarus as the immediate threat, made a beeline to intercept him. The eldest Arkenstone saw that his assault had garnered the attention of the fiends, and he bounded away, his foes in hot pursuit. They sought desperately to trap him, but Lazarus would not go that easily.

Tired as he was, he evaded the fangs and claws of the ugly beasts, hacking and slashing at their weak spots when he could. Half a dozen died at his hand, which served only to enrage them and intensify their efforts, more joining the melee. From the corner of his eye he could see Neslyn and Zafer, holding off what spiders remained behind while they worked diligently to free their comrades.

Suddenly, Neslyn and Zafer succeeded in releasing their subdued friends, and they cried out triumphantly. The spiders shrieked in fury and turned the full force of their rage against their escaping prey. Lazarus seized the opening and cut down those nearest him, racing to join up with the rest of the group.

Azrael and Neslyn unleashed a frightening barrage of magic against their adversaries, momentarily halting their assault. Acrid smoke filled the air, choking their lungs and making them light-headed. In the midst of the confusion Lazarus rallied his cohorts. He picked up one end of the stretcher, Zafer the other, and they raced away. Lazarus prayed that they were heading in the right direction.

It seemed that their foes were endless. For every one that they killed, two more took its place. He could only hope that once they were clear of the forest, the monsters would not continue to pursue them. If they were lucky, the magnetism of the Krullstone would not exceed their reluctance to venture outside their own habitat. *If we could just get free of this nightmare, we have a chance of surviving*, he told himself silently.

They ran for miles until their lungs filled with fire, and their legs felt like jelly, and then they ran some more. After their latest experience they were content to run until they collapsed from exhaustion or at least until they cleared the forest. It was better than risking another encounter with the monstrous tenants of the Morah Weald.

Night fell, darkening the world around them, and the forest closed in. There were no sounds of pursuit, but for the dwindling group that was more unsettling. At least if they could hear them, they could tell where they were.

They slowed their pace to a brisk march, unable to keep up the run any longer. Lazarus was practically asleep on his feet, but he refused to stop, even for the briefest of times. He was adamant about not staying another minute in this hellish place. Already he had lost one of his friends to the forest, and he would probably lose a second before long. He swore that he would not lose another.

Stopping was not an option.

Hours later the trees began to thin, and the night sky peeked through. The twinkling stars had never been a more welcome sight. Lazarus felt like it had been a whole lifetime since he had left the Solaris Plain, and now he looked out over the moonlit plains with newfound respect and fondness. They breathed a collective sigh of relief as the trees broke and finally gave way to the tall, wavy grasses of the plains. A cool breeze wafted out of the south, which seemed to revitalize them and uplift their spirits.

The tattered and worn group kept marching through the night, despite their fatigue. They watched the sun rise as they walked east, and when the first rays of daylight crested the horizon, they felt as though it was burning away all the tragedy and trauma that had been heaped upon them. Zafer took the lead, and Lazarus brought up the rear, constantly glancing nervously behind them for any signs that they were being followed, but there were none. As far as the eye could see the plains were empty.

They came a to a small bubbling brook and stopped to have their first drink of fresh water in days, gulping greedily at the delicious liquid. Lazarus remembered the supplies and horses that they had left behind before venturing into the forest, salivating at the thought of real food. To their amazement, Zafer was able to figure out that they had come out of the Morah Weald far south of where they had gone in, and they turned north. They all prayed that their stash was unspoiled.

It was just after midday when they finally spotted the grove where they had left their extra gear and horses. The sight lightened their feet, and they hurried on to reach it.

Moments later they were standing within the grove, rifling

through the supplies they had left there. They laid Aurora Skall on the ground under the shade, and Neslyn examined her once more while Lazarus and his brothers checked on the status of their goods.

The horses were in good condition and had not strayed from the enclosure, which meant that they would not have to walk home. Most of the food they had left behind had spoiled in their absence, but there was a good portion of cured beef strips that were still edible. Lazarus rationed some and set them aside for the trip home, and the rest he distributed among them, which they devoured ravenously.

Once their stomachs were filled their exhaustion finally caught up with them. Emeris lay down next to Aurora and was instantly asleep. Weary of body and spirit the others of the group tossed themselves to the ground and joined him.

XX UNEXPECTED COMPANY

KAIRAYN PLODDED WEARILY onward across the southern expanses of the Solaris Plain, eyes fixed on the path ahead of him. The sun was bright and harsh, scorching the plains and all those upon it. Heat wafted up off the grasslands in waves, blurring their vision of the horizon, making him see things that weren't there.

He had been delirious and weak, laid up by the poison of the hellhounds and the injuries he had received in the battle. Urgor had bound and treated his wounds and nursed him back to health. The Druhedar had lashed him to his horse and kept them moving until he had finally come to his senses.

Kairayn couldn't even remember anything since the demons had attacked. The fever had finally broken yesterday, and slowly but surely he was regaining his strength. Yet even though the fever had left his blood and the haze had cleared from his brain, fire still burned within his soul. An insatiable flame that cried out to be smothered in the blood of his enemies.

Another day and they would reach the Morah Weald. Their food was beginning to run short. He was sure they would not have enough supplies to last, but the plains seemed fruitful enough to support them, and there was no shortage of water. The trick was just to keep moving, and soon enough the journey would find its end.

If the demons didn't find them first.

Urgor told him that there had been no contact with the vile things who hunted them since the attack in the highlands that had claimed the lives of the rest of their comrades. All was quiet as they moved across the plains, growing ever nearer to their destination.

As they rode, Kairayn thought about what he would do once he was back in the Durgen Range, face to face with the cause of all his sorrows. He hated the demons and their masters now more than ever, not only because they were responsible for the death of almost a dozen of his countrymen and made his life in general miserable, but also because they had nearly killed him, too, and that made him angry beyond reason. He didn't mind brushing elbows with Death, but he didn't welcome it either.

They camped that night next to a bubbling stream, the calming sound of the water rushing over the rocks and soothing his fiery hatred, if only slightly. Urgor kept his distance from the Slavemaster, trying not to set off his fragile temper. They slept peacefully and undisturbed. Kairayn wondered if perhaps the demons had forgotten about them or if they were just letting them get comfortable before swooping in for the kill.

Morning found them unharmed and rearing to go. They ate their small rations without interest or feeling sated and set off into the west. The heat quickly grew unbearable, and the two Orcs did their best to ignore it. The dark line of trees that was the Morah Weald loomed up before them as they approached, and it became clear that they would reach the old forest before nightfall.

They spurred their horses onward, anxious to start a new leg of their journey and put the calamity of their previous experiences behind them. Kairayn wondered how much of a chance just the two of them would stand. He figured if anything they would be better off, harder to track and find. Maybe the Daemon Lords already believed they were dead, if they were lucky. Maybe that was too much to ask for.

Kairayn stopped suddenly, studying the ground. Urgor halted a few paces ahead and turned. "What is it?"

"Tracks," Kairayn said simply, hopping down off his horse. "Human tracks."

Urgor dismounted and came over to stand next to him. "What can you tell?"

Kairayn followed the prints for a few steps before turning back to trace them in the other direction. "They came from the southwest, out of the forest I suspect. They are headed north, eight separate sets of prints, two of them carrying something heavy. The tracks are indistinct and exaggerated. They're very tired."

"Can we catch them?" the mage asked.

"These prints are half a day old; we can catch them when they stop for the night if they can go for that long. We must hurry."

Urgor might not know what their true goal was — though Kairayn was sure that the mage had figured by now that they were after more than just paltry knowledge — but Kairayn knew that these humans had just come out of the Morah Weald. That probably meant that they had ventured into Valinar in search of the same thing he had been dispatched to find, and his gut feeling told him that they had found it, which meant that they had done the work for him, and all he needed to do now was find a way to relieve them of it.

Their tracks told him they were tired and weary from their journey into the unknown. By his guess the trip had not been pleasant, and it appeared that they had suffered casualties. He would bet that the burden they carried was one of their own. Even though the humans outnumbered them four to one, Kairayn was confident that with the element of surprise they would have little trouble removing the Krullstone from the humans' possession.

Of course, the first step was running them down and making sure they had the Krullstone. He hoped his gut was right. It would save him a lot of time and effort.

They pushed their horses harder, careful not to lose the trail they followed and watching carefully ahead of them to be sure they did not overtake their quarry too soon. At one point Urgor thought he saw a group of figures far off in the distance so they slowed their pace a little. Kairayn wanted to take them at night when they would be confused in the dark. It was absolutely imperative that the humans not know he was tracking them.

Little more than an hour later they spotted the humans again. Kairayn noticed the straggling group almost at the same time as Urgor, and instantly the two stopped. They quickly dismounted to conceal themselves as much as they could.

The humans were moving very slowly. Kairayn grinned in spite of himself. They were exhausted, apparently wandering at random across the plains.

It was a few hours past midday when the humans finally stopped. At first Kairayn thought they had somehow lost them as they disappeared into a grove of trees. The two Orcs waited relentlessly for them to reemerge, and several hours went by. Impatience crept into Kairayn's mind, and slowly he began to creep up on his prey.

He got as close as he dared, Urgor sneaking along next to him, and sat to wait for nightfall. Kairayn was convinced now that they would rest in the grove of trees for the night, if not longer. When darkness fell, he would make his move. He looked up into the sky to locate the sun and guessed that he still had at least four hours until dusk. He thought briefly about moving in now but decided against it. It was better to wait for dark when he could be certain that most of his quarry would be sleeping.

Kairayn whispered to Urgor his plan to wait and ambush under the cover of night. The mage nodded in agreement and settled comfortably among the long grass they were hidden in. Kairayn lay back, looking up into the clear blue sky.

He closed his eyes and tried to clear his mind of all the clutter that filled it to nearly bursting. Slowly his brain calmed itself, and he fell into a peaceful state of thoughtlessness. It was a welcome reprieve, and Kairayn let himself be cradled by the serenity of the plains, listening to the birdsong and breathing deeply of the fresh, clean air.

Time drifted lazily by like the occasional tuft of white cloud in the vast blue sky as it floated on the prevailing winds. Soon enough the sun dipped below the horizon, and the sky began to darken. Kairayn sat up and checked on Urgor, making sure that the Orc was awake and ready to move. He waited until full dark had taken hold of the land to tiptoe up to the grove where the humans had stopped earlier.

Without a sound the two stole up to the camp, stopping at the rim of trees to spy on their would-be victims. Kairayn saw only one on watch, a burly looking man with a wicked looking battleaxe. The rest were fast asleep, wrapped up in their blankets in a rough circle.

Kairayn got Urgor's attention, motioning toward the guard. Slowly, silently he drew a dagger from its sheath at his waist. Urgor readied himself and circled around to where the lone guard sat, sleepy-eyed and inattentive. They would have to be quick.

Kairayn took a step forward and signaled to Urgor to move in. Somewhere to his right a twig snapped. Kairayn froze in anticipation. Then all hell broke loose.

ও   ও   ও

It felt like it had only been a few minutes since he had fallen asleep when through the foggy haze of Lazarus' brain he heard Layek's familiar voice calling.

"Laz," he said softly. "Laz, wake up."

Lazarus rolled over and looked up at his friend. "What's going on?"

"Aurora's awake."

Instantly Lazarus was up. He walked briskly over to where the sorceress lie, still on the stretcher. Emeris was at her side, holding her hand and whispering desperately in her ear.

Neslyn was there as well, feeling Aurora's pulse and wiping the sweat from her forehead. She was barely breathing, and her skin was pale as death. The rest of the group was gathered not far off, their faces masked in concern.

When she saw Lazarus approaching, Neslyn stood and met him. The look in her eyes told him what he already suspected. A slight shake of her sad face confirmed it.

There was nothing she could do to help Aurora Skall. The sorceress would not last much longer.

Lazarus knelt next to Aurora and Emeris. He grasped Aurora's hand, and her eyes snapped open. "Be still, Aurora," he whispered.

Her eyes met his, and his heart sank. She knew she was going to die.

"Lazarus," she breathed, her voice barely audible. "Give me a moment alone with Emeris, please."

Lazarus nodded in consent and rose, sympathetically gripping Emeris shoulder as he stepped away. He joined the others, and they stood there together shifting uncomfortably. It was frustrating and heartbreaking to watch a close friend die slowly and not be able to help in any way. At least she could talk to Emeris one last time. At least there was some sense of fairness still left in the world.

Lazarus and the others could not hear what was being said, but it didn't matter. They didn't need or want to. Emeris was sobbing and shaking his head. Lazarus felt pity for the man; nothing could prepare a person for a moment like this, when he would have to say goodbye to his other half before losing her forever.

Abruptly Emeris stood and walked away, stumbling over his own grief. Vinson and Layek immediately went after him while Lazarus rushed to Aurora's side.

"It's okay, Aurora," he comforted her, taking her hand in his. "Breathe easy."

"Commander. Watch after Emeris. Promise me." She closed her eyes against the strain of speaking. "He will need you now more than ever."

"You have my word." Lazarus clenched his jaw. "I'll look after him. You just rest now."

Her eyes closed, and this time she did not open them when she spoke. "No regrets, Lazarus. It has been a pleasure."

Her hand went limp. A final breath escaped her lips, and then she died.

Lazarus held her hand for a moment, fighting back the pain he felt at having lost yet another friend. He stood and walked away from her body to the border of the copse, his temporary castle from the nightmare the world outside had become. The sun was sinking slowly into the horizon behind him, the heat shimmering off of the plains in waves. For just a brief moment it seemed as if it all could just be a horrible dream that he had yet to wake from.

Sighing heavily he resigned to the reality of his situation and turned back to where the rest of his companions were standing mute around Aurora's body. "Bury her here," he commanded, stone-faced. "May she rest in eternal peace. We'll move on in the morning."

He walked off to find where Emeris had gone. He found him near the stream, alone for the moment, and Lazarus took a seat on a rock next to him. The bubbling of the stream was soothing, and they were content just to listen. It was a long time before either of them spoke.

"Emeris, I don't know what to say. She was a good woman and a good friend."

Emeris sniffed. "I loved her. She was my life. Without her I am nothing."

"That's not true, Emeris. Your place is here with us, with your friends. Do not dishonor her memory by giving up."

"You have no idea what it's like," Emeris sobbed. "She was everything, and now it has all been taken away."

"I do not pretend to know the pain you feel. But I do know that she would have wanted you to go on with your life. I do know that we need you."

"I miss her so much!"

Lazarus placed a comforting hand on his shoulder and squeezed. "Pain fades with time. The loss of her presence can never be replaced, but if you let it, the void will be filled. She was a good woman; remember her well and honor her sacrifice. Your friends are here for you, and if you ever need anything, all you have to do is ask."

Emeris stopped crying after awhile and stared vacantly out into the distance. "Do you think she has gone to a better place?"

"I know she has," Lazarus answered him without hesitation. "She smiles down at us from a place without pain or fear or struggle. She watches over us and waits until the day when we can join her."

"I hope so."

"We should think about getting some food and some sleep. It's still a long way back to Illendale, and who knows what we'll run into on our way."

Emeris grew suddenly serious and intense. "I hope the demons come looking for us. I may not be able to get Aurora back, but I can get even with those responsible for her death."

"It is said," Lazarus replied, concern evident on his face, "before you seek revenge, first dig two graves. Be careful you don't sell your life too cheap."

Emeris didn't answer, and together they headed back to the camp where the rest of their companions were waiting, chewing absently on what passed for their evening meal. Zafer and Neslyn had managed to round up some berries to go with their salted beef strips. It wasn't much, but anything was better than starving.

Lazarus ate his food without interest. He insisted that a watch be set, and he outlined the order in which they would take their turns. It was barely dusk when they turned in for the night. Exhausted and ragged from their harrowing journey, disheartened by the loss of their friends, and weary from the long road behind them, they were asleep in minutes. The grove offered them a feeling of safety and isolation from the outside world, and their sleep was untroubled.

Lazarus, however, did not sleep right away. He lay awake staring up into the canopy overhead, remembering how far they had come and contemplating how far they had yet to go. He was in the middle of pondering how they would ever manage to get close enough to the Daemon Lords to destroy them when Neslyn appeared out of the darkness next to him.

He jumped in surprise at her silent approach. "You should be asleep. You must be exhausted," he whispered.

She laid down on her side, quite close, and whispered back to him, "Not as exhausted as you are. How many days since you had any sleep now?"

"What's on your mind?" Lazarus countered, ignoring her question.

"I can't stop thinking about Emeris and Aurora. It must be so terrible to lose someone that close to you."

"I can only imagine and pray that it never happens to me," Lazarus replied somberly. "I wouldn't wish that on anyone."

"It just occurred to me that I don't ever want to feel that way. I don't want to lose you." She looked deeply into his eyes, pressing close against him.

Lazarus' heart sped up. "What do you mean?"

"I am in love with you, Lazarus Arkenstone."

Lazarus was stunned into silence. He hadn't dared hope for this moment, and now that it had come he was overwhelmed with fear. Emeris' heartbroken visage flashed before his eyes, followed promptly by all of the bad things that could happen. These were dangerous times. It was hard enough watching his friends die, but could he survive it if the one he loved was taken from him as well?

He didn't think so.

"Neslyn," he was shaking as he spoke, "I care for you a lot, but these are dangerous times. I don't think I could bear it if I lost you."

"You're not going to lose me," she protested, tears welling up in her eyes. "Please tell me if you feel this as deeply as I do, regardless of your fears. I have to know, Lazarus."

When he didn't say anything for several minutes, she sighed in sadness, fighting to hold back her tears and hide the pain of his refusal to confess his feelings for her. She rolled away from him and sat up.

"You let your fear rule you. You would forsake something great for it. Foolish."

She moved to stand up, and Lazarus grabbed her arm, pulling her back down. Caught by surprise, she lost her balance and fell into his arms.

Lazarus pulled her close to him and kissed her hard on the mouth.

"I love you, too," he whispered.

Neslyn kissed him back, wrapping her arms around him tightly. They fell asleep holding each other close.

ço   ço   ço

Layek was fighting to keep his eyes open against the weight of his eyelids. It seemed to him that lead had been attached to them. Every second that passed was a battle against the weariness that had seeped into his bones.

He was so tired. The rest of his companions were fast asleep, dreaming of happier times and far away places. He sighed. If only he had a nice cold cup of ale to soothe his weary body. This heat was insufferable, lasting well into the nighttime hours, persisting as though the sun had never set at all.

He thought briefly of waking the next watch a little early. It was better than falling asleep on duty. He let the thought roll over in his mind and eventually let it go.

No, let them sleep, Layek told himself. They were as exhausted as he was, and if he could ease their burden just a little by sacrificing a few moment's of sleep, he would gladly do so. Especially for Lazarus and his brothers.

They weren't quite the same since they had found the Krullstone. It wasn't something easily identified or obvious. More like something just under the surface, waiting to break free. He had seen the devastation on Lazarus' face when Aurora Skall had died earlier. That made a total of five of his charges who would not be returning home. Lazarus hated it when soldiers under his command fell in battle; he took it very personally and often blamed himself for their deaths. But when it was your friends dying around you, it scarred you somehow — a slow eating away of the soul that eventually left you hollow and empty.

Layek looked over at his friend curled up with the Elf girl. He smiled in spite of his worry. At least there was some silver lining in this dismal business.

Suddenly, a twig snapped nearby. Somewhere off to his left, way too close for comfort.

He lifted himself from his seat and grabbed his battleaxe. He took a cautious step forward, scanning the darkness for any sign of movement or anything out of place.

He never saw what hit him.

Something big and heavy hurled out of the blackness and crashed into him with jarring force. The air was knocked from his lungs as he tumbled to the ground. His weapon fell away. He tried to cry out to warn his friends, but his voice refused him. Spots danced before his eyes, but he could still make out the vague shape on top of him.

It was as big as he was, all thorny and spiked, with two massive protrusions extending from its forearms. Evil eyes glowed wicked red, its breath hot and fetid.

Layek fumbled for the knife at his belt in desperation as the creature drew back to deliver the killing blow. Slipping it from its sheath, he buried the blade in the demon's throat and threw it off of him, the fiend gurgling unpleasantly and grasping at its neck.

Layek rolled to his feet, scooping up his axe as he did so. He circled rapidly, searching for more attackers, gasping for breath. Glowing red dots began to appear from the darkness, first a handful, then more until it seemed there was an endless sea of them.

Layek's heart sank. The demons had found them once again.

He tightened his grip on the battleaxe. His breathing slowed, and his mind calmed as he slipped into that place of complete concentration deep down inside. That place where it was kill or be killed. He felt the fury rise within him.

He roared in defiance at the monsters that threatened. The demons growled in response and started forward.

Instantly the rest of the group came awake, reaching for weapons and shouting in confusion. The demons charged into them with lightning speed, setting upon them before they had time to react. The company fought back desperately, Neslyn and Azrael launching magic wildly across the clearing, incinerating their attackers as they emerged. Emeris heedlessly charged into the demons, hacking like a madman. Layek was surrounded by a host of grayish bodies; Aldric was struggling to stay on his feet as a wave of the demons besieged him.

Lazarus wrenched free his runesword, igniting the magic within with a thought. Almost as quickly as he could get to his feet the demons were on top of him. He slashed and stabbed at his attackers, and several of them exploded into ash, but where one fell, more came to fill the gap.

Energized by the magic of the sword as it coursed through him, he counterattacked, driving the demons away from him. He heard an unfamiliar cry rise up out of the din and turned to locate it. To his complete and utter amazement, a lone Orc battled through the melee.

Momentarily caught off guard by the strange sight, he was mobbed and brought to the ground. He fought against the hands that pummeled him to no avail. He twisted his head to try to find his friends. What he saw made him go cold. Most of his friends were buried in a sea of dark, surging bodies. They were hopelessly outnumbered and completely overwhelmed.

"Vinson!" Lazarus yelled in desperation. "Use the stone! Vinny!"

Suddenly the demons atop him were ripped away. There stood Aldric, lost in a berserk rage as he cut through them like a scythe through wheat. His brother hauled him to his feet, and together they began to carve a path through the forest of demons to their beleaguered friends.

Neslyn was the only one still on her feet, throwing fire into the faces of the demons to keep them at bay. Her face was bathed in a sheen of sweat as she pressed the attack. Lazarus' heart ached seeing her stand alone, but there was no chance he could reach her.

The demons surged, and the two brothers were torn away from each other. Lazarus saw Aldric go down in a tangle of bodies. He screamed in anguish but was pulled away by the surging mob. He felt a stabbing pain in his leg and dropped to one knee.

He lashed out in frustration. The magic of the Quietus Edge burned through his veins, intensified by his anger and desperation. He felt himself slipping away into a mindset he had never experienced, a dark place where there was no emotion, only cold, hard determination. A monster lurked there, and Lazarus was afraid to set it free.

Then something amazing happened.

There was a bright flash of light, and a triumphant cry emerged from Vinson's throat. His hand was sheathed in the Krullstone's gauntlet, the stone glowing so bright that it was like day in the thicket. Vinson's eyes were hard as steel as he glared at the hordes of stunned demons surrounding him.

He raised his hand menacingly, and the light forked out of the gauntlet like tendrils of smoke, twisting and weaving.

Those demons that were closest were engulfed, becoming little more than a dark cloud within the light. Slowly they were drawn back into the stone, streamers of discoloration in an otherwise perfect sea of white.

Then they disappeared in a burst of smoke. The silence of it all was frightening.

At that moment other strands of light swept forth, engulfing and expanding, drawing the essences of Vinson's foes back into the stone. Vinson's eyes shone like beacons, but Lazarus could see the fear in them, contained just behind the magic's façade.

The demons broke and ran, scattering in every direction. Lazarus and the others stared in awe as Vinson sent the light forth, consuming everything it came in contact with.

Vinson chased them from the clearing and pursued them out onto the open plains. Dozens upon dozens were destroyed by the Krullstone's power. In minutes there were no demons left.

He stood there, hand outstretched for what seemed like an eternity. He turned to face his mesmerized friends, eyes clouded by the magic's fire. For a moment he looked as though he might turn the power of the stone onto his friends. Then he seemed to regain control of himself. The light flared briefly and disappeared back into the stone, and Vinson sagged with fatigue.

Lazarus rushed forward and caught his brother as he fell to the ground. His face etched with worry, he laid him gently in the dry dirt, cradling his head. The others crowded around to glimpse what had become of him. Neslyn pushed her way forward and knelt beside Lazarus, feeling for signs of life.

"He'll be fine," she whispered breathlessly. "He's just weakened by the magic's use. Tomorrow he should be right as rain."

"Did you see that?" Zafer asked, dumbfounded.

Lazarus ignored the question. "Is anyone hurt? Is anyone missing?"

He took a quick headcount and breathed a sigh of relief. Death had spared them this night. Neslyn looked to their wounds, surprisingly minor given the circumstances. She eyed Lazarus with deep concern as she examined the puncture in his leg; her eyes told him that she was scared. He had never seen that before.

Lazarus ordered a search of the immediate grounds to determine the status of their possessions and horses. Several of their horses were dead, which meant half of them would be walking home. That would slow them down considerably, Lazarus thought in dismay.

"Hey! Over here!" Zafer called out from the trees. "As if we didn't have enough surprises tonight!"

They rushed over in a knot to see what the Elf had discovered, crowding around him like curious children. There on the ground, unconscious and wounded, was an Orc. Lazarus remembered then seeing the Orc fighting against the demons and told the others what he had seen.

"So what do we do with him?" Layek questioned gruffly.

"We should leave him here," Aldric put in icily. "Let him take care of himself."

"We'll take him with us." Lazarus put up his hands to fend off the protests of his friends. "We cannot just leave him here to die. We might as well kill him ourselves. And since he cannot defend himself I cannot allow that."

Lazarus knelt down to get a closer look. "Take his weapons and tie him up. He may have some useful information at least. Neslyn, look to his wounds."

The princess looked at him like he had gone mad. He stared her square in the eye and finally she gave in. She knelt down to examine the Orc while Layek stripped away his weapons, the others fanning out to see if there were more of their enemies skulking about. They found the body of a second Orc not far off, mutilated almost beyond recognition.

"Do you think the Daemon Lords will know we have used the Krullstone?" Aldric asked Lazarus at one point as they packed up their equipment.

Lazarus thought for a moment about this. "Yes. Given that the creatures of the Morah Weald could sense the Krullstone's presence without it being used, I would have to conclude that the Daemon Lords would easily be able to sense its location when it was used. After all, they dwarf the monsters of that forest in power and knowledge."

"We haven't much time then," Aldric stated simply.

Lazarus decided that they would finish out the night in their campsite, presuming that it would take the demons some time to rally another strike against them. They would need the rest for the days ahead. Now their journey had become a race against time; they must reach the safety of Illendale before the demons caught up with them again and finished them off for good. The Orc was tied securely to a tree, and they placed Vinson on the same stretcher they had used for Aurora only hours earlier.

They set a double watch for the remainder of the evening and returned to their sleeping rolls, although few of them slept for very long.

XXI BETRAYAL

DAWN FOUND LAZARUS and his companions exhausted and spirit-worn but otherwise no worse for wear. Vinson was still unconscious so they strapped him to one of their few remaining horses, along with the bulk of their gear and the wayward Orc, and began the long walk east.

Their eyes continually scanned the horizon for any sign of movement, and they jumped at every suspicious sound or whenever an animal darted from its cover at their approach. Weapons were kept handy and immediately accessible.

The sun rose quickly in the sky and the heat with it, sapping their energy and scorching their skin. Wearily they marched across the plains, stopping only occasionally to rest and refill their water stores in the numerous streams and brooks that crossed their path.

Vinson came to shortly before noon, groggy and disoriented. They untied him from his position atop the stallion and set him down. They gave him water and let him get his bearings before explaining to him what had happened since the night before.

He accepted the story without question. Neslyn looked him over to be sure he wasn't hurt, much to Vinson's irritation. He insisted that he was perfectly all right and didn't need to be looked after. Oddly, he grew even more disturbed by their myriad questions about the Krullstone and how it felt to use it, brushing them aside with short, gruff answers. They left him alone to sort out his own thoughts after that.

Lazarus insisted that they not linger too long and so set out once again, Vinson walking along with them as though nothing had ever been wrong. It seemed to the rest of the company that he was stronger than when he had fallen unconscious after using the stone. He didn't seem tired or fatigued at all like the rest of them were, and on several occasions he had to slow his pace so that they could keep up. He found his stride eventually, and they moved smoothly along in silence.

As they walked, Lazarus took the opportunity to pull his brother aside. Trying not to draw attention, he grabbed Vinson's arm and held him back, letting the others put some distance between them so they could talk in private.

"How do you feel?" Lazarus asked of his younger brother.

"Like a million gold pieces," he replied. "I can't explain it, but I feel energized, strengthened somehow."

"That's the Krullstone. When you used it against those demons, it looked like they were drawn back into the stone."

"I know. I can feel them inside me. I can't describe it, but they're all there inside my head. Sometimes memories that aren't mine surface. I hear strange thoughts and voices inside my head that don't belong to me. It's like a dark stain on my soul. Even though I have destroyed the demons, part of them lives on in me."

The elder Arkenstone said nothing.

"At the same time," Vinson continued, "I feel like a part of me is missing. Like a man with missing fingers, only something missing from inside of me instead."

"Are you sure you're okay?" Lazarus asked.

"I said I was fine!" Vinson blurted harshly. "I'm sorry. I don't know where that came from."

"It's okay. I know where it comes from." Lazarus looked his brother square in the eyes, concern on his face. "I want you to promise me something."

"Don't worry, I'm not going to do anything foolish."

"I know. But I want you to promise me that you will not use the Krullstone again unless absolutely necessary."

Vinson regarded him solemnly. "I promise. I'm not all that eager to add to the new residents in my head."

"Good," Lazarus replied with relief. "With any luck you won't have to."

Lazarus picked up his pace to catch up with the others, but Vinson placed a hand on his shoulder to hold him back. Lazarus was surprised by the strength he found there.

"What do you think will happen if I use the stone on the Daemon Lords?" Vinson asked softly. "It scares me to think about it, but if these lesser demons have such an effect on me, what will their masters do?"

"We'll burn that bridge when we come to it," Lazarus responded, not having any other answer. "Maybe you just weren't prepared for the side effects of the stone's magic. Perhaps they will fade with time. Next time you'll be better prepared to resist them."

"I hope you're right." Vinson didn't sound convinced.

They plodded wearily onward, concentrating on putting one foot in front of the other. Slowly the sun arced its way across the sky as though a great hand were holding it back, the hours creeping past.

Late in the afternoon the Orc began to regain consciousness. They didn't know how long he had been awake when he growled deeply and demanded that they release him. They stopped in their tracks and eyed the Orc suspiciously. He returned their stares with one as cold as winter.

Layek and Aldric scouted ahead until they found a suitable place and led the others to it. The two had found a small gully surrounded by trees, which had a stream flowing through it for fresh water and a towering elm that offered shade from the tyrannical sun. It would conceal them from anything on the plains above and offer some security for the travel-worn company.

Lazarus had the Orc tied to the tree and after a while brought some food and fresh water and knelt beside him. "Hungry?" he asked. The Orc nodded, and Lazarus adjusted the ropes to allow him the use of one hand without releasing him from his bonds to the tree. Lazarus handed him a water skin and a handful of dried beef strips. Drawing a dagger from his waist in case he tried to escape, he sat down facing the Orc. He waited patiently as he devoured his food and gulped down his water.

"What is your name?" Lazarus asked after the Orc had finished.

The Orc regarded him coolly but did not answer. Lazarus returned his stare, refusing to back down from his own prisoner.

"You know I could have left you for dead back there. Or I could have just let you starve; we need the food for ourselves."

Still the Orc said nothing.

"Very well then," Lazarus sighed, raising himself from the ground. "I'll make sure you are given more water. I'll check back later in case you change your mind and decide you do want someone to talk to."

Lazarus retied the ropes around the Orc and walked away. He walked right past the others of the company who were resting and conversing idly in the shade and headed up the steep embankment of the gully. He sat beneath a stubby little tree, facing out to the west.

He sat in silence, trying to clear his head of the frustration he felt. He had saved the Orc's life, fed him, and kept him in good health. The least he could do was give Lazarus the courtesy of a name. Lazarus gritted his teeth. Surely this Orc was holding some information he could use against his enemies, which was probably why the Orc had refused to talk to him. If he had been in the Orc's place, he would have done the same, he supposed.

Still, it didn't make his frustration go away or answer any of his questions. Why had the Orc been fighting against the demons? Weren't they supposed to be on the same side? Had the Orc been double-crossed by the demons once they had known the Krullstone had been recovered? Or had they been tracking his group separately and by chance had run into each other as each tried to ambush them? Too many questions and not enough answers. Answers only the Orc could provide him.

He stayed out there for a long time, savoring the sights and sounds of the plains, calming his weary and overworked mind. With a sigh he heaved himself from his seat and started back to the camp. Now that he had had some time to think about it, maybe the Orc would be willing to talk.

Lazarus was just starting down the slope of the gorge when he heard commotion coming from the camp below. He broke into a run, worried that perhaps the Orc had escaped or that the demons had found them again.

He was wrong on both counts.

What he saw when he broke through the brush enraged him and worried him beyond his already stretched patience. Vinson was apparently trying to interrogate the prisoner, but when the Orc had failed to respond, he began beating him mercilessly. Neslyn, Zafer, Layek, and Aldric were arguing with Emeris and Azrael over the fate of the Orc, pushing and shoving each other violently. At any moment it appeared the argument would break out into a full-scale fight.

Lazarus rushed down into the fray, jumping in between them and separating them from each other.

"Stop this insanity right now!" he bellowed. "What in the name of the gods is wrong with you?"

They stopped their bickering and lowered their eyes, ashamed and unable to meet Lazarus' own fiery glare. Vinson continued to hit the Orc, heedless and unaware of Lazarus' arrival.

"Tell me what you know, you pile of filth!" Vinson shouted vehemently. "Speak or I'll crush you like the insect you are!"

Vinson hit the Orc again, knocking him sideways. Blood leaked from the Orc's mouth and nose, and bruises were already beginning to appear on his skin. Lazarus darted to his brother and grabbed him from behind, locking his arms behind his back.

Vinson fought back violently, angrily trying to shake his brother off of him. Lazarus didn't remember his brother being this strong. It was all he could do to hang on.

"Stop it, you fool!" Lazarus shouted. "What the hell is wrong with you?"

Layek stepped in, and together they subdued Vinson while the others looked on to see what would happen. Layek, being much stronger than Vinson, forced Vinson to his knees. Vinson struggled in vain.

Lazarus knelt before his brother, the fury of his temper fully unleashed. "Calm down right now, or I'll knock you upside the head so hard you'll wake up in a new age!"

Vinson stopped struggling, but the fire didn't fade from his eyes. "Why are you defending him? He's an Orc! Our enemy last time I checked. It's his fault our friends have died and his fault that we had to make this journey in the first place. We should have killed him when we found him!"

"What's gotten into you? He is a prisoner. An unarmed prisoner. It is our duty to care for him so long as he is alive."

"Traitor," Vinson seethed with anger. "Why don't you just carry him back to the Durgen Range so he can kill more of our friends?"

Lazarus flushed with rage. "Captain Arkenstone!" He never addressed his brothers formally, but Vinson had crossed the line, and Lazarus was not about to be talked down to by his own blood. "You will control yourself! So long as you are in my unit you will obey my orders, or I will have you court marshalled for sedition! If you or anyone else raises a finger against this prisoner without my express permission, I will personally take pleasure in watching you suffer. Is that clear?"

Lazarus searched the faces of his comrades. One by one they nodded their assent. He turned his eyes back to Vinson. He seemed to come back to himself and lowered his eyes in disgrace.

"Where has your honor gone, brother?" Lazarus asked Vinson quietly. "I never thought I would see the day when you raised your fist against someone who could not defend himself."

Vinson did not answer, keeping his eyes glued to the ground before him.

"Layek," Lazarus called sharply. "Get him out of my sight."

Layek lifted Vinson off the ground and led him away. The others turned to go, except Neslyn, who came over to Lazarus' side.

"What happened, Neslyn?" he asked her sadly.

"I don't know," she answered. "One minute all was quiet, and the next, Vinson just lost it. We tried to stop him, but Azrael and Emeris stepped in. Are you okay?"

"I don't know. Something's wrong with Vinny. He's not himself. He would never do something like this."

Neslyn hugged him impulsively, and he hugged her back. They

held each other for a few minutes before Lazarus pulled himself away. He turned to look at the Orc who was watching them from the ground where he had fallen a few feet away.

"Neslyn, do what you can for his wounds," Lazarus directed as he pulled the Orc to a sitting position.

Neslyn checked the Orc over, using her magic to heal the wounds he had sustained. When she finished, she looked at Lazarus intently, her eyes glittering with admiration. "I was right about you. It takes a lot of conviction to do what you just did." She studied him a moment longer. "I'll go check on the others."

Lazarus watched her walk away. "Neslyn," he called after her. "Thanks."

She flashed that dazzling smile of hers, and Lazarus turned his attention back to the battered Orc. He lifted him up and moved him back over to the tree he had been tied to earlier, setting him down to rest. "I'll have some water brought up for you," Lazarus said as he checked the ropes binding the Orc. "Are you hungry?"

The Orc studied him coolly. "No, thank you."

Lazarus was taken aback by the Orc's sudden decision to speak. "What is your name?"

"I am called Kairayn. I am Slavemaster to the Druhedar. Why did you stop them?"

"There is no honor in attacking a person who cannot defend himself. There is no excuse for it."

"I would not have done the same for you," Kairayn stated bluntly in a deep, gravelly voice.

"One must be careful that he does not become the enemy he fights against."

There was an awkward silence between the two as they sized each other up.

"I haven't told you who I am yet. I am Commander Lazarus Arkenstone, Phoenix Legion."

"Why are you all the way out here?" Kairayn asked. "You're way outside your borders."

"I could ask you the same thing, but I think we both know the answer to that question." Lazarus hoped the Orc would take the bait.

Kairayn bit. "The Krullstone. You must have found it, otherwise you would not be returning home."

The confirmation pleased Lazarus. Even though Kairayn had not admitted to being in search of the stone, it was apparent that was his goal by the way his eyes lit up at the mention of it.

"Tell me why the demons were trying to kill you back there. Aren't you supposed to be allies?"

Kairayn fixed him with his stare. The Orc sighed and decided, for reasons Lazarus did not fully understand, to confide in his honorable, yet human, captor. "The truth is, I was sent to find the Krullstone by the High Summoner. Apparently the demons didn't take too kindly to us sneaking behind their backs."

"What did you expect, Kairayn? Demons are not to be trusted under any circumstances. I would've thought that your High Summoner would be smarter than that."

"What do you know about it, human? It is a means to an end. Once we have finished using the demons to fulfill our destiny, the High Summoner will send them back to where they came from." Kairayn was disgusted just thinking about them.

"Do you really believe that? After all that you've seen? The demons won't ever leave," Lazarus stated matter-of-factly. "Once they have eliminated any threat to their supremacy they will destroy you. I think you've already gotten a taste of that."

Kairayn looked him over contemptuously. "I no longer wish to speak with you."

"Very well," Lazarus replied, content. "I will see to it that food and water are brought to you. You should know, Kairayn, that I have been shown a vision. A vision in which either the demons or your master, Grubbash Grimvisage, will destroy this world. What then of your precious destiny?"

Lazarus stood up and walked away. He smiled faintly. Deep down inside Kairayn knew as well as he did that the demons would never leave. He must know as well that someone as greedy for power as the High Summoner would use the Krullstone as soon as the oppor-

tunity presented itself. Lazarus could practically see the wheels turning
in the Orc's mind as he mulled over the obvious truth of the situation.
The seed had been planted. What would happen when it blossomed?

It seemed probable to Lazarus that Kairayn knew little, if
anything, of the High Summoner's invasion plans. The Slavemaster
would have had to leave the Durgen Range weeks ago in order to catch
them here on the plains. That being the case, Lazarus wasn't quite sure
what to do with the Orc. Obviously, he couldn't set him free. That
would be far too dangerous a risk. On the other hand he couldn't hope
to glean much more information from him, except perhaps the details of
where the Daemon Lords were hiding. Their food supplies were
stretched as it was, and having an extra mouth to feed would only strain
them further. His only hope, he guessed, was in convincing the Orc of
the error of his ways and getting him to help them slay the Daemon
Lords. It was a long shot, but he didn't have many other options.

It was growing dark, and he coolly met the questioning stares of
his companions when he rejoined them. For many long moments he just
stood there, surveying his comrades, judging by their looks the manner
of their attitudes.

"Captain Dallen, Azrael," he spoke suddenly, a hint of anger
creeping into his voice. "The two of you have disgraced yourselves by
your actions today. I am very disappointed. For your punishment you
will both take an extra watch tonight. If there is so much as a scratch
on the prisoner when I wake in the morning, you will both pay in blood.
Clear?"

They nodded solemnly.

"Good. Now go. Darkness is already upon us."

The two walked away dejectedly. Lazarus knew that they now
realized how wrong they were, having had time to reflect. He was sure
also that they were remorseful for their behavior, but it was of supreme
importance that they, along with everyone else, understood that it would
not be tolerated, and such actions would be met with extreme punishment. It pained him to scold his friends so, but it was necessary to
maintain order and control.

"Where is Vinny?" Lazarus asked.

"He's down by the creek," Layek answered. "It took a while to calm him down, but I think he's finally come around."

"What's gotten into him, Laz?" Aldric asked quietly. "It's not like him."

"I know, Aldric. It's the stone. It's having a strange effect on him."

"You can say that again," Layek quipped. "I'd say it's chewed him up and spit him out."

"Stuff it, Layek," Lazarus shot back. "This is no time for your jokes."

Lazarus found his brother sitting on a rock twenty feet down the bank of the small river, staring blankly into the waters as they rushed by.

"It's getting dark, Vinny. You should come back to the camp."

"I can't go back there," Vinson said soberly. "I am so ashamed."

"Whether you like it or not, you have to come back. You can't just abandon us."

"I'm sorry, Laz. I let the stone get the best of me."

Lazarus put a reassuring hand on his brother's shoulder. "You've got to get your head straight. We're barely holding on to a precarious balance here, and I need your help to keep it all together."

"I won't let you down again, Laz." Vinson breathed a sigh of relief.

"Now why don't you come back with me and get something to eat? You've got to be hungry as a bear."

The two stood and strolled lazily back to the camp where the others were already preparing for sleep. No one said a word as Vinson and Lazarus approached and began to prepare their bedrolls. Lazarus looked around and didn't see any sign of Emeris or Azrael, and it was a good thing. His anger still smoldered within, and with an effort he forced it back down.

Neslyn came over to him and set her bedroll next to his. Together they lay, looking up at the stars and holding each other close until at last they fell asleep.

ɠ   ɠ   ɠ

The doppelganger watched Lazarus coldly as he settled in for the night. So smug. It focused its cruel eyes on the commander, snuggling with the Elven princess.

His day would come.

For now, though, there was work to be done. It watched closely as the rest of the group drifted off to sleep one by one. The moon rose slowly into the night sky, its silvery fullness frigidly illuminating the glade with its pale glow. Crickets chirped noisily nearby, and flying insects buzzed around its ears. The doppelganger swatted irritably at them as it bided its time.

The appearance of the Slavemaster was fortuitous indeed. All it had to do now was set the Orc free and steal the Krullstone from the one they called Vinny.

Clouds were gathering on the horizon, dark and menacing. Rain was on the way. That was good; it would hide the Orc's tracks as he made his escape and make it nearly impossible to follow him. Just one more circumstance in its favor.

Things were coming together perfectly.

The doppelganger spied out the watch. Slowly, silently it began to weave the spell that would incapacitate the unwary humans.

In moments the web had been laid. The doppelganger looked closely at the man on guard, watching his breathing slow until his head slumped. The others of the party were out like snuffed candles; none of them would be waking until he was ready for them to.

Swiftly the doppelganger was up and moving. Silent as death it crept up on the sleeping members of the group, singling out Vinson from the dark masses on the ground. Careful not to trip or step on any errant limbs, it knelt over Vinson's sleeping body. Delicately the doppelganger searched the man's body for the Krullstone and found it clutched tightly in his hands. It slowly pried the gauntlet from his fingers and stepped away.

It headed straight for the tree where the Orc was restrained. Clouds blocked the moon, and darkness closed in as it approached the captive. He was still asleep from its magic when it knelt next to him. It brought one hand up and spoke the arcane words that would wake him from his slumber, warmth spreading from its palm into the unconscious Orc.

The Orc's eyes snapped open. He gasped in surprise at seeing who had awakened him, and loathing filled his eyes. "You," the Orc whispered, hate thick on his tongue.

"Easy, Orc. What is your name?"

The Orc did not answer, only stared at it, pure venom on his face.

The doppelganger chuckled wickedly. It let its face revert briefly to its original form. It watched as the hate faded and was replaced by surprise and a hint of fear.

"Do not fret, little Orc," the doppelganger whispered conspiratorially. "I am not here to kill you. On the contrary, I have come to set you free. Now do you wish to tell me your name?"

"Kairayn."

"Ah, yes. The Slavemaster. You are the one I need." The doppelganger deftly sliced the ropes securing the Orc. It extended its hand and helped Kairayn up.

"Why are you helping me when all the other demons have been trying to kill me?" Kairayn asked suspiciously, rubbing at his wrists.

"We serve the same lord, Slavemaster. Here." It withdrew the Krullstone from within its robes and handed it to the Orc. "I believe this is what you came to retrieve. You will return this to the High Summoner without delay. He is expecting you. Dawn is in a few hours; I strongly suggest you make haste."

Kairayn stared at the demon dumbfounded. He glanced down at the gauntlet in his palm, wondering if this really was the Krullstone or just a ruse. The doppelganger walked briskly away without saying anything further.

It took several minutes for Kairayn to come back to himself. He couldn't believe this incredible stroke of luck.

Smiling broadly, Kairayn snuck down into the camp. He could not see the doppelganger, but he was in search of something else entirely. He couldn't exactly wander out into the wilderness completely unprepared. Quietly Kairayn rummaged through the packs laying on the ground until he found what he was looking for. A short sword and a brace of daggers, which he stuffed into his belt, a handful of dried beef strips the humans had fed him earlier, and a full water skin. He thought briefly of taking one of the horses to speed his escape, but when he went to check on the animals, he found them all still in the thrall of the doppelganger's spell, fast asleep. He decided not to risk alarming the animals by waking them and returned to where the rest of the party was sleeping.

He put everything back the way he had found it, reasoning that it would take them longer to realize he was missing if nothing was out of place, giving him that much more of a head start. Satisfied, he turned and slipped off into the night, thunder rumbling ominously in the distance.

ა   ა   ა

Lazarus awoke in the morning with water dripping on his head, completely soaked through. Apparently it had started raining some time ago. Dark clouds loomed overhead, discharging water down upon him steadily. The color was drained from everything, leaving the land cast in dreary gray that sucked the energy from him.

Though the sun was completely hidden behind the gray mass of clouds, the heat still persisted, and his clothes clung to him in a sticky mass. Woodenly he rose and strapped on his gear, enjoying a brief moment of silence before waking the others. They ate a meager breakfast, their usual diet plus some berries that Neslyn rummaged up. Lazarus checked on their horses while the others prepared themselves for another long day of marching. It wasn't until Layek went to check on their prisoner that they realized something had gone terribly wrong.

"Lazarus!" Layek shouted. "We've got a problem!"

Everyone rushed up to see what was going on, Lazarus fearing the worst. He was already considering punishments and how he would discover who had harmed their prisoner when he reached the tree where Kairayn was supposed to be. His jaw fell open when he saw that the Orc was missing. His ropes lay severed in a heap at the base of the trunk.

Layek and his brothers looked at him knowingly. The traitor. It was the obvious answer to how the Orc escaped. He didn't even bother to ask who was on watch last night; it didn't matter. He knew already that there was no way to tell which of them had set the prisoner free.

Lazarus sighed in resignation.

Then Vinson started shouting in distress. "The Krullstone! It's been taken! That damned Orc stole the Krullstone!"

The blood drained from Lazarus' face. He saw equally troubled looks mirrored on the faces of his companions. If the Orc was able to make it back to the Durgen Range with the stone, they were all doomed. All of their sacrifices and hard work would be for nothing. If the Orc escaped them, the demons would win.

"We must go after him," Lazarus said to no one in particular. "He cannot be allowed to escape."

"Well," Aldric interjected. "Let's not stand around socializing about it."

They moved quickly to pack up the remaining gear, realizing as they did that the Orc had also stolen provisions and weapons from them. Zafer charged about, vainly searching for any sign of which direction the Orc had traveled, but the rain had washed away every trace.

"He would be heading south back through the highlands," Lazarus concluded. "It's the only way he could have gone."

No one bothered to argue with him. He was right, of course, and in any case none of them had any better ideas. Lazarus gave two of their four remaining horses to Aldric and Zafer with orders for them to ride out ahead in search of Kairayn. Their chances of finding him were better if they divided their resources. The Orc obviously had several hours' head start, and it would take a miracle for them to catch up with him in this weather.

And so the chase began.

The rain persisted for several days as they sped south across the grasslands, and there was no sign of their quarry. They reached the Mirrormere and skirted its eastern shores, presuming that Kairayn would follow the straightest route back to the Durgen Range.

The landscape slowly began to change, the grasslands and groves reluctantly giving way to the rocky, ridged countryside of the Tersal Highlands. Spires of rock replaced leafy trees, gorges and canyons opened where fields of grass had once held dominion, and scrub brush ruled over the uneven terrain. The Serpentspine formed a dark, craggy line to their left as they marched southward, and travel slowed as they made their way over the rough land.

Lazarus hoped that they had not accidentally passed their quarry as they sped to intercept him or that they had guessed incorrectly and were headed entirely in the wrong direction. There was nothing he could do to assuage his doubts, for now at least, and he had no choice but to continue on as planned. It was their best hope in any case.

Days slipped past uneventfully as they continued the search for Kairayn and the Krullstone. The rain finally let up, and the clouds slowly broke apart and drifted away into the limitless sky. The sodden earth gradually began to dry out, and Lazarus decided it would be a good idea to widen their search.

They established a base camp and divided up into search groups. Lazarus took Neslyn with him; Aldric, Vinson, Zafer, and Layek took the horses and split up, while Emeris and Azrael guarded the camp and surveyed the surrounding area from atop a high rise nearby. It was a dangerous decision if Lazarus was mistaken and Kairayn was ahead of them; the delay in finding his trail might mean they would never catch up to him before he reached the safety of the Durgen Range. It was a calculated risk that had to be taken. Doubt was beginning to creep into the minds of Lazarus and his companions, and now was a time they could not afford to be second-guessing themselves.

Fortunately, the gamble paid off. The searchers returned to their camp around midday as they had agreed to do and settled in a circle to consume their lunch. Aldric was the last to arrive, so late that Lazarus was considering sending out a search for him. The youngest Arkenstone came charging up the slope of the hill through the heavy brush and screeched to a halt in front of his waiting friends, showering them with rocks and dirt.

"This had better be good," Layek muttered in displeasure.

"Better than good," Aldric said excitedly as he leapt from his mount. "I've found him!"

Everyone started talking at once, demanding to know how far ahead the Orc was, how Aldric had crossed his trail, and which direction he was headed. Aldric stood stock still and let them trip over each other's words for a minute, his face split nearly in two by his bemused grin, until his friends quieted down.

"The Orc is several hours ahead of us by my best guess, heading south. I came across his trail a couple of miles to our east."

Vinson jumped into action, reaching for his gear. "Let's go! We can catch him by nightfall if we hurry!"

"Hold up a minute, Vinny," Lazarus cautioned. "Let's not forget that we only have four horses. We're exhausted, and he has the Krullstone. How are we going to take it from him?"

"It doesn't matter!" Vinson shouted in exasperation. "We can't take it at all if we don't catch up to him!"

"And we can't use it if we're dead!" Lazarus shouted back. "Calm down, and let common sense and logic guide your actions."

Vinson took a deep breath. "You're right, Laz. What do you propose we do?"

"Obviously, we have to catch him off guard. We have to incapacitate him before he has a chance to turn the stone's power against us, even kill him if necessary."

"Then we should wait until he sleeps," Layek said.

"But we need to keep a close eye on him," Zafer pointed out, "so we don't lose him."

"Without being seen," Lazarus added. "Zafer and Aldric will take two of the horses and watch him while the rest of us bring up the rear. Once he has let his guard down we swoop in and relieve him of the Krullstone."

"Surprise attack," Vinson stated plainly. "We had better be damn sure he's out."

"That shouldn't be a problem," Neslyn assured them. "Once he is asleep I can get close enough to make sure he won't wake."

"Let's get it done then." Lazarus motioned for them to rise. "Zafer. Aldric. Make sure you mark your trail well. We'll follow behind as quickly as possible."

The two mounted their horses, speeding off into the distance. Lazarus and the others pushed as fast and as hard as they dared. They were tired and hungry, but Lazarus kept his friends moving with constant words of encouragement, refusing to show any signs of fatigue or weakness.

Zafer and Aldric left plenty of signs for them to follow, skillfully marking out the trail so those who came behind would know which way to go. Occasionally one or the other would backtrack to check on them or inform Lazarus of their progress. The day progressed in a blur as the rough countryside flew by them. The sharp line of the Serpentspine rose darkly out of the highlands as they grew ever nearer to its rocky face.

Afternoon faded slowly into dusk, and long shadows began to stretch across the land, filling in the gorges and valleys of the highlands quickly. Lazarus was beginning to think it time to stop for the night, his feet sore and feeling like lead weights. It had been some time since either of their two scouts had returned, and he thought certainly at any moment they would show up. He was right, though the manner of their appearance did not soothe him in the least.

Aldric and Zafer came galloping up at full speed only moments after the sun had dipped below the horizon, reining in their horses at the last moment.

"We've got a serious problem," Aldric said curtly as he jumped down off his horse.

XXII COMPLICATIONS

DAYS AFTER HIS escape from his human captors, surrounded by the spires and folds of the Tersal Highlands, hungry and exhausted, Kairayn trotted on. He knew the humans would be hunting him. Once they discovered that he had stolen the Krullstone from them, they would be quick to pursue. With the aid of horses, it would not be much trouble to run him to ground. His only hope was that they exercised some caution in confronting him, knowing that he held the Krullstone and the power to destroy them.

Of course, he didn't know how to use it, but perhaps the humans would be intimidated by its mere presence.

Little did the humans know that he was aware of their presence. Two of them had been shadowing him all day. He had been lucky, catching just a brief glimpse of one of them as he topped a rise a few hours earlier. It appeared that they were waiting for an opportunity to catch him off guard.

He hurried on, intent on keeping as much distance between himself and his pursuers. They would be hesitant to attack him as long as he was awake so the important thing was to keep moving. Kairayn pushed his way forward, fueled by his determination not to fall into their hands again.

Hours crept slowly by until at last the sun swept across the horizon as it faded into night, bathing the sky and the tufts of white cloud in brilliant gold and orange.

Then Kairayn topped a rise strewn with rocks, and he looked out across the ridged countryside of the highlands. For a moment he thought his eyes were deceiving him. There, settled comfortably on top of a mound not far away, was a fortress constructed of wood and flying the flag of the Druhedar. Further off in the distance, some miles to the east, there were thousands of tiny yellow dots, like the cooking fires of a massive army.

Elation surged through Kairayn. Could the invasion already be underway?

It didn't matter. The important thing was that he was saved from certain capture and perhaps death. As long as he could reach his kinsmen before the humans caught up with him, all would be well.

He rushed heedlessly forward, stumbling over rocks and roots, branches slapping at his face and arms as he ran. He tumbled through a tangle of thorny bushes, ignoring the scrapes and cuts. He reached the bottom of the rise and charged through the stream there, starting up the slope of the next hill.

He sensed the fort drawing near with each step he took. Kairayn ran blindly on and tore into a line of heavy brush that blocked his path. He muscled his way through to the other side, breathless and drained, and stopped short.

A scout team comprised of about a dozen Orcs stood there waiting for him, weapons drawn. Kairayn took a deep breath and stood still, waiting to see what they would do. The captain stepped forward, a scarred, husky Orc who looked Kairayn up and down with suspicion. Finally the Orc spoke, signaling for his comrades to lower their weapons. "*Greb dokreg nar*," he greeted in a rough voice.

"Hail and well met," Kairayn answered. "You'll never know how glad I am to see you."

"Who are you and what are you doing out here?" the captain returned.

"Kairayn, Slavemaster. I travel under orders from the High Summoner. I must see your commander immediately."

The Orc winced slightly at the mention of the High Summoner. He turned and motioned for Kairayn to follow him, the others falling into step close behind. The rough wooden gates of the keep opened quickly to accept them, Orcs crying out in welcome to their returning comrades.

Kairayn noticed the freshly cut wood and the rough manner of its construction. It couldn't be more than a few days old, and judging by the design, it was just the first step in a permanent outpost. It was large enough to house several hundred soldiers and the entire necessary support infrastructure.

Tents and cooking fires filled the courtyard of the fort, and the scent of food wafted across the still air, making Kairayn's mouth water. *Food and rest will have to wait*, he reminded himself sternly.

The captain escorted him to a squat stone building. The burly Orc knocked twice on the wooden door before opening it and disappeared inside. Kairayn followed quickly on his heels.

The room was bare except for a large table and a set of chairs; there were no windows or decorations of any kind. On the far side of the table sat a short Orc with his hair tied in a long flowing topknot like Kairayn's and yellow eyes that seemed to look right through him.

Kairayn instantly recognized him. "Vargas. Well met."

"Kairayn." The Orc rose from his seat and the map he was perusing to extend a hand in welcome. "It has been a long time, old friend. What are you doing out here in the middle of nowhere?"

"I should ask you the same thing. I left Grimknoll weeks ago under the direction of the High Summoner. I was on my return journey when I came across one of your scout parties. I saw the fires of the army to the east. Has the war begun then?"

"You could say that." Vargas motioned him to the vacant seat. Kairayn accepted gratefully. Vargas bid the Orc captain to leave them and to have some food brought in for Kairayn. Moments later they were alone, and Vargas explained to Kairayn how it was they came to be there.

He told Kairayn all about the gathering of the Orc armies and the coming of the demons, how the army — nearly a quarter million strong — had marched into the highlands and was now turning toward Illendale. Vargas' company had set up this outpost on orders to watch the Sowel Pass and make sure that the humans did not send any soldiers across the mountains to flank them. His unit had set up this keep only a few days ago.

"Who commands this army heading east?"

Vargas' expression grew dark, and his eyes narrowed. "The Daemon Lords marched with the armies, one with each. Gurgor led this army, a test of loyalty from the High Summoner. The Daemon Lord Satariel had him executed a week ago."

"What?" Kairayn exclaimed angrily. "Who's in command now?"

"The Daemon Lord Satariel now commands the army."

Kairayn thrust himself up from his chair. "Unacceptable! Those damnable abominations!" Lazarus' words echoed in his ears. *Demons are not to be trusted. Once they have eliminated any threat to their supremacy, they will eliminate you.* "I must leave immediately."

"With a good horse you could probably catch them in a day, two at the most." Vargas looked at his friend earnestly. "Do not cross the Daemon Lord, Kairayn, or you will share Gurgor's fate."

"We cannot simply allow these demons to assume dominion over us. They are here to aid us, not rule us. Do not worry; I still have a couple of tricks up my sleeve."

"I will furnish you with a horse, supplies, and an escort, but I beg you to wait until morning. You look exhausted."

"Indeed. See to it then. I will leave at first light." Kairayn stood and clasped hands with Vargas before heading out into the courtyard.

The captain who had escorted him to the keep was there standing by and without a word ushered Kairayn toward a fire where a hot plate of stew was waiting for him. He ate his fill and drank twice as much ale before allowing himself to be shown to a tent.

Kairayn trundled off to bed, his head full of thoughts of the demons taking control of the Orc Empire and enslaving his people. Anger welled up inside, and he swore that so long as he lived it would never happen. Lazarus' words still echoed in his mind, and he realized now how right the human was. The demons were not here to help the Orcs; they were here to serve their own dark intentions. Grubbash had been too quick to act and had not adequately considered the nature of their being.

Kairayn ground his teeth in frustration. Grubbash should have known better. He should have known better.

∰   ∰   ∰

"What's going on?" Lazarus asked, trying to ignore the weariness in his body.

"Orcs," Zafer said as he dismounted. "A whole fortress of them, not to mention an entire army of them marching east. They have taken in the one we pursue. There's no way we can reach him now."

Lazarus' heart sank. He could see the others were already thinking what he felt. Hope was lost. If Kairayn had managed to reach his kinsmen, there was no chance they could take the Krullstone from him.

"How did the Orcs get here?" Layek asked in confusion. "I thought they were supposed to be invading Illendale, not the Tersal Highlands."

"Simple," Lazarus answered solemnly. "Occupy the highlands so that when they do invade, they can attack us on two fronts. This does not bode well for Illendale. The invasion cannot be far off."

"So what do we do?" Neslyn asked.

"We have to go after the Krullstone!" Vinson blurted out quickly. "There is no other choice."

"How, Vinson?" Zafer inquired. "The stone is now surrounded by who knows how many Orcs. We cannot fight a whole army."

"What choice is there?" Vinson shot back. "Without the stone there is no hope!"

"Everybody calm down!" Lazarus shouted. "Now, how many Orcs are we talking about?"

"We don't know," Aldric told him. "The army must be tens of thousands strong, judging by the fires we saw. It's impossible to tell how many occupy the stronghold."

Lazarus thought for a moment. There was no way they could

fight their way through a whole garrison of Orcs, and the chances of them sneaking in past them were slim indeed; they were weary and on the verge of starving. They couldn't just give up on the Krullstone, but they couldn't wait out in the wilderness forever either. Surely the Orcs were close to implementing their plans to invade Illendale. It seemed to Lazarus that the only option was to divide their resources.

"We need to split up," Lazarus said suddenly. Shouts of agreement and protest quickly rose up from his companions, and he raised his hands for silence. "Just hear me out. We can't take the stone away from the Orcs within the fort, but Kairayn won't keep the stone there for long. Soon enough he'll try to move it, and we need to be here when that happens. On the other hand, it is important that somebody warn our people of the threat they face and prepare a defense."

"You speak true, Lazarus," Zafer said. "So who goes and who stays?"

"I am not going anywhere!" Vinson declared. "The Krullstone is my responsibility, and I will get it back!"

"Easy, Vinny," Lazarus said. "You'll need some company. Aldric and Layek, the two of you will accompany him until an opportunity to retake the Krullstone arises."

"You mean you're not going to make some excuse for why we should go back to Illendale?" Vinson asked in surprise.

"I would stay with you if I could, Vinny, but someone has to warn Illendale of this army, and I command the Phoenix Legion. Just take care of yourselves and hurry back as quickly as you can."

"Thank you, Laz," Vinson said.

"Layek," Lazarus called out. "You'd better take good care of my brothers."

"You know it."

"We'll camp here for the night. At first light we'll head out. The horses and what little supplies we have will stay here with you, Vinny."

Zafer hunted a few rabbits, which they quickly prepared and consumed. It was the best food they had had in weeks, but they ate it mechanically, their minds stuck on other, darker thoughts.

Despite their edginess they slept soundly. In the morning the eight remaining members of the original company from Kylenshar awoke refreshed. They ate a simple breakfast comprised of fruits and nuts foraged from their surroundings before gathering up what little gear they had. They said hasty goodbyes, wishing each other well and good fortune, promising to meet up as soon as possible. Vinson and Aldric thanked Lazarus one last time for his lapse in protectiveness before turning their horses to the southeast and speeding off.

Lazarus watched them for several minutes as they rode away, his chest tightening in a knot of emotions, until they disappeared into the folds of the highlands. He wordlessly signaled to his charges, and together they turned toward the dark line of the Serpentspine Mountains.

They marched steadily, resting when they needed it and trying desperately not to let the unnatural heat get to them. Lazarus noticed the line of snow at the top of the ever-nearing mountains, realizing it was far higher than it should have been this time of year. Of course, it should have been a lot colder, too.

There wasn't any food left so they scavenged what they could and continued on their way. They made good time, and by the third day they had reached the western access to Sowel Pass. It should have been blocked with snow this time of year, but the unseasonable weather had kept it open.

Lazarus and his companions waited until dawn to traverse the path that led through the forested pass, though they were anxious to reach the city of Perthana where they could sleep in a clean bed and have a good meal. The plentiful trees offered shade and eased the monotony of their march. Birds and small animals darted through the trunks in flashes of movement, and the sound of the breeze rushing through the limbs overhead soothed and calmed the travelers. Lazarus led them up the gentle slope, and soon the sheer rock walls of the pass closed in about them, the mountain watching them like an ageless sentinel.

The sun was high overhead, burning down upon them with a vengeance when they reached the keep that guarded the center of the pass. The tree line broke two hundred yards from the walls to reveal a towering stone structure with walls easily sixty feet high and solid as the mountains themselves. Battlements and parapets poked out from atop the walls like the ridges on a dragon's back, the pennants of the Third Legion fluttering slightly in the breeze. The pass was narrowest at this point, the cliff walls rising hundreds of feet above them. The battlements of the keep stretched across the entire expanse, requiring any travelers to pass through its gates to access the land beyond. This fortress had stood for nearly as long as Illendale itself, built to protect against invaders from the west.

Lazarus was instilled with a sense of pride as he stared up at the towers. He thought of the immense effort it would have taken to construct such a structure and the amazing things men could achieve when they worked together. It was a little odd, he thought, that he could not make out the figures of anyone on watch on the walls. A knot tightened in his stomach, but he accredited it to his undernourishment.

As they neared the gates a cold pit opened within him. There were no sentries inside, and the massive, reinforced wooden gate stood slightly ajar. Even in times of peace this gate remained sealed shut. These days it should have been barricaded and well guarded. They should never have gotten this close without being confronted by those stationed here to keep watch.

Lazarus drew up short of the gate, his trepidation and uneasiness growing with each footstep. The Elves looked at him in puzzlement, not realizing as he did how out of place everything was. Neslyn brushed up against him and squeezed his hand in reassurance, but he gently pushed her back.

He put his back to the gate and peeked inside the opening. Nothing seemed unordinary except that there were no people about. There were always soldiers posted at this keep, and there was always someone watching the gate and walls. Lazarus reached over his shoulder and slid free his katana sword.

Holding the weapon protectively before him, he stepped inside the gate, the others following close on his heels, weapons drawn, and fear evident on their faces. Lazarus stood for several long minutes in the shadow of the gate, staring out over the courtyard lined by groves of trees on either side. There were no signs of a struggle or any movement, and it appeared that the tenants of the fortress had simply abandoned it. Lazarus knew that this was simply not possible. He explained to the others what was going on. He ordered a quick search of the grounds in two groups; he and Neslyn would take the barracks building situated in the center of the courtyard while the others would search within the main keep.

Neslyn gripped Lazarus' hand tightly as they darted quickly across the yard toward the two-story stone structure that served as the main barracks. Lazarus immediately saw that the door had been broken in, and anxiety built within him. Instinctively he knew what had happened here, but his mind just wouldn't accept it.

It didn't take long to find proof of what Lazarus had feared from the beginning.

In the main dining hall, strewn about in gruesome fashion, were the bodies of nearly two dozen men. Blood was splattered everywhere, and the bodies lay as though they had had no time to defend themselves from their attackers. Weapons were still sheathed on the dead; plates of food and mugs of ale sat half consumed on the tables. Neslyn gasped in horror and surprise. Lazarus bent down to inspect the grisly scene, tracking slowly across the floor of the room.

Demons.

The tracks, perfectly preserved in the pools of blood, were unmistakable. Slowly Lazarus backed out of the room and led Neslyn out into the courtyard. Zafer, Emeris, and Azrael came running up shortly after, reporting similar findings.

Everyone within the keep had been slaughtered. There were no bodies other than the soldiers of the Legion, which suggested they were caught completely by surprise. The only way for the demons to get through the gate without raising the alarm was if the keep was betrayed from within.

Lazarus quickly ushered his friends through the smaller eastern gate and away. Outside the keep the trees and welcome shade returned, and the path began to slope gently downhill. The mountains surrounded them completely and blocked out the sun as it sank into the west, deepening the shadows. The mountains began to separate, and through holes in the canopy they could see out across the Illendale valley.

For as far as the eye could see the land was covered in serene grasslands and pockets of forest. To the right they could catch glimpses of the Myrrh as it wound its way out the Serpentspine and the dense thicket formed by the Riparian Wood. Looking out across the valley one could almost believe that this world had been created perfectly, that struggle and strife were nothing more than a figment of the imagination and that harmony reigned supreme.

The five companions knew better. The horrors of their long journey had left an indelible imprint upon their minds, and the faces of their lost friends haunted them constantly. They hurried on despite the marvelous view. The sun was going down rapidly, and they were running out of time.

The grade of the trail began to get steeper, and branches slapped at them as the darkness closed in. They began to see lights twinkling far off in the distance, beckoning to them, inviting them to share in their warmth. Lazarus picked up the pace, pushing his companions hard to reach the city.

It was well into the night by the time they finally reached the outskirts of Perthana. The trail became a road, packed hard by years of travelers, and the trees began to give way to slat-boarded homes, shops, and taverns. The buildings multiplied, and they began to see others upon the road, tense forms shrouded in shadows that cast furtive glances in their direction before hurrying off into the night. Several times they saw squads of red-garbed Crimson Guard shuffling past on patrol.

They made their way through the mostly empty streets and toward the main gates to the city. Most of Perthana was enclosed within a high wall, and the city itself ran right up to the jagged slopes of the mountains. The entire place was built like a fortress due to its close proximity to the borderlands.

They arrived at the main gate and found it closed and under heavy guard. Lazarus was glad to see that there was at least some security after what he had witnessed in the pass earlier, but at the same time it seemed that the number of soldiers present was overkill. There were dozens of them on top of the walls, peering out from the towers, and at least a dozen that they could see before the massive portal. The great iron portcullis was lowered, barring all entrance.

Lazarus strode directly up to the gate, making no attempt to hide his approach. His cohorts followed after, secretly questioning the judgment of walking up to a bunch of soldiers on obvious alert in the middle of the night.

Torches burned brightly from their sconces around the gate, and as soon as Lazarus and his companions entered the wide halo of light, the guards jumped to attention, snatching up weapons and scrutinizing them with cold, hard eyes. When the guards saw that they were humans, they relaxed visibly, and a portly man with a long beard and scars criss-crossing his face stepped forward.

"No entry into the city after dark," the man told them curtly as they approached. "Come back tomorrow."

"I must speak with your commander, Sergeant," Lazarus replied, unaffected by the man's rough attitude.

"Who are you?" the sergeant huffed. "State your name and business!"

"Commander Lazarus Arkenstone, Phoenix Legion. These are my friends."

The man was taken aback. "My apologies, sir. We've been on high alert as of late, and I have strict orders. I'll have some of my men escort you to the barracks."

"Very good, Sergeant." Lazarus was oblivious to the man's excuses. All he could think about now was a hot meal and a clean bed. The sergeant knocked on a side door that led into the wall. A narrow faceplate opened up, and the officer barked for them to open the door. The sound of heavy locks releasing snapped sharply on the air, and then the iron door grated open. The sergeant ushered them inside.

Several more guards sat around a small table within the room, and they glanced up interestedly from their card game at the new-comers. The escort led them out of the room through a door at the rear and then through a series of hallways that took them out of the wall and into an open courtyard. A dozen or more slat-boarded buildings filled the yard, and in the center of them was a slightly more copious two-story building. The building was distinguished as the headquarters by a pair of stanchions that flanked the path leading up to it, flying the flags of the Crimson Guard and the division housed there.

Without pausing the guards led them up the short steps and through the front door into a waiting room where a single sentinel sat on watch behind a desk. The watchman had drifted off to sleep sometime earlier, and the slam of the door brought him awake with a start.

"Who goes there?" he asked groggily, trying to rub the sleep from his eyes.

"Commander Arkenstone. Where is the Captain of the Guard? It is urgent that I speak with him."

"He has turned in for the evening, sir. You'll have to come back in the morning."

"Then wake him!" Lazarus snapped. "I cannot wait."

The guard was stunned for a moment by Lazarus' sudden outburst, but his tone had motivated the man to action. "Very well, sir. But Captain Webster will not be pleased. Wait here."

The guard ambled off through a doorway. A few minutes later he reemerged, followed closely by another man, presumably Captain Webster. He did not look happy at all. He was still buttoning up his shirt as the two entered the room.

Captain Webster was a tall man, half a foot taller than Lazarus, with bulging muscles and chestnut hair. Sapphire eyes glared out from beneath a heavy brow at the group who had broken his slumber, his jaw tensed with anger.

"This had better be good," the captain said in a smooth, deep voice.

"Captain, I am Commander Arkenstone of the Phoenix Legion. I come with grave news."

Webster's eyes lit up with recognition. "Let's have it then," he mumbled, still discontent about being disturbed so late.

"Tell me first why you are on such high alert."

"Do you not know?" he asked skeptically. "General Markoll is mobilizing the army to defend against invasion from the Orcs. They say that the Queen's Advisor has had a vision. Rumor says that the Orcs have enlisted demons into their service and that their armies are invincible. The Phoenix Legion, along with the Second and Third Legions, is camped at the Myrrh already, where they expect the Orcs to try to attempt a crossing. The Dwarves and the Goblins are at war again, and the Trolls have marched their army against the Elves. Strange creatures have been seen wandering the countryside, and murders have become an almost nightly occurrence. A curfew has been enacted, and security is tighter than ever."

Lazarus whistled. He looked over at Neslyn to see what she was thinking. "That's a lot of information. What news do you have of the Elves?"

"They were supposed to send soldiers to support us," Webster told him. "I have a cousin in the guard at Kylenshar. He tells me that an envoy from the Elves arrived a week ago and broke the news that they wouldn't be able to send any aid so long as the Trolls continue their offensive. So far as I know, no cities have been taken, only border clashes between the armies."

Neslyn let out a sigh of relief.

"Captain Webster," Lazarus said as he straightened himself, "I need several things from you."

"Of course, Commander. Anything you need."

"First, we'll need a place to sleep for the night and a good meal. Also we need horses and supplies. A messenger needs to be sent to General Markoll. Last and of the utmost importance, you must send a contingent of men into the pass to secure the keep there immediately, tonight if possible."

"I will do as you ask, sir." Webster looked at him in confusion. "But why send more men to the fortress in Sowel Pass? There is already a garrison stationed there."

"We came through the keep on our way here. Everyone has been murdered. There is no one left to defend the gate, and we have witnessed an army of Orcs marching through the Tersal Highlands.

When the invasion begins, the Orcs will try to flank us through the pass."

The captain's face turned pale. "I will see that it is done as soon as possible. What of your message to the General?"

"I will write it myself, but it is for his eyes only. Your messenger needs to be someone I can trust."

"It will be done," Webster said.

Lazarus thanked him, and the two clasped hands. The captain called for the guard on duty and instructed him to lead them to their sleeping quarters and see to it that they were fed. The guard led them to the mess hall and served them a delicious meal of fresh fruits, cheese, and bread. It wasn't hot, but after their harrowing journey they thought it was the best meal they'd ever eaten.

The guard waited patiently as they devoured their food, and when they were finished, he led them to a small shack at the back of the grounds. It was unoccupied but elegantly furnished; their escort said they only used it when officers from other legions were visiting. There were several beds in the back rooms, enough for all of them.

Graciously they thanked the guard and released him. They dropped their gear and fell onto the beds without even bothering to undress. In moments they were fast asleep.

Lazarus and his companions slept in late, well past when he would have liked to rise. It was long after breakfast, and the grounds were alive with activity when the five travelers finally got out of bed. They found fresh clothes had been set out for them, and breakfast had been prepared on a table against the wall.

Hungrily they gulped down the generous portions of food. They brought water from the well outside and washed themselves in a tub in one of the rooms, then dressed, refreshed and ready to face another day.

Lazarus met Captain Webster first thing, preparing and sending off his message to General Markoll. Afterward, they were taken to the supply house where they collected fresh gear and horses. Lazarus inspected the equipment, and when he was satisfied that they had everything they needed, he bid farewell to Captain Webster, and they rode out.

"Where are we going?" Neslyn asked him after they had left the walls of the city behind.

"To meet up with the Phoenix Legion," he replied. "I must be there when the invasion begins. It is my duty to defend my homeland, and my men need me."

"What about my homeland?" she snapped back.

Lazarus stopped his horse and turned to face her. The others stayed back a little, giving them enough room so they wouldn't feel crowded but still close enough to hear what they were discussing.

Lazarus looked upon her softly. "Neslyn, I know you are afraid for your people and your country. The only thing I can do to help them is to fight the Orcs, here and now, where our only hope of victory in this awful business lays. You can bet that the demons are behind the invasion of your homeland, too. Go to your people if you must; I will understand. However, please understand that I cannot go with you."

Neslyn stared at him, her eyes betraying the weariness she felt inside. "I love you, Lazarus, and I will not leave you. Just promise me that there is an end to all of this."

"There is, and we will find it together."

It was hotter than ever, and they took turns between walking and riding to rest the horses, taking frequent breaks themselves. Spirits were high as they went, the small group taking in the fresh countryside air, watching the tufts of white cloud sail by, listening to the birdsong that filled the air.

Lazarus wondered briefly at how stressful it must be for Zafer and Neslyn to learn that their people had fallen under attack. War was a tough concept to swallow as it was, but having been at peace for so many years, it must be doubly hard. Eventually he decided that it must be the same for them as it had been for him when he had learned of the dark plot to destroy his homeland, and he let the matter slip from his mind.

The serenity of their surroundings soon melted away all their cares and worries, healing the rifts in their souls and calming their frayed nerves. The path was easy and smooth, and soon they entered into the vast Riparian Wood. Oaks, elms, yew, and all manner of leafy trees wrapped them up in their cool and peaceful shade.

Night closed in quickly once they were inside the shelter of the forest, and they camped just off the trail. They built a fire and ate a hot stew filled with beef and vegetables. Later they sat around the fire, sighing contentedly, enjoying the serenity of the woods and listening to the night sounds that rose up out of the darkness until one by one they drifted off to sleep.

In the morning they broke their camp quickly at Lazarus' insistence and began the day's march. If they got an early start, he reasoned, they could reach the river by midday. The shade underneath the canopy of limbs above them kept the temperature down, which made the march that much easier and pleasant, and just as Lazarus had said they reached the legion's camp just after noon.

The camp was set in between the trees which ran right up to the river, about a quarter mile further on. Row upon row of tents were nestled between the trunks for as far as the eye could see, and smoke from cooking fires wafted through the air, bearing the smell of freshly prepared food. Standards marked the location of individual units among the assembly, and the sound of work filled the air like fog. Men scurried about everywhere, dutifully carrying out the tasks set to them by their officers.

Scouts sat watch and shouted out to their comrades, announcing their arrival as they approached. A squad of guards strode up and saluted sharply, recognizing Lazarus in an instant.

"Afternoon, sir," the lead man said in a gravelly voice. "Good to have you back. Brought some fresh recruits with you I see," he said, eyeing the two Elves behind him.

"Hail and well met, Burhan," Lazarus replied. "It's good to be back. I must see Captain Reich right away; can you lead us to the command post?"

"Aye, sir, I can. But Captain Reich is in the field, scouting our fortifications down by the river. I'll send a man to inform him of your arrival."

"Very good, Lieutenant. As I understand it the Second and Third Legions are camped here as well." Lazarus looked for any of their standards among the rows of tents.

"Indeed they are, sir, on the flanks," Burhan said.

"I see. Send for Commanders Hakan and Booker," Lazarus ordered him. "I would like to speak with them as well."

"Yes, sir!"

Burhan spoke with his men for a moment, and three of them took off running to fetch those Lazarus had called for. Burhan led them down a well worn path through the maze of tents to a clearing in the center of the camp where the headquarters were located. Huge banners fluttered in the breeze, declaring its location. A dozen guards in full armor and pikes stood guard outside the massive tent.

The lieutenant led them inside, promising to provide them with refreshments before he excused himself to return to his post. Burhan was true to his word, and moments after the five friends had seated themselves a pair of servants bearing trays laden with food and drink came in through the flap. They consumed their lunch slowly as they waited, taking the time to savor and enjoy the meal.

Half an hour passed before the men Lazarus had requested arrived. They came in together, talking among themselves. The three were a well-muscled group with tanned skin accented by numerous scars. Had it not been for their uniforms, it would have been easy to mistake them as common highwaymen, but between them they had more than a half-century of experience in the Legion. Together, the three officers would make a formidable opponent, one who would make Lazarus think twice about before engaging.

They greeted Lazarus and his companions warmly, with Lazarus offering introductions of the two Elves. Once the formalities were out of the way, Lazarus got right down to business.

"Commander Arkenstone, it's good to have you back," Captain Reich said. He was a tall tree trunk of a man with blond hair and blue eyes. His good looks had earned him more than a few ill-conceived nicknames among the soldiers, though none would dare use them to his face. He was brash and brave with an eye for details.

"Thank you, Sterl. Now, what's our situation down here?"

Captain Reich took a deep breath. "Well, we have three full legions, twenty-one thousand men in all. Our scouts have reported that the Orcs have amassed a huge army outside the city of Draxx, a day's march south of the river, perhaps more. According to our reports their army numbers into the hundreds of thousands."

Sterl walked over to a table strewn with maps. He pushed them aside to reveal one marked in several places. He pointed to indicate the positions. "We have fortified The Narrows here where we expect the Orcs to attempt a crossing. We've spent the last few weeks building a bulwark and abatis twenty yards back from the banks. The far shores have been booby-trapped, pitfalls and the like. We've built dozens and dozens of catapults, and as soon as we learn that the Orcs have begun the march, we are prepared to oil the far shore and set it to the torch when they arrive."

"You have done well, Captain," Lazarus said once the captain had finished. "It looks like we'll have a few surprises for them when they get here."

"Thank you, sir."

"Still the odds do not look good at all, do they?" Lazarus looked grimly at the marks on the map that indicated the Orc army.

"We'll give them hell, Lazarus," Booker stated passionately. "They'll wish they had stayed home." Booker was the youngest, a few years behind Lazarus, but nevertheless he was an able leader with a sharp mind and a cunning intellect. He had proven himself early in his career with his daring tactics.

"Who's watching the rest of the river, though?" Lazarus asked, tracing the line of the Myrrh on the map. "We don't know for sure that this is where they'll attempt a crossing."

Commander Hakan leaned forward in his chair. He was the eldest among them, an aging man in his mid-fifties and balding at the temples. His eyes burned with conviction and determination, though, and despite his seemingly hard appearance he was quite amiable. As a leader he was superb; his knowledge and skill in the arts of war and strategy were renowned throughout the land. "Most of the Fourth Legion is garrisoned at Kalimith in case the Orcs shift directions. It is highly unlikely, though. With the abnormal heat the mountain snow is melting off pretty quickly. The river has swelled dramatically. They would need hundreds, thousands of boats to cross anywhere but here at The Narrows, and even then it wouldn't be a sure shot. Half their army would probably drown. Even here crossing the river is no walk in the park."

Lazarus smiled grimly. "Well, at least there's some good news. When can we expect reinforcements?"

"General Markoll is gathering the rest of the army in Kylenshar," Commander Booker explained. "Last we heard he should have the other three legions ready to march within a week, along with three reserve legions."

"Well, I hope they hurry," Lazarus replied. "We'll be hard pressed to hold that many Orcs and their demon allies for long. Captain Reich, I want the cavalry patrolling the river from here to Kalimith. Best not to leave anything to chance. Other than that it looks like we're as prepared as we can be."

"I'll see to it, sir," Sterl promised. "We'll set up check points along the banks and have every available horse on patrol."

"Very good. Now all we can do is wait."

The others agreed. The three officers stayed for a while, and they drank ale and shared stories of their travels. A couple of hours and many drinks later the officers took their leave of Lazarus to return to their duties. Even though it seemed that all was in preparation, there was always something that needed attention, especially in a camp of so many men.

Lazarus saw to it that the two Elves were comfortable and taken care of, while Emeris went back to command his cavalry units, charged with setting up the patrols along the riverbanks. Emeris had become taciturn and reticent since Aurora's death, distancing himself from everything and everyone. Lazarus tried to engage him on several occasions, but the man just didn't want to talk. All he wanted was revenge; Lazarus could see it in his eyes, and it worried him. He needed his officers calm and collected, not bent on mindless destruction. He would have to watch him closely.

After he had seen to his friends, Lazarus took to walking around the camp, familiarizing himself with its layout, renewing his acquaintance with his men, and just letting his presence be known. He took the time to wander down by the river to inspect the defenses. The guards on watch paid little attention to him except when he addressed them directly, keeping their attention focused on their task.

This became the routine for Lazarus and his friends, wiling away the hours by keeping busy as they waited for the inevitable assault. Secretly they each hoped that the day would never come, but they knew deep down that it was only a matter of time before their fears became reality. Lazarus thought often of his brothers and hoped that they were doing well, reminding himself constantly that Layek would watch over them and make sure they stayed safe.

Neslyn and Zafer kept him company most of the time; he and the Elven princess had become nearly inseparable. They went everywhere together, often holding hands and giggling at some private joke. Lazarus felt like it had been forever since the last time he was this happy and deeply regretted that his happiness was overshadowed by the current circumstances.

While on one of his many walks with Neslyn through the forest, a runner came tearing into the camp, exhausted and frantic. Everyone came running to see what the commotion was. Lazarus arrived just as the man began to catch his breath.

"What is it, man?" he asked. "Speak!"

"The Orcs," he gasped for air. "The Orcs are coming!"

XXIII SATARIEL'S DEMISE

IT WAS WELL into morning when Kairayn finally awoke. It was a clear blue day with a light breeze blowing out of the west, the heat already stifling. It disturbed him that he must waste this time when there were much more important things to be done, but he really had little choice. His body had been dangerously close to total exhaustion, and he needed to be at full strength when he faced the Daemon Lord Satariel.

Thinking of the Daemon Lord brought his rage bubbling to the surface. It was obvious now that Commander Arkenstone was right. They were here to serve their own dark needs, not the will of the Orcs. Kairayn briefly considered the wisdom of confronting a being as powerful as Satariel. These demons needed to be put back in their place, and being that it was he who held the Krullstone, the duty fell on his shoulders.

He ate a speedy breakfast and hurriedly gathered up the supplies he would need. By all accounts he should reach the army marching east by nightfall so he didn't need much. Vargas, true to his word, provided him with an escort of half a dozen brawny Orcs as an added precaution. It was just past noon by the time everything was finally put in order, and Kairayn and his entourage were ready. The wooden gates of the fort creaked open; Kairayn said a quick farewell to Vargas and charged out into the rolling hills of the highlands.

He set a rapid pace, leading his cohorts through the valleys and gorges of the highlands where the horses would not tire so easily. His anger burned hotly within, a boiling cauldron ready to spill over at any moment. He held it in check, saving it for when it would serve him best, when he would face the Daemon Lord and his minions. There was no fear, only grim determination.

His troop talked idly amongst themselves as they rode, but Kairayn kept himself carefully distanced, wrapping himself in an invisible barrier as thick and hard as forged steel. The others let him be, content to mingle with one another rather than disturb their strange new leader.

The landscape floated by as surely as the changing of the tides, and the sun began to slowly relinquish its hold on the land to its paler twin. The heat rose up from the ground in visible waves that distorted vision and played tricks on the eyes, clinging to the terrain and its inhabitants like an oily substance that could not be washed away. Shadows lengthened and deepened until finally the basins and dells became lakes of impenetrable blackness.

Through the inky murk the Orcs pressed on, their progress slowed considerably as the trail they followed became more treacherous in the darkness. Kairayn had torches fetched to light their way, as well as signal their approach to the Orcs they pursued so that they would not be mistaken for the enemy. He had been through too much to be cut down now by his own people due to a case of mistaken identity.

Over the rims of the ridgelines they could see a muted glow rising up into the night sky. They were getting close now. They topped a small rise, and Kairayn brought them to a halt. Thousands of twinkling lights lit up the valley floor they looked out upon, which was surrounded on all sides by steep inclines. The army was huge, filling up the natural bowl from rim to rim. Orcs wandered everywhere, from cooking fire to cooking fire, and yet the sound of clinking glasses and raucous laughter was strangely missing. Great black spots of emptiness blemished the camp in places, and occasional cries and grunts emanated from within them. Kairayn guessed that that was the resting place of the demons who traveled with the army, and he felt his anger rise in response to the realization. Something was definitely amiss within the camp, and Kairayn knew exactly what it was.

They waited on the ridge above for ten minutes before the skirmishers set out to guard the camp appeared from the darkness around them. Only half a dozen stepped into their small circle of light, but Kairayn would bet there were at least three times that many waiting just beyond sight. The two groups eyed each other suspiciously for a few moments before their leader took a tentative step forward.

"What is your business here?" the large, scar-faced Orc said, his voice low and menacing.

Kairayn looked down at the Orc. "I am the Slavemaster, Kairayn," he replied.

"My Lord." The Orc slammed a fist to his chest in salute. "Hail and well met. How may I serve?"

"You can start by telling me who is in command of this army."

"My Lord," the Orc looked around uncertainly, "the Daemon Lord Satariel now commands the army."

Kairayn kept his anger in check. "And why does the demon lead? Where are our own commanders?"

"Gurgor of Demal was executed for treason just last week, along with all of his staff. Some of our brothers went to contest the Daemon Lord's command several days ago. None of them have been seen since. None dare to face the Daemon Lord; he's just too powerful."

Kairayn grimaced. "At least tell me you have food in this camp, if not courage."

"Of course, master." The Orc scowled at the insult. "Follow me."

The sentinels lowered their weapons and turned off into the night. Kairayn spurred his horse forward and fell into step behind the leader. The rest of his team followed suit, and in single file they began to descend into the valley. The light of the campfires slowly drew closer as they made their way down the slope and through the brush until the group was engulfed in the warm glow of them.

Orcs sat before the fires, their stares lost in the dancing flames as they silently contemplated their lot. Once again Kairayn was reminded of the jovial and boisterous, almost festive, atmosphere that generally dominated an Orc war camp and how blatantly absent it was here. As they passed, some of the Orcs looked up at them, their eyes full of fear.

Kairayn glanced to his left at one of the great pools of darkness. Watch fires were kept at the edges of the emptiness, and the closest Orc never moved within fifty paces. His anger burned hotly within, threatening to erupt like a volcano at any minute. Instinctively he reached down to his belt pouch where the Krullstone was safely tucked away. He reached inside and felt the warm pulse of the talisman. Like an old friend calling him home, it beckoned him, beckoned him to taste the power it had to offer.

Slowly he withdrew the hand. The time was not yet ripe.

Their guide led them through to an unguarded tent. The Orc pulled back the canvas flap and ushered them inside. Within they found an affluent sanctum well decorated with banners and trappings of gold and silver. The tent itself was large enough to house two dozen Orcs, but it had been compartmentalized into several different rooms. No comfort had been spared, and yet Kairayn doubted that whomever it belonged to spent enough time in it to warrant its existence. In the war room he found a large table spread with maps of the land and studied them for a moment.

"This used to be Commander Kurek's quarters," their host informed them. "We found his mangled body earlier this evening after he went to confront the demons. Make yourself at home, Master Kairayn. I will have food brought to you shortly."

Kairayn waved the Orc off, and he disappeared quickly through the entrance. Only a few moments later several Orcs reentered with the promised meal — fresh mutton with bread and cheese and cold ale to wash it down with. He devoured the meal hungrily, and when it was finished, Kairayn pushed back his chair and sighed contentedly.

The Orcs who had brought the food returned to remove the waste, and Kairayn was about to dispatch his escorts to their own devices when a shrill scream pierced the night air. It was so loud that it tore through the thick canvas of the tent like a tornado. It lingered on the air for several long moments as thick as smoke on a breezeless summer night.

The silence that followed seemed hard as steel — no sound would ever shatter it. Kairayn held his breath.

Finally one of the servant Orcs spoke. "Demons. Every night they go on the hunt. More often than not it's us that gets hunted."

Kairayn was not surprised to find that the demons preyed upon his countrymen. It was the realization that none of them would do anything about it that shocked him. Once again his hand slipped into the belt pouch where the Krullstone was safely tucked away. Fury surged through him like fire in his veins, and his vision blurred red.

In that instant he very nearly jumped up and charged out into the darkness to face the demons here and now. His reason held, however, and somewhere deep in his mind cold hard logic urged him to think twice. The night was the ally of his enemies, it told him. Best wait until daylight to face them where he would have the advantage.

The Slavemaster took several long deep breaths and forced his wrath deep down inside where it could be called upon when needed.

Before he slept, though, he made sure that there was an ample supply of guards outside his tent.

Aldric, Layek, and Vinson watched as their companions disappeared into the distance. For all three it was as though a vital part of themselves was walking away, a part that might not ever return. They were invigorated by the thrill of the hunt, yet they were left somehow hollowed by their experiences, and the separation from their companions only deepened the wound. They stared after them long after they had melted into the highlands.

It was Layek who broke the extended silence that followed. "Do not be troubled, young Arkenstones; we will see them again soon enough."

"I sure hope you're right," Aldric intoned forlornly.

They turned away finally, returning to their camp hidden within the brush to watch the fort. It was still early in the morning, the sky clear and the sun bright, and they watched expectantly for any sign of activity. They chewed idly on a meager breakfast and tried to pass the empty hours without dwelling on their anguish too much.

Slowly the hours slipped by. The three companions began to grow restless, and to ease the tension they started standing watch over the Orcs' stronghold one at a time while the other two took walks to ease their muscles and their minds. It didn't help much, but it was all they had.

By noon Vinson was practically tearing his hair out. He began ranting about the possibilities by which Kairayn could have slipped past them. Aldric and Layek tried to calm him, but he only became more irritated. Finally they gave up and decided to ignore him altogether. Tensions mounted, and tempers began to run high.

Then suddenly something did happen. They were so annoyed and preoccupied with ignoring each other that they almost missed it completely. It was Aldric who noticed it first. Slowly, the gates to the Orc fortress swung open, and seven mounted Orcs bolted out into the hills.

"Finally," Aldric vented. "A little action!"

The Orcs were pushing hard and disappeared quickly into the hills. The three friends rounded up what little gear they had and leapt upon their horses to give chase. Layek led the way, circling them around through the brush so the occupants of the fortress would not spot them until they came across the tracks of the ones they followed. They moved cautiously, making certain to stay fresh on the trail but not getting so close that the Orcs might notice them.

For the rest of the day they followed the Orcs through the ravines and gullies of the highlands. Even though they were steadily falling behind their quarry, their earlier frustrations were forgotten as they gave chase.

The sun waned and finally fell behind the ridgelines, dousing the hollows in murky blackness. The trail became harder and harder to discern, although the Orcs made no effort to hide it. It wasn't long before they were blindly leading their horses on.

Layek picked up the pace, taking them up onto the ridges where they could see best. He was now continuing on instinct alone. Just when they thought they must have lost the trail and taken a wrong turn somewhere, Vinson spotted torchlight ahead of them and to the right.

The blackness around them deepened, and they dismounted. In the distance they noticed a bright glow rising up into the night. The Orcs they were following stopped on a hilltop perhaps twice removed from themselves. For a long time they just stood there, not moving. The three companions stopped to watch, waiting to see what would happen. It wasn't long before the torches vanished, and the three were left staring into nothingness.

For a short while they stood and watched. Finally they crept forward, moving slowly and taking care not to make any sound or draw attention to themselves. They crawled on their bellies to the top of the hill that the Orcs had occupied only moments earlier and looked down into the valley.

Layek gasped in disbelief. "I didn't think there were this many Orcs in the whole Empire. There must be a hundred thousand down there."

Vinson and Aldric just stared. Thousands of fires masked the valley in a soft glow. Orcs ambled like ants back and forth between fires. Great pools of emptiness marred the haphazard order of the camp. It didn't take a genius to figure out that that was where the demons made their abode. The sheer size of the army was frightening in and of itself, but with the added strength of their demon allies, it was downright petrifying. For what seemed like hours they sat crouched atop the hill, looking out across the valley. Fear rose up in the three companions as each considered how it was that they were going to steal the Krullstone away from so many or how it was possible for their countrymen to defend against such overwhelming numbers in the event that they failed.

It was Vinson who broke the silence first. "We have to get in there somehow," he whispered. "First let's get off this hill so we can talk."

The three crawled back down to where they had left their horses in a gully heavily overgrown with brush. Layek rummaged through their supplies and brought forth some stale bread for them to chew on. It wasn't nearly enough to satisfy their hunger, but for this night it would have to do.

"You can't seriously be considering going in there," Layek said to the two brothers between bites.

"We don't have a choice, Layek," Vinson replied flatly. "We have to get the stone back."

"Did you even look at the size of that army down there?" Layek breathed in amazement. "There is no way to get through that many Orcs, not to mention the demons who are sure to be lurking about."

"We were looking. That's exactly why we have to go down there," Aldric countered. "We don't stand a chance against an army that size without the stone."

"You're both crazy! I wish Laz were here. He'd talk some sense into you two!" Layek flailed his arms in frustration.

"There's no other choice, and you know it." Aldric folded his arms and stared hard at the big man. "With or without you, we're going down there."

They stared at each other for a long time in silence, testing each other's determination. There was an absence of the usual nighttime sounds that deepened the stillness even further.

Finally Vinson broke the stalemate. "How would you like to be an Orc for a couple of hours, Layek?"

Layek was taken completely off guard and couldn't help but chuckle at the absurdity of the question. Vinson was quite serious he found out, once he had explained his idea. Apparently Vinson knew a spell that could alter their appearance to that of Orcs, perhaps long enough for them to sneak in and steal the stone. Layek wasn't very enthusiastic about it, but then again, the two brothers weren't really giving him a choice. He could go along or be left behind. Since the former would be a betrayal of the trust given him by Lazarus, he would just have to play along and pray that this foolhardy plan worked.

Once Layek had agreed, Vinson set his magic to work. It took only a few short minutes for him to complete the ritual. When it was done, they looked at each other, astonished to find that they had taken on the countenance of burly Orc warriors.

"I can't believe that worked," Layek grumbled discontentedly. "I can't believe I'm going along with this in the first place."

"Stuff it, Layek," Aldric told him. "You sound more like an Orc than the two of us so you're going to have to lead. If anyone confronts us, just act like you're somebody important. Act upset, too. That'll help."

"Great." Layek looked less than pleased. *At least the part about being upset wouldn't be a problem.*

The three climbed over the hill and down to the fringes of the camp before they saw any Orcs. All of a sudden, two Orcs jumped out in front of them, brandishing wicked looking poleaxes.

"Step aside!" Layek growled. When the two watchers hesitated, he added, "Go back to your business, or I'll feed you to the demons and have your hides for floor mats!"

That was enough for them. Instantly they moved to the side and let the three pass. Layek didn't even look back.

"Was that the Slavemaster?" Vinson heard one of the Orcs whisper. He smiled smugly. He knew this was going to work.

They made their way through the multitude of fires, careful to stay out of the glow. Few bothered to even give them a second glance as they meandered aimlessly about. They had no idea which direction to go or really any clue what to look for. Layek assumed they would be searching for a tent fit for someone of high rank, but the more they wandered the more lost he became. There was no order to the layout of the Orc camp, and everything looked exactly the same. Eventually he lost all sense of direction. He was sure they were walking in circles. Sweat began to bead on his forehead, and his breathing became ragged and heavy. At any minute he expected an alarm to sound and Orcs to swarm over them like angry bees.

In a dark spot between campfires Layek finally brought them to a halt. "I have no idea where we're going or where we are for that matter. I think we're going in circles," he whispered to his two companions.

"I think we should search over there." Aldric pointed discreetly off to their left.

"No," Vinson whispered back. "We've been that way already. We need to go right."

"Let's face it," Layek intoned dismally. "We're lost."

"Well, we had better think of something quick," Vinson wheezed. "This spell won't last forever."

Suddenly out of the darkness a solitary Orc stumbled up to them, bumping into and leaning heavily on Layek.

"*Dragu chokmal gurka mog?*" the Orc sputtered.

His speech was slurred, and his eyes were heavy with drunkenness. The three companions were caught completely off guard and stood looking dumbly at the Orc. He repeated the question when they did not answer him right away.

"The ale wagon is over their, friend." Layek pointed. The Orc looked at him quizzically. "That's not what ... Hey! You're not Orcs!"

Layek hit him as hard as he could.

The Orc flew backward, crashing to the ground and remained motionless. The scuffle didn't go unnoticed, however, and other Orcs rose up from nearby campfires to see what was going on. Shouts of alarm rose up into the night, and Orcs scattered, searching for weapons. A knot of burly guards ran at them from their right.

Aldric drew forth his runesword, Shadowsbane, and cut down the first three before the others even knew what was happening. The rest broke and ran, shouting for help as they went. Others were approaching now, weapons drawn, bloodlust intensified by strong drink and clear as day on their faces.

"Run!" Layek shouted as he axed the Orc nearest him.

Orcs charged about in confusion all around them. Layek bolted, followed closely by Aldric and Vinson, cutting through the Orcs wherever they stood in the way, all thoughts of the Krullstone forgotten. They pulled their cloaks close to hide their true identity as much as possible, and it seemed to work, at least a little. They did their best to run in a straight line, but often they were forced to stop and fight. The darkness favored them, though, and many times they saw Orcs fighting each other as they ran, confused by the sudden alarm and dim light.

Vinson saw a place ahead where the campfires abruptly ended. Believing they had reached the edge of the camp, he changed course, shouting to his friends to follow. They ran headlong into the pitch black, stumbling over stone and brush. The sound of pursuit died away, and finally they stopped.

"Are we outside?" Aldric asked, gulping for air.

"I think so," Vinson answered. "I don't hear anything chasing us."

The three fell silent and cocked their ears. Slowly their eyes began to adjust to the darkness. Then something shot out of the black, hurtling at them with frightening speed.

Aldric shouted in warning, but it was too late. Something huge barreled into them, knocking them all aside. Aldric's runeblade flared to life, magic coursing down its length and surging into him, casting a meager blue glow that lit up the immediate area. He saw the snout of the beast that had assailed them as it entered his small ring of light.

A chill ran through him as it emerged from the night. He knew this thing; he had encountered its kind before at the inn in Pilban. The Lurker hissed menacingly. Suddenly Aldric realized what had happened. They had not escaped the camp. Instead they had mistakenly stumbled into one of the great black holes they had seen from atop the hill when they scouted the camp.

They had inadvertently jumped out of the cooking pot into the fire.

A second, slightly paler glow joined Aldric's as Vinson brought his own runesword to bear. The Lurker lunged, and Aldric slashed out of instinct. The blade struck the demon square in the head, and it burst into ash.

Low growls issued forth from the darkness surrounding them. Layek was on his feet again, blood running down his forehead where the Lurker's claws had struck him. More demons appeared, slowly circling. The companions stood back to back, waiting for the assault. Demons of all shapes and sizes appeared, all claws and teeth and leathery skin. Most they didn't recognize and didn't really want to.

"We've got to get out of here," Layek whispered to the two brothers. "We're dead if we don't make a run for it. On my signal, break. Stay together."

Slowly the demons continued to orbit. The three turned with them. Glowing eyes blinked out at them from the black, and the demons hissed in hatred. An imp appeared from the darkness, grinning wickedly.

Layek never hesitated. "Now!" he shouted as he brought his axe down and cleaved the imp's head in half.

Layek leapt over the falling corpse and engaged those lurking behind. The attack caught them by surprise, and they fell back at its fury. Vinson and Aldric followed after, slicing through the demons as if they were made of paper, the magic of their blades giving them a surge of new energy.

A dozen or more fell in the first instants, and then the demons broke and ran altogether. Layek turned sharply to the left and took off at a dead run, the Arkenstones a step behind. Demons jumped out at them from the darkness as they ran, and they cut through them without missing a step.

Without warning a cadre of small screeching demons launched themselves from out of the brush. There was no time to react, and altogether they went to the ground in a heap. Aldric cried out in pain as claws ripped into him. He thrashed wildly and swung his sword in a sweeping arc, turning four of the little terrors into dust. He regained his feet and charged into the demons.

Vinson and Layek were up as well, hacking away at the multitude of assailants. A massive bear-like demon rounded a tree and caught Vinson with a sweeping blow that knocked him to the ground. Layek was instantly on the beast, chopping vehemently with his bloodstained axe until it toppled over lifelessly. Vinson struggled to his feet, one arm held tightly against his side, blood flowing freely from the torn flesh.

"Don't stop!" Layek shouted.

He ran up and put an arm around Vinson, helping him on. Aldric brought up the rear, holding back the rush of monsters. They struggled forward. Vinson lost his footing and went down. Layek lifted him, seemingly effortlessly off the ground, and carried him. Aldric brought his sword arcing down, cutting two more demons clean in half. The last turned and fled, shrieking into the black.

Aldric turned and ran after Layek and Vinson. Somehow the big man had put some distance between them, even with the added weight of his brother. Suddenly his foot caught, and he tumbled head over heels to the ground. The magic of Shadowsbane flared and winked out. He cried out and jumped back to his feet.

Frantically he scooped up his fallen weapon and searched the darkness for his attacker. Nothing appeared. His breathing sounded loud and harsh in the silence of the night; the blood pounded in his ears with the strength of kettledrums. Growls and hisses emanated from the darkness all around him. Layek and Vinson were nowhere to be seen.

He took a few cautious steps forward, whispering for his companions. His stomach tightened in a knot of fear. He tried to calm his reeling mind, tried to think his way through the dilemma, but he could not. He was alone, surrounded and lost. Not knowing what else to do, he dashed off in the direction he believed the other two had been running. The minutes trickled past, and still there was no sign of his companions.

A scraping of claws on rock warned him of the attack. He ducked, and something heavy sailed over his head, landing with a grunt in the brush to his left. Shadowsbane flared to life, illuminating his attacker, and he cut it down where it stood. More demons hurtled out of the darkness, and he desperately fought them off.

When they all lay dead at his feet, the magic of his sword died out and left him standing in the dark once again. He ran on, growing desperate. If he didn't find the others soon, he was as good as dead. Maybe they were already dead. He picked up his pace, dashing head-long into the darkness. He ran for what seemed like miles.

Frustrated and exhausted he stopped and sat down in the dirt next to a thicket of tangled trees and brush. To the east the sky was brightening with the coming of the sun. Despair washed over him. The darkness had allowed him to survive this long, but once it became light enough to see clearly they would have him.

Hope slowly drained out of him. Wearily he shut his eyes against the inevitable. That's when the hand shot out of the undergrowth behind him and clamped down over his mouth like iron, dragging him back into the blackness.

ço   ço   ço

Kairayn felt the hand grip his shoulder as he slept. In one fluid motion he brought the knife from under his pillow and up to the throat of his attacker. He opened his eyes and peered up at the Orc standing over him. He recognized his guard and immediately removed the blade.

"What is it?" Kairayn asked, a hint of anger creeping into his voice. "I gave orders that I was not to be disturbed."

"Forgive me, My Lord," the Orc replied shakily. "There are intruders in the camp."

Instantly Kairayn was up. "Where? How many?"

"On the east end. Somehow they snuck past our sentries. They've been raising hell for about an hour. We don't know how many. At least a dozen according to reports, but we can't seem to kill or capture them."

Something clicked in Kairayn's mind, and he knew instantly who had invaded his camp. At first he thought it had been the demons, but it didn't fit the pattern. It had to be Lazarus Arkenstone and his companions. Only they would be willing to try something as crazy as this. They were trying to steal back the Krullstone.

"Take me there," Kairayn muttered, strapping his weapons in place.

The Orc nodded, and when Kairayn was ready, he led him to where the disturbance had been. More than twenty Orcs lay dead, scattered across an area within bowshot of his tent. He followed the tracks that were pointed out to him and stopped when he reached the border between Orc and demon territory.

"You mean to tell me that they went in there willingly?" Kairayn asked in disbelief. Nobody could be that foolish.

"Yes, My Lord," his guardsman answered. "There were sounds

of fighting, but we dare not go in there at night."

Kairayn growled in dissatisfaction. There was nothing to be done if the humans had mistakenly wandered into a no man's land. Gods have mercy on their souls because the demons would not. It was no way for a man of honor like Lazarus Arkenstone to die, but he had made his own bed, and now he would have to lie in it.

Thinking about the demons reminded him of the task at hand. He looked to the east where the first tinges of purple and red signaled the coming of dawn. The time for action was near, and there was still much to be done. He called over his guard and ordered him to gather the commanders. The guard dutifully complied and hurried off into the gloom. Kairayn walked back to his commandeered quarters, carefully working out the details of his plan as he did.

When he reached his tent, he sent the guard at his door to fetch him some breakfast and sat down in the war room. He stared blankly at the myriad maps and charts on the table for many long minutes before reaching down into his belt pouch to pull forth the Krullstone. He turned it over in his palm, studying the strange markings engraved upon the gauntlet and stared deeply into the multi-faceted stone. He could feel the power pulsing within but had no idea how to call upon it. He slipped the glove onto his hand, finding it to be a perfect fit. He flexed his fingers inside. The stone began to pulse with light, and Kairayn sensed the depth of its power. Gently he called to it, trying to coax the magic from its dormancy into life, but nothing happened. He tried again; still nothing. He traced over the runic markings with his free hand and felt the magic within slowly stir.

There were voices outside his tent. Others were coming, probably the commanders whose presence he had requested. He ignored them. He was enthralled with the magic of the stone. The commanders entered and came into the room, staring wide-eyed at Kairayn and the stone.

Suddenly it flared to life, and Kairayn felt the magic flow through him. It felt like fire coursing through his veins, exhilarating and energizing. Then the magic took form, emanating out of the gauntlet in a thin streamer of light.

A cry emerged from the other Orcs in the room as they shied away, all except for one. Kairayn watched as the Orc changed shape, twisting and writhing until the grotesque form of a demon appeared. It hissed in hatred. Shouts of alarm rose up from the other Orcs present, and the demon suddenly launched itself at Kairayn.

There was no fear in the Slavemaster. The magic coursed through him, giving him strength of will harder than steel. He lifted his gloved hand and sent the thread of light hurtling at the demon. The beam caught it in midair, engulfing it completely in its glow. The thing screamed in fear and pain. Kairayn willed the magic forth, harder and stronger, and the demon began to dissolve. A black stain began to appear in the light, and as the creature dissolved into nothingness, the stain was drawn back into the stone.

The magic flared out, and Kairayn rocked backward with the force of the backlash. He felt the essence of the demon sink down inside him like a blemish on his soul. He squirmed in discomfort for a few moments before the feeling subsided, and he came back to himself once again. He looked around the room, seeking out the faces of the commanders.

They stared at him in awe for several silent minutes before one captain regained his composure. "We've been trying to locate the spy within our camp since we left the Durgen Range," he said in a grating voice. "How did you do that?"

Kairayn could feel the demon's presence within, lurking in the corners of his mind. He smiled in spite of himself. He felt invigorated, somehow more alive, stronger, sharper. He found that he could recall memories and knowledge from a life that was not his. The stone had worked. The side affects would take some time to get used to, but it had worked.

"Welcome," Kairayn bid his guests with a wicked grin. "Please, make yourselves comfortable, and I will explain what is required of you."

Kairayn explained to those gathered what he was planning. They were at once amazed and fearful when he explained his intended use of the Krullstone, but once he had finished expounding his ultimate plan he had them eating out of the palm of his hand.

When he had finished, he dismissed the commanders to their duties. He took some time for himself after that, reflecting on how the use of the Krullstone had changed him and steeling himself for the coming confrontation. Outside the day had dawned, and clear light filtered through the gaps in the tent flaps. An hour or two passed before his personal guard returned to tell him that all was in readiness.

Kairayn rose from his seat, strapped on his weapons, and donned the Krullstone. With his guards in tow he emerged from his tent, confident and assured. The camp was buzzing with activity as Orcs scrambled to break camp. Many were strapping on armor and weapons and marching off in organized units.

He had instructed the commanders to assemble their warriors and surround the demons' camps. He would confront the Daemon Lord Satariel, and if his followers tried to resist, the Orcs would slaughter them all. Kairayn was confident in his plan; they had a clear advantage in numbers, and with the added power of the Krullstone at his disposal, he was absolutely certain that victory would be theirs.

Without further delay he trotted off to the area where he had been told Satariel kept his quarters. It took little more than a few minutes to reach the clear border between camps. Kairayn stopped at the edge and scanned the area.

"Is everyone in position?" Kairayn asked of his assistant.

"Indeed, master. All commands have checked in, and everything is prepared."

Kairayn nodded. With a deep breath he stepped over the threshold. The line of Orcs stretched out to either side followed suit. Another step followed the first and then another, until he was briskly making his way through the scrub. Suddenly he stopped.

Kairayn took a moment to survey the landscape. Then he turned his head skyward. A roar escaped from his mouth, so loud and ferocious it echoed across the valley, causing birds to take flight and small rodents to flee in fear.

"Come forth, Lord of Deception, and meet your doom!" Kairayn bellowed. "I call you out!"

Aldric awoke to the sound of Kairayn's yell, though he did not know what was happening. With a start he sat up, wincing with pain from his wounds and cramped muscles. Instinctively he reached for his sword, squinting against the glare of full-blown daylight. Layek was there next to him, and he calmly reached over to stay his hand. His head was wrapped in a makeshift bandage torn from his travel cloak, and his face was caked with blood.

"Easy, Aldric," he said soothingly. "We're safe. For now anyway."

Then Aldric remembered the events of last night. He remembered their daring foray into the Orc camp and their subsequent flight after they had been discovered. He had been separated as they battled through the demons, and just as he had given up all hope for survival, Layek had grabbed him from their current cover. With the aid of Vinson's magic they had remained hidden there throughout the night, miraculously evading detection.

"What's going on?" the younger Arkenstone asked as he peered through the branches of their makeshift cover. "That's Kairayn! The Orc we captured. What's he doing out here?"

"Apparently he's come to face the Daemon Lord Satariel," he heard Vinson whisper from behind him. He held his arm, which was bandaged above the elbow, close to his body. A stain of red showed through.

They watched in silence as the Orc continued to shout for the Daemon Lord, growing more and more agitated as the minutes crept by. Orc warriors flanked Kairayn on both sides in a defensive ring, and it appeared to Aldric that the entire Orc army had turned out for the spectacle. Kairayn was the closest to them, little more than a stone's throw away, facing slightly to the left of their hiding place. Minutes turned into an hour, and still nothing appeared from the scrub surrounding them. Orcs began to shuffle nervously as they waited for something to happen.

Finally something did happen.

Out of the brush creatures began to appear. First only a few cautiously emerged, tentatively venturing out into the open. Then dozens of all shapes and sizes began to emerge. Some walked on two legs, some on four, some slithered. They stopped perhaps twenty yards from Kairayn, emitting growls and shrieks of rage.

Suddenly a massive crow swooped down and settled on a rock directly before the Orc. Before their very eyes the crow began to change form. A cloud of smoke rose up from the bird, obscuring their view completely. The haze grew and thickened, but they could see the vague outline of something huge. A great roar broke from the fog, shaking the ground and causing the Orcs to take a step backward in fear. Kairayn never moved.

The cloud dissipated, and the three companions all gasped in surprise. They knew the Daemon Lords would be intimidating, but this was far beyond their expectations. Before them stood a creature that dwarfed them in size, standing more than twice the height of Kairayn. Vaguely humanoid in form with blood red skin and wicked looking horns that protruded from its forehead and jaw, Satariel was terrifying in appearance. Aldric cringed in spite of himself. Eyes that burned with hatred and contempt surveyed the gathering, and clawed hands flexed maliciously in preparation.

"Who dares disturb me?" the Daemon Lord demanded in a tone that caused those around him to flinch in fear.

"I do," Kairayn stated boldly. "Terrorize my people no more, demon, for I am the harbinger of death!"

Satariel laughed, a booming sound that rang out across the land, devoid of humor or joy. "Little Orc. You are insignificant. I sense the power you hold, and while it is great, it is no match for my own. Indeed you are the harbinger of death, but I'm afraid it is your own."

"Come then, Deceiver," Kairayn yelled defiantly. "Come see what I have for you!" The Slavemaster raised his gloved fist, and light flared between his clenched fingers. Fire burned hotly in his eyes.

"The Krullstone!" Vinson whispered harshly. "He's learned how to use it!"

Satariel growled in anger. Fear flickered in his eyes for a

moment, and then it was gone. Energy crackled in his fists, and without warning a lightning bolt launched itself at Kairayn. The Orc deftly jumped aside as the bolt exploded into the ground where he had been, sending a shower of dirt and rocks into the air. Again the Daemon Lord struck. Kairayn was too quick for him, though, and once again slipped past the attack.

As Kairayn rolled to his feet, a dark streak shot out of the underbrush and collided with him. The two tumbled to the ground, and Kairayn, using momentum to his advantage, thrust his feet into the demon's stomach, launching it into the air. Still lying on his back, Kairayn sent the magic of the Krullstone careening into the beast, and it disappeared in a haze of white light.

More demons joined the fray, leaping at Kairayn as they shrieked in fury.

The Orc army, momentarily caught off guard, charged into the conflict, roaring their battle cries. Kairayn regained his feet and sent the Krullstone's power sweeping across the attacking demons as they clashed with his kinsmen. Satariel countered with his own magic, gouging the earth with fireballs and chain lightning, swallowing whole units of Orcs.

Smoke and shrapnel sailed through the air tumultuously and mixed with the shrieks and cries of the antagonists in a stomach churning choreograph of pain and death. Demons of all shapes and sizes emerged, tearing ferociously into their enemies only to be pushed back by the vicious, merciless Orcs.

Kairayn disappeared in the haze. Satariel stood his ground like a massive red monolith, swatting and skewering Orcs with his lethal claws.

Then Kairayn suddenly reappeared. Satariel instinctively sensed his presence and turned to face the massive Orc, magic flaring wickedly in the Daemon Lord's palms.

Too late.

A beam of light, thick as a tree trunk, shot out at the Daemon Lord. Like a tentacle the ray wrapped about one arm of the Lord of Deception. The light turned murky and dark and then was sucked back into the stone Kairayn held. Satariel roared in pain and fear, looking down at the empty space where his arm had once been. Now he understood the nature of the Orc's power, and the dread the Daemon Lord felt was nearly palpable.

Again the light snaked forward, entangling a horrified Satariel. Slowly the Daemon Lord began to dissolve into the light, turning it a muddy red as it was drawn into the Krullstone. Kairayn rocked back on his heels with the force of it but held on. Satariel screamed in rage, launching fire in every direction with his one remaining arm, fighting desperately to break free of the killing magic. Smoke and ash filled the air, obscuring their view. The scream became a muddled gurgle and finally died away altogether.

Orc and demon alike stopped in their tracks. Dead silence followed. Nothing moved, not even the wind. It was as if the whole world were holding its breath for fear that the magic of the Slavemaster might be turned upon it. The haze began to clear, and slowly the field came back into view. Kairayn was there, standing stock still. He looked larger than before, emanating an aura of power and strength. Where the Daemon Lord had stood the earth was scorched black as night, and a thin tendril of smoke swirled slowly skyward. The demons that had accompanied their master to the fight looked around in confusion.

Kairayn took a menacing step toward them. "Serve me, vile beasts, or face your master's fate!"

Slowly the demons slipped back into the brush, growling and hissing. Kairayn raised his fist in triumph, and his Orc brethren roared in celebration.

"I can't believe he did it!" Vinson breathed in disbelief.

"One down," Layek replied. "Three more to go."

Vinson became suddenly recalcitrant. "It was my job! The Krullstone is mine!" He pushed himself up into a crouch. "I will have it back!"

Without warning he jumped up, moving toward the open flats where Kairayn still stood. Instantly Layek was on him. The big man knocked Vinson down, pinning him to the ground beneath his weight, careful not to damage his already wounded arm. Vinson thrashed wildly, fighting like a feral animal to break free. Aldric joined in to help Layek hold him tight, speaking soothing words into his ear.

"Let me go!" Vinson rasped. "You don't understand! I must have it back!"

"Have you gone completely insane?" Layek fought to keep his voice down. "There are thousands of Orcs out there right now, one of which can use the stone! You'll be dead, or worse, in less than two minutes!"

"He's right, Vinny. Don't throw your life away. We'll find another way to get the stone back. Please."

Slowly Vinson began to come back to his senses. His limbs went lax, and he stopped resisting. His two friends held him there for several more minutes just to be sure he wasn't deceiving them. Finally they let him go. Gently he brushed the leaves from his clothes and sat up.

"Okay," Layek said cautiously, "how do we get out of this mess?"

"Vinny could use that spell again," Aldric suggested. "We could slip right past them."

"Oh, no," Layek protested. "Not that again. That plan almost got us killed once, and I'm not fool enough to try it again. Anyway, Vinny's not in any shape to be playing such tricks."

"Why don't we just wait them out?" Vinson asked suddenly. "We have good cover here. The Orcs will break camp soon enough and march. We'll just let them pass right on by."

"Once in a while he actually makes sense," Layek said with a lopsided grin.

So they waited. Morning drew into afternoon, and just as Vinson had predicted the Orcs packed up their camp and began to march westward. The three companions had no food or water, and they were forced to simply endure. Afternoon passed into evening, and the land began to grow dark.

Finally satisfied that the last remnants of the Orc army were long gone, Layek led them from their cover into the open night air. He looked cautiously around, scanning the dusky horizon for any signs of their enemies. Convinced that they were alone, the three regained their bearings and trekked back to where they had left their horses and supplies the night before only to find that they were missing.

"I guess the Orcs found them," Aldric offered tenderly.

Layek sighed in resignation. "Looks like we'll be walking home."

XXIV LAMBS TO THE SLAUGHTER

IN THE CATACOMBS beneath Grimknoll a shadow drifted that was darker than the lightless gloom that filled the halls. As if an unsubstantial wraith, Grubbash Grimvisage sped through his one-time sanctuary. As a sorcerer of some power, he had felt the ripples in the energy flows, though he did not yet know what they meant. The unexpected and mysterious occurrence had sparked his curiosity, which in turn had led him to seek understanding from those who would know.

Of course, they did not know of his intentions. Serathes and his lackeys would be hesitant to share their knowledge with him.

Thus, under the cloak of his magic, he stole into the underbelly of his own keep to appropriate the knowledge he sought. Serathes would not be pleased, but Grubbash didn't really care. In the weeks following the ritual that had brought them into this world, he had grown less and less fond of the Daemon Lords.

In truth, he could not stand their presence. They really did little to aid in the Orcs' quest for global domination, but then again that wasn't really why they were there. Their purpose would be served when Kairayn finally returned.

Soundless and swift he slipped through the endless maze of tunnels. A horrific stench filled the air, permeating his nostrils down into his very bones. He fought the urge to wretch.

To his great fortune and dismay, the doors to his once-grand haven had been torn off and discarded. Steeling himself to the macabre images he was certain were waiting within, he crept into the cavern. He did not venture far, sidestepping to the left once he had cleared the entrance. There he crouched, searching the gloom.

A gate of crackling magic energy at the back of the hall cast a dim purplish glow over the room, faintly illuminating the numerous piles of bones and half-rotted corpses. A handful of demons of a manner he did not recognize hovered around the portal, murmuring in their bone-grating tongue. In the center of the room sat a great and horrifying throne constructed entirely of skulls. Serathes himself sat upon it, gazing off into the darkness, no doubt lost in his own sinister ruminations.

Grubbash was rewarded for his efforts when, after a few moments of patient waiting, a sudden rift appeared in the fabric of reality. The sorcerer recognized the slice of bluish light as a teleportation gate frequently used by the Daemon Lords and their ilk to travel long distances instantly. He would give dearly to learn that secret, but for now it would just have to wait. In time, all their secrets would be his.

The rift widened, and two large shapes shuffled their way through. Grubbash immediately recognized them as Adimiron and Athiel. With huge, lumbering strides they strode to where Serathes sat. The three lingered for several long minutes, apparently waiting for something.

Adimiron broke the silence first. "It is true then. Our brother has fallen."

"Indeed," Serathes' deep voice floated through the still air. "The one called Kairayn has succeeded in retrieving the Krullstone. He has used it against our brother and slain him."

Athiel seethed with anger. "I should have gone myself to eliminate this whelp before he became a problem! Now it is too late!"

"My assassins will handle him," Adimiron hissed. "The Krullstone will be ours."

"Patience, my brothers." Serathes silenced them with a wave of his clawed hand. "Let us first see what will become of this Kairayn. He leads his army against the humans; once they are crushed he may return here, and then we shall play."

"This is not a game, Serathes!" Adimiron's voice was laced with fear. "Have you forgotten about the Hated Ones? If the stone falls into their hands, we are finished!"

Serathes leapt from his chair with a speed that defied the laws of physics. One clawed hand wrapped around the Bloody One's throat, the crunch of bones echoing across the room. "Do not question me! You forget that it was I who freed us from the Void! I have engineered our return and I alone! Everything is proceeding according to my design. Do not forget your place, brother."

At the front of the room, the High Summoner grinned in satisfaction.

୨   ୨   ୨

Lazarus leaned back heavily into his hard wooden chair within the war room. "How many?" he asked of the man who stood at attention before him.

It was early afternoon, the bright sun burning down on the banks of the Myrrh River from its perch atop the sky. Immediately after learning that the Orcs were marching, Lazarus had ordered his scouts into the field to gather as much information on their foes as possible. The scout captain had just returned. The Orc army was on the move, pushing hard for The Narrows that they guarded.

The invasion had begun.

"Their army numbers more than two hundred thousand, sir," the soldier stated. Quickly he began to rattle off divisions and regiments, giving a complete account of their enemy's strengths. "They will reach the banks of the river by dusk today."

Commander Booker whistled sharply. An aide marked the positions on a map spread over the table next to Lazarus. For many long moments they stared in awe at the map. The Orc army dwarfed their own, outnumbering them by more than ten to one.

"We'll never be able to hold them off." Commander Hakan's

brow furrowed in frustration. "They'll sweep right over us."

"On an open field I'd have to agree with you," Lazarus responded. "But let's not forget we have the river between us and them."

"Yes, but even with the high waters The Narrows won't slow them down much." Commander Booker shook his head.

Captain Reich rose from his seat in the corner of the room. "With the fortifications we've constructed on the banks, we'll have a clear advantage. It won't be so easy to get past those. All we have to do is hold the line."

"Easier said than done, Captain," Booker said, letting a wry smile slip. "Of course, if it were easy, this wouldn't be the army."

For the next couple of hours the commanders of the three legions strategized. The scouts kept a sharp eye on the Orcs' progress, and constant updates were sent back to headquarters. Soldiers were rallied and sent to take up their positions on the banks of the river. Lazarus had the cavalry units double their patrols along their flanks to ensure the Orcs did not attempt a crossing further down or upriver. Construction began on a series of new traps devised by Lazarus and Captain Reich.

Hours later everything was ready. The camp was abuzz with activity as men scurried back and forth. The sound of wood being chopped echoed through the air and mingled with the clank of metal armor. Rocks were brought up for the catapults and hauled down to the river. Spears and arrows were being crafted by the hundreds to supply the front lines.

Lazarus peered through the thicket of commotion, trying to locate Neslyn and Zafer. He searched for only a few moments before he saw them walking briskly towards him. A mix of excitement and fear shone in their eyes as they approached.

"I have to get down to the river," Lazarus told them as they stopped. "The two of you should be safe enough here."

"Oh, no, you don't!" Neslyn was furious. "If you think we came all this way and went through so much just to sit on the sidelines when it came down to crunch time, you've got another thought coming."

"Neslyn," Lazarus said soothingly, "I can't protect you down there. I need you here where I don't have to worry about you."

"You inconsiderate oaf!" she practically shouted. "Only a knucklehead like you would even suggest such an idiotic idea!"

"But I ..." Lazarus trailed off as she stormed away.

Zafer looked at him apologetically, shrugging his shoulders before chasing dutifully after her. Lazarus sighed in resignation. At a time when he should be worried more about what was at risk and the lives that were certainly about to be lost, he found that he was not. It was the Elven princess who dominated his thoughts. He found that the risk of losing this battle, losing the war, even losing his own life were insignificant next to the thought of losing her. His heart ached at the possibility and felt like even the thought might break it in two.

With a heavy heart Lazarus walked down to the river.

The Narrows was a section of the Myrrh River where the waters came down out of the Serpentspine into a shallow bed. It was only about a half mile long, and the banks on either side were raised several feet over the water level. On their side they had constructed a wall of spiked timbers and a bulwark the length of The Narrows. Trees lined the north bank, a wall in and of itself. The bulk of their army would be hidden there in an attempt to conceal their true numbers. In the cool waters of the river, soldiers were preparing new traps in the deeper pools and eddies.

Lazarus looked out across the river to the open field there. The sun was drifting rapidly toward its resting place in the west, each passing minute bringing the carnage and destruction of war ever closer. Men began to settle in for the evening, taking what comfort they could in the quiet moments before the maelstrom. There were no fires, as Lazarus had ordered, so the men of the Legion ate their dinner cold. The sweet smell of burning tobacco wafted across the banks of the river, and water bubbled affectionately over the rocks and sand.

He looked around for Neslyn and Zafer, but they were nowhere to be seen. At least she was wise enough to stay back from the front ranks. Again he inspected the state of their defenses, checking in with his captains to ensure all was as it should be.

Once he was satisfied that there was nothing more to be done, he went in search of some food. He walked back to the command post where he chewed disinterestedly on his meal of bread and stew. He washed it down with cold ale but never tasted a drop. Outside the light grew dim, and the shadows began to grow like twisted plants from some hellish nightmare. Sounds died away with the light, and silence blanketed the land as life paused to see what would become of the men gathered here.

Reports came in from the cavalry teams that Orc raiding parties had attempted to cross the river further east but that most of them were drowned in the roiling waters of the Myrrh, and those who did make it were cut down once they reached the far bank. Commanders Booker and Hakan stayed for some time, consuming meals of their own before excusing themselves to be with their men on the riverbank. Lazarus remained, enjoying the peace and quiet of the empty tent.

For a short time he drifted off into a daydream, a bright and happy memory from his childhood before all this dark business began. He smiled unconsciously at the fantasy and chuckled lightly to himself. Inwardly, he marveled at the changes he and his brothers had gone through since that time and wondered briefly what changes the near future would bring them.

He hoped they were good ones.

Suddenly a young soldier burst through the tent flaps into the command post. His boyish looks led Lazarus to wonder if the man was even old enough to be in the army, let alone die for his country.

"Commander," he addressed Lazarus, "news from the front. The vanguard of the Orc army has reached the river. Our scouts report skirmishes with cavalry units less than a quarter mile from the Myrrh. The bulk of their army will reach us within two hours' time." The boy's voice was thick with fear, and Lazarus could see the hope fading from his eyes.

"Very good. Send in my aide, and then you may return to your post." The young man saluted and turned to leave. As he was pulling back the canvas flap, Lazarus added, "Don't worry, lad. We've got more than a few surprises for the Orcs. They'll wish they had stayed home before the night is through."

"Yes, sir," he replied doubtfully before disappearing out the door.

Moments later the aide Lazarus had requested slipped in. Lazarus had his armor brought to him, and as he slowly donned the chainmail he steeled himself for the coming onslaught. Nightmares would emerge from the darkness, chaos would reign supreme on the battlefield, and men would die. He let the knowledge wash over him and allowed it to settle in the corner of his mind. The battle plan they had devised played out in his mind's eye, and he offered a silent prayer to whatever gods would heed his call.

The Commander of the Phoenix Legion checked his weapons, tightened the last strap on his armor, and strode purposefully out to war.

ço   ço   ço

Getting out of the highlands didn't turn out to be as easy as Vinson had thought it would be. Three days after Kairayn had used the Krullstone to destroy the Daemon Lord Satariel, when he and his brother along with Layek should have been climbing Sowel Pass, they found themselves barely a few miles from where they had hidden during their encounter with demons. The delay was mostly due to the fact that the highlands were swarming with Orcs by day and demons by night. At every turn they were required to disguise their trail, and frequently they had to stop altogether to avoid detection. The fact that their horses had been lost only contributed to the holdup.

"If that army reaches the pass before we do, we'll never get home," Layek commented darkly as they looked out at the throngs of Orcs who marched east.

Dusk was settling rapidly upon the highlands, the heat rippling off the disfigured landscape in waves. The sky was clear and blue, and a chill breeze gusted out of the north, raising goose bumps on their exposed skin.

It was a dismal state of affairs for the three humans. They had eaten little in the past few days. Most of their supplies had been lost with their horses, and what little they had thought to carry with them had been consumed long ago. They scavenged for berries and nuts as they traveled but unearthed little. Fatigue was setting in, and it was becoming harder and harder to put one foot in front of the other. The skeletal branches of the trees around them seemed to rattle with glee as they passed, delighting in the misery of the three companions.

Aldric gazed off into the distance beyond the massive cloud of dust stirred up by the Orcs, through the Serpentspine Mountains to where his homelands lay. He wondered if Lazarus was suffering from comparable misfortune. "We ought to just go around them," he suggested. "We could move a lot faster if we didn't have to dodge Orcs or demons at every turn."

"Do you have any idea how long that would take, Aldric?" Layek asked harshly.

With every hour that passed, each of them became more irritated. Without an outlet for their frustrations, they frequently vented on each other.

"Maybe you'd rather hang out in the Tersal Highlands until the war is over," Aldric shot back venomously. "Or maybe you'd rather just surrender now."

"Stop it!" Vinson spat at them both. "Don't forget that the enemy is out there." He pointed toward the dust cloud that hovered before them. "Fight them, not each other. Unless you've got a better idea, Layek, I have to agree with Aldric. We've got to get ahead of the Orcs."

"You're right. I'm sorry."

The tension faded, and all three relaxed visibly.

"I'm open to suggestions, but I just don't see any other way," Vinson stated calmly. "We can't delay anymore."

"Let's give it a try then," Layek sighed. "Maybe we'll get lucky and find some food along the way or a good bottle of ale."

At least Layek hasn't completely lost his sense of humor, the two brothers thought. Hungry and worn they turned north and began to trek slowly across the highlands.

ও   ও   ও

The thin slice of the crescent moon shone down upon the banks of the Myrrh, blanketing its shores in a muted white glow. The serene lighting created an illusion of asylum from the chaos of the world, a false sense of security. Deep in the surrounding forest some creature screamed as it fell prey to the nocturnal hunters who stalked the shadows at night. Its final cry cut off sharply and was swallowed by the darkness.

Lazarus looked out across the river warily. It was well past midnight. Already the Orc cavalry had assaulted them three times, and three times they had been driven back. His own losses had been minimal despite his reluctance to spring the traps they had arranged for their guests. No, Lazarus wanted to save those for when the Orcs came at them with their full strength.

He could see their fires from here. Distant sounds of laughter wafted across the bubbling waters of the river as if the Orcs didn't have a care in the world. It wasn't the Orcs who worried him at this hour, though. Night was the ally of the demons. So far, none had been sighted, but Lazarus knew they were out there, and it was only a matter of time before they appeared. Scouts watched the river for miles both upriver and down. If anything tried to slip through, he would know.

A shadow streaked across the moon, temporarily dimming its silvery light. On reflex his hand strayed to the hilt of the sword strapped to his waist. There was an abrupt shriek as the shadow plummeted to the ground. The ringing of weapons and the sounds of battle flared off to his right and died just as quickly.

An Orc war drum beat suddenly. Once. Twice more.

The sound shattered the night like a rock through a pane of glass. Men shuffled uneasily as the sound repeated. The Orcs were marching. Apparently the invasion couldn't wait until morning.

Lazarus grabbed the nearest soldier to him. "Wake Commanders Booker and Hakan. Tell them the Orcs are preparing an offensive. Go!"

The man sped off, and Captain Reich strode up, a pair of

lieutenants in tow. "Your orders, sir?"

"Load the catapults and ballistae and bring up our reinforcements. Double the guards at the watch posts up and downriver in case they try to flank us. Hitch the teams to the ropes and have them wait for my signal. I want the archers set up just behind the tree line ready to go."

"Yes, sir! Like lambs to the slaughter, they march blindly to their deaths." Captain Reich saluted sharply and wheeled away.

Across the river the war drums rolled and went silent. All eyes turned to watch. After several minutes of tense silence, the drums began again, only this time they were accompanied by the sound of boots marching in time. Lots of them. The tempo of the beat increased, and the earth shook with the coming of the Orcs.

Men began to shuffle uneasily as the massive army drew near, hundreds of torches lighting their approach. Officers paced the ranks of the Phoenix Legion, steadying their men with encouraging words.

A hundred yards from the southern bank of the river the Orcs stopped. The drums went silent as the two armies faced each other in the darkness, assessing each other's strengths.

The Orc army was frighteningly massive. Their fires lit up the field upon which they stood, illuminating their chaotically ordered ranks for as far as the eye could see.

Lazarus slowly slid free the Quietus Edge, the metal ringing with gleeful anticipation as it cleared the scabbard. "Steady men," he said calmly. "Archers, at the ready."

Behind him a line of archers stretched the length of his command, stacked five deep just inside the tree line. At his command the regiment slipped forward, almost soundlessly. Arrows were notched and readied.

The Orc ranks split, and siege machines came into view. Catapults rolled forward slowly, creaking and rumbling their deadly intent as they came.

Suddenly a deafening roar broke from the horde of Orcs so ferocious and feral it rattled the bones of the human defenders. The war cry lasted forever it seemed. Then the Orcs charged.

It was so sudden that it took Lazarus a few seconds to realize what was happening. "Steady!" he shouted above the thundering noise. "Ready on the ropes!" He lifted his sword high above his head.

The front ranks of Orcs thinned out as pitfalls and snares claimed handfuls of them. The siege weapons rumbled forward and unleashed a hail of boulders and arrows that filled the darkened sky.

"Cover!" Lazarus yelled as arrows rained down around him.

Screams rose from the ranks as the deadly missiles found their mark. Boulders crashed all around them. The river splashed in fury as the Orc offensive poured into it. Lazarus watched as they sped forward.

"Hold!" he instructed his men. "Hold the line!"

Fueled by the lack of resistance, the first wave of Orcs barreled into the icy waters of the Myrrh. Black shapes led the charge, teeth and claws gleaming wickedly in the moonlight.

Lazarus watched them come. He felt the magic of the runesword calling him, tugging at his soul. Still he waited.

The distance between them closed quickly. A hundred yards. Seventy-five. At twenty-five yards Lazarus brought his sword down.

Soldiers all along the line caught the signal and spurred forward teams of horses who were hitched to thick ropes that stretched out into the river. Driven by the fear of the things that came after them, the teams sprinted ahead, throwing dirt and rocks behind. The ropes went taut, and a great wall of spikes sprang up from the tumultuous waters of the river.

The demons and the Orcs who followed were unprepared for the sudden appearance. Unable to slow their charge and thrust forward by the mob who followed behind them, the front ranks of the demons were impaled upon the deadly barrier. Orcs pressed up against those before them, crushing many of their comrades as they were pinned against the wall.

The charge stalled. Confused Orcs milled about in the river and on its banks. The barricade began to groan and crack under the force of those who pressed against it.

"Archers, draw!" Lazarus raised his sword as the line of bowmen behind him notched their arrows and drew back. "Loose!"

The twang of bowstrings sounded, and missiles whistled through the air. Catapults and ballistae released their payloads. A murderous rain of lethal artillery ripped into the masses. Hundreds of Orcs fell screaming as the arrows struck them, while the boulders and giant spears of the larger weaponry slew them by the dozens.

Chaos reigned supreme among the Orc ranks as they desperately sought an escape from the slaughter. The soldiers of the combined legions let loose volley after volley until bodies choked the ford like the shavings on a carpenter's floor. Return fire from the Orcs intensified as those in the rear tried to bring aid to their comrades.

Lazarus surveyed the carnage. The screams of the wounded filled his ears, drowning out the rush of the river. A young soldier ran up to him and started to report, but halfway through his first word an arrow struck him in the temple. The boy died instantly.

"Lieutenant Daniels!" Lazarus yelled over the din. A tall man appeared next to him, thin and wiry, carrying an ash longbow. "Send a care package to our southern friends. I want those siege machines and catapults burned to the ground! I want it done yesterday!" He pointed across the river.

The man nodded and fled back into the woods. Moments later, torches were struck, and all along the lines of archers flames sprang up. Ceramic jars filled with burning oil were loaded onto the catapults, and bowmen set pitch-coated arrows to the flame.

Fire rained down upon the Orcs. The dry grasses and timber on the south shores caught instantly, and the flame spread like a thing possessed. A second volley followed the first, and within minutes the Orcs' siege machines had become infernos, lighting up the night sky as though it were day. Fireballs exploded among them, incinerating Orcs and demons by the handfuls. Smoke and the smell of burning flesh saturated the air, filling the nostrils of those still living.

The front ranks crumbled and fell apart. Orcs stampeded back across the river, frantically clawing their way through the massacre, trampling their comrades in their desperation to escape.

Cheers rose up from the defenders. Smiles creased grimy and blood-streaked faces as men reveled in their victory.

Not so for Lazarus. Looking out across the killing field, the magnitude of bloodshed appalled him. He wanted to wretch or scream at the insanity of such wanton destruction.

Healers looked to the wounded, and the Legion's dead were removed to be properly buried. Lazarus had the soldiers repair the damage to their main defenses, but the barricades in the river were rendered useless, shattered by the weight of so many. Nervously they kept one eye to the south.

Lazarus walked up and down the ranks, checking on the well-being of his men. He comforted the wounded and offered encouraging words to those who weren't. Bodies clogged the river, and Lazarus ordered his men to remove them from the northern banks. The dead Orcs were thrown upon a pile of timber and burned. At one point he found a section of men who had taken to impaling the heads of their slain enemies upon pikes. "Take those down immediately, soldier," Lazarus commanded in disgust.

"Why, sir? The Orcs would do the same with our heads. The demons would do much worse. We should extend the same respect to them as they would to us."

Lazarus' eyes burned into the man. "Do not question me, soldier. It is true that our enemies would do these things to us. If we sacrifice our honor in retaliation to our enemies' ways, then we shall become as barbaric and evil as they are. Remove this wickedness immediately."

The man nodded, shame glimmering in his eyes. Lazarus moved on. For several hours all was quiet. The moon drifted ever closer to the horizon, and men's eyes grew heavy with sleep. The fires died down, and gray smoke hung over the battlefield, stinging the lungs and obscuring vision. Sounds were muted and indistinct as they floated wraithlike through the hazy darkness.

Nothing could be heard from the far side of the river. Lazarus cautiously dared to wonder if perhaps the Orcs had tasted enough death for one night. On second thought, he sincerely doubted it. Looking up he could see clouds drifting over the mountains, covering the moon, deepening the darkness.

Wandering through the camp he could not find any trace of Neslyn or Zafer. His heart ached in the absence of the Elven princess. It hurt him more that she did not understand that he was trying to protect her. For now, though, there was nothing he could do about it.

To the east, the first tinges of purple on the horizon signaled dawn's coming. Something was missing, he realized with a start. It was too quiet, too peaceful. A cold knot formed in the pit of his stomach.

Hurriedly he ran down to the river. He arrived at the center just in time to see dark shapes scrambling unchallenged over their defenses. The watch had been torn to pieces.

Demons.

"To arms!" Lazarus yelled as he ripped the Quietus Edge from its scabbard. "Fight for your lives!"

The magic of the runesword flowed into him as Lazarus charged headlong into the beasts. Shouts of surprise and alarm rang out across the camp as sleeping men stirred into action. Confusion gripped the defenders.

Lazarus leapt atop the bulwark, cutting down his enemies as they came, roaring defiantly. Behind him his men rallied, crying out as they fought to drive back those who had broken through. Arrows began to rain down on them as the Orcs across the river joined the assault.

Then Neslyn appeared from the fray, Zafer at her side. The two Elves fought their way to where Lazarus stood, and alone they faced the onslaught.

Lightning shot down from the sky, exploding into the demons. Fire sprang up as sorcerers on both sides let loose an apocalyptic string of magic. The Legion's own archers began to respond, launching a barrage of missiles back at their enemies. The flare of the Quietus Edge served as a beacon for the men of the Phoenix Legion, and with a ferocity that rivaled that of the demons they began to press them back into the river.

Without the element of surprise the demons began to waiver. Lazarus led his men forward, Neslyn and Zafer at his side, pressing the enemy until finally they turned and fled.

War drums sounded on the southern banks. A deafening roar

rose up into the predawn sky, and the Orcs charged into the river just as their demon allies were beginning to break.

With a thunderous clash of metal and flesh, the two armies collided. The defenders held for several minutes, but by weight of sheer numbers the Orcs pressed them back. Reluctantly the humans gave ground, leaving a trail of bodies behind them as they went.

Back to the ramparts the humans fled. There they held, fighting desperately against the waves of Orcs. Bodies filled The Narrows until one could walk from one side to the other without getting his feet wet.

Lazarus ran up and down the lines, seeming to be everywhere at once and always where the fighting was thickest. Twice the Orcs broke through their lines. Instantly Lazarus was there, rallying his men to close the breaches. The death toll mounted, and the cries of the wounded rose up in a symphony of anguished voices.

Night gave way to daylight as the combatants vied for supremacy. Through the morning the battle raged, the tides of death shifting back and forth. The sun rose and the heat with it, sapping the strength of both armies.

Finally the Orcs fell back. There were no cheers this time, only relief that for the moment the fighting was over. Appalled, Lazarus looked out across the bloodbath.

The men of the Phoenix Legion began preparing for the next assault. The dead and wounded were carried to the rear, and breakfast was prepared and distributed to the men. Lazarus' heart grew heavy as he watched his men work. Of the seven thousand men in his command, less than six were still in fighting condition. Still there was no word from General Markoll. When the Orcs returned, there were no more reserves to call upon.

"Captain Reich," he yelled, and the man materialized next to him. "Send messengers to the cavalry units. I want every available man to return here."

Captain Reich acknowledged the order and disappeared. Lazarus found a comfortable-looking spot beneath the dappled shade of a leafless maple. He lowered his exhausted body to the ground and leaned back heavily into its trunk. His eyes closed, and he allowed himself a few moments of rest.

"Sleeping on the job?" Neslyn's voice reached out to him from his haven of calm.

"Just making the most of what time I have," he replied smoothly. The princess seated herself next to him, and he felt her hand cover his. "I hope you're not still mad at me. I hope you understand that I was only trying to protect you."

She squeezed his hand. "Of course, I do," she said softly. "And I appreciate it. But you need to understand that I go wherever you go. Our fates shall be the same no matter what comes."

He squeezed her hand back and smiled. He felt her slide close and nestle her head into his shoulder. He held her tightly and felt the warmth of her body ooze into his. He opened his eyes and found that she was staring intently at him. Her hair was tousled, and dirt and sweat streaked her skin. Her robes were frayed, but there was still fire in her eyes. Lazarus found that she was as beautiful as he had ever seen her.

"Do you really think the Orcs will be back after the death we dealt them?" she asked, her voice barely a whisper.

"It's inevitable. They are driven by things darker and stronger than death."

As if on cue shouts and cries split the stillness. The ring of metal on metal rose up from the riverbanks like a specter from a nightmare that would not end.

Instantly Lazarus was on his feet and running toward the sound. Neslyn rose with him without a word, grim determination set in her eyes.

The scene at The Narrows was total chaos. The Orcs had once again come at them in full force. Arrows whistled with deadly intent. Boulders crashed thunderously into the ground, sending showers of debris and dirt into the air to mingle with the cries and shouts of the combatants.

The flanks were holding, but in the center where the Phoenix Legion fought desperately to hold on, Orcs were already beginning to overwhelm them. Lazarus watched in fear as the line began to buckle under the weight of the army pressing against it.

Through the melee a massive pair of one-eyed monsters emerged, bearing spiked clubs the size of a man. Smaller demons followed in their wake, and the ranks of Orcs shifted to allow them passage. They slammed into the beset soldiers with almost comical slothfulness.

Swinging their gigantic clubs with supernatural strength, they hammered into the men, tearing a hole right through the ranks. Soldiers shied away in fear.

Lazarus sprang into action. Without hesitation he barreled into the demons, runesword arcing viciously. Slashing lightning quick, he felled the first demon. The second followed soon after. More followed in the monsters' wake, however, and Lazarus turned to face the rush. The damage had been done.

Virtually alone he stood against the onslaught. Demons came at him from every side. He dodged and weaved between them, hacking and slicing in a lethal dance. Vaguely he was aware of Neslyn's presence as she fought beside him.

It seemed like they were the only two defenders left. There wasn't another soldier from the Phoenix Legion within sight. Lazarus called to them and could hear their rallying cry as they attempted to force the Orcs back through the gap.

The weight of their attackers pressed down on them. Lazarus felt like he was being suffocated. He could not turn the Orcs back. For every one he slew, three more took its place. The magic of the Quietus Edge surged through him, giving him strength, and he felt that dark place within call to him.

Beside him, Neslyn went down in a tangle of limbs and bodies as the Orcs overwhelmed her magic. Desperately she called to him for help.

Lazarus snapped.

Roaring with a fury so intense that it seemed to shake the earth itself, he struck. Orcs fell away as he sliced through them. With strokes as quick as thought he cut them down. A dozen lay dead or dying within the first few seconds.

Bodily he lifted the Orcs from atop his love and cast them aside as though they were nothing. Alone he stood over her and faced the onslaught. Warily the Orcs eyed him, unsure what to do in the face of Lazarus' wrath. All that came within range were struck down.

Lazarus charged into them, determined to drive them back, lost in the magic of the runesword. At once it both consumed him and drove him forward. All around the lines were collapsing as the soldiers of the Legion gave way to the unstoppable Orc war machine.

Surrounded and hopelessly outnumbered, Lazarus refused to give in. He fought like a man gone mad, violently striking out as he writhed and twisted through the maelstrom. Bodies began to pile up around him. Zafer appeared through the horde and pulled Neslyn to her feet. She was bloodied and bruised but seemed otherwise unharmed. Over the din he heard Zafer's call for him to retreat.

Never! A voice within him cried. *No retreat! No surrender!*

With a cry of rage Lazarus redoubled his assault on his enemies. Leaping through the air he beheaded two with a single sweep of his sword. Upon landing he tucked into a roll, emerging onto his feet in the midst of a horde of screeching demons. Immediately they set upon him, reaching with razor-sharp claws and murderous intent. Almost faster than the eye could follow Lazarus cut them down, their bodies bursting into ash as the magic of the Quietus Edge surged through them.

A blow took his legs from beneath him, and Lazarus fell flat onto his back. A dozen rapid strokes brought his nearest attackers tumbling to the ground. Instantly he was on his feet again, cleaving a path through his enemies and leaving a trail of lifeless bodies behind.

Reinforcements from the flanks arrived and rushed into the fray, colliding with the Orc offensive with a crash of metal and flesh. The Orcs stalled, temporarily held back by the surge. Lazarus raised his sword above his head and cried out. Men all along the lines took up the call, and for a moment it looked like the tide might turn once again in their favor.

Dodging the thrust of a spear, Lazarus grabbed the shaft and pulled the owner to him. Using the unsuspecting Orc as a shield, Lazarus borrowed its own spear to impale those approaching from behind. Ducking the swoop of a blade, he hurled the dead Orc into his attackers, bowling them over. He turned his attention back to his own men.

Behind him things were not going so well. The fresh troops had helped in slowing the Orc assault, but they could not seem to turn it back. The Orcs pressed forward with a determination and ferocity that was disheartening. Lazarus' shoulders sank as the cold realization of the eventual outcome washed over him.

Then something amazing happened.

Out of the chaos a horn sounded. At first Lazarus didn't recognize it through the haze of his killing spree. Horsemen began to appear through the trees. New waves of arrows took flight from behind their lines, covering the Orc assault in a blanket of arbitrary death.

"General Markoll!" Lazarus heard someone shout over the cacophony. "The General comes!"

Confused by the sudden appearance, the Orc offensive stalled. Fearlessly the cavalry swept thousands strong into them. With the swiftness of a raging river, they tore through the Orc lines.

Broken and shocked, the Orc offensive fell apart. Scrambling, they turned and ran. The cavalry pursued them to the far banks of the river, showing no mercy to their enemies.

When the pursuers reached the south bank, another horn sounded, and they halted. There they stood and watched as the Orcs sprinted all the way back to their camp.

ဏ   ဏ   ဏ

Hours later Lazarus stood back in the trees looking out over the river. Neslyn lay sleeping at his feet, scraped and bruised but otherwise no worse for the wear. Zafer sat next to her, worry lining his face. "Just a few scratches are all. She'll be fine, Zafer," Lazarus said soothingly.

"Thanks to you," he replied. "I am forever in your debt. If you had not been there to ..."

"I did what anyone would have done in my place, nothing more," Lazarus cut him off. "Friends look after each other. No debt is owed."

Zafer did not look convinced, but he let the matter drop.

On the banks the soldiers of the six legions General Markoll had brought to reinforce them were taking up their positions. The Phoenix Legion, along with the other two, had been moved back from the front lines to rest and regroup.

Lazarus excused himself from the two Elves and went down to the lines to seek out the General. It didn't take him long to find the man, who was barking out orders to his men as they scurried back and forth.

"Good morning, General," Lazarus greeted, saluting sharply. "You really saved our bacon back there."

The General smiled. "Timing is everything, Commander Arkenstone. If it hadn't been for your efforts, though, I'd be defending Perthana right now instead of the Myrrh."

"Did my messenger find you?" Lazarus remembered suddenly the undefended pass north of them. More so, he worried for his brothers who would be returning through that pass.

"Indeed he did. Elements of the Crimson Guard out of Perthana have been dispatched to secure the keep."

"Sir, if the army in the highlands intends on coming through that pass, you'll need more than a few peacekeepers to defend it," Lazarus stated. "The Phoenix Legion would like to volunteer for this duty."

"Don't be in such a hurry, Lazarus," Markoll chuckled. "I know you expect your brothers to return there, and I was planning on sending the Phoenix Legion anyway. There are some people I want you to meet first. I think they might prove useful to you."

Markoll led Lazarus through the bustle of soldiers to the front lines where a pair of Dwarves was overseeing some modifications to the defenses. Upon seeing the General and his escort, they uttered a few hasty instructions and stepped down to greet them. From afar, they could easily have been mistaken for children. Up close, however, Lazarus found they were far from such.

The first and taller of the two stood barely more than half his height. His scruffy beard hung down several inches past his chin, and he had a gold hoop in one ear. Scars decorated every inch of visible skin. His eyes were black as coal and sharp as a hawk's. He wore chainmail over his leather tunic and a leather cap on his head, with a maul as big as he was strapped to his back. Daggers lined his waist. He looked rough and gnarled, the sort you wouldn't want to meet in a dark alley.

The second, just slightly shorter than the first, was only marginally more inviting. Dark eyes peered out from beneath thick, bushy eyebrows, and brown, slightly graying hair snuck from beneath his skullcap in stringy wisps. A short beard, frayed as an old rope, rested on his chin. This one was only lightly armed, a brace of daggers and a spiked mace on his belt. Leathery, worn skin added to the appearance of something as old as the mountains, but his eyes were warm and inviting. A smile tugged at the corner of his mouth.

"Lazarus, meet Kagan Ochak and Vani Carchim," Markoll introduced them in turn. "They've marched all the way from Arendal with five hundred warriors and a detachment of engineers. Kagan leads the warriors. Vani is their head engineer."

"Good day," Kagan said gruffly, offering his hand.

"'Lo there!" Vani said enthusiastically. "Looks like you've been having some fun down here."

"Hardly the way I would describe it." Lazarus took their hands in turn, wincing slightly at their iron grips. "Glad to have you with us. As you can see, we need all the help we can get."

"Vani and Kagan will be traveling with you to Sowel Pass," Markoll informed him. "The skills of their engineers will be better put to use there."

"Excellent. The company is most welcome."

The two Dwarves nodded and then excused themselves to finish their work. Markoll led Lazarus away out of earshot of the rest of the soldiers.

"You're only sending the Phoenix Legion, aren't you?" Lazarus' question was more a statement of fact.

"Yes," Markoll replied. "The keep in the pass was designed to defend against a superior force. Down here at the river we have no such luxury. I need every available man to defend this spot. Lazarus, you have to hold the pass at all costs. If that army gets behind us, we're done for."

"I understand," Lazarus replied. "They won't get through us."

"I know I can count on you. Now get to it."

The two shook hands and bid each other farewell. Lazarus gathered up his captains and delivered their new orders. The Dwarves met them at the edge of the camp, and shortly after midday all was in readiness. The cavalry was sent ahead to prepare the keep for the rest of the Legion's arrival under Emeris Dallen's leadership. Lazarus watched as his men advanced in a long line toward the mountains west. Less than three quarters of his legion would be making the march.

Darkly, he wondered how many of those left would live to see their homes again.

XXV DELAYING THE INEVITABLE

IT WAS WELL past midnight when the Phoenix Legion was finally settled within the keep at Sowel Pass. Lazarus stood atop the walls staring out into the blackness of night. Clouds drifted across the sky, and the light of the moon came and went with them. Crickets chirped in the silence, and for the moment calm prevailed over the madness that gripped his world.

Torches burned brightly on the walls of the keep to ward off intruders, and Lazarus studied the men who stood watch over the empty expanse leading up to their fortress. His eyes were heavy with sleep, and every bone and muscle in his body ached.

As he watched the night slip slowly by he wondered what had become of his brothers and his friend. None had returned through the pass since Lazarus and his companions more than week earlier. He hoped beyond hope that nothing adverse had befallen them, but with each passing day the chances of them ever returning grew slimmer.

Already he had scouts scouring the highlands below the pass for any sign of his family. It was too early, of course, for any word to be returned to him, but he kept waiting anyway. Until he knew they were safe, sleep would be elusive.

He heard footsteps approaching from behind him. Captain Reich's smooth voice reached out through the still night air. "You should at least try to get some sleep, sir." When Lazarus didn't answer him, he added, "If they're out there, sir, we'll find them. You're not helping them by making yourself suffer."

"Very well then. Wake me as soon as you have any news."

Captain Reich nodded his agreement, and Lazarus trundled off. It felt lonely within the sparsely decorated bedchamber. Scenarios and nightmares played out in his mind's eye, and it seemed that every time he closed his eyes the visions only became more vivid. He thought often of his brothers and Layek and prayed silently that all was well with them.

It was a long time before he fell asleep.

∾   ∾   ∾

"Commander Arkenstone!" Somebody pounded on the door to his bedchamber. "Commander Arkenstone! Please wake up, sir! I have urgent news!"

Groggily Lazarus roused himself and rubbed the sleep from his eyes. "Just a minute! I hope this is good," he muttered as he searched for his boots.

"It's your brothers, sir! They've arrived!"

Lazarus forgot the boots, snatching up his shirt instead as he dashed for the door. He yanked it open and bolted into the hallway, nearly barreling over the young messenger on the other side. "Take me to them immediately," he said without stopping.

The soldier struggled to keep up as Lazarus sped down the hallway. He took the steps in leaps and bounds and burst out into the courtyard. The bright morning sunlight blinded him temporarily, and he lifted his hand to shield his eyes. The messenger took the lead and trotted off.

There, hunkered down in the shade beneath the arch of the gates, sat three people. Lazarus recognized them instantly. He broke into a dead run, and within seconds he was skidding to a halt before them.

They looked up from the stew they were ravenously consuming to look upon him, smiling brightly. There was a haunted look within those eyes that Lazarus hadn't seen before. He wondered if the same look had been ingrained within his own visage.

"You'll never know how glad I am to see you!" Lazarus blurted. "What took you so long? I expected you days ago!"

"Well, it's a good thing we showed up when we did. It seems you can't even dress yourself properly without us to look after you," Layek managed between mouthfuls.

Lazarus looked down and realized that he had not yet buttoned his shirt, not to mention he was without the boots he could not seem to find earlier. He couldn't help but laugh. The three stood up, and Lazarus embraced each of them heartily.

As it turned out the encroaching Orc army had proved to be quite difficult to slip past, and it had taken them much longer than it normally would have to cover the distance. They explained everything to Lazarus — all about their foray into the Orc camp that first night and their subsequent misfortune as they stumbled into the demon's territory. They described in great detail and excitement the death of the Daemon Lord Satariel and Kairayn's rise to power. It was a miracle that any of them had survived.

"I knew I should not have let you go alone."

"Easy now, Laz. We had it all under control." Layek tried to smooth things over.

"We're here now anyway," Aldric cut in, heading off an argument before it started. "That's what matters. And the Orcs still have the Krullstone."

"We cannot help that now," Lazarus replied forlornly. "For now we must look to defending this ground. If Kairayn commands that army, then he will bring the stone right to us. Perhaps an opportunity to reclaim it will arise."

"So what's next then? Wait here for the Orcs to appear?" Layek asked uncertainly.

"First things first, Layek. The three of you need to finish your food and then get some rest. You look exhausted."

They tried to protest, of course, insisting that they felt fine, but Lazarus would not hear of it. He sat with them while they finished their meal before sending them begrudgingly off to bed.

It was late morning by then, and Lazarus watched contentedly at the bustle of activity around the keep. In the forested part of the pass to the east, Vani Carchim was working hard with his engineers on some new siege weapons for their defenses, better than any he had seen before, Vani had told him. At the western reaches of the pass Kagan Ochak, along with his warriors and a contingent of men from the Phoenix Legion, was preparing traps for the enemy. The close proximity and steep grade of the walls of the pass made it virtually impossible to come through any way but head on and provided ample opportunities for the Dwarves to create rock slides and pitfalls of the most terminal variety. Cavalry units scouted the Orc army as it crawled across the highlands towards them, keeping tabs on their movements and collecting invaluable information regarding their troop make-up.

Lazarus sighed contentedly. Despite all the tragedy and bloodshed, he felt relieved and peaceful. His brothers and best friend had returned alive. There was little more he could ask, except perhaps the salvation of his people, but for now he would not dwell on it.

He climbed up the flight of steps up to the top of the wall. From that vantage point he stared out over the highlands far below. The ridges and hillocks spread out before him in a rainbow of lush greens and browns, accented by the purplish hues of the higher peaks. A light breeze blew in from the west, cool and refreshing.

In the near distance he could see a massive cloud of dust rising into the sky. His thoughts tugged back to the immediate task at hand. The gates to the keep creaked open, and Lazarus looked down to see a unit of scouts returning from the field. With a sigh he tramped down the stairs and into the courtyard.

Captain Reich was already there, debriefing the scouts as they dismounted.

"What have you got, Captain?" Lazarus asked.

"Well, sir," Sterl replied, "we've got two days before the biggest army ever assembled comes knocking on our gates."

"So what's the bad news?" Lazarus joked.

"Be serious, sir. At last count there's more than three hundred thousand bloodthirsty Orcs and demons just bursting at the seams to join our little party here."

"Well, then. We'll just have to prepare a little welcome gift for them. How soon can we mobilize?"

"You're not serious, are you?" Sterl was beside himself. "You can't actually intend on riding out there to meet them on open ground. That's ludicrous!"

"Which is exactly why it will work," Lazarus replied with confidence. "It's the last thing they would expect."

"You're absolutely crazy."

Lazarus smiled. "Meet me in the war room."

Half an hour later Lazarus sat within the war room of the keep within Sowel Pass. Maps decorated the walls and were rolled up and neatly stacked on shelves. A large, square table dominated the whole room; half a dozen chairs were scattered about it.

He reclined easily within the head chair, looking out across the table at the other leaders gathered before him. Layek, Vinson, Aldric, Sterl Reich, and Emeris Dallen were all there. They sat looking at him, dumbfounded by his audacious plan.

"You're going to get us all killed," Layek grumbled.

"It's crazy enough, it just might work," Aldric chimed in. "They won't be expecting an attack."

"That still doesn't change the fact that they outnumber us more than fifty to one," Sterl Reich pointed out.

"They don't know that," Lazarus rose from his chair. "The Orcs have no idea how many of us there are. We can use the cover of night to hide our true numbers. Surprise and confusion will offset their advantage in size. Strike at their heart, their food, and war machines. We hit them hard and fast and fade back into the darkness before they even know what's going on.

"You're right, Sterl. We can't face them on an open field. Not for long. A quick strike will demoralize the Orcs. We may just be delaying the inevitable, but it will buy us some time and make them think twice about who they're dealing with."

Aldric studied those seated around him. "I agree with Laz. We cannot just sit here and wait for the Orcs to arrive at our gates. The time for action is now."

"Thank you, Aldric. Are there any other objections?" Lazarus looked them each in the eye, trying to transfer some of his conviction with his stare.

"Well, I can't very well let you go alone, now can I?" Layek grumbled. "Of course, I'm in."

The others nodded their agreement, albeit reluctantly.

Lazarus gathered them close in around the table. In great detail he walked them through exactly what he had planned. For more than an hour they discussed the raid, fine-tuning the particulars. The excitement grew as they heard his intentions. A mighty blow could be dealt to their enemy. One that, with any luck, the Orcs might not ever fully recover from.

Of course, there was the chance that something could go terribly wrong. Lazarus carefully steered the conversation away from these thoughts and instead focused his comrades on what could be done to minimize their own risk while dealing as much damage as possible to the Orc war machine.

As they shuffled out the door, Lazarus grabbed Emeris Dallen by the elbow and held him back. Since Aurora Skall's death on the Solaris Plain he had grown taciturn and introspective. Lazarus had not heard him speak for a week. He was worried for his friend. He understood that a certain amount of grieving was normal, but he feared his friend might be falling off the deep end. When he looked into his eyes, there was an emptiness that had never been there before.

"Emeris," he began cautiously, "you seem a little off. Are you well?" His friend looked up into his eyes. There was pain there beyond measurement. "Maybe you should sit this one out."

The big man's stare hardened. When he spoke, his deep voice was barely a whisper. "She was everything, Laz. Without her there is no reason to live. All I have now is vengeance. Those who took her from me deserve to suffer as I do, and now is my chance to bring justice upon them. You cannot deny me this. I must go."

Lazarus stared at him for many long minutes. He felt a pang of guilt and sorrow as he realized the truth of how his friend was coping with the loss of Aurora. Emeris had transmuted his pain into hatred so intense that it dwarfed the love he had lost. He had become a shadow of the man he once was, a shadow hell-bent on the complete annihilation of those he felt were responsible for his torment.

His friend had been irrevocably changed by the death of his mate and not for the better. There was fire in his eyes as he spoke of revenge, something Lazarus could understand. He would want the same were he in the that position.

"Just be careful out there, Emeris," Lazarus said finally. "Remember there are those still living who care about you. Remember that the lives of those men you lead into battle depend on you. Don't do anything foolish." As an afterthought he added, "All wounds heal, Emeris. It just takes time."

"Not these wounds," he whispered, tears springing into his eyes. "Death is the only release."

He trudged off, not waiting for a response. Lazarus watched him go with a heavy heart. Though he understood what his friend was going through, he did not know how to help him. All he could do was give him time.

ᕲ   ᕲ   ᕲ

Scouts kept watch over the Orc army throughout the night and the day after, carefully monitoring their movements. Special attention was given to the way they made their camp and how they conducted the defense of it.

All day had been spent prepping the Legion. The cavalry's horses were outfitted with leather shoes to muffle the sound of their passing. Three out of the four infantry companies that comprised the Phoenix Legion would also make the journey, and Lazarus instructed them to tightly strap down their weapons and armor to minimize the amount of noise they made.

By late afternoon everything was ready.

Lazarus looked out at the formations. He studied the faces of the men he saw there and wondered how many of them would not be returning. He felt the weight of responsibility settle on his shoulders. They had determined yesterday that the first three companies of infantry and the cavalry would fit the bill nicely. The fourth company would remain behind to defend the keep. Four thousand seemed such a small number compared to what they were facing.

He gave the order, and the column of men began to move out. It was an eerily silent procession. Men watched from atop the walls and towers of the keep, grim-faced and mute. The sound of booted feet marching in time seemed distant and oddly detached.

Emeris rode at the head of the cavalry; he might as well have been carved out of stone. Neslyn, Zafer, and Azrael sat on horses next to him, refusing to be left behind. Layek, Vinson, and Aldric each rode with their respective companies.

By now, the thought of keeping his brothers here where they would be safely away from danger didn't even cross his mind. They had been through and seen enough. His brothers had proven that they no longer needed him to look after them. His pride had to give way so they could stand on their own two feet.

With the two Elves and the sorcerer in tow, Lazarus spurred his horse forward and slipped into the ranks of soldiers. They passed between the great stone arch of the main gate and continued on down the gentle slope of the pass.

The sun was already beginning to set as the line of troops snaked down out of Sowel Pass, shading the cloudy sky in brilliant hues of orange and red. They marched several miles into the highlands before Lazarus called them to a halt within a dell just large enough to hide the whole of their army.

He gathered up his officers and gave orders for the Legion to hold its position. He would ride ahead with the scouts to survey the enemy camp. He had to see it with his own two eyes. Neslyn and Zafer insisted on tagging along, but Lazarus didn't argue with them. The danger would be minimal.

Lazarus followed the trail through ravines and gaps for a couple of miles. When his scouts indicated, they dismounted at the foot of a rounded mound of jagged rocks. Beyond, the night sky glowed muted yellow.

Anxiety mounted as they climbed the hill. They slipped through the scrub and bare trees like ghosts until they reached the top. Before them lay a wide valley dotted by the characteristic rises and knolls of the Tersal Highlands. To the west the sun had fallen below the horizon, and the brilliant fire of sunset was fading into deep purple and blue.

Lazarus held his breath.

He had heard the reports, and though he was expecting such a large gathering, words just could not describe its magnitude. The basin was filled to capacity. Everywhere the eye wandered there were fires and tents and wagons of supplies. The light of their fires filled the sky, so much so that it was almost like day within the dell. Huge black pools of shadow occupied several sections of the camp, home to the demons Lazarus knew from his brothers' harrowing account of their foray. Orcs hovered around the campfires like moths, drawn to the light and the companionship it offered.

Once he recovered from the initial shock, Lazarus carefully surveyed the layout of the Orcs' camp. According to his reports their picket lines were just outside the halo of light that permeated the encampment — too close to raise the alarm in time once the assault began. At several points he could see the guards standing just outside the glow, hardly paying attention. Lazarus tried to count units and divisions, but there seemed to be no particular order to the arrangement of the camp.

Standards and banners were strewn about, supply wagons and siege machines abandoned haphazardly between groups of tents. It was impossible even to tell where the command center was located. How the Orcs managed to even march this far was beyond him. It seemed there was no discipline or order to their army.

Good fortune for the Phoenix Legion.

Lazarus and his companions retraced their steps to where the rest of the Legion was waiting anxiously. Men looked up as they passed by, a mix of fear and excitement shining in their stares. Layek and his brothers were waiting for him upon his return, and they greeted him restlessly.

"I don't suppose seeing it for yourself has changed your mind?" Layek asked hopefully.

"Not in the least," Lazarus replied quietly. "We came all this way, we might as well make the most of it."

Sterl Reich approached with Emeris Dallen a step behind. They nodded in greeting and looked questioningly at Lazarus.

"From here we go our separate ways," Lazarus said. "Remember to wait for the signal. We've got a few hours yet; let sleep and drink settle on them before we make our move. You all know the plan; stick to it. Be safe out there."

Lazarus embraced his brothers and shook hands with the others before dismissing them to their duties. The army began to split up into their different units and melted away into the darkness. With the cavalry and third company following, Lazarus rode straight at the Orc army.

Atop the rise overlooking the camp Lazarus stopped his men. The infantry organized into a phalanx backed by lines of archers. Horsemen formed up on both ends of the line.

Thankfully the clouds drifting overhead obscured the moon. The darkness was complete, and there would be no armor glinting to give them away. Lazarus became mindful of the time. Below, within the camp, Orcs were beginning to drift off to sleep, and the sounds of laughter and idle conversation slowly died away. Messengers arrived to report that the other two companies were ready and awaiting his signal. Half an hour went by, and still Lazarus held back. Timing was everything.

Yawns began to tear through the ranks of his men as the hours crept by. Below all was quiet. Lazarus' heart began to beat steadily faster in anticipation.

Now.

Quietly Lazarus whispered his orders into the ear of the messenger next to him. The man melted into the darkness as though he had never been there at all.

The sound of flint being struck cut through the silence, and a flame sparked. All down the lines of archers the flame traveled until hundreds of tiny fires pierced the night. There was a creak of bow-strings as they were drawn taut.

Behind him wizards began to whisper their arcane words of power. Suddenly the twang of bowstrings echoed down the lines, and flaming arrows filled the night sky, sailing through the air like a swarm of fireflies.

A shout of warning rose up from the valley as the sentinels below realized what was happening.

Too late. Silent, fiery death rained down on the Orc camp. Screams and cries multiplied as the arrows found their targets. Tents and supply wagons burst into flames, and the dry grasses that covered the valley floor quickly spread the blaze.

A second and then a third volley followed, amplifying the conflagration. The sorcerers unleashed their magic, and lightning bolts and fireballs began to tear through the camp. Thick smoke rolled across the valley as the wind took up the flames and pushed them further into the camp.

To the north and south Lazarus could see similar occurrences as the rest of the Legion joined the attack. Arrows whistled through the air as the archers continued to inundate the Orcs with death. Alarms resounded through the camp as Orcs scrambled from their slumber to face their attackers.

Only they couldn't tell which direction the attack was coming from.

Smoke began to fill the bowl of the valley, like a river fills a lake, screening out the surrounding areas and stinging the eyes of the Orcs.

A new sound rose above the din as the first and second companies charged into the camp from opposite sides. Cries of surprise and confusion filled the air as the soldiers swept down on their foe, plunging deep into the encampment, killing everything they came across.

From his viewpoint, Lazarus could see the action. The edges of the camp were in complete disarray, but in the center calm still prevailed. Units were forming up and beginning to push through the turmoil to the outer limits.

To his right Sterl Reich shifted nervously. Just as planned the flanks suddenly collapsed. With expert precision the soldiers melted back the way they had come, leaving death and agony in their wake.

Orcs stumbled around, mystified, searching for an enemy. As they came across their comrades in the smoky haze, more often than not they confused them for the enemy. Orc beset Orc ruthlessly, blinded by smoke and confusion.

Exactly what Lazarus had hoped for.

He called to Sterl, and the man bolted into action. Drawing his sword, the bold young captain leapt to the head of his phalanx. Archers released a hail of arrows overhead and on the flanks.

Slowly the formation began to march down the hillside. Lazarus gave the signal, and the cavalry charged forward, swooping down on the Orc camp like a bird of prey. The sound of hooves rumbled across the valley as the horsemen drove right into it.

Orc formations broke apart as they tried to reorient to defend against the new assault. Riders dipped low from their saddles, thrusting the unlit brands they carried into the flames.

The command split into a dozen units, slicing a path through the milling Orcs, torches carried high. They bore down on the nearest siege weapons and supply wagons, hurling the flaming wood onto them.

Light flared like a great beacon as the flames licked greedily at the towers and catapults, transforming them into raging infernos, sending thick black smoke roiling over the battlefield. The cavalry wheeled away, cutting a path through the futile resistance the scattered Orcs offered.

Lazarus watched anxiously. Though the destruction and death his brave men were inflicting upon the Orcs was immense, it was barely a drop in the bucket. Their attack, thus far successful, had hardly even scratched the surface of the massive camp.

From the center where calm still prevailed, the Orcs had organized a counterattack. Already it had reached the places where his cavalry was creating chaos and beginning to engage them.

"Right on cue," Lazarus whispered. A smile tugged at the

corners of his mouth.

From somewhere in the darkness a horn sounded.

The cavalry began to waiver and finally broke. Lazarus held his breath as the horsemen charged back out of the camp the way they came, enraged Orcs hot on their tail.

Heedless of what lay ahead, fixed only on reaching the fleeing humans, they ran headlong into the wall of spears formed by Sterl's company, camouflaged by the smoke and darkness.

Suddenly the fleeing cavalry spun about and charged back into the faces of their enemy. Totally unprepared for this, the Orcs were lost once again to uncertainty.

Orcs fell by the dozens as the combined forces of the cavalry and infantry tore into them. The lines shattered, and the Orcs scattered in fear. The men of the Phoenix Legion pressed the attack, driving them back across the borders of their camp.

Lazarus watched with grim satisfaction from his perch. The Orcs were in full retreat. Their assault had broken like waves upon rocky shores, leaving behind the bodies of hundreds of their kinsmen.

Through the haze and flickering firelight he could see that the Orcs were mobilizing the rest of their army. The demons had yet to make an appearance, but that would not last long if the Phoenix Legion remained.

Enough was enough. Lazarus gave the signal, and the horn sounded once more. Abruptly the men abandoned their offensive and turned to retreat.

Quickly they sped away from the battle, covered by a new barrage of arrows from their comrades on the slopes above. Those few Orcs who thought to give chase were cut down by the torrent, and the men of the Phoenix Legion melted into the night.

Lazarus waited until the last of his men had pulled back. He stood for several long minutes, staring at the utter anarchy left in the wake of his men. Fires burned uncontrollably throughout the encampment, and the screams of the dying rose up into the night sky like specters at haunt. Smoke filled the air and rolled across the valley in thick clouds. Siege machines and supply wagons lay in ruins everywhere. In many places the melee still raged as the confused Orcs mistook each other for the enemy.

Briefly he wondered if they had stirred up the hornet's nest rather than demoralize or hurt their enemy. Looking out across the destruction, he seriously hoped not.

ᴖ   ᴖ   ᴖ

Fire reflected off of the doppelganger's eyes as it stared down at the carnage below. Next to him, Commander Arkenstone watched as well, lost in his own thoughts. The man played a dangerous game, and the doppelganger had to respect that. Lazarus was a worthy adversary, and though the man had known of his presence for some time, he had yet to discover its true identity.

It remained only to ensure that the Krullstone did not fall into the hands of the humans again. The Slavemaster Kairayn would soon hear his master's call to return the stone, and then its job would be finished.

The doppelganger couldn't wait to see the surprise on Lazarus' face when it allowed him to see the truth. It would relish the moment forever.

Of course, it didn't have to kill him, but those were the stakes of the game. It was a treacherous path they tread, and all those who wandered it knew the eventual destination. It was only a matter of time. For Lazarus Arkenstone that time was almost up.

XXVI SACRIFICE

LAZARUS PACED BACK and forth within the war room. It had been two days since he had led the brave soldiers of the Phoenix Legion in the daring raid against the Orc army. The attack had been executed flawlessly. They had inflicted severe damage to their enemies while sustaining only minor injuries themselves. In total he had lost fewer than fifty men. Many of the Orcs' siege machines had been destroyed and scores killed.

Unfortunately, the incursion had not had the effect he had been hoping for. The Orcs had not delayed their march as he had intended them to do. Instead they had pressed on harder than before, stopping only once they had reached the mouth of the pass.

They had arrived yesterday. Now the only chance they had to engage the Orcs was to wait until they attacked the keep again or ride out and meet them head on. Both ways offered little hope for victory, the former more so than the latter.

Now the Orcs sat unchallenged and unchecked at the border of his domain, waiting. For what, he could not tell, but it could not be good. All day the sound of construction could be heard from the camp, echoing up the mountain pass into the ears of the beleaguered defenders. His companions tried to tell him it was perfectly normal, that they were simply preparing for the daunting task of scaling the keep's walls. Under normal circumstances he would have agreed with them, but on this occasion he could feel in his gut that something was amiss.

The Orcs had a darker, more sinister plan in the works.

Lazarus made the most of the time available. He had sent for reinforcements, but given the size of the Orc army at the Myrrh, he doubted any aid would be forthcoming. He ordered the construction of more catapults and ballistae, but as far as he was concerned they were as prepared as they could be.

Demons had begun attacking them during the night, scaling the walls or flying over them altogether. Watch fires burned everywhere to ward them off, but there was little else they could do except fight them when they appeared.

He walked outside, more for a change of scenery than anything else. No matter where he went, he was as nervous as a long-tailed cat in a room full of rocking chairs. His mind raced, ceaselessly running through the possible scenarios. Ultimately, who knew what the Orcs would throw at them?

There were few doubts in his mind that it would be everything they had.

Night fell on the besieged fortress. Lazarus walked up and down the walls and parapets, drawing more than one troubled glance from the soldiers posted there. He stopped and stared out across the blackness, trying to glean some hidden knowledge from the muted glow in the pass below him.

A shrill cry pierced the stillness, and the alarms drowned it out. The brief sounds of fighting echoed across the keep and then went silent.

So it begins.

He knew what the night brought with it.

All at once chaos erupted along the walls. He was moving even before the watch raised the alarm, before the sounds of battle and shrieking cries of the attackers had echoed off the sheer rock walls of the pass. The gut wrenching screams of the Howlers washed over him, signaling their arrival into the fray.

Pulling the Quietus Edge from its scabbard, he began to run, seeking out the nearest point of conflict like the roots of a tree seek out water. He didn't have to go far.

Dark shapes scrambled over the wall to his left, and instantly he turned to intercept them. The blue flare of his runesword illuminated the intruders, catching them by surprise and freezing them in their tracks. Lazarus barreled into them, scattering them like dust in the wind. Several swift strokes and they burst into ash, sending the survivors fleeing back over the wall.

Lazarus scanned the darkness, searching for the place where he was needed. The sounds of battle echoed across the blackness as the keep came alive, and the defenders rallied. Suddenly Layek's ferocious battle cry pierced the night. Lazarus located the sound in the midst of a dark stain on the rampart a hundred paces down where the torches had gone out. A mass of demons had overwhelmed the defenders and was scrambling over the wall in droves.

Only Layek and a handful of men stood between the demons and the inner reaches of the keep.

ဢ　　ဢ　　ဢ

Layek felt it long before it became apparent in the grim set of the faces of those who stood next to him — that subtle shift in the tide of battle that signaled that the scales had tipped in the favor of their enemy.

The demons' attack had not been nearly as random as it had seemed. They had struck in just enough places to spread out the Phoenix Legion's defenses, and then in one massive thrust thrown everything they had at the weakest spot. The shift was so sudden that the defenders hadn't even realized where the real threat was.

Layek grimaced at the jumble of claws and teeth as they hissed and spat at him. He was a brave man. But even the bravest man couldn't stand alone against hell for long. Tightening his grip on his battleaxe and widening his stance, he took a steadying breath. The demons inched forward, jaws snapping in anticipation.

All at once the demons sprang. Layek's scream of defiance echoed off the canyon's wall, almost fierce enough in and of itself to turn the enemy back. Yet where his valor failed, his battleaxe succeeded. Smooth, swift strokes cut the monsters down like razor-sharp scissors through thin paper as they approached.

Layek let himself be drawn into the whirlwind of bloodlust that possessed him. A sweep of his weapon sent a handful of darkened bodies to the blood-slicked stone. Lowering his shoulder, Layek bowled into those who followed after, knocking them away as though they were nothing. He put his back to the stone fortification and faced the rush of demons as they came at him. A swift backhand from his gauntlet-clad hand sent a screeching nightmare plummeting to its death over the wall. A black streak of talons raked his arm, tearing through the armor and into the flesh there, but he ignored the pain. Pivoting on his planted foot, Layek brought his axe to bear and beheaded the beast.

As he pummeled and hacked his way through the melee, he became vaguely aware of the flare of three separate runeblades as they lit up the night. Once again he felt it, felt it even before it registered in the shrill, aggravated cries of the demons all around.

The tide had shifted again.

ဌ ဌ ဌ

After the demons had been driven from the walls, Lazarus took to pacing the battlements of the fortress. The demons continued to pick at them, but without the element of surprise they couldn't muster a strong enough offensive to gain a foothold. Each time they attacked they were driven mercilessly back. The night crept on into the small hours with no end in sight.

He continued on this way, back and forth, constantly in the thick of the latest assault. That was until Sterl tracked him down and insisted that he go to sleep, claiming he would need to be well rested to lead them when the next attack came. He was right, of course.

He trudged wearily to his bed, doubtful that sleep would be any more forgiving than reality. Lazarus flung himself upon his bed and closed his eyes. Even here, in the silence of his bedchamber, he could hear the cries as the demons emerged from the darkness to assail his soldiers again.

It was a long time before he fell asleep, and even then his

dreams were troubled. Death and misery haunted him at every turn, chasing him through the landscape of his subconscious.

Dawn found Lazarus grateful, if not more rested. He stretched and dressed himself, gnawing on his cold breakfast more out of necessity than desire. Grabbing his weapons and strapping them on, he stepped out into the quiet halls of the keep. Briskly he made his way to the ramparts.

Everything seemed in order. The night watch was just turning over its duty to those next in line, stillness still gripping the warm morning. To the east the sun had yet to make its daily appearance, and a slight breeze blew out of the highlands to the west, causing the banners to flutter and flap on their stanchions.

Soldiers saluted him in greeting as he made his rounds. At the mouth of the pass all was quiet. A cold feeling settled in Lazarus' gut as he surveyed the land beyond his keep.

It was too quiet.

Even before the drums sounded in the distance, Lazarus was motioning the guard nearest him to come closer. The pounding bass of Orc war drums rolled into them like thunder.

"Wake the captains and raise the alarm," Lazarus ordered him, a sense of urgency creeping into his voice. "Quickly!"

The man scurried off, yelling out to his countrymen as he went. Horns sounded, and a bell rang in the north tower. The sleepy keep exploded with activity as men snapped awake and rushed to man the walls. Layek, Vinson, Aldric, Sterl Reich, Emeris Dallen, and Aman Desoto appeared next to him within minutes.

Fear shone in some of their eyes, grim determination in others. Questions formed on their lips.

"The Orcs are on the move. We haven't much time before they arrive. Layek, I want you up on the north tower. Emeris, you'll take the south. Sterl, have the Dwarves shore up the gates with heavy timbers and get the oil ready. I will cover the center while Vinny and Aldric will supervise the artillery and reserves. Aman," Lazarus faced the young woman, Aurora's replacement as leader of the sorcerers, "position your wizards all along the walls. Don't let them get too bunched up."

"You're too important, Laz," Layek huffed. "We can't afford to lose you. You should stay away from the front lines."

"No way am I going to sit down in the courtyard while all the action is up there!" Aldric's anger slipped a notch. "Vinny and I should be up on those walls. I think we've earned it."

"Very well then," Lazarus sighed. At least he had tried. "You two take the wall, and I will command from the courtyard."

In the distance, the cadence of the drums increased, and the mountains began to tremble with the weight of the Orcs. Men scrambled back and forth, hastily taking up positions. The sound of booted feet rumbled up the pass, echoing off of the canyon walls and multiplying until it filled the ears of the defenders in a deafening thunder. Rocks and dust showered down in the distance where their traps were triggered.

"Here they come!" Layek shouted over the din from the north tower.

In the pass below, swarms of Orcs began to emerge from the tree line, which was cut back five hundred yards from the walls. Lumbering siege towers loomed up over the forest canopy as they were pulled forward by the advancing horde.

At four hundred yards they stopped.

The drums ceased, and defender and attacker glared at each other. Many tense moments passed until a vociferous roar ascended from the throats of the Orcs, shaking the mountains around them with its fury.

"Steady," Lazarus called as he climbed the wall for a better view. "Stand firm!"

It seemed a very long time before the sound died away. An anxious silence fell over the pass, and the defenders waited on edge for the onslaught to begin.

Then without warning the Orcs charged. A howl rose up from the lines, and the siege towers creaked into motion. Banners waved mercilessly in the breeze. A battering ram snaked its way through the ranks. Ladders appeared among the mob as they closed in on the high rock walls of the keep.

"Three hundred yards!" Layek called out the distance from his vantage point. "Archers at the ready!"

The catapults launched a volley of boulders at their advancing foes. They bounced and rolled through the front ranks, crushing dozens of Orcs underneath them. Kagan watched from the walls and yelled directions to the crews below as they reloaded and targeted their weapons.

"Two hundred yards!" Layek raised his arm. "Fire!"

Bows twanged, and arrows took flight at the big man's command. Before the first volley had even hit the ground, Layek had already loosed a second.

The first ranks were cut to pieces as the deadly missiles fell earthward. The familiar *whump* of catapults firing followed, and two of the dozen siege towers collapsed into rubble as the massive rocks crashed into them.

"One hundred yards!" Vinson called from atop the long wall between the north and south towers. "Ladders! Prepare for ladders!"

Lazarus hurried back down to the courtyard. He would rather have been up on the wall, but somebody had to watch from below and direct the reserves when a breach opened or weak spots appeared. Vani Carchim greeted him with a grim nod. The creaking ropes of the catapults as they were successively tightened and loosed filled his ears, nearly drowning out the sounds of battle. Nearly.

On the north tower, Layek was yelling directions to the archers. "Aim for the siege towers! Bring them down!"

Hundreds of flaming arrows launched, leaving a trail of black smoke. Several of the siege towers were engulfed in flame. Shrieks and cries filled the air as Orcs were burned alive within the towering infernos.

Ladders slapped against stone as the Orcs covered the last stretch. The ringing of metal on metal and the sounds of combat flared up all along the walls.

The defenders held their ground, retaliating viciously. Ladders were thrown down, only to be replaced once more. Several of the siege towers butted up against the wall. Ramps tumbled down eagerly, and

Orcs began spilling from them onto the walls and into the bristling swords and spears of the Phoenix Legion. A great boom split the sky as the battering ram went into action.

Lazarus shouted out to his men, sending reinforcements to wherever they were needed. He felt altogether useless down there on the ground.

Arrows sailed through the air like a swarm of stinging insects, biting at the defenders. The crack of a thunderclap sounded, and a bolt of lightning sent shards of rock flying where it struck the wall. The Orcs had brought their own sorcerers forward. It appeared Kairayn was resolved to taking the keep in a single day.

But there was hope yet. Lazarus wasn't about to give up that easily.

Flames shot skyward as Sterl Reich doused the battering ram with oil from the wall above the gate, archers from the towers launching their flaming arrows to finish it off. Thick black smoked drifted lazily skyward from a dozen places where siege equipment burned uncontrollably. Though pressed, the men held their enemy in check, refusing to give a single inch.

A low rumble rose up through the rock like thunder rolling off the horizon. It built upon itself until the ground shook with the magnitude of it.

Suddenly, a great explosion rocked the courtyard.

A cloud of rock and dust bloomed from the south face of the mountains fifty yards within the main wall. The great, bulbous mass of a slate gray serpent thrust its way into the open, tremors rippling out as it struck the ground. Boulders bounced across the yard, scattering men as they struggled to dodge the debris.

Blood sprayed across Vinson's chest as he slashed the throat of the Orc who stood before him. As the body fell he lurched forward, skewering the next in line. Grabbing that Orc's spear, he vaulted out onto the edge of the wall, knocking back the ladder propped up against it and sending those Orcs scrambling to reach the top plummeting to their deaths.

Standing atop the battlements Vinson took a split second to observe how the rest of the Legion was faring. He felt the rumble of the stone beneath him and heard the explosion as it ripped through the fortress. The shockwave nearly sent him tumbling over the edge, and he quickly jumped back down.

He had no time to discover the source or the severity of the blast, however. Ducking to the side, he dodged the sweep of an axe meant to separate his head from his shoulders. Shadowsbane snaked out, gutting the owner of the axe. The magic of his runesword surged through him, giving him strength and focus.

A shrill cry pierced the pandemonium of battle, sending a chill down Vinson's spine. Looking up from his murderous rampage, he spotted the massive serpent as it began to advance on the men in the courtyard. He saw Lazarus, standing tall amidst the mayhem, barking orders, sending men scurrying into action. Vinson's own command was buckling under the assault of the Orcs, as were the others along the wall. The defenses had been breached in more than a dozen places, and the Orcs were quickly gaining momentum in their attempt to sweep the Legion from the walls.

Suddenly Aldric was beside him. "We can't hold out much longer! We're being overrun!"

As if to emphasize his statement another siege tower butted up against the wall, ramps lowering, spilling Orcs onto the causeway. The great hammering noise of a battering ram joined the cacophony as the Orcs resumed their attempts to batter down the gates.

Vinson felt his anger swell. Emeris joined them just as a horde of soldier demons crested the fortifications and drowned his unit in a sea of black, writhing bodies. "We need to regroup! Everyone on me," he shouted above the roar of battle. "No retreat, not a single inch! We stand here!"

Howling like a madman he charged into the demons, his runesword cutting a path, with Aldric at his side, for those who came behind. Suddenly Vinson was struck and went down. He rolled as he hit the stone, severing the arm that had snared him with one fell swoop. Leaping back to his feet he turned, searching for his comrades. Somehow he had become separated from the rest of them, a crush of Orcs and demons between. Weapons struck at him wickedly, more than he could count. He tried to fend them off, but he could sense that at any moment he would be a split second too slow, and that would be the end for him.

Then Emeris was there, hacking and slashing through the enemy, driving them back. Their eyes met, and Vinson smiled gratefully at the rescue. But Emeris did not smile back.

Instead, Emeris' hand shot out and grabbed him by the collar, yanking him aside just in time to avoid being impaled by the wicked-looking pike of the Orc behind him. The blow nicked his sleeve, and squarely met Emeris' armor in the center of his chest, punching right through into the flesh beyond.

Vinson cried out in agony as he watched it happen. He stabbed at the Orc until it fell away, but it was too late. The others of their company rushed forward to fight the enemy back, and Vinson caught Emeris as he fell forward.

"Emeris! No!" Vinson cradled him in his arms. The man's eyes were distant, his skin pale as blood gushed from the wound.

Emeris took a shallow breath, wincing at the pain. "Leave me, Captain Arkenstone."

"I will not leave you to die!"

"I died on the plains with Aurora. I go now to join the one I should never have left."

Emeris closed his eyes and his breathing stopped. Vinson gritted his teeth in frustration as his rage began to boil over. There was a sudden, thunderous crash as the main gate buckled and collapsed.

Then Aldric was there next him, his blood and sweat-streaked face a mask of determination as he hauled his brother to his feet. "He's gone, Vinny!" Aldric shouted in his ear. "We have to fall back! The keep is lost!"

ကော ကော ကော

"What in hellfire ..." Lazarus muttered as he turned to see what was happening.

The beast reared up, balancing on its hind section, swaying back and forth.

As far as Lazarus could tell, it had no discernable features or orifices, and yet it seemed to pan its head back and forth, like it was surveying those it had ambushed. An ear-piercing shriek split the sky like nails scraping on a chalkboard magnified a thousand times.

Lazarus winced as the sound washed over him.

"An Ettarok!" Vani cried as he ran up to Lazarus, his face twisted in a mix of fear and surprise. "Impossible!"

Lazarus grabbed the Dwarf by the arm. "What is it? How do we kill it?"

Men were scattering frantically. The Orcs surged forward, seeing the defenders momentarily taken aback. Slowly the thing began to inch its way forward, its maw opening wide to reveal a black empty hole filled with jagged stalactite-like teeth.

Vani looked at him with despair. "I don't know. The Dwarves run into them only in the deepest reaches of the earth and even then only extremely rarely. One has never been seen above ground. One hasn't been seen anywhere in a thousand years!"

"There's got to be a way!" Lazarus shouted back. "Get those ballistae turned around!"

Men and Dwarves leapt into action. Slowly the massive weapons began to turn while the ugly monster crept ever closer.

The first volley launched when the creature was a hundred yards away. Giant spears, thick as tree trunks, sped toward the target. Most flew wide or bounced harmlessly off of the thing's thick hide. One did manage to pierce the armor, and the bone-jarring screech that followed curdled the blood of the defenders.

The pounding of a battering ram on the main gate accompanied it. Atop the walls, several more siege towers had been brought to bear, and the defenders were having a hard time holding the Orcs back.

Lazarus dispatched what men he could to support them.

On the walls above he caught sight of Neslyn, hair flowing

wildly as she bombarded her enemies with her magic. Zafer was there next to her, bow singing as he strove to defend her from the hordes.

Azrael appeared next to Lazarus, launching a frightening barrage of lightning bolts at the giant worm. A second volley of bolts from the ballistae followed quickly after, whistling with deadly intent as they flew.

The beast reared back and shrieked in pain as the missiles struck, dozens of them burrowing deep into its flesh. Tendrils of smoke rose up from where the magic had struck it, green ichor oozing from the wounds in little rivers that ran down its body.

It teetered precariously for several moments, stubbornly refusing to give up the life it had already lost. Finally, it did topple over, slamming to the ground in a thunderous crash.

A cheer rose up from the men of the Phoenix Legion — a very short-lived cheer as they realized the true purpose of the Ettarok.

"Gods help us," Lazarus whispered.

From the mouth of the newly-formed cave came Orcs, pouring out by the hundreds. They made a beeline straight for the walls of the keep, intent on trapping the defenders between them and their comrades. Timbers cracked as the beating on the main gates grew more insistent, and the Dwarves ran to reinforce them.

"Fourth company, to me!" Lazarus shouted, lifting his sword high above his head, the metal ringing clearly as it cleared the scabbard. Men materialized all around him, forming up in tight lines facing the onslaught as it hurtled toward them. The Orcs were spilling out of the gaping cavern in droves, the front ranks nearly reaching the guardhouse at the center of the courtyard.

"For Illendale!"

The battle cry rang out across the lines as Lazarus led the charge down the gentle slope.

With a terrible crash the two forces collided, bodies flying as the humans plunged deep into the Orcs' ranks. Lines shattered and broke apart as Orc and Man met. Chaos gripped the battlefield, shouts and cries filling the air. Banners waved lazily in defiance of the anarchy that engulfed the courtyard.

Lazarus hacked and cut at his foes; every ounce of his strength and skill went into fending off the overwhelming numbers set against them. For every Orc struck down, ten more waited to take his place. Their own numbers were dwindling rapidly.

All around him the battle raged, his men struggling desperately to hold back the tide. Breaches formed all through the ranks as his men were systematically overwhelmed. From somewhere behind him he heard the groan of the gates as they buckled under the pressure of the battering ram.

There was no time to look back, however, and Lazarus focused on staying alive within the confusion of battle. Orcs slipped past his men in a steady stream, and slowly they were becoming surrounded.

A knot of fear settled in his stomach as Lazarus realized the eventual outcome. Lifespans were measured in seconds on a battlefield. They would be ground to dust under the weight of the Orc army, relegated to history as the would-be defenders of the world.

Men fell all around him. He tried to rally his troops, but the roar of combat drowned out his voice. Those closest to him formed a defensive ring, men standing shoulder to shoulder. Bodies littered the ground everywhere, the dirt red with the blood of friend and foe alike.

Briefly, Lazarus surveyed the field.

The walls were lost, completely overrun. The gates had been shattered. The Dwarves fought bravely to defend them but were quickly losing ground. There simply were not enough men to match the devastating power of the Orcs and demons. Everywhere Lazarus could see, Man and Dwarf alike were falling back.

Then he saw something he had hoped never to see in the whole of his lifetime.

Just below the great northern tower, along with the remains of their company, Vinson and Aldric fought side by side. Their unit had been cut off, Orcs closing in from every direction to finish them off. Between him and them a sea of Orcs milled about, roiling and churning as it struggled to reach those it sought to kill.

Suddenly Aldric was struck and went down.

Vinson stepped up to defend his younger brother, fighting

valiantly against the impossible odds, brutally slaughtering those who ventured too close.

Then Vinson himself was struck.

He dropped to one knee, still fighting but obviously hanging on by a thread. His men fought desperately to defend him, but Lazarus could see that there was no hope.

For Lazarus Arkenstone, time froze.

Each second seemed like an eternity. The battle still raged around him as Man and Orc fought for supremacy. Sounds grew muffled and distant, replaced within his mind by a seemingly never-ending cry of agony.

Lazarus dropped to his knees.

The scene before him took on a frightening familiarity. He had seen this before somewhere, somehow. A memory tugged at his mind, demanding recognition, screaming to be recalled. From deep within his subconscious it rose up with such terrifying force that the revelation rocked him backward.

Then he remembered Melynda's vision, the images flowing through his mind's eye. He had all but forgotten it, swept up in the events leading to this point in time, relegating it to the deepest, darkest corner of his mind. He cursed himself silently.

Idiot! I should have known! I should have seen it coming, should have sent them away to someplace safe!

Horrified, Lazarus watched as the rest of the vision unfolded before him, taunting him mercilessly with the promise of its fulfillment. His eyes filled with tears. He squeezed them closed, trying in vain to shut out the images.

His worst fear was coming true.

Then other memories began pushing their way to the fore. They came in the form of voices, bits and pieces of conversations he had heard before.

"It's only a vision ... future is not set ... not set in stone."

Something snapped within.

He slumped forward as the mental blocks and barriers, all the defense mechanisms and excuses that had sustained him throughout his life, disintegrated. The whole of who and what he was began to fall away into the chasm that opened inside. His beliefs, his hopes and fears, his dreams and desires, everything, leaving him hollowed and empty.

Then anger welled up from deep within. Anger that quickly built upon itself, filling the emptiness inside him.

Fire raced through his veins, burning, consuming everything that was left and leaving only cast-iron determination. Only the hardened core, as solid as the mountains upon which he stood, remained.

Vinson and Aldric will not die today.

The thought rose up through the fire. Numb with the shock of his transformation he reached down within for that part of him that was unbreakable, that part that refused to give in to the dictates of Fate.

No! I will not succumb! Today Fate will bend to my will!

What little was left of who and what he was crumbled away, and Lazarus Arkenstone was recast in the steel of his determination. His blood boiled as his fury magnified beyond understanding, building until it burst forth from his throat in a ferocious cry. The sound echoed off the rock walls of the pass, rising up over the cacophony of the battle that raged around him like a hungry beast freed from its cage.

In that instant Lazarus Arkenstone was reborn. He emerged a killing machine driven by a fury that would not be deterred from its goal.

Lazarus sprang to his feet, scooping up his discarded sword as he did. "Vinson!" he yelled. "Aldric!"

He had lost sight of them in the melee that surrounded him. The overwhelmed soldiers of the Phoenix Legion were losing ground steadily now, unable to withstand the massive Orc army.

Lazarus drowned out the clash of metal on metal and the screams and cries of the wounded that filled his ears. He was an island of calm in a stormy sea, and soon all he could hear was the steady thrum of his heartbeat as it pounded in his chest. From somewhere deep within, a voice filled his mind.

I am invincible.

Then he charged.

Impossibly quick, given strength and speed beyond that of mortal men by the fire that coursed through his veins, he tore into the ranks of the Orcs with a fury that bordered on insanity. Smoothly, effortlessly he flowed from sword-form to sword-form in the manner he had trained for half of his life, cutting a path through the hundreds of Orcs milling about.

A fierce cry rose from the men behind him as they counter-attacked, fighting desperately to catch up to their leader. But the ranks closed with Lazarus' passing, stalling the resurgence. Lazarus found himself alone, surrounded by his enemies.

He never hesitated.

Spears and swords cut at him from all directions, but he was too quick. He ripped through those who stood in his path as though they were made of paper, leaving a trail of blood and death in his wake. Some of the attackers found their way past his defenses, biting at his armor and flesh, but he ignored them. He was a blur, a shadow streaking across the battlefield that refused to be contained by the wall of Orcs surrounding him.

From somewhere behind him, seemingly miles away, he heard the Phoenix Legion's call for retreat sound. It meant little to Lazarus. He would not be denied.

A squad of vicious looking horned demons appeared from the masses, growling with anticipation as they made their way toward him. Lazarus reached over his shoulder and withdrew the Quietus Edge from its sheath. Without missing a step, a sword in each hand, he barreled into them. Blue fire raced down the length of the blade as its magic flared to life, filling Lazarus with its exhilarating power.

He parried the lead demon's attack and thrust the runesword into its exposed midsection. It exploded into ash. Lazarus whirled and brought the sword down in a sweeping arc, catching three more of the monsters, and they disappeared in a burst of flame. He sliced through those remaining and sped forward.

He was close now.

There, part way up the slope that led up to the sheer walls of the pass, ten paces from the east wall of the main keep. He could see the grove of ageless oaks and cottonwoods where Vinson and Aldric had been forced to stand and fight.

Then he saw his brothers.

Aldric lay on his back at the base of a dying cottonwood, unmoving, eyes closed. Vinson stood a few feet before him, fighting desperately to fend off the swarm of Orcs who assailed them, his left arm soaked in blood and clutched protectively at his side. A dozen or so men fought beside him. A few other pockets were scattered about, remnants of the company assigned to man the walls, cut off by the marauding Orcs when the fortress had been breached.

Lazarus' pulse quickened and his pace with it.

Suddenly Vinson was struck, a crossbow bolt lodged beneath his right shoulder. He dropped to his knees, his weapon fell from his hand, and he doubled over.

An Orc rose over him, its axe glinting wickedly in the sunlight as it reared back to deliver the killing blow.

"Vinson!" Lazarus screamed.

The passage of time seemed to slow to a crawl.

A hulking ogre stepped into Lazarus' path, swinging a giant club. He ducked the attack and rolled, slashing with blinding speed at the beast's knees and stomach. The ogre lurched forward, and Lazarus jammed his katana into its throat. Blood sprayed out, and the creature toppled, clutching at the blade still lodged within its neck. Lazarus deftly sprang onto its shoulders as it fell, vaulting over the Orcs separating him and his brothers.

He landed only a couple of feet from Vinson just as the Orc brought its axe down. Lazarus thrust out his runesword, caught the shaft of the axe, and flung it away. Artfully he spun and lopped off the Orc's head at the shoulders.

Lazarus knelt down to feel Vinson's pulse. With an effort his brother lifted himself onto his knees. He looked up into Lazarus' eyes for the briefest of moments, and then Vinson crawled to where Aldric lay and collapsed, his breathing heavy and labored.

Lazarus rose to meet the rush of Orcs charging at him. He twisted and turned, dodged and weaved, parried and counterattacked, flawlessly executing the savage dance of Death. He was death incarnate, cutting through his enemies like so many blades of grass.

For what seemed like an eternity Lazarus stood alone against the Orc horde. Dozens died at his hand. Demons came forward and were consumed by the fire of the Quietus Edge. The magic of the blade surged through his veins, exhilarating, intoxicating. Arrows sailed past him as archers from the walls joined in the contest to bring him down.

Lazarus roared in defiance, losing himself in the insanity of his wrath. Bodies littered the ground all around him, piled two and three deep in places, and blood soaked the rocky earth beneath his feet.

Still the Orcs kept coming.

Then he heard the familiar twang of Zafer's bow as the young Elf emerged from the trees, firing arrows into the crowd with deadly accuracy almost quicker than the eye could follow. An earth-shaking roar filled the air, and Layek appeared from the fray, scattering Orcs like leaves in a strong wind. He moved quickly to Lazarus' side, keeping the Orcs at bay with his massive battleaxe.

Neslyn materialized from the grove, fierce and feral looking, her forest green robes shredded and singed, her amber hair matted and tangled with perspiration. Bolts of energy flew from her hands, casting her attackers aside as she fought her way to where Lazarus stood. Arms flung wide and head bowed in concentration, the Elven sorceress erected a wall of flame to encircle them, twenty feet high and equally as wide, incinerating the closest Orcs.

"We haven't much time," Neslyn's voice wavered. She looked exhausted.

Arrows fizzled as they tried to break through the barrier. The angry shouts of Orcs and demons on the other side broke through as they sought to penetrate the wall.

"Quickly! Inside!" Lazarus shouted over the din, motioning for the door that led into the keep.

Lazarus heaved Aldric's unconscious body over his shoulder and sprang for the door, the others a step behind. He reached the portal, threw it open, and darted inside. Neslyn came on his heels, followed by Layek carrying Vinson, and Zafer brought up the rear.

Lazarus slammed the door shut and threw the iron crossbar into place.

"That was the craziest, stupidest, and most amazing thing I have ever seen!" Layek managed between gulps of air. "Whatever possessed you to do something so senseless?"

"You know, it won't take them long to figure out what happened to us," Zafer advised.

Lazarus ignored both of their comments and walked swiftly to the far wall of the sparsely furnished room where a rack of weapons rested. Pulling the rack aside and spilling the weapons across the floor with a loud clatter, he grasped an iron ring hammered into the stone at waist level, previously hidden by the rack. Grunting with effort he heaved. There was the sound of stone grating on stone as a section of the wall swung outward, revealing a black, empty hole.

"This cave runs through the mountain to the valley below," Lazarus said, fatigue washing over him. "It will take you all the way to Perthana."

Lazarus felt a throbbing pain in his side and put his hand over the gaping wound there to slow the flow of blood. With his other hand he reached up and pulled the arrow he hadn't even realized was there out of his shoulder, wincing with pain.

Just a little more time. That's all I need.

"You mean …" Layek trailed off as he realized the grim truth, evidenced on Lazarus' pale, drawn face. "Oh, no," he whispered.

"It's too late for me, old friend."

There was a great pounding on the door as the Orcs without began battering it down. The ironwood door shook in its fastenings, but the crossbar held it in place. For now.

"Take them, Layek, and escape while you can," Lazarus said, indicating his wounded brothers who lay unconscious on the floor. "I will not see my brothers die today, not while I yet draw breath."

He clasped hands with his friend for the last time. Layek walked over to where Vinson and Aldric lay and picked them up. Tossing one over each shoulder, he moved toward the escape tunnel.

The hammering on the door grew more insistent.

Neslyn rushed to face Lazarus. "This is insane! Don't do this! I have the magic; I can heal you!"

Tears streamed down her face as Lazarus took her hands in his. "There is no time, Neslyn. You must look after my brothers now. Whatever happens, they must live." He smiled sadly. "In another life perhaps we'll see each other again. I wish there was more time in this one that I could give to you. I love you."

"No! There's still time! I ..."

Lazarus put a finger to her lips. "My wounds are too great. I've gone about as far as I can. You must go."

Neslyn shook her head, sobbing uncontrollably. She searched his eyes, unspoken emotions passing between them as she realized the inevitability of his fate. Then she turned and fled down the darkened tunnel.

There was an ear-splitting crack as the door began to buckle.

"Go!" Lazarus bellowed to Zafer and Layek. "Now!"

Zafer bowed to Lazarus, expressing his deep gratitude, and ran after Neslyn. Layek paused by the dark orifice.

"Lazarus," he choked on emotions struggling to break free, the pain of his loss clear as crystal in his voice. "It has been an honor."

Still carrying the unconscious brothers he fled.

"Godspeed," Lazarus whispered after him.

The pounding reached its apex, and the door disintegrated, groaning in protest as iron hinges were torn from their fastenings. Orcs poured in through the breach, and Lazarus turned to face the onslaught. He was dizzy and lightheaded from loss of blood. His limbs felt leaden and useless. Still he fought on, conscious only through sheer strength of will, killing the first wave before they had time to react.

Dozens more followed after, slowly forcing Lazarus toward the tunnel entrance. Some tried to flank him, but he wheeled left and right, cutting them down where they stood. Hopelessly outnumbered, Lazarus retreated to the black hole his friends had fled into only moments ago. He knew that if he did not find a way to stop them, his companions would not be able to outrun the Orcs.

He clashed swords with the lead Orc and with a heave forced

him backward, toppling those behind like dominoes. Three leapt over the pile, and Lazarus lashed out, sending them to the cold stone floor where they lay bloodied and still.

Suddenly he remembered the peculiar potion Vani Carchim had given him only yesterday. The Dwarf's words had seemed odd then, but now they made perfect sense.

"If ever you find yourself in a bind, toss this at your enemies' feet. Make sure you give yourself a little room so you can watch the fireworks and not be part of them."

His vision began to blur. His time was almost up.

With the last of his strength he rushed the regrouping Orcs, barreling into them with such ferocity that they were forced back to the cave's entrance. Half a dozen Orcs died in the unexpected assault, and the survivors turned to flee from the fury of this man who refused to die.

Lazarus' strength failed, and he dropped to one knee, his head spinning. Blood slicked the floor, and he found it impossible to regain his feet. He reached down and removed the glass bottle with the mysterious red liquid from his belt pouch. The Orcs rallied, led by a black-robed Druhedar. Power flared maliciously at his fingertips as he charged in to finish off Lazarus.

Lazarus tossed the small bottle at the feet of the mage.

White light filled the tunnel as the glass shattered on the rough stone floor. Fire followed, billowing out in a thick cloud, consuming all it came in contact with. The shockwave hit Lazarus in a rush of heat and light, sucking the air from his lungs and launching him backward through the air. He sailed weightlessly for several seconds until he crashed into the rock wall. The unmistakable snap of bones filled his ears, followed by a rush of pain.

He sank to the floor.

A thunderous rumble filled the passageway like an angry storm as the ceiling crumbled, sealing the tunnel entrance in a shower of dust and debris.

Nothing will get through that, Lazarus thought, miraculously still conscious.

His body was a throbbing mass of pain, his breathing ragged and shallow. Smoke burned his lungs, and darkness reigned supreme in the tunnel.

I did it.

He smiled faintly, a tugging at the corners of his mouth that barely registered on his dirt and blood-streaked face. He chuckled briefly, coughing up blood as he did so.

Lazarus knew he was a dead man. At least now he could meet Death with the satisfaction and pride of knowing that he had outdone Fate. He had overcome impossible odds to save the lives of the people he cared for most. He had given all that was good and right a chance against the evil that threatened it.

I did it!

The breath left his lungs, and for Lazarus Arkenstone everything went dark.

XXVII THE SEIGE OF PERTHANA

FROM ATOP THE battered and broken walls of the fortress within Sowel Pass, Kairayn watched as the last remnants of the Phoenix Legion fled before the might of his army. Their little stunt in the highlands had angered him greatly, and now he smiled in spiteful amusement as the last vestiges of their paltry resistance crumbled.

Even now, high up in the mountains, he could almost see the rooftops and smoking chimneys of Perthana. He could see in his mind's eye the sleepy city, unsuspecting of the destruction coming their way. His army would sweep over them as easily as it had swept over the Phoenix Legion.

His power was absolute.

A great and terrible secret had become known to him. The Krullstone did not, in fact, slay those it was directed upon. Rather the life essence was absorbed into the stone and into the one who wielded it.

The voices in his head hardly bothered him anymore. He could feel the dark stain of the Daemon Lord Satariel on his soul, could feel his anger. Often he recalled memories from a life that had spanned eons too numerous to fathom. Forbidden knowledge bubbled just under the surface of his conscious thought, knowledge that had given him the power to summon forth the Ettarok. He could sense the presence of the demons within his army, indeed everywhere on the globe. To the south and east he could feel the dark apparition of Serathes, comfortable within the refuge of Grimknoll.

Yes, his power was absolute. Retribution would be swift upon those who sought to enslave his people. Once the humans had been swept aside he would turn his ire on the treacherous demons.

And then nothing would stand in his way.

෨෧   ෨෧   ෨෧

Footsteps seemed to echo into eternity as the five survivors of Sowel Pass ran blindly down the darkened cavern. Neslyn, sobbing uncontrollably, stumbled in the lead, followed by Zafer with Layek bringing up the rear, carrying the two unconscious brothers.

A great explosion rocked the mountain, dust and silt streaming down from the ceiling, bringing the fleeing band to their knees. In the darkness the soft crying of the Elven princess echoed despairingly.

"Is anyone hurt?" Layek called out, feeling his way forward. He gently set the two brothers on the hard stone floor and crawled forward on his hands and knees. He repeated his question to the black surrounding him.

"I think the answer to your question is quite obvious," he heard Zafer's familiar voice answer hollowly. "We all hurt."

"Neslyn?" Layek called. "We could really use some light here. Neslyn?"

A bright white flash pierced the darkness, lighting up the cavern for a dozen yards in either direction. Neslyn appeared before them, face streaked with tears.

"I'm going back for him," she said, a hard edge to her voice.

Layek stared at her blankly for a moment, certain that he had misheard her. "Neslyn, don't be foolish. You know as well as I do there is nothing anyone can do for him."

Her eyes flared with anger. "I will not abandon him to die! He deserves better than that, especially from his friends!"

Layek felt the sting of the words as though she had struck him. "He's dead! There's nothing we can do for him now! Believe me, I wish it could be otherwise, but I have to accept the truth!"

"He's right, Neslyn," Zafer interfered somberly. "There is nothing more we can do."

She glared at the Elf accusingly.

"Listen to your friend, Elf-girl," Layek calmly advised her. "Don't throw your life away. You will honor him best by finishing the quest he started. Focus on what you can affect, not the sorrow that cannot be undone."

There was a long, uneasy pause as she battled with her emotions. She knew they were telling the truth, that Lazarus was already dead. But in her heart, she could not let him go. Tears welled up anew in her eyes.

Without speaking she moved over to where the two unconscious brothers lay. Layek heaved an audible sigh of relief when she knelt next to them, the white glow of her magic sweeping through them.

She moved first over Aldric and then Vinson, lines furrowing on her face with the effort of concentration, experiencing for herself the damage inflicted upon their bodies. "They're alive," she whispered coarsely. "Just barely. I've stabilized them, but we must get them somewhere safe before I can do more."

"Lead the way," Layek urged her. He moved over to them and grunted as he lifted them over his shoulders. "Watch our backs, Zafer. There's no telling what might be coming after us."

It was cool within the depths of the mountain, making their passing easier. They moved slowly, their footfalls echoing softly against the rock, giving the illusion that there were more than just the five of them. Several times they came to places where the cave split in different directions, each time relying on their best guess to guide them. For hours and hours they trudged wearily onward. The rock began to press down on them, and claustrophobia took hold. Their hearts grew heavy, and despair welled up within.

As they rounded yet another in a ceaseless line of twists and turns, the sound of dripping water rose up to greet them. The stench of raw sewage hung on the stale, warm air. The walls and floor became smoother, the rough stone changing to carefully laid and sealed brick.

They passed through an arched doorway and found themselves standing in a sewage tunnel. A thin stream of putrid muck ran down a channel in the center of the hall; walkways were on either side.

Layek huffed in discontent, fighting the overwhelming urge to wretch. "These must be the sewers underneath Perthana. We must be close."

"Let's hope so," Neslyn said, holding up one sleeve of tattered robe to cover her nose.

In single file they carefully navigated the narrow walkways. There was no way to tell which direction led out so they simply wandered the abandoned sewers, randomly choosing between the numerous passageways and tunnels. The stench became ever more pervasive, and they grew nauseated, gasping for air as they concentrated on putting one foot in front of the other.

Finally they found a passage that gently sloped upward. Eager to be free of the crushing ambience of the tunnels and sewers, they quickened the pace, nearly breaking into a run. Many side passages opened into darkness, but they remained on course.

The passage twisted and weaved, growing steeper as they went. Suddenly they came to a dead end with a rusted iron ladder leading up to another level. Quickly they ascended, pulling the unconscious brothers with them.

Passages honeycombed in every direction, but there was still no sign of an exit. Buoyed by their new hope they pushed on, following a series of tunnels until they came to a vast open chamber so large that Neslyn's light could not stretch to the far side.

Walkways skirted the edge of it, and dozens of drainpipes jutted from the walls, trickling more waste into the pool that dominated the center of the cavern. Creatures swam through the filth, slithering away from the light. No one ventured to guess as to what they were.

"There!" Zafer cried, pointing ahead of them. "Stairs!"

Relieved, they jogged to the alcove thirty paces away. A set of stairs that wound up into darkness welcomed them. Without hesitation they began to climb. Twice they reached landings where more tunnels led off into the earth. The band of friends ignored them and continued to clamber upward.

The third landing ended in a passageway that led straight ahead. They took it excitedly. The air seemed to be fresher up here; they knew they must be getting close to the surface.

Not more than a few dozen yards in, the tunnel dead-ended in a set of steps that led up to a closed trap door. Neslyn immediately rushed up to it and pushed, only to find the thick stone slab securely fastened.

Zafer tried to no avail. Then Layek came forward, throwing his full weight against it and heaving with all his might. Still it did not budge.

"Forget it," he gasped. "There's no way we're going to get through that."

"Maybe we should call for help," Zafer offered lamely.

Neslyn shouldered past them. "Step aside. I'll handle this."

Without waiting for the two men to move, she summoned her magic, blue fire lancing forth from her fingertips. The bolts collided with the stone, shattering the rock and sending shrapnel flying back down the tunnel. A cloud of dust and smoke filled the air, causing them to choke and gasp for breath.

"Are you trying to kill us?" Layek shouted as he leapt back. "You'll bring the whole place down on our heads like that!"

Again the Elf sent the fire dashing into the rock. What remained of the slab exploded outward into the chamber beyond, and a rush of fresh, clean air swooped into the tunnel. They sucked gratefully at it and, grabbing up their two fallen comrades, dashed out into the room.

They found themselves in a small, square space of stone and mortar, completely empty save the rubble from the destroyed trapdoor. A single ironbound door served as the only exit.

From the hall without they could hear the clink of armor and the shouts of guards as they converged on the tiny room. The lock snapped open, and the door swung inward. A swarm of soldiers clad in crimson and black rushed in, spears at the ready.

The two Elves and Layek raised their hands disarmingly as the soldiers closed in on them. An officer pushed his way forward, glaring at them. He looked them over, and a flicker of recognition washed over him.

"You again?" the man said in disbelief.

Lazarus drifted on a gray sea of warmth, soft and comforting as a goose-down blanket. There was no pain, no suffering, none of the strife that had plagued him before. He found that he could move, though it did him little good. It seemed that he was suspended in nothingness, a cloud without substance, somewhere between nowhere and everywhere.

Then it hit him. He was dead.

The memory of who he had once been came rushing back. His entire life, every moment of it, paraded before him, somehow torn from the depths and brought to life within the mists that swirled about him. All the mistakes, successes, lies, hopes, every detail was dissected for him to analyze.

The truth of who and what he had been in his former life burned through him, painful at first, and then soothing as he learned to accept his failings and shortcomings as a human being.

None of that mattered anymore.

Welcome, Se'il'an of the Theos'ne. We have been expecting you, though not quite so soon.

"There are easier ways to get into the city, you know," Captain Webster chided the dirty and haggard group before him. "And cleaner. Follow me."

Neslyn sighed in relief at the recognition. Things could have gone sour very quickly if Webster had not remembered them. Captain Webster ordered several of the soldiers to remain and guard the sewer entrance and then turned and led the weary companions out into the hall. A squad of soldiers picked up Vinson and Aldric and carried them off.

"They'll be taken to the infirmary for treatment," Webster told them soothingly. "Don't worry; we'll take good care of your friends."

He waved for them to come along. They followed him wordlessly as he led the weary group through a series of halls and passageways out into the open night air.

They emerged among a collection of squat stone buildings. The whole area was a buzz of activity as soldiers ran back and forth frantically. Torches and watch fires burned all over the walls, and men stood watch all along the length of it.

From somewhere distant the clash of weapons and the sounds of battle flared up. Moments later they were gone.

"Orc raiding parties," Webster explained. "We've been skirmishing with the vanguard since the pass fell. By tomorrow morning the bulk of their army will be here, and the siege of Perthana will begin."

"What about the rest of the army?" Layek asked soberly. "What about the Phoenix Legion? There must be some survivors."

The captain ushered them inside a squat brick building. "General Markoll is in full retreat. He has abandoned the Myrrh in an effort to reach the city before the Orcs do. Wounded from the Phoenix Legion have been streaming in for hours. Every able bodied man is in the field, doing everything he can to delay the enemy's advance."

Layek looked around the room they had entered and realized suddenly that it was full of men. Long tables stretched the width of the hall, and cooks in white cloth were serving food. Immediately he recognized the insignia upon their sleeves.

"Remnants of the Phoenix Legion have been quartered in the barracks building next door. This has become their interim headquarters."

Layek recognized many of the faces within the room. There were a lot fewer than he remembered.

"Major Ogras!" A young lieutenant ran up to him. "Sir, have you seen Commander Arkenstone? Captain Reich has been commanding in your absence, but all the men are worried for him."

Layek grimaced, a sharp stab of pain piercing his chest. "He's dead. He gave his life so that we could escape."

The man was dumbfounded, as if Layek had just proven beyond

doubt that the sky was red instead of blue. "I, uh, I ..." Weakly he gave up, a defeated look seeping into his eyes. "What should I do, Major?"

"Get some food and some rest, lad, for now. Seek out Captain Reich later for your orders."

The young man trudged off, shoulders stooped as if a great weight had been placed upon them. Layek watched him go, fighting to hold back the barrage of emotions that came bubbling up to the surface. He looked over at his Elven companions. He could see fresh tears in Neslyn's eyes.

"I'm sorry to hear that," Webster was saying. "He was a good man. His presence will be dearly missed. Take what rest you can. I'll let you know immediately if I hear anything."

"Thank you, Captain," Layek answered.

Webster grasped hands quickly with Layek and offered a fleeting nod to the two Elves before he slipped out the door. The three companions found an empty table and sat down, allowing themselves to be served a delicious stew with fresh bread. They ate disinterestedly, barely tasting their food as they swallowed it down. White-clad servants, quiet as a whisper, came and took away their empty bowls.

Layek was at a loss as to what to do next. Lazarus was dead. Vinson and Aldric were gravely wounded. He stared down at his untouched mug of ale and thought back to their time in Kylenshar. No more endless nights at the Blue Moon; he would never have to break up an argument between the brothers again, would never again enjoy the closeness and camaraderie of their once invincible little group. Even if peace were restored, life would never be the same.

Somewhere in his mind Lazarus' laughter echoed. A pang of regret struck him. Had he cherished their time together enough? Had he valued the friendship less than what it really had been worth or taken it for granted?

Tears welled up in his eyes, one rolling slowly down his cheek. No. He brushed angrily at the tear. He would not despair. The best way to honor his friend was to finish the quest they had begun together. So many had been lost along the way. He forced himself to remember each of them. None would have died in vain if he had anything to say about it.

A hand fell on his shoulder, and he jumped. Across from the table Neslyn and Zafer were rising, their jaws hanging open in astonishment. He turned to see.

Azrael's familiar voice greeted him. "Glad you could make it."

"Azrael!" Layek leapt from his seat and turned to face the man. "I didn't think you'd made it out! You'll never know how glad I am to see you!"

The sorcerer grinned from ear to ear. "I would've thought you'd know better of me. Of course, I made it. Where are the others?"

Layek felt the now familiar wrenching of his heart. "Vinny and Aldric are in the infirmary. They were wounded pretty badly. Laz ..." he choked on the words.

"Well, where is he? Spit it out man!"

"He's dead, Azrael," Zafer said solemnly from across the table. The sorcerer's smile faded instantly, and a look of genuine disappointment crept across his face. Several minutes of awkward silence followed.

Suddenly Captain Webster burst through the door. "You're friends are awake. Follow me, and I'll take you to them."

Instantly they were all on their feet, sprinting for the door. Webster led them outside, barely able to move fast enough to keep his attaché from running him over. They sped through the barracks grounds, past darkened sleeping quarters and armories, to a slat-board building four stories tall and painted white. It gleamed in the moonlight, a beacon of hope for the small group in the dark night.

Webster led them through the double doors and up two flights of stairs. Nurses and healers passed them in the hallways, and cries of pain echoed down the halls, muffled and distant.

The captain stopped in front of an unassuming door near the far end of a hallway. "They're still pretty weak so don't get them too excited. They need rest more than anything, but they insisted on seeing you. It was all the healers could do to keep them in bed."

He opened the door and the five of them filed in.

"Layek!" the two brothers exclaimed as one. "Where have you

been? Tell these hoodwinks to let us go!"

Layek smiled at them warmly. Some things, at least, would never change. Vinson's left arm was splinted and wrapped, his right shoulder swathed in bandages. Aldric hardly looked better, a roll of gauze wound tightly around his head, a spot of blood seeping through.

"Relax!" he beseeched them, barely able to contain his excitement at seeing them well. "You two clowns nearly bought the farm back there. You need to rest."

"Like hell we do!" Aldric shot back.

Vinson looked around the room, puzzlement stealing into his eyes. "Where's Laz? He's not out there still, is he?"

For several minutes none of them could seem to muster an answer for him. He looked from face to face, trying to read the mixed expressions he found there.

"Vinny. Aldric," Layek began softly. "Laz is gone."

Neither of them said anything; they just stared at him, jaws hanging open slackly.

"Gone? Gone where?" Aldric asked cautiously. "Where did he go?"

Neslyn sat on the edge of the young man's bed, touching his cheek gently. Fresh tears rolled down her cheeks. "He's dead, Aldric. He fell at the keep."

"That's not possible!" Vinson breathed, looking more like a lost boy than a soldier. "He can't be gone. He just can't. You're absolutely positive?"

Layek nodded gravely. "He gave his life to save yours. Ours, too," he added. He gave them a brief account of the events leading up to Lazarus' death. He swore to himself that he would not cry for his friend, but his resolve crumbled in the face of his shattered heart.

Aldric's lip quivered, and tears welled up in his eyes. He tried to speak but choked on the words. Neslyn hugged him tightly.

"Those dirty, despicable, murderous ..." Vinson growled, his voice rising. "I'll kill them all!" He threw off the blankets that covered him and jumped up from the bed. "They won't get away with this!"

"Oh, no, you don't!" Layek grabbed him. "I won't let you

throw your life away like that, not after Laz paid such a high price to save it!" He forced Vinson back down onto his bed.

"Coward!" Vinson yelled up at him. "You would betray my brother's memory by running from his murderers! You abandoned him to die, and now you're too afraid to avenge his death! You would forsake his memory the same way you deserted him when he needed you!"

Layek's face turned red with ire. Zafer immediately stepped between them as Layek descended on Vinson. "Shut your mouth! You didn't have to look him in the eyes and say goodbye! I should have died back there with him, but I gave my word that I would see you safely through! I want vengeance as much as you do, but getting yourself killed is not the way to do it! If you really want to honor your brother's memory, then finish the quest we started!"

"Exactly how am I supposed to do that?" Vinson asked, calming slightly, his breathing labored and heavy. "The Krullstone is in the hands of a quarter million Orcs. Our army is overwhelmed and outnumbered. With the pass and river lost, we won't survive a week!"

"You know," Zafer interjected, "sooner or later Kairayn will take the stone back to the Orc lands. We could intercept him."

"For all we know he could already be on his way," Aldric said quietly. "It's a big land out there, and it's crawling with Orcs and demons. Our chances of finding him are pretty slim."

Layek took a steadying breath. "But we know where he's going. We don't have to find him; we just have to beat him there."

"Getting through the Orcs won't be that easy," Captain Webster warned them from the corner of the room where he had been standing.

"It shouldn't be that difficult," Zafer replied. "They won't be looking for a small group traveling south. We should be able to slip right past them."

"So," Vinson said, swaying slightly as he stood, "when are we leaving?"

"Whoa! Hold on there, Mr. Invincible. You're in no shape to be scampering about. Get some rest first while I get everything together."

It took some convincing, but the two brothers finally agreed to sleep while Layek assembled the equipment they would need. Webster was good enough to offer his assistance. Layek gave him a list of supplies for their journey, and he immediately dispatched two nearby guards to round them up.

As they headed back toward the barracks to get some rest, they could hear the clash of weapons and the shouts of men much closer than earlier.

"It won't be long now," Zafer said faintly.

"By first light according to reports," Captain Webster said. "Good thing the evacuation was completed hours ago."

"How are you planning to get past all those Orcs, Layek?" Neslyn asked.

"The same way we came in," he replied austerely. "Captain Webster, is there a way through the sewers that will take us beyond the walls?"

"Come to think of it, there are several. I'll have the engineers make a map with the route marked for you."

"Thank you for all your generous help, Captain," Layek offered earnestly.

"Absolutely. As I understand it that Krullstone is our only hope. Glad I can be of some use."

Webster guided them to the barracks before excusing himself to his duties, shaking hands warmly with the four companions. They watched him disappear into the shadows before flitting in through the door. A stout clerk sat behind an empty desk just inside. He greeted them quietly and showed them to a set of rooms where they promptly undressed and slipped into the fresh, clean cots. In moments they were asleep.

It seemed like it had only been a few minutes since he had fallen asleep when Layek felt a hand squeeze him firmly. Captain Webster's familiar voice called to him from the murk of his dreams, his firm grip shaking him gently.

"Major Ogras," he called. "Wake up. It's urgent."

Slowly the fog lifted, and he came fully awake, rubbing the sleep from his eyes. "What is it? What time is it?"

"You've been asleep for five hours, sir. Everything for your journey has been prepared, but you need to leave now. The Orcs have reached the city, and I do not know how long we can hold them back."

Layek was on his feet instantly. "Wake the others."

He found fresh clothes had been placed upon the nightstand next to his bed. He dressed quickly and strapped his weapons into place before darting out into the narrow hallway. The two Elves were already waiting for him; Azrael was hunched down against the wall, half asleep.

"Here is the map of the catacombs beneath the city." Captain Webster handed him a folded piece of parchment. "The path has been marked for you, as well as all the exits in case you run into trouble."

Through the walls the muffled sound of combat latched onto them like shackles. His three companions looked at him flatly. "Thank you again, Captain. I suppose we may not see each other again so farewell and good luck."

The sound of battle swept over them like a wave breaking on rocks as they charged into the cool early morning air. Torches were spread all along the walls, and men ran back and forth everywhere, shouting orders and warnings frantically into the flickering yellow glow.

Without slowing they hurried on to the infirmary where they found the two Arkenstone brothers waiting for them patiently. Vinson had his arm in a sling, but the splint was gone, and Aldric still had the bandage wrapped around his head. Their faces were drawn and slightly pale. Layek greeted them warmly, as did the others, and together they sped out into the growing daylight.

Despite the swarm of activity, the city felt strangely empty. All of the residents had been evacuated once news of the impending siege had reached the mountain hamlet. Shuttered windows and hollow doorways stared out into the predawn haze accusingly as they calmly awaited the death that approached them.

Shouldering their packs, Layek led them to the outer wall of the city and into its stone and mortar hallways. It did not take them long to reach the ruined hatch that had brought them out of the sewers, still under guard for fear the Orcs might try to gain entrance to the city through them. It looked more to Layek like the gaping maw of some dormant beast, waiting for them to foolishly enter and allow themselves to be swallowed up, never to be heard from again.

Zafer had the wherewithal to grab several torches and light them, passing them out to Layek and Vinson before descending into the darkness. The path was marked clearly on the map Webster had given them, making their passage easy and quick.

It was eerily quiet down in the sewers, a drastic change from the commotion of the world above that had them glancing frequently over their shoulders and searching the deeper shadows. Gloom hung thick on the air as rats and slimy things scurried away from their shimmering light. The sound of dripping water echoed ominously through the tunnels, the lonely wail of a place long forgotten by the men who built it. Warily, they pressed on.

The twists and turns of the tunnels led them deeper into the earth until they came to a great open chasm that stretched from one side of the tunnel to the other. A narrow, wrought iron bridge spanned the gaping hole. At their feet, a foul river of fetid sewage ran into the rift, disappearing into the darkness in troublesome silence.

One by one they made their way across the disused and ancient bridge, fearful that it might collapse under their weight at any moment. Neslyn brought up the rear, and once they were all safely across they began their trek anew, grateful at least to have the whole width of the tunnel to accommodate them.

As they traveled they began to notice the tunnel sloping gently downward, and the construction of it slowly became rougher and more natural. It seemed like an eternity as the minutes slipped by, each mile an agonizing lesson in determination and willpower over the claustrophobia and monotony that threatened to pull them down. The air became fresher, and they could feel a slight draft blowing into their faces, enticing them forward with the promise of escape from the confines of the cavern.

Half an hour later they began to notice the tunnel leveling out. The draft became more insistent, and they were forced to dodge roots that hung carelessly from the ceiling. It seemed like an eternity, but a few hundred paces later Zafer spotted light ahead. Their pace quickened. The tunnel grew shorter and narrower, forcing them onto their knees and finally to crawl before they burst into the early morning stillness.

Layek called for a rest, allowing his companions to recoup from the long forced march while he figured out where they were. He wandered a ways from where they had emerged, which turned out to be little more than a hole in the ground. From outside one wouldn't even have known it was there.

He snaked his way through the trees until he came to a line of scrub, obscuring his view forward. Gently he pushed his way through the obstruction, emerging on the other side with a gasp of surprise.

There, many miles to the north and still shrouded in the shadow of the mountains upon which it was built, was Perthana. Fires glowed within the city walls, and one could almost make out the tiny struggling figures as they battled to the death. Even here, so far away from the action, the war drums could be heard like thunder rolling over the landscape.

From behind him, Layek heard Aldric's shrill whistle of awe.

"Gods help them," Vinson whispered to no one in particular.

Suddenly Zafer came crashing through the brush. "I can't find Neslyn! She's gone!"

XXVIII RACE AGAINST TIME

NESLYN CHARGED THROUGH the tunnels and passageways beneath the doomed city of Perthana. Her lungs burned, and her legs felt like stone blocks, but she ignored them. Weariness plagued her at every turn, and each second felt like an eternity, but she could not stop. Time was working fiercely against her, and turning back now wasn't an option.

She had lain awake for some time, thinking over what she was about to do while the others peacefully slept. Fortunately for her, Webster had come through on his promise to deliver a map of the tunnels to them. Once he had awakened them, she had had all the time she needed to commit the map to memory while waiting for her companions to ready themselves.

A tinge of guilt washed through her momentarily. Her friends needed her now more than ever. The battle against the Daemon Lords would be brutal, but she could not help herself. Lazarus had proven to be the one, and even in death she could not leave him. Not while there was still a chance. Her course of action had been decided the moment they had fled the keep in Sowel Pass. She could not live without him.

She had to at least try.

It had been easy to deceive her friends. A quick illusion spell had made them believe she was still treading along with them even though she was long gone.

Returning the deceased to life was strictly forbidden to the Elves and in most other cultures around the world. Since Asaru's reign of terror and the undead plague emerged, it had been banned and was considered treasonous by nearly every civilized species. Even the slightest dabbling in the forbidden art of necromancy was punishable by permanent exile, even death under the right circumstances.

Not that the consequences mattered to her.

Long ago, while studying an ancient manuscript, she had come across an incantation to bring to life the recently deceased. She had committed it to memory, never thinking that the day would come when she would actually apply the knowledge. Timing was crucial. The window to return the soul to the body was small indeed, and the chances of success narrowed with each passing minute.

She reached the rough cavern that had brought them down from the high mountain pass yesterday, recognizing its primitive and natural look. Immediately she sped up, knowing her destination was not far off. Hastily she went over the spell, making sure she could remember every part, every minor detail no matter how seemingly meaningless. Even the most trifling mistake could destroy her or create a nightmare she would be forever haunted by.

Stalactites scraped at her, tearing at the already frayed robes she was wearing and stinging where they scraped the skin. The sorceress ignored them. Pain was trivial and fleeting compared to what she would feel if she failed in this endeavor.

Neslyn rounded the final corner and stopped dead in her tracks. The path forward was blocked by tons of rock where the tunnel had collapsed. Guiding her light forward, she searched the rubble.

There, against the wall.

"Lazarus," she whispered, a new wave of sorrow surging through her.

Eyes, glazed over with life's passing, stared blankly back at her from where his body rested against the rock wall, sword still clutched tightly in his hand. She despaired at the sight of him. His body was broken, burned, and butchered in a dozen or more places. A pool of blood spread out from him, more than she would have thought possible.

What struck her most, however, was not the gruesome look of his shattered body but rather the satisfied smirk that adorned his lifeless face.

Tears sprang into her eyes, and she wiped them away angrily. She should never have left him. Now she must undo what should never have been allowed to be.

Slowly, gently she crept up to him and knelt upon the rocky floor, feeling the cold stone press into her. She reached up to caress his cheek, slipping a vial of powder from her belt pouch. She removed the cork and poured a measure into her palm, sprinkling it over his unmoving form.

The light faded as she focused. The mystical powder began to sparkle and glow like thousands of tiny fireflies in the total darkness. Withdrawing another vial of red oil from her belt, she marked his skin with arcane symbols. The markings flared with golden light, illuminating the two in ghostly half-light.

Then she began to chant.

ॐ   ॐ   ॐ

"Gone? Gone where?" Layek asked in frustration. How could they have lost her? She was right there next to him as they came through the tunnels. "She couldn't have just disappeared. She was right next to me the whole time!"

"Where would she have gone?" Aldric questioned. "Why would she leave us?"

Silence followed as each stared at the other, searching for an answer. Then suddenly it hit them. They knew exactly where she had gone. Only one thing would make her leave.

Lazarus.

"She can't possibly think …" Layek began and trailed off.

Azrael stared at them blankly, his face an unreadable mask. "Magic. She used her magic to make us think she was still with us. She's been gone a long time."

"Well, we can't sit around and wait for her to come back,"

Vinson blurted. "I'm sorry, Zafer, but you know we can't. Take the map if you want to and go find her."

"There is nothing more I can do for her," the Elf replied regretfully. "She has chosen to take a path which I cannot follow. She will have to take care of herself now."

"Shouldn't we do something about this?" Aldric huffed. "She can't just go wandering the tunnels alone; she may never find her way out again!"

"We could search forever and probably never find her," Layek reminded the younger Arkenstone. "Time and necessity prevent us from even trying. We should be going."

"Gods, help her," Azrael said darkly.

Reluctantly they began to trudge despondently onward.

Layek kept them in the trees, fearing that they would be too easy to spot in the open. They were in occupied territory now, and they all knew and felt it. Silence eerily gripped the forestland. The usual sounds of nature were abnormally absent, giving the landscape an empty lonely feel to it. Not a creature stirred as they passed, and only the sound of dry leaves and grass crunching underfoot broke the disturbing stillness.

Their eyes darted from side to side as they went, each of them expecting a mob of Orcs or demons to leap from the cover of the brush at any moment. Trees drifted staidly by, unfeeling giants that watched them pass beneath the canopy of their skeletal limbs with inexhaustible patience. Minutes became hours; paces turned into miles. The trees began to thicken, and as the sunlight began to wane, the sound of rushing water began to fill the air.

Layek led the group on, carefully now, knowing that they were close to The Narrows of the Myrrh River. Undoubtedly it would be under guard as the Orcs continued to bring reinforcements and supplies across. If they were lucky, they could find a way to slip through unnoticed.

Unfortunately, luck had not been one of their assets for a long time.

The sun dipped below the horizon, drenching the land in murky shadows and obscurity. The sound of the river gurgling over its rocky bed greeted them like an old friend as they drew near its banks.

Other less welcome noises also reached their ears.

Layek led them up to the edge of the trees, the ground littered with bodies like so many stalks of wheat mowed down by the indiscriminate scythe. Some were of men, many more of Orcs, and more than a few that were distinguishable only as inhuman. Fires smoldered still within the trees and upon the banks of the river, smoke spiraling lazily into the air and hanging in thick sheets on the warm night.

The Orcs had constructed a crude bridge of timber across the constricted vein of water, allowing their wagons to cross unhindered. Booted feet sloshed through the cold water as teams of oxen pulled wagons across laden with the trappings of war. Voices shouted out into the night, guttural and unpleasant.

Slowly and silently, they pulled back into cover of the deeper shadows.

"There's no way we'll slip past that," Aldric whispered harshly.

"We'll just wait until they pass," Azrael told him. "Sooner or later they will all be across, and then we don't have to worry about it anymore."

"And what if it's later?" Layek pressed him. "We don't have that kind of time. They could go on like this all night or forever for all we know."

"Why don't we just go around?" Zafer suggested earnestly, eyes flicking nervously in the direction of the crossing.

"The river's swollen by runoff from the high mountains," Vinson explained. "Crossing anywhere else is too dangerous. We could be swept downriver for miles before reaching the far banks or maybe never reach them at all."

Layek rubbed the scruff on his chin. It seemed like forever since he had felt a razor against his skin. "Not if we build a raft. We could make it all right, I think. Anyway, what choice do we have? We don't have the time to wait them out, and we don't want to fight a whole army of Orcs to get across the river." The others opened their mouths to protest, but Layek silenced them with a wave of his hand. "It is decided."

Although most of them disagreed with the strategy, they had to admit there was no other choice. Time was working against them, and they couldn't afford anymore delays.

Layek moved them further down the banks to avoid detection, and then they set to gathering deadwood for a makeshift raft. They lashed a dozen fallen logs together with leather straps from their packs, and when Layek was satisfied that it was secure enough to see them safely across, they carried it down the steep embankment to the roiling waters below.

They carefully organized their gear in the center of the crude craft and tied it down so it would not wash away in the frothy waters. Then, as one, they shoved the raft into the water.

The cold water bit at their exposed flesh as they entered it, pushing the raft ahead of them, and almost immediately they were sucked into the river's current as it forced its way eastward. Desperately they kicked, swimming frantically to reach the far shore. In the darkness it was impossible to tell how close to their goal they were or how far downstream they were being carried.

The chill gripped them and sank deep into their bones until they thought they might never be warm again.

"Kick!" Layek shouted over the churning current, trying to organize his comrades into some sense of harmony. "As one now!"

The plan seemed to work.

Despite the icy waters, they fell into a rhythm, kicking furiously at the undercurrent that threatened to suck them down. It seemed like hours, and they were all surprised when their makeshift raft struck dry land. With a jolt the wood collided with the muddy banks, and the five companions scrambled out of the river.

"Where are we?" Vinson looked around uncertainly. "How far did the river carry us?"

"No idea," Layek voiced what everyone else knew. "We'll just have to backtrack along the riverbank until we get back to The Narrows."

"Can it at least wait until morning?" Aldric asked. "We're

exhausted."

Layek agreed. They had marched all day, and the swim across the river had taken more energy than they had to spare. It was imperative that they keep their strength up for the coming days. He would not allow a fire so they ate their dinner cold and promptly threw themselves on the ground to sleep.

A few short hours later Layek roused them, the first rays of light just cresting the horizon. Time was of the essence, and they couldn't afford to waste any more than was necessary sleeping. Reluctantly the others rose and gathered their gear. Without a word the five companions set out down the river. Layek led the way, carefully tracking the path through the trees.

❧　❧　❧

Lazarus struggled in his prison of nonbeing against bonds that could not be seen or touched and yet were harder than any metal or stone could ever hope to be. His once-peaceful release had become a nightmare of epic proportions. At first, he had been content understanding his past and present, accepting that he had gone from the world to save his brothers.

Yet the revelations had not stopped there.

Rather, he had been forced to recognize that he had gained nothing in sacrificing his life. His brothers were doomed still, only now they were in far greater danger. When he had taken their place in death, he had altered the course of the future — as he had intended — to spare the lives of his condemned brothers.

Or so he had thought.

Instead of dying in Sowel Pass as Fate had meant for them to, they would die at Grimknoll, far from their homes and utterly alone. They would be betrayed by one they trusted most and then imprisoned, held captive until the Daemon Lords consumed their souls and destroyed the very essence of their being.

He had not saved anyone.

Now he was trapped, locked out of the mortal world in death.

The torturous truth ate at him, rending and tearing at his formless soul until it was raw. The voices had not returned, even though he had called for them. They could help, he was sure, if he could only reach them. He screamed his agony into the void until he felt his spirit might burst, and then he screamed some more.

But no one came.

Nothing would answer his desperate pleas for help. The knowledge that he was utterly alone and helpless magnified his pain exponentially, and he cried out under the torment. Sooner or later, he knew, he would go mad.

He could feel his mind beginning to crack.

There was a sudden surge as his formless being seemed to be pulled in a direction he had not known existed. It lasted for only a moment. Lazarus shuddered with the force of it. Was this how it would end? Was his immortal soul simply going to tear itself to pieces as he slowly lost his grip on sanity?

The pull came again, stronger, more insistent.

Lazarus panicked, struggling, though he knew there was little he could do. His mind screamed.

Not like this!

He simply could not believe that this was the true end of his being. The death of his mortal body had been a doorway to yet another existence, but what would happen if his soul were to whither and die? Fear sprang up within him. Would he simply cease to be?

It came again. Lazarus felt like he had been dropped into a vat of acid — like his spirit was being pulled through a fine filter, dissolving like water as it passed through.

The forceful tugging didn't stop, would not relent. He screamed in agony as the force built, knowing he was powerless to resist it. Everything went blinding white, numbing his mind with excruciating pain.

It lasted only for a moment.

The bright white light quickly faded to darkness, black as pitch, and the pain receded to a dull throb. He took a deep breath, wincing with the agony of doing so. Cold struck him abruptly, colder than the ice at the highest peaks of the mountains or winter's deepest chill. He shivered uncontrollably, his teeth rattling in rhythm with the spasms of his muscles. He felt the hardness of the stone he rested on.

Lazarus' eyes snapped open.

He was dead. He didn't have a body to feel these sensations with.

But they were there all the same. His vision was blurred, and he could make out little other than a faint glowing light before him.

Then he heard Neslyn's shaky voice. "Lazarus?"

The warmth of a hand reached up to feel the pulse in his neck. He realized for the first time that he actually had a pulse.

"Lazarus! Shades, it actually worked!"

He tried to say something, but his tongue was thick and swollen. All that came out was a low moan that echoed the pain and confusion he was feeling.

Neslyn edged closer to him, forcing a glass vial to his lips. A bitter liquid poured into his throat, and he gagged, but the Elven princess held his mouth closed until he had swallowed it all.

"It will help you gain your strength," she whispered, her hands shaking. Impulsively she wrapped her arms around him, squeezing him tight. She kissed him over and over, rocking back and forth gently. Lazarus could feel the warmth of her tears as they poured down her cheeks. "I'll never let you go again."

Lazarus felt wooden and heavy, but he still managed to bring his arms around her tiny waist and hold her against him. He thought for a moment that if he had the choice, he would stay like this with her forever.

He could feel the liquid she had forced into him burning as it worked its way through his veins. His eyes grew heavy, his mind groggy, and slowly he gave himself over to sleep. As he began to drift, he could still hear Neslyn's voice telling him everything would be all right.

ა   ა   ა

In the late watches of the night, Kairayn stared with great satisfaction at the burning city of Perthana. Fire was spreading quickly, unchecked throughout the doomed hamlet, and by tomorrow evening there would be nothing left of the once-proud city but a pile of rubble and scorched earth.

He smiled grimly at the siege towers that were nestled up against the city walls. His army had succeeded in keeping the rest of the legions from reinforcing the besieged city, and now it was only a matter of time before it fell. Already the Orcs and their demon allies had breached the defenses in several places.

Beside him, Bogran dispatched a messenger with a handful of orders for the front lines. "It won't be long now," he said. "By this time tomorrow the city will be ours."

"And what of the rest of their army?"

Bogran faced him. "We can't seem to pin them down. Every time we engage them they manage to slip away and then pop up somewhere else. At least they can't break through our lines to aid the city."

Kairayn grimaced. The enemy general had proven to be a cunning and skillful opponent. He directed his soldiers with the artful grace of a master puppeteer and was absolutely full of surprises. Their nemesis never used the same trick twice. "Once the city has fallen we can focus our full strength on the rest of the legions. They will not be able to stand against us for long."

"Kylenshar should be our next target," Bogran suggested. "Destroy their capital and break their morale; the rest of their empire will fall easily."

"So shall it be."

They watched in silence for a time, an island of calm in a world gone mad. The sights and sounds of war filled their senses, and the two comrades sat soaking it all in. It was good to be back on the battlefield once more where they belonged.

Perhaps, Kairayn thought, next time he would join the front ranks in battle. It would certainly be better than standing back watching as his warriors rose and fell on the field. Honor and glory could only be found on the front lines where the metal meets the meat, where you could look your foe in the eye.

Messengers came and went as the melee raged, keeping the two up to date on the ebb and flow of battle. A triumphant roar broke from the ranks as a gate to the city began to crumble. A thunderous crash countered it as one of the Orcs' many siege towers collapsed into rubble.

The humans were unwavering in spirit. He had to give them that much credit.

Suddenly a black robed Druhedar mage appeared next to him. Kairayn clenched his teeth at the intrusion. Though the sorcerers served their purpose well, he despised them. They were keepers of secrets, dabblers in things better left untouched, and their leader had been the one to bring the ill-favored demons upon them. In the distance he could see the dark shapes of the monsters as they scrambled up the walls in an effort to reach the human defenders, prompting a surge of anger to well up within.

He sighed heavily. They too served a purpose, and despite his hatred of them he could not do away with them just yet.

Next to him, the sorcerer spoke softly, "Congratulations on your victory, My Lord."

"This battle is far from over. Praise me when they have been crushed, and their city lies in ruin."

"My apologies, My Lord. I bring an urgent message from the Emperor. He requests your immediate presence at Grimknoll. I am to personally escort you."

Kairayn had to fight the urge to smack the mage. His tone was so smug, so condescending despite his feigned respect and deference.

"Very well then. I shall depart once the city has fallen."

"My apologies again, Slavemaster, but I have been instructed that we are to leave without delay." There was no repentance in his voice.

Kairayn sighed again in frustration. He made sure the sorcerer understood the discontent in his voice when he spoke. "Fine. I shall need one hour to prepare an escort. I will seek you out here at the command post. Bogran, you have command."

The wizard nodded in acceptance, and Kairayn stalked off. He didn't really need as much time as he had claimed, but he wanted some time to think. It could be a trap, of course, the demons trying to lure him away from the protection of his army where they could dispose of him and take the Krullstone. It could also be a genuine command from Grimvisage, who naturally would be feeling very impatient by now. That didn't rule out an opportunity for the demons to reclaim the stone, though. He would have to watch his back. Or better yet, bring a few trustworthy soldiers to watch it for him.

He fingered the stone within its pouch at his waist, tracing its perfectly cut edges, feeling its warmth. The voices had subsided since he had last used it, but its presence still remained, contained somewhere deep within. Sometimes he would wake from his sleep screaming or drift off in the middle of some conversation as he recalled knowledge and memories from a life that had never been his.

At first he had thought it would drive him insane. The constant bombardment had nearly cracked his mind, and he shuddered to think what might have become of him then. Even now he could feel the dark taint of the Daemon Lord within his veins, fighting to break free from the shackles that had been placed on it. It was a constant battle, Kairayn trying to hold on to his sanity and control of himself while the other fought to take it away. It seemed to get easier as the days passed, though, and in time Kairayn was certain the whole experience would be subdued into nothing more than a memory.

The Slavemaster walked on through the massive camp toward the front lines. He briefly pondered the simplicity of being a soldier and how he had managed to get caught up in this precarious scheme. For a few moments at least he wished he could have been nothing more than another face on the battlefield, just one more Orc in a chaotic sea of death and destruction, searching for the honor and glory that was promised to each of them.

Frustrated, he wiped these thoughts from his mind. He had a duty to his people now and did not have time for flights of fancy. He gave one last look of longing to the illuminated walls of the city where life was as simple as kill or be killed and turned back to reality.

Grabbing the nearest Orc, Kairayn rattled off a series of orders to find and gather the escort he would need for the journey. No matter what the circumstances, he was not about to jaunt off into the wilderness without some company.

Some company he could trust.

The doppelganger stared at the backs of those it followed through the woodlands south of the Myrrh River. The idiocy amazed him. They foolishly thought that they could simply waltz up to Grimknoll and take the Krullstone and then destroy the Daemon Lords.

How naïve.

Even if they managed to get there unharmed, there was simply no way they could get in and out of the stronghold alive. It would make sure that they did not.

This game was getting old, and it grew tired of holding up the charade of friendship with these moronic beings. How they had managed to escape the wrath of the demons in millennia past confounded it. No wonder they had nearly destroyed their own world before.

At least its duty was almost complete. Once Kairayn returned with the stone and these humans were dealt with accordingly, its master would release it from service. Then it would be free to play with the beings of this world as it wished. Free to enjoy an unending battle of wits with whomever it chose.

Of course, once it got bored of toying with these halfwits there would be other worlds, other species to move on to. The demon hordes would ravage this world and then move on to another. It was the nature of their being. They lived solely for destruction and chaos, seeking order and life across the universe and wiping it out wherever they found it.

It had been so for countless eons. It would be so until the end of time or until every world had been destroyed and every people broken. Whichever came first.

Tired as it might be of the game with these frail mortals, it could play for a little while longer. There was always the chance that they might make it interesting. It thought for a moment about killing one of them in his sleep. That would spice things up a bit. Afterward it could watch as the friends turned on each other in their suspicion and doubt.

Beneath the cloak that enfolded it, the doppelganger smiled cruelly.

༺ྀ   ༺ྀ   ༺ྀ

Lazarus awoke with a start, breathing heavily. Had it all just been a dream? His eyes snapped open. Gingerly, steeling himself for the disappointment he was certain was coming, he tested his limbs. He found he could move, could feel the heartbeat within his chest. The rock he rested on dug uncomfortably into his back, and his muscles cried out in distress at the knots in them.

Then it all came rushing back in an instant — his death and the gratification he had felt at thwarting Fate, his brief stint in the nether-world and the agonizing truth he had learned, and his subsequent and painful resurrection.

His pulse quickened.

He became aware of Neslyn, snuggled up against his chest, arms wrapped around him as though she were afraid to part with him even in sleep. She stirred slightly at his movements, a soft whimper escaping from her lips. Lazarus doubted he had ever seen a creature so beautiful in all his life. For several minutes he sat there, feeling the closeness of her, reveling to be in her arms once again. All his cares and worries melted away as he drank her in. The bond between them had been strengthened obviously, but Lazarus felt that there was something more. Something that bound them together in a way he could not define. He could almost hear what she was thinking, almost feel the emotions that she felt. It seemed strange and fitting all at once, like it was destined to be even though what Neslyn had done was forbidden and unthinkable.

It pained him to wake her, so peaceful she was in her sleep. "Neslyn," he called softly to her, shaking her gently. "Wake up."

She stirred slightly, clinging to sleep as though she feared what waking reality would bring. Softly her eyes opened, a sea of green as warm as the sun. Then she seemed to realize where she was, and all at once she jumped awake. "Light! How long have you been awake?" Tears welled in her eyes. "I thought I'd lost you. I have done the forbidden to bring you back, but I do not regret it. I'll never leave you again. I love you, Lazarus."

He leaned in and kissed her long and soft, squeezing her gently. "I love you, too."

After a long silence she said, "Do you think I have done right?"

"Only time will tell," he answered. "I do know that you have saved me from a hell I could not have survived for long. Do not worry over what is done. We have a lot of work to do. Where are my brothers?"

"They have gone to Grimknoll. Layek, Zafer, and Azrael are with them. I snuck away as we came through the tunnels beneath Perthana to come to you."

Lazarus' heart sank. "We haven't got much time. How long ago did you leave them?"

"I don't know," she stated simply. "A day, maybe more."

He rose up from the cold stone floor, pulling the Elf up with him. It seemed forever since he had used his legs. He steadied himself with a hand against the wall and took a few tentative steps.

For having come through hell and death he felt surprisingly good. Too good. He felt stronger, quicker, and sharper, like he was ten years younger. He felt sprightly and dangerously alive, as if the life that flowed through his veins was twice as strong as it had once been. He thought briefly of the consequences of Neslyn bringing him back from the dead and brushed them away just as quickly. There wasn't time to think about that now.

He took a few more steps down the gently sloping tunnel. Neslyn stayed at his side, supporting him with both arms. Suddenly he remembered something. He stopped abruptly and gasped, prompting Neslyn to grab him tighter, lines of worry creasing her face.

"What's wrong?" she asked.

He didn't answer; instead he turned back to rummage through

the rubble. It didn't take long to find what he was looking for. As he pushed the rocks aside his hand came across the cold metal blade of the Quietus Edge. His hands gripped the pommel and tore it free, the blade ringing with glee as it cleared the rocks. He studied it momentarily, as if rediscovering an old friend. There wasn't a single mark on the blade, not a scratch or ding anywhere. Looking closely, Lazarus thought he could see the runic markings glow faintly in the darkness.

He slipped the sword into the scabbard still strapped across his back. "How did you find your way through the tunnels back to here?"

The Elven Princess smiled slyly. "Captain Webster made a map of the tunnels for us so we could find our way through. I took the liberty of memorizing the way."

"Excellent. Lead us to where you left the others. We've got to catch up with them before they get to Grimknoll."

"What's going on? Why the rush?" Neslyn looked perplexed as she started forward down the tunnel.

"I'll explain on the way," Lazarus told her solemnly. "I just hope we're not too late."

XXIX THE BETRAYER UNMASKED

IT WAS STILL early in the morning, the sun barely clearing the horizon and shining down through the trees of the Riparian Wood in dappled rays when Layek and his cohorts reached The Narrows where they had tried to cross hours earlier. The current had swept them several miles downriver, and a growing sense of urgency gripped the group as Layek pushed them hard along the riverbank.

"I told you we should have just waited," Azrael chided as they surveyed the crossing from the cover of the trees. "All that effort for nothing."

"There was no way to know how long that army would have spent crossing the river," Layek countered. "Don't forget who's in command here."

Azrael's face darkened. "I don't answer to you."

"Anytime you feel like it you can go right back home. But as long as you stay in this group you will follow my lead. Is that clear?"

The sorcerer didn't answer. He simply turned away, facing to the south. Wisely, he found it better not to challenge the big man.

Tensions were high at this point; fatigue and stress were taking a toll on the little company. Each of them had lost friends and loved ones along the way and still more that was as yet indefinable. They had been stripped bare and left adrift on a sea of chaos where the only promise was one of more pain and loss.

"There's no sense fighting about it," Zafer tried to calm them. "We're all in this together. To the end."

"Then we had better get moving toward that end," Aldric quipped. "We're burning daylight here."

"Any other arguments?" Layek asked, daring anyone to challenge him again. When nobody answered, he calmed visibly. "Good. It's south then."

Without waiting for the others he stalked off, leaving them to shoulder their packs and hurry after. Layek set a grueling pace, stopping only infrequently for breaks. Water was sparse, the muggy heat drying up the small streams and pools and leaving the earth dry and cracked so they were forced to conserve as much as possible. Their mouths quickly became parched, and it seemed the farther south they moved the more intense the heat grew. Even within the shade of the trees it was unbearably oppressive.

As they forged deeper into the Orc homeland, they began to notice signs of decay and wilt on the vegetation. It became unnervingly quiet, and they realized they had not seen any form of wildlife for some time. Not even the annoying insects that usually accompanied the heat were present. Pockets of decay appeared and were passed by, moaning in disturbing stillness for aid. Several times they came across fetid ponds that bubbled menacingly, a wicked green mist emanating forth. Each time they carefully skirted the strange sickness, covering their noses against the foul smell. A hot breeze kicked up, flinging dirt and dust into their eyes.

Once Zafer noticed a single flower still perfectly preserved despite the untenable environment. They gathered around to stare in awe, marveling at how something so frail could survive in such a place, but when the Elf knelt down to pick it, it crumbled to dust at his touch, the wind sweeping it away.

Twice they were forced to run for cover when regiments of Orcs appeared from the swirling dust. Their appearance was as sudden as a lightning strike, and the five companions watched in mute apprehension as they marched solemnly onward. Looking upon the faces of their enemies as they passed them by, it seemed that they looked as unhappy as the trespassers. Their eyes were cast to the ground, barely glancing up to see what was coming before them. It was an odd and unsettling sight, almost as if these Orcs had no will to continue on, no reason or purpose to march, and yet they shuffled on zombie-like anyway like they had no choice in the matter.

The weary group camped that night beneath the sheltering canopy of a withering grove of ash. They abstained from speaking, a reflection of their dwindling morale and growing fear that the slightest noise might cause the entire region to crumble away beneath them.

Layek would not permit a fire for fear that they might be discovered, but nevertheless they enjoyed the meal of day-old bread, cheese, nuts, and fruit. For the five fraught companions it was the brightest point of the entire journey thus far. As they turned in for the evening, each silently prayed that the following day would bring some sign of improvement over its predecessor, some swath of brightness in the dreary and lifeless wasteland they traveled through, though they did not dare to hope.

More often than they would have liked they heard the guttural growls of nocturnal hunters searching hungrily for a meal. The sounds would appear suddenly, rousing them from their sleep as they rose up through the darkness disturbingly close. Each time they would wake with a start and reach frantically for their weapons, but nothing ever appeared from the murky shadows. None of them ventured to guess what it was that stalked this territory in the dark of night. None of them had to.

At first light they woke, their eyes lined with fatigue and their spirits worn thin.

"Even Caer Dorn wasn't this dismal," Aldric commented, trying in vain to spark a conversation, anything that might fend off the despair that had taken up residence within them.

Nobody bothered to reply.

Even Layek, who had served as their backbone and solid foundation upon which they could lean, had turned reticent. He never said a word. He simply packed up his gear, checked his weapons, and walked off into the desolation. His usual commitment to order and discipline was temporarily forgotten, lost in the struggle to find the strength to put one foot in front of the other.

Cover became sparse as they worked their way southward, the woodlands giving way to the characteristic rolling hills of the Durgen Range. Layek kept them in the low spaces between the hills as much as possible, avoiding any semblance of a beaten path.

Despite the caution given by their leader, the companions were forced to scramble for concealment on many occasions. Several times they could see in the near distance clouds of dust rising up into the sky, and moments later regiments of Orcs would appear. Sometimes the black-clad Druhedar would accompany them; sometimes it was groups of fiendish demons. Always they had the same wasted, gaunt look to them, as though the passion and enthusiasm had been sucked out of them and left them as nothing more than empty husks.

Progress was slow, and their hearts sank lower with each passing mile. By the time they stopped to eat lunch, their spirits were so low it seemed they were treading on them with every step they took. A great weight settled on their shoulders, and they walked hunched over in single file as they struggled to bear the burden of their own fears and doubts.

Suddenly Layek stopped in his tracks. "We need to rest," he stated simply.

The others looked at him questioningly, thinking that perhaps he had broken and was giving in to the despair that gripped the land with an iron fist. Layek didn't offer an explanation; he simply wandered off to the meager shade promised by two deteriorating oaks, too proud to succumb just yet. The rest of them followed bleakly, dropping their packs as soon as they reached the haphazard sanctuary and flopping to the ground.

"What's going on, Layek?" Aldric finally asked.

Layek looked southward, his eyes squinting against the blowing dust. "Something strange is happening to us, something in the air that makes us lose hope, makes us lose the will to continue on. Can't you feel it?" He looked them each in the eye. "It gets stronger as we get closer to Grimknoll. We need to regroup and find a way to combat this, or by the time we get there we'll have nothing left to fight with."

"I don't feel anything," Azrael commented. "Maybe you're just imagining things. We're all a little worn."

"It's more than that," Layek insisted.

"I feel it, too," Zafer interjected suddenly. "It must have something to do with the Daemon Lords. Look at the environment around us."

Vinson nodded in agreement. "He's right. Remember what Laz told us? The very presence of the Daemon Lords alters our environment until it becomes a barren wasteland. As we get closer to the center of the event, the effects become worse. The despair we feel must be a side effect of the change. Or maybe it's a defense mechanism put in place by the demons to ward off intruders."

"It makes sense," Zafer concurred. "Here the earth weeps. Somehow it transfers to us as we pass through."

Layek took a deep breath, feeling better just talking about it. "So what do we do about it?"

"There isn't anything we can do." Azrael became flustered. "Obviously the demons' power goes far beyond anything we had imagined."

"Don't be so pessimistic, Azrael," Layek said. "That's exactly what we're trying to avoid."

Azrael blew out a deep breath. Dark clouds built up within his eyes, like a pent up storm waiting for release. He bit his tongue, however, and turned away from his companions. Now was not the time.

"Well, I don't know about the rest of you, but I feel better already," Aldric said, diverting their attention. "I think just acknowledging what's happening reduces its effect on us."

"True enough," Vinson replied, "but we need to be wary. It's easy to forget what we know and fall back into the trap."

Layek stared after Azrael as he moved away from them. Something was not right with his young friend. Either the palpable despair of this place was getting to him more than the others, or the death of Lazarus was beginning to take its toll. The two had been close. Also, he was a sorcerer, more sensitive to the subtle ebb and flow of nature than the rest of them.

Maybe it was all that and more.

"So we'll just have to watch each other's backs a little closer," Layek said, his voice distant. "Stay sharp."

Hardened to the bleak and oppressive surroundings and their resolve ironclad against the invisible snares, they rose again. Even Azrael seemed to be doing better, though he talked little. With determination as fiery as the heat that stifled them they took up their march where they had left off. They encountered nothing as the days slipped past; it was as if merely thinking positively was keeping their enemies away from them.

As they wound through the hills they could see the bleak gray stones of Grimknoll rising up into the sky far to the south. A sense of foreboding crept into the five companions. They clenched their teeth in opposition.

Layek picked up the pace, anxious to reach their final destination and yet strangely apprehensive at the same time. In his gut he felt that something wasn't quite right, but he ignored it.

"Probably just the demons," he whispered reassuringly to himself. "It's nothing."

The feeling didn't go away.

As they rounded the bases of the rolling hills, they caught glimpses of the fortress called Grimknoll. The dark stones seemed to echo the feeling of despair that hung in the air. Slowly it grew in the horizon, almost like a living giant rising up out of the land from a deep slumber. Towers and parapets stood silent and dark, the blackened windows refusing to reveal any hint of what it held within. They watched it closely, ignoring the spine-chilling feeling as it steadfastly returned their gaze.

To the west the sun slipped below the mountains, shadows scrambling forth from their daytime hiding places to cover the land in a dark stain. The stars winked down at the travelers, a million tiny diamonds that glittered hopefully. Somewhere far away a scream echoed across the land, a hair-raising warning to find safety or face the consequences.

Fired by determination and need the group pressed on, wary now of the hunters who would likely be out stalking the night this close to the keep. Their pace slowed as Layek struggled to find a path through the darkness. Frequently they tripped over wayward rocks and errant deadwood that littered their trail, eliciting muffled curses from its victims.

The domineering heat stifled their breath, seeming to rise despite the fact that the sun had already set. There was no breeze to cool them or even to stir the stale air. It felt like they sucked as much dust as they did oxygen. Their clothes stuck to them uncomfortably, damp with sweat.

Finally Layek signaled for them to halt.

On cat's paws he led them up the rise facing them. Slowly they crept through the dying scrub, fearful that even the slightest noise would alert the enemy of their presence. They crested the hillock, crawling the last twenty yards or so on hands and knees, and stared out at the crux of all that threatened. It was here that this whole business had begun and here that it would end.

"Do you think Kairayn has already been here?" Vinson asked from Layek's elbow.

Layek frowned, a tugging at the corner of his lips that barely registered in the growing darkness. "I have no idea. There's really no way to tell."

"We'd better hope not," Aldric whispered from his other side. "If Grimvisage already has his hands on the stone, it's going to be awfully hard to take it away from him."

"The real question is," Layek mused, "do we wait and see, or do we go in after it?"

Vinson pondered the question for a minute. "It's quite likely that Kairayn beat us here. Even if he left at the same time we did, he would still have gotten here first. He wouldn't need to avoid contact or take precautions. He could already be inside. I say we go for it."

"What if you're wrong?" Layek asked. "Our only real chance at surviving this ordeal and getting our job done is if Kairayn hasn't gotten here with the stone. If he beat us here, we're too late. If he hasn't gotten here and we go in, we lose the element of surprise, and we're as good as dead. I say we wait."

"Who's to say Kairayn would give up the stone?" Zafer whispered harshly from beside Vinson. "He's tasted its power once already; I doubt he'd willingly hand it over."

Azrael nudged in closer from the opposite end. "That's irrelevant. He would have left for Grimknoll as soon as they made it through the pass. His mission was to recover the Krullstone and return to Grimknoll. Why would he delay? I think he's already inside."

For many long minutes they sat there, mulling over the possibilities in their heads, weighing their options.

Ultimately the decision was made for them.

Out of the west, a party of Orcs trudged down the worn path leading up to the main gates. Layek counted four. Even in the thick blanket of silvery light offered by the full moon it was impossible to identify them, but they moved like Orcs. They were cloaked and hooded like they were trying to hide something.

Layek's suspicions were adequately roused. "This could be it."

"Follow them in?" Vinson whispered beside him.

"On my mark. Everyone ready?"

They all nodded. The cloaked figures abruptly turned from the main gate, deviating from the beaten path. They circled around the outer wall for a number of paces and then suddenly stopped. The lead form stepped to the wall, his hands moving gently across its surface. A black hole opened into the wall.

"A secret entrance," Aldric gasped.

The three trailing figures disappeared into the orifice.

"Go!" Layek signaled the others.

Swift and silent they descended down the hill, crossing the last hundred yards at a dead run. Like shadows they blazed across the open space separating their hiding spot from the keep. Adrenaline flowing like water and breathless, the five slammed up against the wall.

Warily they scanned the darkness, half expecting an alarm to sound. For several tense moments they stood there, weapons held ready, crouched protectively against the stone and mortar.

"I think we're clear," Aldric whispered from the rear.

Layek nodded and slowly stepped toward the spot where the mysterious figures had disappeared moments ago. Feeling his way along the wall, eyes searching the shadows for any sign of movement, he moved into position where the secret entrance had opened.

He signaled to the others.

With a discipline that would have made Lazarus proud they spread out, securing the area. Slowly Layek ran his hands along the wall, searching for the seam or hidden latch that would allow them entry. The walls were smooth, not a single crack to indicate where the entrance was hidden. He moved left and then right, searching, knowing there must be a way.

Nothing.

Layek swore beneath his breath. It must be here somewhere. If only he had some light.

"What's the holdup?" Vinson asked anxiously. "Hurry up already. We're sitting ducks out here."

"I can't find it," Layek whispered harshly. "The damn thing's not here."

Vinson looked at him sideways. "That's absurd. We saw those four go in right here." He scrutinized the wall for himself, finding nothing.

By now the rest of the group had wandered over, abandoning their posts to see what was causing the delay. They took turns searching for themselves, each disbelieving the failure of the one to go before him. One by one they stepped back, exasperated by the uncooperative portal. They shook their heads and looked to each other for insight, finding none.

It just didn't seem possible.

Then Azrael stepped toward the wall. "Let me try," he stated simply.

"Forget it. We must have misjudged the location." Layek was already moving down the stones, investigating every scratch and indentation in the smooth stone. "Fan out. We're running out of time."

As they began to circle, Azrael placed his hands on the wall. He bent his head in concentration, whispering inaudibly.

"Azrael," Aldric whispered as he looked back over his shoulder. "What are you …?"

His words trailed off. The others turned to look.

The faintest green glow emanated from Azrael's fingertips where they touched the stone, nearly invisible behind the dark outline of his lanky form. The glow flashed for a split second and disappeared just as quickly. The sorcerer took a deep breath to steady himself and stepped back a pace.

Suddenly the enigmatic entryway swung open, soundless and smooth. A black maw opened wide to admit them, a breath of hot, fetid air rushing out. Cautiously they stepped forward, casting looks of awe at their black-clad friend and peering warily inside. Azrael grinned smugly.

"Good work," Vinson congratulated the sorcerer as he disappeared inside.

The rest quickly followed, sweeping inside before the door could shut them out. If Layek hadn't known better, he would have sworn that the keep had eyes. He could feel them boring into him as he stepped past Azrael into the dark hole. A cold knot settled into his stomach.

It was pitch black in the tunnel. With ears strained for any sound they warily crept forward. Less than twenty paces inside, the door swung closed behind them, locking in place with a dull thud. The five companions froze, fearing the sound might give them away to the keep's inhabitants. Pulses raced as they anxiously waited, but nothing betrayed the dead silence that gripped the passageway.

"We could use a little light here, Azrael." Layek stumbled to the front of the line.

The sorcerer stepped forward, light flaring with a snap of his fingers. With a flick of his wrist the white orb of luminescence floated forward, stopping just behind Layek's shoulder. "Lead on."

Freeing a short sword from his waist, Layek carefully led them forward, hugging the wall. The strange orb followed him closely, casting light half a dozen paces in front of him.

The hall was long and straight; not even a door or side passage broke the uniformity of its construction. Sweat beaded on Layek's forehead. Often he glanced behind to make sure the others were still following. The Arkenstone brothers were right on his heels, their breath sharp in his ears.

Abruptly they came to an ironbound door. Layek pressed his ear to the wood, listening for any sign of occupants on the other side. After a minute he was satisfied that all was clear and reached down to the handle. The latch jiggled freely. Not locked. Gently he swung the door outward. It was well oiled and made no noise.

Like shadows the five friends swept into the room, weapons drawn, ready to quiet anyone there who might raise the alarm. Silence greeted them.

The portal opened into a small square room with doors centered on each wall. A few crates were stacked carelessly in one corner, idly collecting dust. Layek moved to each of the doors and pressed his ear up to them.

Nothing.

"Which way?" He turned to his comrades for direction. "Near as I can tell all the rooms on the other side of these doors are empty."

"Straight ahead. It doesn't look like either of these doors have been used in a while," Azrael said, indicating the two side entryways. "Whoever came in before us did not go either of those directions."

Shrugging his indifference, Layek strode to the far wall. He tried the latch, listening one more time to be sure no one occupied the other room.

Locked.

Suddenly the light flared and went out.

The doors blew open, and a rush of booted feet entered the room. Blinded by the sudden loss of light, Layek flailed about wildly. He was struck from behind and fell, his weapon skittering across the floor. Instantly he was set upon, rough hands pinning him to the ground. From the sound of it his companions were having a similar experience. A brief flash of Aldric's runesword lit up the room as he tried to fight back. Layek caught a glimpse of their attackers. Orcs, clad in ringmail and midnight blue. Through the corner of one eye he saw Azrael standing to one side, totally untouched by their assailants.

"Help us, Azrael!" Layek struggled against his captors. One of them backhanded him, causing him to see stars for a moment. "Azrael!"

The sorcerer looked at him, sheer malice in his gaze.

A sinking feeling filled him as the room was plunged into darkness once more. The sounds of resistance died away. Frustration welled up within him. How had it come to this? How had he not seen the truth? They had all been so easily deceived. He cursed himself silently. He should have seen it coming.

Light flooded the room again.

Layek was hauled to his feet, his head swimming from the blow he had received. He looked around. The others were being brought to their feet as well, battered and bruised, but they seemed no worse for the wear considering their situation. Vinson's eyes smoldered with a fire that threatened to engulf whatever they fell upon.

They fixed on Azrael's dark form across the room.

Just then a door opened.

A black-robed Orc, shorter than the rest of them, shuffled into the room. His arms were folded neatly in front of him. The Orc raised his hooded head, and gray eyes as cold as ice fixed upon the four captives. One protruding tooth was broken off at the midpoint. He smiled as he inspected the newly-acquired prisoners, stretching the scar that ran down his face.

"Well done, I'hanet," the Orc spoke, his voice low and rough. "You have served me well."

"I tire of this game with the humans, Summoner," Azrael replied. "I am happy to turn their lives over to you. Do what you will with them."

"You slimy weasel!" Vinson yelled, struggling against the hands that held him back. "We trusted you! After all these years you sold us out! For what, Azrael? Power? Riches?"

Azrael took a menacing step forward, eyes glowing malicious red. "The truth is not always what it appears to be, Hated One. I am not Azrael."

The four friends watched in horror as the man they thought they had known suddenly began to change shape. The transformation took only a few seconds. When it was over, they stared in awe at the creature before them. Pink flesh and human features were replaced by something far more demonic. This thing was skinny and bony, its brown flesh pulled tight against the skeletal frame. Glowing red eyes stared at them from within their recessed sockets, cold and wicked.

Layek's jaw hung slack. His stomach knotted in anger and disgust. "What have you done with Azrael?" He feared he already knew the answer, but he had to ask anyway.

"He's dead, of course," the doppelganger said matter-of-factly. "Fear not, though. You will soon join him. Once the Daemon Lords have finished feasting on your souls."

Aldric struggled viciously. His captors held him tight. "I'm going to enjoy watching you die, I'hanet. My only sorrow is that I won't be there to see you burn in hell."

The doppelganger laughed mirthlessly.

"Take them away," the hooded Orc snapped to his subordinates.

"Right away, Your Excellency," the lead Orc answered crisply.

The Orcs began to lead them away. Suddenly Aldric broke free of his guards, charging at the doppelganger. The others began to fight against those who restrained them. Lightning flew from the hands of the hooded Orc, striking Aldric head on. He was knocked across the room, crashing into the wall with an audible thud and slumped to the ground unmoving.

Layek flew into a rage, striking one of the Orcs so hard he heard bones snap. The other Orc sucker punched him in the gut, knocking the wind out of him.

Something heavy hit him over the head, and then everything went dark.

℘   ℘   ℘

Kairayn mounted a tall mustang and rode out from the camp outside Perthana. The city had all but fallen to his brave warriors. It would be only a matter of hours before they cleared out the last vestiges of resistance, and the invaders had now set their sights on the capital city of Kylenshar.

Six good warriors would accompany him on his journey, a safeguard against any attempts at foul play. Kairayn didn't trust Grubbash or the demons any further than he could throw them.

The sorcerer who had appeared the night before with his summons to the sanctuary of the Druhedar had been carefully disposed of earlier that morning. Just another victim of the demons' voracious appetite. The mage was simply too dangerous to be left alive. He did not want any surprises along the way, and it would be best if Grubbash and his demon lackeys were unaware of the exact hour of his arrival.

There were still things he needed to sort out before he could come to any decision about the stone. He doubted that the stone was meant solely to keep the demons under their control, although it did serve as an excellent deterrent against betrayal. Having experienced the stone's power firsthand, he could see other possible applications for it and was wary of Grubbash's intentions. He must know by now that Kairayn had used the stone to destroy Satariel. Perhaps the sorcerer had his doubts about whether Kairayn would give it up. The High Summoner might not be averse to killing him for it. He must be cautious, at least until he had determined how he was going to handle matters once he reached Grimknoll.

The road carved a path straight through the woods south of the city, rutted and well packed under the weight of so many passersby. The sun was out in force, the skies clear and blue. They stopped often, taking as many opportunities as they could to rest themselves and their mounts. Kairayn was not in any hurry to face his former master.

Bodies still littered The Narrows from the terrible battle that had been fought for this choke point. The stench was almost unbearable, and Kairayn raised one sleeve to cover his nose until they had crossed over.

They continued southward, slightly unnerved by the absence of noise and life. While his companions might suffer the mystery, Kairayn knew all too well the reason for the change in his homeland. He spat at the bitter taste the knowledge left in his mouth. The heat continued to rise, reminding Kairayn of how a boar must feel on a spit over an open flame. A light wind kicked up, blowing dust into their faces, causing them to shield their eyes to maintain sight of the road ahead.

The land became more blasted and barren as they went, the lush forest and grasslands being replaced with noxious sinkholes and endless tracks of dead or dying vegetation. The ground was dry and brittle, crunching disturbingly under the hooves of their horses. All the while the sun beat down on them mercilessly like a cruel master with an ill-favored student. Kairayn scanned the landscape in disgust. What the High Summoner had been thinking when he had summoned the demons he would never understand. The harsh environment that his native soil had become disturbed him greatly, and he became taciturn and unapproachable. It seemed the only thing that escaped the blatant breakdown of nature was the telltale rolling hills of his homeland. He drew some measure of hope from this fact and tightened the strap on his scimitar.

He swore there would be a reckoning when he reached Grimknoll.

Slowly the gray smudge of the keep against the skyline continued to grow as they moved further south. It was an intimidating structure under normal circumstances, even more so when taken in with the desolate landscape.

Slowly the sun traced its path from east to west, dragging as if immense chains had been wrapped about it to slow its passing. The small group did their best to ignore the onerous heat, looking forward to the coming night and the end of their short journey.

For Kairayn it was the end of more than just a short jaunt. He had been away from home for a long time, and it dissatisfied him greatly to see what had become of it. The dark stain of the tower before him represented the source of all his discomfort and anger.

After tonight all accounts would be settled.

XXX UNLIKELY ALLIES

LAZARUS CHASED NESLYN through the labyrinthine tunnels beneath the city of Perthana. For many hours now they had been dashing through them, following the twisting, weaving cataracts and seeking daylight like the sun might never shine again.

The sorceress had memorized the map well. Effortlessly she picked out the tunnels they needed to follow. She set a vigorous pace despite the fact that she must be exhausted. Lazarus couldn't help but admire her tenacity.

Lazarus was slightly disappointed to find that it was already dark when they finally emerged from the tunnels into the open air. It felt like it had been an eternity since he had felt the sun's rays, and he had been looking forward to feeling them shine on his skin once again.

Gaps in the trees showed them a horrible sight as they worked their way southward. The two lovers stopped for a moment to look back to the mountains and the once peaceful city that had dwelled there. Fires burned uncontrollably everywhere. Orcs were flooding in, the few remaining defenders hopelessly trying to escape the charnel house.

Perthana had fallen.

From here Lazarus knew that the Orc armies would march straight for the capital, seeking to crush the human resistance once and for all. Part of him ached that he would not be there to fight alongside his people, but he knew the only hope was for him to succeed in destroying the Daemon Lords, and on that the salvation of his brothers depended.

He just hoped they could hold out long enough.

By now Kairayn would be on his way to Grimknoll as well, seeking to bring the Krullstone back to his master. Lazarus could not allow that to happen. He knew there was the possibility that the Orc would not give up the stone, but it made little difference to the outcome if he was not there to influence it.

"Let's go," he whispered. "We haven't a moment to lose."

They increased their pace, resolving to run through the night to make up the time they had lost in the tunnels. The landscape passed by them in a blur, the two barely bothering to look anywhere but where their feet fell. Morning came and went without them stopping, and before long midday was upon them. Lazarus called a halt as they passed through a grove of yew trees for lunch, more to allow Neslyn a chance to eat and rest than himself.

Oddly, he did not feel the least bit fatigued. He gratefully accepted the meager ration of dried meat and bread that the Elf offered him, though he was not hungry. He vowed that he would not take food from her again unless he needed it. Her stores were limited as it was, and he could not allow her to sacrifice her own well being for his. She had done enough for him already.

Unnatural silence gripped the woodlands as they made their way south. No birdsong, no flashes of color as wildlife fled at their approach; not even the sound of wind through the bare tree branches disturbed the quiet. It was as if the whole earth was holding its breath, hiding in a dark corner somewhere until such time it could explode forth again and claim dominion. Sunlight filtered down through the skeletal limbs from a cloudless blue sky, and even here under the cover of the forest it grew hot.

They ignored the lifeless feel of the forestland and the tyrannical heat. Their passage was easy and unhindered as they deftly maneuvered between the thick stands of cedar, oak, and ash. They stayed off of the main roads and trails to lessen the chances that they might come across Orc patrols or reinforcements, but more than once they were forced to move into deeper cover when scouts appeared, no doubt sweeping the forest for stragglers or any sign of an attempt to flank their army.

The two travelers took to the deeper shadows, slipping soundlessly through the trees. A light breeze kicked up, rattling the branches above their heads, whistling forlornly as it gusted eastward, cooling their sweat-drenched bodies. Darkness gathered and thickened, a blackness that spread like a stain of ink, skipping twilight completely and plunging the land into sudden night.

Lazarus pulled Neslyn after him, intent on covering as much ground as possible. Though determined and resilient as she was, the Elven princess's stamina was fading quickly. The rigors of the ritual that had returned him to life and the grueling swiftness of their march were beginning to catch up with her. He risked a quick glance back. The set of her face belied the measure of her fatigue, long auburn tresses matted to her head with sweat. Her hazel eyes burned hot and feverish. She would not stop so long as he kept going.

Though he worried for her, Lazarus could not stop yet. They would be less likely to meet any resistance at The Narrows in the darkness, he reasoned, and if they could slip past undetected under cover of night, Lazarus was confident that they would have a straight shot to Grimknoll from there. Once across they could stop to rest.

In the distance, growing closer with each step they took, the low roar of the river rose up out of the night. Lazarus homed in on it like a beacon, a single ray of light in the darkness that promised to guide them home.

Lazarus grew familiar with the woods even disguised in the darkness as they were, having become well acquainted with them when he had fought to keep the Orcs from crossing. It seemed like a lifetime ago when he thought of it, the sharpness of the memories already becoming dulled and gray with the passage of time.

Abruptly the trees thinned and came to an end. They stopped at the edge of the forest, looking out across the open space that led down to the banks of the Myrrh and the short stretch dubbed The Narrows. Bodies littered the ground, both man and Orc alike, in a thick, macabre carpet. Hot coals smoldered where fires had burned not long before, trailing thin tendrils of smoke. The stench of death was heavy on the air, and scavenger birds picked at the fleshy remains of the fallen, cawing and screeching in bloody satisfaction at the grim buffet set out before them.

Lazarus felt the bile rise from his stomach, wrath quick on its heels. With some effort he forced down both. Neslyn raised one arm of her frayed robe to shield her nose, gagging involuntarily.

They stood there for several minutes, still as statues, until Lazarus was satisfied that a rear guard had not been left in place.

"They're throwing everything but the wash basin at us," Lazarus muttered darkly. "If we don't stop this, nothing will."

Neslyn merely nodded dourly, her eyes fixed on the horrors before them.

Lazarus took a tentative step into the roiling rapids of The Narrows, feeling the icy water soak through his boots. He hesitated for only a moment, relishing the relief the cold water offered from the day's oppressive heat, and then plunged impetuously into the river. Neslyn followed, attached to him as surely as his shadow.

Silver moonlight reflected dully off of the water as the two swiftly crossed, casting them in grayish tones, a pair of ghosts passing mournfully by. Upon gaining the far bank they immediately retreated from the main path back into the wilderness, safely away from where unfriendly eyes might spy them out.

Stars shifted slowly in the darkened skies above, a kaleidoscope of tiny gems twinkling down, cold and distant. They proceeded for several more miles before Lazarus finally called a halt.

Together they huddled in the shadow of an upturned boulder, drawing up close to each other. Neslyn reached into her small pack and produced a meager ration of dried beef and a sorry hunk of cheese, offering half to her companion. Honoring his earlier promise Lazarus declined the food, settling simply for a deep draught from the waterskin she carried.

Lazarus offered to take the first watch, and Neslyn graciously accepted, curling into her robes next to him. She was asleep almost immediately.

Lazarus watched the rise and fall of her chest, marveling at how peaceful and beautiful she was in her sleep. He pondered for a time how it came to be that a person of her sophistication and elegance could become so involved with a simple soldier, a man with blood and guilt on his hands that even time might not wash away.

Whatever the reason, he decided it was a blessing he would cherish for the rest of his days.

He watched the stars then, the silence deepening until he could almost reach out and touch it. His breathing, though slow and relaxed, sounded harsh and jagged in his ears. At first, he found it odd that all signs of life were missing until he recalled something Melynda had told him an eternity ago.

The Daemon Lords were the antithesis of order and life. They and their brethren existed solely for the purpose of destruction. They fed on the misery of other life forms, relished in the obliteration of anything resembling goodness and order. Their arrival had upset Nature's delicate balance, which explained the strange and unseasonable weather. There was more to it than that, though, Lazarus intuited. It seemed that the demons fed on the very energy that bound nature together, slowly siphoning away the mana that formed the basest building block of everything that existed. It was only logical that as the force that bound this world together — and perhaps the whole universe — eroded, creation would slowly break down, order decaying into chaos.

His thoughts drifted to his brothers, miles away and out of reach, walking into a trap they hadn't the slightest clue existed. If he did not reach them in time, they would be doomed to a fate worse than death. They would fall victim to a betrayal so profound it would shatter the will of even the most determined of heroes. Time and existence would eventually forget their sacrifice, and it would be as though they never were at all.

Frustration welled within him, and Lazarus gritted his teeth against it. Silently he swore to himself that it would not be so. He had thwarted the machinations of Fate once before; he could do it again.

Lazarus glanced at Neslyn as she stirred in her sleep. A soft whimper escaped her lips. He wondered if she was plagued in sleep by the same demons as he was in waking.

With a sigh he heaved himself up off the ground and took to pacing their little camp to ease his tension. He tried distracting himself from the haunting within, staring blankly out into the darkness and up into the infinite sky above. He practiced controlling his breathing, counting the heartbeats between to occupy his brain.

Everything he tried failed miserably. Always his mind wandered back, and with each passing minute he felt more useless and forlorn.

Finally he could stand it no longer. He didn't have the heart to wake Neslyn, who was sleeping so deeply and getting some much needed rest. He watched her for several minutes, trying in vain to steal even a fraction of the peace she exuded.

Gently he reached down and lifted her from the ground. The princess curled into his chest as if taking shelter from a fierce storm. Lazarus was amazed at how weightless she felt cradled within his arms, a fragile collection of soft curves and robes, her scent nothing more than a whisper of a dream.

For a moment he dreaded the changes that his resurrection had brought. He was not the same man he had once been, and whether it was from the hardships endured or his transcendence of death he did not know. These newfound traits would serve him well in the near future, but he wasn't so sure the changes were all a good thing.

Only time would tell.

For now he would just have to make do. With a final look around to ensure that he wasn't leaving anything behind, Lazarus began to walk.

ço   ço   ço

Thick gray smoke rose up into the air, filling the sky and blocking out most of the sun's light, covering the ground in an impenetrable fog. Fires burned uncontrollably across the fields and forestlands of the Illendale valley, consuming everything in their path, searing the once-beautiful land in indiscriminate hatred. Sounds wafted eerily through the haze like wraiths, shouts and cries, growls and grunts, disembodied and without origin. The shadow of death lurked everywhere, flitting menacingly across the scorched landscape with evil intent.

Dean Markoll steadied his Clydesdale, Agamemnon, as he surveyed the appalling destruction laid out before him. All around men ran back and forth, desperation so palpable you could cut it with a knife. Fires crackled and hissed with dark satisfaction not too far away. The screams of the wounded and the tormenting stares of the dead plagued him like a swarm of flies would a manure heap.

He wished with all his heart that he could wake from this nightmare. At any moment he expected to jerk upright in his bedchamber, bathed in sweat, and the memory of these disturbing events already beginning to fade.

Unfortunately, that would not happen.

As surrealistic as it seemed, this was what reality had become. There would be no welcome waking. With each passing day he feared that death would afford the only release from this atrocity. It was as if all the nightmares of men had been ripped from their collective subconscious and set upon the physical plane, free to roam and terrorize as they pleased.

The clash of weapons grew distinctly louder in his ears and drew him sharply back to reality. Shouts and cries echoed across the field as battle was joined to his left. Markoll wheeled his horse toward the sound, pulling free his broadsword. The battle was over before he reached it, however; half a dozen dark bodies lay dead, eight of his own soldiers alongside them.

Another pack of demons.

Small skirmishes such as this one were being played out all across the valley as his legions tried to slow the advance of the Orc hordes, a daunting task on open plains when his army was outnumbered more than ten to one. This being the case, he could not engage the Orcs directly and risk annihilation. Hit and runs, tricks, and shadow games had become the order of the day. They had set fire to the grasslands, using the smoke to hide their movements while the prevailing winds blew the flames into their attackers. They never struck the same place twice and never went toe to toe with their enemy for more than a few minutes at a time.

His daring tactics had paid off in blood, though they had failed to slow their enemy. The Orcs and demons had taken sickening losses as they forced their way forward, heedless of the damage that was inflicted upon them. If he could not slow them, General Markoll rationalized, he could at least keep them contained.

It was a simple goal. Distract them from the less defensible cities and lead them directly to Kylenshar. He was confident that with the combined might of ten legions he could hold the city for some time despite their disadvantage in numbers. This might buy them enough time for the two remaining Arkenstone brothers to complete their quest or for their allies to come to their aid.

These were slim hopes, but for now they were all he had.

"General," a messenger approached him and saluted. "Sir. The right flank is falling back as you ordered. The Orcs are in hot pursuit. Captain Reich stands ready on the left, but he reports that there has been no activity there for some time."

"That's because they are expecting us to attack the left flank," he replied. "Send word to Commander Hakan to have his cavalry attack the right flank, full charge."

"Yes, sir!"

Markoll signaled for another messenger. A gaunt-looking sergeant bolted into action. His eyes shifted uneasily. "Don't worry, lad," Markoll soothed him. "We're going to give them more than they bargained for. Has there been any contact along the center?" The sergeant shook his head no. "Excellent. Bring the commanders to me, quick as you can."

The sergeant ran back to the post he had come from, gathering a group of young boys barely in their teens, if Markoll guessed correctly, and began dispatching them. Within ten minutes the commanding officers for each legion, eighteen men in all, were huddled around the modest fire that served as his headquarters. He met their steady gaze with one of his own, nodding at the group as they waited patiently for him to speak.

Finally they could wait no longer. "What's on your mind, General?" Burhan voiced what each of the men present was thinking. "No sense beating around the bush."

Burhan didn't mean to be disrespectful, Markoll knew. They were all on edge these days. "As you all know, we cannot hope to hold the Orcs on the open plains. Their numbers are just too great. The best we can hope to accomplish out here is to delay the enemy as much as possible, perhaps demoralize them, before we retreat to make our final stand at Kylenshar. If we stay out here too long, sooner or later the Orcs will find a way to outflank us, and if that happens, we're finished."

He paused to read the thoughts reflected in the eyes of his peers. He found a mixture of defiance, fear, and anger. "I propose a full retreat to the walls of Kylenshar." Groans of dismay and curses erupted from the congregation. "Wait until you have heard what I have planned before you make judgments."

The General explained his idea to them, drawing images in the dirt to help them visualize what it was he wanted. Heads nodded, and smiles creased the worn and weary faces of the men before him as they realized the wicked massacre he intended.

"This is the last trick," Markoll concluded. "After this they won't give us another opportunity to surprise them. We'll have no choice but to retreat to the capital."

"I think it's worth it," one captain said. "If it works."

Others nodded their agreement, and Markoll dispersed them to their respective commands. Within minutes men were trickling past him, adjusting their positions to fulfill his orders. The trickle became a flood, and the General stood like a statue as he watched the throngs of weary-eyed but determined soldiers march into position.

Some met his steely gaze with looks of hope and admiration; others continued past without so much as an upward glance, concentrating on putting one foot in front of the other. He counted the units and divisions as they sped past his makeshift command post, thinking all the while that they were too few, wondering in despair how it had come to this.

He recognized the banners of the Phoenix Legion, tattered and worn, fluttering disinterestedly as the men-at-arms who bore them hastened through the haze. A pang of sadness surged through him. They had lost their beloved leader in their desperate battle to hold Sowell Pass, and now barely a quarter of their original number remained. Still, despite their staggering casualties, they pressed on with an iron-willed determination and irrepressible spirit that made Markoll's heart swell with pride at the sight of them.

Reports of the army's progress began to trickle in. The cavalry had fully engaged the enemy and was now involved in a pitched battle. The Orcs were responding in kind, massing reinforcements in preparation for a counterattack while still wary of expected attacks on their other fronts. Runners from eight of the ten legions brought word that they were in position.

Everything was falling into place.

Markoll patted his horse, soothing the beast for a moment before spurring him off into the gloom. The sounds of fierce combat called out to Markoll like a beacon, guiding him to where he was needed. Men looked up to him as he passed their well-ordered lines, spears and armor glinting dully in the half-light.

A young scout, scars criss-crossing his weathered skin, ran up and saluted. "Sir, the cavalry is pressing the attack with support from the fourth and seventh legions. Their lines are holding, but Commander Hakan advises pulling them back or risk them being cut off by enemy reinforcements."

Markoll smiled grimly. They were falling right into his trap. "Very good. Pull them back, full retreat. Send word to Hakan to wait for my signal. Standby on the flanks."

The man ran off again. Markoll slid free his sword and spurred his horse forward, slipping between the ranks of men until he stood at the front lines. The sounds of battle from somewhere in front of him slowly died away, and eerie silence gripped the fog-drenched landscape. Men began to shift nervously within their ranks. Markoll imagined the lines of soldiers stretched out for more than a mile on either side of him, forming a horseshoe with the open end pointed toward the enemy that was surely coming for them. A knot tightened in his stomach, the way it always did before battle was joined.

Battle meant one thing to him. Win or lose, men would die.

Of course, this time defeat wasn't an option. No matter how many died today, tens of thousands more lives depended on the outcome. It seemed strange to him that the lives of so many should be placed within the hands of a comparable few, but such was the nature of war. All he could do was fight against those who would threaten the right to live that every creature was inherently blessed with.

"Steady, men," Markoll called out.

Suddenly men began to appear from the haze, running from the fury of those who came behind them. They slipped through the ranks and formed up once again behind those already gathered. Spears were lowered in preparation. Archers notched arrows into their bows and drew back, symbolic of the building tension within every man present.

A low rumble grew in the ears of the defenders of Illendale. The earth trembled under the weight of the thousands of feet stampeding over it. The smoky haze swirled and parted briefly, revealing a tsunami of enraged Orcs charging heedlessly into battle. A fierce cry rose up from the attackers as they spotted those they had been pursuing.

"Hold!" Markoll yelled above the din.

Then suddenly the Orcs were upon them, breaking through the haze and crossing the distance between them with frightening speed. A thunderous crash of metal and bodies resounded across the plains, deafening in its ferocity. The lines buckled under the weight of their attackers but held. Demons, all teeth and claws, came windmilling into them, screeching their hatred.

Arrows filled the sky as the archers released their deadly payload, cutting into the ranks of the Orcs following on the heels of the first wave. Shouts and cries pierced the air, the chorus at the heart of the dark symphony of warfare.

Unexpectedly Agamemnon lost his footing, and Markoll found himself tripped up in a tangle of limbs. Instantly he was set upon, a handful of murderous gremlins spotting the fallen leader and closing in for the kill. Those men closest cried out in dismay and rallied to him, pulling him from the jaws of certain death. Lacerated and battered, Markoll regained his feet and remounted, promptly retreating to the rear. It did not take him long to find the group of runners who stood waiting for his orders.

He grabbed the nearest one by the shoulder, the others gathering around wide-eyed and fearful. "Both flanks charge," he shouted against the cacophony. "Send the signal to execute. Bring up the reserves to reinforce our center. Go!"

Markoll didn't wait for them to respond. There wasn't time for it. The Orcs had rushed into his trap sure enough but with a strength and ferocity he had not anticipated. They were spread dangerously thin, and if they did not tighten the noose now all could be lost.

Horns sounded in the distance as he returned to the front lines, the signal for the other elements of his army to implement their orders. Once again the lines began to buckle, breaches opening up in several places. New battle sounds erupted as the flanks joined the fray. Far in the distance, the war cry of the cavalry could be heard, sweeping in from the south, cutting off the enemy's escape route.

The tide of battle shifted quickly as the Orcs realized their mistake. They had been so eager to catch their prey as they retreated that they had run headlong into the waiting jaws of the humans. The cavalry had executed their phase of the plan perfectly, charging in on the Orcs' unsuspecting rear and cutting off their means of retreat and reinforcement.

Their advance faltered. Markoll shouted words of encouragement to his men, hacking and slashing their way deep into the ranks of the confused Orcs.

Within an hour it was all over.

In the end, thousands of Orcs lay dead. Markoll looked over the bloodbath, suppressing the familiar reflex to wretch at the sight of so many lost. The cost to his army was great as well, though not as extensive as the casualties inflicted upon their enemies.

Later, looking out across the killing field as his soldiers retreated, he watched from atop a small hillock. The Orcs were moving cautiously but determinedly forward, their movements mostly concealed by the drifting smoke and haze. A great buffer of picket lines and scouts that stretched for miles in either direction eliminated any chance of catching them off guard again.

There was no stopping them now.

ᕲ   ᕲ   ᕲ

Layek paced his cell restlessly, too frustrated and angry to sit still. If he sat down, he would go crazy, he was sure of it.

They were the prisoners of Grubbash Grimvisage and his Daemon Lord masters, secreted away deep within the cellars of the forbidding fortress of Grimknoll until such time as their captors saw fit to dispose of them. It was only a matter of time, he knew, and wondered darkly why they had bothered to keep them alive this long.

Crossly he forced the thought from his mind. Thinking hurt his head more than the knock he had received. He looked over to where Vinson, Aldric, and Zafer lay sleeping on decaying straw palettes only a few feet away. It was a restless and disturbed sleep, haunted by nightmares and dark musings that the old soldier knew all too well.

They were lost.

A slot at the base of the iron door leading into their cell opened, and a tray of food slid inside. Stale bread and water, the same as they had been offered an indeterminate number of hours before. They would not touch this one any more than they had the last. Their jailors could not be trusted. They would take far too much pleasure in torturing them with poisoned food.

Despair welled up within him, a sinking feeling in his soul that could not be dispersed. There was no hope for them now. He had personally scoured every inch of their cell for anything that might offer them a chance at escape. There wasn't even so much as a crack in the wall. The weight of the earth pressed against them, threatening to drive them mad.

Lazarus was dead. Azrael had turned against them, had turned out to be an imposter of unfathomable evil. No one would come to their rescue. There was nobody left. Neslyn perhaps offered some ray of hope, however dim, but she had been lost in the catacombs beneath Perthana. Who knew where the winds of time had taken her now? Anyway, the chances of her making it to Grimknoll, let alone mounting a rescue by herself, were so slim as to be nonexistent.

No. They were all dead men.

From almost the exact same spot his brothers and friends had occupied, Lazarus peered out across the blackness of night at the dismal fortress of Grimknoll. He watched the keep with the intensity of a vulture waiting for its prey to die, covered from view by the brush.

Neslyn had fallen asleep hours ago, but not so for Lazarus. Even after the long days of their march, almost no food, water, or rest, he still did not feel tired. He tried to force himself to sleep, rationalizing that it was necessary to keep sharp and ready for what lay ahead.

It was no use. He was simply too restless. Besides, somebody had to keep an eye on the castle lest an entrance appear while they weren't watching. He thought that at some point someone must come or go and perhaps provide them with an opportunity to gain entrance, but all was quiet. It frustrated him to no end. His brothers were in there somewhere, waiting to die, and his patience was wearing thin.

Perhaps Kairayn was already inside, he thought. Fear reared its ugly head within his mind at the prospect. If the Orc had beaten him here, then all was lost. Lazarus found it increasingly hard to sit still. The urge to rush the gates and force his way inside was almost overwhelming, but he knew that he was a dead man if he did.

He couldn't help anyone dead.

Neslyn stirred next to him, startling him and causing him to jump. Something had better happen soon, or he was going to go crazy. He felt his sanity bend as his mind wandered through the endless possibilities of what might be, slowly losing its grip on reality as his fears taunted and goaded him.

Suddenly he noticed movement below.

At first he thought that it was nothing more than a trick of light, a hallucination of what he wanted to see instead of something that really was. Then it appeared again, nothing more than a shifting of shadows anyone would miss if they blinked.

His heart pounded. The shadow moved again, fluid and silent. Lazarus held his breath as the phantom made its way up to the dark walls of the keep. He was surprised when it began to angle away from the gates. The shadow stopped suddenly, almost disappearing in the gloomy backdrop of the keep as it moved along the gray stone. Then a black hole opened up in the wall, and the shadow disappeared inside.

Instinctively Lazarus knew this was what he had been waiting for. The dark figure must have been Kairayn, sneaking undetected into the keep. He took a deep breath.

It was now or never.

Without taking his eyes off the spot where the figure had entered, Lazarus reached over and shook Neslyn awake. She stirred and rose groggily, questioning his motivation for waking her, but he didn't bother to reply. He simply rose and bolted down the hillside.

ა   ა   ა

The air inside the narrow tunnel was stale, the closeness of the rock creating a stuffy atmosphere that threatened to suffocate Kairayn. Sweat beaded on his forehead as he shuffled silently forward. His heart pounded in his ears, his breath a harsh rustling in his chest. His borrowed knowledge had proven to be correct, and he had gained access into the haven of the Druhedar without resistance.

It had almost been too easy.

He couldn't help the feeling that he was being watched, that somehow he wasn't alone in the passageway. He brushed the sensation aside. Of course, he was alone. Even through the darkness he could see far enough ahead to know that nothing accompanied him through the gloom.

The Krullstone wrapped about his right hand tightly, its snug fit comforting in the blackness, its dormant power ready to be called forth at the first sign of trouble. Kairayn tightened his fist and pushed forward, jaw set in grim determination.

His plan was simple. Steal into the keep undetected and find the High Summoner. Once Grimvisage had been located he would convince the sorcerer to do away with the demons once and for all. If the sorcerer betrayed his people by refusing, he would kill Grubbash and do what was necessary himself. It was absolutely imperative that his presence remain unknown until it was time to strike. By now the demons must be aware of the destruction of Satariel and who was responsible. If he was detected before the time was right, he would surely be killed.

He reached the door at the end of the passage and stopped. For a moment he thought he heard something scrape against the stone in the passageway behind him. The breath caught in his throat, and he turned, reaching for the scimitar at his waist. For several minutes he stood there, unmoving, waiting.

Probably just rats, he thought, and turned back to the door behind him. Gently he reached out and took the handle in his palm. It turned easily. He pushed, and the door swung inward. On cat's paws he crept into the unfurnished room.

Through the darkness he could make out the three doors set against each of the other walls. All were closed. He stepped cautiously into the room, first one foot and then the other until he stood in the center. For the first time Kairayn caught the scent of burning oil and instantly froze.

The room had been unlit when he entered, but it hadn't been that way long. The hair on the back of his neck stiffened. His eyes darted from one end of the room to the other in anticipation, and the fist holding the Krullstone came up in preparation.

Several tense minutes passed.

Finally, when nothing appeared, he let out his breath and began moving forward again. He reached the door on the opposite wall and grasped the handle, leaning in to listen. He turned the knob.

The door exploded outward, knocking him across the room.

Stars danced in front of his eyes as he struggled to his knees. Smoke burned his lungs as he fought to bring in air. The ringing in his ears nearly drowned out the sound of clawed feet scrambling towards him.

Numb fingers groped feebly for the sword at his waist. Kairayn raised his gloved right fist, calling forth the power of the Krullstone in a desperate attempt to save his life.

Clawed hands tore into him, ripping the Krullstone away. Blows began to rain down upon him, and he thrashed out wildly. His vision grew dark as unconsciousness threatened to consume him. Despair gripped Kairayn as he realized how futile his resistance was. He had walked blindly right into their trap.

It was over.

Suddenly out of the corner of his eye, he caught a trace of movement through the fray. The demons howled in surprise as a flash of blue illuminated the room. Briefly, Kairayn caught a glimpse of a lone figure as he tore into the demons, steely-eyed and ruthless. His breath caught in his throat as recognition seeped through the thick blanket dulling his senses.

Then Kairayn blacked out.

When he came to, Kairayn found himself still lying on his back on the cold stone floor of the barren room. A faint white glow emanated from the hand of an elf-woman and doused them both in a thin wash of light. He recognized her from a time before, seemingly an eternity ago. Then a man's faced pushed into view, hovering over him, and a wave of shock gripped him.

Lazarus Arkenstone.

The last time he had seen this man he had been his prisoner. How had he come to this place? More importantly, why had Lazarus saved his life? Suspicion boiled to the surface.

"Relax," Lazarus whispered, apparently recognizing the Orc's discomfort. "If I meant you harm, I would simply have let the demons have their way with you."

"Why have you come? You should not be here!" Kairayn forced himself to a sitting position. His eyes scanned the room. A dozen piles of black ash littered the ground. The Krullstone was nowhere to be seen.

Lazarus stood and offered the Orc a hand. "You know why I have come. We share a common enemy. We can help each other."

"*You* are my enemy," Kairayn replied, pulling himself off the ground without the man's help. "Why would you want to help me?"

"You are mistaken. I am not your enemy. The true fight here is not between Man and Orc but rather against an evil older than our world. An evil that threatens to destroy all of the races."

"I care nothing for the other races," Kairayn shot back, a hint of anger seeping into his voice.

Lazarus grinned. "Perhaps. But you do care about your own people. They risk destruction as much as any. Your master has been twisted by his pursuit of power. He has betrayed your people, and the error of his ways will destroy us all if we do not do something to stop it."

"You are confused, human. Our dominion over this world is all but assured, as is our right. Sooner or later you will realize this truth."

"It is you who are mistaken, Kairayn," Lazarus replied with calm insistence. His gaze belied the iron strength of his conviction, and Kairayn found it hard to meet his stare. "You can feel the threat to your people's continued existence. I can see it in your eyes. My brothers saw it when you destroyed the Daemon Lord Satariel. Whether you admit it or not, you realize that the demons have betrayed your race and that they must be destroyed. Your ideals of supremacy, right or wrong, must be set aside. Will you help us?"

The man was right, though Kairayn would never confess to it. He had come here to destroy the demons. That still didn't explain why he was still alive. Lazarus was naïve if he truly believed that they were not enemies. Kairayn's brethren had killed hundreds, thousands, of his countrymen. There must be a hatred buried somewhere behind the iron mask of his face. It was almost insulting that his enemy had saved his life. It might be better to die instead. "You don't need me. You have the Krullstone. Why not kill me and be done with it?"

"There has been enough blood shed between our two races. Besides, you know the keep. It appears, for the moment at least, we need each other."

Kairayn thought for several minutes, refusing to release the man's stare. Like it or not, Lazarus was right. They needed each other, at least until he could relieve the misguided human of the Krullstone's burden.

"Fine. Follow me."

XXXI INTO THE ABYSS

"WE CAN'T JUST give up!" Vinson shouted at his fellow captives. "There has to be a way out of here!"

"We've searched every inch of this cell," Layek barked back. It's over!"

"He's right," Zafer calmly replied, the only one among them keeping his temper in check. "There's nothing in here we can use."

Aldric glared hotly at the Elf. "Then we wait until one of our captors comes back. We ambush the first one through that door and make a run for it."

"To where?" Layek's face was red with frustration. "We don't even know the way out. That would just get us killed!"

"We're dead anyway," Aldric shot back. "We have to at least try, Layek. No one's coming for us. If we don't do something to free ourselves, then we surely will die down here. I can't believe you would just give up like this."

The four companions glared at each other for many long minutes. Frustration and despair had gotten the best of them, reduced them to squabbling amongst themselves, the only ones present upon which they could release their anger. For hours they had yelled and screamed, several times nearly coming to blows with each other.

"It's your fault for leading us in here!" Vinson pointed an accusing finger at Layek.

"If Azrael hadn't betrayed us, we would have been fine!" The big man took a menacing step forward, his fists balled at his hips.

"Everyone shut up!" Zafer shouted, stepping between them. He cocked an ear toward the door, listening intently. "Someone's coming!"

For the moment, their petty arguments were swept aside. Aldric and Vinson slid up to the door on either side, backs to the wall, tensing like cats waiting to pounce. Zafer stood his ground before the portal, Layek a step behind. The sound of booted feet echoed hollowly through the hallway without, growing heavier with their approach. Muffled voices spoke briefly outside the door, guttural and unintelligible. Something weighty thudded dully as it hit the ground, and the sound of keys jangling pierced the ensuing silence.

The four captives held their breath. The snap of locks being released sounded like thunderclaps in the ears of the prisoners. Then the door creaked open, and a single figure stepped into the room, torch held high in one strong hand.

Layek's voice seethed with poison. "You!"

ço   ço   ço

In the days following their retreat from the valley, the armies of Illendale took refuge within the capital city of Kylenshar. Dwarven engineers had been working hard in their absence, preparing traps in the fields below the walls and strengthening the defenses of the city. As many as could be had been evacuated from the city before the Orcs came rampaging through.

It hadn't taken them long to rush to the city's gates.

Dean Markoll let his gaze sweep across the bloodstained battlefield. An endless sea of tents, roaring campfires, the wreckage of siege equipment, the bodies of the dead, all the flotsam of warfare. The sheer magnitude of the wanton destruction sickened him. He tore his eyes away from the repugnant scene and walked down the blackened and scorched walls of Kylenshar.

To the east the sun was cresting the horizon, desperately trying to burn through the haze of smoke that filled the air. The Orc camp was stirring below, organizing for another assault. It wouldn't be long now. In the last two days alone his casualties numbered into the thousands. The Orcs had suffered greater losses, of course, but death did not seem to deter them in the least. Markoll wondered if today they would break through the walls and finish them. Yesterday's three-pronged attack had nearly broken them, taxing the limits of their capabilities. The south gate might hold until noon if they were lucky.

That is if their enemies didn't breach the walls before that. Demons of every size and shape imaginable joined the Orcs in their assault. Furies, harpies, ogres, gremlins, bloodreavers, and other nightmares seemed to grow more numerous by the day. All through the night the demons picked at them, and twice already they had been betrayed from within. It was only by some miracle that they still held on.

Hope was a commodity in short supply. Markoll held no illusions to the eventual outcome of this conflict. Sooner or later they were all going to die. Those who had escaped the slaughter here would only live as long as it took the Orcs and their demon allies to hunt them down. The enemy grew stronger every day while they grew weaker.

War drums sounded in the distance.

Markoll hurried back to the south wall to watch their advance form. Their own warning trumpets sounded the alarm, and men scrambled to their posts. Catapults were hastily loaded and large barrels of boiling oil brought up in anticipation of the coming attack.

Arrows began to pepper the walls. Men ducked for cover, yelling out in warning to their comrades as balls of fire and boulders began to rain down on them as well. Markoll's own archers and artillery returned fire, launching a barrage of missiles into the sky.

A great cry rose up from below them. Thousands upon thousands of Orcs charged, ladders at the fore. Siege towers and a battering ram lumbered into view, seemingly oblivious to the hail of projectiles pouring down on them. Smoke filled the air as new fires broke out behind the walls of the city.

Markoll drew his sword from his waist as the first of the ladders slapped against the walls, Orcs scrambling up like angry ants charging out of a hill. For every ladder that was thrown down, three more went up in its place. A great boom rang across the battlefield as the battering ram began its assault on the gate, tremors shaking the walls. He looked up and down the lines as he slashed through an Orc's exposed belly, sending him tumbling back down the ladder.

The Orcs had already gained footholds in half a dozen places. Slowly but surely they were being pushed from their defensive positions back into the city. If they lost the outer wall, they would retreat to the castle to make their final stand, but there was little hope that it would hold for long. He could feel their precarious grip begin to slip.

Quickly he ran to the nearest breach and charged into the fray. He buried his sword into the chest of the first Orc, and without missing a step scooped up the Legion's fallen banner. Waving it high in the air, Markoll called out to his men. They surged forward, sweeping the remaining Orcs off the wall.

A harpy swooped down and raked him with its claws, screeching in fury. Markoll leapt atop the battlement and speared the beast through the neck with the pennant, and it fell gurgling to the stone. His men cried out victoriously.

Suddenly an arrow pierced his armor, shooting pain up through his leg where the projectile had lodged itself. A second missile buried itself in his shoulder, throwing him off balance. He toppled into the arms of his horrified men, gasping against the burning sensation.

"Go!" he roared at them as he pulled the dart from his shoulder. "Get back into position!"

Then he heard the rumble and quaking of a siege tower as it rolled up to the wall right where they had just thrown the enemy back. The wooden ramp slammed down, and dozens of Orcs poured onto the walls, ferocious and bloodthirsty.

Markoll struggled to his feet, snatching up a fallen sword as he did so. The pounding of blood in his ears strangely drowned out the sounds of battle. Through his peripheral vision he witnessed several other siege towers ramming up against the wall.

Gritting his teeth, Markoll turned to face the rush.

಄   ಄   ಄

Kairayn barely had time to open his mouth before the four prisoners leapt on top of him, fists hammering. His desperate cry for cessation was muffled as he was forced down onto the ground. Barely twenty minutes since he had formed his fragile alliance with Lazarus and now he was going to be pummeled into oblivion by the very ones he had come to rescue.

It figures, he thought.

"Stop!" a voice commanded. "Stop it!"

The blows ceased, and the hands holding him down released their grip. Kairayn lifted himself gingerly off the ground, eyes like lances as they stabbed at his attackers. They didn't even notice him. The four captives were staring slack-jawed at the figure standing in the doorway.

Several long minutes of silence passed.

Finally Layek spoke, his voice shattering the stillness like a brick through a glass window. "Laz! How can this be? You died at the pass!"

"It's another trick," Vinson declared. "Lazarus is dead."

Kairayn growled. "You fool! What purpose would such a trick serve at this point?"

"Peace, Kairayn." Lazarus placed a soothing hand on the Orc's shoulder. "They have every right to be suspicious." He faced his brother. "You're almost right, Vinny. I *was* dead."

"Oh, no," Zafer muttered woefully. "Neslyn, what have you done?"

The others looked at her as though discovering her for the first time. Defiantly she stared them down, daring any of them to challenge her.

"I did what was necessary."

"I don't believe it! It's just not possible!" Vinson was incredulous. "It's just another demon, like Azrael, come to torture us with the mockery of our fallen brother!"

"Anything is possible if your mind is open to the possibility!" Neslyn snapped back.

Lazarus took her hand in his. "Easy, Neslyn. Vinny, you are

right to doubt my identity. Give me the chance, and I will prove it to you." Vinson said nothing, his eyes fixed on his brother. Lazarus slid the Quietus Edge from its scabbard strapped across his back, the smooth metal glinting dully in the dim light. "You know this sword. It is one of three we took from the vault beneath Caer Dorn. Take it and call forth its magic."

Lazarus held it out to his brother. For several moments Vinson hesitated, staring intently in his brother's eyes, trying to determine the truth of what he was. Slowly he reached a hand forward and gripped the the hilt. In one swift motion he brought the sword up to Lazarus' neck, resting it delicately against the artery.

Lazarus didn't flinch.

Closing his eyes, Vinson willed forth the magic of the runesword. The dormant blade flared to life, blue fire sweeping up its length. The others took a step back with bated breath.

"You all know that demons cannot withstand the power of this sword," Lazarus spoke calmly, looking his brother squarely in the eyes. "If I am not who I claim to be, then the magic will destroy me."

Slowly he reached up and gripped the sharp edge of the runesword with his hand. Then he squeezed. Blood oozed from his hand, staining the blade red.

"Enough!" Neslyn cried. "Are you satisfied now?"

Vinson let the blade slip from his numbed fingers, and it clattered to the floor. Layek rushed forward, his smile broad as the sea, and wrapped his arms around Lazarus in a bear hug, lifting him completely off the ground. Aldric and Zafer crowded around, wonderment painted brightly on their faces.

"I can't believe it!" Vinson breathed. "Laz, I'm sorry. I'm sorry I doubted you."

"I would have done the same if I were in your shoes," Lazarus replied simply, reaching out to embrace his brother.

"We're wasting time here," Kairayn grumbled. "We'd best keep moving if we want to see the end of this business."

Lazarus nodded in agreement, kneeling down to collect up the Quietus Edge. Ushering his friends from the cell, he dragged the corpse of the guard into the room but not before Layek stripped the Orc of his weapons. He closed the door of the cell quickly and turned to Kairayn, motioning for him to lead them on.

Without a word he hurried down the passageway. They hadn't gone far when Aldric suddenly stopped them. "Wait one second," he muttered and disappeared through a cracked door into an adjoining room. Moments later he appeared again, arms full of weaponry. "Can't exactly go running around this place unarmed," he said with a devilish grin. "I thought we might want to have our old weapons back."

He passed them around to the others. Kairayn took off again, and the others hurried to catch up as they strapped their weapons into place. The Orc led them down the hall for a way and then turned abruptly onto an adjacent passage. They took several more twists and turns before coming to a large, empty chamber with vaulted ceilings. A handful of doors bordered the circular room, all exactly alike. Kairayn didn't miss a step, leading them directly across the chamber to one particular door.

Suddenly a figure detached itself from the wall.

Its skin seemed to be the same color and texture as the rough stone; only the blur of movement as it hurtled at them gave away its presence. Before anyone had a chance to react, Lazarus pulled free his sword and slashed through the demon's midsection. It screamed in fury and burst into ash.

A handful of others began to appear, their skin turning a sickly gray as they dropped their camouflage. Lazarus shouted out in warning and charged into the nearest ones, bowling them over. Two fell to his blade as the others joined the fray. Neslyn launched lightning from her palms, incinerating several more in mid-attack. Zafer's bow sang its deadly song as more demons poured into the room. Alarms began to sound as the three brothers and their comrades fought the massing evil. Neslyn threw up a wall of fire, cutting off their entrance to the chamber. Flames licked hungrily at the thick support timbers, and smoke began to fill the air, burning the lungs and stinging the eyes of the combatants. Then Kairayn went down in a flurry of limbs and claws. Vinson rushed to his rescue, pulling him free from the melee.

Lazarus spotted a cadre of black-clad Druhedar near the back of the room. He tore into them, runeblade arcing with deadly intent, and in moments they all lay dead.

Around the room the demons were giving way to the small band, fleeing in terror from whence they came. Or to gather more of their ilk.

Kairayn ran to the door he had previously indicated. Blood ran down his face from a nasty gash. "We must be quick!" he shouted at them. "It won't take them long to come back for us."

They dashed through the doorway into the dark stairwell beyond. Kairayn slammed the door behind them, but there were no visible locks to secure it. Pitch black engulfed the landing, and the seven companions froze for a moment. Neslyn produced a ball of light with her magic, the white radiance spilling out and chasing the darkness away.

There was only one way to travel from here. A single stairway wound down into the blackness, not quite wide enough for them to go two abreast. Hot, fetid air rushed angrily up to assail their nostrils.

"Mind the ledge." Kairayn began down the steps. "Stay close."

They hugged the rock wall as they wound downward into the earth. It was dead silent in the passageway, and it seemed their footfalls echoed into eternity. They kept a constant watch on the stairs behind them, expecting the demons to come charging down at any moment and sweep them into the black abyss that opened to their right.

For what felt like hours they continued their downward spiral. The construction of the cavern gradually changed from crafted stone to rough earth, and the air grew harsher with each step.

Finally they reached the bottom, huddling close in the darkness. It was unnaturally hot, like walking into a furnace. No one dared to speak, fearful that any word would shatter the fragile balance of the corridor and bring the whole place down on top of them. Slowly they began to move forward again, wary of what was likely lurking in the dark there, biding its time, waiting for the chance to strike.

"We must get to the sanctuary," Kairayn whispered. "That's where the Daemon Lords will be."

They rounded a corner and came face to face with a pair of Druhedar. Neslyn and Kairayn went down with the two surprised sorcerers in a tangle of black robes and limbs. The mages recovered first, leaping up and running screaming down the hall.

Lazarus yanked free his runesword and flung it after them. It caught the first mage square in the back, causing his lifeless body to topple over on top of the other.

The Orc squirmed frantically as Lazarus leaped over his two fallen comrades to where the Druhedar lay. Lazarus pulled his sword from the dead body and kicked it over, revealing the cowering mage. He brought the sword up to his throat. The mage blubbered and begged for his life, anything that might convince the man before him to have mercy and spare his life.

Although Lazarus pitied the Orc, he could not let him live. He lifted his sword, seeing the sorcerer's surprise as the blade was removed, and brought it down hard. The body twitched once or twice, then lay still.

Vinson paced cautiously over to his brother, the others in tow. The disappointment in his eyes was plain as daylight. "You've changed, Laz."

"Not all for the worse, I hope," he replied, unable to meet his brother's eyes. Though it had been necessary, he had killed an unarmed foe. A month ago he would have let the Orc live. There would be plenty of time for remorse later. For now, he had a job to accomplish. "Lead on, Kairayn."

The halls were eerily silent as Kairayn led them through the maze of catacombs beneath Grimknoll. At any moment they expected to round the corner and find a horde of nightmares waiting for them. All they knew was that somewhere ahead the tunnel would end, and the fight for their lives and the deliverance of their world would begin.

It was a strange procession, the single Orc leading his Elven and human charges on through the inky black, unsure of what to expect and yet certain it would surpass even their darkest nightmares. The air was muggy and stifling, like all of the sun's heat had been captured and released within the labyrinth beneath the keep. They sweated freely, gasping raggedly for breath as their heartbeats pounded in their ears.

Suddenly Kairayn stopped, cocking his ear to one side. The others looked at him curiously, but he didn't offer an explanation. Deftly he crept forward, stopping in front of an unassuming door twenty paces further on. Lazarus huddled in close as he placed an ear up to the door. Fell voices conversed within, barely discernable.

"What do you mean escaped?" one voice growled angrily. "How is that possible?"

A second voice hissed in response. "Their friends have come for them. They have breached the keep and affected a rescue. The one who bears the stone is aiding them."

"Kairayn would not help the humans."

"He would if he knew the game you are playing. You should have let me kill him weeks ago."

"Find them!" the first voice shouted. "Find them and kill them! If the Daemon Lords discover what is going on here, we will both share a fate worse than death. Bring the stone to me once you have eliminated them."

Kairayn stiffened. He knew that voice. He could tell by the uneasy shuffling behind him that some of his companions recognized the voice as well.

Lazarus had been right all along.

Rage bubbled to the surface. His own master had betrayed him. Roaring in fury Kairayn threw his shoulder into the door, shattering it into a million pieces. He rushed inside, his allies close on his heels.

"Traitor!" he yelled as he charged, brandishing his scimitar maliciously. "Now you die!"

Grubbash Grimvisage threw up his hands, throwing a bolt of energy at Kairayn and striking him squarely in the chest. Kairayn sailed backward, tumbling into Layek, Zafer, and Vinson, and the four collapsed in a heap.

A lightning bolt followed quickly behind, but Lazarus was too quick. Runesword flaring to life, he leapt in front of his incapacitated companions, catching the bolt on his blade and deflecting it harmlessly away. Slowly Kairayn and the others regained their feet, fanning out behind him.

"You're supposed to be dead!" the demon hissed wickedly.

Lazarus narrowed his eyes, hatred burning intensely. "I was. I have come back to settle accounts between us, hellspawn."

There was a flicker of fear in the doppelganger's eyes, gone an instant later. Hissing venomously, forked tongue flicking from its mouth, it crouched, coiling up like a serpent preparing to strike.

Lazarus took a step forward. To his right Grubbash readied himself.

All at once they began moving. Zafer released a pair of arrows from his bow so quick that they were flying through the air before anyone realized what had happened. Grubbash hurled a fireball, and the group scattered. It crashed into the wall behind them, spraying a shower of rock and cinders all around.

Lazarus sprang at the doppelganger. His sword arced downward at the waiting demon. A flare of power on the demon's fingertips warned him of the impending attack, but it was too late. The blast struck him dead center in the chest, launching him back across the room where he crashed into the wall, rubble collapsing on top of him.

Flinging blue fire of her own, Neslyn rushed to his side. Vinson cried out in fury as he closed in on the doppelganger. Zafer went down as a large piece of rock struck him in the head. Smoke and dust filled the air, choking the combatants, reducing visibility to almost nothing.

The doppelganger retaliated against Vinson's onslaught, driving him back with a torrent of lightning. Aldric rushed to his aid, leaping over the debris at their betrayer. At the last moment the doppelganger saw him and turned his magic on the younger Arkenstone. He parried the attack and crashed headlong into the demon. His sword clattered away uselessly as the two rolled across the floor, hands locked together as each fought to subdue the other.

On the other side of the room, Layek cornered Grubbash, deftly dodging the storm of fire the sorcerer threw at him. He descended on the Orc with his axe, bringing it down at his head with deadly force. The mage abandoned his spells, reaching up to grasp the shaft of the weapon, stopping it just inches from his face.

Their eyes locked, the hatred between them strong enough to burn holes through lesser beings. Layek put his weight on the Orc, slowly bringing the blade closer to its target. Unexpectedly Grubbash released the axe, dodging his head so that the weapon smashed into the stone floor. Layek was caught completely off guard and fell forward on top of the mage. Grubbash pulled a small dagger, hidden within his robes, and plunged it into Layek's shoulder.

The big man reared back as he howled in pain, and Grubbash kicked up with both legs, bowling him over. The mage scrambled to his feet, only to find Kairayn towering before him.

"Wait, Kairayn!" he begged as his old friend brought up his sword. "It was all just a ploy! I never intended to kill you! I had to make it look like I was on the demon's side!"

"Save it," Kairayn snarled. "Explain it to your new friends when you meet them in hell!"

Kairayn plunged the sword deep into the mage's chest.

Grubbash gasped as the blade slid home. Blood bubbled up through his mouth, stifling his final curse. Kairayn pulled the blade free, spraying blood over him, and Grubbash Grimvisage fell lifeless to the floor.

Kairayn looked around, trying to find his allies in the haze and smoke. Across the room the doppelganger hissed in dissatisfaction as the others began to surround it. He held Aldric before him like a shield, one clawed hand gripped tightly about his throat.

Lazarus and his friends held their ground, cautious to attack lest their companion be killed by the monster but unwilling to let it go. Amazingly, the resilient man was still standing. The blast he had taken from the doppelganger should have killed him. His already ragged clothes were burned and singed through to the skin, his chest exposed, but not a mark was on him.

"It's over, demon!" Lazarus shouted. "Let him go!"

Slowly the doppelganger inched along the wall, trying to force its way out of the trap. Kairayn moved in, cutting it off from escape.

"Stupid Orc!" it snarled at him. "I should never have helped you!"

So infuriated was the demon that it failed to see that it had stopped right on top of Aldric's fallen runesword. Aldric, who had remained silent the whole time, inconspicuously slipped a foot beneath the blade.

"Now back off, or I kill the whelp right here!" the doppelganger spat.

Kairayn took a menacing step forward. Instantly the demon turned to face him. That was all the distraction Aldric needed.

The young man kicked up and snatched the sword out of the air with his free hand, striking the doppelganger with his other elbow. Surprised, the creature loosened its grip, and Aldric spun, calling forth the power of Soulreaver.

With a single slash Aldric struck, cutting clean through the demon's arm. Roaring in pain it retaliated, digging its claws into the flesh just below the neck. Aldric cried out and fell backward.

Before the others could even react, Neslyn stepped forward, blue fire sparking on her fingertips. The demon strained in fury as her magic drove into it, slamming it up against the wall. The cry became a shriek of pain as the Elf pressed the attack. She screamed back, funneling all her energy into the assault and burned the monster to ash.

XXXII RECKONING

DEAN MARKOLL REFUSED to give in and die. Wounded in half a dozen places and barely standing, he continued to cut at those who would seek the destruction of his people. His men rallied to his side, fighting back with a grim ferocity that stunned their enemies.

The walls were breached in a dozen places. The south gate had been reduced to rubble. For hours the battle had raged back and forth, neither side able to turn the other.

It wouldn't last forever.

While for the moment the bravery and tenacity of his soldiers was enough to hold the enemy at bay, they were slowly being crushed under the weight of the Orcs' massive army. Every man in reserve had been thrown into the battle in a last ditch effort to turn the tide, but it seemed that the enemy's strength was inexhaustible.

Twice already the Queen had ordered him from the front lines so his wounds could be tended. Twice he had ignored her order. For a second he looked up to the tower in the castle from which she would be watching.

Live or die, he was needed here.

A pair of brutish demons, clad in plate armor, lumbered to the front lines, tearing into his troops. They shied away, unable to penetrate the thick armor. Slowly the whole line began to give way. Their tenuous grip was slipping.

Orcs poured onto the walls, slowly forcing them back. A trail of bodies littered their retreat as more and more of his men went to join

their comrades in whatever realm lay beyond this life. A line of spear-
men pushed to the fore, thrusting and stabbing at the juggernauts. Half
a dozen good men died before the beasts were brought down. The line
surged forward again.

Markoll lagged behind, dizzy from the loss of blood. He
shouted encouragement to his men as he leaned against the blood-
slicked rampart, fighting to catch his breath. A healer ran up to him,
hands probing his wounds, seeking the extent of the damage done.
Warmth flowed through him and a sense of peace as the magic flooded
into his system, stemming for the moment his gradual slide into the
waiting arms of Death.

The wind gusted, bearing the scent of Death upon it. All around
Markoll was death; the faces of the fallen stared accusingly at him, their
gaze boring into him like an auger. If by some miracle they managed to
survive this conflict, he wondered how he would live with himself
knowing what had been sacrificed, knowing that so many had perished
as a direct result of his decisions.

His head swirled, and for a moment he thought he might pass
out.

Suddenly a bannerman cried out from the bastion. "Look!"

Markoll instantly perked up, following the line that the soldier's
finger indicated. A dark stain swarmed across the field to the east, forming two separate fronts. The General squinted against the haze and smoke
that blanketed the battleground, spying out the banners flying proudly in
the wind. Hope surged anew within him as recognition took hold.

"It's the Elves!" the guardsman shouted, drawing the attention
of both man and Orc alike. For a moment the fighting stopped. "The
Elves have come!"

The Elves charged into the flank of the Orc war machine. Their
cavalry cut deep into their lines and wheeled away as their infantry
marched in. Markoll, however, was preoccupied with the second front,
which seemed to move with a slower, more determined purpose. With
brutal ferocity the dark line collided with that of the Orcs. Then Markoll
caught the flash of strange markings on the battle standards.

Trolls. The Trolls had come to fight as well.

From the towers and walls of Kylenshar, both armies watched in stunned silence as the combined armies of Elves and Trolls began to push with undeniable insistence against the Orc hordes.

Then all at once the battle erupted again upon the walls. But the tide had finally turned. The soldiers of Illendale pressed forward against their attackers with renewed hope and fervor, driving them back despite their superior strength.

No longer were the Orcs pressing the advance but instead were fighting in desperation to hold their position. The arrival of the Elves and Trolls had shaken their morale to the core. Fear was almost as palpable and deadly as the blades with which they fought. Markoll rejoined the fight, his own passion stirred.

The Orcs began to give way, slowly at first, and then all at once they turned and fled. Back down the walls they gushed, back through the shattered gates of the city, fiery-eyed defenders hot on their heels. All across the field the Orcs were retreating, the vast sea that was their army drawing in upon itself like the ebbing tide.

Markoll charged after them with his men, swept up in the euphoria of salvation. So shaken were the Orcs that they continued to fall back for several miles from the city walls. As night began to descend upon the land — the sky flaring in an inspiring array of red and gold on the horizon — the combined armies of the allies ceased their attack, content to allow the Orcs to sit and stew in their defeat. Skirmish lines were drawn in the blackened soil of the fields outside of Kylenshar, ready to explode into furious battle upon dawn's arrival.

Camp was struck, and a delegation from the Elves came before Markoll to cement their alliance and formally declare their intentions. The General could hardly contain his excitement and gratitude as the handful of graceful ambassadors approached, resplendent in their gilded armor and lissome gait. He greeted them warmly, taking their hands each in turn as he introduced himself.

"Hail and well met, General," the lead Elf replied. "My countrymen and I have come to stand with our human brothers against the evil that threatens us all. We are proud to join you in battle. My name is Tellyr Laen."

ဢ   ဢ   ဢ

In the silence that followed the death of the High Summoner and the doppelganger, Lazarus and his companions looked to their wounded. Amazingly they had escaped the confrontation with relatively minor injuries. Zafer had been knocked unconscious by a large flying piece of rock but was otherwise unharmed. Layek, Kairayn, and Aldric suffered a few lacerations, but none were serious enough to warrant immediate medical aid.

"Laz, you should be dead after a shot like that," Vinson told him matter-of-factly.

Lazarus shrugged his shoulders. "I guess it's against the rules to die twice in the same week." His attempt at humor went largely unnoticed. He simply had no explanation for him. "I guess I just got lucky."

Far in the distance, echoing ominously off the rock walls of the catacombs, they could hear the sound of the keep's inhabitants stirring to pursue the invaders. A sense of urgency washed over them as they hastily clawed through the rubble and into the hallway beyond the chamber.

As they ran blindly through the tunnels, Lazarus reached down to his belt where the Krullstone was secured. He was torn about what to do with the artifact. According to Melynda's prophecy, Vinson was to be the one to wield it in the final battle, but Lazarus had witnessed first-hand the changes it had brought about in his brother the first time he had used it against the demons on the Solaris Plain. It disturbed him greatly that the side effects of the stone had yet to be fully identified and understood. This led him to the conclusion that perhaps he should be the one to wield it. There were obvious risks involved with this idea. Would he be able to call on the stone's power as easily as his brother had, or would the consequences be direr than any of them could comprehend until it was too late?

Ultimately, he guessed, the appropriate choice would be made clear to him when the time came.

His train of thought snapped when he suddenly ran headlong

into the back of Layek, who had stopped dead in his tracks. Lazarus noticed that the path they followed seemed somehow darker, the stone walls roughened and scarred by its most recent denizens.

A low hiss emerged from the tunnel ahead. Wicked eyes glowed blood red in the darkness a dozen paces in front of Kairayn. There had to be at least a dozen pairs. Lazarus didn't have to look over his shoulder to know that the demons were behind them as well; he could feel their eyes on his back.

Lazarus tightened his grip on the Quietus Edge.

Shrieking in crazed hatred the demons rushed, nothing more than a shadowy blur of slashing claws and razor sharp teeth. All at once they were moving, magics flaring to life as they burned a path through their enemies. Lazarus covered their backs, cutting down the demons as fast as they could approach. Neslyn shouted in defiance, casting fire down the hall in both directions, revealing their attackers in brief flickers of light.

At first they advanced quickly. The demons were no match for the magic the group wielded, and they were forced to retreat or face destruction at their hands. The companions surged into the breach, encouraged by Kairayn's insistence that they were nearing their objective.

They came face to face with a cadre of brutish soldier demons, spiked joints bristling wickedly. Aldric and Vinson hacked though them, dragging the others behind.

Nearly blind in the murky blackness of the catacombs, they ran on. Demons continued to assail them from the rear, chasing down the small band with growing urgency and ferocity. More and more often they were forced to turn and fight.

Layek was struck, sending him tumbling to the ground. Instantly he was set upon, demons screeching in delight at having finally crippled one of them. Lazarus rushed to his friend's aid and hauled him from the fray, scattering the attackers. The big man reached down and pulled free the dart protruding from his thigh, gritting his teeth against the pain.

For a moment their eyes met. Lazarus' chest tightened at what he saw in his friend's gaze.

They charged on. Passages opened to either side, but Kairayn did not deviate from their course. Layek began to fall behind, limping badly from the wound he had received, struggling to catch his breath. Lazarus put Layek's arm around his shoulder and helped him along, the other's labored breathing heavy in his ear.

The distance between them and the rest of the group widened until they disappeared around a corner, leaving the two shrouded in inky blackness so thick they could taste the foulness of it.

Suddenly Lazarus' foot caught, and the two stumbled to the ground. Layek grunted as he struck. He forced himself up to a sitting position, which seemed to Lazarus to require far more effort than it should have for his mighty friend. From the tunnel behind they heard the familiar sound of claws scraping on stone.

"Leave me, Laz," Layek rasped. A cough rattled up from his chest, doubling him over with pain. "I'll watch your back, keep them from getting through. Go finish this."

From what seemed like miles away the sound of their friends calling for them to catch up reverberated down the tunnel. Lazarus met Layek's steady gaze. The poison was working its way through his system too quickly. His eyes betrayed the truth long before Lazarus was willing to accept it.

Tears sprang into his eyes.

"Go on, Laz. I'll handle this. They need you more than I do. There's nothing you can do here."

He knew it to be the truth as soon as he heard it, but he couldn't bring himself to abandon his friend, not after all they had been through together. His resolve began to crumble. The fear and doubt crept back into him, wrapping around him like an iron vice. He found he couldn't speak, only shake his head in fervent denial.

Another cough racked his friend, a spatter of blood staining his sweat and dirt-streaked face. "I'll be fine. Just make sure you come back for me."

Impulsively Lazarus reached and took Layek's big hand in his own. He embraced his friend emphatically for a moment. Then he pulled him to his feet. Layek leaned against the rock wall for support, hefting his battleaxe, testing its weight against his own waning strength.

Then Lazarus turned and ran down the hall.

It didn't take him long to reach the others, his agility boosted by molten hot anger, so blinded by his rage that he nearly ran over his companions as he rushed down the passageway. Neslyn grabbed and turned him about, the obvious question forming on her lips. One look into his eyes gave her the answer she sought. The rest of the company shifted uneasily as Lazarus pushed his way forward.

The hallway before him had been widened, the door to the chamber beyond ripped from its fastenings and thrown carelessly aside. Strange markings were carved into the walls everywhere he looked, glowing a sickly and malicious green as if they had a life of their own. The ground leading up to the entrance was littered with bones and rubbish. The room beyond was shrouded in darkness blacker than pitch, and a pervasive silence gripped the area, adding to the overwhelming sense of foreboding and imminent doom. The smell of death and decay assaulted their nostrils, suffocating in its intensity.

Lazarus could feel the evil emanating from the darkness, waiting just out of view to swallow them whole. Fearlessly he took a step forward, glancing at the taut faces of his companions as they followed after him. Bones crunched beneath his boots, and his hand strayed down to the pouch where the Krullstone was encased. It pulsed with power, responding to his touch.

Cautiously he ventured into the blackness.

About twenty paces in half a dozen braziers flared to life. The shadows retreated to the corners, dancing angrily upon the walls. The six comrades shielded their eyes against the sudden brightness, momentarily blinded.

When sight finally returned, they found themselves within a massive, circular chamber carved roughly into the bedrock with huge columns rising up to support the ceiling. Carcasses and bones covered the floor from end to end, bizarre markings scratched onto every available surface. In the center was a raised dais upon which sat a massive throne crafted from the skulls and bones of the owner's victims.

It was the figure entrenched upon the throne, however, and those standing next to it that caught their eyes and stole their breath. Standing more than ten feet tall, with blood red skin, the three Daemon Lords emanated an aura of pure evil. Vicious claws extended from hands and feet, long razor-sharp fangs gleamed from behind snarling lips, and eyes burned with the hate-filled fires of hell. The one to the left of the throne had numerous spikes that protruded from its joints and spine, spurring visions of slaughter and carnage. The one on the right was shrouded in darkness that even the light from the flames could not penetrate, its features obscured and indiscernible. The one seated upon the throne was obviously Serathes. He was not quite so adorned with horrifying features as the other two, but there was something indescribably frightening about him. The claws of one hand tapped idly on the bone arm of his throne.

From the hallway behind them emerged a horde of demons. More appeared from behind the spiraled columns. Dozens of red-glowing eyes blinked open in the darkness beyond the light's reach.

"Welcome, little humans," Serathes' deep, booming voice greeted them. "We have been waiting for you."

Layek tightened his grip on his axe. A sharp pain racked his chest. He shut his eyes and gritted his teeth against it. It was more than the poison working its way through his body. It was the pain of having come so far, only to leave his friends when they needed him most. There was no regret in the knowledge that his life would end sooner rather than later. His only regret was that he would not be there to protect those he cared for most when they faced an evil older than their world itself, that his friends — no, his family — would have to face that evil alone.

The thought angered him beyond comprehension, drowning out the pain of the poison coursing through his veins. He could hear the foul things that stalked these hallways creeping up on him, wary still of the foe before them. He could almost feel their fetid breath on his neck.

Some would say that there was a choice before him, but he knew he could not sit on his backside and wait for Death to claim him while his friends waged war against the greatest threat to this world since the empires of old had destroyed themselves.

Layek waited.

The scrape of claws on stone told him the time was now or never at all.

Suddenly he leapt up, throwing the hunters of the darkness back in surprise. He gave them no quarter, and charged into their ranks howling like a madman. Again and again his battleaxe felled his enemies as he chopped away at them like a lumberjack might a stubborn tree. Without light to guide him, Layek simply kept swinging, using the cries of dismay and agony of his rivals to determine where to attack.

Claws and teeth struck at him, but Layek was heedless to the damage they caused. His only concern was in killing as many of these foul beings as he could with what little time was left to him.

He reached a point where a cross tunnel intersected with the one he defended and stopped. Here he would make his stand. So long as he breathed nothing would pass to flank his comrades. Dropping to one knee, Layek fought to regain his breath against the burning in his lungs. He felt the black well of unconsciousness rise up within, and he crushed it under the weight of his wrath.

A Druhedar Master suddenly lit up the catacombs with his magic, temporarily blinding him. Layek knew instinctively that they would attack him from every angle possible while he was disoriented. He hefted the weight of the axe against his own waning strength. Talons raked his right side, warning him of the enemy's presence.

He swung his weapon in a mighty upward thrust. The blade sliced clean through the blurry nightmare beside him and crashed into the ceiling of the adjoining tunnel with a metallic thud. Swinging in a wide arc, he then struck at the support walls on either side of the passageway. The stone cracked and buckled, a small shower of dust streaming from the ceiling as the demons rushed him again, frantic now to escape the trap Layek was laying for them. A final blow brought the stone crashing down, filling the hallways with debris and crushing those trapped within under a shower of earth and rock.

Layek retreated, covering his mouth with his arm to ward off the choking clouds of dust. The battleaxe felt like a lead weight, dragging him down toward the floor. With great effort he flung it down the corridor. The weapon buried itself in the Druhedar Master's chest, nearly slicing him in half and knocking him into those who followed behind, sending them all tumbling to the floor. Reaching to his waist, Layek pulled the broadsword from its scabbard. It was no runeblade, but the edges were sharp enough.

Leaning against the wall as his sight began to blur, Layek braced himself for the attack he knew was coming. The shrieks of his enemies filled his ears as his sight failed completely. He lashed out and felt his blade strike home. Several bodies thumped to the ground as more demons scrambled over the pile, roaring in rage at the man who simply would not die.

Layek returned their snarls with an equally ferocious one. Willpower encased in iron kept him standing, and instincts sharper than his weapon kept the demons dying all around him.

Something solid collided with his knee, crushing bone and dropping him to the floor. A heavy body smashed into his chest and knocked him onto his back. Layek pulled a knife free from his belt and jammed it into the creature's skull, rolling it off of him as it died. He forced himself into a sitting position.

The waiting arms of Death tugged at him with insistent force, and Layek had to chuckle despite the mind-numbing pain that racked his body. Apparently he would die sitting on his duff.

"Your time is at an end, Serathes," Lazarus said through gritted teeth, his rage barely contained. "Your destiny is at hand."

Serathes chuckled mirthlessly. "Stupid human. Nothing can stop me now. Even the Krullstone you carry cannot help you. Yes. I know of your little trinket. Thank you for bringing it to me. It will serve me well as I lay waste to your pitiful planet."

"You lie! Your deception betrays your fear!" Kairayn yelled in fury.

"Do I?" The Daemon Lord smiled, revealing rows of jagged teeth. "Why then do your people serve me, foolish Orc? It is because they understand the true nature of the universe. Power and dominion are available only to those who reach out and take it for their own. Your people have embraced their destiny. Your betrayal will be your undoing."

Lazarus inconspicuously slipped his hand down into the pouch containing the Krullstone. "Your tricks will not serve you here, demon. They only delay your demise so enjoy the last few moments of existence left to you."

"Silence! I grow tired of your arrogance, heir of Icarus. For millennia your bloodline has been a thorn in my side. Today I will make extinct your wretched line. Since the beginning of time we have plotted the destruction of your world. My brothers and I have devastated hundreds of planets just like this one, and hundreds more have yet to follow in its wake. Still, none will bring me as much pleasure as the annihilation of this earth. Once already we nearly succeeded. The entire history of your race has led up to this moment. Every step of the way we were there, silently guiding your pathetic race toward its doom. The bill has come due, Hated One, and I will collect it!"

One massive arm lifted, fire crackling to life in his palm. With a heave Serathes launched it at them. Lazarus shouted in warning to his friends and ducked to the side. It detonated right where he had been standing, sending a shower of debris in every direction and knocking the small band to the ground, scattering them across the room. Instantly the demons moved in.

Lazarus regained his feet quickly, the magic of his runesword flaring to life. All around him demons reared up. From what he could see, Zafer was the only other one of them still standing, longsword snaking out with deadly results as he fought to hold back the hordes. Lazarus shouted for his brothers desperately. There was no answer.

Then suddenly Aldric and Vinson appeared from the melee, twin lances of blue fire cutting a swath through the demons. Neslyn's feral cry rang off of the domed ceiling as she emerged from the crowd, lightning and fire springing from her hands in deadly arcs. Kairayn's wrathful roar joined that of the Elven sorceress.

The six fought their way to each other, standing back to back in a loose circle against the encroaching masses of nightmarish creatures. For a long time Lazarus lost track of the Daemon Lords and thought perhaps they had fled to safety. Then he spied them as Adimiron and Athiel moved in to join the battle.

The two massive Daemon Lords barreled at them, wielding swords of fire. Their battle cries were loud enough to drive a man mad, shaking the very foundations of the cavern. Dust and debris rained from the ceiling. Lazarus fumbled for the Krullstone within its pouch.

This time he was too slow. Athiel plowed into their defensive ring, scattering them. The Krullstone flew from Lazarus' hand, skidding across the floor. A howl of exhilaration surged through the demons as they rushed after it.

Neslyn released her full fury, launching thick fountains of fire into the demons. Vinson charged after the fallen stone, wildly hacking a path through their enemies, Kairayn and Zafer at his back.

The massive form of Adimiron rose up to block Lazarus' view of the others. He tightened his grip on his sword and leapt at the demon. From the corner of his eye he caught sight of Aldric as he danced sprightly through the barrage of magic Athiel threw at him to engage the Daemon Lord.

His momentary distraction cost him. Adimiron, hardened by eons of combat, struck the instant his attention shifted. One great hand caught him in the midsection, knocking him to the floor. Instantly the demon was on top of him, fiery sword coming down with blinding speed.

Their blades met with an earth-shaking crash, their faces so close they were almost touching. Lazarus kicked out, knocking Adimiron off balance and rolled out from underneath him. Regaining his feet, he barreled into the demon, sword arcing in a series of deadly strikes. The Bloody One matched him blow for blow.

Across the room, Aldric lost his footing and went down.

Lazarus' breath caught in his throat. Athiel was instantly on top of his brother, clawing and tearing at the fallen man. Aldric's cry of pain pierced Lazarus' heart as surely as a blade.

Again, his distraction cost him. While his head was turned, his attention focused on the safety of his brother, Adimiron lashed out. His fiery blade went through the flesh of his stomach, cutting right through and emerging on the other side. He gasped in shock and pain, his eyes turning to meet the Daemon Lord's toothy grin.

Aldric's anguished cry echoed in his ears. Fire rose up within, unquenchable rage boiling to the surface. He reached out with his free hand and took hold of the monstrous figure before him, pulling him close with a strength he had not known he possessed. Adimiron reached up, one clawed hand clamping about his throat like a vice, strangling him.

Lazarus' vision went red with fury. Adimiron sneered in victory.

Too late the Daemon Lord realized what was happening. Lazarus brought his sword-arm to bear, swinging up beneath Adimiron. The blade caught the demon mid-torso and tore up through his blood-red flesh. Like a hot knife through butter, the magic of the Quietus Edge sliced all the way up through the skull, nearly cutting the Daemon Lord in half.

Adimiron reared back, disbelief and agony a stark contrast to the hideous features of his cloven face. The Daemon Lord unleashed a cry that tore at the soul and sanity of every being within earshot. Slowly, he disintegrated into ash.

The fiery sword that held Lazarus impaled vanished. For a moment, as if suspended in time, he did not move. Then he collapsed to the floor, his sword clattering uselessly onto the stone.

On the other side of the room, Vinson finally reached the Krullstone. With a triumphant cry he slipped the gauntlet over his hand, turning to help his embattled friends.

Serathes appeared from the fray, features twisted in rage. The others cried out in warning, but Vinson was too slow. The Daemon Lord unleashed a string of lightning, catching him a glancing blow and sending him sailing across the room. He crashed into a pile of debris and did not move.

Fires burned in every corner of the chamber, filling the air with smoke. The rock rumbled in protest with each new errant blast that struck its hardened skin. Rubble crashed down from the ceiling and littered the floor.

Neslyn erected a wall of fire, blocking the only entrance to the chamber. Eyes burning, she turned to launch a barrage of magic against the advancing Serathes. Serathes responded with his own magic, and the two engaged in a death struggle for supremacy in which neither was willing to back down. Kairayn and Zafer fought to break free of the few remaining demons, but for the moment she stood alone.

Out of reach of any of his companions, Aldric continued his battle against Athiel. Blood seeped from his numerous wounds, but he ignored the pain. He dodged around one of the massive stone pillars as the Daemon Lord threw fire at him.

Running full speed, he charged the monster. He had to be quick. He wheeled away sharply as the demon redirected its fire.

Aldric vaulted off of a large boulder that had fallen from the roof. A bolt of lightning grazed him as he sailed over Athiel's head, knocking him off course. He landed with a grunt, tumbling through the wreckage that blanketed the floor.

He came to a stop on his back, struggling to catch his breath. Stars danced before his eyes. Desperately he tried to focus. In the back of his mind, buried under layers of pain and fatigue, he could feel the approach of the one they called The Deceiver.

Aldric closed his eyes, slowly drawing breath into his aching lungs.

The crunch of clawed feet on the debris gave away Athiel's position long before he came to a stop, hovering over the still body of Aldric Arkenstone. Rasping in delight, the Daemon Lord knelt down, claws stretching toward its victim.

Suddenly Aldric was moving again.

Before the demon could even react Aldric thrust up with his sword, slicing clean through the emaciated flesh of its arms. The appendages plummeted to the floor and disintegrated.

Aldric leapt to his feet as Athiel recoiled in surprise. Their eyes locked, the enmity between them as bright and intense as the sun. Sweeping his sword up, he slashed across the demon's chest and then brought the blade back around to its neck, slicing clean through the bone and muscle.

Athiel's head bounced off the floor and rolled away, bursting into ash as it came to rest. The rest of the demon's body fell forward, falling away like sand through an hourglass as it did so, disappearing completely before even hitting the ground.

Looking around, Aldric could see the battle was not going well. Though they had slain Athiel and Adimiron, along with most of the lesser demons, Serathes was proving to be an indomitable foe. Lazarus lay not far from him, his body still. On the other side of the room, Vinson was buried under a pile of rubble. Neslyn was going head to head with the Daemon Lord, but her strength was waning.

The Elven princess took a step back under the force of the other's attack, dropping to one knee. Serathes pushed even harder, sensing his opponent was near the point of breaking.

Suddenly out of the darkness a flock of arrows sailed into Serathes. They buried themselves in the flesh of his chest and torso, taking the demon by surprise. Zafer appeared from the shadows, firing more arrows in rapid succession, loosing his missiles faster than the eye could follow. Kairayn's sudden cry of fury announced his attack as he charged at the Daemon Lord.

Serathes quickly recovered and turned to meet the onslaught. Kairayn pounced on him like a hungry cat, hacking and slashing at the monster's exposed flesh. Zafer quickly rushed to join him.

Without the magic of the Krullstone or the runeswords he and his brothers carried, Aldric knew they were no match for the demon. Digging down deep he found a well of strength and determination and dashed into the fray.

It felt like an eternity as he sped across the cavernous hall.

The Elf and the Orc nimbly dodged the slash and stab of the Daemon Lord's lightning quick claws. One misstep, though, and it would be over for the one on the receiving end. Aldric's breath seized in his throat, and he ran on.

His thoughts proved to be prophetic.

Just once Kairayn was too slow. There was an audible crack that echoed off the walls of the chamber as one massive hand caught the brave Orc across the chest. Kairayn was launched across the room. The sound of bones shattering split the air as the he crashed into a pillar, the force of his collision so great that the stone broke and gave way. Kairayn landed just beyond, rock and debris crashing down on top of him.

Leaping high in the air, Aldric shouted in bloodthirsty rage at the beast. With crushing force Aldric brought his runesword down, its magic flaring to life. He plunged the weapon deep into Serathes' chest.

Serathes roared in pain. Aldric held his grip on the blade, clinging to the Daemon Lord like a leech as it thrashed wildly about. Aldric was struck a glancing blow, knocking him from his perch. He tumbled away, his body seemingly lifeless as it lie on the ground.

Lazarus stirred from unconsciousness just in time to see the whole thing. Zafer continued his attack, with Neslyn backing him up, flinging lightning bolts in rapid succession. All to no avail.

Serathes was simply too powerful for them.

Instantly Lazarus was on his feet, a streak of lightning as he bridged the gap between himself and the battle. Serathes never even saw him coming. As the monstrous being reached back, preparing to sweep the two Elves aside, Lazarus struck. A quick slash, severing the tendons and muscles of the legs, brought the demon to its knees. Lazarus' stroke turned upward, full of all the rage and fury bottled inside him, and struck Serathes just above the elbow, the fire of the Quietus Edge burning through flesh and bone.

The Daemon Lord roared in surprise and pain.

Serathes lifted his ruined stump, staring at where the rest of his arm should have been. Then he began to laugh, a maddening cackle that opened a cold place in the pit of Lazarus' stomach.

With his good arm the Daemon Lord reached down and grasped his fallen appendage. Then, rising once again to his feet as though nothing had happened, he placed the loose limb back into its rightful position. Bone and sinew fused together, a sickening weaving of flesh. The gleeful laugh became a snicker of contempt for those who stood against him. Slowly he worked the arm back and forth, testing it until he was satisfied.

Lazarus' heart dropped with his jaw. Even the power of the runesword was no match for this ancient being. Serathes began to step menacingly towards him, fire in the demon's eyes as he moved in for the kill, knowing that the pesky beings before him posed no threat. Lazarus scanned the ruined hall for the Krullstone. It was the only hope left to him.

Neslyn redoubled her efforts, throwing every bit of magic left to her at her enemy. Serathes brushed the attacks aside as if they were nothing. With one great clawed hand he gestured, and the sorceress was thrown back into the wall. She slumped to the ground slowly and did not rise again.

Enraged and beyond reason, Zafer rushed. Without a thought for his own safety he clambered up the demon's ridged back, hacking and stabbing as he went. Lazarus charged in to aid his friend, but one sweep of the Daemon Lord's massive arm sent him tumbling away.

Lazarus struggled to his knees.

Horror struck him as Serathes reached over his shoulder, grasping the Elven warrior in the palm of one mighty hand. Swiftly the demon swung his arm around, slamming Zafer into the ground. The monster lifted his leg and with brutal force brought his massive foot down on top of the hapless Elf.

A shrill, nerve-racking scream filled the cavern. Moments later it died away.

Lazarus screamed in fury, his blood boiling, blinded by rage. He caught sight of Vinson briefly, blood soaking one whole side of his face, his jaw slack and eyes widened in stunned shock.

Without a thought as to what he intended he leapt at Serathes, so quick that the demon didn't even have time to react. Grasping the runesword still lodged in his chest, Lazarus called forth the magic. Fire ripped through Serathes once again, the painful cry that erupted from its mouth shaking the very foundation of the chamber. New showers of dust and rock plummeted from the ceiling above them.

Pulling free Soulreaver, Lazarus swung it down and buried it deep into the flesh of its neck. Again and again he hammered away at the loathsome beast, determined to hack its head clean off.

But Serathes would not have it. Shaking vehemently, he reached up and swatted Lazarus away once again. The runesword flew from his hand, spinning off into the darkness. Rocks and wreckage scraped at his flesh as he rolled to a stop. Instantly he was back on his feet, determined to attack once more.

Then Vinson rose to his feet, tightening his fist around the Krullstone as he did so. Bracing himself against a nearby pillar, he called forth the stone's power. It came easily, almost eagerly rising to its master's call.

Serathes sensed its awakening immediately.

With hardly a backward glance, the demon knocked Lazarus aside, turning toward the true threat to his power. Giant steps shook the hall as Serathes raced toward Vinson, his speed belying his massive size.

Still, the Daemon Lord was too slow by half.

Lazarus forced himself to his knees, screaming his brother's name.

Familiar white light flared from Vinson's outstretched arm, brighter than daylight, pure as the driven snow. Shadows vanished as the light engulfed everything that was dark in the chamber.

Serathes cried out in fear and frustration, his hateful demon's eyes settling on the small form before him.

With a ferocious shriek, Vinson unleashed the Krullstone's power. Channeling all of his hatred and rage, the flare of light materialized into a thick beam and rocketed out, slamming into the lone Daemon Lord.

Serathes was stopped dead in his tracks by the force of the ray, leaning into it as though he might a strong wind. A dark stain appeared within the ray of light. Serathes' growls of rage were drowned out by Vinson's own as he gave himself over to the power of the stone.

Slowly the beam of light spread over the demon's blood red

flesh, engulfing him. The sound of a thousand tortured voices finally set free filled the cavern as Serathes was drawn into the light and absorbed by the stone.

Vinson rocked back on his heels with the effort, throwing every ounce of energy he possessed into the destruction of his foe.

Serathes' form disappeared entirely into the blinding glow. Vinson's cry turned from one of satisfied victory to intense anguish. The light drew back into the stone, the black blemish of evil starkly clear.

In the blink of an eye it was all over.

Vinson's voice faded into silence. He wavered, swaying dangerously. Lazarus bolted instantly to his brother's side, catching him just as his eyes rolled back into his head, and he collapsed into unconsciousness.

Around him the cavern began to rumble and shake, the earth groaning in discomfort at the sudden shift in the balance of power. Silt and dust filtered down from the ceiling. Large rocks and boulders followed not long after.

Lazarus briefly checked his brother's life-signs. He was weak but still alive. Reaching down, he lifted the hand that bore the Krullstone. He was shocked to see that the stone had changed from brilliant clear to slate gray. Gingerly he slid the gauntlet from his brother's hand and let it fall to the earth.

Hoisting his cataleptic brother onto his shoulder, Lazarus crawled to where Neslyn lay, her breathing shallow. He tapped her lightly on the cheeks, struggling to wake her. The crack of stone as it fell earthward filled his ears until he thought they might burst.

Grimknoll was falling apart.

Elation surged through him as the Elven princess stirred, her eyes opening slowly. She moaned softly, her eyes fixing upon his.

"Is it finished?"

Lazarus smiled warmly. "It is finished. But we must go. Quickly. Can you move?"

She tested her joints and nodded. Lazarus pushed himself to his feet, pulling her up with him. Anxiously he searched the room until his eyes found Aldric sprawled out little more than twenty feet away.

Still carrying Vinson, he struggled over the wreckage of their battle to where Aldric lay, and without even straining with the effort lifted him onto his other shoulder. Steadying himself, Lazarus trudged back to where Neslyn had been but found no sign of her. Desperately he scanned the room.

She materialized from the dusty haze next to him seconds later, arms laden with the three runeblades, lost and forgotten during the struggle with Serathes.

Nodding his approval, he motioned for her to lead the way. Lazarus hoped against hope that they could find their way free of the catacombs before they collapsed on top of them.

They sped out the gaping portal and down the long series of tunnels and passageways. They came across Layek's body not far from the entrance to the temple, maimed and mutilated, sitting next to the wall, a thin smile on his face. For as far as they could see, the floor was carpeted with the bodies of the demons who had tried to break past.

A profound mix of sadness and guilt at having left his friend behind, then an immense pride for the bravery and valor and sacrifice he had made, washed over Lazarus as he looked down at him. He promised himself there would be more than enough time for mourning later.

Neslyn led on, her memory proving to be flawless. The keep continued to disintegrate as they finally crested the long flight of steps leading up from the dungeons of Grimknoll, and they dashed desperately for the exit that would lead them to freedom.

As they broke through the final doorway to the open air, the stone at last gave way, and the whole of the keep crumbled down into the earth.

Lazarus and Neslyn trudged to the top of the nearest hill and turned to watch as the stone parapets and towers fell away before them. The earth seemed to open up, the giant maw of an angry beast grinding the keep into rubble, leaving a great crater where the citadel of the Druhedar had once stood.

For many long minutes they stood and stared.

A breeze kicked up, fresh and cleansing, cooling their weary, blood-streaked bodies. To the east the sun was just beginning to crest the horizon, painting the cloudless sky in swaths of red and gold brilliance. For the first time in a long time, Lazarus felt like everything was going to turn out right.

Neslyn snuggled in close as the two watched the sunrise. She turned and met his eyes, leaned up, and kissed him. It was a long time before either of them broke away.

Lazarus smiled as wide as the sky. "Come, my love. It's a long walk home."

Epilogue

A CHILL FALL wind swept across the square where Lazarus sat undisturbed upon a stone bench, leaves scraping along the smooth rock pavers as they were dragged to and fro by the breeze. The morning sun filtered down idly through thin wisps of cotton-lined clouds, bathing the plaza alternately in shadowy gray and warm yellow glow.

It had been nearly a year since the battle at Grimknoll and the destruction of the Daemon Lords. Nature had restored her balance in that time and, it seemed, was coming back stronger than ever. Already the high mountain peaks were mantled in heavy snow. A flock of birds, flying in formation, winged southward across Lazarus' view, migrating for the winter to warmer climes.

The Orcs had been driven out under the combined might of Men, Elves, and Trolls, withdrawing into isolation within their own lands. With the death of Grubbash Grimvisage their society had spiraled once again into anarchy. It would be a long time before the enmity between Man and Orc faded and the two could coexist in peace, but for now the separation was enough to appease both sides. After the death of their masters, many of the demons brought forward from the abyss in those dark times had been hunted down and killed, the survivors melting away into the wilderness.

Perthana was rebuilt in great splendor, a shining jewel at the base of the Serpentspine and a monument to the indomitable spirit of mankind. In the center of the newly reconstructed city a great court had been fashioned, replete with breathtaking gardens populated with every imaginable variety of flower and tree, extending for acres all around. The greatest gardeners in all the lands were brought to tend them, constantly striving to keep the manicured flowerbeds and hedge-lined pathways in perpetual beauty.

In the center of these gardens, where Lazarus now sat, was a paved square, dubbed the Hall of Heroes, where statues of all the heroes of the war had been carved from the purest alabaster and marble. All thirteen members of their original party were represented, their spirit entombed forever in unblemished stone, a permanent tribute to their sacrifice and valor. At the end of the row of impressive effigies a great wall of black marble had been constructed with the names of every man lost in the fighting etched into it, an eternal reminder of the heroism of their people.

Lazarus rotated on his seat and faced the statue directly behind him. Rising up a dozen feet into the air, Layek's stone image stared down at him. The resemblance to his dead and gone friend was remarkable. Gazing up at the smooth facets of the carving, he could almost hear his jovial laughter.

He sighed heavily as he reminded himself that his friend would not be coming back. Between measured breaths he took stock of what had been lost on their long, arduous journey and also of what had been gained. So many good people lost along the way. Friends and family whose comforting presence would no longer be felt except as a warm memory, and even that would fade as the years passed. Aside from the obvious physical changes he felt, the full ramifications of his resurrection had yet to be realized. Likewise, Vinson was still trying to come to terms with the effects of the Krullstone's use. It had taken months for him to recover, and only the future would reveal what was ultimately in store for him.

Mankind may have recovered from the destruction and terror of the war, but he doubted that the desolation he felt within his heart and soul would ever fade. He had simply seen and done far too much to ever go back to the life he had lived before any of this had begun. The old adage claimed that all wounds heal with time, but Lazarus doubted that an eternity would ever repair the scars he bore. He realized now that he would never have all the answers, and for the first time in his life he didn't care.

The very existence of their world had been saved, all of them given a new chance at life. Lazarus mused that the determination of whether the price paid for their salvation had been worth it would be decided on how those who had survived carried on.

A smile creased his worn face. He intended to make the most of what time he had been given. Even after so much loss, a love had been gained that he had never dreamed would belong to him. The silver lining was there; sometimes you just had to wipe the dirt off to see it.

Footsteps approached from behind him, thumping noisily on the stone tiles of the plaza. Lazarus rose from his seat and turned to face the newcomers.

"Laz, you old goat!" Aldric called out, Vinson right behind him.

Lazarus couldn't help but chuckle. "What took you so long?"

"Got lost in the gardens." Vinson gave Aldric a playful shove. "Seems junior here read the marker stones wrong."

"It was your idea to go left, not mine," Aldric protested.

"How are you two ever going to get along without me if you can't even navigate a garden? I can't babysit you forever, you know." Lazarus clapped them both on the shoulder. "Walk with me a ways."

He noticed that the lines and scars on their faces were deeper and more numerous than he remembered them being a year ago. He wondered if his own features compared. It had been a long time since he had been able to look at himself in the mirror. Demons and ghosts still haunted him, and he presumed, some of them always would. Looking his brothers in the eyes, he could see it was the same for them as well.

"So, Commander Aldric, how are things with the Phoenix Legion?" Lazarus asked as they strolled down the pathway.

"So many new recruits, I don't know how I'm ever going to train them all. I wonder how you ever managed, Laz."

"You're sure you won't stay?" Vinson pressed.

"Yes, I'm sure," Lazarus stated simply. "Too many old ghosts here. It's time for a fresh start. I could use a vacation anyway."

"Ah, yes. Laying down the sword to take up the plow," Vinson joked. "I bet they have good farmlands over there, far away in the Elven lands."

"Who said anything about farming?" Lazarus retorted. "There's plenty of things left to do in this life besides being a farmer."

They reached the long wall of names and stopped. From the far end of the courtyard, Lazarus spotted Neslyn's lithe figure strolling toward them. She was positively radiant, the sun's rays playing on her ageless face, her robes billowing in the breeze. She was a revelation of beauty, a stark contrast to the dark history the two had shared since their meeting so long ago.

She smiled as she drew near. "Vinson, Aldric. Are you well?"

The two brothers nodded in greeting, returning her smile warmly.

"No chance we can convince you to stay?" Aldric questioned her. "There's plenty of room for another princess at the palace, you know."

Neslyn giggled in spite of herself. "Why don't you come with us? You'd like Elysium, plenty of adventure there, too."

"I cannot. Too much work to be done here, and somebody has to do it."

There was a long, awkward moment of silence between them. Everything that had needed to be said already had been.

"I guess this is goodbye, then," Vinson said finally.

"So long but not farewell, little brother. We'll be seeing each other again."

"Take care of yourself, Laz." Aldric hugged his brother emphatically.

Lazarus took Vinson into his embrace. There were several more moments of silence as they looked each other over, etching the memory of the others into their minds.

Then Lazarus took Neslyn by the hand, and the two walked down the pathway. Vinson and Aldric watched them go until they disappeared behind the line of hedges.

THE END

Watch for Scott S. Colley's
upcoming epic series

BLOODLINES

entering your world
SPRING 2012!

KRULL STONE

PUBLISHING

Springville, Alabama
www.krullstonepublishing.com
www.worldofmythica.com
www.scottscolley.com

ALTAR OF THE
ANCIENTS

TENNIA FLATS

SARMONT
PLAINS

CAER
DORN

MORAH WEA

CLOUDSPIRE MOUN

URSAI PENINSULA

THE GREAT SEA

NIT

THE

IRRULAN

STEPPES

SUARIM
MOOR

TH
BLA
DE

T'LAS MOUNTAINS